Mistakenly Married?

Mistakenly Married?

A multicultural, age gap, forced proximity, friends to lovers, drunk vegas marriage, sports romance.

Galactic Wrestling Association Book 3

Leah Mae Wright

Copyright

Contents

Copyright iv

Contents v

Dedication vii

Author's Note viii

Introduction x

Prologue 1

Chapter One 24

Chapter Two 46

Chapter Three 74

Chapter Four 109

Chapter Five 139

Chapter Six 164

Chapter Seven 202

Chapter Eight 230

Chapter Nine 262

Chapter Ten 287

Chapter Eleven 328

Chapter Twelve 363

Chapter Thirteen 394

Chapter Fourteen 419

Chapter Fifteen 448

Chapter Sixteen...478

Chapter Seventeen 506

Chapter Eighteen 531

Epilogue...546

Coming Next in the GWA 559

Coming Next in Heart's Destiny 560

Books by Leah Mae Wright.................................562

About The Author...564

Dedication

To all my high school and college math teachers. Ya'll were right. I did have to use the Pythagorean Theorem again while writing this book to figure out the distance between diagonal ring posts to estimate how far Josh is able to jump across the ring.

And to my physics and biomechanics professors in college. Because of you, I know it's possible to estimate the various amounts of speed and force used in every athletic scene in this book. Unfortunately, my memory loss after my concussions encompasses the majority of the classes I took with each of you. So, I apologize for not remembering the formulas you taught me to do more than guesstimate.

Author's Note

As you're reading this book, you will notice some words that appear to be misspelled or used improperly. For some of those, specifically the misspellings, that is my artistic license for spelling things phonetically for how they sound when Liam is speaking in Irish or putting on an Irish accent for his wrestling persona. If you have problems reading them, please try to "hear" them in an Irish accent so they'll make more sense.

You will also notice that the Irish terms of endearment Liam uses with Rylie are spelled phonetically when she hears them and spelled correctly in Irish when the scene is from Liam's point of view. My apologies to my Irish ancestors and the entire Irish population of the world if I've totally butchered the language. You can blame it on my Wright ancestors, who came to the US from Ireland about two-hundred years before I was born, for not passing the language down through the years, so I had to rely on what I could learn online.

There are also several terms in this book that have different meanings in the professional wrestling industry, which people outside the industry might not know. For those who might need it, you can refer to the _Glossary of Professional Wrestling Terms_ (_https://dl.bookfunnel.com/eg7nfwo6hb_) while reading this book if you come across a term that doesn't make sense as the GWA characters are speaking.

Also, while reading this book you'll notice that Josh Parker drives a seafoam green, 2017 Chevrolet Colorado Z71 Hurley truck while they're in his hometown of San Diego. As I was doing some research online to find out what modern surfers might drive to replace the wood paneled station wagons and VW vans of the past, I found this concept vehicle that was presented at the 2016 SEMA show and spotlighted on Car and Driver's website. (_https://www.caranddriver.com/news/a1534185/g narly-brah-chevrolet-colorado-z1-hurley-concept-is-a- surfers-dream_) From what I can tell, this vehicle was never produced for the mass market or sold. But it was too perfect for Surfer Josh to drive, so I've used my creative license as an author to imagine he bought the first, and possibly only, one ever produced. My apologies to all the surfers who wish they could buy one now.

Introduction

What happens when the Galactic Wrestling Association celebrates a little too hard after a successful show in Las Vegas? Too much drinking that leads to a night several of the wrestlers have completely forgotten. Especially when one of their meddling, matchmaking mommas instigates an excursion to take pictures at a local wedding chapel.

The photographic evidence on social media of thirteen inebriated performers stopping at a wedding chapel caused quite an uproar, making them wonder if some of their angles needed to be rebooked. But with all of them waking up in their own rooms at the hotel the next morning, with only vague memories of what had happened, they all believed they'd stayed outside the chapel, as the pictures indicated.

Until a few weeks later, when Rylie Long checked her mail while the GWA was in her hometown for a show, and learned that what happens in Vegas doesn't always stay there. Finding out she'd actually married Liam Connery that night in Vegas was a shock. She hadn't wanted to let on to anyone in the company that she had a little crush on the older wrestler. Now she had to figure out if she wanted to take advantage of their situation to see if her little crush could turn into more.

When Rylie took her marriage license to the arena to inform her boss, several of her coworkers suddenly scrambled to check their mail to find out their marital statuses as well. Apparently, Rylie and Liam weren't the only GWA wrestlers who got mistakenly married.

Teagan Shields and Josh Parker also got married while drunk that night, as did Aiken Pearson and Brent Crockett. Now they all had to figure out how they wanted to handle the legalities of their situation, while the GWA bookers reworked their angles to try to control the celebrity gossip. Would any of them stay married? Or would they get divorced? Or have their marriages annulled? And how did the fact that none of them had their legal residences listed in the same state as their spouses, or the state where they got married, factor into their options?

Taking the time to meet with attorneys and determine the requirements for each of their situations was difficult with them traveling with the GWA. Especially when their coworkers conspired to keep them together by pairing the three couples in the bridal party for Dean and Allissa's wedding, so they couldn't go home for their Thanksgiving break.

DISCLAIMER: This multicultural, age gap, forced proximity, friends-to-lovers, drunk Vegas marriage, sports romance contains profanity, graphic sex scenes, and references to infertility issues. It is intended for adult readers (18+) who are not easily offended.

Prologue

As she sat in the VIP room reserved for the **Sin City Showdown** after-party with her daughter's coworkers, Windy Walters didn't understand why the GWA boss was so opposed to a few of the wrestlers going to take pictures at one of the local wedding chapels. The young couples that she could tell clearly belonged together didn't need to fight his negativity on top of already fighting their feelings for one another. *So what if the pairings don't go along with the storylines he has scripted for the next few months? The GWA is a form of live theater, not a reality show where the storyline is loosely based on real life. The actors don't have to date the same characters off screen that they pretend to fall for on screen.*

Hell, Victoria Vicious and Dean Dangerous aren't dating in the scripted world of the GWA, but Rick doesn't seem to have a problem with my Lissie dating dashing Dean in real life. So, why's he so adamant that these other couples shouldn't follow their hearts and take the plunge while they're here, where there's an Elvis impersonator on every corner waiting to marry them off?

Not understanding the reasoning behind Rick's objections, Windy waited until Rick and his wife left the party, pretending to go to her room for the night at the same time. While she'd rather stay at the party to keep getting the wrestlers drunk enough to go along with her plans, she had to go upstairs to her room to ditch the bodyguards Rick had hired for her because of the packages Allissa's stalker had sent to her house in Dead End, Nevada. Once she was sure the boys who would ruin her fun were in their rooms for the night, she snuck back down to the front desk to set everything up. Then, she met back up with her best friend Kandi in the VIP room to convince her new friends to head over to the Clark County Marriage License Bureau before it closed.

She felt like she got lucky with the timing of everything, since the GWA show had to go live on the east coast at seven p.m. Eastern Time, which meant it had to start at four p.m. Pacific Time in Las Vegas, Nevada. Even though it was a three hour show, they were done wrestling by seven p.m. local time. Though from what she understood from Lissie, the wrestlers all tended to run on Eastern Time anytime they were working a televised show, since TV airtime where the GWA was based dictated their schedule. The good news for her was that meant the after-party started before eight, which gave her plenty of time for the fuddy-duddies to get tired of partying and go off to their rooms by ten p.m., which was when the parties usually got started for Windy and her best friend Kandi.

Even having to wait in the room for half an hour to make sure the coast was clear, and then spending another half an hour organizing the limo with the front desk, we should still have plenty of time to get to the marriage license bureau by midnight.

"Okay, I have us one of those stretch Hummer limos reserved and pulling up to the front of the hotel now," she informed her daughter's coworkers as she walked back into the VIP section of the club in the hotel. Looking around at how several of the couples had pushed the tables and chairs to the outside of the space to make their own dance floor in the VIP room, instead of having to go mingle with the public in the other part of the club, made it obvious that they hadn't stopped drinking in the hour since she'd feigned leaving. *Oh, good, they're all nicely lubricated and letting go of some of their inhibitions. Though I'm not sure I'd pair them up with the guys they're dancing with right now.* "So, who's coming with to take some pictures?"

If only Lissie and Dean hadn't left earlier, so they could get married now, too.

"We're in," Magnum called out, standing from his seat at one of the tables, and motioning to his tag-team partner, Trojan, and their manager, Chastity, who were both up dancing together.

"We're in, too," Amethyst spoke up for her and her tag-team partner, Emerald, as well as their dance partners, Crockett and Surfer Josh. The girls led their guys over to stand near Windy.

They were soon followed by Blade, Sawyer, and Killer Kade. *Yeah, I'm just gonna call him Kade from now on 'cause I don't like his ring name.*

She'd had a hard time keeping track of everyone's names when they'd introduced themselves with both their real names and ring names, so she'd opted to just think of them by their ring names, since those were what she'd heard weekly while watching her daughter on the GWA television show. And she just referred to Sawyer as Sawyer because she couldn't remember if his ring name was Owen Sawyer or Sawyer Owens. She knew he just reversed his real name, but since the announcers always referred to him as Sawyer while calling his matches, she hadn't heard the ring name enough to remember which was which.

"I don't know about being in any of the pictures," Cruz shook his head. "Rick really didn't seem to want us to do this."

"Yeah, but we've gotta go, 'cause it's our duty as locals to keep our friends from ending up in some of the seedier parts of Vegas," his brother Dane added, dragging Cruz along.

Thankfully, those boys kept it simple by just using their first names for their ring names, so they aren't confusing like some of the other wrestlers.

"You coming, Red?" Crockett goaded, poking at the other wrestler, who'd just signed the bar tab and put his credit card back in his wallet. Crockett was acting like one of the annoying drunks she hated dealing with at the brothel, where she worked managing the bar, but at least he was trying to help her get Red to join them, so she couldn't complain too much about his attitude. "Since you're at least part of a tag team, so Rick can spin it into an angle for Red Velvet versus Protection Detail for Chastity's honor, maybe you can keep the rest of us outta trouble by taking one for the team."

Maybe it's a good thing I wasn't planning on matching Crockett up with any of these girls. They're way too nice to have to put up with being married to an annoying drunk. But with the way he's sticking close to Amethyst, I might have a problem convincing her to swap him out for one of the Protection Detail guys.

"Yeah, I'm in," Red agreed, stumbling a little as he joined them in heading out of the club to the front of the hotel. "But this would probably work better for spinning into an angle if Dark Chocolate was still here with us."

Oh, I probably shouldn't have kept swapping my full shots of Irish whiskey for his empty glasses, Windy worried. *I just wanted to get him drunk enough to loosen up and reveal the fact that he's obviously hung up on Chastity, not so drunk that he can't consent to getting married. Maybe we should stop for some coffee to sober him up a little? I mean, in the condition he's in now, if he's able to stay upright to walk down the aisle with her, he probably won't remember it in the morning. And that was definitely not my intention.*

"Where the hell does D keep sneaking off to after our shows are over?" Surfer Josh inquired, also slightly slurring as he threw his arm around Emerald, and they made their way out to the limo that was already waiting for them.

Oh, shit, did Kandi not realize I wanted her to help me pair up Magnum and Trojan with Emerald and Amethyst? It looks like she got the wrong guys drunk enough to reveal their feelings while I was up ditching Miller and Knight, since the Protection Detail guys still look mostly sober. And neither one of them seem to be interested in any of the women wrestlers.

Huh? Guess I misread that situation. But maybe this can still work for each of the ladies to find their soulmates if one of the other guys steps up for Amethyst, like Josh seems to be claiming Emerald.

"He swears he's just going to his room to get some extra sleep," Red replied, slightly slurring his words.

"Maybe he's calling a special lady back home?" Chastity suggested, assisting Red when he stumbled as he tried to get into the limo.

"Naw," Red disagreed, leaning heavily on Chastity. "He's pretty much avoided going home to NOLA since our Labor Day break last year 'cause of a fight with his brother. He didn't even go to his condo to stay the night when we went there for GWA shows in October and April, so I doubt he's got a girl there he's callin' or whatever."

I guess at least one of the couples I thought were into each other are actually acting like they might be amenable to getting married tonight. But with the way they're both a little stumbly, we should probably grab some iced coffee first thing, so they can sober up enough to be coherent when we get to the license bureau and the chapel. She insisted on iced coffee when she placed the request with the driver, just in case they spilled it in their inebriated state, so nobody risked burns from hot coffee on what she hoped would be their wedding night.

"Maybe he's just getting old and needs more rest and recovery time than the rest of us," Kade suggested as he followed Red and Chastity into the limo.

"He's almost two years younger than me, ya fecker," Red chastised Kade.

"He has quit hangin' with the ring rats in the last couple of years, too, though, so maybe Chastity has a point about him having a special girl," Crockett pointed out as the rest of them piled into the limo, almost looking less drunk until he broke out laughing for no reason and hugged Amethyst to his side.

Huh? Maybe she can handle him when he's drunk after all, since she seems to have a similar drunk personality, Windy thought when Amethyst broke out in laughter along with Crockett. Unfortunately, her laughter made it impossible for Windy to understand what Amethyst said to trigger Emerald to join the discussion.

"That probably has something to do with how much we pick on him about the ring rats calling him Big D," Emerald giggled, leaning over like she was inspecting Surfer Josh's crotch. "Do you have a big D, too?"

Are they talking about the guys' dicks? As Emerald reached out to stroke Josh's cock and he retaliated by cupping her breast, Windy realized that she'd definitely been wrong about who to pair up with whom. *Maybe Kandi got the right guys sloshed enough to loosen up, after all.*

"Enough talk about Big D, when none of us are getting any big D," Amethyst interjected, fanning herself to stop laughing as she leaned across both Crockett and Blade's laps. "Let's get on with the pictures. Who's gonna pretend to marry me first?"

"You can pretend with the rest of the guys now, but once we get to the chapel, you and I are getting married for real, Princess," Crockett declared, earning a big smile from Amethyst.

Leah Mae Wright

"Deal," she agreed, sitting back up and throwing her arms around Crockett's neck before giving him a smacking kiss.

Well, I guess that settles that.

"We're making it real, too, Em," Surfer Josh informed the group, not waiting for Emerald to agree before he covered her mouth with his.

"Guess we are too, Chas," Red agreed, pecking Chastity's temple. "So we can keep everyone else outta trouble by pitching our marriage as an angle between Red Velvet and Protection Detail."

"Awesome," Magnum agreed, reaching over to high-five Chastity and Red. "Can't wait to work with you guys and hopefully get our first tag title run."

Windy started snapping pictures with her phone, beginning with Amethyst and Blade as they posed for the first pretend pairing. Soon, several of the wrestlers' phones were being passed to Windy and her bestie, Kandi, to photograph the various pairings, as the driver went through a Starbucks drive-thru to get them all iced coffees. Windy and Kandi swapped out phones several times, making sure to upload the best of the pictures to the various social media accounts they found on the wrestlers' phones before giving them back.

"Do we need to go buy some rings to make these pics look more official?" Surfer Josh held up his hand, pointing out his bare left ring finger.

"No," Chastity decided for them, holding up her right hand and pointing to the rings on it. "No point in over spending on whatever costume jewelry we can find now that might turn our fingers green, when we can just use my mom and dad's rings."

They played a game of musical ring fingers to make sure all three girls could wear her mom's rings and all three guys could wear her dad's ring without anyone having problems with the rings getting stuck or looking like it was way too big. They had to take the clear plastic spacer off her dad's ring for all the guys, and Aiken had to put it on Rylie's mom's rings, since she had smaller hands than the other ladies, but they figured out the best way to work it so the rings worked for all three couples. Finally, they all got out of the limo to take more pictures outside both the Clark County Marriage License Bureau and one of several wedding chapels with neon signs lit up to advertise their services.

First, they took pics of each of the ladies with all the guys surrounding them. Well, most of them. Dane and Cruz opted to stay in the limo to make sure nobody else from their hotel could commandeer it and leave them stranded. Then Blade and Sawyer wandered away with a couple of female fans, while Windy snapped more pics of each of the ladies with both the men she'd originally thought they should be paired with, and with the guys who ultimately demanded that they were the guys the girls should actually marry.

Yeah, those pairings will definitely work out better long term than the guys I originally picked for them.

Windy would have taken pictures inside the buildings, too, but apparently only official photographers were allowed. Especially when the three couples who'd gotten their marriage licenses took turns walking down the aisle to make things even more official. Since she was busy swiping her debit card to pay for the licenses and ceremonies, Windy was almost glad for the break from taking pics while the three couples filled out all the legal documents.

"Where do we need to put this paperwork while we're getting hitched?" Surfer Josh held up the photocopy of the official documents for him and Emerald. The chapel had to keep the original paperwork to send into the Clark County Clerk's Office to make everything legal. As part of the services they offered, they would also be ordering the certified marriage certificates and sending them out to each of the brides' and grooms' residences.

"Kandi and I will keep track of all that for you," Windy suggested, as Kandi took the paperwork from Josh. She and her bestie were more than happy to hold onto the photocopies of the documents for each of the three couples about to walk down the aisle in what would eventually turn into a triple ceremony.

Since they were all using the same rings for the pictures, once Crockett and Amethyst finished saying their vows and took their pictures, they'd pass them on to Surfer Josh and Emerald, who would do the same and pass them on to Red and Chastity.

I suppose that makes sense, so they can go to a higher end jewelry store and pick out the rings they want, instead of getting stuck with whatever the chapel has available. And I'm not on the hook for jewelry too, so none of them have receipts or any other proof of what happened tonight, so Rick can't complain about them actually getting married.

"Yeah, you better keep it here," Crockett added, handing her the copy of the paperwork for him and Amethyst. "'Cause Rick will kick our asses if we take it with us when we fly out tomorrow."

"Rick will kick your arse," Red slurred, throwing his arm around Chastity's shoulders after passing over their photocopied paperwork, which got folded with the other two and stuffed in Windy's purse. "But we'll be fine since we can spin our marriage into an angle."

"Are those the couples you thought would get married tonight?" Kandi questioned once everyone had either taken a seat or moved into position for walking down the aisle.

"Not exactly," Windy admitted, as they watched the festivities. "But after seeing them in the different pictures with both the guys I thought they had sparks with, and the guys who actually make these girls glow, I have a feeling these three couples will work out much better than my original plans."

"And what are we gonna do if they don't remember any of this in the morning?" Kandi looked nervous as they watched the first couple walk down the aisle. "You think Allissa's boss will still keep paying for those bodyguards if he figures out we ditched them to marry off his drunk wrestlers?"

"Oh, I'm pretty sure none of them are gonna remember any of this in the morning. So, we'll just pretend we were sloshed too and don't know anything," Windy decided, knowing she'd need those bodyguards when she went back home to Dead End, even if she thought she was perfectly safe while surrounded by a bunch of big, strapping professional wrestlers while traipsing around Las Vegas. "They'll figure out they got married when they get their marriage certificates in the mail. So as long as we make sure we're not in any of the pictures, he'll never know we ditched the bodyguards and came along tonight."

"He's still gonna blame us for making the suggestion earlier," Kandi pointed out, just as Amethyst and Crockett kissed to seal their union.

"But he won't be able to prove we did anything more than make the suggestion." Windy just hoped that Rick wouldn't punish Lissie for her actions. *And maybe I shouldn't have used my debit card to pay for the licenses and ceremonies?*

No, it'll be fine. Since it's not a crime to help people follow their hearts, he won't be able to get a warrant to check my banking records for the receipts for my wedding gifts to the happy couples. And if he does, then I'll point out that I tried to sober them up with coffee first to make sure they were all able to legally make the decisions for themselves.

"You don't think any of them will figure it out if they wake up in bed with their new spouses tomorrow morning?" Kandi questioned as the first ceremony ended and the rings were passed to Emerald and Surfer Josh.

"No," Windy hoped, finally seeing a bit of a flaw in her plan. "They each have their own rooms, so we just have to make sure they each go back to their separate rooms when we get back to the hotel. Though now I'm kinda wishing we hadn't ditched Miller and Knight, so we coulda had their help getting some of these big guys to their beds before they completely black out."

"Yeah, maybe Cruz and Dane are still sober enough to help us with that?" Kandi suggested as Surfer Josh and Emerald walked down the aisle to start their ceremony.

"Perfect," Windy agreed, smiling at her bestie as the second couple started their vows. "And since they didn't come in here or the license bureau, they won't know that any of their coworkers got hitched, as long as we keep the copies of the licenses hidden."

"And we should probably make sure Kade, Magnum, and Trojan are sworn to secrecy about the ceremonies," Kandi added. "Surely, they'll keep our secret to make sure they don't get in trouble with Rick for not stopping any of the weddings."

"Yeah, that'll have to work," Windy agreed. "'Cause there's no way we'd be able to get Magnum up to his room if we were actually successful in getting him drunk enough to pass out and forget everything that happened tonight."

It only took a few minutes for Surfer Josh and Emerald to complete their ceremony with a much less chaste kiss than the one Crockett and Amethyst shared at the end of their nuptials. They quickly walked back down the aisle to pass the rings to Red and Chastity, who brought the heat level up even more by kissing passionately before the Elvis impersonator officiating their ceremony could even start. Getting those two to head to their separate rooms after they were married didn't seem like it would be quite as easy as she hoped.

Since she had to stay behind long enough to schedule a time for her to come pick up all their official photographs later in the week, she missed the debate about which couple should upgrade to the honeymoon suite back at the hotel. But when she finally walked over to the limo for them to all head back, she heard Kandi settling the disagreement among the inebriated couples.

"How 'bout you guys all go to your separate rooms and pack up your stuff, while Windy and I check to see if they have three honeymoon suites available? And if they do, we'll take care of changing your reservations and send a bellman up to each of your current rooms to carry your stuff to your suites, so the guys all have their arms free to carry their brides over the threshold."

Her suggestion was met with a chorus of "yeah," "sure," "that'll work," "perfect," "cool," and "yes," all said simultaneously by the three couples. Then, they all climbed back into the limo, where Kandi started passing out flutes of champagne to toast the three marriages on the drive back to the hotel.

Yeah, hopefully the extra alcohol will hit them soon enough that they'll forget about the honeymoon suites before we have to follow through with Kandi's new plan.

As they followed the wrestlers into the hotel and watched them split off, with the remaining single guys heading back to the club or to the casino, and the three newly married couples heading for the elevators or stairs to go to their rooms, Windy slowed her steps to talk to Kandi before they got to the front desk. "Do you really think they'll let us change the reservations for the six of them? And what happened to making sure they all went to their separate rooms, so Rick doesn't figure out we set this all up?"

"No, we can't change their reservations," Kandi chuckled. "But they're too drunk to realize that. And now they're each headed for their own rooms, where they'll probably pass out before bothering to pack a single thing. So, all we have to do now is go get our beauty sleep, and pretend like we don't know what they're talking about if any of them ask us tomorrow about why they kept waiting for a bellman to come help them change rooms."

"Still, to be on the safe side, we should probably go check each of their floors to make sure they actually make it to the right rooms." Windy wasn't sure how they could possibly make it up ahead of the wrestlers to verify that they went to their rooms, but she had to try something.

"Or we can just go spend a few minutes in the security room with Chuck to watch the cameras on their floors, so we can make sure they're each in their own rooms without getting caught," Kandi smirked, pointing to one of their regulars at the brothel where they worked, who was standing off to the side of the desk in his security uniform.

"Excellent idea," Windy agreed, looping her arm through her best friend's as they walked over to have a brief discussion with Chuck, who let them see a little more than they expected on the security camera in the stairwell.

"Chastity has some great tits," Kandi commented, as they watched Red and Chastity start their honeymoon before making it to either of their rooms. "But it would have been nice if they'd removed more of their clothing before fucking, instead of just dry-humping, so we coulda seen Red's dick."

<div align="center">~~~</div>

Monday, August 19, 2019, 10 a.m., Las Vegas, Nevada

"Oh, Liam," Rylie cried out, coming hard as Liam pounded her into the wall, fucking her with wild abandon in the stairwell leading up to their rooms. She wasn't sure how she got there with her arms and legs wrapped around the man she'd been crushing on since she started working with the GWA, her skirt pushed up to her waist and her blouse opened for him to be able to fondle her breasts as he fucked her, but she was oh so glad to find herself in such a decadent position.

"Foehck, Rylie, comb ahn me cahck," Liam commanded, his strong Irish accent coming out as he thrust in deep, holding still as he joined her in a simultaneous release.

They passionately kissed as the aftershocks washed over them. It was a kiss unlike any that Rylie had ever experienced, feeling electric, like she was being claimed by her soulmate. It was more than she ever dreamed possible, even in her nightly fantasies of hooking up with her older white coworker.

"Hmmm, beautiful, we have to hurry to pack up, so we can meet in the suite to have round two of the honeymoon before our flight out tomorrow." Liam's voice reverted to his normal New Yorker inflection as he lowered Rylie's feet to the floor, helping her adjust her clothing before removing the condom, tying it off, and tucking himself back in his slacks. He tossed the condom in the first trashcan they passed as they exited the stairwell into the hallway leading to their rooms.

"One more kiss, Hubby," Rylie insisted, puckering up for him as he stopped at the door to his room.

"As you wish, Wifey." Liam pecked her lips once more before turning her in the direction of her room down the hall and swatting her ass to get her moving in that direction. "Now hurry and pack your stuff, so I can carry you over the threshold of the honeymoon suite."

Ring! Ring! Ring!

Rylie Long rolled over to shut off the alarm on her phone, regretting using the loudest old-school ringtone she could find to make sure she woke up in time for her almost daily flights. While it was helpful most days when she was up late for a wrestling show and had to get up early the next morning to fly to the next city, the loud ringing wasn't so welcome when she woke up feeling more hungover than she'd ever felt in her life.

"Ugh! Of course, it was only a dream," she muttered, unable to speak too loudly because of the massive headache pounding behind her eyes as she looked around to see she was still alone in her standard hotel room. "All that talk about getting married with an Elvis impersonator as the officiant last night must have influenced my nightly dreams about Liam."

Rylie had developed a huge crush on Liam Connery, the Irish American wrestler who used the ring name Red, soon after her tryout with the GWA back in March. She'd been hired immediately and teamed up with the Canadian tag team known as Protection Detail because of how well her ring name of Chastity went along with Magnum and Trojan and their gimmick of promoting safe sex by tossing out condoms on their way to the ring. Harrison Thorne, who used the ring name Magnum, and Cameron Wentworth, who used the ring name Trojan, had just joined the roster two days before her tryout, and hadn't been on the GWA's weekly television program yet, so it was perfect timing to add her as their manager, in addition to her role as a wrestler. Surprisingly, though, she wasn't attracted to either of the Canadians, whom she was almost contractually obligated to become fast friends with to make their gimmick appear more real to the fans.

No, Rylie had instantly been attracted to one of the guys who worked as Protection Detail's opponents in some of their earliest matches, before they started their Spring feud with the Dangerous Twins and Leigh. It was strange because she normally didn't go for white guys, or guys that were at least ten years older than her twenty-four years. To be honest, before starting work with the GWA, if she'd had to guess which member of the tag team known as Red Velvet that she'd be most attracted to, then she'd have guessed it would be Dark Chocolate Dion Davis, not Red, AKA Liam Connery.

Dion was still almost ten years older than her, but at least he was Black like her, so they wouldn't have had as many cultural differences if they ever dated. Technically, she was only half Black since her dad was white, but her medium brown skin tone made it clear that her mother was African American, so she identified as Black, and growing up had mostly associated with the other Black kids. But within her first week working with the GWA, she'd seen how Dion was way too reserved and always went straight to his room after a show, instead of going out with the rest of the crew. While nobody else seemed to think he was seeing anyone seriously, she thought he had to be going to his room to call his girlfriend back home.

Liam on the other hand was the life of the party and made her feel welcomed into the tight-knit group of performers by including her in everything going on with the GWA, even more than the other women wrestlers. He never acted creepy, like he was flirting or anything like that. But he was always friendly, offering to help her with anything she needed, like lifting her bags up into the overhead compartment on the plane, or mastering a new move when she was practicing in the ring, and inviting her to join the group, both backstage and when they were going out in public. He even opened doors and pulled out chairs for her, like the chivalrous alpha men she'd previously only read about in steamy romance novels.

All the guys in the GWA exhibited similar gentlemanly behaviors, but for most of them, it was only with their girlfriends, wives, or children. *Maybe that's why I'm crushing on him so hard,* Rylie thought as she finally got out of bed and went to find some over-the-counter pain relievers and water to deal with her hangover. *Because he's the only guy to ever do those things for me. Well, besides my dad back when I was a little kid. But he's the only guy to do those things after I became an adult. And probably because it's just his nature and doesn't seem calculated, not like he's only doing those things to try to get laid.*

As she popped the pills in her mouth, Rylie noticed that her mother's wedding set, which she normally wore on her right hand, was on her left ring finger. *That's strange. Maybe I moved the rings last night when we were taking pictures to make the possibility of a Vegas wedding seem more realistic?*

She only vaguely remembered the pictures she'd been talked into taking while they were in Vegas, thinking they must have taken more than just the ones in the limo that she recalled being in with several of the other GWA performers the night before. But that was the only reason she could think of that was feasible for why she'd moved her mother's rings, especially since her father's ring was right where it normally was on her right pointer finger.

Since her parents died right after she turned eighteen, their wedding rings, her mom's journals, and a couple of photo albums were the only items of any value she had left to remember them by. She'd had to sell everything else to pay for their funerals and final medical expenses. Now she wore her mother's rings on her right ring finger and her dad's wedding band on her right pointer finger, or sometimes on her right thumb, only taking them off and stashing them in her locker when she was working.

She kept a couple of pictures of her family from her childhood in her wallet, but really needed to digitize the photos in the albums in her apartment back in Atlantic City, so she could keep them all with her. As it was, the albums were just too bulky to tote around the world while she was touring with the GWA. *I guess I know what I'll be doing while I'm home for our Labor Day break.*

After moving the rings back to her right hand, she didn't think anything more about why they were moved. She just went back to her normal morning routine, getting ready to fly out to the next city on the tour. As she brushed her teeth and washed her face, she wanted to kick herself for getting so drunk the night before that she crashed as soon as she hit the bed, not even bothering to wrap her hair first, much less strip out of anything but the shoes she'd worn to the **Sin City Showdown** after-party.

"Guess it's a good thing we're not flying out 'til noon today, instead of our normal nine a.m. boarding time. I'm still gonna need to hurry and get packed up, but at least I got a couple more hours of sleep than normal, so maybe this hangover won't be as bad as it could have been."

<div style="text-align:center">~~~</div>

Monday, August 19, 2019, 4 p.m., Reno, Nevada

As he made his way to ringside for the daily talent meeting, Liam Connery felt banjaxed after drinking way too much the night before. It'd been a while since he felt so hungover and had so many gaps in his memory after a night out. Yeah, he was still one of the first of the guys to hit the club after a wrestling show, but he'd quit getting hammered when he entered his thirties. At almost thirty-five, he really should have known better than to try to keep up with Windy and Kandi with the shots of Irish whiskey the night before. But apparently, he was dumb enough to believe he had the advantage of his larger size and Irish heritage to be able to go shot for shot with the two women, who had a decade of drinking experience on him.

Da would be embarrassed as hell if he knew two middle-aged women drank me under the table last night, Liam thought as he took a seat at ringside to listen to the boss go over the plans for that night's show. *He'd probably team up with Granda, all four of my brothers, and a few of my uncles and cousins to tease me mercilessly about it, too.*

Liam was the oldest of the five sons of Brian and Cathleen Connery of Belle Harbor, Queens, New York. And the only one of them who

15

Leah Mae Wright

hadn't followed in their father's footsteps by joining the NYPD. Though his middle brother, Rory, no longer worked in law enforcement, having opened Connery's Irish Pub after being injured in the line of duty, Liam still felt like a little bit of an outsider whenever his whole family gathered for holidays because of their lack of understanding of his career choices. Well, that and his lack of desire to immediately settle down in the old neighborhood with a nice Irish girl to give his parents the grandbabies of their dreams. It wasn't that he was opposed to one day having a family and living in the same neighborhood where he'd grown up. He just didn't want to do it on his family's timeline. *And I really don't care if my future wife has a single drop of Irish blood,* he thought as he forced himself not to picture the woman he wanted to one day fill the role of his wife.

He was so fed up with the pressure from his family to settle down that he'd actively avoided going home for the GWA's holiday breaks since the previous Thanksgiving. He'd gone to Heart's Destiny, Texas, that first break for the wedding festivities of one of the GWA's pilots, Anthony Burleson, and found he liked helping deflect other people's family drama more than dealing with his own. Anthony's mom and aunt ran a group of matchmakers that put his mom, granny, and aunts to shame. From that first trip to Heart's Destiny, they'd set their sights on matching him up with Anthony's cousin, Jen, and his tag-team partner, Dion Davis, with her twin, Julie.

While the Burleson girls were nice enough, and certainly very attractive, Liam hadn't felt anything more than friendship and mutual understanding about the constant matchmaking. At the end of that first break, Jen had asked him to come back for the Christmas break, not because of any desire to start a relationship, but because she'd needed the buffer from future setups with guys who might not be as understanding as he was about her not being interested in more than friendship.

Since Dion had come to the same kind of arrangement with Julie, they'd both gone to Heart's Destiny for every holiday break since then, even when they didn't have a wedding for one of their GWA friends to attend. In fact, Liam and Dion were scheduled to go back to Heart's Destiny in a couple of weeks to reprise their roles as buffers for the Burleson girls over their Labor Day break, when Jen and Julie's cousin was getting married, even though she wasn't marrying anyone in the

GWA for everyone in the company to feel comfortable attending, regardless of the fact that they'd all been invited.

He'd felt a little awkward about appearing to be dating Jen, when the whole company had gone to Heart's Destiny for James and Randi's wedding over their Memorial Day break, and again for Rick and Fiona's wedding over their Independence Day break. Especially when Rylie Long caught his eye from across the room at each of the wedding events they'd all attended. But in a way it was nice to have Jen to talk to as a friend to keep him from acting on his attraction to the much younger female wrestler. While he hadn't given Jen any specifics about why he'd needed a buffer as much as she had, he thought she might have figured out his secret the last time he was there.

Not that he could think about any of that right then. He needed to pay attention to what Rick was saying about the matches they had planned that night. Considering he still felt like shit from his hangover, he really hoped that successfully defending the tag-team titles the night before in their match against the Bama Boys, meant he and Dion had the night off. He could really use the time to hydrate and take a couple more over-the-counter pain relievers for his headache, which didn't seem to want to go away.

"I've been dealing with calls all day from our social media department back in New York," Rick started, confusing Liam, since he only posted on his GWA social accounts when he was working as a babyface, and Red Velvet, the name given to his and Dion's tag team earlier in the year, had turned heel back in the Spring, letting the social media department take over posting on their GWA socials. "They've had to take down several pictures from last night, trying to stop the rumors about which of you actually got married while we were in Vegas. But unfortunately, CNZ and a few other celebrity gossip sites grabbed screenshots before our team even knew about the pics to take them down."

Feck! I hope I wasn't so drunk that I posted pics from last night. Liam wanted desperately to take his phone out and look through the photo album to see what he might have done, but he knew better than to do that while Rick was lecturing them about social media etiquette and their responsibility to the company to maintain a professional presence online.

Leah Mae Wright

"There are now all kinds of rumors and speculation online and on the various celebrity gossip shows about who married whom in the GWA last night," Rick continued, looking around at them with that disappointed-dad look that still got to Liam, even though Rick was only three years older than him. "With several of you posting group shots outside of a wedding chapel, and at least one of our female performers sporting wedding rings on her left ring finger while surrounded by several of our male performers, there is now scrutiny about the legality of poly marriages that the Inglemans will have to go through again, even though they weren't part of this fiasco last night."

Liam couldn't help but look over at the women wrestlers on the GWA roster, knowing there were only a few of them who were single to be able to cause such a stir online. Rylie Long naturally caught his eye, where she was playing with the rings on her right hand. *No, it's the left hand for wedding rings, isn't it?*

He momentarily imagined himself pushing a set of rings on Rylie's left hand while standing in front of an Elvis impersonator. He had to look away from her to stop himself from wishing it was a memory of the night before, not just him being susceptible to a little wishful thinking from the images Rick had just put in his head. Unfortunately, when he turned away from looking at Rylie, his gaze landed on Tait and Reid Ingleman, making him feel even more guilty for whatever he'd done the night before than even his wishful thinking about Rylie a few seconds earlier.

Feck! Feck! Feck! Liam cursed internally, hating that his friends were going to be criticized once more for having a commitment ceremony that wasn't legally recognized as a marriage in any way, other than in their hearts and in the eyes of their friends. Yeah, Reid and Tait both called Kori their wife and each other their husband, and Kori called both Reid and Tait her husbands, but the only legal paperwork they'd done was when Tait and Kori each changed their last names to Ingleman, since neither polygamous marriages nor poly domestic partnerships were legal in the United States. *They really shouldn't have to feel like they're under the microscope again because some of us were drunk and stupid last night. I'm gonna have to think of something I can do to apologize to them for any part I might have played in them being thrust back into the spotlight of the celebrity gossip sites.*

Liam only vaguely remembered riding in a limo with Windy, Kandi, and a few of his fellow wrestlers after the party the night before. But he still felt the need to apologize to his friends if anything he did while inebriated put them in a position where they were uncomfortable because of the additional media coverage leading to trolls spewing hate-speech online.

Feck! I hope I passed out in the limo before the pics were taken, since climbing in it is the last thing I really remember from last night. He didn't let himself acknowledge that the only reason he probably remembered that was because he'd leaned on Rylie to help him in the vehicle, since he was so drunk he couldn't see straight at the time.

"Now I need to ask if there's anything any of you remember about last night that might help us get out ahead of a scandal before more pictures, or God-forbid, copies of marriage licenses, hit the internet." Rick implored them with his eyes to disclose what they remembered.

"No, I don't think any of us actually got married," Brandon Braddock, who used the ring name Blade, spoke up. "If so, we would've had some kind of evidence, like receipts for the ceremony or license or whatever. Right?"

"Yeah, I didn't have anything like that in my room this morning," Brent Crockett, who just used his last name as his ring name, agreed with Blade. "And since I'm pretty sure I'd have consummated the marriage if I'd tied the knot, I think it's safe to say waking up alone in my bed this morning is proof enough that I didn't get married."

"Did any of you wake up with visitors to your rooms this morning?" Rick looked over the wrestlers gathered around the ring, most of whom were shaking their heads, including Liam.

"Yeah, Archer's going through a phase where he's afraid there's monsters under the bed," Mountain Man Everest, whose real name was Tanner Everett, chimed in with a smirk. "But I don't think you're asking those of us who're married with kids."

"No, I'm just asking the thirteen performers who were in the pictures we've taken down today," Rick asserted, shaking his head at Tanner.

"You're gonna have to be more specific, Boss," Liam spoke up for himself and the rest of his hungover coworkers. "Some of us don't remember enough of last night to know if we were in the pictures or not. But I can say for sure that the only visitor I woke up with this morning was this massive hangover, and the only receipt I had on my bedside table was from my bar tab, which had enough bottles of Irish whiskey listed on it to cover for at least a dozen of us to be blackout drunk and incapable of walking down the aisle. And that's without even counting the long list of individual drinks and shots."

Damn, I think that's the closest I've ever seen Rick come to wanting to roll his eyes like his daughter does all the time.

"And look on the bright side, Boss," Crockett chuckled, holding up and shaking his phone, which he'd obviously just looked at the pictures on. "At least we were just posing with each other. This coulda been much worse if we'd been posing with a bunch of ring rats instead."

Oh feck! I really hope I passed out in the limo, Liam thought again as Rick glared at Crockett before starting to point out each of the offenders, starting with Crockett.

Unfortunately, Liam realized he hadn't passed out as he hoped when Rick called out his name next, along with all three members of Protection Detail, both of the Precious Stones, whose real names were Aiken Pearson and Teagan Shields, Surfer Josh Parker, Blade, Sawyer Owens, who used the ring name of Owen Sawyer, Cruz and Dane Bennington, and Killer Kade Carrington. He then informed them that they all had to take part in a refresher course with the head of the social media department on what they were allowed to publicly post on their GWA socials.

Feck! I know better than to post anything but narcissistic workout pics when I'm working heel, or positive fan interactions and foodie pics when I'm working face, which is why I let the social media people back at the office in New York handle most of my social media posts. So, what the hell was I thinking last night?

Probably that you wanted to fuck Rylie and you thought pretending to marry her would help you get in her pants. Liam imagined the voice of his youngest brother, Finn, replying to his mental question, as the rest of the people Rick had just named claimed to have also woken up alone.

Finn was five years younger than Liam, and the only one of his brothers who hadn't started getting tired of sowing his wild oats yet, which was probably why Liam imagined him as his inner voice. While he was serious about his job as a police officer for the NYPD,

Finn still took advantage of Liam's celebrity status and their similar looks to score with the ladies. He had so many one-night stands, the rest of the brothers joked that his bedroom had to have a revolving door to accommodate all of them coming and going. Of course, at almost thirty years old, Finn should be getting close to the point where he'd outgrow that habit like the rest of their brothers did, starting to look for serious long-term relationships once they left their twenties behind.

Liam had been the only one of the Connery brothers who persisted in consistently having one-night stands well into his thirty-fourth year of life. But he blamed his lack of serious relationships on his nomadic lifestyle while working for the GWA. At least, he had until March of this year, when Rylie Long joined the company, and his dick decided he no longer wanted any other woman.

Not that Liam had done anything to act on his attraction to the much younger performer. Oh, he hadn't been able to stop himself from being friendly and slightly flirtatious, but he'd never crossed the line to anything inappropriate, making sure he treated her the same way he treated the rest of the women he worked with, as just friends. Regardless of how his boss and coworkers had started falling in love and embarking on committed relationships in the last year, he knew better than to mix business with pleasure. Especially with a coworker ten years younger than him.

There was too much risk of a hostile working environment if things didn't work out between them. And even if they managed to get past the early dating stage to start talking about marriage and babies, like Rick and Fiona or James and Randi, the relationship would derail in just a few years, when he retired and she still had ten or fifteen years left of her career touring with the GWA.

Feck! I hope I wasn't so hammered that I let my dick take charge of the rest of my body last night. Liam had a brief flash of memory, but he couldn't quite pin it down to make any sense of it. *I said something to Crockett about Rick kicking his arse but not mine. Was that because I wasn't stupid enough to take pictures in the chapel? Or because me marrying Rylie could actually be spun into our next angle, once me and Dion finish this feud with the Bama Boys and Protection Detail finishes their angle with the Mountain Men?*

As Rick moved on from the issues the night before and started giving them their assignments for the show that night, Liam decided to wait to find out exactly who he was photographed with the night before and what was being said about him in the dirt sheets before he went to Rick and pitched the idea of a feud between Red Velvet and Protection Detail for Chastity's hand in marriage as a possible fix for the media fallout. *Hopefully, this'll all blow over in a day or two and it won't be an issue.*

"Dude, what the hell did you get up to after I went up to crash last night?" Dion questioned as soon as they were released from having to wrestle that night, finished sparring with a couple of the other guys while their coworkers choreographed their matches, and started walking back to the dressing room to change.

"Hell if I know." Liam shrugged as he pulled his phone out of his pocket to start looking through the photos. After scrolling through several pics of him and Rylie, and noticing that they were always side by side and touching in some manner, even when there were other wrestlers in the pictures with them, he realized that he'd obviously lost more of his inhibitions than he should have the night before. "But after seeing these, I'm pretty sure I'll never get that drunk again."

Dion leaned over to get a better look at the pics as Liam scrolled through a few more. He slapped Liam on the shoulder and chuckled at what he saw. "With the way ya'll were lookin' at each other in those pics, I don't think staying sober will be enough to keep ya'll from eventually hookin' up."

"Feck, man, I hope you're wrong about that," Liam groaned as they entered the locker room.

"Why? It's clear you're gone for her, so why are you fighting it so hard?" Dion clearly knew Liam way better than most people.

"'Cause she's too young," Liam sighed, dropping down on the bench in front of his locker. "Hell, I'm gonna retire sometime in the next two or three years, and I'll wanna start having kids and building a family as soon as I do. She'll still have ten or fifteen years of her career left then. And you've seen how she is after a show. She lives for being in the ring, so there's no way she's gonna wanna cut her career short to start having babies."

"You never know," Dion disagreed, shaking his head as he pulled his stuff from his locker to get a shower after their midday in-ring workout. "Falling in love changes priorities for a lot of people."

"Yeah, and how would you know?" Liam scoffed, grabbing his bodywash and a towel to hit the showers. "I don't see you giving up your plans for a twenty-year career to settle down with the love of your life."

"Maybe not yet," Dion smirked. "But I can definitely see myself retiring early for the right woman."

"Yeah? Does this right woman have a name?" Liam hoped deflecting the conversation to Dion's love life, or lack thereof, would be enough to change the subject.

While retiring early would work if his lady wasn't in the business, he knew pushing to wrestle past his prime to stay with her would be a disaster. He not only didn't want to be an embarrassment to her by getting sloppy in the ring by trying to push until he was too old to perform. But he also didn't want to take the risk that his in-ring skills would decline to the point that he was an injury waiting to happen. He wanted to retire early enough that he was still in great shape and able to keep up with the kids he wanted to have in the future. But he couldn't expect Rylie to give up her dreams for the future he envisioned, which other than the Irish bride, looked a lot like what his parents had and wished for him and his brothers.

"A gentleman doesn't kiss and tell," Dion shrugged, turning away so Liam couldn't read his expression. "But hopefully, I'll be able to tell you I've met my dream girl in the next couple of years."

Liam wasn't quite sure if Dion's vague statement meant he'd already met her, or if he just already had an idea of what he was looking for in the future Mrs. Dion Davis. But as a few of their coworkers, who also had the night off from wrestling, soon joined them in the locker room, he let the subject drop, grateful Dion did the same with his feelings for Rylie.

Chapter One

Rylie Long took advantage of the GWA show being in her hometown to go stay the night in her own bed, instead of checking into the hotel with the rest of the crew. As soon as they landed, she rushed straight to her apartment, wanting to air it out and clean any dust bunnies that had taken over the residence since the last time she was home for the Labor Day break a month before. While her landlord gladly emptied her mailbox anytime it got full and left her mail on the kitchen counter for her in exchange for a little extra money with her monthly rent, which she had set up to automatically transfer to his account at the same time her rent transferred to the Carson Condos account while she was on tour, Mr. Dobson drew the line at cleaning anything.

I'm definitely going to have to make sure someone else comes by to clean if we have any more water pipes burst this winter like we did last year, she thought as she unlocked her front door and let herself into her apartment. The previous winter, when a pipe had burst under her kitchen sink, he'd asked her for towels to sop up the water while he fixed the pipe, but he'd left them there for her to lug down to the laundry room to wash, once the repair was done. To be honest, she'd assumed he'd only asked for the towels to put down, so he wouldn't have to replace the cabinets or flooring from letting the water sit on the wood. *Though I'm not sure how we'll know if there's another issue like that if I'm not here to notice the water leak in the first place.*

After carrying her luggage to her bedroom and changing out of her dress and heels into yoga pants and a t-shirt, Rylie started opening windows before going to the kitchen to grab a dust rag and furniture polish from the cabinet where she stored her cleaning supplies. When she got there, however, she quickly got sidetracked by the stack of mail on the counter, deciding she needed to sort through it first, so she could put all the junk mail in the recycling bin and get it out of her apartment. *It's kinda hard to wipe down the counters with a month's worth of junk mail in the way. But I guess it's better than the five months' worth that I had to deal with over the Labor Day break.*

"I really should try again to convince Mr. Dobson to toss all these flyers and ads out, instead of stacking them up here for me to toss whenever I get home on my next break," she complained to the empty room as she sorted through take-out menus and various sales circulars, stacking them up to go to the recycling bin in the basement of the building. "Since my bills are all set up with electronic statements, he'd never have to bring anything up to my apartment if he'd toss the junk while he's already down there."

At least, that's what she thought, until she came across an official looking envelope with a return address from the Clark County Clerk in Las Vegas, Nevada. With her luck, he would have tossed it out with the rest of the mail, if she'd have convinced him to toss the junk. "Oh, holy hell! What did I do in Vegas? And why didn't I get this when I was home for a whole week last month to be able to figure it out sooner?"

Like the rest of her coworkers, who'd been reprimanded for their drunken antics almost seven weeks ago, she'd assumed that the Vegas photo situation was already resolved. Because the pictures on their phones and social media accounts were all taken in the limo and outside the chapel and license bureau buildings, and none of them found any receipts for a ceremony, marriage license, or anything to show they'd done more than take a few pictures, she hadn't thought it was possible that she or any of her coworkers had actually gotten married that weekend.

With trembling fingers, Rylie opened the envelope to pull out an official document that she'd never even imagined she'd one day see, much less actually hold in her hand. "Oh, fuck! Rick's gonna kill me! Or at the very least, fire me. Shit! Shit! Shit! How the hell did I end up actually getting married in Vegas? And to Liam, fucking, Connery!"

For the last seven weeks, Rylie had desperately tried to figure out if any of her nightly dreams of having sex with Liam were real memories of their drunk night in Vegas because some of the dreams included saying, "I do," in front of Elvis. But since she'd woken up in her own room the next morning, and hadn't felt any different in her vajayjay than she did from regular usage of her vibrator, she'd convinced herself that all the talk about the photos had tricked her mind into dreaming about how she'd wanted the night to have gone. "Holy shit! I guess there was some truth to those dreams after all. At least, to the ones where we got married anyway, if not the sexual dreams."

Forgetting all about needing to clean her apartment, Rylie quickly put the marriage certificate back in the envelope and carried it back to her bedroom to put it in her purse. She shut all the windows she'd just opened before changing back into the business attire she had to wear to meet the GWA dress code for traveling. She then grabbed her purse and wrestling gear to take an early trip to the arena. She needed to break the news to her boss and face the music for her screw up. "I guess I also need to break the news to my husband, too. Unless he already knows. I mean, we *were* in New York yesterday, so he should have gotten his copy in the mail then, right?"

Once she caught a cab to take her to the arena, she pulled the envelope out of her purse to look over the certificate of marriage once more. Sure enough, Liam's address was listed under his signature in one of the neighborhoods she thought she recognized as one of the wealthier areas of New York City. *What the hell? Why wouldn't he have said something at the show last night?*

Not that she had the time to figure that out right then. She wasn't sure if she'd been so flustered by the realization that she was married to Liam that she'd zoned out, or if she somehow got lucky enough to get in the fastest cab in town and made it to the arena in record time. But she soon found herself walking into the arena in an almost trancelike state, so she quickly toted her stuff to the women's locker room, stuffing her purse and gear in a locker and taking a moment to splash some water on her face to help her calm down a little. She checked the time on her phone before grabbing the envelope from her bag once more and going to find the owner of the GWA, Rick Robertson. *Fuck! It's later than I thought, so I must have zoned out in shock while I was in that cab.*

Since the wrestlers weren't scheduled to meet at ringside for another hour and a half, she hoped he'd be somewhere backstage, and not off with his wife and daughter for some midday sightseeing, which all the families who worked with the GWA tended to do quite regularly. First things first, she checked the room where the classroom was being set up, assuming he'd go there with his wife and daughter first. While Fiona and Britney were both there, Rick wasn't, so she planned to check the catering area next, assuming he'd be there, probably meeting with the bookers to plan out the show for later that night. Although she didn't see Rick, she did find both Ethan Abrams and Stone Fields, the GWA bookers, in catering.

"Hey, guys, I need to talk to Rick. You know where I can find him?"

"Yeah, he's around the corner in the alcove set up as his office," Stone replied, pointing her in the direction of where Rick's office had been set up when she'd met with him to sign her contract back in March.

"Thanks!" She didn't wait for them to say anything more, practically running to the office area.

Rylie vaguely registered that Allissa Walters and Dean Hunter were meeting with Rick and a few of the security guys who'd been traveling with them while dealing with Allissa's stalker situation. But she didn't think about how rude she was being by interrupting their meeting, shouting her apology as soon as she was within six feet of Rick's desk.

"I'm so sorry, Boss," she cried out as she came to a stop and held the envelope out to Rick. "I don't know how this happened. I swear, I thought we just took pictures at the chapel in Vegas, not that any of us actually got married! But when I went through my mail while I was at my apartment to drop off my stuff, I found our certificate of marriage. I guess it takes a little while for them to mail it from Vegas."

"Fuck!" Rick swore as he took the envelope from her and removed the marriage certificate. He then looked around at the rest of the people in his office space before looking at the document in his hand. "I'm going to let you guys handle the security situation without me while I deal with whatever fallout we're about to have from our last trip to Vegas."

"We've got it covered, Boss," Cage Dalton, the GWA chief of security, assured Rick as he ushered everyone but Rylie out of Rick's office area.

"I wonder who she ended up marrying," Allissa mused loud enough for Rylie to hear, as the group walked off in the direction Rylie had just come from.

"Who knows?" Dean chuckled and shrugged. "I'm just glad to know it's not one of us about to get their ass handed to 'em by Rick for that mess."

Yeah, I wish it wasn't me, too! Rylie thought as their voices faded with them walking to the one table in catering where she could still see them, but they were just far enough away that she couldn't hear what they were saying.

"Okay, this might not be too bad," Rick finally said after taking so long to look over the certificate of marriage that she assumed he had to have read the entire thing. Twice. "At least Liam is part of a tag team, so we can spin this into an angle between Red Velvet and Protection Detail. We'll have to go back through all the pics from that night and figure out which ones we can use to make it look like he tricked you into getting married and now he's demanding that you honor your vows and drop Protection Detail to be Red Velvet's manager."

"Does that mean you're not going to fire me for being too drunk and stupid and not even remembering that I got married that night?" Rylie was tempted to cross her fingers for luck like she'd done as a little girl, but figured she already looked unprofessional enough right then, so she didn't need to make it worse by acting like a child now.

"No, I'm not firing you," Rick sighed, shaking his head as he pulled his cellphone out of his pocket and sent off a text, presumably to Liam. Although, she supposed he could have texted everyone who'd been in the pictures in Vegas to give them all a heads up that they needed to check their mail as well. "Between the hangovers all you guys suffered the next day, remedial social media training, and now having to figure out the legalities of your situation, I figure you've been punished more than enough."

"Thank you, Boss," Rylie gushed, so grateful to still have a job that she was willing to completely change her gimmick, if that's what Rick wanted to keep her on the roster. "I promise, I won't ever screw up like this again. In fact, I've pretty much avoided alcohol since that night, just to make sure I don't ever do anything that might seem unprofessional in public."

"While I appreciate your efforts, I don't expect you to completely cut out alcohol when you're hanging out with your friends. Just maybe don't get so drunk that you don't remember what happened the next morning," Rick suggested with a very slight upturn of his lips. So slight that Rylie wasn't sure if it counted as a smile or not. "And maybe try to think about that night to warn me if there are others who got married that I need to try to spin into new angles, too."

"I still don't remember what I did that night, so I have no idea what anyone else did," Rylie admitted with a sigh. "Though I do have to wonder why Liam didn't say anything last night, since he should have found a copy of this certificate in his mail while we were in New York yesterday."

"I'd like to know the answer to that myself," Rick confided, "which is why I'll be asking him when he gets here. Along with everyone else who was in those pictures, so they can make arrangements to have their mail checked if we're not going to their hometowns in the next few days."

Well, at least, I'm not the only one who fucked up back in Vegas, Rylie thought as she took a seat to wait for her cohorts to arrive. *Though I really hope it's just me and Liam that got married, so this doesn't turn into an even bigger headache for Rick and the bookers to have to deal with before TV on Tuesday.*

<center>~~~</center>

Teagan Shields, who mostly went by her ring name of Emerald Stone, had a bad feeling when both she and her best friend and tag-team partner, Aiken Pearson, also known as Amethyst Stone, got a text from the GWA owner, Rick Robertson, to come straight to the arena while they were out shopping at the famous Boardwalk in Atlantic City. Rick never suddenly called anyone to the arena early. Oh, he might schedule an early afternoon meeting when it was time to renew a contract, but he never texted at the last minute to schedule something like that. Even when she and several of the other wrestlers had screwed up while out in Vegas and posted pictures to social media that weren't on brand for the GWA or their gimmicks, he'd addressed it in their normal briefing to get their match assignments for the night. So, if Rick was texting them to come in early, something really had to be up with the company to warrant the urgent message to report to him.

I wonder if this has anything to do with Allissa's stalker? Like, maybe he's started sending stuff to some of the rest of us, since he hasn't been able to get close to her?

When they got to the arena and found that all three members of Protection Detail — Magnum, Trojan, and Chastity — were already in Rick's office, her bad feeling got a whole lot worse. Especially when Red, Surfer Josh, Crockett, and Blade followed her and Amethyst into the meeting.

"What's going on?" Since her brash, aggressive heel character was just an extremely turned-up version of her normal personality, Teagan was the first of them to speak, needing to know why they'd all been called to this meeting.

"We'll get to that when everyone else gets here," Rick replied before indicating that they should all pull up chairs to get comfortable for whatever he wanted to discuss.

It didn't take long before Owen Sawyer, Killer Kade, Cruz, and Dane joined them, making her wonder if this meeting had something to do with the Vegas pics they'd all taken a couple months back. *Fuck! I thought we'd already been punished for that with the whole remedial classes for social media. What the hell happened now to bring it back up? And is Rick gonna punish us again for the same thing?*

"Are our Vegas pictures making the rounds on the dirt sheets again?" Apparently, Josh was thinking along the same lines as Teagan, so she made eye contact with him to let him know she agreed with his assumption.

"Not that I know of," Rick sighed, shaking his head. "But apparently, some of you did a little more than take a few pictures that night. Now we need to figure out who all among you actually got married, and get in front of the story before the dirt sheets get copies of the marriage certificates."

"No way," Blade protested, holding up his hands until Rick glared at him with an arched eyebrow. "I mean, we were pretty buzzed, but Sawyer and I bugged out back to the hotel with a couple of ring rats after taking pics in the limo and didn't even go to the chapel, so I know we didn't get married."

"And we stayed with the limo when everyone else decided to go in a couple of places," Cruz deflected, motioning between himself and his brother Dane. "We just went along to make sure they didn't end up in any of the seedier parts of town."

"And made sure the limo didn't pick up another party going back to our hotel and leave them stranded," Dane added. "Which is how we can vouch for Blade and Sawyer, 'cause we made sure they had another ride when they wanted to head back while everyone else was in the clerk's office."

"Well, then the rest of you might want to call someone, who can check your mail at home, to have them look for an envelope like this one," Rick informed them, holding up an envelope addressed to Rylie Long in Atlantic City from the Clark County Clerk in Las Vegas.

Holy shit! Chastity got married? Did she finally get brave enough to put the moves on whichever one of the guys she's crushing on but won't tell us about? Teagan just hoped it wasn't the guy she'd always had a little thing for, but hadn't acted on because she'd never felt her feelings were reciprocated. *No, Josh always seems to gravitate to the white girls, so him marrying Rylie would be as unlikely as him marrying me that night.*

It wasn't that she thought he discriminated when picking his conquests from the pool of ring rats that fawned over him everywhere they went. Truth be told, he was just as flirtatious with her as he'd been with all the other women wrestlers. He just didn't date coworkers, so his hookups were limited to the ring rats that gravitated to him, who were mostly white girls. Just like her rare hookups, back when she still had them, were mostly with Black guys because they tended to hit on her more than guys of any other race. She still felt uncomfortable just thinking about those guys while in the same space as Josh, even though it had been at least a couple of years since she'd allowed one of them to do more than walk her out of a club and give her a brief kiss before getting in separate cabs to end the night. *Come to think of it, he doesn't really seem to have a preference for blondes, brunettes, or red heads when he's flirting at our after-parties, so maybe it could have been him to marry Rylie?*

After being raised by a single mom, who was open and honest with both her daughters about her sex life, Teagan was kind of a sexual free spirit, not really having a preference for a specific race or nationality in her partners. While in her younger years, some people would say she inappropriately dealt with her daddy issues from not knowing her father by seeking out older men for her sexual partners. She liked to think of that time as when she experimented with men who were more experienced, so she could learn what she liked and what she wanted to avoid in her sexual relationships. Now that she was getting closer to entering her thirties, she was much more discerning when picking her sexual partners.

Whereas earlier in her career, she'd hooked up with anyone she'd found attractive who was also into her, now she had to feel some kind of connection with a man, other than physical attraction, before she'd even consider fucking them. At least, that's what she told her friends and coworkers whenever they noticed she was in a dry spell, so she didn't let on that her attraction to Josh was what was really holding her back. And while she very much wanted to be the one in control of her sexual encounters, she absolutely refused to chase after a man. Unfortunately, her indifferent act had led to a few instances of younger guys following her around like little lost puppies, which she wasn't quite sure if she enjoyed or not.

Oh, she'd relished the way a few of them had showered her with attention, but she didn't have the time or patience to deal with needy men. Her desire for control was more about deciding who she slept with, when it happened, and what positions and sexual acts they engaged in together, not wanting to be the dominant partner during the act itself. While it could be fun to role-play once in a while, she wasn't really into playing mistress to a subby boy.

She also wasn't interested in the over the top alpha guys, who wanted her to be submissive to them, either. While she didn't want to play the role of dominatrix, she had too hard a time trusting anyone, especially any man, enough to take care of her when she was vulnerable and at his mercy. So, she didn't want to be with a man who needed total control, either. Which was why the initial attraction she'd felt to Dane Bennington, when he first joined the roster the previous year, hadn't ever led anywhere other than friendship. Their one attempt at going on a date had ended with the most awkward goodnight kiss she'd ever experienced. So, while they still acted flirtatious with one another, it was all an act to run off overly aggressive ring rats when one of them needed a save. Or sometimes it was just to be aggravating, like they were an annoying brother and sister, even though they weren't related in any way.

When Dane had first joined the roster, she'd thought she saw a hint of jealousy from Josh because of how they acted with one another. But either she'd totally misread his expressions, or Josh had gotten over it quickly when he realized that adding another guy friend to her circle didn't affect the way she acted with him. She'd felt a little hurt that he hadn't acted on those jealous feelings she'd thought she saw. But she had more self-respect than to let one unrequited attraction get her down. If a guy wasn't interested enough in her to pursue her, she walked away, even with Josh.

Now she just hoped to one day find a man who was willing to let her take charge when she needed to, but who would challenge her to let him have control some, too. Someone who either also wrestled, or worked behind the scenes in the industry, so they could travel together to build a life as a couple. *And hopefully, when my Mr. Right comes along, my feelings for him will kill any residual attraction I still have to that stupidly sexy surfer.*

"Oh, shit, Chastity! You got married that night?" Amethyst voiced the question while Teagan was lost in thought, bringing her out of her head and back to the moment. "Who'd you marry?"

"I don't know, Red, who'd I marry?" Rylie glared at Liam Connery as she took the envelope from Rick to shove it in Liam's face. "And why didn't you say anything yesterday, when we were in New York, and you should have found your copy of this marriage certificate in your mail?"

Holy shit! Rylie married Liam? And why the hell didn't I see she has the hots for him before now?

It didn't matter that Rylie was glaring and obviously mad at Liam right then. The sparks between them were bright enough that Teagan was pretty sure they could be seen from outer space. When she thought back to the way Liam acted around Rylie since the first day she joined the roster, and the way Rylie responded to his chivalrous behavior, Teagan could clearly see that they'd each developed a little bit of a thing for one another.

Huh? Maybe this is the push they both need to take these sparks to the bedroom?

"What the feck?" Liam snatched the envelope from Rylie's hand and pulled out the document inside to look it over. "No, fecking, way. Why didn't we have copies of the receipts to pay for the license and ceremony, so we'd have known about this sooner?"

"I'm assuming Windy or Kandi paid for them," Rick interjected, "since they signed the documents as your witnesses. But you still should have found your copy when you checked your mail while we were in New York yesterday."

"I didn't go home to check my mail yesterday," Liam admitted, running a hand through his short brownish-red hair as he continued reading over the document in his hand. "But, feck, now I wish I'd have risked the lecture from my da to go home and look at my mail yesterday. If I had, I coulda got my lawyer started on the annulment. Now it's gonna hafta wait 'til our next break, so I can go sign whatever I have to sign in his office."

Oh, shit. What the hell is he thinking? Acting all pissed off like a damn fool ain't gonna fly with a sista like Rylie.

"Not if I can find a lawyer to handle it today," Rylie informed him, looking pissed as she yanked the paper and envelope back from his hands. She then turned back to Rick before continuing. "Do you need me for anything else? Or can I go make some calls to try to find a lawyer's office that's open on Saturdays?"

"Just be back at ringside in time for our normal meeting and to run through your match tonight," Rick replied with a pitying look at Rylie before turning to address the rest of them. "That goes for all of you. Make your calls now, and be back and ready to work at four."

As everyone else scattered, pulling out their phones to call home, Teagan sat there in shock. *Thankfully, we're going to Baltimore tomorrow, so I can check my mail without having to try to find someone else to do it.*

It wasn't that she didn't have family or friends to call on to do it for her. She had plenty of them. Maybe only a few who were blood related, but at least twice that many who felt closer than blood. *And every single one of them is nosy as fuck, and would probably get me in more trouble by posting a pic of the marriage certificate online, if they found one in my mail. Which is why I'm not stupid enough to give any of them a key to my house.*

"You okay, Emerald?" Rick gave her a questioning look, when she didn't leave his office space with the rest of the group.

"Yeah, just thinking about how glad I am that we're going to Baltimore tomorrow, so I don't have to call my mom or sister to have one of them break into my house to check my mail."

"Why would they have to break into your house?" Rick looked at her with confusion in his eyes. "Don't you have someone go by and pick up your mail already? Or have the post office either hold it or reroute it to one of their addresses?"

"No, I have a mail slot right beside my front door, with a box right under it to catch everything while I'm gone. Though if the post office will hold it, I might check into that in the future, just so my box doesn't end up overflowing with junk mail between our holiday breaks." That had been a problem when she went home for the Labor Day break because she'd spent her Memorial Day and Independence Day breaks in Texas at weddings, so she hadn't been home to empty the box since March, the last time they'd had a show in her hometown. Teagan had to wonder what the rest of her friends did if they didn't have a mail slot on their homes like she did.

"Oh, well, then I guess you have a little free time before you need to be back here for the show tonight." Rick looked down at his watch, making it clear that he had other things to deal with, so she really needed to vacate his office.

"Yeah, I'll probably just go hang out in catering," Teagan decided as she stood to leave. "That way I'll be close by in case my name shows up on a marriage certificate that someone else finds when they call home."

"Let's hope it doesn't," Rick ever so lightly chuckled, as she walked out of his office.

"For real," Teagan agreed, not verbalizing the rest of her thoughts. *'Cause I'd hate to have forgotten my wedding night, especially if it was with a certain surfer. And let's be honest, even blackout drunk, I'm sure he'd be the only one I'd willingly walk down the aisle with. Not that I think he'd agree to it, so I doubt I have to worry.*

She wasn't sure what it was about Josh Parker that she'd always found attractive. On the surface, the blond-haired, blue-eyed white boy from Southern California had absolutely nothing in common with a Black woman from Baltimore. But from her first day working with the GWA five years earlier, he'd treated her with the respect of an equal.

Yeah, he really wouldn't agree to marry me if he knew I still think of him as a blond, even though he's argued several times that his hair is sandy brown. Like sand isn't so light brown that it's almost yellow, which is honestly more accurately described as blond instead of brown, regardless of whatever modifiers he adds to it. Maybe next time he decides to rant about not wanting to be stereotyped as an airheaded blond, I should suggest the commentators call his hair sandy blond. I mean that's got to be better than the way his mom described his hair color as dishwater blond the last time he ranted about it when we were in San Diego, right?

Thinking back on the various conversations she'd had with Josh over the years, she couldn't stop herself from trying to figure out what it was that made her start to fall for him. Well, besides how much fun it was to rile him up over trivial stuff like his hair color. Yeah, it had been surprising to find out they shared a love of seafood and TV crime shows, or that they often listened to a lot of the same music. But the same could be said for several of their coworkers, so Teagan didn't think their common interests were really what attracted her to him.

Maybe it was because he'd been the first person backstage at her tryout to compliment her on her skills in the ring. Or maybe it was because he was so easy going and flirtatious with everyone, without making any of the women uncomfortable because they all knew he wasn't trying to get in any of their pants. But she'd been down to fuck with Josh from her very first night working with the GWA. At least, until he'd gently explained his no-fucking-coworkers rule, so they'd just been friends ever since.

I wonder if that rule would still apply if we were married? 'Cause, damn, I'd enjoy the hell outta the conjugal benefits of being his wife. She couldn't stop herself from looking over at him on his phone as he paced around the catering area.

Like that's ever likely to happen. And even if it did, he'd probably be right there with Liam in scheduling time with a lawyer to annul the marriage. Teagan shook her head at herself as she joined Aiken at one of the tables in catering, overhearing news she couldn't believe she was hearing about her best friend and tag-team partner.

Well, shit! If both the other single women in the GWA got married that night, then maybe I did, too, 'cause there's no way I'd let my girls have all the fun without me. Oh, I really hope I'm right about drunk me only being willing to walk down that aisle with Josh. If not, then I'm going to have to schedule the earliest appointment with a lawyer I can get on Monday and hope we can get it annulled before I have to be on the GWA plane to Virginia.

Hell, if Josh isn't willing to change his rules even if we got married, then maybe I'll need to schedule that appointment anyway, even if I got lucky enough to have married my crush in Vegas.

~~~

Aiken Pearson felt more nervous about making the phone call to her dads to have them check her mail than she'd been in the meeting with her boss, even when he'd dropped the bomb on them that at least one couple had gotten married in Vegas back in August. After everything Theo and Shawn Pearson had to go through to get their union legalized as a gay couple, Aiken was afraid they'd be disappointed in her, if she'd gotten married on a drunken whim when they weren't there to walk her down the aisle. She was especially afraid her costume designer papa, Shawn, would be hurt by not having the opportunity to design her wedding gown, the way they'd always planned since she was a little girl.

As the meeting broke up and her coworkers shuffled around making phone calls, she took a few moments to just breathe and do a short walking meditation, trying to figure out how to break the possible news to her dads. Finally, after taking a seat at one of the tables in catering, she dialed their home number, hoping they were both at home. *Maybe I should've called Daddio's cell and let him break the news to Papa if they're off on different film sets today.*

Theo Pearson, the dad she called Daddio and the man who'd legally adopted her in Vietnam when she was only a little over a year old, was a motion picture director and producer, and the least dramatic of her dads. So, if she could only get ahold of one of her dads, she hoped it would be him.
~~~

Shawn Pearson, the dad she called Papa and the man who'd had to wait until Theo had gone through all the legal processes for a single-parent adoption in Vietnam and officially moved Aiken home to Los Angeles before he could start the process of a second-parent adoption to become her legal parent in the state of California, on the other hand, was dramatic enough for all three of them. Unfortunately, as a costume designer who didn't have to be on set daily, he was also the most likely to be at home on a Saturday.

She recalled the stories they'd told her about meeting on a movie set, when Shawn worked as an assistant costume designer, and Theo said he'd fallen for the gorgeous Black man because he had more stage presence than all the actors on the film combined. Later, when it was just the two of them, Theo had explained to Aiken that by "stage presence" he meant "diva attitude," but he never worded it that way in front of Shawn, so he wouldn't think it was anything but a compliment, the way it was intended.

Papa is definitely gonna show his "stage presence" if I got married in Vegas, she realized as the phone started ringing. *But maybe the fact that I don't remember it will be enough for him to forgive me. And depending on who I mistakenly married without him, or the dress he's been designing and modifying for years, present for the ceremony, maybe I'll end up getting it annulled, and eventually giving him another opportunity to do all the wedding planning I know he's looking forward to doing with me?*

Aiken didn't let herself think about the possibility of wanting to stay married if she'd drunkenly tied the knot. While every single one of the guys that she'd been photographed with that night were exceptionally hot, after five years working with the GWA, they'd all been pretty much relegated to the friend zone.

Oh, she'd thought about hooking up with several of them when she first started working with the company. Some more than others, like the sexy lumberjack, Brent Crockett. But then she saw the fallout of a bad breakup, when a couple still had to work together to fulfill their contracts. Tension backstage was at an all-time high back then, with everyone walking on eggshells to keep from getting caught in the crossfire of one of their separating coworkers' arguments. She, along with everyone else in the locker room, had been thrilled when neither of their contracts were extended, and they left the GWA, just a few months after she'd started.

Since then, Aiken had forcibly stifled any attraction she felt toward any of the guys who worked for the GWA, which greatly disappointed her papa. And even though she often joked around with her coworkers about there being a dearth of male ring rats compared to the women who hit on the guys all the time, she also didn't feel comfortable hooking up for a one-night stand with the men who occasionally hit on her, so she usually took care of her own needs with a vibrator. Not that she wanted to mention that to either of her dads, even though she knew Papa would be proud of her for taking charge of her sexuality.

Her dads had always been great about being open to discussing sex with her, but since neither of them had girl parts, or were interested in having sex with girls, they hadn't been much help in explaining her body to her or helping her figure out what she wanted in a sexual relationship. Luckily, she'd had sex-ed class before she started having periods, so her teacher had already gone over all the information she needed to tell her dads what to buy in advance.

Unfortunately, that same sex-ed teacher hadn't been as thorough when discussing the actual act. She'd focused more on telling them they should abstain as long as possible and teaching them how to properly put on a condom for when they felt they were in love and no longer able to abstain. Needless to say, neither Aiken nor her high school boyfriend had a clue how to make it pleasurable for her when she finally lost her virginity.

Her experiences with her college boyfriends weren't much better. It wasn't until she started reading steamy romance novels that she learned a few things that sounded like they'd work for her. But by then, she was well ensconced in her professional wrestling career and not in one place long enough to find a steady boyfriend, so she'd only sort of tried them on herself with toys, instead of following Papa's advice to date one of her colleagues.

Maybe if I did get married that night, it'll be to one of the guys Papa thinks is hot. Then maybe he won't be as upset by it? But that'll only work if I'm also attracted to the guy and he reciprocates the attraction to want to give staying married a try. Which I'm not sure is possible with the players on the GWA roster. I doubt many of them

Leah Mae Wright

would be willing to quit spending every night with a different ring rat to stay faithfully married to me.

When the answering machine finally picked up, Aiken disconnected the call and let out a sigh of relief. *Awesome! Now I can call Daddio's cell. And hopefully, when he checks my mail, he won't find anything to upset Papa.*

She quickly scrolled through her contacts to pick the right number, feeling relieved when Daddio picked up after only one ring.

"Hey, Baby Girl. What a wonderful surprise to hear from you today." She could hear an engine running and traffic noise in the background, and assumed he was in his car, which meant he was using his Bluetooth over the car stereo and anyone in the car with him could hear her.

"Hi, Daddio," she chirped, intentionally sounding more cheerful than she felt at the moment. "Are you in the car? Is Papa with you?"

"Yes, we're both here, Aikey Baby," Papa chimed in, sounding just as chipper as she was pretending to be at the moment. "Just on our way home after brunch with friends. Where are you and what are you up to today?"

"I'm in Atlantic City," she informed her dads, trying to figure out how to tell them why she was at the arena over an hour before she was due to report for work. "I, um, am already at the arena…"

"It's a bit early for you to be there isn't it?" Daddio sounded concerned, obviously picking up on her underlying tension, even though he couldn't see her to recognize her nervous tells.

"Yeah, technically I've got about an hour before I'm supposed to be ready for rehearsal," she explained, using the term they'd understand due to their movie backgrounds, instead of the match run-through, or sparring practice that more adequately described what she did in the afternoons before the GWA's nightly shows. "But several of us were called in early for an update on the situation from Vegas a few weeks ago."

"An update? What kind of update?" Daddio questioned as Papa squealed, "Oooh! Did some of you enjoy the honeymoons for your pretend weddings and are finding out that what happens in Vegas sometimes shows up at home nine months later?"

"Are you asking if our daughter is pregnant?" Even without being able to see them through the phone, Aiken knew Daddio was glaring at Papa as he barked out the question.

"I am not pregnant," Aiken assured her dads, just as Emerald, her best friend and the other half of the Precious Stones, joined her at the table. "And since we're all on birth control, I doubt any of my coworkers are either."

"Well, then why else would you need to get an update on that situation from Vegas?" Papa's tone of voice clearly indicated that he was rolling his eyes at both her and Daddio. "Unless more pictures leaked out that we haven't seen yet."

"No, there weren't any new pictures that leaked out." Aiken took a deep breath before elaborating. "You remember Rylie, the new girl who joined the roster in the Spring?" Aiken waited for her dads to confirm they remembered meeting her when the GWA was in Los Angeles the week before the Vegas show before continuing. "Well, she's from here in Atlantic City. And when she went to her place, instead of the hotel with the rest of us, she checked her mail and found an envelope from the Clark County Clerk's office in Las Vegas with a marriage certificate inside. So, now the rest of us need to have friends or family members check our mail to make sure we didn't also get married that night."

"Married! You got married without us there to walk you down the aisle? Or wearing the dress I'm designing just for your wedding day?"

Aiken had to pull the phone from her ear to save her eardrum from Papa's dramatics. "I don't know if I got married or not. I don't remember it if I did. Geez, Papa, I don't even remember leaving the VIP lounge that night, or taking any of the pictures. But since we've all seen them online, I know there's a possibility that I did. And if so, then I've got to deal with it before I can even think about planning my real wedding, if and when I ever meet my Mr. Right."

"So, what do you need us to do, Baby Girl?" Daddio asked, thankfully stopping the dramatics just as he turned off the car.

Wow, talk about perfect timing, if they just got home.

"Just go through my mail and see if there's anything in there from the Clark County Clerk's office." Aiken lived in the guest house on her dads' property, so she knew it wouldn't be difficult for them to go through the basket in her living room that their housekeeper put her mail in while she was on tour. "If so, then I need you to open it and tell me who I married."

"I'm on it," Papa exclaimed, just before she heard a car door slam.

"Give me a second to switch from Bluetooth to speaker mode, and I'll follow him in there to make sure he doesn't scatter the rest of your mail in his haste to find the envelope," Daddio reassured her with a sigh. A few seconds later, she heard his car door shut a lot quieter than Papa's had before he spoke again. "You still there?"

"Yes, Daddio, I'm still here," she smiled, imagining the scene at her home in West Hollywood. She knew Theo was calmly walking from the garage to the guest house on the other end of the property, while Shawn had already sprinted there and was probably already frantically flipping through her mail.

"Oh. Em. Gee. Theo! Our baby married the hunky lumberjack we've been drooling over since she first started working with the GWA!" Papa's shouting was so loud that, even though she didn't have her phone on speaker, Aiken worried Crockett might have heard his tirade from the other side of catering, where he was on the phone and staring at her.

From the way her eyes bugged out, it was obvious Emerald had heard every word from across the table, so it was theoretically possible that some of their other coworkers had also heard him.

"Crockett?" Aiken barely croaked out the name, unsure if she was loud enough that anyone could hear her over the way her papa was squealing on the opposite side of the country through her phone.

"Yes, Aikey Baby! Brent Crockett is listed on this marriage certificate as *your husband*!" Papa confirmed, still not regulating his voice. "I mean, I'm still upset that you got married without me and Daddio there, and not wearing the perfect dress. But I can forgive all that, since you clearly share my taste in men, and gave me the hot, hetero version of Daddio as a son-in-law."

Aiken had to laugh at Papa's description. Yeah, Daddio and Crockett both had medium brown hair and green eyes, but that's where the similarities between the two men ended. Daddio was clean cut with a slight build and a quiet, staid personality. In addition to having long hair and a beard for his lumberjack gimmick, Crockett was taller, more muscular, and way more boisterous than Daddio.

"Oh, Theo, can you imagine how drop dead gorgeous our grandbabies are gonna be?!" With the way Papa kept gushing about his buff and burly son-in-law, Aiken didn't have the heart to tell him that she wasn't sure if they'd stay married or not.

Thankfully, Surfer Josh walked over and sat down beside Emerald, giving her a reason to get off the phone.

Oh. Em. Gee! Did Emerald marry her secret crush?

"Um, okay, now that I know, I guess I need to go, so we can talk and figure out what this means for us."

"Okay, love you, Baby Girl. Let us know if you need anything from us." Thankfully, Daddio understood her need to get off the phone, disconnecting the call before Papa could start trying to talk her into planning some kind of reception for the next time they were in Los Angeles.

"Yeah, yeah, I get it," Josh huffed into his phone, shaking his head, and looking exasperated by whoever he was talking to. "But it'll have to wait until my next break, 'cause the only time I'll be in San Diego between now and then is on a Sunday, and I won't have time to meet with anyone before flying out on Monday morning. Just put it in my top desk drawer and I'll pick it up then if I need it."

He got quiet for a moment before practically shouting, "No! Do not take a picture of it! I don't need a digital copy now. And if it ends up online, you're fired."

He paused again as the person on the other end of his phone spoke. "Because I'm about to talk to her to find out who she's got checking her mail, so I'll know that if it's leaked it'll only be by you or them. And considering what I know about her, I don't think she'd send anyone to check her mail that would post it online. So, it'd have to be you who leaked it."

He pulled his phone from his ear and looked at the screen before blowing out a harsh breath and dropping the phone in the front pocket on his shirt. Josh then turned to Emerald and grinned. "Hey, Wifey, please tell me the person you have checking your mail is trustworthy, so I can fire my PA if our marriage license ends up online."

"I'm checking my own mail tomorrow when we first get to Baltimore," Emerald replied, apparently before all his words registered in her brain. Her eyes bugged out as she looked up from where she'd been playing a game on her phone to gape at Josh in shock. "Wait. Did you just call me *Wifey*?"

"Yeah, according to Sarah, my PA, we got married in Vegas," Josh informed them with an ornery grin spreading on his face. "So, I figured *Wifey* was the moniker you'd like best. But if you really hate it, I can always go with *my blushing bride*, or *the old ball and chain*, or *my old lady*."

"How 'bout you just stick to calling me Teagan or Emerald. That way I don't feel the need to hurt you." Emerald glared at Josh. "Rick's gonna be pissed enough to find out we got married, we don't need to add domestic violence charges to our list of transgressions before either one of us has actually seen the marriage certificate to verify it."

"Yeah, I'm gonna go and give you guys some space before the violence breaks out," Aiken chuckled as she stood to go talk to her husband about what they needed to do. She didn't give them a chance to reply before she walked over to where Crockett was pacing and looking through his phone. *Oh wow, Crockett is my husband!*

"I guess you found out we're married?" Crockett asked as soon as she walked up, not looking exactly thrilled about the revelation.

"Yeah," Aiken replied, feeling somewhat awkward discussing it when she still had Papa's descriptions of him running through her mind. *Stop! Aiken Thi Pearson, you can't start lusting after him just because he's temporarily your husband and you totally agree with Papa that he's the hottest guy on the roster.*

"I'm sure your dads are pissed at me for taking advantage that night," he sighed, still looking down at his phone. "But I swear, I don't remember doing anything inappropriate…"

"I know you didn't take advantage or do anything inappropriate," Aiken assured him, reaching out to place her hand on his forearm in what she hoped he'd take as a comforting gesture. "And my dads aren't pissed at you. Disappointed at not getting to walk me down the aisle maybe, but not pissed."

She decided not to mention how Papa had been excited at the prospect of having him as a son-in-law. Things between them felt uncomfortable enough, so she didn't want to make them worse by mentioning Shawn's crush on him.

"Well, you can let them know that I'm looking into what we need to do to get it annulled," Crockett informed her, finally putting his phone back in his pocket and looking up at her. "My dad thinks us being so drunk we don't remember getting married is sufficient for meeting the requirements for grounds to annul, but he's not sure if we need to file in Oregon, California, or Nevada because of the residency requirements."

"Oh, okay," Aiken replied, unsure how she'd break the news to Papa that Crockett wanted an annulment. "Just let me know what you find out, so we can figure out when's the next time we'll be in whatever city where we need to file."

With that, she turned and briskly walked to the women's locker room, needing a little time alone to process the irrational feelings of rejection she had running through her right then.

Geez, why does it hurt so much that he wants an annulment? It's not like we were in a relationship and he's breaking my heart by breaking up with me. We're just friends and coworkers, so it shouldn't matter that he wants to make it like the marriage never happened. So, why do I feel so crushed that he doesn't even want to try dating to see if we can make things work between us before jumping straight to dissolving the marriage?

Get it together, Aiken! Do not cry over a marriage that wasn't even on your radar two hours ago! Or at the very least, don't cry until you get somewhere private, so nobody sees what a fool you are to think you could actually be woman enough to tame the biggest player on the roster!

Chapter Two

Josh Parker barely slept the night before after finding out he'd married Teagan Shields in Las Vegas almost two months ago. That was partially because of the fit his personal assistant had thrown when she found out he wasn't single and available anymore, and partially because of not knowing how he wanted to handle the situation with his new wife. Well, maybe not exactly that he didn't know what he wanted with Teagan, but more that he didn't know how to make it happen. Unfortunately, before he could think about transitioning his friendship with Teagan into a romantic relationship, he had to deal with the unrequited feelings of his PA. He couldn't exactly pursue a relationship with his new wife, to whom he'd always been attracted from the first moment she came to a GWA show for her try-out match, when his personal assistant was living in his home and acting like a jealous lover.

When he'd first done his lifelong friend, Ben Nash, a favor by hiring his baby sister, Sarah, to house sit for him while he was on tour, he'd thought it would just be a short-term thing to give her a place to stay when she lost her job. Then she started taking care of things around the house and convinced him to hire her as his PA, when there was an issue with his flight arrangements for a holiday break that he couldn't handle himself while on the GWA plane without cell service. Next thing he knew, she was taking calls from his business advisors and financial planners, and keeping him from missing any important correspondence when he didn't check his email every day.

He'd never once gotten the impression that she was interested in him as anything more than a boss, who paid well and let her live in his guest room for free. He'd certainly never seen Sarah as anything more than Ben's little sister, who'd needed an easy job. He'd also never thought she'd act the way she did when he called her to have her look through his mail, either.

Since he had most everything set up for electronic statements and automatic payments, he didn't get much more than junk mail at his house in La Jolla. Other than Christmas cards and various announcements and invitations from his family, whenever one of his cousins graduated or got married, most everything else was sent to his email. So, Josh just assumed Sarah tossed the sales papers and take-out menus with coupons that he'd never use, unless they were something she'd use while she was house sitting, before putting the cards and such on his desk, where he often found them when he went home on a holiday break or when the GWA had a show in San Diego.

When he'd called her to ask about an envelope from the Clark County Clerk's office, he'd assumed it would be no big deal for her to look on his desk to see if he had something. He didn't realize that she'd actually gotten the envelope from the mailbox a little over a week ago and had already opened it, which was why she'd been in a bitchy mood the last time he'd talked to her, when he'd asked her to send flowers to his mom for her birthday on October first.

Apparently, she'd figured out that the marriage happened the same weekend as the picture scandal had blown up and had already made some phone calls to lawyers about what he needed to do to get it annulled.

Damn, come to think of it, she'd been bitchy a couple weeks after the pictures came out, when I got home for our Labor Day break, too. But then I'd joked around with Ben about getting in trouble for faking wedding pics on my GWA socials while I was home that week, and she seemed to think it was funny.

Now I can see that she'd only chilled out about it after she found out we all thought it was a joke and didn't think we'd really gone through with getting married. And because she thought it was a drunk mistake, she thought I'd want her to do the preliminary research on how to get an annulment.

I mean, if it was anyone but Teagan that I'd wed, I'd probably be grateful for her finding out what I'd need to do to dissolve the marriage. But damn, me not wanting to annul the marriage to Teagan doesn't give Sarah the right to threaten to send pics of the marriage certificate to CNZ and claim to be my jilted girlfriend to get her fifteen minutes of fame.

After only talking to Teagan for a few minutes the day before, Josh had called Ben to get him to make sure his sister didn't do anything stupid. He'd also gone in and changed all his passwords on his online accounts that Sarah had previously had access to, so she couldn't do any damage by posing as him in an email. He'd sent messages to his financial planner, lawyer, and other business advisors to let them all know that she was no longer authorized to do anything on his behalf, but he wasn't sure if any of those messages would be seen before Monday. He hadn't officially fired her yet, but he'd made it clear to Ben that it was happening, just as soon as he heard back from his attorney about what steps he had to take to make it official and legally evict her from his house.

He felt a little bad for deciding to fire her regardless of whether she posted his certificate of marriage online or not, after telling her that he'd fire her for posting it. But the more he thought about it, the more he realized that Sarah's attitude and insolence couldn't be tolerated, or she'd likely make Teagan extremely uncomfortable, if he somehow convinced his wife to give him a shot and brought her to his house when they were in San Diego in a little over a month.

I've hated myself for over five fucking years for following my stupid rules about not dating anyone I work with, and immediately friend-zoning Teagan when she first joined the GWA roster. But I'm not about to make that mistake worse by continuing to keep her in the friend zone now that we're married. What he'd actually hated was how guilty he'd felt every time he spent any time with a ring rat, when he'd actually wanted to be with Teagan. Even flirting with other women, in whatever club he ended up in after the GWA's almost nightly shows, felt too much like cheating on her, so he'd pretty much quit hooking up with any of them.

The only times he let anything go past a little bump and grind on the dance floor was when Teagan left the club with another guy. But even then, he might finger-fuck a ring rat, or let a ring rat jerk him off in a nightclub bathroom, but he never took them back to his room to actually fuck them. If he couldn't have Teagan's pussy, he didn't want anyone else's, so those random encounters weren't nearly as pleasurable for him as he imagined her hookups with other guys were for her. They were just his way of trying to keep from thinking about what she was doing with guys who weren't him, when he'd normally have gone back to his hotel room to jerk off to fantasies of her.

Surely, marrying her that night is some kind of sign that we can make it work, and won't implode our careers by trying to have a relationship, Josh hoped, thinking maybe being married to Teagan was the push he needed to break his self-imposed rules and go after the woman he really wanted to be with for the rest of his life.

The only time he'd been tempted to break his rule about not fucking coworkers was about a year before, when the Bennington brothers joined the company. Teagan and Dane seemed to have developed an instant connection, which for the first few weeks Josh thought went beyond friendship. He'd been irrationally jealous of how they'd flirted with each other almost constantly. But then one day he'd overheard Dane talking to his brother in the locker room about what a disaster his date with Teagan had been the night before. Hearing Dane describe their goodnight kiss as feeling like he was kissing his sister eased Josh's jealous feelings. Now he knew the only times they acted flirty with one another were when they were messing with each other like siblings, or whenever really aggressive ring rats were hitting on one of them in a club and they needed a save. It was actually the best breakup he'd seen in his time with the company. If they were ever officially a couple to have a breakup, that is.

Yeah, there've been a few couples I've seen over the years who've screwed the pooch by not separating business from pleasure. But there's also been several more couples that seem to be living the dream of wrestling and having a family with spouses they clearly love unconditionally. If there's even the slightest possibility I can have that with Teagan, I've gotta take the chance and try. And I should probably get started on trying now, instead of waiting until Sarah is completely out of my house before letting Teagan know I wanna see where things can go with us.

With that decided, Josh followed Teagan when they got off the company plane in Baltimore, needing to catch up with her before she left the airport to head to her house. He couldn't believe how fast she was able to walk through the airport while wearing a pair of sexy-as-fuck, red-soled, black stilettos that brough her up from her normal five-foot-seven-inch height to just a couple inches shorter than his six-foot-two.

"Teagan!" Josh hollered to get her attention, when he realized she was going in the direction of long-term parking, instead of the rental car lot like everyone else. "Teagan Shields-Parker!"

"What the hell, Josh?" Teagan spun on her heels, glaring at him.

"What? Do you prefer just Teagan Parker?" Josh grinned as he caught up with her.

"No, I prefer Emerald when we're out in public, so none of the fans can figure out who I am to start stalking me, like that asshole is stalking Victoria," she barked at him. "Besides, until I actually see the certificate with my own eyes and hold it in my hands, I'm not sure I believe it actually happened. And you really shouldn't be giving anyone in the airport hints about anything they can start trying to dig up and cause more issues with Rick and our angles."

"I'm sorry, Emerald, I wasn't thinking…about any of that." Josh ran a hand through his sandy brown hair nervously, glad he kept it cut in a shaggy surfer style so his agitation wouldn't be obvious by messing it up, even though he absolutely hated being referred to as a cliché whenever someone described him as a typical Southern California blond surfer. To him that description made him think of having hair that was bleached out to the point that it was almost white, which wasn't an accurate depiction of his hair color. So, he always thought of his hair as sandy brown, since it was closer to the color of playground sand than the white sand that always seemed to be the most popular in advertisements for the beaches of Southern California. Of course, that always led to heated discussions with his mom, whom he inherited his hair color from, since she referred to hers as dishwater blonde. "I just wanted to get your attention, so I can come with you to see the certificate for myself, too. And I thought we might wanna talk about what happens next if that paper says what I think it will."

"What happens next is that we start calling attorneys tomorrow to find out what we have to do to get it annulled or file for a divorce," Teagan hissed, keeping her voice low as she resumed walking with him tagging along beside her on the walkway between the airport and the parking lot. "If we'll even be able to file for either, since we're never really home to actually meet with an attorney, much less appear in court. And if we do manage to physically meet with someone and file, who knows if we'll meet the residency requirements to file with how rarely we're actually at our homes. Does owning property, paying taxes, and having a driver's license listing my address in Baltimore qualify me as a resident of Maryland, when I'm actually traveling outside the state eighty-five percent of the time? Or will we have to wait 'til the next time we're in Vegas to file there 'cause that's where we got married?"

"I have no idea," Josh replied, knowing Sarah had already compiled the information for the state of California, but he hadn't paid much attention when she was rambling it all off the day before to know if that was where they needed to file or not. "But since it'll be at least our Thanksgiving break before either of us can take some time off to find out, I thought we might wanna try dating or whatever until then before deciding if we want to go to all the trouble of dissolving the marriage."

"Wait a second, Mr. I-Don't-Date-Coworkers." Teagan threw the hand not pulling her rolling suitcase up in his face as she stopped and spun on him once again, somehow not dropping any of her other bags from her shoulders. "Are you telling me that you want us to date? And possibly not dissolve this marriage?"

Damn, she's hot when she's feisty. Josh couldn't help but smile at his sexy wife. "Yeah, I am. I mean, marriage has worked out for more of our coworkers than the few couples I saw implode earlier in my career. And if there's anyone on the roster that I can see being able to make it work with, it's you. So, why not give it a shot and see what happens? Worst case scenario, we kiss once and realize there's no chemistry and end up going through all the legal shit. Best case, we set the sheets on fire in every hotel we stay in from now until we retire, and then split our time between Baltimore and San Diego, so our kids get to know both our families."

"And what happens if we think there's chemistry, but it quickly fizzles out when we annoy the hell outta each other? Do you think we'll still be able to act professional and not jeopardize both our jobs with a messy breakup?" Teagan pulled her keys from her purse and clicked the key fob to unlock her silver Lexus IS 350 as she turned once more to walk a few spaces down to where her car was parked.

As he followed along behind her, Josh looked over her car and appreciated how close to perfect it was for Teagan. *Sexy and sleek, just like her*. The only thing that would make it more consummately her would be if it was emerald green, which he knew was her favorite color and the inspiration for her ring name.

"We're not gonna annoy the hell outta each other," Josh declared adamantly, dropping his bags, and waiting until the trunk opened to take her luggage and load it for her. He put his luggage in the trunk as well, after loading hers. "If we were gonna do that, it woulda happened before now just from being friends and working together all the time. And I really don't think we'll have any problems with chemistry."

"Yeah, well, until I see this marriage certificate for myself, I'm not willing to test my luck to find out."

As Teagan got in the driver's side, Josh joined her in the passenger seat, grateful she hadn't argued about him tagging along to her house. He knew he'd probably have to get a ride to the hotel from one of the guys after they got to the arena later, but he wanted to spend as much time with Teagan as he could now, even though he didn't think she'd be ready for him to spend the night in her bed anytime soon. "Then we'd better go check your mail before we plan our first date."

Teagan rolled her eyes at him as she started the car and backed out of the parking space. "So, did you end up firing your PA? Or are you waiting to see if she posts the marriage certificate first?"

"I haven't officially fired her yet," Josh admitted as she drove. "But I blocked her access to all my online accounts and left messages for my legal and business advisors to find out what I need to do to officially fire her, and get her out of my house, since she's also my house sitter."

Josh stopped short of telling Teagan about Sarah's inappropriate crush on him, but he did fill her in on how he'd ended up hiring his friend's little sister. If firing Sarah ended up turning out as messy as he feared, he knew he needed to start laying the groundwork now to keep Teagan from being too upset by the situation later.

"Wow, and you really think your friend's sister is gonna stab you in the back by posting it online?" Teagan gave him an incredulous look when she stopped at a red light. "I'd think after you stepped up to give her a job and a place to live, she'd have more loyalty than that, especially since you're friends with her brother and have presumably known her for quite a while."

"Yeah, Ben and I grew up together, so I've known Sarah since she was a baby," Josh sighed, remembering back to when he and Ben were seven years old, and Ben complained at school about the new baby crying in the middle of the night and waking him up. "In fact, there were a few years when I was in elementary school that Ben only came to my house to play after school 'cause we hated having to be quiet while his baby sister was napping. It really pissed him off, since she cried like a banshee in the middle of the night and didn't get in trouble for waking him up, the way we got in trouble for waking her up in the middle of the afternoon. Now, I know it's ridiculous to think a baby should be punished the same way a second grader was. But man, it felt like a major ordeal back then."

"Second grade?" Teagan arched an eyebrow as she turned into a neighborhood. "So, you were what? Seven or eight when she was born?"

"Yeah, seven," Josh confirmed, nodding as he looked out at the single-family homes in the neighborhood Teagan was weaving their way through.

"Then I guess it makes more sense that she might not be close enough to her brother to care about screwing you over online."

Josh knew he should probably mention the inappropriate crush then, but he just couldn't do it. Luckily for him, Teagan pulled into a driveway at a cute little brick house, giving him an excuse to change the subject. "Wow, I expected you to live somewhere bigger and flashier than this."

"It's actually bigger than it looks from the street," Teagan informed him, shaking her head at him as she put the car in park.

"It must go pretty far back then, 'cause it looks like a cute little cottage from here." Josh couldn't imagine the one-story home could possibly have more than one bedroom. "How many bedrooms and bathrooms do you have?"

"Three bedrooms, four bathrooms," Teagan smirked as she turned off the car and got out. "And I know it looks like it's just a single story, but it's actually a three story, with the master bedroom and bathroom taking up the entire top level since the attic was finished out to be livable. And the basement is underground, so not only can you not see it from outside, but also there aren't any windows, which makes for a great theater room."

"Nice." Josh quickly followed her as she walked up to the front door, leaving their luggage in the trunk of the car for the time being. "I guess I just expected the outside of your house to be as ostentatious as you are in the ring as Emerald Stone, and then the inside to be as comfortable and down-to-earth as you are when you let us see the real Teagan."

"Yeah, well, all you get here is Teagan." She shrugged as she unlocked her door. "Emerald only appears in Baltimore at the airport and the arena."

"Cool," he chuckled as he followed her inside, unsure what else to say without sounding like even more of a douchebag than he already was by rambling about her house.

As they walked into the open floor plan of the living room, dining room, and kitchen space, he had to agree that it certainly felt bigger inside than it appeared from the outside. The two-tone taupe walls were accented by white cabinets and trim, which looked exceptionally sharp on the decorative beams attached to the ceiling, which was painted to match the darker taupe lower portion of the walls. The granite countertops and mosaic-tiled backsplash in the kitchen perfectly matched the taupe and white of the rest of the room, while bringing in the darker brown of the wood floors and a few shades of gray to tie in the stainless steel appliances. The same could be said of the wood dinette set and various side tables, and the comfortable looking brownish-gray sofas and chairs that filled the rest of the space.

Teagan sat her purse and keys down on an end table before turning and pointing to a wooden box, which appeared to be about a quarter full with sales flyers and was pushed against the wall behind the door, right under the mail slot. "Thankfully, we only have a month's worth of mail to go through, so it shouldn't take us long. I normally dump it out on the dining table to sort through."

"Guess we'd better get to it." Josh locked the front door after shutting it. Then he picked up the box and carried it over to the dining table to help her sort through it all. Only instead of dumping it and risking making a mess with all the different sized envelopes, sales papers, and flyers, he tried to push it into somewhat of a stack and lift it out in chunks, so they each had a stack to go through, instead of both trying to go through the same messy pile.

Once the box was empty, Teagan carried it back over to put it back in place under the mail slot before sitting down in the chair beside him to start sorting. It didn't take but a few minutes of them working in silence before they had most everything from the box stacked in a junk mail pile to go in the recycling bin, a few envelopes in a separate stack for Teagan to go through later, and the envelope from the Clark County Clerk's office in Teagan's hands for her to open right then.

"Damn, I guess it really is true." Teagan's hands were shaking as she opened the envelope and pulled out their combination marriage license and certificate of marriage.

Josh leaned over closer to her, so he could read it at the same time she did, needing to verify it with his own eyes. *Thank fuck! Sarah wasn't lying yesterday when she read my bride's name to me over the phone.*

Sarah pranking him about whom he'd married had been Josh's biggest fear in the whole situation. He'd have been fine if neither one of them got married in Vegas, but he'd have been devastated if Teagan had married anyone but him, or he'd married anyone but Teagan.

"So, I guess we need to start planning our first date, Mrs. Parker." Josh draped his arm over her shoulders as he turned and grinned at his wife. "You wanna take me to your favorite restaurant in town for lunch? Or would you rather eat here after giving me a tour of our Baltimore home? Maybe make out a little in that theater room after I carry our luggage up to our bedroom?"

"You are not seriously suggesting sleeping here tonight?" Teagan glared at him incredulously as she dropped their marriage certificate on the table. "Don't you think we should maintain our separate hotel rooms while we try this dating thing for a little while, so nobody gets their hopes up that we'll end up staying married?"

Too late. My hopes are already up.

"I mean, you know Randi, Fiona, and Kay are all gonna flip when they find out we're married," she went on, reminding him of the matchmaking tendencies of the newly married women who worked with the GWA. "And they'll get Shauna, Holly, and the rest of their whole happily-ever-after club on board with treating us like a couple, when we're not even sure we have the chemistry to make it work."

"Fine, I'll just carry your luggage in, then," Josh conceded, before wagging his eyebrows seductively. "But I think we can disprove your lack-of-chemistry theory with that make-out session I just suggested."

"Yeah, you're gonna have to earn a make-out session," Teagan scoffed, turning in her seat to face him. "I'm not taking you down to my theater room until after you prove we have chemistry with a single kiss, right here, right now."

"Hmmm, bossy, I like it," Josh smirked as he turned in his seat to face her, adjusting his arm around her shoulders to cradle the back of her head in his hand, being careful not to mess up her braids. With his other hand, he tipped her chin up, savoring every moment as he leaned in and kissed his wife for the first time that he could remember. At least, he assumed he'd kissed her during their wedding ceremony and just didn't remember it, like most of the rest of that night.

As he brushed his lips over hers, he felt a shock of electricity pass between them that momentarily triggered the memory of feeling that same kind of jolt while kissing Teagan when they were standing in front of an Elvis impersonator. But unlike that first kiss that was just ceremonial, Josh took his time with this kiss, needing to prove to her just how much chemistry they had together. He moved his mouth over hers for several long seconds before licking along the seam of her lips to coax her into opening her mouth for him to truly taste her.

Teagan didn't let him control the kiss for long, gripping the lapels of his jacket to pull him in closer before winding her arms around his neck and running her nails through his shaggy, sandy brown curls. She not only opened for him, but she also plunged her tongue into his mouth, returning his ardent passion lick for lick.

Within seconds, she was out of her chair and straddling his lap, grinding her pussy against his hard-as-steel cock as they frantically tore at one another's clothing. She somehow managed to loosen his tie enough that she pulled it out of the knot at his throat at the same time she ripped his light blue dress shirt open, sending the buttons flying across the room. Without breaking their kiss, Josh shrugged off the shirt and navy-blue jacket at the same time, needing his arms free to shove her burgundy dress up her thighs and over her hips. He only stopped pushing it up when he got to the band that was tied around her waist.

"Let me help you with that," Teagan insisted, breaking their kiss as she moved her hands down from where she'd been caressing his chest to undo the ties at her waist.

"Yes, ma'am," Josh agreed, lifting her off his lap and placing her on the table, so he could unfasten his belt and slacks to give his cock more room while she removed her dress. As much as he wanted Teagan, Josh didn't think he needed to actually remove the rest of his clothing because he didn't think she was ready for more than a little foreplay. So, he planned to kiss every inch of her she was willing to expose, hoping to eat her pussy until she came on his tongue and fingers before dealing with a massive case of blue balls the rest of the day.

Fuck, I can't wait to find out if her pussy tastes as sweet and spicy as she smells. What is that scent? Vanilla? Brown sugar? But there's something else, too, that adds that earthy, spiciness I love. Something that keeps the sweet vanilla base notes from making me think of a bakery.

He thoroughly enjoyed the view as she revealed the sexy, sheer matching bra and panties that did absolutely nothing to hide her gorgeous umber tipped tits and the neatly-trimmed little landing strip of black curls between her legs. He couldn't resist leaning forward to trail his lips along the rich mahogany swell of her breasts over the top of her burgundy bra as he reached around her to unfasten it. Just as he got it unhooked and was planning to lower the straps down her arms so he could suck on her diamond hard nipples, Teagan stopped him by pulling his hair to lift his mouth from her chest.

"Oh, no, don't you dare stop with just unfastening your pants," she protested, shaking her head at him as she stood from the table and took a step away from him before dropping her bra to the floor. "You need to finish stripping and get a condom on that big dick. Now!"

"Fuck, Teagan," Josh groaned at the loss of having her in his arms, unable to believe she was ready to take his cock when they'd only been kissing for a few minutes. "Are you sure? Don't you wanna let me get you off with my mouth and fingers first?"

"Next time," she panted out, bending to push her panties to the floor and stepping out of them without taking off those sexy-as-fuck, red-soled, black stilettos. "Right now, I just need you to fill me up with your cock."

Josh didn't need to be told twice, standing from the chair as he reached into his back pocket for his wallet. He opened his wallet and got out the condom in it with one hand, while shoving his navy-blue slacks and boxer briefs down with the other. He then toed out of his dark brown oxfords and navy-blue socks before stepping out of his pants and underwear to stand naked before his wife as he tore open the condom package and rolled it down the turgid length of his dick.

"How do you want me first, Josh?" Teagan teased him as she strolled naked around the room, running a hand over each surface as she named it. "On the table? Or maybe on the counter, since it's a little taller? Or would you prefer to fuck me against the wall? Or maybe bent over the back of the sofa, so you can play with my ass while you fuck me from behind?"

"Maybe I'd rather sit on the sofa and have you ride me," Josh suggested, thinking that position would allow her to take him as slowly as she needed to stretch to accommodate him, but only if that was what she wanted for their first time, too. He stroked his cock as he stalked around the room behind her, eager to get her back in his arms, knowing he wanted to take his time, no matter how they made love this first time. "So I can suck on your sweet tits while we consummate our marriage."

Teagan's eyes flared wide at the realization of what they were about to do. "I guess if we do this, we won't be able to get an annulment, huh?"

Josh shrugged, unwilling to mention that because they were inebriated when they got married, they could technically have kids together and still get an annulment in California. At least, that was what he thought he remembered Sarah telling him the day before, but he wasn't sure if her info was accurate or not, so there was no point in mentioning it right then and ruining the mood.

If it was up to him, they wouldn't ever need to look into their options because they wouldn't ever want to dissolve their marriage. But it wasn't just up to him, so he had to give her another opportunity to back out. "It's not too late. We can still wait and just date for now if you want."

No matter how much his cock disagreed with his words, Josh would gladly get dressed and spend some time winning her over before they had sex, if that was what she wanted. He'd have to get mostly dressed and go out to get a shirt he could actually button from his luggage before they could leave for their first date, but he wasn't embarrassed about going outside shirtless, if it didn't bother her.

"No, I don't wanna wait," Teagan decided, stopping in front of the sofa, and pointing for him to sit down. "After that kiss, I know I'll regret it if we stop now."

Josh followed her lead, sitting down where she directed him. "I don't want you to do anything you'll regret, Tea. But I don't want you to feel like I'm pressuring you for anything, either."

"Oh, please," Teagan scoffed as she moved to straddle him once more. "You're not pressuring me for anything. Hell, if either of us are pressuring the other, it's me pressuring you, since I was the one who wanted to fuck you the first night we met."

"Yeah, that feeling was mutual," Josh chuckled, as she rubbed her wet pussy along the underside of his cock. "I was just too much of a chickenshit to go against my rules after Rick signed you to the roster that night. If you hadn't gotten a contract immediately after your try-out match, I woulda given you my dick as a consolation prize."

"Oh, like that wouldn't have been awkward when I kept practicing and came back for another tryout the next time the GWA was anywhere near Baltimore," she laughed as she reached down and lined up the head of his cock with the tight opening of her dripping wet pussy.

"Maybe it woulda been the push I needed to get my head outta my ass and break my rules with you?" Josh suggested, starting to lose his train of thought when Teagan slowly sank down on his dick, taking him one slow inch at a time. He ran his hands over the smooth sepia skin of her thighs as his eyes locked on where she was joining their bodies, rejoicing in the feel of being inside her for the first time. "Instead of wasting five years, when we coulda been doing this all along."

"I'm just glad that us getting married pushed you to break your rules with me now," Teagan confided as she ran her hands over his chest, making him tingle everywhere she touched him. "Now, shut up and fuck me already."

"Yes, ma'am," Josh grinned as he gripped her hips and held her still for him to thrust up into her perfect pussy, only giving her a couple more inches before backing off and repeating the process to let her gradually open up to take all of him. He leaned forward and kissed her once more, needing to taste her more than he needed to talk things out right at that moment.

She returned his ardent kiss until he worked his dick all the way inside her. Then Teagan gripped his wrists to pull his hands off her hips, nipped his lower lip with her teeth, and took control once more. She rode him like she was the World's Surf League Women's Champion and he was the most bitchin' wave to earn her the title.

Loving the feel of her tight pussy squeezing his cock, Josh reveled in letting her show off her sexual skills, moving his now empty hands up to play with her bouncy boobs. He couldn't resist them any longer, dipping his head to suck one nipple while lightly pinching the other. He bucked his hips in sync with her movements, hoping to make this first time last so he wouldn't look like a two-pump chump to his wife.

Hmmm, my wife, he thought as he grazed his teeth over her nipple before releasing it and kissing his way to her other breast. "Yeah, ride me, Wifey."

"You sure are bossy, Hubby," Teagan teased as she scraped his scalp with her nails to grip his hair and guide his mouth to her nipple. "You really need to keep your mouth full, so you don't distract me with all that talking while I'm trying to use your big dick to get myself off."

Oh, no, sweetheart, Josh thought as he planned for how he could take control of their lovemaking. *I'm not just a human dildo for you to use to get off. I'm your man. The man responsible for all your orgasms from now on.*

Josh didn't stop sucking on her sweet tit as he wrapped her in his arms and flipped her to the side, essentially performing a mini-belly-to-belly suplex to lay her on her back on the sofa with his body covering hers. The new position allowed him to take charge as he plowed into her, circling his hips to make sure he rubbed her G-spot with his cock every time he ground his pubic bone on her clit.

"Oh, fuck, Josh," Teagan panted as she wrapped her legs around him, poking him in both ass cheeks with the heels of her shoes. "Yes, just like that. Fuck me."

Josh didn't care that her stilettos stabbed him each time he pulled out before plunging back inside her slick sheath. Fucking Teagan felt so amazing that he wouldn't have even cared if he ended up having to have Doc, the GWA's resident physician and athletic trainer, stitch up the stiletto holes in his ass afterward, so he wouldn't bleed through the board shorts he wore in place of wrestling tights for his match that night. All that mattered to him at that moment was making his wife come on his cock.

Josh tweaked her nipples as he kissed his way up her chest and neck, blowing in her ear before commanding, "Come for me, Teagan. Come on your husband's cock." He didn't miss a beat as he continued plunging into her pliant pussy, even when her inner walls tightened with the first waves of her release.

"Oh, fuck, yes, Josh," Teagan cried out, digging her nails into his back as her whole body spasmed in orgasmic bliss.

No matter how much he wanted to hold out to give her at least one more orgasm before he came, Josh couldn't maintain control when her pussy squeezed down tight on his dick. He felt his balls drawing up and that distinct tingle in the base of his spine that signaled he was too close to hold back any longer. Each contraction from her release triggered a responding spurt of his cum into the condom separating them.

"Fuck, Teagan!" Josh came so hard that he feared the condom couldn't hold it all, unconsciously reaching down between them to clamp his hand around the base to keep it from leaking before he found the energy to pull out and roll off of her.

"Yes, you need to fuck Teagan on the regular," she giggled as the aftershocks washed over them. "But first we need to get up and get dressed, so we can grab some crab cakes at Jimmy's for lunch before we have to be at the arena."

Before Josh could catch his breath, Teagan pushed him off of both her and the sofa, sending him tumbling to the floor between the sofa and the coffee table before jumping up and starting to gather her clothes. "Yeah, I'm gonna need a little recovery time before I can go out and get another shirt from the trunk of your car first."

And fuck, after that, I'd rather stay here and eat your pussy instead of crab cakes for lunch. But, what's that saying Dad's always going on about when Mom ropes him into doing stuff? "Happy wife, happy life." I guess my first task for following Dad's example to make my marriage work is going to eat crab cakes at Teagan's favorite restaurant. At least, I know our shared love of seafood means she'll be taking me somewhere we'll both enjoy.

So, like the good husband he wanted to be, Josh got up and put on the pants she tossed at him before going out to bring in both their luggage for the night. After carrying everything but their wrestling gear up to the master bedroom, he found a shirt that still had all its buttons before going to his wife's favorite Baltimore restaurant, where he officially met his new in-laws.

~~~

As he walked into the locker room to change into workout clothes before reporting for match run-throughs at ringside, Brent Crockett felt like the world's biggest jackass. That feeling had started after the brief conversation he had with Aiken the day before, when they first found out they were married. He knew they'd both been shell-shocked at the revelation, but he still felt like he should have spoken a little kindlier to her when they talked about how to handle the legalities of their situation after that drunk night in Vegas.

She'd tried to cover it up, but he'd clearly seen her eyes start to glisten with tears when he'd mentioned getting an annulment. She'd walked away from him before he could think of how to backtrack to ask how she wanted to handle the situation before making the decision. Then she'd pretty much avoided him ever since, sticking with the other ladies backstage all night and not going out with the rest of the crew after the show. He hated that he'd hurt her by passing along the info his dad had given him without thinking she could possibly want to do anything else.

He wasn't intentionally trying to be an ass. But after growing up as the only son of a single dad because his mom took off when he was just a little kid, Brent hadn't ever thought he'd ever get married, so he wasn't prepared for how to behave like a husband. Hell, considering he'd modeled his dating life after his dad's, which was virtually nonexistent, he had no idea how to even act like a boyfriend. And even though he felt like he was friends with all the women on the GWA roster, he mostly treated them like he did the other guys he
~~~

worked with, so he wasn't sure how to treat a woman he'd married while drunk in Vegas.

He'd never done relationships. He had hookups with ring rats and random women he met, but he never even spent the night with any of them. He'd always been a single, carefree guy, who had sex when the urge struck, and the women he was with always understood their hookups were a one-time thing with no strings attached. And if the woman wasn't on the same page, it didn't happen.

In fact, it'd been several months since he'd hooked up with anyone. His last hookup had been in the back room of the local bar with a ring rat who'd come to town at the same time as the whole GWA, when he was in Texas for Rick and Fiona's wedding, which was over a month before his own Vegas wedding night seven weeks ago. The sex wasn't bad, but it wasn't great either. The most memorable part of the whole hookup was having to give her the money for a new phone after he'd stepped on hers in the middle of having sex and ground it into several pieces under his size twelve work boots, which he'd pulled from his gimmick clothing to wear with his jeans that night.

Looking back over the years he had to admit most of his sexual encounters were pretty much the same. A physical release with no emotions or feelings involved. To be honest, they were mostly forgettable, which was probably why he'd slowed down on the one-night stands and fucked his hand a couple times a day instead. *Damn, it must be a sign that I'm getting old when I start thinking that jerking off is just as satisfying as fucking a ring rat.*

Now that he knew he was married, he also knew he couldn't hook up with any of the ring rats at the club after the GWA shows anymore either. While he was too young at the time to remember specifics about his parents' fights before they split up, he couldn't help but think his mom had to have cheated on his dad and ended up running away with her other man. After seeing how devastated his dad was after their breakup, Brent couldn't fathom hurting anyone like that. So, whether he'd intended to get married or not, he wouldn't cheat on his wife, even if that meant he only fucked his hand until they could legally end their union. *Guess it's a good thing I'm just as happy with the release I get jerking off as I am when I fuck some random chick. But damn, it might be nice if I could fuck my wife while I'm not getting any other pussy.*

Leah Mae Wright

Fuck! With as drunk as we all were that night, could I have actually fucked Aiken afterwards and just don't remember it? Or was I so sloshed that I ended up with whiskey dick and couldn't consummate the marriage? If that's the case, then it's just another reason we could use for getting an annulment.

But not if she actually wants to see if we could make a marriage work, he realized, thinking about how Aiken seemed to observe the married couples who worked with the GWA with a look of longing on her face. *Shit, the way I've seen her get that wistful expression on her face whenever she looks at the families playing with their kids backstage, I bet that's what she wants for her future — marriage, babies, and happily ever after. That's probably why she never hooks up with any of the guys who flirt with her when we all go out after a show, 'cause she knows it'll only be a one-night stand and not the start of the relationship she wants with her Prince Charming.*

But, hell, I'm not exactly cut out to be her Prince Charming either, no matter how fucking hot I've always thought she is. While she's great at working heel as Amethyst Stone, when she's just being herself, Aiken is too much of a sweet little Disney princess for an asshole like me. He was so pissed at that realization that he flung his locker open, causing the locker door to bang into the locker beside it.

"What the fuck, Crockett?" Blade Braddock snapped at the sound. "What's got your panties in a twist today?"

"Nothing, man," Brent replied, yanking the rubber band out of his long hair, and shaking his head before starting to change out of the suit he wore to and from the plane and hotels that day. "Sorry, didn't mean to scare ya like that."

"You didn't scare me," Blade scoffed, swapping his dress shirt for a t-shirt as he, too, changed for going to the ring. "Just wondering if you're gonna work as stiff with me in the ring as you are with that locker, if Rick follows through with that plan to have you turn on me to team up with Josh and steal the Precious Stones, since ya'll married the girls who've been in my corner during my feud with the Valors."

"No way, man." Crockett didn't think that plan would work. "For one, doing that would turn you face and Josh heel, not the other way around like he mentioned, which won't work for your gimmicks. And for two, trying to turn me and both of the Stones face would make the roster way too face heavy, if it would even be believable that turning

on you would make us babyfaces. I don't know how he's gonna break you and the Stones apart without killing your current angle, but when he does, it'll end up with me versus Josh, and the girls being torn between their sisterly bond and each sticking by their man. And that's only if the dirt sheets find out we got married. As long as we keep it under wraps, and quietly get the marriages annulled, he shouldn't have to change any of the current booking."

"Yeah, but what happens if my PA leaks my marriage certificate, like I'm afraid is gonna happen any day now?" Surfer Josh interjected as he started unbuttoning his white dress shirt. "Or if we decide to stay married?"

Wait. Wasn't he wearing a blue shirt earlier?

"Are you and Emerald thinking about staying married?" Brent watched his friend closely, trying to figure out if the guy who'd always adamantly declared he'd never date a coworker was seriously thinking about staying married to a woman they worked with. *Yes, he definitely had a light blue shirt on when we were on the plane this morning. But that was before he went home with Emerald to verify that what his PA told him about the marriage certificate at his house was true. What the hell happened at her house for him to have to change before coming to the arena?*

"We're gonna try dating for now," Josh confided with a shrug, trying to act nonchalant, even though his smirk looked awfully smug. "Since we can't do anything about meeting with lawyers until our next holiday break anyway, we thought it might be better to see if we like being married before deciding what to do."

Holy shit! I bet he had to change his shirt earlier 'cause he got lipstick on the blue one while making out with his wife at her place after looking at their marriage certificate.

"Is that why you changed clothes since the plane this morning?" Blade chuckled, proving he was on the same wavelength as Crockett with his thoughts. "'Cause you messed up the others during your conjugal visit with your wife this afternoon?"

"A gentleman doesn't kiss and tell," Josh replied. Too bad his giant grin gave him away without him having to tell them any of the details. "Ain't that right, Dean?"

"Absolutely right," Dean Dangerous agreed, as he walked past Josh, just as Josh removed his shirt and hung it in his locker.

"Especially when the scratches on your back tell us all we need to know about what you were up to with Emerald earlier today."

"While you're lookin', Dean," Josh chuckled as he unfastened his belt and slacks, preparing to strip them off, "you mind checking the stiletto holes in my ass cheeks, too? Teagan got the bleeding stopped earlier, but I need to know if I should have Doc sew me up, so I don't get color through my shorts in the ring."

"TMI, Dude!" Dean quickly turned away from Josh, who'd just dropped trou to change into his workout shorts. "Seein' as how she married you, Emerald needs to be the one to advise you about needing stitches for your sex injuries."

Brent was among the guys who chuckled at the ridiculous antics of their coworkers, even though he was secretly jealous of how Josh and Teagan were handling their unexpected marriage. *Fuck! Aiken wears those sky-high stilettos, too. And I really wouldn't mind seeing them propped on my shoulders while I was fucking her. But unlike me, I doubt Aiken can fuck without feelings getting involved. And I don't wanna take a chance on hurting her worse than I already have by trying to have a fling until we can get with our lawyers in a couple of months.*

Just before Brent and the rest of the guys finished changing to head out to the ring, the GWA owner joined them in the locker room. "Hey, I need to talk to you guys before we go out and meet with the ladies."

Rick waited for everyone in the room to finish changing and gather around before he elaborated. "As some of you already know, we're adding another team of bodyguards to cover Allissa and Dean as of today. While her stalker's threats only seem to be escalating to include Dean as of the pictures we received yesterday, I'm concerned that he might branch out to one of the other ladies, if he feels like they might be easier to get to than Allissa because of the added security. So, I want you all to be extra vigilant in watching out for all our wives and children, as well as the single women who work with us."

"Since these guys got married in Vegas, I think Allissa is the only single woman working with us now, Boss," Dean pointed out, slapping Brent and Liam on the back. "Not that she'll stay single for the rest of the year if I get my way."

"Yes, well, from the way everyone was talking yesterday, I'm sure the Stones and Chastity are all expecting to be single again soon,"

Rick countered, "so I'm sure they'll stick to their normal routines and try going off by themselves, which could be dangerous."

Brent remembered seeing Aiken getting in a rental car by herself at the airport that morning, and suddenly wanted to kick his own ass for not insisting she ride with him, Blade, and Red Velvet. *Hell, as little as she is, we wouldn't have had a problem fitting her in the back seat between me and Blade for our short drives between the airport, hotel, and arena. And she'd have been extra protected with all four of us surrounding her. I know she probably won't let me ride back with her tonight, but maybe I can convince the guys to follow her back to the hotel after the show, so she'll still be protected, even if she's alone in her rental.*

"I'm not trying to play matchmaker and suggesting you guys start dating your wives or anything like that," Rick continued. "But maybe use our travel time between airports, hotels, and arenas to carpool with them to discuss your plans for dealing with your legal issues, so they aren't left vulnerable for whatever this guy might try."

"Emerald and I are going to try dating, anyway, so that won't be a problem for me," Josh informed the boss and the rest of the male talent for the GWA, who hadn't already overheard his bragging earlier.

"Chastity and I aren't, though," Liam interjected, shaking his head. "So, she's gonna be pissed when she finds out you want me to babysit her."

"Yes, well, that's why I wanted to talk to you guys now, without the women, so we can figure out how to keep them all safe without making them think we're treating them as incapable of taking care of themselves."

Fuck! Maybe I should suggest dating for Aiken and I, too, so I can watch out for her without pissing her off. But if I do that, then I'm going to be so fucking tempted to act on my attraction to her and enjoy the physical benefits of us being married. And I really don't want to hurt her if things go too far between us, and then I still feel the need to end the marriage once this stalker situation is resolved.

"Don't worry, Boss," Magnum, the largest member of Protection Detail, interjected, slapping a hand on Trojan's shoulder. "We'll keep living the gimmick with Chastity, so she'll be safe, no matter what happens between her and Red."

So that just leaves Amethyst unprotected, Brent realized as Rick turned to look directly at him, neither of them noticing Red's reaction to the two Canadians volunteering to protect his wife. *Unless I step up and fulfill my duties as her husband.*

"What the hell? I guess I'll be asking my wife to date me," Brent declared, unable to think of any other options that wouldn't make her mad for being obvious that they didn't think she was capable of defending herself. "And hopefully, all this extra security will pay off, so this stalker can be caught before we go on our Thanksgiving break to have time at home to check into our options for dissolving the marriages."

"Yeah, you might wanna amend that to our Christmas break," Dean chuckled. "'Cause I'm still hopin' to convince Allissa to marry me over our Thanksgiving break, and ya'll better all be there."

Thanksgiving break? Christmas break? Either way, this stalker needs to be caught before we get time off to go home and start the legal paperwork. If he's not, then I guess we'll have to look into the time limits on annulments, or if we'll have to file for divorce when we finally end things.

And now I have to figure out how to "date" my wife, without actually doing any of the kissing, touching, or fucking that I usually do on dates. Then again, do my random hookups actually count as dates, when they only last an hour or two while we're at whatever club where I met them?

Looking around the room, he couldn't help but wonder which of the guys might be able to give him some platonic date ideas, so he wouldn't be tempted to take things too far with Aiken. *Since he has to deal with bodyguards tagging along with him and Allissa all the time, maybe Dean can give me some ideas? Or maybe one of the guys with kids can give me some ideas based on what they do with their families, so there'll be kids around on our dates to keep me from being tempted to make a move on my wife?*

~~~

Liam felt like an even bigger heel than he portrayed in the ring as he tossed and turned in his bed after the show that night. He just wasn't
~~~

sure if it was because Rylie still wasn't talking to him after the idiotic way he responded the day before, when she dropped the bomb on him that they'd gotten married in Vegas. Or because he was jealous as fuck of Surfer Josh and Crockett both deciding to date their wives, even though it looked like Crockett was going to have his hands full convincing Amethyst to give their marriage a shot based on the way she'd shut him down at ringside earlier.

After trying to call my attorney, and then having Dion talk me down, though, I was much more cordial the rest of the evening. Not that she noticed, since she basically avoided me like the plague. But since she didn't try to yell and scream at me anymore, she's obviously calmed down about all this, too. So, I doubt I'm losing sleep because she's still pissed. No, it's probably because I'm jealous as fuck that I can't date my wife like the other guys.

After seeing the scratches on Josh's back as proof that he and Emerald were doing a lot more than just dating, Liam was pretty sure he was especially jealous of him, since there was no chance in hell of getting to have a sexual relationship with his own Vegas bride. *And I'm probably a little pissed at the smug way Josh bragged about his sex injuries in the locker room. Jealousy combined with anger can definitely cause a sleepless night, right?*

Then again, Liam could also be suffering from insomnia because he felt guilty as fuck for having kissed Jen Burleson while he was in Heart's Destiny over the Labor Day break, when he didn't know he'd married Rylie two weeks earlier. But regardless of the reasoning, Liam couldn't force himself to fall asleep while he felt like the world's worst cheating asshole.

Thank feck, we didn't do more than kiss that night in the storeroom at Tully's for Ian and Charlotte's bachelor and bachelorette party, Liam thought, mentally beating himself up for having followed Jen in there that night a little over a month earlier. *I mean, kissing is still cheating, but it's not as bad as if I'd actually fucked someone other than Rylie since we got married.*

He still didn't know what he'd been thinking when he'd responded to Jen's uncharacteristic flirtatiousness that night. But for some strange reason — probably a combination of drinking a little too much, going too long without having sex with anything but his hand, and wanting to find a way to quit lusting after his too young coworker —

he'd flirted back when she rubbed up against him on the dance floor. Then, when she'd surprised him as he was coming out of the men's room, he'd willingly followed her into the storeroom at the end of the hall. When she'd told him she wanted to explore the chemistry she felt between them, he'd desperately tried to feel it the way she described.

Unfortunately, their first kiss had fallen flat, when they both tried to angle their heads in the same direction and ended up head-butting one another instead. Their second attempt wasn't much better, even with Liam taking the lead and holding her head in place, so they could actually kiss without injuring one another. It wasn't a bad kiss per se, but it wasn't the explosive chemical reaction he regularly dreamed about having with Rylie, either.

Liam imagined it felt as personal and intimate as two actors kissing for the hundredth take on a movie set, when the director kept making them reshoot it because of how insincere it appeared. And the kissing did absolutely nothing to arouse him. Even with Jen pressing her body into his like she wanted him to fuck her right then and there, Liam's dick remained as flaccid as if he'd been kissing his granny.

Not that it matters that it was a bad kiss. Or that we stopped after those two piss poor attempts. Or that I didn't know I was married to Rylie at the time. Kissing another woman is still fecking cheating.

Even though he doubted he'd ever get to have sex with his wife, having been raised in an Irish-Catholic family, he couldn't in good conscience even think about doing anything of a sexual nature with anyone other than Rylie as long as their marriage was valid. *But feck, even if I go to confession and ask for forgiveness for that very brief disaster of a make-out session with Jen, Da will still disown me for it if he ever finds out about it.*

Hell, he'll probably wanna disown me for getting married in Vegas, instead of having a church wedding in Belle Harbor, even though we're only married on paper and not actually a couple. So, I need to stick to the plan to get this marriage annulled and never let anyone in the family find out about it.

Feck! Since I haven't been home to check my mail in over a year, it might be too late to keep any of them from finding out.

Granted, he had a cleaning service go in and clean his house, including sorting through his mail and forwarding anything that looked important to his attorney's office, so his family shouldn't have seen the certificate of marriage. But since he hadn't heard from his attorney that he'd received it in the mail, and the women who worked with the cleaning service he used went to church with his family, it was entirely possible that the envelope from the Clark County Clerk had been passed to his ma or granny, instead of being forwarded to the attorney as it was supposed to be.

But if they gave it to Ma or Granny, then surely one of them would have already called me to set something up to meet my bride, right? Or maybe not, since they weren't the ones to set me up with her. I don't really think they'll have a problem with me marrying a woman who isn't Irish, but they might not be happy to not have at least met her before I married her.

And they could be waiting on me to call home and mention her before they say anything about knowing. Maybe I should call one of my brothers to try to get an idea of whether anyone's mentioned knowing something? But that'll just set off their detective skills and clue them in to start investigating what I've done. And I'll still be disowned when they tell Da or Granda.

Fecking feck! Hopefully, I'll hear from Boyle in the morning that he has it in his office and just hasn't had the chance to call me, since it was late on Friday when it finally made it to him after being forwarded. If that's the case, then he should be able to get started on the annulment in the next couple of days.

Unfortunately, every time he thought about following through with the legal process to dissolve his marriage to Rylie, Liam felt another piece of his heart break off and shatter to the floor. Especially when he thought about the look on her face the day before, when he'd acted like a jackass from the bombshell of finding out he'd married the only woman who'd been able to arouse him for the last six-plus months.

He'd thought at first that she was upset because he'd stayed at the hotel in the city with the rest of the GWA, instead of dealing with the family inquisition by going to sleep in his own bed for the night, thinking she hated that they'd wasted a weekday when he could have met with his attorney to start the annulment process. *Not that going home would have guaranteed I'd find the marriage certificate, since it was most likely forwarded to Boyle Kelly at the Kelly Legal Group, instead of still being at the house.*

But then when he mentioned the lawyer and annulment and having to wait until their next break to do anything about it, the slight irritation he'd seen in her eyes had morphed into pure anger. Now he wasn't sure if her anger was because he'd raised his voice from the shock of the situation, or because she felt hurt by him automatically jumping to the annulment decision without consulting her about how she wanted to deal with their mistake of a marriage.

No, she wouldn't be angry about that…unless she's as attracted to me as I am to her.

No, that's not possible. Regardless of what Dion claimed he saw yesterday, she doesn't really act like she's into me any more than she's into any of the other guys. If anything, the way she's living her gimmick by riding with Magnum and Trojan between the plane, hotels, and arenas, and always sitting with them whenever we all go out in public, she's probably into one of them way more than she'd ever be into me.

But they weren't the ones with her in the pictures from Vegas, his inner voice, which sounded an awful lot like his best friend Dion after their similar discussion the day before, reminded him. *You were the one right beside her in all those pics, even when the rest of the guys surrounded her.*

"That was because I was drunk and uninhibited with my desire to be close to her," Liam muttered to his empty room, feeling like he was going crazy because he was trying to argue with his inner voice.

And she was also drunk and uninhibited that night, when she stuck close to you, his inner Dion voice quibbled back. *So, maybe you should try giving your marriage a shot, like Crockett and Surfer Josh.*

"Feck! If only she wasn't ten years younger than me!" Liam was only a little over a week away from his thirty-fifth birthday, which was the age when professional wrestlers started to retire because of how taxing the pseudo-sport was on the human body. If he was really lucky, he could avoid any catastrophic injuries for a few more years, but he absolutely refused to keep trying to wrestle in his forties and fifties, when he wouldn't be capable of putting on the best performance in the ring. He'd seen too many of the old-school wrestlers push past their prime when he first got started in the business. And Liam had no desire to beat up his body to the point that he looked like he could barely walk down to the ring before giving a half-assed performance in a match. "With her just starting in the GWA, she's got at least ten or fifteen years before she'll be ready to retire from the ring and start a family. So, even if we tried to date and see if we could have a real marriage, like Crockett and Josh are doing with their wives, we'd still have to divorce in a couple of years when I retire."

Knowing they were doomed to fail didn't stop him from wanting her, though. Just thinking about the possibility of what could happen between them if they tried being a couple for the time he was still wrestling caused an immediate response in Liam's cock. Already unable to sleep, he couldn't resist stroking his dick while imagining what it would be like to fuck his wife. So he immediately banished his inner voice from his head and did just that.

"Feck," he groaned as he shoved his boxer briefs down to his thighs and gripped his thick cock. "What I wouldn't give to strip her out of those full-coverage bodysuits she wears in the ring to suck on those sweet tits while buried balls-deep inside her."

Envisioning Rylie's voluptuous body spread out naked on his bed, with him kissing, licking, and touching every square fucking inch of her glorious bronze skin, and bringing her to climax with his hands and mouth before finally plunging his cock in her wet and willing pussy, it didn't take long for Liam to reach his release while jerking off. "Feck! Rylie," he moaned as he covered his stomach with rope after rope of his cum.

"Too bad that fantasy won't ever come true," he mused once he caught his breath, getting out of bed to go clean up in the bathroom.

Chapter Three

Monday, October 7, 2019, Richmond, Virginia

As she exited the company plane with plans to head to the hotel first thing, Aiken was still reeling from the about face Crockett had pulled the day before when he'd cornered her right before the GWA talent's daily ringside meeting to ask her to try dating him before deciding what to do about their marriage. She'd been so surprised by his change of heart that she'd told him she'd have to think about it for a little while before making a decision. Then she'd taken advantage of the way the whole women's division of the GWA rallied around Allissa, after finding out they'd doubled her security, to avoid him for the rest of the night.

She just didn't understand why he'd gone from immediately talking about an annulment, when they first found out they were married, to suddenly wanting to date her the next day. *Does it have something to do with what Emerald told us about hooking up with Surfer Josh yesterday? Like maybe, Josh was bragging in the locker room, so now Crockett thinks this marriage is a free pass to get me in bed? I mean, what other reason would he have for suddenly changing his mind like that?*

As she caught up with Emerald at the rental car office, she decided to ask her bestie's opinion once they were alone in their car on the way to the hotel. She would have asked her while they were on the plane, but they spent most of the flight brainstorming ideas for ending their current angles and coming up with a way to work their marriages into their upcoming storylines. Then when they finished their discussions with the bookers, Emerald moved to sit with Josh for the rest of the flight. "Which one of us is renting the car today?"

"Oh, um," Emerald cringed, barely glancing at Aiken before turning back to look at Josh, who was already at the counter. "I'm riding with Josh today. We made plans for another lunch date before going to the hotel."

"Oh, okay." *Guess that means I'll be doing like I did yesterday and renting a car for just me.* Aiken internally winced at how being the only person in a car went against her desire to be environmentally friendly by carpooling as much as possible.

In addition to her environmental reasons for carpooling, typically, everyone in the GWA always had at least two, and quite often four, people in every vehicle, so their large crew didn't completely wipe out the rental company's stock of cars at the airport. With the women's division being so small, and most of them being married and traveling with their husbands and families, the Precious Stones had carpooled with Victoria Vicious until Allissa started dating Dean.

When she first started with the company, Chastity rode with them too. Until there were pictures of the four of them getting out of the same car, and Rick suggested heels and babyfaces quit riding together to protect kayfabe. Now Rylie, as the only single babyface in the women's division, rode with the rest of Protection Detail.

Oh, I guess that's not true anymore, since she married Liam. But I guess since we're trying to keep the dirt sheets from finding out about our marriages, Chastity is going to have to continue riding with Protection Detail, instead of her heel hubby, Red.

But wait, what does that mean for Emerald and Surfer Josh, since she's a heel and he's a face?

As she looked around at the other members of the GWA crew who were in line to get their rental cars, she realized that they weren't the only couple who'd married across the aisle with gimmick opposites. Babyface Holly the Hottie was married to heel tag-team wrestler Mountain Man Everest. And the heel GWA champion Crusher Cooper was married to backstage reporter Tiffany, who'd worked as a babyface when she wrestled before moving to the announcing team due to an injury that ended her in-ring career. *I guess marriage trumps kayfabe?*

But won't Emerald and Surfer Josh suddenly riding together tip off the paparazzi that maybe some of those pics from Vegas were actually of couples who got married? If we're really trying to keep the dirt sheets from finding out about our marriages until we can work them into our gimmicks, shouldn't they be avoiding each other in public?

Before she could ask Emerald about how they'd be fodder for the dirt sheets if anyone caught her and Josh riding together, Crockett walked over and lifted the straps for Aiken's garment bag and gear bag off her shoulder. "What are you doing?" Aiken protested, tightening her grip on the handle of her rolling suitcase, so he didn't take it from her as well.

"Carrying some of your stuff out to our car," Crockett replied, easily transferring her bags over to rest atop his. "I know how your eco-friendly heart must have broken yesterday when you were the sole occupant of your rental car, so I figured I'd save you from having to endure that again today by bringing you along with me and the guys."

"Which guys?" Aiken questioned as she had no choice but to follow along when he started walking away with her bags.

"Red Velvet," Crockett informed her just as they caught up with Liam and Dion in the first aisle of cars right outside the rental office. "I figured you'd be more comfortable riding with them than with Blade and Sawyer, who are probably going trolling for ring rats before hitting the gym this afternoon."

"You don't think the papzz seeing me arrive at the hotel with three guys is gonna get them started with more speculation about the Vegas pics, do you?" While she hadn't been in any of those pics with Liam, and Dion hadn't been in any of them at all since he'd already gone to his room for the night, she still thought the way Rick was planning to use some of the pics of Red and Chastity from Vegas to start a feud between Red Velvet and Protection Detail would lead to more speculation about her if anyone photographed her riding with the three of them now.

"Feck! I hope not," Liam groaned, as Dion opened the tailgate on a black SUV for them to load their luggage.

"Yeah, I doubt there are any paparazzi in Richmond, Virginia, to take our pics today," Crockett scoffed, shaking his head as he loaded her luggage into the SUV, including the rolling suitcase that she hadn't even realized she'd let go of a second earlier. "We probably won't have to worry about celeb spotters for CNZ in any of the sleepy southern towns we're in this week. Maybe next week when we get to Florida, but even then, the papzz will probably only be out in Miami."

While Aiken knew he was right about the rabid paparazzi only being out in force in certain cities, like they'd been in New York City on the previous Friday, and how he expected them in Miami when they arrived there on the eighteenth, and that the vultures were always the worst in Los Angeles, she still didn't believe they only had to be vigilant about being photographed in those cities. Even average people in small towns had camera phones nowadays, and they could easily email their inconspicuously obtained shots to someone at CNZ by clicking on the celeb-spotting link at the bottom of the webpage. So, in her opinion, they needed to be mindful of their actions at all times to keep from ending up making headlines they didn't want.

"We'll probably have a bunch in NOLA for the *Halloween Horror* weekend, too," Dion added as he got behind the wheel of the SUV after all their luggage was loaded. "But they're usually more focused on who they can catch partying on Bourbon Street than following us from the airport to the hotel or wherever."

"Is that why Xavier's isn't on Bourbon Street?" As she climbed into the backseat right behind Dion after Crockett opened the door for her, Aiken wondered about the club Dion co-owned with his brother, where the wrestlers had all partied a few times after GWA shows in New Orleans during her time with the company.

"Exactly," Dion grinned at her through the rearview mirror. "We're still in the Quarter to get plenty busy, but by not being on one of the more famous streets, we don't attract as many of the obnoxious drunk tourists."

"And you have that private entrance to the VIP balcony, so we don't have to deal with any papzz that hang around out front," Liam pointed out, getting in the front passenger seat.

"Are we having the *Halloween Horror* after-party there? Or are you still avoiding your brother?" Crockett asked after closing her door and walking around to get in the back passenger seat.

"Yeah, Dare's gonna hafta get over his hissy fit," Dion chuckled. "'Cause I already called his assistant manager and reserved the balcony."

They talked a few more minutes about plans for the *Halloween Horror* after-party before Crockett turned to her to start pleading his case for Aiken to date him once more. "We can consider the after-party in New Orleans a date if you want, but I'm hoping you won't need three more weeks to think before you agree to go out with me, so we can be on, like, date number twenty by then."

"Crockett," Aiken exasperatedly sighed his name, not in the mood for the hard sell he was obviously gearing up to give her.

"Please call me Brent," Crockett interjected before she could get another word out. "We're married, for fuck's sake, so you should at least use my first name instead of my last, especially since I also use it for my ring name."

"Fine, Brent," Aiken huffed, hating how much she loved being able to use his first name, when he pretty much insisted that everyone else call him Crockett. "I have been thinking about it, but before I can decide, I need to know why you changed your mind."

Please don't say it's so you can have sex without cheating, she mentally beseeched him. Even though she was attracted to him, she didn't want to have sex with him just because they were currently married. Could they date and eventually develop strong enough feelings for one another that she'd want to have sex with him? Yes, absolutely. But she didn't want to do it out of convenience with no emotions involved. If orgasm was the only end goal, she wasn't interested. She had her vibrator for that, and didn't need to risk her heart on a man, who possibly still intended to dissolve their marriage as soon as they had time off for their next holiday break.

"I didn't really change my mind," he insisted, reaching over to take her hand in his much larger one. "But you took off so fast Saturday that I didn't really get the chance to go over all our options with you, so we could discuss them before making a decision together."

"Yeah, well, the way you immediately jumped into the annulment requirements, it seemed like you'd already decided that's what we should do," she argued, wishing having him holding her hand didn't feel so amazing, so she could pull her hand back and think clearly. "So, the dating scenario you sprung on me yesterday felt like you'd done a one-eighty."

"Shouldn't you guys discuss this in private once we get to the hotel," Liam groaned, rubbing his temples like he had a headache, "instead of torturing us with the pussy-whipped-Crockett show?"

Brent reached up and slapped the back of Liam's head. "Dude, just because your bride wants nothing to do with you, doesn't give you the right to spout off your negative bullshit to mine. And wanting to date my wife doesn't make me pussy-whipped. It just means I wanna see if our friendship could develop into more before deciding how we want to handle the legal stuff."

Aiken almost felt like Brent was defending her and was halfway to agreeing to date him. Until Dion chimed in with his two-cents and voiced the same suspicion she'd had earlier, making her second-guess Crockett's motives.

"Ya sure it's not 'cause you're jealous of Josh and Emerald banging like bunnies since they found out they're married?" Dion chuckled, grinning at them in the rearview mirror. "'Cause if that's the case, ya need to back off. Amethyst deserves better than to be treated like a convenient road-lay until you can dissolve the marriage and go back to banging ring rats."

Aiken appreciated how Dion stepped in like a protective big brother on her behalf. "Thanks, D," she smiled at him through the rearview mirror, after stopping herself from using the Big D moniker that she and Emerald had started using to joke around with him after some ring rats had commented on his big dick one night at a club. While she'd probably still use it on occasion whenever they were all goofing around, she didn't want him, or either of the other guys in the vehicle, to think she was anything but serious in thanking him for standing up for her.

"Considering I'm asking her to go to lunch and on sightseeing dates, not back to one of our hotel rooms to fuck, I think my intention to be a perfect gentleman and get to know one another better is pretty damn obvious," Brent barked, clearly irritated by Dion's implications.

"And considering you didn't mention what activities we'd do on these dates until now, your intentions weren't obvious at all," Aiken informed him, fighting not to roll her eyes at her clueless husband.

"Well, now you know," Brent shrugged. "I heard Cooper say something about going to the Edgar Allan Poe Museum today, and I thought that might be an interesting first date before grabbing a late lunch on the way to the arena. What do you say?"

"Dude, if you're gonna take a woman on a date to a museum devoted to a poet, you should probably pick one that wrote romantic poetry, not Poe," Dion chuckled, shaking his head.

Liam mumbled something about "horror seeming appropriate" under his breath that Aiken couldn't quite comprehend. *I guess I should be grateful that I'm not having to deal with being married to someone as pissy about it as Red. Although, I do feel sorry for Chastity. Hopefully, she'll be able to get her marriage annulled quickly and be able to move on to find her real Mr. Right soon.*

"Poe actually wrote a poem titled **Romance**," Brent pointed out.

Aiken was surprised to hear that Crockett knew of a poem by Edgar Allan Poe other than **The Raven**. She only vaguely remembered the poem he'd mentioned from her high school and college literature classes, but didn't think he was academically inclined enough to have studied more than Poe's most famous works.

Not that she knew him well enough to know what he'd studied in college, or even if he went to college. While she knew he had a preference for strawberry protein shakes and indie rock bands that she'd never heard of, she really didn't know much about him as a person apart from his in-ring persona. While she considered him a friend, whenever they hung out together it was always with several of their coworkers and never one on one.

Of course, if I get to know him a little better by going on some one-on-one dates with him, he could prove me wrong about how intellectual he is, she decided, thinking back to what she remembered of the poem he'd just mentioned. *Considering all I really remember about that poem was how confusing it seemed and that I thought it was inappropriately named because it wasn't all that romantic, he might just surprise me by being able to explain it to me.*

"True," she finally commented, deciding to give Brent a chance by going on a date with him that afternoon. "But I think maybe back in his day, romanticism meant something other than the love poems and romance novels we think of nowadays."

"The best way to find out would be to go check out the museum once we get checked in at the hotel," Brent suggested, smiling hopefully at her.

"Sure, I'll agree to go check out the museum with you this afternoon," Aiken agreed, returning his smile, as Dion pulled into the hotel parking lot. "But since neither one of us rented a car, you're going to have to figure out how we're going to traipse all over Richmond without hauling our gear bags to the museum and wherever we go for lunch before going to the arena."

"We can leave our gear bags in the car," Brent declared with a smirk. "And after getting a cab to the museum and lunch, we can meet up with Dion to get them out at the arena right before our afternoon meeting. Right, D?"

"Sure," Dion agreed, chuckling. "I can't wait to hear how romantic ya'll think the Poe Museum is after your date."

"And if it turns out to be too much of a pain in the ass to meet up to get our bags later, then we'll just start renting a car for the two of us," Brent added, pointedly glaring at the two members of Red Velvet as they all got out of the SUV.

Is Dion implying that Brent is trying to romance me with this date? Or is he just teasing Crockett for not really knowing anything about Edgar Allan Poe? I mean, Brent does seem to know some of Poe's lesser known works, so I'm sure he knows what to expect at this museum. So, I highly doubt he's thinking we'll be reading over love poems, or anything that might arouse me to the point that I'd let him get in my pants, or anything like that. But then again, I don't really know that much about Brent to know that for sure. But I guess this is a good first step to learn more about him. And we'll see if the two of us are compatible or have any chemistry before making an informed decision about our marriage.

~ ~ ~

As she walked into the locker room to clean up after the afternoon meeting and getting sweaty while running through her match with Shauna Valor for later that night, Teagan couldn't help but think about how her relationship with Josh seemed to easily transition from just friendship to dating and fucking. Her inner skeptic couldn't help but wonder if it was too easy because they weren't taking things seriously enough. *Shouldn't we have taken more time to talk things out and plan for our future, instead of jumping straight into fucking each other's brains out within minutes of seeing that marriage certificate? Are we just blinded by lust right now? And making a mistake that could end up fucking up our careers when the lust starts wearing off?*

Teagan still couldn't believe how easily she'd gone from being cautious and wanting to go over all their options for dealing with the legalities of what they'd done in Vegas, to jumping straight to taking advantage of the sexual benefits of being married to Josh Parker. Yeah, she'd known she wanted him from the first day they met, but in all the time she'd known him she hadn't thought a single kiss could fry her brain cells to the point that she couldn't think about anything but the urgent need to get him inside her.

And when they came together that first time, it was the most explosive, carnal, amazing sexual experience of her life up to that point. She'd even loved the way he'd flipped her onto her back and took charge, making her feel like he needed to fuck her as much as she needed to fuck him. It was that primal need she'd never felt with anyone else that drove her to let him stay at her place the night before, and why she hadn't balked when he checked them into the same room at the hotel when they first got to Richmond. And already fucking him in both of those beds hadn't quenched her thirst for him in the slightest. If anything, the way the sex just kept getting better made her want him more.

Like I can possibly get enough of being woken up by him going down on me like he did this morning...

"Oh, yes, Josh," Teagan had moaned, thinking she was dreaming up the exquisite feel of his mouth and tongue on her pussy. Considering the only guys who'd ever gone down on her in the past had barely given her a cursory lick or two before expecting her to reciprocate with a half-hour long blow job, she knew the way Josh took his time with long slow licks alternated with soft sucks on her clit and targeting her G-spot when he fucked her with his tongue could only be a figment of her imagination.

I mean, even though he showed me that he knows how to target my G-spot with his dick, I doubt his tongue is long enough to reach it. He'd have to have a tongue as long as that old rock star, who was famous for sticking his tongue out on stage, like a decade before I was born. But damn, if he could do this, I might need to start listening to classic rock.

Teagan's strange dream thoughts were quickly forgotten when Josh lifted his mouth from her pussy long enough to growl, "Come, Teagan. Let me taste your sweet cream."

His guttural words combined with the way his hot breath wafted over her delicate flesh quickly helped her realize she

wasn't dreaming. Holy shit! This is really happening, *she'd thought just before he pushed her clit hood out of his way with one hand, thrust two fingers from his other hand past her lower lips to hit a bullseye on her G-spot, and suckled her bundle of nerves with the perfect amount of pressure to send her over the edge.* God, why didn't I let him do this yesterday when he said he wanted to?

"Oh, yes! Josh!" Teagan *cried out as her core clenched with her release. Instinctually, she gripped the shaggy strands of his dark blond hair, holding his head in place so he couldn't stop until she indulged in every moment of pleasure she could possibly glean from her stronger-than-normal orgasm.*

As Teagan came down from her peak, she finally released Josh's head, feeling a little bad for not thinking about his needs as she climaxed. Damn, girl, let the poor man breathe. You should reward him for giving you your first oral O, not try to suffocate him for it.

"Good morning, Mrs. Parker," Josh chuckled as he pushed up off the bed, crawling up beside her before rolling over to reach for the bedside table, where he'd apparently left a condom within easy reach. "I hope you don't mind that I woke you up an hour before we actually have to get up to head to the airport. But I was hoping you might have some ideas for some couple's exercises to replace my normal morning cardio."

Teagan couldn't help but smile at the way he waved the gold and black condom package around while impishly grinning and wagging his eyebrows at her, even though she wanted to roll her eyes at the way he kept calling her Mrs. Parker. "Yeah, I might have an idea or two."

She reached out and plucked the condom package from his hand, deftly ripping it open and rolling it down his impressive erection. He wasn't the biggest man she'd ever been with, but he also wasn't the smallest. If she had to guess, she'd say he was packing a solid eight inches with the perfect amount of girth to make her feel stretched out without being painful.

"But just to make sure you get your heart rate up into the cardio zone, you've gotta catch me before you can fuck me," she taunted him before jumping out of bed and running for the stairs.

She only made it to the landing halfway between the main floor and the top floor, where her bedroom was located, before he caught her, looping his arms around her waist to pick her up and spin her around. He sat her down on the bottom step, which headed back up to her bedroom from the landing, obviously thinking about needing to accommodate their seven-inch height difference to fuck her from behind.

"Spread your legs, bend over, and lift your hips, Tea," Josh commanded as he released his hold on her waist. "And you might wanna brace your hands on one of the other steps, so you don't face plant on them while I take what's mine."

Teagan didn't stop to take a moment to think about how his dominant tone affected her, she just blindly obeyed. Which was probably good, since she barely had time to follow all his instructions before she felt the latex covered head of his cock pressing into her.

Josh might have implied that he was going to be rough with her, but he took his time working his way inside her on that first stroke, making sure she was wet and ready before he pulled out and plowed back into her. He gripped her hip with one hand, while reaching around to rub her clit with the other, already seeming to have learned that it took more than just penetration to get her off.

Teagan used the strength in her arms to push back against him, almost doing an unusual form of a push-up to match the rhythm of her hips to that of his thrusting cock. Their coupling was intense. Primal. Carnal in a way she'd never experienced before. Fucking Josh felt so amazing that she was even turned on by the way he grunted and growled out more dirty talk than she usually liked to hear.

It wasn't that she had a problem with the dirty words, per se. She just normally had to concentrate to achieve her orgasm and was easily distracted by how most men used dirty talk as a lame attempt at stroking their own egos by overexaggerating the size of their dick or their sexual ability.

Josh, however, never once referred to the size of his cock, or made her feel like what they were doing was all about him. Instead, he praised her beauty and responsiveness while using the raunchiest words to tell her how she made him feel. He made her want to reciprocate the praise, but she didn't want to ruin the mood because she wasn't nearly as erotically eloquent as him.

But even though she didn't return his delectably dirty words, she reveled in them, finding that with Josh she didn't need to concentrate to achieve an orgasm. In fact, Josh gave her two more, on top of the oral O he'd awoken her with, before he finally plunged into her pussy as deep as he could go, holding himself there as he shot his load into the condom.

"Fuck! Teagan!" Josh repeated her name several times as he came, punctuating each with a twitch of his dick inside her.

I still can't believe how fast he was able to recover and carry me back upstairs this morning for round two in the shower, Teagan thought as she let the memories fade to the back of her mind. *But even as amazing as each time with Josh feels, I still can't help but wonder if we're letting our lizard brains take charge, when we should be acting more rationally about our relationship. Should we maybe back off on the sleepovers for a few weeks? And just focus on our more platonic midday dates, like the escape room we did today, to get to know one another better before clouding our feelings with sex and diving head first into married life?*

Though I suppose we did get to know each other a little better on both of our lunchtime dates so far. Maybe a little more today, since Mom and Kijana were both with us yesterday at Jimmy's. But even then, he was getting to know more about me from the stories they told him about my childhood.

After Teagan and Josh unexpectedly fucked on her sofa the day before, she'd taken him to the restaurant where she always met her mom and sister for lunch whenever she was home for a GWA show. Thinking about seeing her family the day before reminded her of the advice her mom had always given her about men.

Mom always said I should take my time getting to know a man before getting serious. Not that she seemed to think that after meeting Josh yesterday. Hell, neither did Kijana and she's the queen when it comes to making guys work for her attention. Though I guess they figured I've known him for five years already, so they probably felt like I already knew him well enough to know I wanted to marry him, which is probably why the whole drunk-in-Vegas thing didn't faze either of them.

Technically, her mom and sister had met Josh and a few of the other wrestlers when they came to watch her wrestle the first time she was back in Baltimore after signing with the GWA. But since they both complained about how nerve-racking it was to worry about her getting hurt when they watched her perform, they hadn't been back to a GWA show in years, which was why the introductions the day before had seemed like the first time they were meeting.

Leah Mae Wright

She hadn't planned on breaking the news of her Vegas wedding that she couldn't remember to her family, but Josh hadn't given her much choice. When they'd first arrived, she'd suggested they sit at separate tables and pretend like they weren't together while out in public, so they could keep the dirt sheets from figuring out they were married. But he'd refused, rather adamantly, especially when her mom and sister called her over to their table. Instead of keeping things private while they dated to see if they could make their marriage work, he'd insisted on meeting his new in-laws at the first opportunity, not seeming to care what kind of scene they made.

Of course, her mom and sister had both fawned all over him, welcoming him to the family with open arms. *With as loud as they were, I'm surprised it was only our pictures that ended up on the gossip sites today, and not the news of our "wedded bliss," as Mom put it yesterday. But I'm sure it's only a matter of time before they start with more speculation about Vegas, especially if we keep being photographed every time we go on these midday dates he's insisting on planning.*

What the hell is he thinking with making us into a public spectacle, anyway? I mean, he's totally acting freaked out about the possibility of his personal assistant leaking a copy of our marriage license to the gossip sites, so shouldn't he be insisting we keep a low profile, too? Aren't these pictures of us just gonna make whatever she claims seem valid?

Josh hadn't come out and admitted it yet, but based on the things he'd said about his personal assistant, Teagan was pretty sure there was more between him and Sarah than just business. Considering his ardent stance with her about not banging anyone he worked with, she didn't think he'd ever slept with his PA. But at the very least, it sounded to Teagan like Sarah might have harbored feelings for him that she'd hoped would one day lead to his ring on her finger. And finding out he'd married another woman could easily trigger someone with unrequited feelings into posting lies online about being his jilted lover, which was what Teagan was more worried about than Sarah posting a copy of their marriage license.

That would affect his status as a babyface in the eyes of the fans way more than our marriage leaking out to the public before Rick works it into our storylines could screw up our future angles. So,

86

shouldn't he be more worried about stuff like that and trying to keep a low-profile, instead of pushing for these public dates?

Speaking of people acting out of character, what is up with Kijana wanting to plan a wedding reception for us the next time we're in Baltimore? Did she and Josh drink the same spiked soda yesterday at lunch, since neither of them seemed to understand that we're supposed to be hiding our marital status from the dirt sheets? Teagan pondered as she gathered her bodywash, shower puff, and towel, placing them on the bench beside her before covering her hair with a shower cap to keep from getting it wet. She'd patted off any sweat on her scalp with a paper towel as soon as she got in the dressing room. But knowing she'd just get sweaty again in the ring that night, she figured it was best to wait to wash her braids in the shower after the show, not wanting to wet her hair twice in one day.

I mean, I know Rick's going to try to capitalize on all the speculation by switching up our angles on TV over the next few weeks. But I think he wants to control the narrative by trickling out the news of who married whom to tease the dirt sheet trolls for a little while. Not have someone leak the news before we get a couple of months of in-ring drama out of it.

Shit, maybe that's why I'm so nervous about how seamlessly Josh and I have gone from friends to lovers? Because I'm afraid someone else will break the news to CNZ and the rest of the gossip mongers online before we can work our new angles, and Rick will decide to swerve the fans by pulling the plug on them, or booking us to act like we're romantically interested in other people instead.

"Hey, Em, you okay?" Amethyst plopped down on the bench a couple of feet away from Teagan, arching an eyebrow in her direction before beginning to go through the things in her locker.

"Yeah, I'm fine," Teagan replied, trying to figure out how to share her thoughts about her marriage without sounding like a bitch, since she was the only one of the three Vegas brides who was actually enjoying the conjugal benefits. She felt bad enough for being on such an orgasm high the day before that she'd told the girls all about finally fucking Josh. That braggadocian bitch wasn't who she wanted to be with her friends. She'd much rather be supportive of her BFFs, whose husbands had immediately jumped on the annulment bandwagon, instead of sounding like she was gloating about how many orgasms she was getting from her hubby, or whining about how her relationship with Josh seemed too easy.

But damn, I'm sure enjoying fucking my hubby every chance we get, and especially going for record numbers of O's when we can take our time in bed at night. Sex with Josh was by far the best she'd ever had, and she really wished she could talk to her best friends about it. *But maybe I can catch Randi and Allissa later when Aiken and Rylie aren't around. I bet they can tell me if it's so fucking fabulous because of my feelings for Josh, or if it's just because he challenges me in a way I never knew I wanted before. Then maybe I'd be able to figure out if we actually have a shot at making this marriage work, or if I should just plan to date more dominant men when we finally fizzle out.*

"You seemed totally cool with us starting this tension-between-us angle when we rehearsed it earlier, but now you have this pissed off look on your face that makes me wonder if you'd rather do something different than what Rick's booking for us?" Aiken pointed out the expression Teagan got when she thought about the possibility of her relationship with Josh ending, mistaking it for her being angry about their upcoming angle in the ring.

"No, that's not it at all," Teagan vehemently denied as she double-checked that her braids were all completely covered, trying to figure out how to conceal her true reason for feeling irrationally angry without outright lying to her bestie. "I mean, I'm going to miss teaming with you, but I'm actually looking forward to the awesome matches we're going to put on once the Stones are split up to stand by our men."

"Then what's with the angry expression?" Chastity interjected as she also covered her hair to prepare for hitting the shower. "You went from smiling when you got here this afternoon, like one of those annoying bubbly cheerleaders that drove me nuts in high school, to sporting a pissed-off bitch face now."

"I just can't help but worry about my ability to pull off working babyface," she lied, knowing she'd done a great job being the good girl while working in the indies before switching to being a heel when she started working in the GWA. She knew it was a lame excuse, but it was the best she could come up with at the moment. "That is, if Rick doesn't scrap this whole idea to swerve the fans if our marriages leak to the dirt sheets before he plans to release the info as part of these new angles."

"Considering he flew in the social media people to scour our phones for Vegas pics that weren't previously published to start building the new angles online before TV tomorrow, I doubt he'll scrap his current plans," Amethyst asserted, shaking her head as she grabbed what she needed from her locker to go rinse off in the shower before changing for the show that night. "Especially since he seemed cool with the pictures that were posted of you and Josh today."

"I was surprised he was cool with those," Chastity added as they each shut their lockers and headed for the showers. "But I guess he's handling you guys' situations differently than he is mine."

Yeah, so was I, Teagan thought. *But I guess it makes sense that he's okay with pics of us looking flirty with each other, since we're not actually wearing rings to show that we got married. They'll just feed into the whole tension thing between me and Amethyst, since it looks like I'm starting to fall for one of the "good guys," instead of hanging out with the other heels.*

"I know, right?" Amethyst agreed with Chastity as they each stepped into side-by-side shower stalls to keep talking while they stripped and cleaned off. "After the way he insisted you keep riding with Protection Detail and act annoyed by Red's ringside flirtation, I thought for sure he'd want us all to distance ourselves from the guys to keep the gossip sites from figuring out which of us got married. But after he changed his plans for our angles today, I don't feel so bad about possibly being photographed while on my date with Crockett this afternoon."

"Whoa! Why didn't you tell me before now that you decided to date him?" Teagan knew Crockett seemed to be wavering on the annulment plan and had asked Amethyst about trying to date the day before. But the last she'd heard, her bestie wasn't sure it was something she wanted to do. *Hell, if dating works out for them and they decide to try staying married for a little while too, maybe we'll be able to discuss our sex lives after all.* "And where'd you go on your date?"

"I just decided on the ride to the hotel this morning," Amethyst admitted, raising her voice to be heard over all three showers, as they each turned them on and adjusted the temperature before stepping under the spray. "We went to the Edgar Allan Poe Museum and then for lunch."

"The Poe Museum? That seems like a strange place for a first date," Chastity commented, sounding like she was as confused by the location choice for Amethyst and Crockett's date as Teagan felt.

"Was he trying to ensure," Teagan teased in as close to a poetic refrain as she could come up with immediately, "that you'd go out with him, nevermore?"

"No," Amethyst laughed. "He overheard Cooper talking to his sons about going to the museum today and misunderstood the assignment Fiona gave them to compare Poe's poem *Romance* to his other works. He apparently hasn't ever read any of Poe's work, so he thought it would be a bunch of love poems. But then when we got there and saw the boys asking questions to try to do the assignment, he quickly realized that Fiona was trying to point out that Poe wrote during the Romantic era, but his gothic themes aren't what we think of as romantic nowadays."

"So, he thought he was taking you to a museum full of love poems?" Teagan questioned her friend as she finished rinsing the soap off her body and turned off the shower. She couldn't imagine how embarrassed Crockett must have felt when he actually read some of Poe's work on what he'd tried to plan as a romantic date. "How'd he not know anything about Poe before then?"

"Apparently, either he didn't read any of his poems in high school, or it was so long ago that he forgot reading them," Amethyst replied as another shower turned off.

"He's not that much older than us, is he?" As she dried her body and gathered her things to go back to her locker to slather on her lotion and get dressed, Teagan thought back and realized it had been over a decade since she'd learned about the works of Edgar Allan Poe in her high school English class. She was only a few months older than Aiken, having just recently celebrated her twenty-ninth birthday in September, while Aiken's wasn't until February the next year, so she'd probably learned about Poe at about the same timeframe Teagan had.

"Just a couple of years," Amethyst replied, stepping out of the stall right behind Teagan and Chastity. "He turned thirty-one this year."

"So, he's the same age as Josh," Teagan realized as they walked back over to their lockers.

She was surprised to see that Kay had joined her sister in the locker room, along with the last person from Heart's Destiny that Teagan expected to see at a GWA show so far outside of Texas. Cait Campbell was so quiet and shy that she'd barely spoken to anyone but the Burlesons whenever Teagan had seen her at the various events for the two weddings she'd attended in the small town earlier that year.

"I don't think age has anything to do with it," Chastity shook her head as they each opened their lockers to return their toiletries to their bags and go through their daily ritual of lotion application before starting to put on their gear for the show that night. "I'm younger than all you guys and I barely remember enough about reading *The Raven* in high school to get Emerald's 'nevermore' reference earlier."

Teagan remembered that they'd missed celebrating Rylie's twenty-fifth birthday on September first because of their Labor Day break and had ended up combining their birthday celebrations on Teagan's birthday, September twelfth. "You don't think your big age gap is why Red has such a problem with you two being married, do you? Like maybe being married to a hot young thang like you makes him feel like a dirty old man?"

"Red is Liam, right?" Cait questioned Kay as they stopped walking halfway between the lockers and the toilet stalls. "Does Jen know he got married? Or rather, do Hazel and Susan know, so they'll quit trying to fix him up with Jen?"

Teagan looked over at Chastity, realizing how uncomfortable her friend looked at hearing about the Burleson matriarchs trying to match up her husband with one of their daughters. *Damn, I really should have paid attention to our audience before asking her about the tension with Red.*

"No, we just found out about some of the Vegas wedding pics being legit a couple days ago," Randi answered for her sister. "And Rick wants the marriages kept under wraps for now, so he can book them into our shows."

"I'm still planning to discreetly inform Hazel and Susan, though," Kay added as she and Cait finally continued walking, obviously only in the locker room for a bathroom break while all of Kay's kids were in the classroom area being supervised by the teachers. "But I figured it was best to do that in person, so I can emphasize the need to keep the information private."

After putting on her emerald green metallic booty shorts and bra top that she wrestled in most often, Teagan donned her matching warm-up pants and jacket, socks, and sneakers, opting to wait until after eating dinner in catering to get into her knee pads, elbow pads, and wrestling boots. As she dressed, she noticed how her fellow Vegas brides had clammed up while they had an outsider in their midst.

Yeah, I'm not sure what Cait's doing here either, she thought as she made eye contact with both Amethyst and Chastity to reassure them that she had their backs. *But Randi and Kay are part of our crew, so if they brought her here, we've got to trust that they'll make sure she keeps our secrets to herself.*

As soon as both ladies left the toilet stalls and were washing their hands, Teagan shut her locker and walked over to the mirrors near the sinks, where she could touch up her makeup while also making sure they could hear her. She slouched more than usual in an attempt to try not to be too intimidating, since she was more than half a foot taller than the petite pilot's wife. While Cait was maybe an inch taller than Teagan, she still felt like she might intimidate the obviously introverted woman if she didn't tone down some of her innate brashness. "When you're telling the Burlesons about our marriages, make sure they know Surfer Josh, Crockett, and Red are all off limits for their matchmaking from now on."

"Of course," Kay smiled over at her. "That's the whole reason I asked Rick for permission to tell them in the first place. But don't be surprised if the Matchmaking Mommas include you and your new hubbies in their schemes next time ya'll are in town, especially if they get word that any of ya'll are considering annulments, so they can try to prevent them."

"Why would they include us?" Amethyst inquired as she joined them in the huddle by the sinks and mirrors, dragging Chastity along with her. "I thought they were just trying to marry off their kids?"

"Oh, yeah, it started off with wanting to marry off their kids to get grandbabies they can dote on," Kay agreed, chuckling. "But the whole town, or at least the older generations in town, are all obsessed with the folklore of being a place where soulmates connect. They love *true love* so much that they don't care if you're related to them or not. They just want everyone to fall hard and fast in love, and live their happily ever afters."

"Even those of us that they haven't paired up?" Teagan wondered, unsure how to take the news that she and Josh might be pushed together even more if Dean was able to convince Allissa to marry him at Thanksgiving, the way he'd claimed at Rick and Fiona's wedding back in July, and they attended the festivities. *What could they possibly do to try to matchmake us when we're already embracing married life? Unless…they could derail our attempt to back off on the sleepovers like I was thinking earlier by working with Dean's mom to have us share rooms with our husbands anytime we stay at the bed and breakfast.*

No, they wouldn't do that. I mean, it would totally work fine for me and Josh, but Aiken and Rylie would both be really uncomfortable with living in close quarters like that with Crockett and Liam, when they're all still possibly planning to annul their marriages.

Huh? Look at me thinking positively about me and Josh really making a go of this married thing. Teagan smiled as she looked over at her friends to observe their body language during this discussion, trying to figure out if either of them were feeling optimistic too, since hearing they might be matched up with their hubbies whenever they went to Dean and Allissa's wedding. *Well, Rylie would probably be extremely distressed if she got stuck rooming with Liam, since she already looks more than a little uncomfortable right now with just talking about possibly being pushed at him. But if that wistful expression on her face is to be believed, Aiken looks like she might be open to taking things to the next level with Crockett. Maybe his Poe museum date wasn't such a bad idea for them after all.*

"Knowing Hazel, she'll probably claim the credit for you guys getting married," Cait chimed in, surprising Teagan as she spoke, lightly elbowing Kay. "How much you wanna bet that she'll say her attempts to match the guys up with the wrong women are what pushed them into dragging the right women down the aisle while in Vegas?"

"Yeah, I'm not betting against that," Kay laughed, shaking her head. "'Cause that's absolutely what she's gonna say when she hears about the Vegas weddings."

"You don't really think she'll do anything to push my girls into their new hubbies' arms, though, do you?" Randi questioned her sister as she touched up her makeup in the mirror. "I mean, she didn't really do anything to help James and I along when we first got together, other than going along with pairing us up in your bridal party."

"Please," Kay scoffed at her sister. "She kept Mom and Dad occupied all week, so you could spend time with James without them hassling you."

Since Teagan hadn't met Randi until she joined the GWA crew on the plane the day after that Thanksgiving break when Kay married Anthony, she had no idea what the Heart's Destiny matchmakers had done to help Randi and James get together. But when she'd gone to the small Texas town for all the events surrounding James and Randi's wedding, and then Rick and Fiona's wedding, she'd clearly seen their influence in all the seating charts and games, especially the games at Kay's baby shower.

Thinking about that day as the other ladies discussed the various matchmaking attempts they'd witnessed, she realized that the matchmakers had paired her up with Dane Bennington, instead of pushing her toward one of the local guys. *Huh? Maybe they were pushing for everyone to find love, regardless of whether it was with one of their kids or not. But then again, they also paired Josh up with Becky Burleson that day. And most of the men who showed up for the baby shower were GWA wrestlers, with only a few locals who were already attached to other women, so maybe they just ran out of local guys to match us up with?*

When she thought back to James and Randi's reception, she realized that they'd paired each of them up with a different local of the opposite sex. Josh had still been paired up with Becky, but Teagan had been paired up with Luke Walker, while Aiken and Rylie had been paired with his brothers Landon and Leo.

Then at Rick and Fiona's reception, they'd changed things up again to have all three members of Protection Detail sit with the Precious Stones, Bennington brothers, and Allissa, so they were all sort of paired off with fellow GWA wrestlers. While they were still matching up Red Velvet, Crockett, and Surfer Josh with the Burleson girls and one of their friends, they had changed the lineup to pair Becky with Crockett and Josh with the bubbly blonde Sierra Sadler.

And he actually went to Anthony and Kay's wedding, so I'm sure he was matched up with someone then, too. I wonder if he hooked up with any of his "dates" in Heart's Destiny? And since he's clearly closer to the Burlesons than I am, did he go back for Charlotte and Ian's wedding over our Labor Day break? If so, who was he matched up with then? And did he sleep with her? Teagan hated the flare of jealousy she felt rising up inside her at that moment, knowing she'd had no claim on him back then to have a legitimate reason to be jealous, even if he'd hooked up with someone over their Labor Day break, when they didn't know they were married.

"Uh-oh, Em's getting that pissed-off bitch face again," Amethyst pointed out, drawing Teagan back into the conversation that she'd basically tuned out.

As she looked around at the other women, she realized that Chastity had a similar expression. "Yeah, I'm sure I'm not the only one who's wondering what happened when our husbands were pushed toward the Burlesons and who knows how many other women in Heart's Destiny," Teagan grumbled, unsure how to stop her jealousy over Josh from before they were legally tied to one another.

"Um, I can't say for sure for everyone else in Heart's Destiny," Cait muttered sheepishly, turning to look directly at Chastity before continuing. "But I know none of the Burleson women have hooked up with your men. Jen has specifically told me that she has absolutely no interest in Liam. They just worked out a deal to hang out as friends whenever he's in town to try to keep the Mommas from playing musical matchmaking chairs with them, the way they do with almost everyone else."

Cait then turned to look directly at Teagan before adding, "And none of them can get past the fact that Surfer Josh and my Josh have the same first name. In fact, it's kind of a joke at our book club meetings that since my Josh is either related to or has been friends with every woman in town since childhood, they'd all be too grossed out to cry out his name during sex. And it's too weird to even think about trying to use his wrestling name then, so I don't think you have to worry about anything having happened there either."

"Well, that's good to know," Teagan laughed, imagining screaming "Surfer Josh" as she orgasmed and agreeing that it would be too weird. "But for the record, I don't think of anyone but my man when I scream 'Josh' during an orgasm, so you don't have to worry about me confusing him with your man."

"And I don't think of anyone but my cowboy when I do the same," Cait laughed, lightening the mood. "But just to make sure there's no confusion when he gets here after looking for Allissa's stalker today, I'll stick to using his SEAL call sign of Cowboy, since he's used to me calling him that half the time anyway."

Ah, so that's why they're here today, Teagan realized, thinking maybe they might make some progress with calling in a former Navy SEAL to help track Allissa's stalker. With the way Cait blushed as she explained that they'd had to resort to nicknames when Josh Burleson's son, who was also named Josh, showed up in town, Teagan had to wonder if the reserved woman called out Cowboy as often as she did Josh in the throes of an orgasm. But she didn't want to embarrass the other woman any more by calling her out on it, so she redirected her attention to her fellow Vegas brides.

Unfortunately, even though she and Rylie both seemed to relax a little with Cait after her reassurances about their men, Aiken still looked skeptical about what might have happened when Crockett was in Heart's Destiny. *Damn it! Maybe if I point out why we shouldn't be bothered by any of that, it might help all of us quell our inappropriate jealous feelings.* "Not that it really matters what happened when the guys were matched up with any of the women in Heart's Destiny, since anything that might have happened was before we were married, when we had no claims on them."

"You're right, Em," Amethyst smiled at Teagan. "All that really matters is what happens from now on."

"Like more dates to places like the Poe Museum," Chastity teased, bumping shoulders with Amethyst.

"Yes, even if I do have to teach Brent the difference between my idea of romance and the Romantic era of literature," Amethyst agreed, chuckling. "And you flaunting what your momma gave you to show Red how he's missing out by not jumping on board with Brent and Josh's idea to date their hot wives before making any decisions about annulments, at least until our next holiday break."

"Oh, no," Chastity disagreed, holding up her hands and shaking her head. "He's made it clear he's not interested, so our marriage will just be part of our gimmick until we can meet with our attorneys to find out our options and sign the paperwork."

"But isn't he the guy you've been crushing on but didn't want to talk about?" Randi interjected.

"Yeah," Rylie sheepishly admitted. "But like Emerald said earlier, I think he has a problem with our ten-year age difference."

"Oh, please," Kay scoffed, shaking her head at Chastity. "Age is only a number, and our hearts don't care about counting. I'm almost eight years older than Anthony, and our age difference doesn't matter. Neither does Rick and Fiona's, and he's ten years older than her, too. So, you're gonna hafta come up with a better excuse than that. Not that I think you can, since it seems like you really want a chance at enjoying being married to your husband."

"Look Chas, I know he's been acting like an ass since finding out you guys got married," Teagan added, wanting to support her friend while she had the backup of half the GWA women's locker room and a couple of their non-wrestler friends. "But before that, it was obvious that he was into you, too. So, I agree that you should push a few of his buttons to go after the relationship you want."

"I don't know," Chastity stammered, looking down at the floor instead of making eye contact with any of them, acting like she was embarrassed and unsure of herself.

"I'm not talking about sneaking into his hotel room for him to find you naked in his bed," Teagan pointed out.

"I don't know, that might be the best way to get his attention," Kay chortled, grinning mischievously.

"Maybe eventually, but not for a first move," Teagan disagreed, grinning back at the oldest woman in their little huddle. "I'm thinking something more subtle at first. Like pulling your top down to expose a little more cleavage when you're flirting with him as part of the angle you're starting between Protection Detail and Red Velvet on TV tomorrow. And going back to the way you acted around him last week, before you found that marriage certificate. Friendly and fun-loving, instead of guarded and grumpy, like you've been since Saturday."

"You really think that'll work?" Chastity lifted her gaze from the floor to lock eyes with Teagan.

"It can't hurt," Teagan said in unison with Cait, surprising them both. When they looked at each other in shock at sharing the same thought at the same time, they both chuckled before turning back to Rylie.

"Seriously, the friend route worked for me and Josh, uh, Cowboy," Cait confided with a shrug, making Teagan realize the need for the different designations of their men's names whenever she was talking with the women from Heart's Destiny. "It took a few months longer than I would have liked, but we both had some major obstacles to deal with before he was able to move home for us to take our shot at a relationship. You guys don't have a thousand miles and a boatload of baggage between you to deal with like we did, so it shouldn't take you near as long to work things out."

While she didn't know what baggage, other than his surprise kid, had kept Cait from her Cowboy, Teagan realized then that she didn't want to let any of the drama his personal assistant might cause come between her and Josh. *And I really don't want to put up any other barriers between us, like the stupid idea I had earlier to back off on the sleepovers. We can still spend time getting to know one another better without having to miss out on the O's. And who knows, maybe that physical bonding time is just as important to a marriage as the emotional bonding time of our deep discussions over lunch and when we're driving to and from the arenas, hotels, and airports every day.*

"Okay, I'll try being more friendly and flirty," Chastity conceded. "But if we haven't managed to work things out before we go back to Heart's Destiny whenever Dean convinces Allissa to marry him, then you guys better enlist the help of those Matchmaking Mommas to help me seal the deal."

"Absolutely," Kay, Randi, and Cait chimed in unison.

"And since my in-laws convinced Allissa's mom to stay in town to help plan the wedding," Randi added, "ya'll better be ready to spend your Thanksgiving break in Heart's Destiny being fixed up with your hubbies."

Teagan didn't think she and "Surfer" Josh needed much fixing up to make their marriage work, at least for the short-term. But she'd gladly take any help the older generation of ladies in Heart's Destiny could give her for turning their short-term lust into a more long and lasting love, like they all seemed to have found with their spouses.

Maybe with the help of all my GWA friends and their matchmaking families in Heart's Destiny, I just might be able to have it all with my sexy surfer after all.

~~~

Tuesday, October 8, 2019, Virginia Beach, Virginia

Rylie couldn't believe she was actually considering taking the advice of her fellow women wrestlers and their family and friends, who were in town for the GWA shows the past couple of days, and was seriously contemplating flirting with Liam even more than Rick suggested for the promos they were planning for that night's live TV broadcast. But after the initial suggestion was made in the locker room the day before, she'd observed each of the other ladies with their men while they were all having dinner in catering and hanging out backstage during the show, especially Cait once Josh Burleson arrived, since she hadn't ever seen them as a couple before.

Oh, she'd noticed that they were seated together at Rick and Fiona's wedding reception, but her brief glance in their direction at that event in July made it seem like they were only seated at the same table because Cait's brother and Josh's sister were engaged. So, Rylie had assumed that was the primary reason Cait hung out with the Burlesons whenever she attended the various wedding events that week, as well as the week of Randi and James's wedding earlier in the year, not that she was secretly harboring feelings for Josh Burleson.

Wow! I totally get what she was saying about all the women in Heart's Destiny not being interested in Surfer Josh because of the same name thing. Hell, with both of them at the arena the last couple of days, I'm even having to make sure I differentiate between Surfer Josh and Josh Burleson in my head, so I don't get confused by my own thoughts about the two couples.

Since Cait hadn't come to the bachelor and bachelorette parties or danced with anyone but her nephew at the receptions, Rylie had assumed she wasn't dating anyone and was too shy for the local matchmakers to try to fix her up with one of the wrestlers while they were all in town those weeks. But after talking with her a little more
~~~

the past couple of days, while Cait was hanging out backstage and her boyfriend was scoping out the airports and hotels to help look for Allissa's stalker, Rylie had learned that she'd had a crush on Josh Burleson since the first time she met him at a Christmas party the year before. Cait had filled her in on how they'd built a friendship whenever her Josh was home on leave, as well as how he and the rest of the Burlesons were helping her deal with agoraphobia after being shot in a drive-by out in California a few years back.

They'd also discussed how Cait felt extra safe at this show, even knowing there was a stalker targeting one of the GWA performers, because it was being held on the base where Josh Burleson had been stationed for years as a Navy SEAL. Rylie had to admit that she liked having that extra feeling of security anytime the GWA booked a show on a military base, which apparently Rick did several times a year to entertain the members of the armed forces and their families for free.

It wasn't just the newest woman she'd made friends with that made her envious of her friends' couple statuses, either. Pretty much every woman she knew and could glance around to see backstage had paired up with the men of their dreams. Rylie was the only woman in the GWA, or their close circle of friends, who was sitting with her gimmick partners instead of her legal husband. Even Emerald and Amethyst were sitting with their new spouses as they all sat down to dinner in catering. While Emerald and Surfer Josh were more openly affectionate than Amethyst and Crockett, the latter couple still seemed to have a connection with one another that fueled the laughter they shared over inside jokes, which they almost seemed to convey to one another through looks more than words.

Randi, Kay, and Allissa had even commented on seeing that connection and expounded on how they felt it with their men, so they knew that those two Vegas couples were highly likely to make their marriages work. It also wasn't just the relatively recent couples that provided inspiration for Rylie in what she longed to feel in a relationship one day. Watching several of her coworkers, who were in long-term relationships and raising families, sneaking in kisses and innocent ways of touching their partners throughout the day also showed Rylie that her childhood dreams of a fairy-tale love were more than possible.

Between all that talking with the women she counted as friends, and observing the dynamics of all the couples around her, Rylie had somehow channeled her jealousy over what they all seemed to have found with their partners into a form of hope that she could develop that same kind of loving connection with Liam. Even his claims of wanting to have the marriage annulled as soon as they could meet with an attorney on their next holiday break weren't strong enough to prevent her from wanting her happily ever after to be with him.

She couldn't stop herself from daydreaming about the possibilities as she quietly ate her dinner, only half listening to the conversations going on around her. But if she ever wanted to have a chance at living out those daydreams, then she had to figure out how to break down the walls he'd put up between them to get him to truly see her and what they could be together, so they could explore what they really felt for one another.

And she knew he felt something other than anger toward her because she'd seen it in his eyes when they were practicing their promos earlier and he hadn't been able to cover up how his eyes roamed her body. Granted, Rick had specifically directed him to exaggerate the movement of his head to make it obvious he was looking her over from head to toe, but since he wasn't looking directly at the camera, nobody instructed him on making his eyes flare with appreciation as he did it. With their positions in relation to the camera and the other wrestlers, Rylie was pretty sure she was the only one who'd been able to see his eyes at the time to see his reaction to the tank top she wore to practice the promos and run through the match she had that night with Amethyst.

While technically neither of their current angles had them feuding with each other, they often had to wrestle against people they weren't working a specific angle with on TV nights to build up the anticipation of the major fights on pay-per-views. Often these bouts with less animosity between opponents were used for their primary rivals to do a run-in to help build the tension leading up to their pay-per-view match. But her match with Amethyst that night was specifically to help set up the angle between Protection Detail and Red Velvet because Red Velvet would be coming out to sit at ringside, so Red could flirt with Chastity.

Leah Mae Wright

He certainly seemed more than a little attracted to me while we were practicing earlier, both backstage and at ringside. And I didn't even pull my shirt down more than normal like the ladies suggested.

Since it wasn't possible to pull the front down on any of the mock-turtleneck full-coverage bodysuits that she wrestled in, when it was time to change for the promos, she'd opted to put on the warmups she normally wore over her ring gear while she was hanging out backstage, only without the bodysuit underneath, so she could pull the zipper down in the front to reveal a little more cleavage for the vignette they were opening the show with before going back to the locker room to get ready for her match. Now, she was just waiting for the families to clear out of catering, and for either Rick or one of the production assistants to give them their cue to get in their positions to start the backstage portion of their performance, once their cameras went live for the GWA's weekly TV show.

As soon as the kids went back to the classroom and everyone who wasn't supposed to be in the background of the vignette had moved off to the side of the room, Rick directed the three members of Protection Detail to sit at a specific table. Then he positioned several of the other performers at the various tables around them to make it seem like they were still in the middle of dinner time, but were maintaining kayfabe by having the heels and babyfaces on opposite sides of the room.

From the corner of her eye, Rylie could see Rick off in the corner behind the camera as he watched the monitor while the opening credits ran, the same way everyone at home would see the show opening. Then he gave the signal for a couple of the local women, who were there for a try-out match that night, to walk over and start flirting with Protection Detail.

"Are these seats taken?" Rylie couldn't remember the name of the busty blonde, who sat down on the other side of Magnum without waiting for him to answer, but it didn't take much acting talent for her to roll her eyes at the over-the-top performance of her role as a distraction for the big guy, who according to the storyline was supposed to be protecting Chastity from the advances of the other men in the company.

"We're such huge fans of yours," the bubbly brunette, who was dressed in a cheerleader gimmick to match her blonde partner, gushed as she took the seat on the other side of Trojan, placed her hand on his forearm, and comically batted her eyelashes. "And hope you can give us some tips on how not to be nervous during our try-out match."

"Of course we can, sweetheart," Trojan replied, playing his part perfectly.

Yeah, I bet both Magnum and Trojan are planning to console those girls with their dicks later, if their wrestling skills are as bad as their acting and they don't get GWA contracts, Rylie thought as she followed the script, stood from her seat, and walked over to the dessert table, pretending to try to choose between a variety of fruits and cookies. She knew her gimmick partners were two of the biggest players in the company. Yeah, they watched out for her and always checked her room for intruders since Allissa's stalker had been able to find out her room number to bypass the front desk and send her flowers at the hotel in San Francisco the weekend of the *Gateway to the Gold* pay-per-view. But she also knew that once they left her in her room for the night, they both went trolling for ring rats. *It's a good thing they got that condom sponsorship deal as part of their gimmick, 'cause even our hefty GWA salaries wouldn't be enough to cover the massive number of condoms they go through each week, even if they only personally use half as many as they throw out to the fans.*

"'Ey, Chastity," Red greeted her as he and Dark Chocolate walked up, already in their tights for wrestling that night.

Rylie had to fight not to obviously enjoy the eye candy that was Liam Connery in spandex pants and his ring jacket, which was a blinged-out tuxedo jacket with tails, sans shirt. *Just glance at him, don't look too long. Okay, just don't look too interested. Play it cool,* she told herself when she couldn't help but turn her head in his direction to get a glimpse of the smooth, lightly tanned skin covering his sculpted pecs and six-pack abs, which were peeking out between the open lapels of his jacket. *He's supposed to be showing his interest in me, not the other way around. But damn, it's hard to hide my attraction to him when I want to lick his abs way more than I want to take a bite of the cupcake we're using in the promo tonight. Or better yet, I'd rather spread the cupcake frosting on his abs and lick it off. But I probably shouldn't improvise quite that much. Just what I have planned is going to be a little close to crossing the line on how salacious Rick wants the GWA's programming to be. Actually licking him would blast right past that line and might get me fired.*

Once again, Liam's eyes roamed over her from head to toe, causing her whole body to tingle from the lusty look in his eyes as he noticed her half-zip pullover was completely unzipped.

Wow, I guess the girls were right about the need to show some extra cleavage, Rylie realized before turning her head back toward the table to feign being more interested in the food than the man standing beside her.

As she peered around Liam to see what was on the opposite end of the table from where she was standing, she noticed Dion in his position at Liam's back. It was like Dion was keeping himself between Liam and Protection Detail, so the guys wouldn't notice Liam flirting with her, but at the same time he appeared to be focused on loading a plate with every chocolate cookie option on the table.

Damn, Dark Chocolate must really have a sweet tooth. Or at least he wants the fans to think he does, anyway.

"Oh, um, hi, Red." Rylie tried to act coy as she pretended to finally notice Liam and turned away from the table to fully face him. But it was hard not to smirk when he seemed to involuntarily lick his lips while his gaze lingered on her tits.

"Ye know ye don't 'afta put up wit dose guys ignorin' ye, right? Dere are other teams ye could manage dat wouldn't toss ye over for a couple o' ring rats like dat." Red tilted his head in the direction of the table where she'd been sitting, where Magnum and Trojan were really playing up the distracted schtick by cozying up with the two girls that she couldn't believe Rick was paying five-hundred dollars each to practically crawl in the guys' laps for a few minutes of TV time.

Not that she could pay enough attention to what was going on across the room to really comment on any of their acting abilities, when Red turning on the Irish accent he used for his gimmick instantly soaked her panties.

"Oh, I don't know about that." Rylie leaned back and rested her hands on the edge of the table, thrusting her chest out just a little more, which Liam apparently noticed since his eyes dropped from her face to her cleavage once more. "I hired them to protect *my virtue, not theirs.* And they've done a pretty good job of that so far. So, I don't really have much of an incentive to switch teams now."

"Ah, but I might 'ave jus de thing ta entice ye ta pick a new team." Red pulled a bakery box from behind his back, opening it to reveal a half dozen red velvet cupcakes topped with swirls of cream cheese frosting and red heart-shaped sprinkles. "Red Velvet cupcakes."

"Hmmm, are they tasty?" Rylie leaned in closer to Liam, showing her interest in this new dessert option.

"Ye'll 'afta try 'em ta find out." Liam lifted one of the cupcakes from the box before placing the box down on the table. He then peeled the paper off one section and held it out for her to take a bite.

Instead of biting into the cake portion like they'd planned when practicing this scene earlier without the food, Rylie stuck her tongue out and licked from the side of the cupcake through the frosting to the very top of the swirl, where she closed her lips, in a manner similar to how she imagined closing her lips over the head of his cock if she ever got the pleasure of giving him a blow job, to take off half the frosting and sprinkles. She then closed her eyes and made a big production of savoring the flavor, moaning sensually as she swallowed it down.

"Hmmm, very tasty," she teased as she opened her eyes and licked her lips. She closed the open box on the table before picking it up and turning to walk away in the opposite direction of the table where she'd been sitting with Protection Detail, looking over her shoulder to deliver her final line. "Thanks for my special dessert, Red Velvet."

Red gaped at her as she walked out of camera range, opening and closing his mouth as he floundered for how to respond while still holding the cupcake that was now missing half the frosting.

As soon as the red light on the camera went off, half the people in the room erupted in laughter, including Dion, who'd apparently had to turn his back to the camera when she had her eyes closed, so it wouldn't be obvious that he was smiling at the way she'd changed things up.

"Fuck, I'm sorry," Dion chortled, slapping a hand on Liam's back. "I know I missed my line there at the end, but I figured it was better to skip asking if that meant she'd manage us than to accidentally say what I was thinking right then."

"What were you thinking right then?" Rylie wondered aloud as she returned the box of cupcakes to the dessert table.

"Did she skip the chocolate cake 'cause she's only interested in the creamy white guy with red on top?" Dion mussed Liam's short reddish-brown hair as he teased his tag-team partner.

"Glad I'm not the only one who thought it was odd that he'd basically insinuated he wanted her to eat both of ya'll," James Hunter chuckled. "Especially after the way ya'll ragged on me about the Chocolate Cream Pie promo last year."

"Good job salvaging that, Chas," Dean added, praising her performance as he nodded in agreement with his brother while pointing and smiling at Rylie. "Way to make it obvious that you were only flirting with Red."

"Yes, excellent job improvising, Chastity," Rick agreed, nodding. "Even though this feud is between tag teams, we definitely need to make sure the lines are clear about who's flirting with whom. So, instead of having both you guys go out to ringside for Chastity's match later, I think we should just have Red go out there to cheer her on. You still need to make eyes at her and get in the ring to congratulate her when she goes over. But instead of discussing the match with D, stay quiet and more contemplative as you watch, and let your appreciation show in your facial expressions."

Rylie knew Rick wanted to protect the Inglemans by preventing as much speculation as possible about poly-partnerships in the dirt sheets covering the happenings in the GWA, so she was glad her little improv in the scene could be perceived as helping with that goal. But since she'd actually done it to tease Liam with the image of her giving a blow job, she still felt a little bad about accepting everyone's accolades for her quick thinking.

But I'm not about to tell any of them that while Liam's standing right here, she thought, trying to come up with a way to quickly excuse herself to go get ready for her match.

"Kinda like that lusty look he got when she licked his…cupcake?" Dean chuckled.

"Or the fish-outta-water look when she walked away from him?" James questioned.

"Yeah, but nothing else blatantly graphic, so hopefully, the FCC will overlook Chastity imitating a sexual act on a cupcake so early in the evening and won't fine us," Rick groused, even though he was smiling bigger than Rylie had ever seen before from their stoic boss.

"Yeah, I got it, Boss," Liam declared, no longer looking in her direction.

"Yeah, I, um," Rylie stuttered, pointing over her shoulder with her thumb in the direction of the locker rooms, "better go get changed for my match. We're still up fifth on the card, right?"

"Yes," Rick replied, even though she didn't wait for his answer before turning and beelining toward the women's locker room.

She'd barely made it to her locker when she was surrounded by most of the women who wrestled for the GWA, minus Holly and Shauna, whom she knew were waiting in the gorilla position to go out for their tag-team match with the chesty cheerleaders trying out that night in the second match on the card, along with Kay and Cait.

"That was awesome!" Randi fist bumped her as the other ladies all voiced their agreement.

"I can't believe you were brave enough to really flash your titties at him like that on live TV." Emerald pointed at Rylie's chest, as Rylie took off her warmups to put on the iridescent white bodysuit she wrestled in most often.

"Oh, please," Allissa scoffed at Emerald's comment before fighting not to laugh as she made the same joke about Rylie's ring name that Rylie had a few times in the past. "She is Chas-*titty* after all."

"Yeah, but she's supposed to be acting all virginal and shit, so I woulda thought someone woulda said something about how low her zipper was before the cameras came on, so Rick could keep the show family friendly," Emerald replied, shaking her head. "But kudos to you for managing to let a little of your inner heel show through."

"Maybe this will lead to turning Chas-*titty* heel when Emerald turns face?" Randi suggested.

"Oh, I wish I didn't have to avoid using any of ya'll's names in my books," Kay chortled. "Especially since I know Rick would never let ya'll say it that way on one of your shows."

"No, I'm still supposed to be a face," Rylie interjected, not even wanting to think about the possibility of being a character in one of Kay's romance novels as she reached back to zip up her bodysuit before sitting down to put on her kneepads and wrestling boots. "Just reluctantly accompanying my heel husband to ringside once it's revealed that he tricked me into marrying him in Vegas."

"They're not planning to imply he's forcing himself on you as part of this storyline, are they?" Cait appeared concerned as she voiced the question. "'Cause I don't think any of the kids need to see something like that."

"No, that's not part of the plan," Rylie assured her new friend. "It's all supposed to be lame, cheesy attempts at flirting to woo me away from Protection Detail, so they can have a series of pay-per-view matches where they swap my management services back and forth along with the tag-team titles. Rick said he's going to use this feud to eventually turn Protection Detail heel and Red Velvet back to babyfaces, since Red will be my doting, faithful husband, while Magnum and Trojan will be shown for the players they are. But that will be sometime next year, and even then, I'm not turning heel with the guys."

"I bet that's why he's focusing on only women's tryouts recently," Amethyst added, nodding like the plans their boss was making finally made sense to her. "He's not just trying to expand the women's division, so we have more variety to our matches. He needs to find someone to act as Dion's love interest for this angle to work at turning Red Velvet."

Damn, I hope Liam doesn't welcome any new women Rick hires the same way he welcomed me to the company, Rylie thought, feeling jealous of her imaginary rivals for his attention. *'Cause I don't think I can handle seeing him with someone else, even if he's just treating one of them like the friend I used to be to him.*

As the ladies around her all discussed the possibilities, Rylie couldn't help but hope that working closely with Liam over the next few months would bring out the man he'd been before they found out they'd gotten married. Even if things didn't work out for them to stay married, or ever take a shot at being a real couple, Rylie missed the friendship she'd had with him, and hoped they could at least get some of that back. *And hopefully, he won't decide to fall for the next woman Rick signs to the roster before the ink's even dry on our annulment papers.*

Chapter Four

Brent couldn't believe how much the online speculation about which of the GWA performers had gotten married in Las Vegas had increased in the last week, as had the pictures in the dirt sheets of everyone in the GWA. It didn't matter if they were walking through an airport, entering a hotel or arena, or out in public sightseeing or having a meal. Every person on the GWA roster kept being photographed everywhere they went. It was crazy how they'd all seemed to somehow move up in the rankings of celebrity status all at the same time. They were being watched so closely by every Tom, Dick, and Harry with a phone camera that Brent no longer felt safe taking Aiken on dates in public places.

Hell, that probably has more to do with the way Rick's responding to the increased scrutiny more than me wanting to protect her, though. Right? I'm probably just confusing the way I'm picking up on Rick's suspicions as me feeling as protective and obsessive about Aiken as he is about his wife and daughter. I'm not really starting to have feelings for her, other than the lust that's always kinda been there.

Considering Rick was getting paranoid because of the daily pictures and threats being sent to them from Allissa's stalker, he'd put a moratorium on as many of their public appearances as possible. He still wanted the guys to make sure the ladies never went anywhere alone, but he'd asked both Brent and Josh to limit their "dates" with their wives to the hotels and arenas as much as possible. He'd even vetoed going sightseeing with the GWA families, which was what Brent had planned for most of his "dates" with Aiken. The families were even having to skip their usual outings until Rick could arrange even more security personnel to accompany everyone in the GWA, no matter where they went.

Because of these new restrictions, he'd spent a lot more time alone with Aiken than he'd intended. Instead of being able to keep their conversations limited to whatever they were learning about the various places where they went sightseeing, they'd spent that time actually talking and getting to know one another over their midday dates.

Learning about her family and sharing stories of their childhoods over lunch dates in hotel restaurants only seemed to amplify his attraction to her. She was intelligent, way smarter than he considered himself to be, as well as compassionate and fun loving. She laughed at his stupid jokes, and came up with some of the best ideas for ways to prank their coworkers. He was afraid he was really starting to like her for more than just how beautiful she was, and he didn't know how to handle that. At least, not until the stalker was dealt with, so he could distance himself from her to keep from acting on the massive desire he had to claim his conjugal rights.

Needless to say, there were only so many times he could arrange meals in the hotel restaurant, or workouts in the hotel gym, before he took things too far with his wife. Especially when she insisted on wearing those sexy as fuck, form-fitting workout shorts and tank tops for their exercise sessions, like the purple set she was wearing right then.

Fuck! What the hell was I thinking when I suggested a lower body workout for today? If I keep watching her bend over for those deadlifts very much longer, I don't know if I'll be able to resist walking up behind her to rub my dick against her tight little ass. But hell, since she's a foot shorter than my six-foot-three, I'd have to set up a step bench with a few risers under it to be able to fuck her from behind. And I doubt sweet little Aiken would be down for that here in the hotel gym, where any of the guys could walk in at any moment.

Fuck! I need to get that fantasy outta my head. I'm only dating her to keep her safe until that fuckhead stalker is caught. Not because I really think we should stay married. And if I don't feel up to all that love and babies stuff I'm pretty sure she wants, then I really shouldn't give her false hope by acting on the attraction and lustful fantasies I'm having.

As she cycled through a circuit of dumbbell squats, lunges, and stiff-legged deadlifts, Brent couldn't take his eyes off her firm, toned ass in the short shorts that reminded him of a less flashy version of the shimmery booty shorts she wore to wrestle. His total lack of focus on his own workout made him grateful the hotel had a Smith machine for him to safely do his own set of squats, when he couldn't focus on his form the way he'd need to if he was using a traditional barbell loaded down with weight plates.

Thank fuck, I remembered to wear a cup for this workout, so she can't tell how my dick is trying to pitch a tent in my sweats. Now if I can just think of something else to deflate this erection, so I don't end up with permanent cup impressions on my cock.

Maybe I can come up with something we can talk about to get my mind off of how much I want to fuck her? I mean, she's gonna figure out that I'm only sticking so close to her right now to keep her safe if we don't keep using these dates to get to know one another better, right?

"Okay, I have to ask." Brent finally broke the silence between them as he racked the three-hundred pounds he'd been squatting after losing count of his reps. "I know your ring gear is purple because of your gimmick, but with as often as you wear purple when you're not dressing for the gimmick, I have to wonder if it's your favorite color. Is that why you picked Amethyst as your ring name, 'cause it's purple?"

"Actually, I picked Amethyst because it's my birthstone," she panted without stopping her exercise. "Amethysts being purple gemstones dictated the color of my ring gear, but I added so much purple to my wardrobe, so I can consider some of my more casual clothes as gimmick wear and don't always have to dress up to meet the company dress code for traveling. My favorite color is actually pink. What about you? What's your favorite color? And why did you pick a lumberjack gimmick?"

Pink, huh? Yeah, that sounds about right for a Disney princess like Aiken. Then again, I bet she has some sexy as hell pink parts. Hell, if I ever get the chance to see how pink her nipples and pussy get when she's turned on, I might just pick pink as my favorite color, too.

"I don't really have a favorite color," Brent shrugged before retrieving his water bottle and taking a drink, needing to redirect their topic of conversation, since his first attempt at picking a subject to break the silence hadn't done much to help him get his dick under control. He then adjusted the weight plates on the Smith machine to drop down to two-hundred-and-fifty pounds for a set of lunges as he elaborated on his gimmick choice. "And I picked my gimmick because I come from a long line of loggers. But when I'm walking to the ring carrying an ax, I probably look more like my ancestors from the eighteen-hundreds, who did the backbreaking labor of actually using axes to cut down trees, than my dad, who worked his way up to middle-management, so he could spend more time behind a desk than out in the woods. Especially since he doesn't remember ever using anything more primitive than a chainsaw, even when he first got started logging as a teenager."

"Well, that makes a lot more sense than what I originally thought when I first met you," Aiken giggled as she racked her dumbbells and took a quick water break. "I thought you were taking advantage of having the same last name as Davy Crockett. But he was a frontiersman and not a lumberjack, so I thought you must have mixed him up with Paul Bunyan."

"No," Brent chuckled along with her. "I might not have done well enough in school to learn about Edgar Allan Poe, but I know the difference between Davy Crockett and Paul Bunyan."

He still felt like an idiot for not knowing anything about the famous poet, other than recognizing his name as someone who was as well known for his writing as William Shakespeare and Mark Twain. He'd never been much of a reader, hating most of the stuff he'd had to read in his high school English classes. Even now, the only time he picked up a book was if a famous athlete he liked watching put out an autobiography. But when he'd heard Cooper Stafford talking to his sons, Connor and Cody, about a poem titled *Romance*, he'd thought the museum about the poet would be an appropriate place for taking his sweet, if unintentional, bride on a first date.

Thankfully, she'd laughed off his lack of knowledge and seemed to think his attempt at being romantic for their first date was endearing, even though he'd failed miserably. They'd still ended up having a good time, and the outing had worked a lot better at helping him stay close to her without being tempted to act on his attraction to her than it probably would have if he'd taken her someplace dedicated to sappy love poems, like he'd originally thought.

"You seem quieter than normal today," Aiken pointed out, as he stepped back under the bar and started his set of stationary lunges. "Is that because of how heavy you're lifting and needing to concentrate to count your reps? Or are you getting bored with me already?"

Neither, Brent thought as he tried to regulate his breathing with the movement. *It's because I can't focus on anything but staring at your sexy ass in those short shorts.*

"I'm definitely not bored with you, Amethyst." Brent smiled at her as he stood to his full height and switched the position of his feet, hoping he'd actually completed the ten reps he'd planned for each set in this workout before switching sides. "But it is harder to concentrate to keep track of my sets and reps while trying to carry on a conversation, and not making you feel like I'm objectifying you when I keep looking at you, instead of checking my form in the mirror."

"Really?" Aiken arched an eyebrow at him curiously. "Your eyes look more like they're glazed over, like you're lost in your thoughts instead of looking at me, which is why I thought you were bored."

"No, I'm not bored," Brent chuckled self-deprecatingly as he hooked the bar on the rack once more to take a break between sets, still not a hundred percent certain he'd done exactly ten reps on either side. "You haven't been talking much either today. Is that because you're bored?"

"No, I'm not bored. I'm just..." Aiken's voice trailed off as she turned away from him, picked up a single thirty-pound dumbbell, and started doing a set of plié squats. "I'm just not sure what we're doing. I mean, I've enjoyed our midday dates, but I'm not sure how they're going to help us decide whether or not to dissolve our marriage, when it feels more like we're just hanging out as friends and not as a couple."

Fuck! I was afraid she was gonna start expecting more than just friendly dates. But how am I supposed to tell her that I'm more than willing to spend all our date time fucking, like Josh and Emerald are, but I'm still gonna wanna dissolve the marriage as soon as we can schedule an appointment with an attorney?

I don't want to hurt her by letting her know that these dates are just my way of staying close to keep her safe because Rick wants us all on guard while dealing with this stalker situation. But damn, she'll be even more hurt if I let us cross the line to a sexual relationship, when I know we're not going to end in the happily ever after I'm sure she's dreaming of.

But fuck, she looks hurt now because she obviously thinks I haven't made a move 'cause I'm not attracted to her, which is so not the case. Maybe I can stall her a little by telling her I want us to go slow?

"Sorry, I haven't really done the whole relationship thing before," Brent shrugged before getting into position to start a second set of lunges, "so to keep from screwing it up, I figured we should go slow and start out building our friendship first before trying for more."

"I suppose that makes sense," she agreed as she sat her dumbbell down on the floor between her feet for a break between sets. "But we've been going on these dates for a week now, without even holding hands or kissing to see if we have any chemistry. I mean, yeah, friendship should be the foundation for a strong marriage, but even a great friendship isn't enough if there's no chemistry. So, it seems to me that we could save ourselves a lot of time on awkward friend dates by testing our chemistry at least once."

Fuck! I'm gonna have to kiss her to keep her from putting herself in danger by going off on her own instead of hanging out with me. And if I kiss her, I'm liable to lose control and push things too far.

Aiken paused long enough to take a drink of water, continuing once she put her water bottle down and picked up her dumbbell once more. "But I understand if I'm not your type or whatever. You don't have to try to force yourself to develop an attraction to me that's not there. We can just plan to meet with our attorneys when we go through L.A. and Portland next month."

"No!" Brent shouted as he fumbled to re-rack his weights, surprising himself with how vehemently his whole body protested that plan. Especially since he'd had the same thought, when he realized they'd be in both of their hometowns on weekdays only two days apart in less than a month. With the way his heart rate picked up, he was afraid he couldn't blame such a visceral reaction on his dick's desire to fuck her, either. At least, not completely. "Wanting to go slow has absolutely nothing to do with not being attracted to you. If anything, it's the exact opposite."

Aiken put the dumbbell back down without finishing the set she'd just started, turning to look directly at him, instead of continuing to only make eye contact through the mirror on the gym wall. "The opposite? How?"

"I'm extremely attracted to you," he admitted, yanking the rubber band out of his hair, so he could run his hand through it nervously, even though he knew he'd just have to put it right back up to keep it out of his way while lifting. "Hell, I'm so attracted to you that I have to wear a jockstrap whenever we workout together to keep from popping a boner every time I look at you. And I'm pretty sure our chemistry is gonna be explosive. So, I've been trying to take things slow to keep us from burning out fast like my parents did."

Fuck! I so did not mean to admit any of that out loud, he thought, closing his eyes momentarily and missing the way she looked down at the bulge under his heather-gray sweatpants.

While Brent didn't believe Aiken was the type to flake out and leave the way his mother had, he wasn't so sure about himself. He'd been young when she left, but he still remembered the way his mom and dad fought right before then. He hadn't completely understood it as a kid, but now looking back, he could see that his parents had the same kind of explosive chemistry he feared he had with Aiken.

His parents had barely known each other when a night of passion led them to get married because he was on the way. Their sexual combustibility was only enough to sustain their marriage for five or six years because they never took the time to build the foundation of friendship, which Brent recognized as the basis for the most stable marriages he'd witnessed in recent years among his friends, coworkers, and their families.

And even though his dad had provided the stable parental presence in his life, Brent knew he got half his DNA from his obviously flaky mom, which made him question his own ability to stick it out and fully commit to a relationship. Hell, he hadn't ever committed enough to spending a full night with a woman before, so dating Aiken for a full week still felt like an anomaly to him. One he wasn't sure he'd be able to maintain long term.

While he still didn't think there was much, if any, chance for him and Aiken to stay married and have the same things their friends were recently finding, Brent still wanted to build that friendship with her.

Even if it didn't lead to the happily ever after he knew she wanted, he felt like it was the only way they'd be able to navigate the legalities of dissolving their union without making things awkward and risking one or both of their careers with the GWA.

"You told me your mom left right after you started school, but you didn't really get into details the other day." Aiken reached out and took his hand, lightly pulling to get him to follow her over to an empty weight bench, where she sat down without releasing his hand. "Maybe it would help us both understand now, if you tell me a little more about what happened back then."

"Not much to explain," Brent sighed, plopping down beside her, and feeling staggered by how comforting it was to hold her dainty hand in his much larger, rougher one. "They confused lust for falling in love at first sight, and got married a month after meeting because I was on the way."

At least, that was what Brent thought happened after finding the scrapbook his mom had left behind when she took off, looking through it as an adult, and noticing the dates she'd documented for when various events happened. Since his dad didn't really like to talk about his mom, Brent had to figure out their dynamic for himself, once he was old enough to understand the clues.

"They never really took the time to get to know each other outside the bedroom, so when the lust wore off, they fought for a few weeks, and then she left."

"So, now you think we need to be friends first to be able to make our marriage work once the honeymoon period is over?"

He couldn't tell if Aiken intended for her statement to come out as a question, or if he just heard it that way. But either way, he couldn't respond, so he just sat there, looking down at their joined hands. *Fuck! If I agree with her, then I'll be giving her false hope for the two of us. But if I disagree, then I'll kill any chance of us remaining friends and keeping our careers unscathed by our mistake of a marriage.*

When she just sat there quietly, though, he knew he had to say something. "I just don't want us to make the same mistakes my parents did. And as much as I'm sure we'd both enjoy all the benefits of being married, sex complicates things. It makes feelings seem stronger than they are, which can lead to more pain if things don't work out. But if we take things slow and focus on our friendship, then neither one of us will get hurt, and we can stay friends, even if we decide not to stay married."

"Okay." Aiken nodded once before tilting her head thoughtfully. "But I wasn't really talking about jumping straight to sex. I know we're nowhere near ready for that. I just meant we could test our chemistry by showing one another affection in other, more innocent ways. I mean, I hug my girl friends all the time, and have even kissed guy friends platonically, at like New Year's and stuff. So, it seems like we should be able to do those things without going faster than you feel comfortable."

"And holding hands," Brent added to her list of signs of affection that they could start using with one another, smiling, and lifting their joined hands to make his point. "Yeah, we can definitely start doing those things."

"Great," Aiken smiled before leaning up to brush her lips across his cheek right above the line of his beard. "Now we'd better hurry up and finish this workout, so we have time to go clean up without being late getting to the arena."

As she stood, he lightly tugged her hand to stop her from walking away from him. "I think we can do a little more than cheek kisses."

He reached up with his free hand to cup her face, gently pulling her back down so he could get a small taste of her luscious lips. The instant their lips touched, he felt a strong jolt to his systems, like he'd been struck by lightning. It felt like the universe was trying to send him a message about him and Aiken that Brent wasn't sure he felt ready to hear.

He desperately wanted to part her lips and plunge his tongue inside to truly enjoy kissing his wife. But that wouldn't exactly fit with the message of taking things slow that he'd just sold her on, so he kept the kiss sweet and chaste, releasing her after only a few seconds of brushing his lips over hers. He knew that if such a sweet, innocent kiss incited such a feeling of being awestruck by his beautiful bride, then he wasn't prepared for how he'd feel if they exchanged anything more carnal between them.

Aiken appeared as dazed as he felt by their chemistry when they parted. Then she dazzled him with her brilliant smile. "Actually, I think we should probably go ahead and clean up our equipment, so I can have a little extra time in the shower before we have to leave for the arena."

"Yeah, me too," Brent agreed, wondering if she'd be using that time to touch herself, as he planned to use it to jerk off.

They quickly put away the weights they'd used, wiping everything down before he walked her up to her room. As soon as he checked her room for any unwanted visitors, he practically ran down the hall to his room, eager for that shower to fantasize about his wife while yanking his cock.

Unfortunately, as soon as he got his hotel room door open, his phone rang with his father's ringtone. *Guess I'll be taking a quick, cold shower instead,* he thought as he answered the call. "Hi, Dad. What's up?"

"Not much. Just checking in to see how things are going with you and your new wife."

Harlan Crockett didn't normally inquire about his son's love life nearly as often as he'd started "checking in" over the last nine days. So, Brent had to wonder if his unintentional marriage was giving his dad thoughts of being a grandpa. *I should have realized those stories about his friends showing off pictures of their grandkids were hints about him wanting a grandkid of his own.*

"Wanted to see if keeping her safe from this stalker has changed your mind about setting up an appointment with the lawyer when you're in town next month."

"Yeah, maybe," Brent confided, unsure if his change of heart was just because he didn't think the stalker would be caught by then, or if he was starting to feel more for his wife than he wanted to admit, even to himself. "I can't really push her for an annulment and still expect her to stay close to me so I can protect her."

"No, that's…" Harlan's voice trailed off momentarily as he seemed to think about his words before finishing his sentence. "…true. But that wasn't really why I thought you might have changed your mind."

"Oh? Why else would I change my mind?" Brent stepped into the ensuite bathroom, knowing he'd need to jump straight in the shower as soon as the call with his dad ended. He put his phone on speaker mode and laid it on the bathroom counter, stripping off his t-shirt.

"Well, I don't know if you realize this, Son, but you come from a long line of Crockett men, who only fall in love once in their lives. And when they fall, it's usually hard and fast."

Brent was so surprised by his dad's statement that he momentarily froze with his shirt only halfway off. Both arms were still trapped in the sleeves, and the collar of the shirt was still around his neck, with his face covered by the inside-out garment.

"With as protective as you're acting toward Aiken, I thought maybe this whole stalker situation might have revealed your true feelings for her, which I think you acted on when your inhibitions were down from drinking too much in Vegas."

Brent somehow managed to wrestle his way out of his t-shirt, so his dad could hear him without his voice being muffled by the garment. "Wait a minute. You think I married her because I…what? Secretly harbored feelings for her that I only let out when I was too drunk to keep hiding them?"

"Exactly," Harlan agreed, sounding quite confident in his opinion. "And you're not the first of us to take advantage of a situation to get to marry the woman you love, even if she didn't really return the devotion."

"Really? You recently get married and not tell me about my new step-mom?" Brent shoved his sweatpants to the floor, toeing out of his sneakers so he could fully remove the pants and his jockstrap.

"No, not recently," his dad chuckled. "But I did push your mom to marry me, even though I knew she didn't love me half as much as I love her."

"Loved, you mean," Brent scoffed, shaking his head even though his dad couldn't see him. "Since she left us over twenty-five years ago and never once looked back, that should really be past tense."

"No, I said exactly what I mean," Harlan claimed, sounding way more certain of his feelings than Brent expected. "I still love your mom. Always have. Always will. Why do you think I've never been able to do more than scratch an itch with another woman? And won't ever get serious with anyone else?"

Holy shit! Brent flopped down onto the toilet, his knees buckling at the realization that he'd been wrong in his assumptions about what his parents felt for one another. Or at least, possibly wrong about what his dad felt for his mom. He was still pretty sure that his mom never really loved his dad, or him, or else she wouldn't have been able to walk away from them so easily without any further contact. *Could this mean he might be right about my feelings for Aiken?*

No, just because he thinks he's still in love with Mom, doesn't mean he really is. Or that he has a clue about my feelings. Feelings that I'm not even sure I'm capable of experiencing. He's probably just looking back through rose-colored glasses and letting his faulty memories influence what he thinks is happening with me and Aiken now.

"I don't know, Dad," Brent quavered, shaking his head in disbelief. "Before this happened, I've always just thought of Aiken like one of the guys, so I don't think I'm feeling what you think I'm feeling for her. Hell, even the *dates* we're doing to keep her from going off by herself with this stalker on the loose are things I'd do with any of my friends. It's not like we're sleeping together or anything like that."

No matter how bad I want to fuck her.

"Maybe not yet," his dad chuckled. "But you keep taking care of her like you are, and you'll get there eventually. In the meantime, I think I'm going to wait a couple more weeks before scheduling that appointment to give you time to come to terms with your feelings."

Brent really didn't want to argue with his dad, especially since he was afraid his dad might be at least partially right. "Whatever, Dad," he chuckled, removing his socks, and standing to start the shower. "Listen, I've gotta hurry and shower to get to the arena on time, so I'm gonna let you go. Take care."

"You, too. Love you, Son."

"Love you, too, Dad." Brent swiped the screen of his phone to disconnect the call, noting the time from his phone's display. *Fuck! I really am gonna hafta take a cold shower now.*

~~~

Just as Josh finished changing out of his workout clothes from the sparring session he did in the ring in place of a match run-through since he had the night off from wrestling, his phone rang from where he'd stashed it at the top of his locker. Considering he was expecting a call from his attorney, Cal Talbot, about the outcome of his efforts to
~~~

terminate Sarah Nash's employment and evict her from his house, Josh jumped up and grabbed the phone, swiping the screen to answer without even looking at the caller ID. *Fuck, I hope it's Cal with good news for me.*

"Parker," he barked into the receiver as he put the phone to his ear.

"Good afternoon, Josh. It's Cal."

"Please tell me it's done," Josh pleaded with his attorney. "And that you verified that she doesn't have pictures of the marriage license on her phone that she can post online."

"As you know, we notified her last Monday that her employment was being terminated and she had seven days to vacate the premises. You also know that she didn't allow me access to your home when I personally delivered the legal documents last week and that I had to wait that same seven-day period before I could gain entry with local law enforcement to have her removed from the house," Cal explained in his bland no-nonsense tone.

"Yeah, yeah, I know all that." They'd covered all the legal requirements when they talked the week before, along with why his dad couldn't be the Parker Security Services' employee that accompanied Cal to reset the security codes on Josh's alarm system and change his locks, so Josh didn't understand why Cal was reiterating it all again. He made a rolling motion with his free hand, wanting the attorney to get on with his update, even though he knew Cal couldn't see him through the phone. "Now tell me that you've got good news for me about how that went today."

"I do," Cal agreed, but Josh could hear the hesitation in his voice. "But I also have some bad news. The good news is that Sarah Nash has vacated your property. But unfortunately, she wasn't here when we arrived to change the locks, so I wasn't able to verify that she hasn't photographed your certificate of marriage."

"Fuck," Josh groaned, hating that they still had to worry about Sarah breaking the news on CNZ or one of the other gossip sites before he and Crockett could finish out their current angles and move from just some light flirtation with their wives to the feud Rick had planned for them to culminate at the *Saint Valentine's Day Massacre* show in four months. "Please tell me she at least left it in my desk and didn't take it with her to turn over to a reporter."

"Oh, yes, she left it on your desk," Cal confirmed, even though his voice didn't sound as upbeat as Josh thought it should with that news. "But it was torn to shreds, so we'll need to order another copy from the clerk's office for me to get all the information I need from it to add your wife to all your accounts and update your will and other legal affairs. And she basically trashed the rest of your house, so we're going to have to bring in a cleaning service and replace a lot of your furnishings."

"Great." Josh plopped back down on the bench in front of his locker, using his free hand to rub his temples with his thumb and middle finger. "I guess I'll call my mom and dad when I hang up with you, so I can forewarn them that they'll need to coordinate all that once you give them the extra override key you had to have today."

"Are you sure you want them to handle that? I can coordinate it for you after the police finish photographing everything to prosecute Ms. Nash for the property damage. And with all the bills going through my office, it'll be easier to sue her for reimbursement, since I'll already have all the receipts to back up the claim."

"Yeah, I'm sure," Josh chuckled ruefully. "And I'm not pressing charges for the property damage."

"I don't think you understand just how bad the destruction appears to be," Cal started, obviously about to try to change Josh's mind.

"Oh, I'm sure it's about as bad as it could possibly be," Josh scoffed, shaking his head, even though, again, his lawyer couldn't see him. Josh could easily picture Sarah throwing every breakable dish in his kitchen against the wall, along with every decorative item she could get her hands on. And if she couldn't break something with her bare hands, she'd probably gone and bought a few cans of spray paint to deface all the furniture, walls, and probably even a few appliances and bathroom fixtures, too. "But if we have her arrested for it, she'll either get a slap on the wrist and not learn her lesson, or she'll end up in jail and unable to work to pay any restitution. But if my parents come over and see what she's done, they'll make sure Sarah's parents know all about it. She still might not be able to find a decent enough job to be able to completely reimburse me for whatever I have to replace at the house. But I can one-hundred percent guarantee you that between Mom, Dad, and Mr. and Mrs. Nash, Sarah will be properly supervised while she cleans up the mess she made and will be put on a payment plan to cover it a little at a time. And having our parents involved will be a much worse punishment than whatever a judge might sentence her to."

The more he thought about it, the more Josh realized he should have looped his parents in the week before. Unlike Josh's friend Ben, who kept trying to bail his sister out without informing their parents of any of her issues, Connie and Cole Parker were more than capable of helping their friends, the Nashes, show their daughter some tough love. Remembering back to how his mom had shared his most embarrassing moments with everyone she knew when he was a teenager, Josh almost felt sorry for what Sarah was about to go through, now that Connie Parker had access to social media.

"And if she hasn't already shared pics of the marriage certificate, I'm sure my mom can keep her from possibly leaking it," Josh chuckled, imagining his mom posting pics of Sarah cleaning his house with a sign pinned to her shirt proclaiming what she'd done, kind of like those animal shaming pics that started going viral online a few years back. "Although, now I'm almost hoping she's already leaked it, so Mom can follow up with a bunch of Sarah shaming pics on social media to refute whatever false narrative she might be spreading about her relationship with me."

"Sarah shaming pics?" Cal sounded confused by Josh's words.

"Yeah, you know, like those pet shaming pictures you can find pretty much all over social media of dogs and cats next to signs saying how they misbehaved?" Josh explained, chuckling at the images in his head as he elaborated. "Like pictures of dogs with signs that say things like, 'I got excited to meet our visitors and peed on my human's new mother-in-law.' Or of cats with signs that say things like, 'I jump on the counter and push full glasses of wine off onto the carpet.' Only my mom would post pics of Sarah amid the destruction of my house with a sign pinned to her shirt that says, 'I threw a hissy fit like a spoiled child when my boss got married. And destroyed his house after lying about him and spreading rumors online because I was mad that he's never been interested in me.' I'm sure Mom would just have to suggest posting pics like that online to get Sarah to delete any pictures she might have taken of the marriage license with the intent to share it with CNZ."

"Maybe we should put your mom on the ballot next time we vote for a new judge," Cal chuckled.

"I speak from experience when I say her creative punishments are very effective," Josh laughed along with him. "And if you can convince her to run for a position with the criminal court, her creative court rulings might help reduce prison overcrowding, too."

"Okay, well, since I'm heading to their place now, I'll let your parents know what's going on and how you want to handle everything."

"Cool, then I'll wait 'til after dinner to call them," Josh decided, knowing his mom had insisted he'd better have his bride available to talk to them the next time he called, after he made the mistake of calling to inform them of his marriage when he was alone in his hotel room in Atlantic City on the first day they found out any of them had tied the knot in Vegas. "That way you have time to meet with them first, and I have time to get Teagan somewhere private where we can both talk to them this time."

They soon signed off on the call. Then Josh stuck his phone in the pocket of his slacks and closed his locker. Since he wasn't wrestling that night, he'd changed back into the same business casual gray dress pants and green button-down that he'd worn to travel from Savannah, Georgia that morning, hoping to be able to leave the arena early since Teagan also wasn't scheduled to wrestle that night.

When he sat down beside her in catering, however, he realized that his wife still had to make an appearance at ringside during Blade and Amethyst's match against Vaughn and Shauna Valor. They were currently using their house shows to test fan reactions to their match options for the *Halloween Horror* show coming up at the end of the month. Since it was going to be the blow-off match to end their feud, so they could start working on splitting up the Precious Stones for the new angle between Surfer Josh and Crockett, they knew it had to be a mixed-tag match, but Rick hadn't decided yet which of the Precious Stones would be wrestling and which would be at ringside for the pay-per-view.

When Josh heard that Amethyst was wrestling on the card that night instead of Emerald, he'd immediately jumped straight to all the ideas of ways he and Teagan could take advantage of them both having the night off, not realizing that Emerald still had to be at ringside for the match. And while technically, he could still sneak off for some private time with her while they were waiting for her to have to go down to the ring, the fact that she was dressed in a sexy emerald green catsuit for the show would make sneaking off for a quickie backstage next to impossible.

Damn it! Sneaking around to find a spot backstage where we wouldn't get caught woulda been fun. But maybe we should try that for our midday date tomorrow, since Rick has us limited to staying in the hotel or arena for those now?

Josh had only been able to take her out to some great eateries for lunch and on cool dates, like the Red Door Escape Room in Richmond, Virginia and the True Crime Tour in Raleigh, North Carolina, a few times before Rick started getting worked up about all the pictures in the dirt sheets. So, while they still spent that midday time talking over meals and getting to know one another even better than they already had, they'd only spent half that time in the hotel restaurants or gyms, opting to spend the other half of it connecting more intimately in bed.

Since they'd already been friends, Josh felt like he'd already known a lot about Teagan, at least on a superficial level. And while their private talks definitely made him feel like he was getting to know her on a much deeper level, he felt like all the time he spent making love to her was essential in building his bond with Teagan and strengthening their relationship enough that she wouldn't ultimately decide to end their marriage.

Fuck! At least, I hope I'm doing everything right to get her to fall so deep in love with me that she won't ever want us to end. I don't think I'll survive it if this shit with Sarah scares her off of wanting to be with me. But maybe I should up the romance a little bit to make sure I convince her that we're meant for one another.

Obviously, I don't need to change anything about the sex, 'cause that's already better than I've ever even imagined. But maybe I need to do more outside the bedroom to be romantic, like buying her flowers or jewelry or something?

Shit, we don't even have wedding rings! How is she supposed to know that I want us to really make a go of this marriage if I haven't even put a ring on her finger? I wonder if I can get a jewelry store to bring a selection of wedding sets to our hotel for us to pick out something she'll like?

No, it needs to be something more special than whatever I can get some random jeweler to bring to us. Something like my great-grandma's emerald ring, so she'll know how special I think she is that I want her to have a family heirloom. One I hope she'll one day pass down to one of our kids or grandkids. And it's perfect that it's an emerald ring, since her ring name is Emerald. Yeah, that's definitely the ring I should give her. Too bad I won't be able to pick it up before next month when we're in San Diego.

"Everything okay?" Teagan arched an eyebrow curiously at him, making him worry slightly that she was picking up on his momentary fear of losing her. "I was beginning to wonder if one of the guys had hidden your clothes or something, since you took so much longer to get back out here than everyone else."

"Everything's fine," Josh smiled, glad she hadn't been able to read his mind, and instead, had followed her thoughts in a different direction, knowing the prank she'd described had been overdone in the last few years among the GWA crew. "Great, actually. I'm only late getting out here for dinner because I was on the phone with my attorney, finding out Sarah has officially been evicted."

"That is great news," Teagan grinned back before taking a sip from her water bottle. "Was he able to verify that she didn't take any pics of the marriage license or share them with anyone?"

"Unfortunately, no," Josh sighed, shaking his head. "She'd already vacated the premises before he got there with the authorities to change the locks. And she completely trashed the place before she left. So, now we have to come up with some other ways of making sure she doesn't share the pictures, if she took any before she tore the certificate up and left it amongst the rubble."

Teagan's eyes widened as she stabbed her salad with her fork rather aggressively. "He had the cops with him to see what she'd done, though, right? So they can hunt her down and arrest her for destroying your property?"

"Yeah, Cal said the cops are photographing everything, but I told him I don't want to press charges."

"Why the fuck would you tell him something stupid like that?" Teagan screeched, dropping her fork before putting the bite on the tines in her mouth.

"Because having her arrested won't do a thing to keep her from sharing whatever pictures she took of our certificate of marriage and spreading a bunch of lies about being my jilted lover," Josh admitted, hating that he had to bring up Sarah's crush on him as part of his explanation. "But having my parents talk to her parents, so they can get her the mental help she needs, just might."

"No, it won't," Teagan scoffed, rolling her eyes at him. "She's a grown woman, not a little kid. Having Mommy and Daddy try to ground her isn't going to do a damn thing. But spending a little time in jail, or out picking up trash on the side of the road in an orange jumpsuit, should teach her there are real consequences for her stupid actions."

"Trust me, that'd just piss her off more and give her more incentive to post shit online," Josh disagreed, shaking his head at his wife.

"Well, since she is *your jilted lover*, I guess you'd know what will piss her off," Teagan hissed, clearly not missing his piss-poor way of mentioning Sarah's unrequited crush on him, like he'd briefly hoped when it wasn't the first thing she reacted to.

"She is *not* my jilted lover." Josh sighed, hating that he was having this discussion in the middle of their coworkers in catering. "I said she'll probably spread *lies* like that if I escalate things by having her arrested."

"Whatever," Teagan huffed before picking up her fork and going back to aggressively eating her dinner.

After spending the last nine days dating his wife, Josh could tell from her body language alone that she didn't agree with his decision. From her pissed off expression, he was pretty sure she wasn't finished with the discussion about Sarah's claims of being his former love interest, either. And he knew he was in for an uphill battle to prove those claims were nothing but lies. But instead of arguing with him about it right then, she dropped the subject, so that was as close to a victory as he thought he'd get for the time being. He just had to hope that he'd be able to bring her around to his way of thinking when they got to their room later that night.

Surely spending half the night worshiping her body will show her that I'm only interested in her, and be all the proof she needs that I was never interested in Sarah. But maybe I should up the romance factor with a candlelight bubble bath followed by a total body massage before I worship her with my mouth?

Deciding to go along with her dropping the subject, Josh informed her of the call he had to make later that evening. "I have to call my parents after dinner to come up with a plan for getting my place cleaned up before we get there next month. Will you have time to at least say 'hello' to them before you have to go out to the ring?"

"Maybe," Teagan shrugged between bites, not looking all that excited about getting to know his parents a little better, now that they were her in-laws. "But we're the second match on the card tonight, so it'll have to be just a quick reintroduction before I leave you to discuss everything else with them."

"That's fine," Josh agreed, thinking it might not be in his best interest to include her in the part of the discussion when he asked his mom about giving her his great-grandmother's heirloom emerald ring anyway.

It'll be much better to surprise her with it while we're in San Diego next month. Then we can go pick out wedding bands that match the ring, instead of taking the chance on looking at them now and picking something that won't line up with it on her finger, since I can't remember exactly what it looks like.

<div align="center">~~~</div>

Tuesday, October 15, 2019, Orlando, Florida

"Dude, you need to chill the fuck out," Dion instructed Liam, who'd just tossed his phone on top of his gear bag and slammed his locker shut. "You ever think maybe you can't get ahold of the attorney because you're not supposed to?"

"I know he's not the right kind of attorney to handle an annulment," Liam huffed as they finished putting away their stuff and walked toward the exit of the locker room. "But I'm just trying to get a referral to someone else in his firm that can handle it, so I don't understand why he can't return a fecking phone call."

Liam was really getting frustrated with the lack of response he was getting from his attorney's office in New York. He'd called and left messages at least once a day for the last week and a half, and he couldn't believe Boyle Kelly hadn't returned a single one of them. Granted, the attorney Liam kept calling specialized in entertainment law and contracts, not family law, which was what he thought he'd need for an annulment. But since he kept the Kelly Legal Group on retainer for reviewing all his contracts with the GWA and any other businesses he partnered with for various commercial endorsements and investments, Liam still thought Boyle was the best person for him to contact to get a referral to a family law attorney.

Just in case the messages he'd left weren't clear that he was just looking for a referral, Liam had also emailed his lawyer the day before, explaining the whole situation in detail and specifically asking for a referral to a family law attorney. Since their offices took up several floors of one of the skyscrapers in Manhattan, he assumed the Kelly Legal Group was a big enough firm to have lawyers that specialized in different fields, so he hoped it would just be a matter of forwarding his information to another attorney in their office. But at this point, Liam would be happy if Boyle just gave him a name of someone he'd either gone to law school with or met at a legal conference or whatever, as long as he had some inkling that they specialized in the right form of law and were decent at their job.

Yeah, he knew he could do an online search for family law attorneys in New York City and could probably come up with several thousand names he could call and try to get an appointment with for the next time he was in the city. But Liam didn't have the time or ability to vet that many potential lawyers while touring the country with the GWA, so he kept holding out hope that his contract attorney would know someone he'd vouch for to make this process easier.

"That's not what I meant," Dion sighed, shaking his head as they made their way to catering for a protein shake while waiting their turn to shoot promos that afternoon. He looked around to make sure they were far enough away from everyone else that nobody would overhear their discussion before elaborating. "I meant that maybe you're not supposed to get an annulment. Or maybe that you don't really want an annulment, so you're stalling in finding an attorney to handle it by only calling Boyle when you know he's not available. Lord knows you've had a thing for Rylie since you first saw her, so maybe ya'll are destined to embrace the love at first sight and stay married."

"Like you know anything about love at first sight," Liam scoffed, shaking his head at his tag-team partner before chugging down the prepackaged chocolate protein shake he'd just pulled from the tub of ice on the end of one of the serving tables. "Although, with the way you keep going on about me needing to stay married, maybe I should call Mama Marcel and ask her to please stop whatever you have her doing to a voodoo doll of Boyle, so he'll return my calls again."

"I know enough about love at first sight to recognize it when I see it," Dion chuckled, a wistful expression crossing his face that made Liam wonder if his best friend was holding out on him with regards to having found a woman he thought could be his special someone. "But I haven't mentioned any of this to Mama Marcel, so I don't think you have to worry about her pulling out a voodoo doll to run interference between you and Boyle."

"No, I know that," Liam sighed, moving off into a corner out of the way as several of their coworkers approached the table. Once he knew they were no longer within hearing distance of anyone, specifically Rylie, he shared his actual concern with his best friend. "I'm actually more worried that maybe Ma or Granny intercepted the marriage license before it was forwarded to Boyle's office and have maybe convinced him not to return my calls."

"Oh, damn, I didn't even think about that possibility." Dion's eyes widened as his expression turned to one of surprise. "But you text your family regularly. Surely if they had, someone would have said something to you about knowing. Especially since I know they all blew up your phone this morning for your birthday."

"Yeah, they all texted this morning, but only because it's my birthday. And they only sent happy birthday wishes, not anything that might indicate they know about Vegas," Liam sighed before clarifying how often he normally spoke to his family. "And I wouldn't say I text them *all* regularly, just Granda. But our once- or twice-a-week text sessions are usually him correcting my Irish after watching one of our GWA shows. And if Granny asked him not to let on that they know, he'd never let it slip."

"True," Dion chuckled, validating Liam's thoughts, as he thought back on all the times Dion had gone home with Liam and spent some time getting to know the whole family.

"And other than holidays or birthdays, I only call or text with everyone else about once a month, or maybe once every other month, so other than thanking them for the birthday wishes this morning, I haven't talked to Ma, Da, or any of my brothers or cousins since we found out."

"Well, maybe you should call one of them," Dion suggested. "Maybe whichever one of your brothers is most likely to be in good with your ma and granny for going on dates with the girls they're picking out, but will also be loyal enough to you to spill the beans if they know you got married."

"Maybe," Liam pondered, dropping the conversation as a few more of their friends joined them. *But which one of my brothers should I call?*

Quinn and Rory are the two most likely to be letting Ma and Granny help them find the right woman to settle down, but they're a lot less understanding of my nomadic lifestyle, so I don't know if either of them would tell me if they'd heard anything about my Vegas wedding if I called them. While Aiden and Finn are a little more understanding of my career, that's really only so they can use their relation to me while picking up women. And even though Aiden is less of a player than Finn, I know neither of them have agreed to let Ma or Granny fix them up yet, so they might not have a clue if anyone from the family intercepted the marriage license. But Quinn and I used to be pretty close, so maybe he'd give me a heads up?

In addition to pondering which brother to possibly reach out to, Liam also had to consider Dion's earlier words about why he was having so much trouble getting in touch with his attorney. *Could I be subconsciously calling Boyle when I know he's most likely to be out of the office or in meetings because I don't really want to annul the marriage? Is that why I've only called Boyle's private line, instead of calling the main switchboard to ask for a family law attorney in the practice? No, 'cause if I was trying to sabotage my efforts to find a family law attorney, then I'd have kept calling exclusively and I wouldn't have sent that email yesterday. There has to be some other reason why Boyle hasn't returned my calls, like Ma or Granny meddling, since I know they're both friends with his wife.*

Yeah, right. It's all on you, Bro. If Ma or Granny knew you got married, they'd have already called to tell you to bring your bride home for the wedding feast they'd be planning. Liam heard the voice of his brother Quinn as his inner skeptic. *Just like me, you're really starting to feel like it's time to settle down. And Rylie's the woman you want to settle down with, so you're really just dragging your feet on finding a family law attorney to keep from having to end your marriage. Why don't you quit fighting your feelings so hard and channel that energy into fighting for what you really want instead? Your beautiful wife.*

Quinn was the second oldest Connery brother, only two years younger than Liam and the brother he was closest to growing up. He was also the brother who was most adamantly searching for his future bride, even if that meant going on dates with the women their mother tried hand-picking as her future daughters-in-law. Knowing how much his brother longed for a love like their parents shared to be able to start his family, Liam was confident that Quinn would tell him to try to make things work with Rylie, if he ever confided in his brother about his attraction to her.

Still, he couldn't stop himself from mentally engaging in a debate with his inner voice, as if he was actually talking to his brother. *You're only saying that 'cause you're so desperate to find a wife. But before you judge me, maybe you should try one more time to make things work with Erin Lynch.*

Yeah, we both know that ship has already sailed, Liam imagined his brother replying, knowing Quinn still had the hots for his high school sweetheart, even though she refused to give him a second chance after he got tired of sowing his wild oats. *But how 'bout you learn from my mistakes, and don't waste your shot with the woman you want to be your soulmate the same way I did.*

No, Quinn hadn't married Erin and then had it annulled, the way Liam was planning to do with Rylie. He'd just broken up with her when they graduated high school, so they were both free to date other people while they were off at college. Then when they'd both come back to the old neighborhood after college, she'd turned him down every time he asked her out, saying he'd lost his chance with her when he'd chosen to see how many coeds he could bang without a girlfriend holding him back.

Since his cock basically went into hibernation around any woman but Rylie, Liam knew his issues with her weren't because of a wandering dick like Quinn's had been fifteen years ago. But he couldn't help but wonder if insisting on an annulment now would ruin his chances of reconnecting with Rylie in ten or fifteen years, when she finally retired from wrestling.

Feck! Maybe my inner Quinn voice is right. Maybe I am dragging my feet on finding a lawyer, so I can make sure I'm not ruining my chances with her sometime in the future, when she's finally ready to settle down. But how the hell am I supposed to figure that out?

By askin' 'er what she wants, eejit. For some reason, whenever it was stating the obvious, Liam's inner voice always sounded more like his Irish Granda Neilan, who still sounded like he'd come straight off the boat from Ireland, even though he and Granny Breena had moved to the United States over sixty years ago. It didn't matter whose persona his inner voice initially took on in Liam's mind, the wisest words, and often the best insults, always sounded like Neilan Connery, even if he'd originally imagined talking to one of his brothers or a friend he wasn't related to, like Dion. Liam based the accent of his wrestling persona on Granda Neilan, who at eighty-six years old still critiqued Liam's use of Irish slang whenever he used it on the GWA's weekly television show.

Unfortunately, he didn't have time to argue with his inner self about why he couldn't ask Rylie what she wanted to happen between them because Caleb Quinn, the producer for the GWA's weekly television show, called out for the next group to pre-record their promos, instead of doing them live on the televised show that night. "Red Velvet and Protection Detail, you're up!"

Guess I'll be channeling Granda for this promo, instead of imagining I'm having a telepathic debate with him.

Liam and Dion both left catering to walk over to the interview set, which was in a backstage area as far away from the classroom and catering as possible, so they didn't have any extra voices accidently interrupt them. They stopped just out of camera range to watch while Protection Detail started their interview with Tiffany, which he and Dion were supposed to interrupt.

Liam had to wonder if Rick had changed his mind about doing these promos live because of getting fined for the one they did the week before. And if so, were they fined because of Rylie showing too much cleavage, which he'd thoroughly enjoyed seeing, even though it distracted him to the point that he couldn't improv when Dion missed his line, or because of the way she basically gave him a preview of the view he'd have if she ever gave him a blow job, which he also thoroughly enjoyed seeing, even though it caused him to get an erection in his wrestling tights for the first time in his entire fifteen-year-long wrestling career.

Hell, it coulda been because my wrestling gear didn't exactly conceal the boner I got from being up close and personal when she put on that show.

Liam didn't normally have to wear a jockstrap under his tights to wrestle, so he hadn't thought about needing one for the vignettes they shot live the previous week. But since he'd struggled like a teenager for the last week to keep his erection under control every time they worked a show with either him flirting with Rylie, or Rylie coming out to ringside while he was wrestling, as if she was weighing her options for switching teams, Liam had started wearing one regularly now.

Since Rylie was dressed in a smokin' hot red pencil skirt, which ended a few inches above her knees, with a matching blazer over a fairly low-cut white camisole, for her role as Protection Detail's manager, instead of the turtleneck bodysuits she wrestled in, which covered everything but her hands from the neck down, it was definitely a good thing Liam had put on a cup to keep his cock contained. The power-suit look definitely worked on her, making Liam positive that he wasn't the only man who'd watch this promo and picture her sitting on a desk with the skirt pushed up to expose her pussy and her sexy red stilettos propped on his shoulders as he fucked her.

Liam got so caught up in the fantasy that he couldn't comprehend what the guys were saying and almost missed his cue to step into the frame when it was time for Red Velvet to interrupt the interview. He only managed to step forward at the correct time because Dion slapped a hand on his back to push him forward.

"We all know Red's not really interested in Chastity for her managerial skills," Magnum grumbled into the interviewer's mic.

"He's just trying to get in our heads, so we won't come after the tag-team titles now that we've knocked the Mountain Men back down to the size of anthills."

"Ah, I'm definitely interested in more dan Chastity's managerial skills," Liam interjected in the Irish lilt he put on for his character, enjoying the fact that he was literally being paid to ogle her long legs and curvaceous body for this angle. "Especially when she shows de interest is mutual by dressin' in red joehst fahr me." To make his point, he tugged on the cuff of his red tuxedo jacket, which had red glittery trim around the lapels and tails to match the glittery stripe down the outside legs of his wrestling tights, which were designed to look like flashy tuxedo pants.

If only her interest was real, instead of just scripted.

"Are you wearing this red outfit for Red?" Trojan turned to glare at Chastity. "I thought you were dressed in the colors of the Canadian flag in honor of our Canadian Thanksgiving yesterday."

"I didn't really think about anyone or anything in particular when I got dressed for our meetings today," Chastity denied, shaking her head so vehemently it was almost comical. "I mean, I wore my red ring gear yesterday when I wrestled because of it being Canadian Thanksgiving, but I just grabbed the next business suit in my wardrobe today, not thinking about the color at all."

Liam had to fight to contain his smile at how well she was playing her part. He'd admired her in-ring performance since her first night trying out for the company. But her character was mostly seen and not heard in her first few months on the GWA roster, so working this angle with her was the first time he was really getting to see her acting ability outside the ring.

"We'll discuss all the red that's recently been added to your wardrobe later," Magnum barked, his miffed expression conveying his disappointment in Chastity. "Right now, we need to make it clear that Red needs to back off and quit drooling all over our manager."

Yeah, that's never gonna happen. Especially since eyeing her up and drooling over her are all I can do without crossing the line and claiming her as mine. And since I know being mine isn't what's best for her career long term, I have to keep my hands…and other body parts…to myself. So, I have to just be grateful that Red gets to flirt and drool over Chastity, while I keep Liam from acting on how I feel about Rylie. And maybe one of these days, I'll figure out how we can go back to being friends and hanging out, even when we're not acting in our GWA roles.

"If ya'll have such a problem with my partner showing an interest in your manager," Dion interjected, stepping forward a few inches to be more visible on camera, since he and his tag-team partner were so close to the same size and Liam standing immediately to his right blocked most of the camera's view of Dion, "why don't you step in the ring with us at **Halloween Horror**, so we can show Ms. Chastity why she should cut you chumps loose and come manage the champs?"

"Only if you're putting the titles on the line," Trojan replied, aggressively bowing up to Dion, even though he was two inches shorter than the six-foot-four of both members of Red Velvet.

Liam knew it worked for Trojan to be the cocky mouthpiece for Protection Detail, since his six-foot-seven, three-hundred-pound partner could come rescue him anytime he challenged opponents bigger than his six-foot-two, two-hundred-and-twenty-pound frame. Even with Liam and Dion both being six-foot-four, and two-hundred-and-forty pounds and two-hundred-and-fifty pounds respectively, if they added the two members of each team together, Protection Detail had an inch and thirty pounds on Red Velvet. Luckily, size didn't really matter in the scripted world of professional wrestling.

"'Ow 'bout we make it a winner-takes-all match," Liam suggested, smirking at the guys in Protection Detail before redirecting his gaze to Chastity and looking her over from head to toe once more. "If ye win, ye get our titles. If we win, we get Chastity as our manager."

"Deal," Trojan declared for Protection Detail, pointing to Rick, who was standing outside the camera's view. "Book the match, Boss. Winners take all at **Halloween Horror**."

"I'll get our legal team started with drawing up the contract," Rick called out, setting them up for a contract signing center ring on the go-home show a week later, even though he didn't actually step into the shot, since there were already so many people taking up the limited interview space, with the four large men crowding the two smaller ladies from both sides.

"As your manager, don't I get a say in whether or not my services are on the line?" Chastity put her hands on her hips and looked indignantly back and forth between Trojan and Magnum.

"Yeah, no," the men of Protection Detail growled in unison.

"Don't worry, Swee'heart, only yeer managerial services are on de line in de match. Ye'll get all de say in when ye're ready ta be me Mot." Liam grinned at Rylie in full view of the camera as the Protection Detail guys ushered her away from the interview. *Hopefully, Granda will approve of the Irish slang for "my Girl."*

"Well, there you have it, folks," Tiffany addressed the TV audience, speaking into the microphone while looking directly at the camera. "Protection Detail versus Red Velvet at **Halloween Horror**, with the winners walking away with the tag-team titles *and* Chastity's managerial services."

As Rick approved the scene without them having to do a second take, Liam wished he could go congratulate Rylie on her stellar performance, the way he'd done after all her matches up until the day they discovered they were married. There were a lot of things Liam wished he could still do with Rylie, like hanging out backstage and critiquing everyone else's matches, or going out after the show was over. But even though he missed the easy friendship they'd developed in the seven months she'd been with the company, he didn't trust himself not to back down on the annulment if he tried to maintain that friendship now.

Maybe we can find a way to be friends again once the legal stuff is dealt with, Liam hoped as he watched the woman he wanted to love walk away.

Later that evening, after their promo aired, and while he was sitting in catering, celebrating his birthday by sharing his favorite Irish apple cake with his friends and coworkers, Liam's phone buzzed, signaling he had a text. When he pulled it from his pocket, he wasn't surprised to see it was from his Granda.

Granda: Me Mot was the wrong term to use. Mo Ghrá, my love, would've been better.

Yeah, it would have, Liam mentally agreed, wishing he could use the same term of endearment for Rylie that his Granda used for his

Leah Mae Wright

Granny. *But then the whole family would know how I really feel about her.*

Liam knew better than to text his true thoughts back to his Granda. But he also couldn't bring himself to lie to him by saying it was all just a work for the show, so he'd chosen to use the more common term to save the more meaningful one for his future wife. Instead, he replied in a way he hoped wouldn't set off any red flags for his family, whether they already knew he'd married her or not, and also wouldn't be a blatant lie.

Liam: I'll try to remember that for next time.

138

Chapter Five

Saturday, October 26, 2019, New Orleans, Louisiana

"Whaddya know, he can take a piss without the Avengers babysittin' him," Liam quipped as he and Dion joined Dean at the urinals in the men's locker room, trying to keep the mood light after witnessing his friend propose that morning. He knew Dean and Allissa were trying to keep their lives as normal as possible while dealing with her stalker, but he also knew the stress had to be getting to them, too. So, he hoped teasing Dean about the extra bodyguards following him and Allissa around would keep his friend's spirits up while pointing out that his lady love was well protected.

"The Avengers?" Dean chuckled as he finished urinating and zipped his fly.

"Yeah, I've decided your bodyguard team is the new secret identity of the Avengers," Liam explained, quickly relieving himself, as Dean walked over to the row of sinks to wash his hands. "Since your brother is named after Iron Man, and the two new guys are Thor and Hulk, it was easy to see through their cover."

"It's Thor and Bishop, not Thor and Hulk," Dean chuckled as he soaped up his hands. "Though I suppose he is big enough to play the Hulk without much CGI work needed."

Considering at six-foot-six and two-hundred-and-eighty pounds, Bishop was bigger than at least three quarters of the men on the GWA roster, Liam easily agreed with the lack of CGI work necessary for the big bodyguard to be able to play the role of the gamma-irradiated character if he were ever cast in a Marvel movie.

Before Liam could finish assigning Avengers' identities to the other bodyguards while zipping up and walking over to wash his hands, a blood-curdling scream came from the direction of the women's locker room.

"Fuck!" Dean, obviously realizing it was Allissa who was screaming, turned away from the sink without even rinsing the soap from his hands.

"Wait!" Dion stopped him, having just walked over to the sink beside Dean.

"That bastard is making his move to kidnap Allissa. I'm not gonna wait to go rescue her!" Dean tried to push past Dion, so Liam stepped up to help hold him back.

"I'm not tellin' you not to go rescue her," Dion argued, nodding his head toward the back of the locker room, where the training rooms were located in this arena. "I'm just tryin' to get you to go in the other way. The bodyguards will all be going in through the main doors from backstage. But if we go in through the training rooms, we can surround him."

"And unless you plan on blinding him by gouging his eyes out with soapy hands, you might want to rinse off, so you can get a good grip on him," Liam added, not bothering to wash his own hands, like he normally would after urinating.

Dean did a cursory swipe of his hands under the faucet before brushing his hands over his pants to half-ass dry them, not seeming to care about water damage on his biker leathers, as the three of them ran through the locker room and out the back door. Since there wasn't an athletic event going on at the time, the training rooms were all empty as they ran through them to get to the door leading into the women's locker room.

They slowed their movements then, hoping to sneak up behind the stalker and assess the situation before taking action. Not that three six-foot-four, two-hundred-forty-plus-pound professional wrestlers could really sneak anywhere.

"Please, you don't have to do this," Liam heard Allissa pleading, as they made their way past the showers at the back of the locker room, trying to keep their boots from squeaking on the tile floor.

"Lower the weapon and turn yourself in, man," the bodyguard they all called Linc commanded, clearly trying to settle the situation peacefully.

"No, you lower your weapons, so Allissa and I can leave," the psycho countered as Dean, Liam, and Dion came around a bank of lockers to see the situation unfolding near the bathroom stalls.

They could clearly see the top of Allissa's head over the shoulder of a balding man with salt and pepper hair around the sides and back of his head, who looked to be an inch or two under six feet tall. Liam didn't recognize the man at all, but he could tell it wasn't Ron Langston, the prime suspect that their boss had insisted everyone know to watch out for at all their shows since this stalker situation started in the spring, not long after Ron was fired from his position with the GWA.

From what he could tell, the man was waving a gun around, and apparently, holding Allissa in front of him like a human shield to keep the bodyguards from shooting him, since all four of them also had their weapons drawn. The bodyguards were all standing in the area just past the toilet stalls, where Liam knew the sinks and mirrors were since the rest of the layout seemed to be exactly like the men's locker room, with the exception of having two rows of toilet stalls instead of one, since a row of urinals took the place of the second row of toilets in the men's locker room.

"We're not going to let you leave here with Allissa," the bodyguard named Wright argued with the stalker. "So, if you want to walk out of here at all, you need to lower your weapon and let her go."

Instead of following the directions of the bodyguards, the stalker showed how crazy he was by ranting and raving about first meeting Allissa in 1993, which Liam knew was before she was born, since they'd just celebrated Allissa's birthday a few days earlier, and he'd found out she was a year younger than Rylie.

Feck! Where's Rylie right now? Liam looked around, trying to make sure she wasn't in the locker room, where she could be caught in the crossfire if the stalker and bodyguards ended up in a gunfight. *Oh, thank God! I think she's out on the arena floor for the second session of autographs and stuff with the other babyfaces.*

Liam missed a lot of the lunatic's tirade because of thinking about the woman he'd married in Vegas, but he still followed Dean as he slowly creeped up behind the stalker's back. *Don't think about Rylie right now,* he admonished himself as he noticed Dean using the hand signals they all used in the ring to direct him and Dion which way to go and what wrestling maneuvers he was planning to try to disarm the guy. *I've just gotta do the same thing for Allissa and Dean that I'd want someone to do if it was me and Rylie in their place.*

Unfortunately, nobody had taught the bodyguards the hand signals used in professional wrestling, so they didn't understand what Dean was trying to do. Because they didn't understand Dean's plan, they tried to wave off the three wrestlers and alerted the stalker to their position behind him.

Feck! Why didn't any of us think to coordinate our hand signals with theirs, so we could work together better?

"Who's back there?" The stalker spun around as he screeched out the question, bringing Allissa with him.

Allissa's eyes widened in fear when she realized the stalker now had his gun aimed directly at Dean. "No, don't shoot him. I'll do whatever you want. Just don't hurt Dean."

"Like hell you will, Darlin'," Dean growled as he gave the go signal for Liam and Dion.

As Dion charged toward Allissa to body press her out of the stalker's hold, Liam followed Dean when he lunged for the stalker. When they all moved suddenly, Allissa elbowed the asshole in the gut and twisted out of his hold around her waist, making it easier for Dion to extract her from the stalker's grasp. Unfortunately, her unexpected movement caused the stalker to spin with her and flail his arm out in an arc toward Allissa and Dion, just as he pulled the trigger.

Hearing the gunshot and assuming the bodyguards would open fire on the assailant, Liam decided on the fly to change tactics. Instead of going for a leg sweep on the stalker to throw him off balance while Dean went for a wrist lock to get control of the gun, Liam tackled Dean to the ground to get his friend out of the line of fire. He then heard four more loud bangs of obvious gunfire as he and Dean crashed into the door of one of the toilet stalls.

They got lucky that the door wasn't locked and gave way for Dean to take the back bump on the floor without injury. Well, other than having the wind knocked out of him by Liam landing on top of him. Liam felt a little guilty for that, but he figured it was better than getting shot by friendly fire.

Not taking the time to get up off of Dean before looking to see if the coast was clear, Liam glanced over his shoulder in the direction

Dion had tackled Allissa toward the stalls on the opposite side of the room. He could clearly see that the stalker laid there in the middle of the space, bleeding out from the four gunshot wounds inflicted by the Avington Security team. When he lifted his gaze past the obviously dead stalker, he could see that Allissa was trapped under Dion, who was out cold and bleeding from his head.

"Fuck!" Dean screamed as he pushed Liam off of him to scramble over to Allissa and Dion. "Allissa, Darlin'!"

"Oh, shit," Liam mumbled as he quickly jumped up to run over to help his best friend and tag-team partner.

Liam vaguely recognized that two of the bodyguards worked to secure the stalker and his gun, while a third bodyguard called for assistance from the police and an ambulance. The fourth bodyguard was right by Liam's side, insisting, "We've gotta be careful with his spine as we roll him, so we don't make any possible spinal damage worse while freeing Allissa and assessing for any other injuries either of them have sustained."

Liam followed the bodyguard's directions as he and Dean assisted the man, who obviously had some medical training, in carefully rolling Dion off of Allissa to assess their injuries, hoping they didn't exacerbate any they already had from the shot the stalker got off and their impact with the ground.

"I'm not hurt," Allissa assured them as Dean ran his hands over her, obviously trying to feel for any injuries. "But Dion hit his head really hard on that door frame."

"Yeah, that blood's not coming from where he hit his head," the bodyguard Liam now recognized as Linc informed them as he applied pressure to the right side of Dion's head, while Allissa pointed at the cut on the back left side of Dion's head, which wasn't bleeding nearly as much as the one Linc was treating. "He was also grazed by the bullet the perp got off when you all went rogue, instead of letting us keep trying to negotiate."

It didn't take long before the space was full of police officers and paramedics, who quickly took over assessing injuries. Once they got Dion secured in a neck brace with gauze covering both of his bleeding wounds, they moved him to a gurney to take him out to the waiting ambulance and get him on his way to the hospital. As soon as Dion was stabilized by the paramedics, Dean insisted they check Allissa out while he held her on his lap, clearly too distraught to let go of her for a second if he didn't have to.

"I'm so sorry, Darlin'," Dean choked out. "If I'd have known it'd go down like this, I never would have suggested tryin' to piss him off to get him to make a move."

"This is not your fault, Dean." Allissa insisted, soothing her worried fiancé as much as possible. "Kidnapping me was always his plan, so it could have happened just like this, whether you tried to piss him off or not. So don't you dare take an ounce of blame for how it happened. You, Dion, and Liam are my heroes for jumping in to save me when you weren't even armed. And you damn well better not feel guilty for saving me from that psycho."

Feck! I wish I could lean on Rylie like that. Liam felt an overwhelming need to see her right then, needing to reassure himself that she wasn't in any danger and hadn't been hurt the way Allissa almost was a few minutes earlier. *But I can't, 'cause even though she's technically my wife right now, she's not really mine to take comfort in 'cause we can't have a real relationship like Dean has with Allissa.*

He tuned out whatever was happening between his friends and followed the directions of a police officer to step out of the women's locker room. The officers insisted on separating each of them to take their statements and allow the crime scene investigators to confiscate their blood-spattered gimmick clothing.

Thankfully, because they assumed they'd be going out to celebrate Dean and Allissa's engagement after the fan expo, Liam and Dion had carried in a change of clothes to meet the GWA's dress code for traveling and making public appearances, instead of just wearing their gimmick attire all day. While technically, they could wear nice jeans and Red Velvet t-shirts for things like the fan expo and going to a club after any of their shows, because they expected it to be a special occasion, they'd brought the dressier versions of their business casual traveling attire to wear to the impromptu engagement party planned for that night.

Now, he just had to convince the cop taking his statement and clothing to let him go back into the men's locker room to get them and change when he turned over his jeans and Red Velvet t-shirt. "I have extra clothes in the men's locker room. Can we go in there to do all this?"

"Sure," the officer agreed, just as Rylie ran up to them. The officer barely stopped her from throwing her arms around Liam. "Sorry, miss, we can't let you contaminate the evidence. You'll have to wait out here to talk to your friend after we get his statement and clothing."

"He's not just my friend," Rylie declared, not stopping following them, as they got to the door of the men's locker room, where a crime scene investigator joined them. "He's my husband. I promise I won't touch him to contaminate whatever evidence is on his clothing, but I am coming in there, so I can see for myself that he's not injured while he removes your evidence from his body."

Feck! It shouldn't feel this good to hear her claim me as her husband, Liam thought, even as he soaked in the affection radiating off of Rylie like the love-starved sponge he felt like right then.

Liam knew it was wrong to take advantage of their unintentional marriage to keep her where he could see her while he was going through the adrenaline crash, which was bound to hit him anytime now since the danger had passed. But as he felt himself going into a mild state of shock, he needed someone to help him get through the rest of the day. With his best friend unconscious and in an ambulance on the way to the hospital, and the rest of the guys he considered as his wrestling brothers paired off and taking comfort with their women, Rylie seemed like Liam's only option to help keep him grounded, so he could make it to the hospital and back to the hotel for the night without getting in a car accident from being so distraught.

"Since the locker rooms are mirror images of each other, once I'm changed, my wife can help me with marking where everyone was standing as I go through my statement to give you more of a visual of how it happened," Liam informed the officer without turning his gaze from Rylie, hoping she could see in his eyes how grateful he was to have her there with him. And hoping she didn't mind him reciprocating the claim of their marital status, just because he needed to hear himself say it at least once.

"Very well," the officer agreed, allowing her to enter the men's locker room with them.

Liam quickly walked past the sinks, urinals, and toilet stalls to the locker area, where he and Dion had stashed their belongings earlier.

The crime scene investigator carried over a hard-sided silver case about twice the size of a standard briefcase, which Liam assumed was his forensics kit that contained everything he needed to collect evidence from a crime scene, placing it on the bench beside where Liam had stopped to open his locker. Once the CSI photographed Liam wearing the clothing, he asked him to remove each garment in a specific order. He took possession of everything but Liam's boxers and socks, since they didn't appear to have any blood on them, bagging and labeling each item just like they did on that television show, *CSI*, which surprised Liam since the NYPD officers in his family constantly ragged on the show for being inaccurate. The crime scene investigator even swabbed his hands for evidence, even though Liam told him that the only thing he might find would be where he hadn't had time to wash his hands after urinating before they heard Allissa's cry for help.

Once the CSI was finished processing Liam and his clothing, the officer waiting to take his statement allowed him to take a quick shower and get dressed. Liam then walked the officer through the events, starting with where he, Dion, and Dean had each been standing when they heard Allissa scream, and ending with having Rylie and several other officers and crime scene investigators, whom the first officer called into the room to assist, do a bit of a reenactment of how the incident had ended, only without anyone actually falling to the ground, or any of the officers discharging their weapons. After the officers documented his statement and the crime scene investigators took notes about the differences in the locker rooms to be able to go into the women's locker room with a better understanding of the events while gathering the rest of the evidence, Liam and Rylie were informed that they were free to go.

"Um, I rode up here with Dion. Can I get his stuff from his locker and take his vehicle to his brother at the hospital?" At least, Liam assumed Rick had already called Darius to inform him that Dion had been injured. If Dion's only living relative wasn't already at the hospital when he got there, Liam would make the call himself to make sure both Darius and Mama Marcel, the woman Dion thought of like a second mother after she finished raising him after he'd lost both his parents, knew where he was and what had happened.

"Yes," the officer nodded. "Considering the vehicle and belongings in this locker room aren't evidence in the case, I'm sure it's fine for you to take them to your friend's brother."

"Thank you." Liam shook the officer's hand before opening up Dion's locker to grab his bag, glad his best friend was a creature of habit and had left his keys in the locker as usual. He looped both Dion's bag and his own over his shoulder, then took Rylie by the hand, needing to feel connected to her in some small way as they walked out of the men's locker room. "You don't have anything in the women's locker room that we need to try to get, do you?"

Thinking of what she might need to get out of a locker before they could leave made him wish he'd have put his rosary in the bag he brought to the arena instead of leaving it in his bigger suitcase back at the hotel. While technically he could pray for Dion without it, he felt like he needed something to hold onto to keep him grounded until he found out his best friend's prognosis.

"No, I left my purse in the car when we got here and didn't plan on changing until after going back to the hotel once the expo was over. If Trojan and Magnum aren't at the hospital when we get there, I can get it back from them whenever we get back to the hotel later."

"Feck," Liam swore, feeling that crash hitting him hard and not trusting himself to get behind the wheel. "That means I need to find someone else to drive us, 'cause you don't have your license on you."

"My license is right here." Rylie held up her free hand to show the wristlet phone case she carried everywhere but to the ring when she wrestled, even when she didn't carry her purse with her while hanging out backstage during the GWA's shows. "So, if you need me to drive, I can."

"Yes, yes, I definitely need you to drive." Liam sighed with relief, handing over the keys to Dion's Escalade, and barely holding it together long enough to get in the vehicle before losing his shit and bawling like a baby.

Liam couldn't remember ever crying in his life, even at his maternal grandparents' funerals. But the realization that his best friend was lying in the hospital with a bullet wound to the head hit him harder than anything else ever had. He didn't feel like he could even take a full breath until he got to the hospital and verified that Dion was still alive.

Rylie didn't say a word as she set up the GPS on her phone to guide their way to the hospital, presumably having verified which one Dion had been taken to at some point when Liam hadn't noticed. Once she had it in the cup holder with the electronic voice giving them turn-by-turn directions, she reached over and took his hand, giving him more comfort than she probably realized as she drove.

Liam clung to her hand, futilely wiping away his never-ending tears with his other hand. He kept running through the events in his head, trying to figure out what they could have done differently to prevent Dion's injuries. Unfortunately, as he did so, he kept seeing Rylie in Allissa's place and imagining her being the one injured or killed instead of Dion.

The thoughts were too much for his fragile psyche, rendering him practically catatonic by the time they got to the hospital. Somehow, he managed to move to get out of the vehicle and walk with Rylie into the emergency waiting room. But he clung to her the whole time and never said a word. Luckily for him, Rick had indeed called Darius, since there was no way Liam was capable of making that call after all.

Feck! I'm the biggest asshole on the planet. Liam mentally berated himself. *After the way I've acted the three weeks since we found out we're married, I don't deserve to lean on Rylie and have her take care of everything for me the way she is now. She deserves someone so much better than me. Someone strong enough to take care of her, instead of acting like a pussy the way I am right now. But feck, I'm not man enough to get through this on my own.*

~ ~ ~

Brent felt shell-shocked as he and Aiken made their way into the hospital after leaving the arena. Seeing Dion wheeled out of the locker room on a gurney struck him hard. Not only because it proved that everyone around them was vulnerable, no matter who among them a stalker was actually targeting, because he knew every single person on the roster would have done the exact same thing Dion did, if they'd been in the men's locker room to hear Allissa call for help, himself included. But also, because Dion was literally the friendliest guy in the business. Yeah, he was a big prankster, but he was also the peacemaker they all relied on to help settle disputes backstage. So, in Brent's opinion, this stalker must have been the biggest asshole on the planet if Dion couldn't talk him down to settle things peacefully.

When Brent first started with the GWA a little over eight years ago, it was Dion who first befriended him while they planned their choreography for his try-out match. After the match, Brent knew it was Dion's endorsement that earned him his contract with the GWA because he'd been so nervous that he didn't feel like he'd performed to the best of his ability. But since Dion had been with the company for five years by then, he took Brent under his wing and helped him with strategies to overcome his nerves to have better matches, as well as taught him how to navigate the ins and outs of the behind the scenes stuff they all had to deal with as professional wrestlers. Needless to say, Brent couldn't imagine the GWA without Dion Davis, so he was really concerned about the extent of his friend's injuries.

Of course, when he first heard the commotion, Dion wasn't the first person he worried about. No, that spot in his mind was reserved for Aiken. And having her be the first person he thought of finding when he heard gunfire made him wonder if his brain wasn't the only one of his organs where she held a special place.

He'd been sitting in catering and waiting for Amethyst to get back after staging her disagreement with Emerald during the babyfaces' fan interaction portion of the expo when it all got started. Due to the sound of the music blaring through the arena for the fan expo, as well as the sounds of excited fans whooping and hollering, he hadn't heard Allissa cry out for help. It wasn't until he heard the gunshots that he even noticed the four bodyguards who'd been standing by the women's locker room door were no longer there. He wasn't sure how he remembered where Aiken was while he was freaking out. But somehow he realized she was on the arena floor and not in the women's locker room, where he'd heard the shots. So, instead of running toward the danger to help protect Allissa and whoever else was in the women's locker room, he immediately got up and ran to find Aiken, making it as far as the gorilla position before he was stopped by one of the extra security guys that had been brought in for the pay-per-view weekend.

Brent was frustrated with not being allowed out of the backstage area to find her. But thankfully, it didn't take very long at all for the security personnel to separate the GWA talent from the fans, and escort Aiken, and the rest of the performers who were out on the arena floor, back to where he was waiting for her. He'd immediately pulled her into his arms and hadn't let her out of his sight since.

Since he and Aiken were among the group of performers who hadn't witnessed anything, they were able to evacuate the building almost immediately after Dion was wheeled out by the paramedics. So, they'd led the caravan of wrestlers to the emergency department waiting room, where they still sat waiting to hear the status of their friend.

"I just can't believe this happened," Aiken sniffled, fighting back tears as she held hands with both him and her best friend, Teagan, who was flanked on her other side by her Vegas hubby, Josh.

"D's tough, though. He'll pull through just fine." *I hope*. "I'm sure." Brent tried to console his wife, swapping out his left hand for his right to hold hers, so he could wrap his left arm around her shoulders and pull her close. He wasn't sure if the gesture was more comforting for Aiken or himself, but either way, they both needed it right then. Especially since he wasn't as sure of Dion's chance for recovery as he'd just indicated to his wife and their coworkers within earshot.

"But he was already bleeding through the bandages," Aiken whimpered, releasing Teagan's hand to pull out a tissue from the box being passed around the room and dabbing at her wet eyes. "And did you see how much blood was on Liam's clothes when he came out of the women's locker room? That was a lot of blood. And we didn't even see how much was on everyone else, or the floor of the locker room. What if he's lost too much blood to make it?"

"Head wounds bleed a lot," Brent pointed out. *But cuts to the head don't normally spatter all over bystanders, like the blood on Liam's clothes, which looked more like something you'd see from being too close to someone who was shot. Not that I'm gonna share that information with Aiken right now.* "That's why we were taught to cut our foreheads back in the day when blading was standard practice in wrestling. But just because it looks like a lot, it doesn't mean he's really lost a lot of blood. And I'm sure they've got plenty to give him here if he needs it."

"And if not," Josh added, comforting Teagan in much the same way Brent was comforting Aiken, "there's enough of us from the GWA here willing to donate that I'm sure one of us will match his blood type to give him more if he needs it."

"Exactly," Brent agreed, wondering if they should ask someone about the process of donating blood.

Before he could suggest going to the desk to ask, their conversation was disrupted by the arrival of Dean and Allissa's families, who all rushed to the nurse's desk and loudly asked if either of them had been brought in with injuries.

"Dion's the only one who was transported via ambulance," Josh called out to the family, obviously realizing the nurses couldn't answer any of their questions, since Dean and Allissa hadn't made it to the hospital yet. Once they'd all stepped away from the desk to gather in the middle of the seating area, where half the GWA roster was congregated, he continued. "The paramedics and cops didn't say much about what happened, but they did reassure us that D was the only one from the GWA that was injured, and said his wounds appeared to be mostly superficial. Apparently, the only reason they brought him here was because he was knocked out, so we're hopeful that his worst injury is a concussion."

"Are you talking about my brother?" Darius, Dion's brother, questioned as he joined them. Brent recognized him from the club the Davises co-owned, where they usually had the after-parties for any shows they did in New Orleans, but he hadn't seen him walk into the waiting room. "I just got a call from a cop, who said he'd been shot. What the hell happened?"

"Yeah, Dare, we don't know exactly how he was injured," Brent explained. While he was trying to be as hopeful as Josh that Dion would fully recover after only a mild concussion and a few stitches, he knew better than to give his brother any information that might or might not be accurate. "And since none of us are family, they won't tell us anything. But since you're D's brother, maybe they'll let you go back and find out more."

"Yeah, thanks guys." Dare gave them each a chin lift before walking over to the desk and speaking softly with the nurse.

It wasn't long after that before Dean and Allissa finally arrived, along with three more Avington Security guys, in addition to the ones who'd already set up outside the waiting room to keep the paparazzi out. They quickly settled their family members' fears about their injury statuses before briefly talking to Dare. When Darius was instructed to follow a nurse back to see Dion, Dean and Allissa finally settled in the chairs on the other side of the waiting room with their family members.

Once everyone was seated, Brent noticed Liam had come in at some point, too. While he wasn't surprised to see Dion's tag-team partner there, he was shocked to see him clinging to Rylie. It was almost like he was finally embracing their marriage, instead of continuing to fight his feelings for his new wife.

Damn! I bet actually being back there when this stalker shit all went down has made him start thinking about what really matters to him. And apparently, Rylie means more to him than he's been letting on.

Hell, I wasn't back there to witness any of this shit, but it's still making me think about everything I need to do to keep Aiken safe. Fuck, that's gonna be a never-ending job, even if this stalker is no longer an issue.

As he sat there holding his wife against his side while they waited to hear Dion's status and prayed that he was going to be okay, all he could think about was how it could have been Aiken who'd been the target and possibly injured or killed. And even though this stalker was no longer a threat, she could still be the prey of another. As long as they continued working with the GWA, and were spotlighted by celebrity gossip sites regularly, none of them were truly safe from the fans, who all too often crossed the line over to fanatics, psychotically fixating on them for whatever reason that only made sense in the deranged mind of a seriously disturbed person.

He also couldn't stop thinking about how his need to protect her felt almost visceral, like protecting Aiken was as essential to him as breathing. Thinking back over the conversations he'd had with his dad in the last couple of weeks, all of which seemed to focus on how Brent had already subconsciously fallen for Aiken, he started trying to figure out exactly how he felt about his wife. Combining those thoughts with reviewing everything he'd learned about her in the last three weeks made it very clear in Brent's mind that his dad could quite possibly be correct about his feelings for the woman he'd only thought he'd mistakenly married that night in Vegas.

Is this love? This constant need to be with her? To touch her just to feel connected to her, even when we're keeping things platonic and aren't anywhere close to having a sexual relationship? To protect her from anyone or anything that could hurt her in any way? To be the man she shares everything with? Does all that mean I'm falling in love with her?

I know it's more than just lust that I feel for her, but does that mean I've jumped straight into love? Could I maybe just feel a deeper form of liking her? Like more affectionate and caring than just how I like my other friends, but not all the way to full-blown love? Yeah, that's gotta be it. I just like her more than my other friends.

And really want to fuck her. But that's okay. That's just lust, not love. I'm sure what I'm feeling for Aiken is the standard way people feel when they have friends-with-benefits relationships. Since that's probably closer to what my mom felt for my dad, I'm sure I'm capable of feeling that level of caring for Aiken, even if I'm never able to fully fall in love.

Besides, I don't think it's even possible to fall in love with someone in only three weeks, so I'm sure it's not really love. While technically, they'd been married for almost ten weeks, Brent didn't think the first seven weeks counted, since they didn't know they were married then, and he hadn't thought of her any differently than he did the rest of the crew until he learned of their marriage.

And what the fuck am I supposed to do about these friends-with-benefits feelings? I still don't have a clue how to be a boyfriend, much less a good husband. Hell, I doubt she'll even want me to be her husband when she realizes I'm not capable of loving her the way she wants from her Prince Charming. But I can't just walk away and not at least try to see if this deeper way I care for her can eventually turn into love.

I mean, Dad claims he's still in love with Mom, so it's possible that I got enough of his genes to be capable of really falling in love, too. But I won't ever know which one of them I'm most like if I don't at least try to let myself fall in love. Which means I need to cancel any appointments with lawyers to talk about our options. At least, for now.

Despite the fact that he still didn't think he was what she needed in a life partner, Brent knew he wouldn't be able to stand watching her move on to someone else if they went through with the annulment. Even if their relationship never progressed to the point of them actually sleeping together, he couldn't stand the thought of seeing her kissing anyone else. And the thought of anyone else getting to fuck her, when he hadn't, made him crazy. To the point that he wanted to tighten his hold on her, both literally and figuratively. He barely stopped himself from squeezing her tighter against him as he pondered his next move with his wife.

Fuck! I don't just want to cancel all the plans to dissolve our marriage. I want to give myself the chance to actually fall in love with my wife by making this marriage real in every way possible. Now what the fuck am I gonna do to convince her that we should stay married and actually start living together as husband and wife? Hell, the only thing I can think of is to start kissing her for real, instead of keeping our kisses limited to the chaste pecks we've been exchanging the last couple of weeks. But even if she's receptive to that, I'm still gonna hafta take it slow, and not push for sex until I know she's ready. And hopefully, by the time we get to that point, we'll both start feeling like we're actually falling in love.

Brent looked around the waiting room at the various couples all leaning on one another, hoping his friends in solid, committed relationships could provide him with some inspiration for how to man up and be the husband Aiken needed. *Maybe I can catch a few of these guys alone in the locker room to get some advice on how to romance my wife?*

"Any updates on Dion's condition?" Rick's bellowed words brought Brent out of his own head, making him realize that he was still holding Aiken close, as she quietly leaned on him.

Damn, I hope the way she seems to be trusting me to take care of her today means she's started feeling more than basic friendship for me, too. Even if I know there's no way she's fallen in love with me in the last three weeks, I hope we're both feeling pretty much the same deeper form of caring and affection for one another, so we're on the same page with regard to our relationship. I definitely don't want to be the only one feeling more; 'cause if that's the case, then trying to push for more could scare her straight into a lawyer's office to file for an annulment.

"Not yet, Boss," Dean replied for everyone else in the room, raising his voice so everyone around them could hear him. "Last we heard, he was stable and going for tests. But Darius is the only one who's been allowed to go back to see him, since the hospital doesn't consider any of us family."

Guess that's what the nurse said to Dare earlier, before taking him back to be with his brother.

Rick nodded in acknowledgment of Dean's words before walking over to the desk, probably to see if he could get an update on Dion since he owned the GWA and the incident happened while they were all there for work. As he walked away, Byron Avington, the head of Avington Security, walked over and sat on the coffee table in front of Allissa and Dean. Crockett didn't bother trying to strain to hear their soft-spoken conversation, preferring to check on his wife and their friends instead.

"You okay, Princess?" Brent wasn't sure why he suddenly started using the term of endearment as he brushed his lips over the top of Aiken's head. "Anything I can do for you?"

"Just keep holding me," she whimpered, turning her head to look up at him and give him a sad smile.

"That I can do," he reassured her with a soft upturn of his lips before she leaned her head back on his shoulder. He still wasn't sure which of them took more comfort from holding onto one another, but he relished the feel of having her in his arms and knowing she was safe there.

He then glanced over at Josh and Teagan, who were basically mirroring his and Aiken's positions in the curved grouping of four chairs taking up this corner of the waiting room, so the girls could take comfort from their husbands while still holding on to each other as well. When his eyes met Josh's over their wives' heads, they seemed to come to a mutual understanding that they'd back each other up in supporting their women.

Maybe we should try talking Rick into turning Josh heel, instead of having us feud and splitting up the Precious Stones. I mean, he's gonna need to come up with another heel tag team if Red Velvet has to be out for a few weeks while Dion recovers, so if Josh and I team up, then he'll be pulling one heel and one face from the singles roster to keep his numbers even. And if we're all heels, then the four of us can travel together, so the girls will still have each other to lean on as well as us.

He glanced over at Liam and Rylie once more, noticing that they were still holding hands and obviously comforting one another as well. *And maybe if we're all able to make things work in our marriages, we can have a double, or triple, ceremony to renew our vows on our first anniversary, so Aiken's dads will get to walk her down the aisle after all.*

Brent felt more than a little bad about marrying Aiken without her dads knowing about it in advance. While he still didn't remember much after leaving the **Sin City Showdown** after-party, and knew he probably wasn't the primary person responsible for any of them walking down the aisle, after Aiken told him more about her dads and how Shawn especially wanted to design her wedding dress, he felt like he owed them for cheating them out of that experience. Originally, he'd thought annulling the marriage was his recompense, so they could do all that stuff when she got married for real. But now that he'd started coming to terms with his feelings and realized he really wanted to try staying married, he knew he'd just have to give them the ceremony they'd missed as a vow renewal, once he convinced his wife to give him a real chance at being her husband. Even if that meant they had to go through the ups and downs of learning how to be a married couple over the first few years of their union.

Before he could start to think about how to talk to Aiken about the next steps for their marriage to get them in a place where she'd be ready to agree to a vow renewal, Rylie stood from her seat, whispering something to Liam before he let her go so she could walk over to kneel down in front of Aiken and Teagan. Looking back and forth between Brent and Josh, she whispered, "Can I get you guys to help me with Liam? He's completely shut down and hasn't said a word since we left the arena, and I'm starting to get really worried about him."

Josh lifted his chin at Brent to signal his agreement, which Brent returned to let Josh know he was in. Josh then turned to slightly smile at Rylie, stating, "Yeah, we'll talk to him."

Brent squeezed Aiken into his side quickly before releasing her, so both he and Josh could stand to walk over, and hopefully, bring Liam out of his state of shock. He wasn't quite sure what to say to his friend when they got over there, but he hoped the words would come to him.

"Hey, man, how are you holding up?" Thankfully, Josh broke the ice as he took the seat Rylie had just vacated, leaving Brent to sit on the table in front of the chairs where the other guys were sitting.

Fuck, I hope this thing is sturdy enough to hold my weight, Brent thought, wishing Josh had sat on the table since he was ten pounds lighter than Brent.

Liam looked really dazed, with his eyes almost glazed over. It took him a couple of minutes of opening and closing his mouth like a fish out of water before he finally spoke. "I, uh," Liam stuttered out, shaking his head. "I don't know."

"Anything we can do for you?" Brent asked, feeling completely useless at consoling anyone but Aiken.

"Just tell me he's gonna be okay." Liam's voice sounded more dejected than Brent had ever heard him in the past. "There was so much blood. And I can't stop seeing it over and over, only with Rylie in Allissa's place and then being the one killed instead of the stalker."

"There's always a lot of blood from a head injury," Josh reiterated the words Brent had shared earlier and were continuing to be whispered in all the conversations around them, trying to be positive when Liam obviously needed it. "But D's strong, so I'm sure he'll bounce back in no time from the concussion he's bound to have from hitting his head, regardless of you walking out of the locker room with half a pint of his blood on your clothes."

"Yeah, it wasn't D's blood on my clothes," Liam informed them, shaking his head again. "Allissa's the only one of us who probably had D's blood on her, since he covered her body with his when the gunfire started. All the blood on me, Dean, and Dion's back was from the stalker when all four of the Avington guys shot the son of a bitch. Well, Dion might have some of his own blood on his back from when that asshole's bullet grazed the right side of his head, and then he turned his head to the right, trying to avoid the frame around the toilet stalls when he tackled Allissa to the ground, so the wound could have dripped blood on his back then."

"You sure it just grazed him?" Brent was glad he was sitting down when he realized that Dion had literally been shot in the head. *Holy fuck! No wonder he was still unconscious when they wheeled him outta the locker room. He'll be lucky as fuck to survive that, and will probably have more than just a concussion to show for it if he does.*

"Yeah, I'm sure," Liam sighed, nodding his head. "I got an up-close view of both his wounds when we had to roll him off of Allissa to assess her injuries. I also saw where the bullet lodged in the door of the toilet stall three down from where Dion and Allissa landed. And that bullet could have only come from the stalker's gun because none of the Avington guys were aiming in that direction. They all hit center mass on the stalker, so if any of their shots were through and throughs, then the bullets would be lodged in the lockers straight back, not off to the side like that."

Holy fuck! Brent mentally repeated the silent curse once more. *D's lucky as hell if he came that close to a bullet in the brain and got away with only a graze. But then again, it was obviously deep enough to knock him out, so maybe not. But wait, Liam said he saw "both his wounds." So, what the hell happened to give D multiple injuries?*

"If the bullet just grazed him, what was the other wound you saw?"

"The bullet that flew between him and Allissa hit him about here as he was extracting Allissa from the clutches of that psycho." Liam pointed on his own head to show the approximate location on the right side of Dion's head, just above his ear where the bullet grazed him. "But in his haste to get out of the line of fire, he got too close to the frame around the toilet stalls and turning his head away wasn't enough to keep him from hitting the back of his head as they went down. Allissa said it was the gentlest back bump she'd ever taken, probably because all his momentum was somehow focused on that frame, which cut his head here." Liam pointed to another spot on his own head, not quite halfway around on the opposite side of where the bullet wound was located, just behind his left ear. "It was actually the hit to the head that Linc said knocked him out, even though the bullet wound bled worse."

"Yeah, that's the one we saw that appeared to be bleeding through the dressing they put on to transport him," Josh commented, reminding Brent of what he saw when they moved the gurney through the backstage area.

They sat silently for a couple of seconds before Brent went back to Liam's original statement about seeing it over and over in his head, only with Rylie taking Allissa's place, and then things ending differently with her either being injured or killed. *Fuck! Even not witnessing it or knowing exactly what happened, I've been worrying about Aiken possibly being in a similar situation one day. So, I bet those images have to be ten times worse for him, especially since he's been fighting his obvious attraction to Rylie. Not being the one to protect her has to be killing him inside.*

"You know the only way to stop those images of Rylie in one of their places is to quit fighting what you feel for her, so you can be by her side to keep her safe, right?" Brent pointed out to his friend the same thing he'd just had to face for himself with Aiken.

"Yeah, but unfortunately, what's best for me isn't what's best for her," Liam sighed, looking longingly over Brent's shoulder, presumably at his wife.

"You don't know that for sure, Bro," Josh disagreed, shaking his head. "And if she's anything like Teagan, she'll be pissed as hell if you keep unilaterally making the decisions and don't even ask her what she wants to happen between you two."

Damn, I hope I haven't been doing that with Aiken, Brent suddenly worried, looking back on how he'd pretty much dictated their dating plans for the last three weeks. *No, she told me when I was keeping things too much in the friend zone and wasn't giving her the affection she needs. So, I'm sure she'll tell me if I start to go too fast with her, now that I've realized I want a hell of a lot more than just friendship for our future.*

"I agree with Josh," Brent declared, hoping to nudge his friend in the right direction with his wife. "You could be exactly who she wants to spend the rest of her life with, but you won't know that unless you give your marriage a real shot. Leaning on her like you've been doing today is a good start, so let her help you deal with everything running through your head, and drop all the annulment talk for a little while."

"Yeah, definitely don't bring that up again," Josh added, nodding along as he encouraged their friend to change his tactics. "Use the next few days to get back to the easy friendship you had with her before finding out you married her. Then once you're both feeling comfortable with one another again, start upping the romantic gestures to woo her a little before asking if she thinks you guys could possibly stay married."

Before they could finish the discussion and be assured that Liam would take their advice, Allissa broke out in what appeared to be hysterical laughter, drawing the attention of everyone in the room.

"Allissa, Darlin', are you okay?" Dean's voice rose, conveying how worried he was about his fiancée's behavior.

"No," Allissa cackled, shaking her head as the concerned expressions spread around the room. She was literally laughing so hard she was crying, trying futilely to wipe away the tears before she elaborated loud enough that everyone could hear her. "I grew up without a dad because my mom didn't like any of her regulars enough to want to find out who he was, so we didn't get stuck with any of the losers in our lives. And because she wasn't very discriminating in choosing her partners, my biological father may very well be the psycho who's been stalking me and just tried to kidnap me at gunpoint with plans to take me back to his house and rape me. My life is like a cheesy soap opera that's too outlandish to even sound believable. So, I'm gonna follow Randi's advice and laugh my ass off to keep from crying."

Damn. Brent was too shocked by Allissa's words to think anything other than the expletive in response to what she'd just revealed.

"Do we need to put her in the bed next to my brother for a psych eval?" Dion's brother Darius surprised them all by suddenly appearing beside Rick, while they were all focused on Allissa.

"Oh, Darius, is Dion okay?" Allissa jumped up from her seat, throwing her arms around Dion's brother.

"Yeah." Darius grunted as he caught Allissa and returned her brief embrace. "He can't remember shit, but he's awake and gonna be fine."

Thank God!

"What can't he remember?" Brent questioned, wondering if that symptom was just standard concussion stuff, or made worse by the damage from the bullet wound.

"When can we see him?" Liam asked at the same time.

"How soon will he recover?" Josh added as they all stood and rushed over to surround Dare.

As soon as Aiken was by his side, Brent took her hand and pulled her against him, needing that connection, even though it was still very platonic. Apparently, he wasn't the only one who needed to feel connected to his wife, since Josh clasped Teagan's hand and Liam clung to Rylie's.

"I'm not sure about all that." Darius held up his hands to get the questions to stop. "The doctor said he has retrograde amnesia and a pretty bad concussion, but he didn't give me any idea about his recovery time, or if he'd get his memory back to be able to give the cops his statement about what happened today or not. They're gonna keep him in the ICU for a couple of days. I guess they have to do some more tests and watch him to make sure he doesn't have a brain bleed or something more serious pop up. And it's only family allowed to visit him in the ICU, just like in the ER. But I've got his phone 'cause he's not allowed to use it right now with the concussion, so I'll keep ya'll informed via text."

Amnesia and a concussion? That doesn't sound too bad. So, I guess the bullet did just graze him and wasn't as life threatening an injury as it appeared with how he was bleeding through the bandage they put on his head.

But, is amnesia one of the symptoms of a concussion? Like maybe he'll get his memories back once he follows the concussion protocol for a couple of weeks? Or is it a separate type of injury? Like maybe it's from the traumatic events of the day and he won't ever remember exactly what happened? Either way, Brent was relieved to hear that Dion would most likely recover enough to rejoin the rest of the GWA on tour, even if he didn't remember the events of earlier that day.

"Oh, thank feck," Liam sighed, wrapping Rylie in his arms like he couldn't stand the thought of letting her go right then.

Hopefully, that means he's going to take our advice from earlier and keep leaning on her to help him get through the traumatic events of the day.

"Is there anything we can do for you? Like, go grab you some food or something?" Allissa offered, as the rest of the group nodded along to show they each wanted to do something for him too.

"You don't have to do anything like that," Darius smiled. "I'm actually on my way to the cafeteria right now to grab a bite to eat while they're transferring Dion up to the ICU. But ya'll can come with and finish filling me in on what happened, if ya want."

"Yeah, now that we know Dion's going to make a full recovery, I think it would be best if we send everyone else back to the hotel for now," Rick interjected, obviously not comfortable with having the entire roster of the GWA take over the hospital cafeteria, the same way they had the emergency waiting room. "Dean and Allissa can finish filling Dare in on what happened today, while the rest of you work with the security teams right outside to lure the paparazzi away from the hospital."

"Um, we drove Dion's vehicle over here from the arena. Do you need us to leave it here, Darius?" Rylie turned her head toward Darius while still embracing Liam.

Since Brent had to drive Aiken back to the hotel in their rental car, he shut out the rest of their conversation and focused on his wife. "What do you say we go coordinate with the security guys to lead the papzz all over New Orleans before heading back to the hotel?"

"Sounds good," Aiken agreed, smiling at him as they cleaned up the tissues she'd used, grabbed her purse, and started to walk toward the doors. "But I'm not sure even us holding hands as we walk out of here will be salacious enough to distract them from trying to get pics of Dion in his hospital bed."

"Then maybe we'll give them a little show first to get them to follow us," Brent grinned, wagging his eyebrows at his wife, as he decided to start implementing his plan to progress their relationship. "How do you feel about a public make-out session in the hospital parking lot, Mrs. Crockett?"

"I'm cool with that," Aiken grinned back as they exited the building. "If you're okay with Papa framing whatever pictures they take today and hanging them in the living room with the rest of the pictures of what he considers the milestones of my life."

"Oh, I really can't wait to see all these pictures when we get to Los Angeles in a couple of weeks." Brent stopped her just before they reached the line of security guards blocking the paparazzi from entering the emergency room, knowing they'd have to get at least one of them to follow them when they left the hospital. He tapped the closest man in an Avington Security shirt on the shoulder to get his attention. "Hey, can I get you to escort us to our car, and then to the hotel, after we get the attention of as many of these reporters as we can, so they'll follow us away from the hospital?"

"Absolutely," the man in the Avington Security uniform agreed. "But how are you going to get them to focus on you and not keep trying to get into the hospital?"

"Just give us an opening in the human wall you have guarding the doors, and you'll see."

As the man stepped aside for him and Aiken to step through, Brent made sure they were well within the line of sight of the majority of the papzz before pulling Aiken into his arms and dipping her back to kiss her, as if they were reenacting that famous V-J Day photo of the sailor kissing a nurse in Times Square, or were acting in one of the classic black-and-white films she'd told him about watching with her dads as a kid.

Unlike all the sweet, innocent kisses they'd shared in the last couple of weeks, Brent didn't hold back his desire this time. When Aiken's lips parted as she gasped in surprise at being dipped, he swooped his tongue in to deepen the kiss. *Fuck, she's even sweeter than I expected.*

She responded perfectly too, clinging to his shoulders with both hands and tangling her tongue with his as she returned the passionate kiss. But no matter how much he enjoyed their explosive chemistry, he couldn't completely shut out the sounds of cameras clicking and questions being shouted at them and the rest of the GWA talent coming out of the hospital. So, Brent reluctantly pulled back, smiling at the sexually stunned look on Aiken's face as he returned her to an upright position.

Yeah, her papa isn't gonna be the only one framing some of these pictures.

Chapter Six

Rylie was exceptionally worried about Liam as she sat beside him in the waiting room at the hospital, where Dion had been taken, along with pretty much everyone else who worked for the GWA. Like everyone around her, she was also worried about Dion and his recovery. But she knew Dion was in good hands with the doctors and nurses treating his injuries, while Liam just seemed to have her to take care of him right then.

To be honest, she couldn't believe how she'd reacted to this tragedy and jumped into her role as his wife to help him through it. For the last three weeks, she'd been mostly avoiding him whenever she wasn't required to interact with him in her role as Chastity. Yeah, she kept trying to be a little flirty with him during their spots on the GWA's shows, but she limited her flirtatious behavior to her role as Chastity. When she was just Rylie backstage, on the plane, or anywhere else they crossed paths, she was cordial, but never actively sought him out for any reason. It wasn't that she didn't want to try to get back to the easy friendship they'd developed when she first started with the GWA. It was just that she didn't want to feel like a fool for still crushing on him, or have anyone around them think she was acting like an infatuated child, when he'd been acting like an asshole since finding out they were married. But as soon as the Avington Security teams had separated the GWA talent and staff from the fans at the expo, escorting the talent to the catering area backstage while taking the fans out to a lobby on the opposite side of the arena, so they could all be cleared by the police to leave the building, she'd felt an urgent need to make sure Liam wasn't among the injured.

As the families and couples gathered in small clusters, she'd felt like the odd woman out among all the single men on the roster. Yeah, they were all checking on her, but their concern for her felt more brotherly or friendly than anything. Then, when she saw Liam being escorted out of the women's locker room by a police officer, looking slightly shell-shocked and covered in blood spatter, she couldn't stop herself from breaking away from the group of unattached performers to go check on him.

Realizing he'd risked his life to go help Allissa had only increased her attraction to him, even though it also scared her to the point that she was afraid she might have a heart attack from how hard her heart was beating out of her chest. That was probably because he'd come out of the locker room just a few minutes after the paramedics had wheeled Dion out on a stretcher, with one of the paramedics asking her partners for more gauze while applying pressure to the blood-soaked bandage already covering the wound on the right side of his head.

Seeing him covered in what she assumed was Dion's blood, she'd wanted nothing more than to examine every inch of Liam's body to make sure he wasn't injured in any way. It didn't matter that he'd acted like a jackass for the last three weeks. She still cared for him and needed to know he was okay. It took all her willpower to stop herself from running over and wrapping him in her arms. But thankfully, she understood the officer's warning about contaminating the evidence on his clothes and held herself back. Still, she couldn't stop herself from asserting her wifely right to stand by her man, even if it was only a legal technicality until they could meet with their attorneys to dissolve the marriage.

My mother would be so proud of how I'm following in her footsteps, Rylie thought sarcastically. Her African American mother had also married a white man, Rylie's father, who'd moved from Atlanta, Georgia, to Atlantic City, New Jersey, to be with her after meeting her while there for an educators' conference. Whenever asked about why she hadn't moved to be with her husband, Rylie's mom had always replied with, "My name might be Tammy, but it's not Tammy Wynette. My man stands by me." *Yeah, but you stood by Dad a lot too, Mom. And hopefully, Liam will appreciate me standing by him now when he needs me. And might actually start to act more like the man I was falling for before finding out we got married. So maybe eventually, we can explore our options for actually being a couple and staying married, instead of just snapping at each other, as we go through the court process to dissolve our marriage.*

He certainly seemed to act more like his old self when he insisted she accompany him into the men's locker room and included her in helping to demonstrate the incident. Because of that, she'd enjoyed seeing him strip down to his underwear while relinquishing his clothing to the crime scene investigator and the officer taking his statement. Though considering the circumstances, and the bruises she saw forming on his arms from Dean landing on them when they both hit the floor, she did feel a little guilty for appreciating how he filled out those boxers. Which was why she'd waited with the officer when Liam was allowed to go back to the showers to clean up and redress. *But damn, I wouldn't have minded getting to see the whole package. Especially if I'd have gotten to see how much that bulge grew if I'd have been able to go back and soap him up.*

She was so proud of how he'd stoically run through everything with the officers and handled being processed as part of the crime scene back at the arena. But the way he'd broken down once they were alone in Dion's SUV, and then basically shut down completely when they got to the hospital, had her concerned about how he was processing everything that had happened earlier that day. His uncharacteristic behavior made her glad that she'd taken the card for the crisis counselor, which one of the officers had handed her while Liam was walking them through his version of events earlier.

Now I just have to figure out how to convince him to actually call the number and talk to them. Considering he didn't even say anything to Dean and Allissa when we got here earlier, I'm not sure what it'll take to get him to open up again.

She looked around at the other GWA wrestlers, who'd filled every seat in the waiting room, and wondered if any of them might be able to get through to him, since they'd worked with him much longer than she had and presumably had much closer friendships with him. Obviously, she couldn't ask the Dangerous Twins to talk to him. While Dean was busy taking point on comforting Allissa, James and Randi were right there beside him, as well as running interference with the rest of the Hunters, who all wanted to rally around their soon-to-be new member of the family.

That meant she needed to run through the rest of the roster to figure out who might be closest to Liam to be able to get through to him. With Liam being friendly with practically everyone, it was hard to figure out who that might be, other than Dion, who was clearly his best friend. And obviously, Dion had other priorities at the moment. If he was even awake yet.

She knew Magnum and Trojan weren't the best options, since they'd barely been with the company a couple days longer than she had. The Bama Boys and Bennington brothers also weren't her best options, having only been with the company about a year. While there were a few guys who'd been with the GWA as long as or longer than Liam, most of them were married with families, and didn't really hang out with him after the shows all that often. That basically left Crockett, Surfer Josh, Owen Sawyer, Killer Kade, and Blade as her best options for who might be able to get through to him.

Since Sawyer and Blade often went off on their own in search of ring rats, Rylie didn't think they were really close friends with Liam. Kade tended to congregate with the Bennington brothers to do the same, only typically having better luck with the ladies since they were all babyfaces. That left her with Crockett and Surfer Josh, who had seemed to carpool with Red Velvet quite often. At least, they had until Rick pointed out that it wasn't a good idea to have a babyface seen hanging out with three of the top heels in the company all the time, when CNZ decided that GWA wrestlers were celebrities that needed to be spotlighted on their site.

Yeah, Crockett and Surfer Josh are probably my best options for trying to get through to him. Rylie decided, making eye contact with the Precious Stones, who were each sitting and holding hands with their new husbands. *And since they're all trying to make their marriages work, maybe they can plant a few ideas in Liam's brain for us to make a go of being married, too.*

After three weeks of watching her friends date the men they'd married in Vegas, Rylie was extremely jealous of her friends' relationships, and heartbroken that outside their performances in the GWA, she and Liam had basically avoided each other, instead of trying the same thing. While she wasn't sure they could ever actually be a couple like Emerald & Josh or Amethyst & Crockett, she couldn't deny that she was still ridiculously attracted to Liam. And her feelings hadn't been quashed in the slightest by his recent asshole behavior. She knew it was because of her unrequited feelings for him that she'd insisted on making sure he wasn't injured at the arena earlier. And also, why she felt the need to take care of him now, when he clearly needed someone to lean on as he processed the trauma he'd been through. She just hoped she wasn't setting herself up for more heartache, as he went through the various phases of grief to deal with the shocking events of the day.

As she started to stand to go talk to her friends, Liam's grip on her hand tightened, surprising her with how vehemently he didn't want her to leave his side. "I'm just going right over there to talk to the girls for a second. Maybe see if we should coordinate a coffee run for everyone while we're waiting. But I promise I'll be right back and I won't leave this room unless you go with me."

Liam didn't respond verbally, but he released her hand and nodded. She smiled affectionately at him as she stood before walking over to where the Stones sat between their men.

Squatting down in front of them, she whispered, "Can I get you guys to help me with Liam? He's completely shut down and hasn't said a word since we left the arena, and I'm starting to get really worried about him."

"Yeah, we'll talk to him," Josh offered, lifting his chin at Crockett before they both stood and walked over to, hopefully, bring Liam out of his state of shock.

Rylie took Crockett's now empty seat so she could keep Liam in her line of sight as she checked on her other friends, knowing they'd been friends with Dion a lot longer than she had, so they had to be hurting for him even more than she was at the moment. "How are you and your guys doing with all this?"

"We're doing okay," Emerald replied, shaking her head like she wasn't a hundred percent sure of her answer. "Probably way better than Liam, Dean, and Allissa, since none of us were in the locker room when it happened."

"I feel terrible about not being in the locker room with Allissa," Amethyst added, dabbing her teary eyes with a tissue. "We should have continued sticking close to her, instead of advancing our angle during the babyfaces' expo time slot."

"Honestly, when I first heard the commotion, I thought it was you guys fighting over Em going out to flirt with Josh. It wasn't until someone mentioned hearing gunshots that I realized it wasn't a work," Rylie admitted.

"No, we're building the Stones breakup slowly, so we went with more of a subtle, seething conversation, instead of a yelling, screaming catfight," Emerald explained what Rylie hadn't been able to see from the booth where she was signing autographs with Protection Detail, which was on the opposite end of the arena floor from where the Stones interrupted Surfer Josh playing the GWA video game with fans. "The way Rick has it booked for now, that's not supposed to happen until *Christmas Chaos*. But I suppose that could change, depending on how he has to rebook tomorrow's show."

"If we even have a show tomorrow," Amethyst added, sniffling as she wiped her tears. "Even if the police finish processing the locker room and release the crime scene, or just keep the locker room cordoned off but allow us to use the rest of the arena, I don't think any of us will be able to wrestle if Dion doesn't make it."

"Dion's going to survive this," Rylie declared, whisper-shouting so Liam, Allissa, and Dean didn't hear her to figure out that anyone else among them believed Dion might die from his injuries. "According to what Liam told the cops when he had us reenacting the events to give his statement, the bullet only grazed Dion. It was hitting his head on the frame around the toilet stall that knocked him out. So, I have to believe he's just going to need a couple of stitches and to follow the concussion protocol to heal up before he can come back."

"God, Chas, I hope you're right about that," Emerald asserted, pulling a tissue out of the box that had been circulating around the room and dabbing at her eyes.

As they sat there silently for a moment, Rylie looked over to see that Liam was actually talking to Josh and Crockett. "Oh, thank God."

Amethyst and Emerald both looked at her before following her line of sight to see what she was commenting on.

"What's up with you and Red today?" Emerald asked, her curiosity showing in her expression, even though Rylie could still see her worry for Dion. "Are you guys actually trying to make things work now? Or were you just the only one with a valid excuse to get the cops to let you stay with him while he went through his statement and stuff?"

"And what exactly happened that's got you so worried about him?" Amethyst added, appearing hopeful that Rylie could distract her from her fear for Dion with an update on her relationship with Liam.

"I'm not really sure what's happening with us," Rylie confided, sighing over how futile her attempt at being there for him seemed, now that he was clearly opening up to the guys way more than he felt comfortable opening up to her. "I freaked out when I saw him covered in blood and basically asserted rights that I don't really have. But I think your guess that I was just the only one with a valid excuse to stay with him is probably spot on for why he let me get away with it."

"As he walked through everything with the officers, I kinda felt like he was holding up better than I was. But then, when we were told we could go and drive Dion's Escalade over here, he insisted on me driving because he didn't feel like it would be safe for him to get behind the wheel. And when he broke down crying as soon as we got in the vehicle, I realized everything was way more traumatic for him than he let on in front of the cops."

"Red cried?" Amethyst appeared shocked by that revelation.

"And he actually let you see him when he cried?" Emerald's eyes were as wide as saucers as Rylie nodded to answer both their questions. "Chas, you know he's gotta trust you a lot more than he's been letting on if he's willing to let you see him in a vulnerable moment like that."

"I don't know about that," Rylie disagreed, shaking her head. "After hearing everything that happened in the dressing room, I'm sure it all just got to be overwhelming to the point that he couldn't hold it in any longer and had to let it out, no matter who was with him right then."

"What exactly happened? I mean, I know there were gunshots and Dion was knocked out, but what did you mean when you said Big D was grazed by a bullet?"

Considering her love of true crime shows and police procedurals, Rylie wasn't surprised by Emerald wanting a complete recap of what she heard while Liam gave his statement to the cops. So, she did her best to recap, making sure to emphasize what Liam said about Dion's worst injury being that he was knocked out from hitting the back of his head on the frame around the toilet stalls to keep Amethyst from freaking out again and thinking Big D was going to die.

Just as she finished her recap of the incident and was about to change the subject to suggest sending someone on a coffee run, Allissa broke out in what appeared to be hysterical laughter, drawing the attention of everyone in the room.

While everyone else was focused on Dean checking on his fiancée and Allissa ranting about her stalker possibly being her biological father, Rylie looked over at Liam to see his reaction to the outburst. Thankfully, his eyes appeared a little clearer now that he was talking to the guys, even though Rylie felt a little jealous of the fact that he was looking at Allissa instead of her. *It's just because she's the one who was in danger and he had to help rescue her. He's just looking to see how she's doing after what happened today, not looking because he's interested in her. Hell, even if he'd been attracted to Allissa when she first started working with the GWA, I'm sure he wouldn't have stepped on Dean's toes by acting on it once Dean staked his claim.*

Having not met him before, Rylie didn't recognize the voice of the man who commented on Allissa's need for a psych eval. But when Allissa jumped from her seat, threw her arms around him, and addressed him by name when she asked how Dion was doing, she soon realized he was related to Dion. *Wow, I should have noticed the family resemblance to see he's the guy Liam was talking about at the arena earlier, when he mentioned bringing Big D's stuff to Dion's brother at the hospital.*

"Yeah." Darius grunted as he caught Allissa and returned her brief embrace. "He can't remember shit, but he's awake and gonna be fine."

Oh, thank God!

"What can't he remember?"

"When can we see him?"

"How soon will he recover?"

Several of the guys started yelling out questions at once, including Liam, much to Rylie's relief. She followed along with the girls as they all crowded around Darius, making her way over to Liam's side and taking his hand as Dion's brother spoke.

"I'm not sure about all that." Darius held up his hands to get the questions to stop. "The doctor said he has retrograde amnesia and a pretty bad concussion, but he didn't give me any idea about his recovery time, or if he'd get his memory back to be able to give the cops his statement about what happened today or not. They're gonna keep him in the ICU for a couple of days. I guess they have to do some more tests and watch him to make sure he doesn't have a brain bleed or something more serious pop up. And it's only family allowed to visit him in the ICU, just like in the ER. But I've got his phone 'cause he's not allowed to use it right now with the concussion, so I'll keep ya'll informed via text."

"Oh, thank feck," Liam sighed, wrapping Rylie in his arms as his whole body seemed to sag with relief.

She looped her arms around his waist, making sure she was positioned to hold him up if he needed her to, even though she wasn't sure she was fully capable of shouldering his whole weight because of their size difference. Liam was almost a foot taller than her five-foot-five and outweighed her by at least a hundred pounds, but she was determined to be strong enough to support him.

Rylie focused on comforting her husband, as Allissa offered to go get Darius some food, and he informed them all that he was on his way down to the cafeteria. It wasn't until Rick broke in to direct the majority of them to go back to the hotel while leaving Dean and Allissa there to fill Darius in on the details of what had happened that Rylie realized she needed to know what to do with Dion's vehicle before they could leave.

She pulled back slightly from Liam's embrace as she spoke, "Um, we drove Dion's vehicle over here from the arena. Do you need us to leave it here, Darius?" Rylie looked to Dion's brother for what he wanted done, as Liam continued holding onto her, obviously still trying to gather his composure.

"No, I drove my car here, so I'll need ya'll to take his Escalade back to the house." Darius shook his head momentarily before locking his gaze on Liam. "You know the codes to put it in the garage, don'tcha, Red?"

"Yeah," Liam agreed, nodding, and finally releasing Rylie from his bear hug, even though he kept one arm around her shoulders. "And where to leave the keys."

"Cool," Darius smiled, reaching out to fist-bump Liam. "Thanks, brother."

Byron Avington waved them over to the side of the group as everyone else started gathering their things to leave while planning to take several different routes to confuse the paparazzi. "Be sure to grab one of my guys from outside to follow you and give you a ride back to the hotel."

"Will do," she and Liam agreed in unison before walking out to grab the first Avington Security bodyguard they could find.

The man who only introduced himself as Maddox stoically agreed to assist them, waiting patiently for Rylie to get her purse out of Protection Detail's rental car before getting back behind the wheel of Dion's Escalade, since Liam still insisted she drive instead of him. Only this time, she didn't have an address to program into her GPS, so she had to follow Liam's directions, which were clearly not the direct route to Dion's home in the French Quarter.

They didn't really talk as she drove, though he did point out several places she thought might have some historical significance as they passed them. She saw way more of New Orleans than she ever expected while the GWA was in town, but was starting to wonder how many hours they were going to drive around before Liam finally remembered where Dion lived to give her accurate directions, when his phone rang.

"Connery," he barked in a clipped tone as he answered his phone. "Cool. Yeah, we'll head there now."

Rylie wanted to ask who was on the phone and where they were supposed to go next, but didn't get the chance as Liam hung up the phone and dropped it back in the pocket of his suit jacket. "Maddox said we finally lost the papzz, so we can actually go to Dion's now."

Ah, so that's what all that driving around was all about.

Within a few minutes, they pulled up to a historic brick building in the French Quarter, where Liam got out and keyed in a code to open the gate beside it, which opened into what looked like an alley almost too narrow for Dion's large vehicle. He then directed her to pull in, closing the gate behind her before Maddox could pull in behind them. He then hopped back in the passenger side and guided her around behind the building to turn into a quaint courtyard surrounded on three sides by the building she assumed Dion lived in and what appeared to be two separate garages. Liam pointed to the garage closest to the building she assumed was Dion's home to direct her where to park before getting out once more to key in another code in order to raise the door. Once it was open, Rylie pulled in and parked. After getting his bag from the back, he instructed her to put Dion's keys in the glove box and not lock the vehicle.

After securing the vehicle in the garage, they had to walk back down the alley and use the code to open the gate to get out and join Maddox in his SUV, which she thought might be an actual Avington vehicle, instead of a rental like all the wrestlers got when they arrived in town, since it had Georgia plates instead of Louisiana tags.

There was even less conversation on the drive from Dion's home to the hotel where the GWA was staying for the weekend, other than the brief praise Maddox gave Liam for knowing how to evade a tail when they first got in the vehicle.

Once they finally arrived back at the hotel, Rylie assumed she and Liam would go to their separate rooms, feeling like he'd pulled back from her since leaving the hospital, and assuming his talk with Crockett and Surfer Josh went well enough that he no longer needed her to lean on. She was surprised, however, when he followed her off the elevator and all the way to her room.

"Um, Liam, what's going on?" Rylie muttered as she stopped at the door to her room. "Why aren't you going to your room?"

"I just…" Liam took a deep breath before sighing it out. "I'm not ready to be alone yet. So, I was hoping maybe we could sit and watch a movie, or maybe order room service, or whatever. Just until I figure out how to process everything from today and feel ready to be alone for the night."

Rylie wasn't sure about being alone with him in her hotel room, but she couldn't refuse when he was still so upset and not acting like his normal self, either. "Sure," she agreed with a sympathetic smile as she unlocked the door and walked inside. "Do you think it would help to call that crisis counselor the cops recommended and talk through everything?"

"I don't know." Liam walked past her to flop down on her bed, not seeming to realize that he took up all the space in her single queen room. "I know everyone says it's better to talk about stuff to keep from bottling it up. But I just don't feel comfortable talking to a stranger. Ya know?"

"Yeah, I understand that, but this is more like talking to a doctor, not a stranger. Someone who can help you find strategies to be able to deal with your emotions." Rylie actually planned on calling them herself once she was alone in her room to be able to freely talk, but it didn't look like that was going to happen anytime soon.

"I don't need that though," Liam argued, shaking his head at her, as she put her purse down on the dresser and walked around to sit on the opposite side of the bed, as far away from Liam as she could get since there wasn't anyplace else to sit in the smallish hotel room. "I just need to talk to Dion to hear from him that he's gonna be okay, and then I'll be fine."

"Yes, well, since you aren't related to him, that's not an option right now."

"No, but one of these times when I call Dare for an update, he'll be in D's room, so I'll be able to talk to him on speaker, even if he's not allowed to use his phone yet." Liam grabbed the remote off the bedside table and turned on the television, essentially killing their conversation.

As Liam flipped channels, looking for something to watch without asking her opinion, Rylie decided to take a moment to herself. She needed to cool her temper before she blew up at Liam for going back to acting like an ass, instead of appreciating how she'd been trying to take care of him all afternoon.

She grabbed a pair of sleep shorts and a t-shirt from her suitcase before stepping into the bathroom to wash off her makeup and change. There was no point in staying in her Chastity getup when she had no plans to leave her room for the rest of the night.

Having him in my room to watch a movie isn't a big deal, she told herself as she cleaned up and changed. *It's no different than when we have girls' nights in one of our rooms, except I doubt Liam will want to do facials and paint our nails. I just have to make sure I don't think about replacing those activities with anything sexual, just because I'm hanging out with the friend I've been dreaming about fucking for the last several months.*

When she went back out to the main room, she wasn't surprised to see that Liam was looking at the room service menu. She was stunned, however, to realize he'd stopped surfing channels to watch ***CSI: NY.***

Seriously? He didn't get enough of the crime scene stuff at the arena earlier?

Leah Mae Wright

"What do you feel like eating?" Liam didn't bother looking up from the menu in his hand.

"Whatever salad they have with grilled chicken," Rylie replied, not wanting to eat anything that might make her bloated, just in case they were able to gain access to the arena for the **Halloween Horror** show the next day. "I'm not picky about dressing, but I do want it on the side."

Liam only nodded before turning his back to her and picking up the room phone to call down for their meals. She put her clothing in the dirty clothes bag to take down to be laundered the next morning before sitting back down on the bed. It wasn't until after he'd ordered her a chicken Caesar salad and him a burger and fries that he turned to face her.

She barely had the chance to notice the way his hazel eyes flared as he briefly scanned her body before he turned back toward the television. "Sorry, I couldn't find any movies on TV. Normally, I stream them on my laptop and cast them to the TV, but I didn't want to go up to my room to get my computer. So, I figured this was just as good, since it looks like they're running a marathon of shows for the rest of the day."

"Yeah, it's fine," Rylie shrugged, not really having a preference for watching anything in particular. "I'm not as into these kinds of shows as Emerald is, but I can handle it as long as they don't show the over the top blood and guts stuff like some of the ones she watches."

"No, this one's not too gory. But even though my family will all tell you it's completely unrealistic of their jobs with the NYPD, I like watching it 'cause it makes me feel closer to them whenever I get a little homesick with all our traveling."

"You have family who work for the NYPD?" Rylie relaxed back onto the pillow, enjoying getting to know Liam a little better.

"Yeah, three of my brothers are still on the force, while my dad and middle brother both retired. Well, Dad retired after thirty years on the force. Rory left after being shot in the line of duty and now owns Connery's Irish Pub. But I don't know if he had enough years on the force to officially retire, or if it was more like a medical discharge."

Liam seemed to relax more and more as he told her about each of his four younger brothers while they ate. While she thought he needed to talk more about the shooting earlier that day to get past the trauma, she could clearly see how he was comparing what he'd just been through with the jobs his brothers did every day, so she thought their discussion was still productive in helping him heal.

He also compared the events on the television with the actions of the New Orleans Police Department officers they'd interacted with earlier, which she also thought might be his way of processing everything. Unfortunately, she couldn't tell if his comparisons were from his natural resistance that would keep him from developing PTSD from the incident, or if he was just in the denial phase of trauma and grief, which she'd learned way too much about after losing her parents in a car accident when she was only eighteen. But either way, she sat there and let him talk, appreciating the feelings of bonding she felt with him, and only adding her two cents when he specifically asked her a question.

Their conversation was so pleasant that neither one of them seemed to notice how much time passed. Eventually, she took the time to tie up her braids in a silk scarf before laying down as they continued talking. Ostensibly, they were both comfortable enough with each other to drift off to sleep together.

Rylie wasn't sure how much time had passed when she woke up wrapped in Liam's arms. But apparently, he'd turned off the television and lights at some point without waking her up to discuss him staying over.

And got undressed, she realized when she felt the bare skin of his chest under her cheek and hand, and recognized his bergamot and sandalwood scent was stronger without his clothing, making it clear it was from his bodywash and not a cologne that he sprayed on after getting dressed. *Holy shit! How far did he strip down?*

She was tempted to run her hand down his torso to find out if he was still wearing pants, but she was afraid if she did, then she'd wake him up. *And after the way he's acted the last three weeks, there's no way I'm going to do anything that he might consider as me throwing myself at him. If anything is going to happen between us, he has to make the first move.*

Still, she took advantage of laying on her side and cuddling with him to move her top leg against his to figure out that he had removed his slacks. She just wasn't brave enough to hitch her leg up higher to try to feel with her thigh or knee if he'd kept his underwear on or not.

Surely, he kept his boxers on, right? While it is a bit presumptuous to just get undressed and crawl in bed with me, I'm sure he thought the bed was big enough for both of us and just didn't want to walk out after I fell asleep, so he can be here in the morning to reassure me that nothing inappropriate happened between us.

Yes, that's probably it. He's just being a gentleman and not running off in the middle of the night to leave me guessing what happened. And because he's being a gentleman, I'm sure he's still wearing his boxers, or whatever he put on after his shower that I didn't get to see earlier. He probably thinks they're no more revealing than the short wrestling tights he wears in the summer, so it's no big deal for me to see him in them when we wake up in the morning.

So, now I just need to roll off of him, and make sure I stick to my side of the bed for the rest of the night, so he doesn't get the wrong idea when he wakes up.

Rylie barely moved an inch in her attempt to roll away from Liam before he squeezed her tight against him. That's when she realized one of his hands was skin on skin with her ass, where he'd apparently stuck his hand down the back of her shorts and under her panties. *Holy shit! His hand should not feel that good there.*

As she tried once more to roll away from him, he moved the hand that was resting on the middle of her back, taking it down to the hem of her t-shirt before pushing up under her shirt.

"Don't go, Rylie," Liam moaned, caressing up her side until he reached her braless breast. He cupped the underside of her mound and gently pinched her nipple between his thumb and forefinger. "I need you. I know I don't deserve you and am nowhere near good enough for you, but I need you. Please say I can have you, if only for tonight."

Rylie didn't know where his insecurities came from, but she couldn't deny him when she craved him just as much, if not more, than he seemed to desire her at that moment.

"Oh, Liam, yes." Rylie couldn't resist running her hand up from where it rested on his pec to cup his slightly scruffy jaw, as she tilted her head up in preparation for what she hoped would be their first kiss. Well, the first kiss that she could remember anyway, assuming they'd had to kiss during the wedding ceremony neither of them remembered. "I need you too. So bad."

She wasn't disappointed when their eyes met momentarily before he dipped his head and brushed his lips over hers. He didn't keep the kiss sweet and chaste for long, plunging his tongue past her lips to deepen their connection only a moment later.

Rylie returned the kiss with equal passion, wrapping her arms around him, as Liam rolled them to cover her body with his. She felt the steel rod of his erection against her thigh, realizing that he had indeed kept on his cotton boxers, when she felt them rubbing the bare skin of her leg as he seemed to involuntarily rut against her.

Words no longer felt necessary as she ran her hands down the muscular planes of his back. As Liam squeezed her booty in his right hand and fondled her breast with his left, Rylie slipped both of her hands into the back of his boxers for a double handful of his athletic ass.

"Too many clothes," Liam complained as he broke their kiss to slide lower on the bed. He stopped fondling her long enough to push her t-shirt up to give him access for his mouth.

"Yes, definitely too many clothes," Rylie agreed as she used her now free hands to remove the t-shirt, while Liam teased her turgid tips with his teeth and tongue. As much as she loved the way he laved her breasts with his oral affection, she couldn't wait any longer to remove their clothing from their lower halves. So, once the t-shirt was out of her way, she reached down to wiggle her shorts and panties off her hips.

Apparently realizing what she was doing, Liam kissed his way down her torso, sliding off to her side as he assisted in removing the rest of her clothes. Once the garments had all been tossed off the end of the bed, he settled between her legs and showed her that his oral skills weren't limited to just pleasing her mouth and tits.

"Holy, fuck," Rylie moaned in ecstasy when he devoured her pussy like a starving man, running her fingers through his short brownish-red locks.

While she wasn't as virginal as she portrayed while in her Chastity role for the GWA audience, none of the guys she'd hooked up with in the past had gone down on her. So, she couldn't describe exactly how he licked and sucked her, but she did know she'd been missing out before Liam.

I wonder if this is why Allissa and Randi both insist on the full Brazilian every month when we get waxed as part of our spa days? Rylie wondered, glad she'd finally listened to them earlier that month, instead of sticking to her typical basic bikini wax. *Or, more importantly, what does Liam think of me being completely hairless down there?*

Based on the slurping noises he was making as he sucked on her clit, Rylie assumed he liked what he could feel in the mostly dark room. *I wonder if the little bit of moonlight coming in around the curtains is enough for him to see what he's doing down there?* When he inserted first one finger and then two in her pussy, she lost all ability to think about anything but how amazing it felt to have his head and hands between her legs.

"Oh, God, Liam," she moaned, unable to hold back the orgasm he literally sucked out of her. She gripped his head with both hands, holding him in place as every muscle in her body seemed to convulse at once from the outstanding O. "Yes, oh, God, yes, Liam."

When the ripples of pleasure finally started to subside, she released his head, allowing her arms to collapse onto the bed as she caught her breath. While she laid there trying to recover, Liam pushed up off the bed. He rustled around in the dark for a few minutes before she recognized the sound of a condom wrapper tearing. Since she was too wiped out to open her eyes, she assumed the next sounds she heard were him removing his boxers and rolling on the protection. Her assumptions were proven correct when he'd clearly sheathed himself before crawling back into the bed and covering her with his body once more.

"Last chance to change your mind, moh graw." Liam kissed his way up her torso, stopping just as she thought he was about to kiss her lips and planking above her with all his weight resting on his elbows on either side of her head, apparently wanting to give her the opportunity to stop before they actually had sex.

"I'm not changing my mind, Liam," Rylie insisted, reaching down to grip his latex-covered cock and line him up with her opening. Once she felt the tip push slightly past her outer lips, she released his girthy shaft to wrap her arms and legs around him, pulling him down on top of her as his dick slowly sank inside her.

Liam groaned incoherently as he claimed her mouth in a scorching kiss and thrust his hips to fill her completely, bottoming out when his tip hit her cervix, which apparently hadn't receded as far inside her as possible yet. While she couldn't tell in the dark how long his dick was, it was definitely the thickest she'd ever had inside her, causing her to feel a slight sting of pain as she stretched to accommodate him.

Oh, yeah, I was definitely just dreaming about fucking him in Vegas, Rylie realized as she tangled her tongue with his. *'Cause I'd have absolutely still felt him the next morning if we'd actually fucked in that stairwell like I imagined.*

He must have felt her wince momentarily, holding his lower body still to give her time to relax around his cock, even as he continued to kiss her passionately. Unable to withstand his lack of movement for very long, Rylie bucked her hips, signaling that she was more than ready for his next stroke inside her. Thankfully, he seemed to understand her meaning, pulling out slowly before thrusting back in a little faster.

Soon, they settled into the perfect rhythm, syncing up their movements as they made love. Rylie ran her hands up and down his muscular back, as Liam shifted his position to bring his right hand down to fondle her breasts.

When they broke the kiss to breathe, Liam continued to run his lips over her neck and chest, whispering several phrases in Irish that she couldn't understand. The only one she could clearly comprehend was "moh graw," the same words he'd used when giving her the chance to change her mind about having sex. She still didn't know what it meant, but she hoped to remember it to look it up later.

Rylie desperately wanted to memorize every moment of what she hoped wouldn't be the only time she made love with her husband. And she could only think of this coupling as making love because she knew she loved him, even though she was pretty sure he just needed a distraction from the earlier events of the day. But the sensations spreading through her body with every kiss from his lips, each caress of her body with his hands, and each slide of his cock inside her pussy, soon overwhelmed her to the point that she could do nothing but feel.

Leah Mae Wright

She couldn't think. Couldn't speak. But she felt every tingle, every orgasmic flutter, and most especially, the ultimate unbridled pleasure of joining as one with the man who owned her heart.

Liam's rhythmic thrusts drove her to the peak of ecstasy, shoving her over the edge to oblivion. As her inner walls convulsed around Liam's cock, she felt the waves of pleasure cascading out to encompass her whole body. She barely registered that Liam held still deep inside her, calling out her name as he reached his own release, because she felt like she was floating in some celestial realm she'd never experienced before.

I love you, Liam. Wish we could stay together forever in this place of nirvana, she thought as she drifted off to sleep, not realizing her bubble of bliss would be popped the next morning when she awoke alone in her bed.

~~~

Aiken didn't look forward to spending the rest of the evening alone in her room, as she and Brent made their way hand in hand into the hotel. While she knew the trauma of the day didn't really affect her as much as it had others in the company, she still felt like crying whenever she thought about what Allissa, Dean, Liam, and, especially, Dion were going through. And even though she'd heard that this stalker was killed by the extra security the GWA had hired, she didn't even want to think about the possibility of someone else targeting her or one of the other GWA wrestlers, which she would probably fixate on if she spent much time alone.

I suppose I should call and check in with Daddio, so he can assure Papa that I'm fine before this makes the national news, she thought, deciding to do just that as soon as Brent dropped her off at her room. *That will at least keep me from feeling all alone for a few minutes. Though maybe I should text Daddio, so he can reassure Papa before we get on the phone. That way, Papa's freak out won't trigger me to stress over potential stalkers even more.*

Glancing at Brent as they walked through the lobby, she quickly forgot her plans, getting sidetracked by thinking back on the spectacular kiss they'd shared as they'd exited the hospital. While
~~~

she'd thoroughly enjoyed the sweet, mostly chaste kisses they'd exchanged the last couple of weeks, they were nothing compared to how aroused she'd gotten when Brent dipped her back and demonstrated just how explosive their chemistry was in front of all those reporters.

Her nipples had instantly hardened and her pussy had flooded the moment their tongues touched for the first time. She just wasn't sure if her heightened arousal was because it was Brent she was kissing, or if she had a latent exhibitionist streak that she'd never noticed before. But either way, she had to wonder if he'd stepped up the intensity of their affectionate gestures because he was ready to take the next step in their relationship.

If that's the case, maybe I should invite him up to my room to keep me company tonight. Even if he's still not ready to have sex, maybe he'd be open to watching a movie or something to keep my mind off of how horribly this day could have ended and the possibility of it happening again with even worse consequences.

And if my dads call after I text Daddio, then maybe having him in my room to talk to them will help set their minds at ease about my safety, too.

"Um, would you, um, maybe, be willing to stay in my room tonight?" Aiken softly whispered the words as they reached the elevator, feeling nervous about his reaction to the invite. "After everything that happened today, I just don't want to be alone tonight."

"Of course," Brent agreed, smiling softly at her. "Or we could both stay in my room, since I have a king suite, where we'll have a little more space."

His room? Aiken took a moment to contemplate how comfortable she'd be in his space instead of her own. But she quickly realized that it didn't really matter, since they were both hotel rooms and not one of their actual homes, where she might feel like one of them had the home court advantage. *I suppose a man his size would feel more comfortable in the room with the bigger bed, which is probably why the guys all request them when we check in at the hotels daily.*

"That's fine," Aiken agreed, nodding as the elevator doors opened for them to step inside. "And if you have a t-shirt I can borrow to sleep in, we don't even have to stop by my room to get my stuff."

"Yes, I do. If you're comfortable with that. I'm also okay with stopping for your stuff, if that will make you more comfortable." Brent released her hand and escorted her into the elevator with his hand on the small of her back, making tingles spread from where he innocently touched her all the way to her most womanly parts.

Maybe I should go to my room and get my stuff, so I'll at least be able to put on a pair of shorts or sleep pants in case this isn't going the way I think it might. But then again, if we go get all my stuff from my room, aren't we kinda implying that I'm moving to his room for the rest of our stay in New Orleans, and not just for tonight? I don't want to do that if he's really not ready to do more than kiss me like he did in the hospital parking lot earlier.

Although, if we go get my stuff and I put on a sexy nightgown for bed, then maybe it'll entice him enough to want to do more. But while I know I'm ready to take our physical relationship to the next level, I don't want to manipulate the situation or coerce him into going farther than he wants with me.

Ugh! This is probably one of those times the girls mentioned the other day, when I just have to be brave enough to ask him what he wants and tell him what I want, so we can make the decision together.

So, why do I feel so awkward just thinking about asking him if he's ready for us to have sex and start sharing rooms all the time? Why can't I be more outspoken about what I want, like Teagan? It would be a whole lot easier to have this conversation, if only I was a little more like my bestie.

Gathering all her courage, Aiken turned her head to really look at her husband. Brent Crockett really was the most attractive man she'd ever seen. At six-foot-three, he was exactly a foot taller than her, making her feel really petite, even when she wore the six-inch-high heels that made her feel super tall because of how they lifted her up almost eye to eye with Daddio.

She didn't care if he pulled his long brown hair up into a man bun, like he did for workouts or casually hanging out, or if he left it down, like he wore it to the ring or whenever they went out clubbing after a show, she constantly wanted to reach over and play with the soft-looking strands. Though she did prefer both of those messier styles over the super neat, low ponytail look he sported whenever he was in a suit for traveling. She especially liked his hair right then, since he'd stripped out the rubber band, which had been holding up his man bun at the fan expo, to be able to run his hands through the long silky strands while they were at the hospital.

I really hope he leaves it down in bed at night, so I can play with it during sex. If we manage to get to the point where we're having sex, that is.

Since they'd started kissing a little more often over the past couple of weeks, she also realized that she liked the feel of his soft, neatly trimmed beard brushing against her skin, and really wanted to feel it on more delicate places than her face. That was a new appreciation for her, since she hadn't ever been attracted to men with beards before.

Yeah, you're never gonna know what that beard feels like between your legs if you don't show your pussy and tell him what you want. Aiken's inner voice sounded an awful lot like her friend and coworker, Allissa, who'd explained to all the women backstage that since pussies could handle a lot harder impact than balls, her mom had taught her to replace the phrase "grow a pair of balls" with "show your pussy" and to call cowardly people "ball sacks" instead of "pussies." Since her inner voice had clearly taken Allissa's lessons to heart, Aiken figured that was why she heard it in her head in Allissa's voice.

Maybe if I show him my pussy Allissa's way now, then I'll be able to literally show him my pussy later when we're up in his room. Aiken couldn't help the smile that spread across her face at the possibility of following the advice in both the ways it could be meant.

"What's it gonna be, Princess? Your floor or mine?" Brent softly whispered the words as his hand not pressed against her back hovered near the elevator control panel, where he hadn't yet pushed a floor button to make the car move.

"Um, I'm not sure," Aiken admitted with a sigh, looking up into his forest green eyes. "It kinda depends on what we're gonna do in your room once we get there, and if this invitation is just for tonight, or if you're ready for us to start sharing a room all the time after this."

"Oh, um, okay," Brent stuttered out, obviously feeling as uncomfortable with this conversation as she did. When the elevator doors opened once more and an older couple joined them, he seemed to come to a conclusion, pushing the button for her floor. He then leaned down to whisper close to her ear, suggesting, "How about we go to your room to discuss this further?"

"Yes," Aiken agreed, nodding in case he couldn't hear her softly uttered word.

Neither of them said anything more until after the elevator stopped on her floor, they exited the car, and they entered her room, where they could speak in private. Assuming he still needed to respond to her earlier statement before she offered her opinion on their plans for the evening, Aiken placed her clutch purse on the dresser before sitting on the end of the bed to remove the heels she'd worn with the purple mini dress she'd put on that morning. When she got dressed for the fan expo, she'd opted to go with club wear since they were taping a segment that would be replayed on the pay-per-view the next day, planning to wear the same outfit out to celebrate Dean and Allissa's engagement after the fan expo.

Even if she left everything else in her room and only planned to go up to his room long enough to watch a movie, like they'd done on a couple of their most recent dates, she could easily take a few minutes to step into her ensuite bathroom and change into something more comfortable to wear the rest of the night. But she kind of wanted to wait until after they talked a little more before deciding what to change into for their evening together.

"So, I, uh, thought from your initial invitation that you meant for us to spend the evening hanging out like we did before, only not going to our separate rooms once the movie was over," Brent started, pacing around the room, instead of sitting down like she had for their talk. "And I figured my king-sized bed would give us enough room to stack the extra pillows between us, if you're not ready for more than just sleeping in the same space, so neither of us are alone to keep reliving everything that happened today and stressing out about it."

"And I'm totally fine with that, if that's what you want," Aiken interjected, looking over at her suitcase to try to quickly remember what was clean that she could change into right quick. "I just need a few minutes to change into something comfortable enough to sleep in that won't be too revealing for walking through the hotel up to your room."

"But you also mentioned the possibility of bringing all your stuff up to my room and sharing rooms from now on," Brent pointed out, finally stopping his pacing to look at her as he ran his hand through his hair.

I thought he only did that when he was stressed or worried, like when he was uncomfortable talking about his parents a couple of weeks ago, or when he was clearly worried about Dion earlier at the hospital. Is the thought of sharing a room with me stressing him out now? Or is he just nervous about actually discussing what we want to happen between us?

"If we did that, would it just be because you need someone with you to feel safe after what happened today? 'Cause I don't know how long I can handle sharing a bed with you and not touching you. I mean, I can definitely handle it for a night or two, if you need that comfort. But I know myself well enough to know that there's a very real possibility that I wouldn't be able to hold back much longer than that, especially when I'm asleep. And I don't want to take the chance that I might push past whatever boundaries you need set between us."

"Since I definitely need someone with me to feel safe after today, I can see where you might get the impression that I only want us to share a room for the safety factor. But if it was just to feel safer, I could hang out with anyone else who works for the GWA, not just you." Aiken wanted to stress the point that she wasn't just hanging out with him lately so he could protect her like the guys had stepped up to protect Allissa earlier. "While I do feel safe with you, I also know Rick has hired enough security to watch out for other threats that I could offer to supervise a slumber party for all the kids and still be perfectly safe, whether there's another adult in the room with us or not. In fact, if we don't end up having a show tomorrow because of the arena still being locked down as a crime scene, then I'll probably try to get Jax and all the ladies to have an extra spa day this month, so I won't have to spend the day alone in my room. Lord knows, we could all use a good deep tissue massage after the stress of today, Allissa especially."

"Why is Jax the only guy who gets to participate in these spa days?" Brent interrupted her, veering even further off on a tangent than she had in her rambling. "I thought it was a sexuality thing at first, but he's not the only gay or bisexual man in the GWA. So, why's he the only one you gals invite to your spa days?"

"If you ask Jax that question, he'll tell you it's because when it comes to enjoying the spa services, he's a bigger diva than the entire women's division combined," Aiken chuckled, remembering the history teacher's words from the first time he'd joined them for a spa day as she reiterated them to Brent. "But honestly, it has nothing to do with his sexuality at all. He's just the only guy who's expressed interest in being included when we schedule group activities like that or book clubs or whatever. Which is surprising considering how many of you guys must get your chests waxed. You know you're welcome to come whenever we have spa days and stuff, right?"

"Naw, I use a depilatory cream for that," Brent informed her, shaking his head. "It's a lot less painful than waxing and can be done in the shower, without having to schedule treatments with different service providers every time because of our schedule. Though I do know some of the guys have done the laser hair removal thing, especially if they had issues with back hair they couldn't reach themselves to use the cream. But I wouldn't mind being included when you're going for massages, especially if they offer couple's massages."

Aiken was momentarily sidetracked by picturing where all Brent used that cream and missed his sexy smirk when he mentioned couple's massages. Since he had the sleeves of his plaid shirt rolled up to expose his forearms, she could clearly see the smattering of light hair he didn't remove there. But thinking back to seeing him shirtless while he was wrestling, she knew he kept his torso mostly smooth, with only a thin happy trail on the lower portion of his abs. One that she often fantasized about following with her hands and tongue.

Thinking about following that happy trail down under his denim-look printed wrestling tights to see how he manscaped reminded her to go back to the original topic. "Yeah, we'll have to come back to your hair removal routine later," Aiken stated, her voice sounding a little more breathy than normal, even to her own ears. "But as I was saying, yes, safety is one of the reasons I want us to hang out tonight, but it's only a small part of it. There's also a small part of me that needs to be distracted from worrying about the potential for other stalkers targeting anyone else in the GWA. But again, that's just a small part of why…"

"So, what's the big reason why you want us to stay in the same room tonight?" Brent interrupted, his inscrutable expression almost appearing to turn slightly optimistic.

"Because I just want to spend more time with you," Aiken admitted with a hopeful smile as she looked up into his forest green eyes. "And I'm kinda hoping that some of this extra time together will lead to us taking the physical part of our relationship to the next level."

"What exactly do you mean by the *next level*?" Brent's lips turned up in what could only be described as a roguish grin, giving her even more hope that he was ready for them to start spending part of their time together naked. "Are we just talking about adding fully-clothed cuddling to our repertoire of affectionate activities? Or are you thinking maybe second base is our next level? And if that's the case, how long do we need to stay on second before rounding to third? Or hitting a home run?"

"Well, I'm not much of a baseball fan, so I'd rather not feel like I'm sitting through a long, boring game by waiting too long between bases." Aiken countered his roguish smile with a dreamy one of her own. "But I wouldn't be opposed to our cuddling leading to some clothing-optional activities at some point this evening, or in the very near future, if you still want to wait a little longer."

"You mean like skinny-dipping in your pool when we get to L.A. in a couple of weeks?" Brent teased, obviously remembering her mentioning the pool at her dads' house. "Or do you have something else in mind that we can do now without having to leave the comfort of the hotel?"

"Sure, skinny-dipping can be one of the clothing-optional activities we do together," Aiken agreed, until she thought about the possibility of her dads catching them in the act if they tried getting naked in her family pool anytime they were in Los Angeles. "But only if I'm sure there's nobody but you and me around at the time."

"You don't have to worry about that, Princess. I'm kind of a stingy guy, so I'd never want to share even a glimpse of what's mine with anyone else." Brent didn't give her a chance to finish listing her ideas for how they could spend time together without their clothing, as he finally stepped up close to her, running his finger down the side of her face before lifting her chin to tilt her head back, so she had to look up at him. She could clearly see his desire for her in the emerald depths of his eyes, and hoped her brown orbs reflected her passion back to him. "But if you're really ready for us to start spending clothing-optional time together tonight and wanna do all the things I wanna do with you without our clothes on, then I think we should definitely move all your stuff up to my room and plan on spending every night together."

He didn't set a timeframe for how long into the future they'd be sharing their accommodations, but she clearly understood his implied *"from now on"* in her mind. At least, she hoped the fact that he'd completely dropped all talk of checking into the requirements for an annulment when they traveled through their hometowns during the second week of November, since they'd started dating, meant he intended to try to make their marriage work long-term. But she wasn't brave enough to ask him if that was what he meant, too afraid that she'd find out he only wanted to have a fling with her until they could take time over the holidays to deal with all the legalities of dissolving their marriage.

"Okay, then I'll just grab all my stuff and change when we get up to your room," Aiken finally muttered, not wanting to start acting on their obvious mutual desire until they were in his room for the night.

"Okay." Brent took a step back, allowing her to stand and start gathering her things.

Since her toiletries were the only things she hadn't already returned to her suitcases after getting ready that morning, she quickly gathered them and stuffed them in her bags before stepping back into her shoes. Brent quietly watched her, as she moved about the room and made sure she had everything. Then he insisted on carrying all three of her heavier bags, leaving only her clutch and the oversized tote that she used in place of a larger purse and electronics bag for her to carry. She stuffed the clutch in the tote and looped the strap over her shoulder, as they left her room.

When they got up to his room, she was too nervous about the possibility of finally having sex with her husband to notice if there were any differences in their rooms, other than the size of the space to accommodate the larger bed. She wasn't sure why she was as jittery as she'd been on prom night her senior year, when she'd lost her virginity. It wasn't like that was her only previous sexual experience. In fact, she'd actually had several boyfriends since breaking up with her high school sweetheart, including one each of the four years she was at UCLA, earning her Bachelor of Arts in film, television, and digital media with a minor in theater, and two others while working as a professional actor before completing her professional wrestling training with the Blue Thunder Wrestling Academy for a film role, deciding to switch careers to be a professional wrestler, and joining the GWA.

While having a total of seven sexual partners in the last twelve years probably paled in comparison to the number Brent had in that same timeframe, she still considered herself fairly well experienced. *Surely it doesn't matter that all seven of them were in the first seven years I was sexually active, right? I mean, I've used vibrators in the last five years, so it's not like my vajayjay has closed up due to lack of actual male penetration. It's not like I'm revirginized because I haven't had a man-made O in over half a decade. So, I really shouldn't be this nervous all over again.*

After stacking her larger bags with his in the closet of the suite, Brent walked over and took the tote bag from her shoulder, placing it on a side table before reaching out to gently rub his big, strong hands over her shoulders and upper arms. "Relax, Princess. We don't have to jump straight into bed now that we're here. We can still change into more comfortable clothes and order room service while watching a movie. And just let nature take its course in how fast or slow we go at doing anything else."

Feeling reassured by his comforting words, Aiken looped her arms around Brent's waist, resting her cheek against his chest as she hugged him. "Thank you. I don't know why I got so nervous all of a sudden. Yeah, it's our first time together, but it's not like it's either one of our first times ever."

"Good to know," Brent chuckled as he wrapped her in his arms, surrounding her with his intoxicating scent, which reminded her of the smell of a freshly cut Christmas tree. "Since I haven't ever seen you hook up with anyone in all the time you've been with the GWA, I wasn't sure about that, so I was a little nervous about being your first, too."

"I suppose now's the time for us to discuss our sexual histories and stuff, huh?"

"Either now or after room service gets here," Brent replied as he rubbed her back. "Though I have a feeling we might lose our appetites if we start trying to count former partners or get too specific with details about our past experiences. So, maybe we should just stick to the basics of our S.T.I. statuses, contraceptive preferences, and how long it's been since the last time."

"I'm S.T.I. free and on the pill, but I've also always used a condom," Aiken stated, agreeing with the limits he'd set for them sharing their sexual histories, even though she was embarrassed to admit how long it had been since her last time.

"I'm S.T.I. free too, and I've also never failed the monthly tests we take in my entire career in the GWA." Brent informed her of the results of not only his S.T.I. tests, but also the drug tests they all did regularly with the GWA, before she could muster the courage to tell him how long it had been since she'd had more than solo sex. "And I also always use a condom."

She felt his chest expand against her face as he paused to take a deep breath before continuing. "And it's been about three-and-a-half months since my last hookup, which was the week of Rick and Fiona's wedding back in July while we were in Heart's Destiny."

Wow, not that long ago, she thought, even as she counted back to know they'd only been married a little over two months. *Although, that probably feels like a long time for him. But I guess at least I know he hasn't been unfaithful while we were married, even when we didn't know we were married for the first several weeks.*

"How long has it been for you?" Brent's question brought her out of her mental musings, making it obvious that she couldn't avoid telling him any longer.

"Um, yesterday with my B-O-B," she confessed, glad she wasn't making eye contact with him as she finally gave him her real answer. "But if you don't count solo B-O-B sessions, it's been about five-and-a-half years, with the last time being right before I broke up with my last boyfriend, when he got mad that I was trying out with the GWA."

"What's a B-O-B session?" Brent coughed, clearly confused by her answer.

"Battery-operated boyfriend," she explained, turning her face even farther into his chest to cover her blush, even though she was grateful he'd skipped over any questions about why it'd been so long since she'd been with a partner to focus on her masturbation habits. "You know. A vibrator."

"Oh, Aiken," Brent groaned, squeezing her tight, so she felt his cock hardening against her belly. "I'm gonna need to see that."

"You want to watch me use my vibrator?" She'd read a few scenes in romance novels where guys liked to watch stuff like that, but she assumed those were just the fantasies of the female writers, thinking real men wouldn't want to feel like their women were replacing them with a toy. "Why? Wouldn't you rather it was you, um, participating, instead of the toy?"

"Oh, I'll definitely be participating," Brent chuckled, releasing the embrace to tilt her chin up, forcing her to look at him while they talked. "But watching first will show me what you like, so I'll be able to repeat the process without the toy to show you that I'm much more satisfying than a hunk of battery-operated plastic."

"Oh, is that so?" Aiken grinned up at him, enjoying his playful cocky attitude.

"That's definitely so," Brent declared, before dipping his head to claim her lips in a carnal kiss.

As Brent's tongue delved between her lips, Aiken ran her hands up his muscular back, eager to get ahold of his long, flowing locks. She returned the kiss lick for lick as she weaved her fingers through the thick brown tresses, thinking his hair was the only soft part of him.

As the kiss spiraled out of control, Brent literally lifted her out of her shoes, carrying her over to the bed. She wrapped her legs around his waist, rubbing her core against the bulge in his jeans from her desperate need for friction on her clit. He tried to gently place her in the center of the large bed, but with her arms and legs around him, he barely had the control to keep his whole body weight from crashing down on top of her.

Aiken reveled in the feel of his much larger body pressing her into the mattress, especially when he rocked his hips to grind his cock against her mound. They both soon forgot about his request for her to demonstrate the use of her vibrator, getting totally lost in one another as they only pulled apart enough to start removing their clothing.

Aiken wasn't sure her dress survived the rapid removal, hearing a very distinct ripping sound as Brent shoved it up and off her body while kissing his way down. *Guess I shouldn't have bothered taking my time to unbutton his shirt,* she thought right before he distracted her with his mouth on her breasts, as he shrugged out of his plaid flannel shirt.

She'd always been slightly self-conscious about her boobs because they were smaller than all her friends' tatas. She'd even considered getting implants at one point, until she heard some of the women in the locker room, complaining about how uncomfortable they were in the ring while dealing with their larger hooters. Apparently, well-endowed women either had to suffer through the pain of having their tits bounce around while they wrestled, or endure the torture of squeezing their funbags into compression garments under their ring gear.

While she was grateful she didn't have to worry about either of those issues with her A-cups, she'd assumed the men in her past had avoided her chesticles during sex because their small size wasn't appealing to most men. Brent, however, quickly showed her that not all men felt that way, honing in on her sensitive nipples, lightly sucking one while gently pinching the other between his thumb and forefinger.

Instinctively, her body bowed up in pleasure from the exquisite way he teased her, even as she ran her fingers through his hair, trying to ground herself to him. With his free hand, Brent inched her panties down out of his way, so he could cup her mound. She wasn't a hundred percent sure how to interpret his moan when he realized she'd pierced one of her inner labial lips, but she thought the way he increased the intensity as he humped her leg might be a good sign that he appreciated her brief foray into body modification back when she was in college.

She moaned in response, bucking her hips to show him how eager she was for more. He didn't disappoint her, separating her folds to stroke one of his fingers through her slit while flipping the ring in her labia with another. As he inserted a single digit, she couldn't contain her delight. "Oh, yes, Brent. Need you inside me."

"Patience, Princess. I've gotta get a closer look at this little ring first," Brent informed her as he kissed his way down her body. "Maybe I was wrong in thinking of you as the human embodiment of a Disney princess, 'cause I highly doubt any of them have pierced pussies."

"Is that why you've been calling me Princess lately?" Aiken had been curious about his recent use of the term of endearment, but with so much else going on that day, she hadn't taken the time to ask him about it.

"Yeah, maybe." Brent tilted his head toward his shoulder as his lips turned up in an impish smile. "It just kinda came out without me really thinking about it."

Aiken hated to admit that she kind of liked hearing him call her Princess, even if he'd originally done it because he thought of her as being as sweet and innocent as some of her favorite childhood cartoon characters. She didn't get the chance to tell him that, though, because he redirected his gaze down at her piercing and started asking her more about it.

"Why'd you get the side pierced instead of the clit hood? I thought that's what most women get pierced."

"Mine's too small," Aiken sheepishly admitted what she'd only learned about her own body when she went for the piercing, as he pulled his finger from her slit, spread her open, and closely examined her pussy. The piercer had explained that her outer lips basically covered her small clit most of the time, so it didn't matter that she didn't have a clit hood. She actually had to spread her legs to move the lips over far enough to expose her clit, so she didn't have to worry about being overly stimulated by her clothing rubbing over it during normal daily activities. She did still try to avoid any wrestling moves that required her to do the splits, though, just to ensure her matches didn't accidentally turn into orgasmic experiences. "Can't pierce a clit hood if there's not one there."

"Ah, but you could have put this sexy ring a little higher so you'd have the same sensations. While this is gonna feel amazing for me, I don't see how it benefits you off on the side like this."

Not without being at risk of overstimulating my love nub and having mini-orgasms at very inappropriate times. It might be smaller than average, but it's still very sensitive. But I doubt he realizes just how easily a little friction there makes me come. Aiken decided not to explain all the drawbacks to having a constantly exposed clit right then, preferring to focus on enjoying the way he was touching her instead.

"Trust me, it still feels good with you playing with it like you are now," Aiken assured him, unsure if it was the way he played with her jewelry, or the feel of his hot breath on her exposed clit, that was already pushing her close to the edge. "In fact, if you keep doing that much longer, I'm gonna come without you having to do anything else."

"Oh, we can't have that yet," Brent taunted as he stopped playing with her piercing and spread her moisture over her other lips before teasing her opening with his finger once more. "I need to taste you first."

He pulled his finger back without actually inserting it again. Then he repositioned himself, so he could lower his head to swipe his tongue along the rim of her opening before circling her clit with the tip. She reveled in the feel of his soft beard brushing against her inner thighs, almost as much as she luxuriated in the pleasurable way he ate her.

Maybe I should have warned him about how fast playing with my clit makes me come. She barely thought the words before he sucked lightly on her needy nub and sent her soaring. "Oh, God, yes, Brent!"

He lapped up her release as her whole body convulsed in pleasure, licking through her folds before backing away just a bit and inserting a finger once more.

"Fuck, you're so tight, Aiken," Brent groaned against the skin of her inner thigh as he rested his head there to watch as he finger-fucked her. "Even if I'm able to open you up some with my fingers first, you're gonna choke my cock."

Aiken was too breathless from her first orgasm of the evening to reply, trying to catch her breath as she floated down from the high. Her lack of verbal response to his statement didn't stop Brent from asking her what she liked best as he used his mouth and fingers on her, though.

"Do you like it best when I lick your clit? Or suck it?" He demonstrated each as he continued working his finger in and out of her, eventually adding a second digit to start opening her up.

"Yes," she panted, unable to decide what felt best as he worked her up to a second climax. "Both."

"Do you prefer my mouth or my fingers?" Brent kept his mouth targeting her clit while continuing to finger-fuck her with one hand and using the other to play with her piercing once more.

"Oh, fuck, Brent!" Aiken couldn't stop the orgasm from crashing through her, loving the feel of her inner walls clamping down on his long, thick fingers, even though she wished he'd hurry up and replace them with his cock. It took every ounce of breath she had in her to gasp out her next words. "I love…it all. Everything…you do…to me. But I…really need…your dick…inside me. Please, aahh, don't make…me wait…any longer."

"You need my dick inside you, huh?" Brent smirked as he lifted his head, his beard glistening with her arousal. The loss of stimulation on her clit allowed her orgasm to recede and her to start catching her breath. "Fuck, Princess, I can't wait any longer either."

Brent pushed up off the bed, bending over once he was standing to strip her panties the rest of the way off her legs. He then unfastened his jeans, pulling his wallet from the hip pocket before shoving them to the floor. If he was wearing underwear under his pants, Aiken didn't notice, assuming he'd shoved them down with the jeans. Of course, she also didn't know what he'd done with his wallet once he pulled a condom out of it, focusing exclusively on watching him push the foreskin below the head of his cock before rolling on the protection.

Aiken was fascinated, having never seen an uncircumcised penis before. *Is that why his dick is bigger than the other guys I've been with? I mean, I assumed they were all average sized, but his looks a little longer, like maybe not having the foreskin cut off gave him an extra inch or two. If circumcision makes a guy's cock shorter, why would anyone ever have it done?*

Aiken quickly decided to research dick size differences later, as Brent crawled back onto the bed and positioned himself on his knees between her legs. He elevated her legs to rest her feet on his shoulders, lifting her hips from the mattress as he stroked the head of his cock through her folds to coat the tip of the condom with her juices.

"Please, Brent, don't tease me." Aiken wiggled her hips, trying desperately to get him to hurry up and plunge inside her.

"Never, Princess," he smirked as he slowly pushed his dick past her labial lips, dropping his glorious green gaze from hers to watch where he joined them as one.

"Oh, God, that feels so good," she moaned in pleasure as his cock stroked against her G-spot before bottoming out and hitting another sweet spot even deeper inside her, one she hadn't even found with her vibrator.

"Not God, Princess," he chuckled as he slowly pulled out before thrusting back in a little faster. "Brent Crockett, your husband. My name's the only one I wanna hear you crying out when you come, 'cause I'm the only man allowed inside your tight little pussy."

"Yes, Brent, yes," she agreed, trying to rock her hips to match the rhythm of his thrusts, as he reached out to play with her breasts with one hand while moving the other toward the top of her mound.

"Fuck, that ring's gonna be the death of me," he groaned, flicking her piercing with his thumb while stroking her clit with his first finger. "You're gonna hafta tell me the whole story of when and why you got it over dinner later."

Aiken was glad he hadn't asked her to tell him right then. She was too lost in the feelings of euphoria that he was inducing in her body at that moment to coherently say anything more than his name, so there was no way she could think clearly enough to convey the story of her very brief desire to do something wild and rebellious right before her college graduation.

In this position, she couldn't reach to touch him anywhere but his forearms, so she ran her hands over them, while he continued using his fingers on her most sensitive external erogenous zones and his cock on her internal ones. The short hair on his forearms was just as soft as the hair on his head, though she didn't really notice for long as he fucked her into a third orgasm. This one made the other two seem small in comparison, rocking every part of her being until she felt like she was floating outside her body.

"Brent!" Aiken tried to chant his name repeatedly, but she couldn't be sure if she actually vocalized it or just kept repeating it in her mind.

"Oh, fuck, yes, Aiken! Come on my cock!" She was so overwhelmed in her state of nirvana that Brent's words sounded muffled in her ears, even though he appeared to be shouting as he pounded into her one last time and held still as he joined her in orgasmic bliss. "Yeah, that's it, Aiken. Keep squeezing my dick until you milk all my cum out."

Aiken was too out of breath to tell him that she couldn't control the spasms of her inner walls. And honestly, too lost in her own release to comprehend that it was her orgasm triggering his right then. Her climax was so intense that she practically passed out, not even realizing when Brent lowered her legs and collapsed on the bed beside her.

She had no clue how long they laid there recovering, only becoming fully conscious once more when she heard her phone ringing with a very distinct special ringtone. "Shit! That's Papa calling. And I forgot to text Daddio to warn him before they heard about today on the news."

She shoved Brent's arm off her torso before jumping from the bed and running to dig through her bag for her phone.

"Relax, Princess. I'm sure they'll understand that we've been busy, especially when you tell them now that you're perfectly fine." Brent rolled to sit up in the bed before standing and removing the condom to dispose of it.

When she finally got her phone out of the clutch she'd forgotten she'd put it in that morning, she barely stopped herself from swiping to answer the FaceTime call while standing there completely naked. "Shit! Shit! Shit! Why is he calling on FaceTime? We need clothes on before I can answer this!"

Aiken spun around, looking for her dress, knowing she didn't have time to dig through her luggage to find anything else. When it wasn't in her immediate line of sight, she started to panic even more.

Brent came back out of the bathroom and immediately stepped into his jeans. Obviously realizing what she was looking for as he quickly pulled them up and fastened them, he stepped over to the opposite side of the bed from where she was standing, bent over, and picked up the piece of material that used to be her dress. "Yeah, I don't think this is gonna work."

"Ya think?" Aiken scoffed at how he'd stated the obvious while fingering the split down the side of the garment. Just as she was about to ask him to pull her bags back out of the closet so she could find something else to wear, her phone stopped ringing. "Oh, great! Papa's gonna be a basket case by the time I find something else to wear and call him back."

When her phone rang again before she finished her sentence, Brent bent over, picked up his shirt, and tossed it at her. "Put this on for now. It'll be faster, so you can go ahead and answer before he hangs up again."

She quickly dropped her phone on the bed and shoved her arms in the sleeves, glad he hadn't taken the time to unroll them when he removed it earlier, so she didn't have to fight with them being way too long for her arms. She quickly buttoned the second button from the collar and several buttons down. But she didn't take time to button it all the way down before she picked up her phone and swiped to answer the second FaceTime call.

"Aikey Baby!" Shawn squealed before she could say a single word in greeting. "Oh, thank God! She finally answered, Theo!" Papa dramatically turned to Daddio, waving the phone around and making Aiken dizzy from trying to follow the rapid movement, until he finally turned to speak directly to her and centered both her dads in the frame on her screen. "Please tell me you and your hunky hubby weren't shot today!"

"No, we weren't shot," Aiken assured him. "Neither one of us were anywhere near the shooter. But we did spend all afternoon at the hospital, waiting to hear that our friend Dion will make a full recovery from his injuries."

"Show me! I need you to move your phone, so I can see all of you to know for myself that you're still in one piece."

"Yeah, you don't really want her to do that right now, Mr. Pearson," Brent informed her papa, stepping up behind her, so her dads could both see that he was still shirtless.

"Oh my God! Put a shirt on, Brent!"

"You're wearing it, Princess," Brent chuckled, brushing his lips over her temple. "And I'm sure your dads would rather you not take it off while we're FaceTiming them."

"Listen to your hunky hubby, Aikey Baby," Papa instructed her, leaning to the side as if he was trying to look around Aiken to see Brent shirtless. "We'd much rather you keep his shirt on for now."

Yeah, this is so not how I thought having Brent here when they called would ease Papa's fear for my safety.

"But now that we know you're both uninjured, maybe we should switch to a regular phone call," Daddio suggested, looking a lot more uncomfortable than he had when she first answered the phone, "so the two of you can finish getting dressed."

"I agree with Daddio. Give me five minutes to get changed and I'll call you back." Aiken hated feeling like she was hanging up on her dads, but when Brent started speaking, she had no choice.

"Yeah, if you take off that shirt, it's gonna be a lot more than five minutes before either one of us gets dressed again."

Before she could argue with him, her phone beeped to indicate she had a text. When she looked down at her phone she had to laugh at what it said.

Papa: Have fun with your hunky hubby, Aikey Baby. Call us when you come up for air in a few hours, because we all know it'll take a lot longer than 5 minutes. ;)

Chapter Seven

Josh was still reeling from the events of the day before as he and Teagan made their way hand in hand into the arena the next morning to prepare for the GWA's *Halloween Horror* show. He still couldn't believe how close they'd come to a tragic ending to the ordeal with Allissa's stalker. Even knowing that Dion was going to make a full recovery didn't quell his worry about what could happen if another stalker targeted someone else on the roster. Due to his not-so-unfounded fear, he hadn't been able to handle being more than a few feet away from Teagan since it happened, needing to know he was close enough to protect her should someone come after his wife.

Once they got back to the hotel the evening before, they'd holed up in their room, clinging to one another, much like he assumed the rest of their married coworkers did, reassuring themselves that the people they loved were still alive and well. They hadn't really talked much about the events of the day, other than him sharing with her about what he and Crockett had said to Liam to get him to talk to them at the hospital. Teagan had been glad to hear how he'd encouraged Liam to lean on Rylie, as they both hoped their friends would eventually admit to having feelings for one another and embrace the blessing their marriage could be for both of them. After that, Josh and Teagan had mostly focused on using their bodies to reconnect with one another, showing each other how they felt, even though neither one of them seemed to feel ready to say those three little words yet.

Well, Josh felt more than ready to say them, but he didn't think Teagan was quite ready to hear them, so he was still holding them back. He'd done his best to up the romance factor in their relationship by pampering her with lots of bubble baths and massages in their hotel rooms over the last couple of weeks. He'd even upped the ante by surprising her with extra spa services and specialty products he could order whenever they checked-in at hotels with in-house spas or gift shops, trying to show her all the affection he felt for her.

He wished he could order her gifts to be sent to the hotels or arenas in advance, but with the GWA head of security intercepting any packages that were sent to them because of Allissa's stalker, that hadn't been an option. *But maybe I should ask Cage if that's a possibility now, since the stalker is no longer an issue. That way I can start ordering her some sexy lingerie, or some of the sex toys she mentioned one of the women in Heart's Destiny selling online, so we can play with them together.*

No, I probably need to wait a little while before ordering stuff like that, so I can make sure she's in love with me first.

Even though she'd reciprocated the heartfelt gestures he'd started showering her with a couple of times already, specifically insisting on him joining her for couples massages, and they continuously connected physically multiple times a day, he could still see in the depths of her umber brown eyes that she was still a little wary of how real their feelings were for one another. *She's getting there, though, so hopefully it won't be too long before I'll be able to tell her I love her and give her the ring I'm picking up in a couple of weeks.*

In addition to not wanting to scare Teagan off by declaring the love he felt for her so soon into the more romantic phase of their relationship, Josh knew he'd also kept quiet the night before, about his fear that his former personal assistant's antics could easily turn into a stalker situation, in an attempt to protect Teagan from developing the same fear. When he realized that his wife could be the next target if his plans for parental intervention weren't enough to squash Sarah's delusional thoughts about him, he couldn't stop himself from envisioning the horrible things she might try to hurt him, specifically by harming Teagan.

Even after Teagan had fallen asleep in his arms, Josh had laid in bed worrying about the possibility of Sarah turning into a stalker, like the guy who'd fixated on Allissa for the last year. While he didn't think she had the means to travel the way that guy had, Josh also knew she didn't have to follow their tour all over the country to inflict fear or try to get to them. Sarah could all too easily still show up with a gun at his house or the arena while the GWA was in San Diego in just a couple of weeks.

Then again, he'd paid her a very generous salary while she was his personal assistant, along with covering her living expenses while she took care of his house. So, if she'd invested some of her money in the same things she'd helped him invest in over the last few years and hadn't blown it all on frivolous things to maintain the appearance of a lavish lifestyle, then she might have the means to travel the country following him and the rest of the GWA. Those thoughts made him question whether or not he should ask Rick about keeping an Avington Security team with them, just in case Sarah tried to take out the woman he loved.

Maybe Teagan was right about me needing to press charges for what she did to the house? But would that really do anything more than piss Sarah off even worse and cause her to escalate as soon as she's outta jail? If she even spent any time behind bars and didn't just get a slap on the wrist with a fine, or maybe some community service hours?

After their semi-public disagreement about how to deal with Sarah a couple weeks before, Josh and Teagan had discussed the Sarah situation in more detail that night in their room. Unfortunately, other than verifying what he hadn't blatantly admitted earlier about Sarah having an unrequited crush on him, not much had come from that conversation. They'd ended up agreeing to disagree on how to handle Sarah, and basically avoided any mention of her ever since.

No, letting Mom and Dad deal with Sarah's parents to keep her in line is definitely still the best way to go. But I'll give Dad a call later and ask his opinion before I make a decision about whether or not to discuss extra security with Rick and his Avington contact. He might focus more on the tech side of things at Parker Security Systems, instead of providing bodyguards like Avington, but his background and personal relationship with the Nashes will still give him better insight into whether or not I need to have bodyguards with us while we're in town.

As they arrived in catering, where Rick had texted them to all congregate for this earlier than normal pre-show meeting, since they couldn't meet at ringside while the road crew finished taking down the booths from the expo the day before and reset the arena floor to fan seating for the show that evening, Josh pushed all those thoughts out of his mind. Eager to find out how they were going to have to change things up for the show, and especially to get an update on when they could expect Dion to be cleared to wrestle again, Josh dropped his and Teagan's gear bags at the end of one of the tables and pulled out a chair for her to sit before taking his seat right beside her.

To be honest, Josh was a little surprised at how quickly the local authorities had worked to gather all the evidence they needed, so the GWA's **Halloween Horror** show could still happen on time. He'd thought for sure they'd have to cancel the show and have one of the other road crews meet them in Jackson, Mississippi the next day because the ring, all their production equipment, costuming trunks, and even the tables and chairs they carted around for catering and the classroom area backstage would still be locked up with the whole arena being considered a crime scene.

As he started the meeting, Rick explained that they would be meeting a new ground crew in Jackson the next day, but only because the ground crew that was with them in New Orleans had to be up during the day to reset the arena floor, and wouldn't get the sleep they needed to be able to break down the equipment and drive to Jackson overnight like they normally would. He also explained that the women's locker room was still off limits because the crime scene cleanup crew contracted with the city wasn't able to do their thing in such a short timeframe.

"While we have cordoned off the entire lower level around the arena floor to be able to use it all as backstage area for this show, the restrooms normally utilized by the fans with floor seats don't have showers," Rick informed them. "So, while you're welcome to spread out and use them to change, anyone who needs to shower before or after your match will need to do so in the men's locker room."

"So, are we gonna rearrange the card to be able to schedule a designated time when all the guys have to vacate the locker room for the ladies to be able to shower in private?" Vaughn Valor asked, putting his arm around his wife.

"No, that won't work," Rick explained, shaking his head. "We'd have to divide the card between men's matches and women's matches to do that. And that would not only disrupt the flow of the show, it wouldn't work with your mixed-tag match, or for either of the tag teams with female managers."

"We can't just share the locker room, though," Dean protested. "'Cause I'm sure I'm not the only one who doesn't want anyone else to see his girl naked."

Several of the married guys grunted their agreement with Dean, including Josh, causing a few chuckles from his lovely wife and a few of the other women.

"No, you're right, that wouldn't work either," Rick acknowledged Dean's opinion. "But what we will do is schedule the matches so that couples who aren't working matches with their significant others are working back-to-back matches. Then we'll schedule fifteen-minute time slots for private showers for everyone. Couples are more than welcome to shower together if they wish, but you'll still have to keep to the fifteen-minute time limit, so we can get everyone through after their matches. That means none of you will be able to change in the men's locker room, or leave your stuff in the lockers to risk needing to go in there when it's someone else's turn in the showers. But with all the additional restrooms, we should still have plenty of facilities to meet everyone's needs."

There were a few more questions about the possibility of the single guys signing up for the same time slot since there were multiple shower stalls in the locker room, but Josh tuned all that out as he thought about what he'd like to do with Teagan while sharing a shower. *Fuck, I wonder if we can sneak past Rick to sign up for back-to-back time slots, so we can have thirty minutes to fool around?*

"Alright, now that we've got the shower situation all settled, let's go over the changes to the card," Rick continued after shutting down the rest of their grumbling about the showers. "Obviously, we can't have the tag-team title match between Red Velvet and Protection Detail. But I think we should go ahead with the reveal that Red and Chastity got married in Vegas, only instead of playing it up as a surprise to her like we'd planned for the end of the match tonight, I think we should do a couple of vignettes to show that she knew about it, and now feels torn between being loyal to Protection Detail and wanting to be there for her husband while he's dealing with everything that happened yesterday."

"I can definitely do that," Chastity agreed.

"Red, I'll leave it up to you if you think you're ready to talk about yesterday on camera or not." Rick directed his words to Liam, who looked even more shook up than he did the day before in the hospital waiting room, when Josh and Crockett had to bring him out of his shell after Rylie reported that he'd clammed up from the trauma. "We can do the vignettes without you having to do more than sit there if you need a couple days."

Liam nodded, obviously wanting to go with that option.

Fuck! If he goes back to that silent act he started to pull in the hospital yesterday, then maybe I should get Crockett to help me talk him out of it again.

"Actually, not having you speak about it yet might give us enough time to get an update on when Dion might be able to return before we commit to a plan leading into **Christmas Chaos**. But I do think you need to be on the stage with everyone else at the beginning of the show, when I plan on issuing a statement from the company, dedicating the show to Dion, and informing the fans that he's going to be out on medical leave. Allissa, do you want to say anything then?"

When Josh turned to look over at Allissa to see how she responded to Rick's plans, he noticed that she seemed to be as zoned out as Liam. *Fuck! I can't imagine she feels ready to perform on the show tonight, either.*

Apparently, he wasn't the only one who noticed she hadn't heard a word Rick had just said, since Dean leaned over and gently nudged her to get her attention.

"Sorry, Boss," Allissa apologized sheepishly. "I was still stuck on having to go in the men's locker room to shower after my match and missed what you just said."

"I was just saying that we want to issue a statement at the beginning of the show, dedicating it to Dion and informing the fans that he's going to be out on medical leave for a while. Do you want to be the one to address the crowd? Or do you want me to do it?"

"I'd rather you do it, please," Allissa stated, surprising Josh with the strength of her voice. "I'm not sure I can talk about, um, everything so publicly yet. Not and be able to compartmentalize everything to be able to wrestle afterward."

Leah Mae Wright

Damn, I guess she's tougher than she looks. Hell, I don't know if I'd be able to perform today if it'd been me and Teagan in her and Dean's shoes yesterday.

"I understand," Rick reassured her with a sympathetic smile. "I want to give him a twenty-one bell salute to kick off the show and will mention that he was injured while rescuing a fellow wrestler from a stalker, but I won't mention your name, so hopefully the press coverage will drop off and they'll leave you alone."

Allissa nodded in agreement as Rick continued laying out his plans for the show.

"I also think we should drop kayfabe for the salute and have the whole roster on stage to dedicate the show to Dion. He won't be able to see it while he's still in the hospital, but I'll make sure Darius gets a digital copy of the card to show him whenever the doctor allows him screen time again. So he'll know we're all thinking of him and wishing him a speedy recovery."

Rick continued their meeting by running down the new card for the event that night and gave them a new schedule for their promo tapings, since they had to be skipped the day before due to the lockdown of the arena. Since this was his blow off match for his feud with Madman Matt, the only thing that really changed for Josh was that his match was now earlier on the card, so he could perform right after Teagan worked her last mixed-tag match with Blade against Shauna and Vaughn Valor.

Finally, Rick gave them the latest update on Dion's condition, which was that he would be in the hospital for a few more days while they kept testing to make sure he didn't have any residual bleeding on the brain and was just suffering from a concussion and amnesia. *Fuck! I hope following the concussion protocol will help him get his memories back and be cleared to get back in the ring as soon as his stitches are removed.*

Unfortunately, because they were still keeping him in ICU in an attempt to try to prevent any additional ring rats or paparazzi from being able to enter his room, like had apparently happened in the emergency room the day before, none of them would be able to see him before having to fly out of town the next morning to stick to their schedule. Josh was just glad that D and his brother had made up, so they could all call Darius to continue getting updates, knowing Dare would share their well-wishes with Dion, even if they couldn't directly talk to him.

Finally, Rick ended their meeting by announcing that the catering crew was working overtime to feed them both lunch and dinner at the arena that day, so they were all directed to go fill a plate before sitting back down to start choreographing their matches for that night.

"Don't worry, Darlin'," Dean squeezed Allissa to his side as they lined up to fix their plates. "Dion knows how grateful we are for what he did yesterday. And I guarantee, he wants nothing more than for us to go on with the show and keep the ring warm for when he returns."

"Absolutely," Josh and Teagan agreed in unison, smiling at one another before taking a moment to reassure Allissa, as they lined up behind her and Dean.

Once they made their plates, he and Teagan sat with Crockett and Amethyst and all their opponents for the night to start talking through their match plans, leaving the table where Dean and Allissa sat open for their family members who'd just arrived. They were all still in town after coming in to witness Dean propose to Allissa the day before, and Josh thought they were definitely the most qualified to help Allissa overcome the trauma, so she could get through her performance that night.

"How much you wanna bet they're going to push for that Thanksgiving wedding to take Vic's mind off of everything?" Teagan chuckled, referring to Allissa by the shortened version of her ring name, Victoria Vicious, and pointing with her fork at the table filled with Dean and Allissa's family members.

"I'm not dumb enough to bet against that," Josh chortled, shaking his head. "And considering it's at least half Windy and Kandi's fault that we don't remember our weddings, and Mandi was in cahoots with the rest of the Matchmaking Mommas in Heart's Destiny, trying to pair all of us up with locals whenever we've been there for a wedding, I'd say they're also plotting to figure out who else they can fix up that week."

"Oh, you think we can convince them to help us with Red and Chastity? Or do you think Randi and Kay included them when they said they'd talk to the Burleson matchmakers?" Teagan's eyes widened as she looked back and forth between the table where Dean and Allissa sat with their family and the table where Red and Chastity sat with the other two members of Protection Detail and Rick, obviously going over what he wanted in those vignettes he mentioned earlier while they ate.

"Definitely," Amethyst agreed. "And if they haven't already been clued in on the plans, then we'll just have to sneak in a few minutes alone with one of them to clue them in on how we think Chastity and Red really feel about each other."

Josh left the plotting and matchmaking up to the women, knowing he'd go along with whatever Teagan asked him to do later to help with her plans. But for the time being, he had a match to choreograph with Matt, so that's what he focused on while they ate. It wasn't but a few minutes later that his planning session with Matt was interrupted by both of Dean's grandmothers appearing at their table.

"Josh and Crockett, we need you both to stand up, so we can measure ya'll for your groomsmen's tuxedos." Meemaw Hunter pointed to each of them while unrolling a measuring tape.

"Isn't it customary for the groom to ask his friends to be groomsmen in his wedding before any measurements are taken?" Josh asked, deciding he didn't want to know where the flirtatious octogenarian had hidden that measuring tape since she wasn't carrying a purse.

"Nope," she replied, tugging on his sleeve until he pushed his chair out and stood for her to start taking his measurements. "In our family, the bride decides who's going to be in the bridal party and the rest of the women in the family make it happen. Neither the groom or any of his groomsmen get a say in the matter."

"Nor do any of the bridesmaids," Mandi added, taking over his seat beside Teagan before asking if she already knew her measurements.

Windy and Kandi surrounded Crockett and Amethyst, who clearly took advantage of having their attention to recruit them in helping with mending the rift between Red and Chastity. "Oh, yes, we'll gladly be in the wedding," Amethyst gushed. "But you need to make sure Liam and Rylie are also paired up in the bridal party 'cause they need all the help they can get to keep from ending up in divorce court."

"Oh, don't worry, we've already got lots of plans for the two of them," Mandi chuckled while noting the measurements Teagan gave her in her phone. "Starting with making sure they're too busy on ya'll's Thanksgiving break to even have time to call an attorney."

"We just knew to start with ya'll," Meemaw Hunter added as she got precariously close to feeling his family jewels while measuring his inseam, "so they'd know our plans are set in stone, and they won't be able to refuse when we go get their measurements in a few minutes."

Good luck with that, Josh thought as Meemaw Hunter finished measuring him while Dean's other grandma wrote the numbers down. *While they seemed to be working things out to lean on one another yesterday, Liam doesn't look quite so willing to act on his feelings for Rylie today. So, it wouldn't surprise me if he goes right back to being an asshole and avoiding her whenever he isn't required to work with her for their new angle.*

After the women finished getting measurements from the four members of the bridal party at their table, they regrouped to go get Liam and Rylie's measurements, leaving Josh to go back to planning his match with Matt.

Just as they thought they had a plan in place for the basic framework of their match, Teagan leaned over and got Josh's attention.

"Josh, will you and the guys please go try to talk some sense into Red?" Teagan pointed across the room, where Josh saw Liam stomping away. Out of the corner of his eye, he caught a glimpse of Rylie getting up and running off in the opposite direction, looking like she was about to start crying.

"Yeah, guess we need to be a little more aggressive with him than we were yesterday," Josh agreed, turning to nonverbally recruit the other guys at the table to go with him.

"While you're doing that, I'm going to go check on Chastity." Teagan leaned over and pecked a kiss on Josh's cheek before standing and turning to the other women at the table. "Ladies, let's go see what we can do to cheer up Chas."

Hopefully, he'll fucking listen better this time than he apparently did yesterday.

~ ~ ~

Liam felt like a total piece of shit for the way he'd snuck out of Rylie's room in the wee hours of the morning, right after going to dispose of the condom and coming back to bed to realize she was sound asleep. But he knew if he'd have crawled back in bed with her, he'd have been too tempted to make love to her again, so he felt like he had no other choice. Succumbing to his desire for her once was bad enough, making him feel guilty as fuck for not being sufficiently strong-willed to stick to his plan to release her from their mistake of a marriage. If he'd felt the sweet clench of her pussy on his cock again, there'd be no way he'd ever be able to let her go. And if he'd still been in her bed when he awoke a couple hours later after the nightmare of seeing her shot and killed along with the stalker, he most definitely would have made love to her again just to reassure himself that she was alive and well.

But even though he hated himself for leaving her without a word, that loathing was nothing compared to how he despised the way they'd both acted like nothing happened between them the day before, as they barely interacted while discussing their roles in the **Halloween Horror** show. He'd thought for sure that as soon as they saw each other at the arena, she'd try to corner him to ask why he'd left so abruptly. But she didn't say a word to him, as they'd all gathered for their morning meeting. She also hadn't tried to single him out to talk when they all lined up to get lunch before sitting down to plan for the show while eating.

Feck, the way she keeps directing all her comments on the vignettes we're planning to tape this afternoon to Rick, it's almost like she doesn't remember us fucking in the middle of the night, Liam realized, just as Dean's grandmothers finished taking his and Rylie's measurements for their wedding attire. *Holy feck! What if she really doesn't remember it 'cause she wasn't really awake when it happened? I mean, if people can sleepwalk, I'm sure they can sleeptalk. So, she might not even know we made love. Or maybe she thinks it was just a dream, if she has any recollection at all.*

Liam was so lost in his self-recriminations for taking advantage of Rylie during a vulnerable time for both of them the night before that he almost missed Rick offering them some advice for dealing with the Heart's Destiny matchmakers while they were in town for Dean and Allissa's wedding.

"If I'm right in thinking that pairing you up in the bridal party is just the first of their ploys, then you guys should probably spend the next month practicing acting like you're happily married before we go to Heart's Destiny," Rick chuckled, shaking his head. "That way you can keep the Matchmaking Mommas off your backs during our Thanksgiving break."

"Absolutely," Liam agreed, knowing from his previous trips to the small Texas town just how conniving those ladies could be when they decided to set up a couple. At least, if his constant pairings with Jen Burleson for the last year were anything to go by. "Guess it's a good thing we're switching up our angle today to start trying to sell us as a couple, so it won't be too hard to fake being in love at all the wedding events that week."

"Since we're switching all this up to admit that they both know they're married, should Chas still ride with us?" Trojan asked, looking back and forth between Rick, Liam, and Rylie. "I know we're just making it seem like she's torn between us right now, until D's able to come back and we can do the winner-takes-all match. But if they're supposed to be acting like a happy couple, then shouldn't they start riding together?"

Liam wasn't sure if the stricken look on Rylie's face was from his statement or Trojan's, but it was very clear she wasn't happy with the turn of their discussion. *Feck! Or maybe she could be remembering bits and pieces of last night to realize what an arse I am to take advantage of her like that.*

Regardless of why she looked upset, Liam couldn't stay sitting there feeling like it was all his fault a moment longer. "Naw, she doesn't need to ride with me, yet. Except maybe to and from Heart's Destiny to sell the happily-married gimmick while we're there. But we can play it up on TV and in the ring that you guys are trying to keep us apart by insisting that Protection Detail continues riding together. At least, until D comes back and Red Velvet wins her managerial services between pay-per-views. Then she might have to ride with us for a couple of months before you guys win her back." With that, he stood and walked away, needing to step out for some fresh air to clear his head, so he could think back on the night before more rationally.

It didn't take him long to get to the exit that led to the performers' parking lot, but once he got there, the Avington Security guard on the door stopped him from going outside. "We've got arena security out there dealing with some paparazzi right now, so you're going to have to wait if you need something from your car."

"Thanks." Liam lifted his chin at the guy he only knew worked for Avington because of the logo on his shirt, before turning and walking through their expanded backstage area. *I guess pacing inside will have to do for now.*

Since the security guard wasn't one of the team that he'd gotten to know by name over the last few months, he didn't feel the need to let the guy know he was only going for some fresh air and didn't absolutely have to go outside right then. Of course, Liam had only learned the names of Byron Avington and his four sons, the half dozen guys that had been assigned to watch over Allissa and her mom, and Maddox, the guy who'd given him and Rylie a ride to the hotel the day before. So, with there being at least thirty or forty Avington bodyguards working the pay-per-view weekend and him not even knowing half their names, it was highly unlikely that he'd randomly come across one of the twelve guys he'd consider enough of an acquaintance that he'd explain himself to them. Which was fine with him, since he really wanted to be alone to reexamine his actions in the middle of the night.

Was she awake or not? And feck, if she wasn't awake, did I technically rape her, since she might not have been coherent enough to know what she was consenting to?

Liam thought back to the night before, trying desperately to remember if she'd actually woken up when she tried to roll away from him, or had just responded to him, when he spoke to her after she'd tried to change positions, while still sound asleep.

"Don't go, Rylie," Liam moaned as she started to pull away from him, sliding his hand from her mid-back down to the hem of her shirt before caressing up her side until he reached the soft globe of her unencumbered breast. He lightly squeezed her firm ass with one hand, where he'd slid his hand down the back of her shorts, and cupped the underside of her tit with the other, gently pinching her nipple between his thumb and forefinger, reveling in the feel of how her body responded to his touch. "I need you. I know I don't deserve you and am nowhere near good enough for you, but I need you. Please say I can have you, if only for tonight."

"Oh, Liam, yes." Rylie ran her hand up from his chest to cup his jaw as she tilted her head up to lock their eyes on one another. In the low ambient light of the room, he couldn't differentiate between the onyx of her pupils and the rich topaz of her irises, but he still felt like they were connected through their gazes. "I need you too. So bad."

"She was definitely awake then," Liam told himself as he passed through the doorway between their typical backstage area and the lower-level concourse that they'd taken over to have access to more restrooms for changing areas. "It might have been mostly dark in the room, but there was enough moonlight coming in around the curtains over the window for me to see her eyes…" He let his voice trail off as he heard several of his coworkers walking in his direction, not wanting them to overhear him talking to himself. *Which were clearly wide open and appeared to be filled with emotion when she told me she needed me too, even if her pupils were so dilated that only a thin sliver of topaz surrounded them. So, it was definitely consensual, regardless of whether she fell asleep as she was coming down from her orgasm, or right after, while I was in the bathroom dealing with the condom, and she doesn't remember all of it.*

"Red, dude, what the hell just happened to cause you and Chastity to both get so pissed that you stormed off in opposite directions just now?" Josh was the first to speak, just like at the hospital the day before, even though he brought more backup than just Crockett this time.

Liam knew both Josh and Crockett wanted to try to talk him into following in their footsteps with trying to make their Vegas marriages work. But he had no idea why Madman Matt, Vaughn Valor, Blade, and Cruz had followed them to come after him. Yeah, Matt and Vaughn were both happily married and would probably try to offer him some sage advice about how to be a good husband. But Blade and Cruz were both single, and still partook of the wide variety of ring rats to a much greater extent than Liam ever had, so he didn't think they'd come along for anything more than to overhear the juicy gossip.

Feck! I'm definitely not gonna let any of these guys know how I couldn't resist Rylie last night. Cruz might not know me well enough yet to rib me about it, but Blade sure as feck will.

"I don't know what Chastity's problem is," Liam lied, knowing she'd probably been pissed at him for acting like an asshole and unilaterally making the decisions for how they'd portray their marriage to both the fans and their friends in Heart's Destiny. Part of him hated being the reason she was upset, wanting nothing more than to be her hero and fix everything for her. But his more rational side knew that it was better to keep pissing her off, so she wouldn't fight him over the annulment. "I just needed to get some air, after all this planning for how we're gonna sell our angle 'til D comes back made me think a little too much about how close we came to losing him yesterday."

"You sure that's the only reason you stormed off looking pissed?" Crockett arched an eyebrow at him, obviously not buying his lie. "'Cause that doesn't explain why Chas looked like she was about to start crying."

Feck! Liam mentally groaned as he schooled his features to keep the guys from seeing how he was feeling, hating that he was most likely the cause of Rylie's tears, even though he had no idea exactly what he'd done or said to upset her. "I have no idea what's up with Chastity. But I'm sure I just needed some fresh air and a little space to call Dare and check on D."

"Then why are you pacing back here instead of going outside to actually get some air?" Matt chimed in, motioning to the concourse area of the ground floor, which was usually not part of their backstage area, where they were currently standing.

"Because security wouldn't let me go outside." Liam pointed with his thumb over his shoulder at the nearest door, where a different security guard from the one he'd spoken to was standing, since he'd walked farther than he'd realized while thinking about the night before. "Apparently, there's a hoard of papzz out there, so they're trying to get rid of them."

"And where's your phone?" Vaughn pointed to Liam's empty hands. "If you're gonna call Dare to check on D, you kinda need your phone."

"I just hadn't pulled it out yet," Liam lied once more, pulling his phone from his pocket. "I needed to chill for a minute before I make the call, so I don't sound irritable or pissed off, just in case Dare's in D's room."

"Ah, so there *was* something said that pissed you off," Josh smirked. "You might as well tell us now, 'cause if you don't, we'll just go ask Magnum and Trojan to fill us in."

"Nothing was said that pissed me off," Liam argued, shaking his head at his coworkers.

"Really? 'Cause I thought you looked like you might be a little pissed at being roped into walking your wife down the aisle at Dean and Allissa's wedding," Blade teased, holding his hand up with his thumb and forefinger about half an inch apart before waving his hand back and forth between Josh and Crockett. "And to be honest, I don't get why you're not doing like these two and taking advantage of your Vegas marriage to get laid."

"Don't be a dick, Blade," Crockett growled, obviously not liking the other man's implications, but he was standing too far away from him to punch him like he clearly wanted to do right then.

"We actually care about our wives, you ass," Josh added, forming a united front with Crockett. "And want to build strong relationships with them based on more than just sex."

"Yo, Blade, why don't we leave the married guys alone to discuss their relationships, so you don't say anything else to get your ass kicked," Cruz interjected, pushing Blade back the way they'd came. "I really don't wanna take a chance on Emerald hearing any of this, and thinking I agreed with your dumb ass, 'cause she's scary as fuck when she gets pissed."

"Yeah, she is," Josh grinned, lifting his chin proudly at Blade. "And with all the true crime shows she loves watching, I'm sure she knows at least ten different ways to dispose of your body where you'll never be found. So, you might wanna watch what you say from now on."

"Whatever," Blade chuckled as he shook his head and walked away with Cruz.

"Now that they're gone, why don't you tell us why you seem to have a problem with Chastity?" Vaughn redirected the conversation back to Liam. "I thought you were pretty good friends with her until you found out you'd married her, and yesterday it seemed like she was really there for you when you needed her to lean on, so I don't understand why you're at each other's throats half the time now."

"I don't have a problem with her," Liam admitted with a sigh. "She's a good kid, and a great wrestler with a long career ahead of her. But she's way too young for me. I'm at the point in my career where I'm looking at retiring in the next few years to settle down and have a family. I can't do that with someone who's just starting their career, especially when that career is gonna keep her on tour for at least the next decade. Hell, even if she just took a break from wrestling to have a couple of kids like your wife did, I couldn't ask her to stay home with me and the kids 'cause she'd be miserable without being able to fulfill her wrestling dreams."

Realizing how true his statement was about wanting to settle down with a family when he retired, Liam felt a little bad for only replying to his family's calls that morning, when they'd all checked on him after hearing about the shooting on the news, with terse texts to let them know he was fine. While he also let them know about Dion's injuries, he hadn't known how to explain the wedding angle that would be revealed to the world when the **Halloween Horror** show aired. So, while he'd listened to the voice mails they left, he had to limit his replies to only texts, knowing that if he actually spoke to any of his loved ones while in his current fragile mental state, he might have slipped and spilled the news about Vegas.

"And you don't think you can do like my wife does, and travel with her to take care of the kids together while she's finishing out her career?" Matt looked at Liam like he thought he was a total idiot. "Hell, man, even if you're too beat up to keep wrestling, you know Rick will give you a job as a booker, so you won't have to feel like she's the breadwinner in the family."

"And don't even get us started on how great the education is that our kids are getting with the tutors here, especially compared to the shitty schools we went to," Vaughn added.

"Look, as great as the education stuff is that Rick has set up for all you guys' kids, I wanna raise my family in the same neighborhood where I grew up, not on tour." Liam raised his hands in surrender to the guys. "I want my kids to have the same kind of bond with my parents as I have with Granda and Granny. Feck, I want Granda and Granny to still be around to meet my kids when they're born. So, we need to annul this marriage and both find people closer to our own ages, whose priorities line up better, so we can have the lives and families we want."

If my family doesn't disown me for annulling this marriage, anyway. Feck, I might end up having to take that booker job 'cause the Connerys will ban me from Belle Harbor if they find out I wanna end my marriage, even though we got married in Vegas and not the church. He still wasn't sure how he'd explain the angle after it aired without outright lying to his family, but that was a worry for another time. *Maybe having to go to Heart's Destiny for Dean and Allissa's wedding is a good thing, so I can put off actually talking to anyone in the family 'til our Christmas break.*

Before the guys could argue with him any longer, one of the production assistants came by to direct them to each pick one of the various single-occupant restrooms for a personal dressing room for that night's show. They were then instructed to change for their match run-throughs and promo tapings. So, Liam did the only thing he could right then. He picked a room and changed into his gimmick wear, trying desperately to get into the right mindset to sit quietly, holding Rylie on his lap, while she explained to an irate Protection Detail why they caught her in a compromising position with him, that they'd gotten married in Vegas, and she needed to take care of her husband as he dealt with the trauma of seeing his best friend being shot.

Thank feck, Rick said I don't have to talk during any of these vignettes today. Hopefully, I can handle holding Rylie, and pretending to whisper in her ear to have her negotiate a postponement of our match until D's healed, without getting a hard-on.

Teagan was glad she and Aiken recently had their measurements taken by the costuming department of the GWA, when they were in New York at the beginning of the month to design their specialty ring gear for the pay-per-view, so she could just give Mandi the measurements, instead of having to actually be measured by Dean's grandmas, like the guys. She had enjoyed the uncomfortable expression on Josh's face as Patty Hunter subjected him to a much more invasive measuring session than she'd endured at the GWA headquarters, though. And she couldn't wait to tease him about being felt up by an octogenarian the next time they were alone. *Maybe I can help him erase the memories with a hand job in the shower later?*

As soon as the whirlwind of women from Allissa and Dean's families finished taking measurements from Teagan, Josh, Aiken, and Crockett, they all sat back down to finish eating and planning their matches for that night. But even as she tried to focus on talking with Shauna about their portion of the mixed-tag match later, Teagan couldn't help but watch as the matchmakers all swarmed around Chastity and Red. She could tell that both Rylie and Liam were uncomfortable with basically being forced to participate in the wedding, but neither one of them were willing to be blatantly rude by saying "no" to Dean's sweet, elderly grandmothers, even if Patty and Joan were a little more handsy than necessary while taking the guys' measurements.

Yeah, those ladies sure know what they're doing with having the grandmas take the lead, instead of Windy, Kandi, and Mandi. After the way they schemed in Vegas, I bet Red wouldn't have a problem telling Windy and Kandi "oh, hell, no," if they'd been the only ones going to enlist them in the bridal party. Who am I kidding? We're talking about Liam, not one of the other guys. So, he'd say "oh, feck, no" to keep from officially cursing in front of the kids sitting and eating lunch at the other tables, as if "feck" isn't just the Irish version of "fuck" and still just as real a curse word.

Once the older ladies seemed to have all they needed from each of them and went back to the table with the rest of Allissa and Dean's family members, Teagan could see the tension was still high between Rylie and Liam. They didn't raise their voices enough for her to overhear what was being said, however, so she devised a plan to get Aiken, Shauna, and possibly some of their other friends to get Rylie alone later to ask her what was going on.

When Liam stood and stormed off in one direction, and a couple seconds later Rylie ran in the opposite way, looking like she was trying to keep from crying in front of the rest of the crew, Teagan knew she didn't have time to strategize with the other ladies at her table, much less to recruit the rest of their friends.

"Josh, will you and the guys please go try to talk some sense into Red?" After getting her husband's attention, she pointed in the direction Liam had stomped away.

"Yeah, guess we need to be a little more aggressive with him than we were yesterday," Josh agreed, looking to Crockett and the other guys at the table for backup.

"While you're doing that, I'm going to go check on Chastity." Teagan leaned over and pecked a kiss on Josh's cheek before standing and turning to the other women at the table. "Ladies, let's go see what we can do to cheer up Chas."

Aiken and Shauna both joined her as they traipsed through the expanded backstage area to find where their friend had gone off to be alone while she licked her wounds. While Teagan partially understood Rylie's need for privacy, she also knew how much better it was for her to know that her friends had her back. Even if they couldn't do much to fix the situation with Liam, it would still help Rylie to know that she had all of them to lean on as she dealt with her huffy husband.

Luckily, it didn't take long for them to find her. They just had to follow the sounds of sobbing to locate her, where she was sitting on the floor behind the counter of one of the closed down concession stands. They quickly surrounded her, not caring that their dresses were getting dirty when they sat down on the floor with Teagan on her right, Aiken on her left, and Shauna directly in front of her.

"Do I need to text Josh to have him switch from just talking to actually beating some sense into Red?" Teagan put her arm around Rylie's shoulders, trying to comfort her friend, even as she joked about having her husband beat up Rylie's husband.

"No, he's bruised up enough from yesterday." Rylie shook her head as she wiped her eyes, obviously trying to stop the tears. "He doesn't need any more, even though he's back to being an ass today."

"I'm sorry, Chas. I was really hoping the way you guys seemed to be leaning on each other yesterday would last longer than a day." Aiken bumped shoulders with Rylie, barely missing squishing Teagan's hand between them.

"Me too," Teagan sighed. "But is there anything we can do to help you deal with him turning back into an asshole?"

"Yeah, him not being an ass didn't even last a whole day," Rylie scoffed, shaking her head. "Like twelve hours maybe. But considering he snuck out of my room almost immediately after I thought we'd really connected and made love for the first time, apparently, all he needed to feel better and go back to being a fucktard was to get laid."

Teagan was speechless at the realization that they'd finally succumbed to their attraction to one another and slept together. Though she wasn't all that surprised that Liam had snuck out right afterwards, assuming his regrets stemmed from feeling like he'd taken advantage of the situation the day before to get in her pants, as much as, if not more than, from their age difference.

But maybe since they've slept together now, Rylie won't be as opposed to rooming with him the whole time we're in Heart's Destiny as I'd originally thought. After seeing Aiken and Crockett coming out of the same room together that morning, she thought the same might be true of her bestie as well. *So, maybe we should see about getting the matchmakers in Heart's Destiny to help make a little forced proximity happen while we're there after all?*

"Seriously?" Shauna arched an eyebrow at Rylie, obviously offended on her behalf by Liam's behavior, and clearly not feeling as speechless as Teagan. "No wonder you ran outta there crying just now. But I've gotta ask, how'd you manage to keep your cool through both our morning meeting and lunch without slapping the shit outta him for pulling something like that?"

Considering she was three years older than Teagan, had been married to Vaughn for the better part of a decade, and was a mother of two, Shauna seemed like the perfect person to help Rylie keep the peace in her marriage. At least, Teagan had assumed Shauna's life experiences had equipped her to be better at diffusing the situation for their friends than either Teagan or Aiken. But her response just then seemed to suggest she had even more of a violent streak in her than any of the rest of the women in the GWA. *Damn, I wonder if she's ever had to slap the shit outta Vaughn? Not that that big ass bastard would probably feel it if she did, since he's at least a foot taller and a hundred-and-fifty pounds heavier than her. But still, she's got some brass tatas if she's ever tried to physically set him straight.*

"Oh, that wasn't why I was crying just now." Rylie shook her head at Shauna. "I knew he wasn't planning on spending the night before he even stepped into my room yesterday. And we were actually doing pretty good with getting along while planning the vignettes for this evening. It was after Rick said something about how we need to fake being happily married when we go to Heart's Destiny for the wedding to keep the Matchmaking Mommas off our backs, and Liam wholeheartedly agreed that I got upset."

"Because that messes with your plans to get their help in winning him over?" Aiken asked.

"Or because you hate the thought of him faking feelings that are very real for you?" Teagan continued the questioning started by her bestie.

"Both," Rylie choked out, her eyes glassing over once more, but she didn't fully start sobbing and letting the tears flow. "Probably more that I don't want it to be fake. And maybe because him saying he'd be faking his feelings for me makes me question if anything he said while we made love last night was real."

"Well, the good news is that you don't have to fake your feelings for him," Shauna pointed out. "So maybe a week in Heart's Destiny will give him enough of a taste of what married life can be to convince him that you guys should really be together."

"And we can still get the Matchmaking Mommas on board with all our plans for couple's activities that week," Aiken added, "so his faking it won't matter."

"Especially if we bring Randi, Allissa, and Fiona into our plans," Teagan tacked on, unable to stop smiling at how she'd decided to set in motion the plans she'd originally thought the meddling matchmakers would try the week of Dean and Allissa's wedding. "They can get Rick and Mandi to finagle the room assignments at the B and B, so we all have to room with our Vegas hubbies. There's no way he'll be able to resist you when you're sleeping in the same bed the whole time we're there."

"More like I won't be able to hold out and not jump his bones," Rylie laughed self-deprecatingly. "Especially if we have as many rounds of shots at Allissa's bachelorette party as we did at Randi and Fiona's parties."

"Yeah, I swear the only reason we weren't married off one of those nights, instead of in Vegas, was because the Matchmaking Mommas weren't at the bar for the parties to be able to go wake up a Justice of the Peace," Teagan joked, knowing that they couldn't have gotten married at the spur of the moment like that in Heart's Destiny because the county clerk's office wasn't open on weekends, or until midnight any day of the week, in Heart's Destiny, like the one in Las Vegas.

"Don't say that too loud, or you might give Windy and Kandi the idea to share their playbook with Mandi and the rest of the women in Heart's Destiny," Aiken chuckled.

"What do we care? We're already married," Rylie laughed along with them. "The only way they can catch one of us in that trap again would be if we actually manage to meet with a lawyer over our Christmas break, like I know Liam is currently planning, and then go back there for another wedding next year."

"Yeah, I suppose that's pretty safe, since nobody else in the GWA has shown an interest in one of the Heart's Destiny girls," Teagan agreed, even though she wondered if Rylie was kind of hoping to have a re-do with Liam in Heart's Destiny if they somehow managed to dissolve their Vegas marriage.

"I don't know," Shauna quavered, shaking her head. "With as fast as those ladies can throw together a wedding, Allissa might not be the only GWA wrestler to marry a Heart's Destiny local over Thanksgiving, if the Matchmaking Mommas figure out how to make the Vegas playbook work for them. There's still quite a few single guys on the roster they could marry off to the local women."

"After the way they stayed with the limo and didn't do anything to prevent us from falling for Windy and Kandi's schemes, it would serve Dane and Cruz right if we suggest them as the first victims, urh, grooms," Rylie chortled.

"Oh, definitely!" Teagan agreed, remembering how her good buddy Dane had played innocent on the day they all found out they'd gotten married.

Before they could stop laughing long enough to discuss who else they wanted to throw on the mercy of the Matchmaking Mommas, Joel Baker, one of the production assistants, peeked over the counter they were sitting behind to get them all back on track for that night's show. They quickly helped each other up off the floor to head back around to catering and grab their gear bags to change for their match run-throughs and promo tapings.

While they hadn't actually solved any of Rylie's issues with Liam, they had at least gotten her to laugh instead of cry, which Teagan considered a win for the time being. Now she just needed to find her hubby to find out if he'd had any luck with pulling the stick out of Liam's ass during their talk.

Thankfully, when she got back around to catering, where they'd left their gear bags, she saw Josh walking up from the opposite direction. "Hey, Wifey, I claimed us one of the single-user restrooms for our private dressing room," he informed her as he picked up their bags.

As Teagan followed Josh back in the direction he'd come from, she finally noticed that the public facilities of this arena had apparently been converted to include several banks of larger, private, gender-neutral restrooms with wide doors that also allowed for wheelchair access, instead of just the large, multi-stall men's and women's restrooms that were typical in most arenas. While Josh called them single-user restrooms, they were also large enough to be used as family restrooms, like for parents to accompany their children, and had built-in diaper changing stations with solid surface counters that looked sturdy enough to hold the weight of a couple of full-grown adults, which Josh used as a shelf for holding their bags when they entered the one he'd claimed for the two of them.

"Hey, Hubby, why don't you put those on the floor for now," Teagan directed Josh in a teasing tone as she locked the door behind them. "I've got a better idea for how we can use that shelf at the moment."

As Josh moved the bags off the shelf, Teagan untied her black wrap dress. She dropped it on top of her gear bag before hopping up to sit on the shelf, which was the perfect height for Josh to fulfill her counter fucking fantasies. Well, as close as they could get until the next time they were at her house, anyway.

"Hmmm, I like the way you think, Wifey," Josh crooned as he stepped between her legs and reached around her to unfasten her bra.

Teagan reached out and used his green and black paisley tie to pull him in closer, so she could claim his mouth in a passionate kiss. That would be her only act of aggression for this round of lovemaking, since she'd quickly learned that it was always better to trust Josh to take the lead. While she'd thoroughly enjoyed the single orgasm she'd had their first time together, when she'd initially taken charge and rushed them to the finish line, that O hadn't happened until Josh took over control.

In the weeks since then, she'd learned that she didn't always have to have hard and fast to get off. In fact, when Josh took the lead and slowed things down, she actually got multiple, more intense orgasms than she ever had when she was calling the shots. Not that they really had time for him to slow things down and do all the foreplay he loved to torture her with whenever they were in their room for the night. But she trusted that her husband knew this needed to be a quickie, even though she knew from their recent experiences that he'd still insist on making her come twice before he finally finished.

She let go of his tie when he tugged her bra straps down her arms. But as soon as the black stretch Leavers lace balconette bra was removed from her body, she went right back to tugging on the knot, needing the tie out of the way, so she could remove his black dress shirt. Knowing he hadn't brought another dress shirt to the arena, she carefully unbuttoned it, instead of ripping it open and sending the buttons flying like she had at her house.

Josh broke their kiss to trail his mouth and hands down her body. He teased one nipple with his fingers while suckling the other. His other hand delved lower, stroking her pussy through the barrier of her panties.

Damn it! These panties are La Perla! I should have thought to take them off before hopping up here. But since I didn't, he's probably going to rip them off to get them out of his way. And with our travel schedule, I won't be able to go in a store to buy more until the next European tour.

Sure enough, Josh only tolerated playing with the material between him and her pussy for a few seconds before he hooked his finger through the crotch of her black stretch Leavers lace thong and yanked. He quickly proved that even the elastic lace wasn't able to stretch far enough to hold up against his strength.

Maybe I can order a replacement pair online and have them shipped to the B and B in Heart's Destiny, since we'll be there for a whole week at the end of next month. I'll have to remember to ask Mandi later if she'd be willing to hold the delivery for me. And if so, get the mailing address from her.

All thoughts about her lingerie fled her mind as Josh slid two fingers into her pussy while circling her clit with his thumb. Between the luscious way he laved her breasts with his mouth and tongue and the exquisite way he finger-fucked her, it didn't take long before Teagan felt her first climax building.

"Oh, Josh," Teagan moaned, rocking her hips in time with the movement of his hand. She gave up removing his shirt, not wanting him to stop what he was doing with his hands for her to strip it off his arms. Instead, she ran her palms over his broad shoulders and upper back, needing to touch him, even if she couldn't feel his bare skin right then.

"Come for me, Tea," Josh growled, lightly grazing her nipple with his teeth as he spoke.

"Oh, yes, Josh." Teagan couldn't believe she, of all people, got off on having him command her to come. She'd always considered herself the least submissive of all the women she knew. But apparently Josh Parker was capable of bringing out all her previously hidden kinks.

Josh didn't let off even minutely as he used his mouth on her tits and his fingers on her pussy to take her over the edge. Teagan reveled in the waves of her release washing over her, moaning his name repeatedly as he prolonged her climax. It wasn't until she started coming down from her high that he stepped back and started removing his clothing.

Teagan felt bereft as she waited for him to strip off his pants and roll a condom on his cock. They'd had the discussion about their S.T.I. statuses and the fact that she was on birth control a couple weeks before. But they'd decided that it was probably best to continue using two forms of birth control for at least a few months, just in case one of them failed. She'd initially thought it was best to make sure they could work out as a couple before they decided to take their chances on increasing their pregnancy risk by dropping the condoms. But after how close they came to losing one of their fellow wrestlers the day before, she was starting to reconsider their plans.

Now's not the time to talk to him about possibly starting a family, though. No matter how much I worry about his PA going psycho when we're in San Diego in a couple of weeks and ending my chances of having his babies.

"Hey, no thinking right now, Wifey," Josh commanded as he stepped back between her thighs and cupped her face in both hands. "I only wanna see smiles and orgasmic expressions on your pretty face when we're making love, not sad expressions from whatever you're thinking about when you should only be feeling, not thinking."

"Then next time, don't make me wait so long while you're putting on a condom," Teagan teased, wrapping her arms around his torso and smiling, just before he claimed her mouth in a scorching kiss.

As she opened her mouth for their tongues to explore, Josh ran his hands down her body, pulling her to the edge of the smooth, solid-surface shelf, so he could line his cock up with her opening. He pushed inside her gently at first, giving her plenty of time for her pussy to stretch around his girth. But as she wrapped her legs around his waist, he soon sped up his thrusts, giving them both the fierce fervor they required to rapidly reach their peak.

While normally, she'd prefer the way Josh showed off his stamina when they were in their room, she was exceptionally glad they'd perfected the five-minute quickie when they had to hurry while at work.

"Oh, yes, Josh, right there," Teagan cried out, breaking their kiss to keep from biting down on his tongue as the ardent O crashed through her.

"Fuck, Teagan! I love…the way your pussy clamps down on my cock when you come."

The way Josh paused after the first two words of his sentence made Teagan wonder if he'd been about to say those three little words she longed to hear from him, but then changed his mind at the last second. *Yeah, in the middle of our mutual orgasm probably isn't the best time to share our "I love you's" for the first time,* Teagan decided, holding back her own declaration, and only chanting his name as they both convulsed in the ultimate pleasure.

They clung to one another as they basked in the euphoric feelings of how connected they felt to one another every time they simultaneously climaxed. Unfortunately, the drawback of a quickie was that they didn't have much time for recovery before they needed to separate themselves from one another.

"So, did you have any luck beating some sense into Red earlier?" Teagan queried as she hopped off the shelf and removed what was left of her panties, while Josh dealt with the condom.

"Unfortunately, not much," Josh huffed before turning on the sink and washing up from their lovemaking. He wet down a few paper towels and took care of cleaning her up too, which still felt surreal every time he did it. "I swear he's so caught up on how he thinks she needs someone closer to her age that he can't see how fucking perfect they are for each other."

"Well, maybe he'll start to see it when we set up lots of couple's activities and alone time for them while we're in Heart's Destiny next month," Teagan said hopefully, explaining the plans the ladies were working with the Matchmaking Mommas of Heart's Destiny to set up, as they changed into their workout gear to go run-through the final plans for their matches that night.

Chapter Eight

Josh couldn't believe Rick wanted to reveal their Vegas weddings to kick off a feud between him and Crockett only two days after Red and Chastity's marriage had been revealed on the ***Halloween Horror*** show. He'd thought they were going to wait until the ***Christmas Chaos*** show in December to make the announcement of the other two Vegas weddings. But on the plane that morning, Rick had informed them otherwise. Since they'd played up how Red and Chastity had both started remembering what had happened the night they all got blackout drunk back in August, it made sense that the rest of them would start to remember as well. So, Josh supposed it wouldn't work to keep acting like they didn't remember, or pretend the relationships were brand new to make it seem like they were just planning to get married in December. This change of plans for their angle meant they were now tasked with coming up with a reason to book him and Crockett into a one-on-one match that night without revealing anything in the setup, so the ladies could announce their marriages while arguing with one another about who to root for in the match.

Rick had planned to just book the match without giving the fans a reason, much like he did the matches that weren't part of an angle, which they used to fill the GWA's weekly television show with plenty of action while stalling for the pay-per-views for the big feud matches. Of course, the owner of the company still had a lot going on with the added paparazzi following them on tour and having to maintain extra security until all that hubbub died down, so he wanted the other bookers to focus on the vignette the ladies would be taping to kick off their split and the feud between the two couples.

Besides that, Rick was also preoccupied with his and Fiona's plans for expanding their family in the coming months. At least, if the rumors he'd overheard were true, that's why Josh thought their normally meticulous boss might be a lot less concerned about the minor details of every angle in the GWA at the moment. Regardless of why Rick hadn't come up with a reason for them to wrestle that night, though, Josh decided that was something he and Crockett, and their respective wives, could come up with while choreographing the match, which was part of the reason he'd suggested they get there early to use the ring before their coworkers arrived.

And when we come up with it, we'll present it to one of the other bookers, so the boss doesn't have to worry about anything else, Josh decided as he finished changing into his workout clothes to head out to the ring to plan everything with the others. *And hopefully, Teagan won't ask too many questions about why I'm the last one done changing again, so she doesn't ruin the surprise I'm cooking up with Mom for when we're in San Diego in a couple of weeks.*

When he got as far as catering, he found Crockett already talking to the ladies about their cues. The first cue was to alert the production crew to air their vignette on the jumbotron, which would end with Emerald and Amethyst fighting their way down to ringside. And the second would signal it was time for them to get in the ring to cause the double disqualification to end the match.

Cool. Maybe them already discussing the match will keep my sexy wife from asking why I had to wait until she wasn't around to call my parents, so I won't accidentally slip and tell her about the ring. Surely, I wasn't lucky enough to wrap a string around her finger to get her ring size without waking her up last night, only to screw up the surprise now.

"Since we're ending it in a double DQ, I think we should use our typical finishers as the cues," Crockett suggested, as the four of them started walking through the backstage area as soon as Josh joined them.

Josh wasn't a fan of having his Alley-Oop 360 seem like a weak finisher by using it earlier in the match and having an opponent catch their breath too soon for the pinfall. Considering Josh had to make it seem like he'd beat down his opponent bad enough to leave him lying prone in the center of the ring long enough for him to run around the perimeter of the ring before running up the fourth set of ropes to set up the jump into a three-hundred-and-sixty degree spin for the corkscrew double foot stomp off the top turnbuckle and onto his opponent's back, it just didn't seem realistic to have an opponent that out of it recover within three seconds to kick out of the pin. Especially after having the wind knocked out of him from the stomp too.

"The only way that'll work for my finisher is if you roll outta the way at the last second and don't take the stomp," Josh mentioned, pointing at Crockett as they passed the Gorilla position.

"Or since as a face, you'd never want to hurt a woman, we can have Amethyst jump in the ring then and cover his body with hers, so you have to jump over both of them to keep from hitting her with it," Teagan suggested, taking his hand as they walked down the ramp toward the ring. "So, you'd maintain the strength of your finisher while giving us the perfect cue to disrupt the match."

"But in order to make it a double DQ, you'd have to go after her right then too," Josh pointed out. "You think the three of you can get close enough into the corner that I won't accidentally hit any of you while you and Amethyst are catfighting practically on top of Crockett?"

"Only way to find out is to try it," Crockett shrugged.

"Okay, but the first time, I wanna be the only one in the ring, so you guys all see how close in you'll have to be." Josh couldn't believe he was about to attempt jumping up and over three people while spinning around as if he was riding a wave without hitting any of them, especially since one of them was his wife.

"Or how far out we have to be, so you can't reach us," Amethyst added.

"Yeah, but it'll be so much more impressive if he flies over all three of us," Teagan grinned, excitedly bouncing along beside him.

"Damn, Wifey, I don't know if I should be worried that you're such a risk taker for wanting to try this," Josh half-heartedly chuckled. "Or let it go to my head that you have so much confidence in my ring skills."

"Definitely the latter, Hubby," Teagan smirked, popping up on her toes to peck a kiss to his lips as soon as they got to ringside. "Now get up there and show us how far you can fly."

Josh didn't take the time to explain that the Alley-Oop 360 was all about how high in the air a surfer could get while spinning in a circle and basically staying with a wave, not traveling a long distance from where he'd started. He just slipped off his Vibram Fivefingers, knowing he needed to be barefoot, just like it was a real match, to get the most accurate assessment of how far out he could land from the turnbuckle, and hopped in the ring.

While he and Crockett had both felt it necessary to get some extra time for their run-through after not having wrestled against each other for a while, Josh was exceptionally glad to have the extra time in the ring now, when they would normally be taking their wives on midday dates now that the stalker was no longer an issue, since they were planning to add an extra level of risk to make his signature move more difficult. That extra planning turned out to be advantageous, so Josh could have the ring to himself right then, needing to make sure nothing they did on the show that night would put his wife, or their friends, in danger.

He did a quick warm up and stretch to prepare, while psyching himself up to go as far up and out as possible. Once he felt mentally ready, he ran through the move for the first time, landing on his feet approximately a third of the way diagonally across the ring from the turnbuckle. In a twenty-by-twenty ring, that meant he landed approximately nine feet from the turnbuckle toward the center of the ring. Josh couldn't believe how he'd doubled his normal distance with just that little bit of mental preparation.

"Holy shit!" Crockett shouted at the same time Josh had the same thought.

"Oh, yeah, I knew I was right about you being able to jump over all three of us," Teagan squealed, grinning with excitement as she hopped up on the ring apron.

"Could you tell that I intentionally overshot it?"

"No, it looked just like you always do it," Crockett shook his head. "The only reason I could tell it's a lot farther out than you normally land is because I know where you've had me lay in the ring to take it in the past."

"Why don't you hop up here and get in the normal position, so I can run through it a few times?" Josh directed Crockett, who took the stairs up into the ring instead of jumping up like Josh and Teagan both did. "That way I can make sure I can still miss you, even when I'm not as fresh and rested as I was for that first one."

They ran through the move several times with Josh adding extra spin to his corkscrew to make it obvious he was trying to miss actually hitting the move. As soon as the women decided Josh accurately portrayed not wanting to hit one of the Stones with his finisher, they added their part of the choreography, with Amethyst jumping in the ring first to cover Crockett and Emerald following immediately after her to pull her off him and start a bit of a catfight. With each successful attempt, Josh progressively got closer and closer to actually hitting Crockett or one of the ladies. So, they finally decided to make sure the guys only wrestled for thirty minutes before the Alley-Oop 360, just to be certain Josh wouldn't be too winded to safely perform the maneuver without risking any of them getting injured.

By then, everyone else had started arriving for their pre-show meeting, so they all got out of the ring to rest and rehydrate while Rick briefly reviewed the plans for that night's card. *Shit, we didn't think about why we're wrestling each other tonight to give Stone or Ethan the suggestion.*

As Rick introduced the local talent there for try-out matches that night, Josh got the idea that they could start the show with a vignette between him and Crockett, just in case the dark matches didn't quite end right on time for the kick off of the GWA's live broadcast. *We can tape something in catering maybe. I don't know if they'll want me to challenge Crockett or Crockett to challenge me, but one of us getting pissed at the other for eyeing up the Precious Stones should do the trick to set up tonight's match without giving away that either of us married them.*

With that idea in mind, Josh settled in to listen to the rest of the plans for the card that night. He and Crockett both filled everyone else in on their plans to limit the match to less than thirty minutes, so the bookers and television production people could all time out the show for the live broadcast. As soon as Rick released them to start on their match run-throughs and promo rehearsals, Josh held Teagan's hand to keep her from heading straight backstage. "We still need to figure out how we're signaling the production guys to air your promo and you to come to ringside."

"Oh, I thought we'd come down when Crockett hits the Widow Maker, since we're using the Alley-Oop 360 as the cue to go home." Teagan looked at him like she was confused by why he didn't already know that.

Remembering that Crockett suggested using each of their signature moves as the signals for the ladies, Josh felt kind of stupid for not realizing that they'd all thought it was already decided. "Yeah, but we need to make sure we do it in a way that we don't make his finisher look weak, either. So, I wasn't sure if we were just going to set it up with me somehow getting out of the fireman's carry before he falls like a log, and you'd need to know that just the setup is the signal."

"Actually, I was thinking we'd do the full Widow Maker, but land with you close enough to the ropes that you can get a foot over the bottom one to stop the pin," Crockett suggested. "That way there's no confusion, since the fireman's carry leads into so many other moves."

As one of the smaller guys on the roster, Josh didn't use the fireman's carry all that often, preferring more of an aerial style of wrestling to make him seem capable of defeating his larger opponents. While Crockett was only an inch or so taller than Josh, he supposed the extra ten or fifteen pounds of muscle he carried was enough for Crockett to be able to pull off more of the power moves than Josh could. So, it made sense that he might use the fireman's carry several times in a match before he ultimately went for his finisher, if only to tease the fans that the Widow Maker was coming.

"Okay, yeah, if you're cool with that then so am I," Josh agreed, leaning over to sneak in a peck of a kiss on Teagan's lips before she went backstage to go over the vignette she'd be taping with Amethyst.

As the ladies walked backstage, Josh and Crockett took advantage of the fact that the rest of the performers needed to talk over their matches before getting in the ring to run through any tricky spots. Since they were the first ones back in the ring, they quickly practiced Crockett's signature move a few times to make sure they knew exactly where they needed to be in the ring for Crockett to fall backwards with Josh draped over his shoulders, so they'd land with Josh close enough to the ropes to reach out and stop the pinfall, but weren't so close that they risked actually hitting the ropes. Or worse, Josh falling through them and landing on the floor outside the ring.

Once they were certain exactly of their ideal ring positions for both of their major spots, they quickly talked through the basics to choreograph the rest of the match, only practicing anything that one of them hadn't done recently. Then they rolled out of the ring to free it up for everyone else wrestling that night to have a turn running through their matches, hopping over the ring barricade to sit back down in the ringside seats.

"Hey, Stone, I have something I wanna run by you." Josh called Stone Fields, the booker he considered second only to Rick in planning their angles, over to sit with him and Crockett while they watched the Dangerous Twins and Heavy Artillery run through their match.

"Yeah, what's up?" Stone leaned against the barricade, but didn't jump over it to join them.

"I was thinking that we need to do some kind of set up for why we're wrestling tonight." Josh motioned between himself and Crockett. "I know the Stones are gonna set up the feud by announcing our marriages, but since we haven't had a beef with each other in a couple of years, we kinda need a reason to be booked in the main event tonight. So, I was thinking that we could maybe tape another vignette to air as the show opens, with me catching Crockett eyeing up the Stones and challenging him to the match to defend their honor. Then later, when the girls do the whole Vegas wedding reveal, it'll click with the fans that I thought he was eyeing my wife. Or vice versa, whichever way you wanna run it."

"Since the Stones and I are all heels, shouldn't I be the one to act protective of the girls?" Crockett interjected.

"I figured it'd work either way, since we both married one of them." Josh shrugged, not really caring who challenged whom to set up the match. "I just suggested it the way I did because I thought chivalry is more of a babyface trait than a heel trait, so I figured it'd seem more in character for me without hinting anything about our relationships."

"Yeah, I suppose that does make more sense." Crockett nodded before turning to look at Stone. "So, whaddya think, Stone?"

"Yeah, we're already opening the show with the tribute to Dion from *Halloween Horror*, and then re-airing the vignette with Red and Protection Detail, so any fans who didn't buy the pay-per-view will be caught up on what they missed," Stone informed them, even as he nodded like he thought Josh's idea had merit. "But I'm sure we can squeeze in a minute or two for ya'll to set up your match tonight. As long as you both remember, you absolutely can't call them your wives until after Emerald and Amethyst break the news in the middle of the main event."

"No problem," Josh and Crockett agreed in unison.

"Great, then figure out a script," Stone instructed them as he looked at his watch. "And we'll tape it in about an hour, right before we have the ladies tape the segment to air on the jumbotron in the middle of your match."

With that, Stone walked back up the ramp, presumably to let Caleb Quinn, the GWA head of production, know about the addition of another vignette he had to tape. A few minutes later, Dean, James, Tait, and Reid turned the ring over to the next set of performers for their run-through and joined Josh and Crockett at ringside.

"Dude, what's up with you trying to show me up with flying halfway across the ring over Crockett and the Stones?" Tait Ingleman, who used the ring name Missile as part of the Heavy Artillery faction and was known for getting extreme air with his high flying wrestling style, slapped Josh on the shoulder as he took the seat beside him.

"You need to get your eyes checked, Missile," Josh chuckled. "I won't ever come close to flying halfway across the ring like you do. Hell, I only made it about a third of the way across the ring on the first few practice runs."

"Yeah, I noticed it seemed shorter each time, but I wasn't sure if it was because you were getting tired or because trying to turn the three-sixty into a four-fifty or five-forty made it harder to go as far."

"Probably a little of both," Josh chuckled. "But the extra spin is to make it obvious that I'm trying not to hit one of the women, not because I'm trying to make it a four-fifty or five-forty."

"Yeah, I figured that out once the Stones jumped in, but before that I thought it was just you trying to add a little flare to impress your lady."

"Well, duh, obviously I wanna impress Emerald," Josh chuckled. "But since she's the one who suggested this spot, I also had to add a little extra oomph to the jump to make sure I live up to her belief in my abilities."

"Damn, you're really falling for Emerald," Reid stated, appearing to be surprised by the realization. "I thought you were just having a fling until our next break when you could meet with an attorney."

"Nope. I've been all in since I first found out we're married. And while I'd like to think I'm falling even more for her each day, I know that I first started falling for her back when she first joined the company. I was just too stubborn and stupid to act on it 'til I got so drunk I lost all my inhibitions." While he felt safe admitting as much to his friends, Josh wasn't about to say the L word to anyone else before he said it to Teagan.

"What about you, Crockett?" Dean kicked the bottom of Crockett's boot to get his attention. "You just having a fling with Amethyst? Or have you been falling for her like Josh has for Emerald?"

"My dad seems to think I've always had a thing for her, and like Josh just said, I only acted on it when I was drunk enough to let down my shields," Crockett confided with a shrug. "But I honestly don't think I started falling for her until after I started hanging out with her all the time to keep her safe while we were all on alert for the stalker. And I'm still not sure if I'm really falling for her, or if I just think it's more than friendship and lust because we're having the best sex of my life. Or maybe, is it possibly the best ever because we have real feelings for one another and it's not just a random fuck like I'm used to? Hell, I'm still not sure if it's really possible to fall in love in only a few weeks like that or not. But damn, I hope that's what I'm feeling, so I don't ever have to go back to mediocre fucks with ring rats."

"I don't know about these guys," Josh replied, lifting his chin toward the Inglemans and Hunters. "But I think sex with Teagan is better than I've ever had with anyone else because of our feelings for one another."

"Absolutely, real feelings definitely make sex better," Tait agreed.

"And while it can take some people a few weeks to realize they're in love, for others it's possible to fall in love in an instant," James chuckled. "You just have to be open to letting it happen. So, yeah, I think once you finally started paying attention, you could have easily fallen for your wife in the last few weeks. If you hadn't already fallen in an instant and just didn't recognize it, that is."

"How the hell do you know you're in love in an instant like that?" Crockett looked around at their friends, obviously needing more reassurance of the validity of his feelings. Or maybe just some insight into what everyone else felt for their soulmates, so he could figure out if that was what he felt for Amethyst or not.

"When I first saw Allissa…" Dean sighed out his fiancée's name as if he was still in awe at what he felt for her from that very first moment, looking around until he saw her on the opposite side of the ring and smiling like only a man in love could. "I just knew. It was almost like everyone else just disappeared, and I could only see her."

Josh kind of understood what Dean was saying, thinking back to when he first saw Teagan at ringside on the afternoon of her try-out match. She was just wrestling as Emerald then, not having come up with the Precious Stones gimmick until a few weeks later when Amethyst joined the roster. Josh hadn't recognized his instant attraction to her as anything more than lust at the time, but he did have a moment when it felt like they were the only two people at ringside for that pre-show meeting.

"When I first saw Randi, I thought she looked like an angel walking toward me," James confessed, glancing over his shoulder at his wife, who was still sitting on the opposite side of the ring, talking to one of the local wrestlers, who would be working their try-out match with her and Allissa. "But with the way you flirtatious assholes were hitting on her, I didn't think I stood a chance with her. So, when Anthony let me know she was down in the hotel bar later that night, I wasn't about to pass up my second chance with her. And sure enough, the second time I saw her, she still had that ethereal glow that drew me to her, proving she was my Angel from day one, even though I had to get her alone in the car before I could fully block out everyone around us."

Damn, is he describing the same thing I saw when I watched Teagan in the ring that first time? I mean, I didn't think she had an ethereal glow, but I did think her talent shined.

"I think it's a little different for everyone," Reid added, bumping shoulders with his husband Tait. "With Tait, it took a little while before I realized that I felt more than friendship. But that's probably because we grew up together and still had no clue how to define our sexuality yet. Once we figured out we were in love with each other, but were also bisexual and needed a woman to complete us, the feelings were instant when we met Kori."

Josh had been with the company for about a year and a half when the Inglemans joined the roster in 2012, so he remembered seeing Reid and Tait as a couple before they met Kori in 2014. While he'd seen them pick up a ring rat to share a few times in those first two years, Josh had recognized the difference in the way they felt about Kori from the first night they met. It was like overnight the Inglemans went from being the life of the party after every show to rushing straight back to their hotel room to call their girl. They were clearly committed to her immediately after they met, even before they went to Rick to ask if she could travel with them as their shared spouse, when they'd only been able to see her on the tour stops within a hundred mile radius of her hometown.

As a few of the other guys joined them and shared their stories of how they knew they were in love with their spouses, Josh reflected on his own feelings for Teagan. *Damn, maybe it really was love at first sight and I was just too ignorant to recognize it. That's probably why I felt so guilty every time I hooked up with a ring rat that I eventually just couldn't do it anymore, even when I didn't think I had a chance in hell of ever being with Teagan.*

"Okay, so now that I know I'm most likely falling for her, and not just confusing friendship and lust for love, what do I need to do to make Aiken fall in love with me, too?" Crockett's question brought Josh out of his mental musings, keeping him from feeling guilty all over again as he realized he needed the advice from their friends as much as Crockett did.

"You can't make her fall in love with you," Everest insisted, shaking his head. "She either will or she won't, but it's completely up to her."

"But you can be persistent in showing her how you feel," Olympus, Everest's tag-team partner, whose real name was Donovan Kirby, added with a knowing smile. "That's what I had to do with Sarina when she needed a little push to recognize her feelings for me."

"And I think you know I agree with Olympus," Dean added with a smirk. "Especially since ya'll had front row seats for how I've had to work for the last year to win Allissa's heart."

"So, just be persistent in continuing to plan our dates and stuff?" Crockett gave them all a dubious look.

"Yeah, and do little romantic things, like giving her a massage after you get back to your room on nights she's wrestled," James suggested.

"I've already been doing stuff like that and bubble baths with Teagan," Josh confessed.

"And get some rings on those girls' fingers, for fuck's sake," Tait added, pointing back and forth between Josh and Crockett.

"Already got it covered," Josh assured the guys, holding up his hands in surrender. "I'm just waiting to get to San Diego in a couple weeks, so I can pick up my great-grandma's emerald ring for her."

"Oh, excellent move, going with the family heirloom." Dean fist-bumped Josh. "Hope it works as well for you with Emerald as it did for me with Allissa."

"Yeah, I'm not sure if Dad still has anything like that from our family," Crockett sighed. "I might just have to take her shopping to pick out something I know she'll like."

Josh was tempted to ask Teagan to help Crockett pick something Aiken would like, but he didn't want to mention anything about rings to his wife until after he gave her his great-grandma's ring. Luckily, they were called back to change for recording their vignette right then, so he and Crockett had to quickly plan a short script as they walked to the locker room instead of continuing the discussion.

If he doesn't find something from his family when we go through Portland, then I'll suggest Teagan helping him pick something else out. Well, I will as long as Mom gets the ring back from having it resized in time for me to give it to Teagan before then.

~~~

"Oh my dog, ya'll missed out by not staying at ringside to practice your promos!"

Teagan had no clue what Randi was going on about as she and Allissa walked into the locker room, along with the two women who were there to try out for the roster that night. Teagan and Aiken were already changing into the gimmick attire they planned to wear for that night's show, which she considered a cross between flashy rave wear and workout clothes. Since the metallic green, skirted unitard she had on was originally designed for gymnasts or ice skaters to be able to
~~~

perform without flashing their panties, it was one of her favorite outfits to wear whenever she had to do a run-in after kicking off her heels, when she otherwise looked like she was ready to go out, instead of being dressed to actually wrestle on the card.

"What?" Teagan directed her question to Randi, since Allissa seemed to be occupied with showing the new girls where to put their stuff. Normally she'd avoid talking about their relationships with local talent present, knowing that they couldn't be trusted not to leak info about their Vegas marriages until they signed contracts with the GWA. But since they were revealing them that night, she assumed it would be fine if they overheard a little bit, as long as the weddings or their wedding date weren't specifically mentioned. "Did our guys add something else to the match tonight that we need to know about? Something other than the extra vignette Stone told us about already?"

"Oh, no, I don't know anything about that." Randi waved off Teagan's guess for what she and Aiken had missed. "But they did have an interesting conversation with a few of the other guys while sitting at ringside watching the rest of our run-throughs."

"Don't listen to her." Allissa rolled her eyes at Randi as she opened her locker to change out of her workout clothes and into her ring gear. "They weren't talking loud enough for us to hear them, even when we moved from the opposite side of the ring to actually in the ring for our run-through with Juno and Venus." She then motioned to the two new girls, who apparently used a Roman goddesses gimmick for their tag team.

"Oh please, you're too hard of hearing to even understand the right lyrics when a song is blaringly loud, so I'm not surprised you couldn't hear them," Randi argued with her soon-to-be sister-in-law. "But I heard them just fine."

"So, what was so interesting about this conversation, Leigh?" Aiken referred to Randi by her ring name when she posed the question.

"I didn't hear how it started, but the general gist of it was all about how each of the guys knew they were *in love*." Randi covered her heart with both of her hands, batting her eyelashes dramatically. "And once your guys figured out that they've also fallen, there were questions about what they could do to make sure ya'll fall for them, too."

"Yeah, I'm pretty sure Josh wasn't the one asking those questions," Teagan chuckled, shaking her head at her friend's over-the-top dramatics. While she could easily see Josh sharing with the other guys that he'd been attracted to her since the first day she appeared on a GWA show, especially if James and Dean had just shared their love-at-first-sight stories about Randi and Allissa, she didn't think he'd ask their advice for getting her to fall for him. Even though they hadn't yet shared those three little words with one another, all the sweet romantic gestures he'd started showering her with in the last couple of weeks were more than enough proof that he already knew how to win her over. *Hell, he can probably tell from the way we make love every day, multiple times a day, that I'm head over heels for him.*

"Well, it might have been Crockett that specifically asked that," Randi confessed with a shrug. "But Josh was clearly interested in what the other guys suggested, especially when Missile said something about ya'll needing wedding rings."

"Stop!" Teagan held her hand up to Randi in the universal sign to get her friend to shut the hell up. In addition to not wanting her friend to mention anything about the Vegas weddings in front of the two strangers in their midst, Teagan had to look around to make sure Rylie hadn't come back in the dressing room after taping her vignettes with Red and Protection Detail, so their friend who wasn't having as easy a time with her marriage wouldn't get her feelings hurt. Once she verified that Rylie hadn't come back in the dressing room, she continued. "If they discussed plans for rings, I don't want to hear about them."

"Seriously? You're not excited to know your man is planning to give you a ring?" Randi's eyes widened as she gave Teagan an incredulous look.

"No, not when I'm hearing about it from you," Teagan scoffed, finding it ridiculous that Randi would want to ruin whatever Josh planned to surprise her with. "That surprise needs to come from him."

"Come on, Leigh," Aiken huffed, clearly not wanting her potential ring reveal ruined either. "You'd have been pissed if we'd have told you about his plans before James proposed. So, you can't really think we'd be happy for you to tell us what our guys are planning for our special moments before they can surprise us. Right?"

"Sugar! I'm sorry, I wasn't thinking," Randi apologized. "I was just so excited to realize that your guys weren't still considering annulments that I forgot you never really got those proposal moments."

Teagan cringed at the mention of annulments, knowing they were putting too much information out there in front of the women who were just there for a try-out match. *But surely, they won't leak anything they hear before the show and blow their chances at getting signed tonight. Right? So, it's probably okay if we talk about all this with them here now, especially since we're about to go tape the segment revealing our marriages when they'll most likely be right there watching us.*

"Damn, girl, did I not make it clear that Josh and I were really trying to make a go of things between us from the first moment we laid eyes on that marriage certificate?" *Guess I didn't brag about the amazing sex as much as I thought.*

"Well, yeah, but James said something about Rick asking all the guys to watch over all the women and children that same weekend," Randi explained, blushing lightly with embarrassment. "And he made it sound like Josh and Crockett were both using ya'll's dates as a way to keep you safe, and maybe to have a fling until our next break when ya'll can get with your lawyers about ending the marriages. So I assumed, since he's known all ya'll longer than I have, that he might know more than you were telling us. Especially since I didn't know if there were any real feelings there or not, which is why I got so excited when I heard them talking at ringside about falling for ya'll."

Teagan remembered Rick talking to everyone at their pre-show ringside meeting in Baltimore about being extra vigilant when they doubled Allissa's security detail because her stalker had escalated. But even though he mentioned how they all should couple up in their rental cars, he didn't have that discussion with everyone until after she and Josh got to the arena after they'd already consummated their marriage. So, while Randi's assumptions could explain why Crockett had suddenly decided to try dating Aiken, she didn't think Randi's theory was true for her and Josh.

"Yeah, well, you know what they say about making assumptions," Teagan pointed at Randi.

"Yeah, and from now on I won't presume to think my husband knows anything about anyone's relationships but ours," Randi chuckled self-deprecatingly. "And I'll ask ya'll for the scoop on what's going on with your hubbies."

"Just so you don't have to ask, I'll tell you that Josh and I had already decided to date and consummated our marriage before Rick told us about the need to increase security and be even more vigilant." Teagan grinned at her contrite friend.

"And Crockett suggested we try dating before that meeting, too," Aiken added, even though she didn't look completely confident in her words. "And even though I didn't agree until the next day, it was only after he made it clear that he'd planned to ask me when we first found out we'd gotten married that I agreed. But I didn't give him a chance to list out all our options and plead his case for dating on that first day, or else we'd have started trying to make our marriage work even sooner."

Knowing her bestie had fallen hard for Crockett, Teagan wasn't about to share her doubts about him honestly wanting to try dating from the get-go. Even if Crockett had only backed off on the annulment talk after being asked to watch over Aiken by Rick, from everything she'd observed between her best friend and her husband, and also from what Randi just told them about Crockett specifically asking about how to make Aiken fall in love with him because he'd fallen for her, Teagan was pretty sure their feelings for one another were real, no matter how or why they started spending more one-on-one time together.

"Is the GWA locker room always like a live-action soap opera?"

Teagan wasn't sure if it was Juno or Venus who broke the silence that had settled around them, but she couldn't help but chuckle at the way they'd lightened the mood. "Not most of the time. But we do have our moments. I'm Teagan, by the way, but everyone calls me by my ring name, Emerald Stone. And you are?"

"Amoura Valentine," the blonde introduced herself as she sat down to put on her wrestling boots after donning her goddess costume. "But ya'll can call me Venus."

"Your real name is Amoura Valentine?" Teagan thought that sounded like a great ring name, as Amoura nodded to indicate it was her legal name. "And you don't use it for your ring name? It would be perfect for a Cupid gimmick."

"Yeah, more like a stripper gimmick," Amoura laughed, shaking her head. "Or a porn star gimmick. I seriously don't know what my mother was thinking when she named me. And her only defense when I asked her about it was that they'd given her the good drugs when she had me, so she thought it sounded good at the time. If it wasn't my legal name, I could definitely see using it as a ring name, though. But I've heard too many horror stories about stalkers to use my real name for my gimmick, so I stuck with her love theme and picked Venus when I teamed up with Juno."

Amoura motioned toward her tag-team partner, who had also changed into a white outfit with gold trim to match their goddesses gimmick. Their ring attire was similar to the green outfit Teagan was currently wearing, only theirs included gauzy capes and a few extra layers of sheer material forming removable skirts, which they presumably removed before wrestling.

"I'm Juno Johnson," the brunette introduced herself. "And yes, that is my legal name. My mom originally named me June, but then when the movie *Juno* came out the same year she and my bio-dad divorced and she remarried, she legally changed my first name at the same time her new husband adopted me to change my last name. So when Amoura and I met, we instantly bonded over having the two weirdest names in school."

"Your names aren't any weirder than mine," Aiken giggled as she introduced herself to the local talent. "I'm Aiken Thi Pearson, but everyone calls me Amethyst."

"Aiken? Like that singer, Clay Aiken, that my mom used to listen to all the time?" Amoura arched an eyebrow at Aiken.

"Well, it is spelled the same, but I had the name at least a decade before he made it famous," Aiken joked. "And it was actually my papa's last name before he changed it to match Daddio's. When they adopted me from Vietnam, they gave me each of their names, along with a Vietnamese middle name, so I have links to my heritage as well as to both my dads."

"Well, your name might be as unusual as ours, but at least there's special meaning behind it, so I don't think it counts as weird." Juno pointed out. "While I've embraced my name for my gimmick because it's also the name of a Roman goddess, it doesn't change the fact that my mom got it from a movie about a pregnant teenager."

"Yeah, well, I don't think any of your names are weird, just unique, kinda like the rest of us," Teagan interjected, liking these potential new coworkers much better than she had the ones who'd recently tried out for the roster when they were in Virginia Beach. Of course, those two had basically ignored all the female performers in the company, other than Holly and Shauna, whom they'd wrestled in their try-out match, while flirting shamelessly with all the guys, which was probably why Rick hadn't signed them. Whereas, Amoura and Juno seemed to understand the need to be friendly with the women they might be working with in the future.

After a little more discussion about how most of the women on the GWA roster had a hard time finding items personalized with their first names, they all finished changing and left the locker room to tape their vignettes before having dinner. Since they had to wait until the catering staff had the buffet tables set up to tape the guys promo, when they'd set up their match that night by arguing over the way Crockett eyed up the Precious Stones while they were filling their salad plates, they had to shoot the segment that would air on the jumbotron part way through the main event first.

The production crew quickly set up one of the monitors, which the wrestlers usually watched the show on backstage, in the area where they had most of the cameras set up for interviews, placing two chairs beside it for Emerald and Amethyst to sit side by side while supposedly watching the first part of the main event.

"Come on, Josh," Teagan shouted as soon as Caleb pointed to her to begin the segment once the camera aimed at them started rolling. "Kick out! Reach out for the bottom rope. Do something. Just don't let him pin you!"

"I just don't get why you're cheering for Surfer Josh and not Crockett," Amethyst whined, rolling her eyes at Emerald, as they sat facing the camera while pretending to watch a match on the blank monitor screen in front of them. Since the camera was positioned behind the monitor, there was no reason to actually put a match on it as they pre-recorded this interaction to air during the TV main event later in the evening. "I mean, I know you've got a crush on him, or whatever, but he's too much of a boy scout for you to really be interested in him."

"He's not always a boy scout." Emerald sighed, shaking her head at her bestie. "And it's more than just a crush. Chastity and Red aren't the only ones who got married last time we were in Vegas, ya know."

"Oh, yeah, I know," Amethyst replied, rolling her eyes. "Which is why I'm confused by why you're rooting for my husband to lose this match."

"Your husband?" Emerald turned her head to stare at her friend, instead of continuing to watch the monitor. "I was talking about me and Josh. Are you saying you got married that night, too?"

"Yeah, I finally remembered more of what happened after we got so sloshed at the *Sin City Showdown* after-party," Amethyst nodded, a secretive smile spreading her lips. "Well, I remembered saying, 'I do,' anyway, and then consummating my marriage to Crockett. But I thought you were just as drunk as I was and didn't remember anything either. So, are you sure you married Surfer Josh?"

"Yeah, I'm sure," Emerald huffed. "And I actually picked up the certificate of marriage last time we went through my hometown, so I know for certain and don't just think I married him because of some fuzzy memories. So, until you can show me your marriage license, I think you should be rooting for my husband, since he's legally bound to the Precious Stones now."

"It's not mine or Crockett's fault that we haven't been back to one of our hometowns yet for me to pick up our certificate of marriage to show you," Amethyst protested, turning in her seat to glare at Emerald. "Besides, I don't need a piece of paper to know I'm gonna stand by my man. In fact, I think I'll go to ringside, so I can get a better look when Crockett defeats Surfer Josh."

"Oh, no," Emerald argued, grabbing Amethyst's arm to stop her when she stood as if she was about to head to ringside. "I'm not gonna let you go out there and do something to cheat Josh outta this otherwise easy victory."

The two women pushed and shoved each other as they made their way out of the camera's shot, knowing they'd have to recreate the shoving match as they made their way down the ramp later to end the show with the guys pulling them apart in the middle of the ring.

"Perfect! Got it in one. Good job, ladies." Caleb smiled at them as he directed the production assistants and camera operators to reset the scene for the next promo they needed to tape.

"Damn, Wifey, way to set the bar high, so Crockett and I look like hacks when we mess up our lines and have to reshoot our spot more than once." Josh gave her a teasing smile as he pulled her into his arms. "That performance deserves to be rewarded with a kiss. Or maybe a visit to a secluded area where I can properly reward you."

"Oh pul-ease," Teagan scoffed, placing her palms on the lapels of Josh's suitcoat, and acting like she was about to push him away. "You're just trying to get me to go off for a quickie, so you can mess up my outfit and make us have to reshoot our perfect vignette."

"Oh, no, I definitely don't wanna mess up your outfit." Josh shook his head, grinning mischievously. "That's why I suggested going somewhere secluded, so you can take it off first."

"Sorry, Hubby, no time for all that." Teagan smiled up at her husband, even though her four-inch heels brought her up to only three inches away from being eye to eye with him. "Since we have to hurry and shoot your confrontation with Crockett before everyone else gets to catering for dinner."

"Fine," Josh sighed, pouting like an insolent child. "But I still think you need to take pity on me and give me a kiss for good luck while they're resetting the cameras."

"Hmmm, that I can do," Teagan agreed, pushing up slightly on her toes to brush her lips over his.

Just as Josh started to deepen the kiss, they were interrupted by the catcalls of their coworkers. Specifically, Caleb calling out, "Josh, you might want to go wash off that lipstick before we tape this segment when you're supposed to be defending the ladies' honor."

Even Teagan had to laugh at the irony.

Thursday, October 31, 2019, Halloween, Johnson City, Tennessee

Rylie felt ridiculous dressing up as Princess Leia to go out to the club with her GWA coworkers for Halloween. Especially since her

Protection Detail partners were the ones completing the *Star Wars* group costume theme with her and not her husband. After the vignettes they taped on both Sunday at the *Halloween Horror* show and Tuesday for their normal weekly TV show, she'd assumed that Rick would expect her and Liam to appear together at the nightclub where the VIP room was reserved for the GWA Halloween party after their house show. But even though Red had made an appearance at ringside while she wrestled earlier in the evening to show he was supporting his wife, even on the non-televised shows, Liam had made it clear that she was still supposed to ride with Harrison and Cameron, which included not just to and from the airports, hotels, and arenas they visited each day, but also to any public appearances. Well, other than their trip to Heart's Destiny for the upcoming break.

You'd think we'd use these after-parties to practice, so we're prepared to act more like a couple while we're there for Dean and Allissa's wedding, she thought as she double-checked her hair hadn't been messed up when she'd put the hood up on her princess robe after walking outside in the wind.

Since she'd taken her hair out of the braids she normally wore it in the day before, she'd been able to put her natural hair up in two afro buns to mimic the space buns style of Princess Leia's hair in the movies relatively quickly without going to a salon or having Emerald help her, like they often did whenever one of them removed their braids or put in new ones. She could also take it down on her own at the end of the night without damaging her hair, so she could let her scalp breathe for a few more days before installing new braids. The ease of the hairstyle was only one of the reasons she'd chosen the costume. Knowing *Star Wars* costumes were timeless and always popular, she'd also chosen it because she knew it would be easy to find no matter what city they were in that day.

And her assumption had been proven correct when they'd been able to hit up the local mall in the middle of the day to find everything they needed for their costumes. Well, mostly. Harrison had wanted to find a Darth Vader costume, but the costume shop they'd found in the mall hadn't had one big enough to fit him. Therefore, he'd switched to a Han Solo costume, so he could wear his own clothes and just had to find a toy blaster and belt with a blaster holder to complete the get-up. His belt didn't hang as low on his hips as Han's had in the movies, and he didn't have the vest she associated with the movie character, but she supposed the leather jacket he wore worked well enough. With her dressed as Princess Leia and Cameron dressed as Luke Skywalker, their costumes made it clear who Magnum was supposed to be when the three of them walked into the party together.

When they joined the rest of the GWA in the VIP room, Rylie realized that most of their coworkers had clearly planned ahead for their costumes, instead of waiting until the last minute like Protection Detail had. At least, she assumed that was how they had such elaborate costumes without running into any sizing issues for the larger members of the roster.

Apparently, there was a predominant theme for superheroes among the GWA crew, too. With masks in place, she wasn't sure who had dressed as the Hulk, Iron Man, Spiderman, Black Panther, and War Machine, but since they were all hitting on ring rats at the bar, she assumed they were the single guys on the roster. Not wanting to watch as Protection Detail joined in the raucous flirting, she quickly turned away without taking the time to determine who all was actually at the bar.

How'd that many ring rats end up in the VIP room anyway? I thought it was supposed to be reserved for just the GWA. I mean, we all had to give our names to the bouncer at the door to get back here, so they shouldn't have been allowed access. Unless some of the guys brought them back here?

Rick must not be here tonight. If he was, he would have insisted the guys go back out to the main part of the club to hang out with the ring rats, not bring them back here.

Oh, well, at least the only way them crashing our party affects me is that it gives me more practice with calling everyone by their ring names instead of their real names.

When she scanned the room to find the couples who weren't surrounded by fans, she found that they'd all congregated in the seating area on the opposite side of the room from the bar. As she walked over to hang out with her fellow female performers and their spouses, she made note of their couple's costumes, as well. Crockett stood out as an excellent Thor, and she assumed Amethyst was supposed to be Jane Foster from the first *Thor* movie, since she sat on his lap in street clothes similar to what the character wore when she first met Thor.

The Hunters had all chosen DC characters instead of Marvel, but she still recognized them from the popular comic book themed movies she'd originally started watching with her dad as a teenager and continued to watch in his honor every time a new one came out. Dean Dangerous was clearly dressed as Aquaman with Victoria Vicious by his side as Mera. James and Leigh Dangerous, however, had maintained their heel wrestling personas by dressing as the Joker and Harley Quinn, which worked perfectly with Randi's blonde hair and a little spray in temporary hair paint.

Rylie didn't know the names of the characters Surfer Josh and Emerald were dressed as, but that was because they'd bucked the superhero theme and were clearly dressed as characters from one of the crime dramas Emerald loved to watch. They were both in black jeans, t-shirts, and tactical vests with the letters N.C.I.S. stitched on both the front and back. Much like Magnum's blaster and Trojan's lightsaber, the guns on their hips were clearly toys, standing out from their black tactical clothing due to their bright coloring.

"Okay, I recognize all the superhero and villain costumes, but I have no idea who you guys are dressed as," Rylie admitted, pointing back and forth between Emerald and Josh as she took the seat beside Emerald at the end of the table.

"I'm Kensi Blye and Josh is Marty Deeks, from *NCIS: Los Angeles*," Emerald clarified. "I don't really look anything like Kensi…"

"No, you're much hotter than Kensi," Josh interrupted his wife, wagging his eyebrows and grinning.

Teagan shook her head at her hubby, but her smile gave away how much she appreciated the compliment. "But Josh is a dead ringer for Deeks. Well, he would be if his hair was a little darker and he didn't shave for a couple of days, anyway. So I couldn't resist dressing up as the married couple from one of my favorite shows."

"And after she made me watch their wedding episode, I'm kinda glad we got our wedding instead of theirs," Josh joked. "Even if our only memories of it are from looking at the pictures the chapel emailed us, our drunk ceremony wasn't nearly as crazy as Deeks and Kenzie's."

"Aw, Hubby, but you can't really say that for sure," Teagan teased, smirking at Josh. "Since we don't remember it, we can't guarantee that a gay, Russian mobster with a crush on you didn't show up for the festivities."

"Maybe not with one-hundred percent certainty," Josh shrugged. "But since Kirkin wasn't in any of the pictures from the chapel, I think we're safe in saying we didn't have to fight any thugs to thwart their attempt to assassinate him."

Rylie smiled at her friends' playful banter as their mention of the pictures from their weddings triggered her to flip through hers and Liam's in her mind. Since Rick had asked them each to contact the chapel to get any pictures that had been taken that night that weren't on one of their phones, so he could use them with the wedding announcements on their social media profiles now that they'd announced they'd all gotten married on television, some of the memories Rylie had originally thought were just dreams felt validated as real in her mind. While she'd forwarded all the pictures the chapel had sent her to their social media contact in the corporate office, she'd also saved all of them to her private cloud account. She knew it was probably foolish to want to keep them to look back on after her marriage and career were over, but she couldn't help herself. Even if Liam never returned her feelings, she wanted that tangible evidence of the night she'd married the man she loved.

Thinking about their wedding night caused her to look around the room to find her husband. *I should probably go sit beside him to keep up appearances, since there are so many GWA fans in here.*

When her eyes landed on the six-foot-four leprechaun standing at the bar, however, she quickly changed her mind. Red was clearly too busy holding court with a bevy of naughty nurses, sexy schoolgirls, and wicked witches, whose costumes revealed way more skin than they concealed, to realize he was supposed to be acting like a happily married man whenever they were out in public.

I guess I should have picked the slave Leia costume, instead of the classic white robe Leia outfit, if I wanted to get his attention tonight. But, no, I had to think about what was appropriate for wearing backstage with the kids for the other party, as well as what would keep me warmest when the temperature dropped into the upper forties tonight.

Although, I suppose it doesn't really matter which Leia costume I picked out, since even the slave Leia costume had a long skirt that still covered way more than some of the outfits those women are wearing. Hell, I think that Playboy Bunny is in actual lingerie that shouldn't be legally allowed as outerwear in a public place like this. I hope she has a warm coat to put on before she leaves to go home, 'cause I imagine her nipples will cut right through that lace if she goes outside without something else on.

No matter how hard she tried, Rylie couldn't make herself turn away from the train wreck of a scene in front of her. Even though Liam was clearly having a grand time flirting with the ring rats surrounding him and all the single guys who worked for the GWA, she couldn't look away from him. It was like her eyes were drawn to him, whether she wanted to watch his antics all night or not.

Anyone else would look absolutely ludicrous dressed in a shiny green suit and oversized top hat. But no, Liam fucking Connery has to look like the most dashing and debonair leprechaun ever to walk the earth. Why couldn't he have dressed up as that evil leprechaun from the old horror films, instead of combining the pot of gold leprechaun we think of on Saint Patrick's Day with his studly ladies' man gimmick he uses as Red? Like, seriously, did he have that green suit custom tailored like the tuxes he wears to the ring? And if so, why did he save it for Halloween, instead of wearing it on Saint Patrick's Day?

Considering she signed her contract with the GWA on the day before Saint Patrick's Day, that after-party was the first one she'd attended with her new coworkers. In fact, it was Liam who invited her to come out with them that night, so she clearly remembered him wearing a dark gray suit with a light green shirt and a tie covered in shamrocks on Saint Patrick's Day. Of course, back then, he'd also spent the whole night talking to her and the other new GWA crew members, not flirting shamelessly with a bunch of ring rats like he was right then.

"Chastity, you have to try the Witch's Brew Lemonade." Amethyst pointed to the purple and blue drink in front of her, momentarily distracting Rylie when a cocktail waitress came by to deliver their drink orders and presumably to take her order.

"Or the Black Magic Margarita," Emerald added, pointing to the black drink with green sugar coating the rim and a lime floating in it that was placed in front of her.

"Ya'll take the colors of your gimmicks way too seriously," Leigh laughed, pointing out how the Precious Stones had matched their drinks to their gimmicks before holding up her own glass of brown liquid served in a Mason jar. "But seriously, Chas, if you're looking for the best drink to try tonight, I recommend the Apple Pie Moonshine."

Rylie hadn't intended to get totally wasted at the party that night, knowing she'd promised herself that she'd never get so drunk she blacked out again like she had in Vegas. *But if I want to have any chance of surviving more than ten minutes of this party without wanting to run out crying because Liam is hitting on all those other women, then maybe I should try all the specialty drinks tonight. Even if I end up making a fool of myself over my asshole husband, at least then I won't remember it.*

"Yeah, I think I'll start with one of each of the drinks these ladies are having, so I can figure out which one I like best." Rylie motioned to the three drinks her friends had recommended, as well as the red frozen drink in front of Allissa, assuming it was the Halloween version of some kind of daiquiri, which would probably end up being her favorite. "But you guys have to make sure I safely get back to my room alone when they knock me on my ass."

"Don't worry, Chas," Emerald stated, glancing over toward the bar and making a face at what she saw. "We'll watch out for you, so you can let loose tonight."

"Absolutely," Amethyst added, along with Leigh and Victoria, none of them pointing out the elephant in the room, who just happened to be dressed as a leprechaun.

Liam felt like a jackass for not extracting himself from the hoard of ring rats, who'd somehow managed to get into the VIP section of the club, before Rylie arrived. Considering Blade, Sawyer, Kade, Dane, and Cruz were with the girls when they'd surrounded him at the bar in the private room reserved for the GWA, he assumed they'd insisted that the bouncer standing guard at the entrance to the VIP section let them in for the after-party. But he really wished they'd have left them out in the main part of the club. Or at least, waited until he'd gotten his beer and walked away before they all swarmed the bar.

Now he was stuck unable to move without running into a scantily clad woman, or several scantily clad women, while Rylie glared at him from the opposite side of the room for appearing to be a lousy cheater. *Feck! I want to push her away enough that she won't fight the annulment, but I don't want her to think I'd ever pick one of these chicks over her.* But as much as he wanted to make his way through the crowd to go join her, where she'd sat down with several pairs of their happily married colleagues, he knew that wasn't an option he could choose right then.

He not only had to be polite to the female fans to maintain kayfabe and stay in character as Red, but he also had to find a way to sell his and Chastity's marriage to the outsiders in their midst, while maintaining enough distance from his wife to keep from being tempted by her. So, he did the only thing he felt he could at the moment, politely engaging the ring rats closest to him in conversation, while making it clear to them that he was officially off the market, and trying to foist the really aggressive women off on Magnum and Trojan, who'd left Chastity alone with their coupled-up friends to join the melee of women around the bar.

Hopefully, if I successfully start selling this happy marriage gimmick tonight from across the room, then maybe I'll be able to spend the next three weeks conditioning myself to be able to keep it up while moving closer and closer to her. So by the time we go to Heart's Destiny, when I'm gonna hafta be right by her side at all the wedding festivities, then I'll be able to do it without losing control and making a move on my wife.

"Did you really marry Chastity?"

"Yes, I did," Liam smiled as he replied to the buxom blonde dressed as a Playboy Bunny. She was among the group who'd introduced themselves to him when they'd first arrived, but he didn't remember any of their names.

"Then why aren't you wearing a wedding band?"

"Because I can't wear it when I wrestle, and I forgot to get it out of my bag before I left the arena," Liam lied to the brunette dressed as a slutty schoolgirl as he watched Rylie turn away from him to talk to their friends. *And because I don't wanna ask my bride to let me wear her dad's ring again when it's just for the angle 'cause we're gonna annul the marriage.*

Liam honestly wished they hadn't used her parents' rings for their wedding ceremony, thinking rings that meaningful should have been saved for when she married the man she'd spend the rest of her life with, the man she actually loved. But he also wished they'd have bought rings at the chapel that night, so he'd have something tangible to keep forever as a reminder of the time he'd married the woman he knew he'd love for the rest of his life.

Yeah, he had the pictures the chapel had emailed them. But after having them shared with the GWA fans earlier in the week, they no longer felt like something special and private, just between him and Rylie.

He'd also finally heard back from Boyle Kelly to know his copy of the certificate of marriage was now in the lawyer's office, even though Boyle had no clue who all had seen it before his secretary put it on his desk without the envelope it came in. But since Boyle was passing it on to someone else in the firm to start the paperwork on the annulment, Liam wasn't sure he'd ever even hold it in his hand, assuming the official document would become part of his file with the Kelly Legal Group. At best, he assumed he'd get a photocopy of it attached to the annulment papers once everything was officially settled.

Guess that's something I'll have to ask about when they call to let me know the name of the lawyer handling the annulment and set up my first appointment with them for sometime in the week and a half I'll be home for Christmas and New Year's. And I also need to ask if Boyle's secretary ever remembered whether or not that piece of mail was open before she removed the marriage certificate and tossed the envelope, so I know whether or not to be worried about being ambushed by my family when I get home for the holidays.

Liam continued making small talk with the ever changing women around him as he watched a cocktail waitress carry over a tray to deliver four different drinks to Rylie.

Oh, feck! That can't be good. Hopefully, she just couldn't decide which one she wanted and plans to take a sip of each before deciding which one to actually drink, and isn't planning to drink all four of them.

As she picked up a Mason jar filled with brown liquid, and promptly chugged it, Liam realized his hopes were dashed. When she followed it up by pulling a slice of lime from the glass of black liquid and sucking it dry before also chugging the second drink, he knew she was so pissed at him for talking to the fans around him that she was trying to drown her anger in copious amounts of alcohol.

"Hey, Magnum," Liam called out to the closest member of Protection Detail, lifting his chin in Rylie's direction as soon as the bigger man in the tag team turned his way. "Please tell me either you or Trojan are staying sober enough to drive Chastity back to the hotel in a bit."

"Sorry, Red, we dropped the rental back at the hotel and Ubered here, assuming we'd each Uber back to the hotel on our own." Magnum grinned as he wagged his eyebrows at the women around him. "Or with some of our new friends."

Since he'd ridden to the party with Blade and Sawyer, knowing he'd have to Uber back to the hotel alone when they picked up ring rats for the night, he couldn't really say anything about Magnum and Trojan planning to do the same as their other single coworkers. But he really wished Rylie had planned better than he had, especially since she was obviously planning to drink a lot more than he intended to that night.

"I guess you're not as happily married as you claim," the redhead in the naughty nurse costume accused, jabbing his chest with her obviously fake, French manicured, long fingernail, "if you're not planning to spend the night with your wife."

Feck! Liam quickly thought on his feet, realizing he was going to have to get a lot closer to Rylie that night than he'd anticipated. "I never said I wasn't planning to ride with them. I just didn't know what the plan was for all of us getting back, since I had to catch a ride with a couple of the other guys because Chastity had a meeting with the powers that be in the GWA as part of Protection Detail before they could leave the arena tonight. Now, if you'll excuse me, I'm going to go join my wife, who will be Ubering back to the hotel with me later tonight."

By the time he weaved his way through the crowd to get to Rylie's side, she'd downed the purple and blue concoction that was her third drink. He would have thought it would take longer for all that alcohol to be absorbed into her system, but apparently, it worked faster than he expected, since she was already slurring her words as she acknowledged his presence.

"Na-na-na, nice of you to fine, fine, finally break away from your har-har-harumph of sluts to ack, ack, notice your wife, so we can sell our gimmick."

Did she just decide to change from "acknowledge" to "notice" because her brain is already so fried from the alcohol that she couldn't remember the word?

"What's a harumph of sluts?" Liam questioned, unable to keep from chuckling at her adorably drunk show of jealousy. *Too bad it's just because she thinks I wasn't trying to sell our gimmick marriage, and not real jealousy because she thinks I was flirting with those other women.*

"I think she means a harem of sluts," Emerald offered, grinning.

"Yeah, they're not my harem." Liam shook his head, looking around for a chair he could pull up to sit beside Rylie. "They just swarmed around me like bees while I was minding my own business and waiting for my beer."

Liam held up the beer in his hand, which he'd yet to take a drink of, to emphasize his point.

"Bitchy bees," Rylie giggled, reaching for a frozen fruity drink, which he hoped she wouldn't try to drink as fast as she'd downed the other three, so she wouldn't give herself brain freeze on top of being well on her way to a case of alcohol poisoning. "Buzz, buzz, buzz. Buzz off bitchy bees."

"Yeah, I think you might need to switch to water for a little while, Mo Ghrá." Liam intercepted the glass before she could wrap her lips around the straw, flagging down the waitress and requesting a couple bottles of water and an appetizer sampler platter.

"Hey, that's my drink," Rylie protested as he handed both her full fruity drink and his full beer bottle to the waitress to remove any alcohol from within her reach.

"I don't think it's yours anymore, Chas," Emerald consoled her, making sure to move her mostly full glass with a lime floating in it closer to Josh, so Rylie couldn't reach it. "But Red's ordered you something else, so you can quench your thirst in a minute when it gets here without drowning your liver in too much alcohol."

"But my libber likes too much alky-hall," Rylie whined.

"And I'd like my wife to not die of alcohol poisoning," Liam countered, squatting down to scoop Rylie up into his arms, so he could sit down in her chair with her on his lap, since he couldn't find another empty chair nearby. He knew he'd be fighting a hard-on the rest of the evening, especially if she kept squirming the way she was right then. But at least he'd be able to keep her from getting up to go to the bar, or reach for one of the other drinks at the table. *And hopefully, the water and food will help sober her up enough that I won't have to worry about needing to stay and watch over her once I get her back to her room later. 'Cause there's no way I want to take a chance on falling asleep in there and freaking her out when I wake up in the middle of one of the nightmares I've been having this week.*

Several of their friends gave him knowing looks, but they didn't say a word about him suddenly acting like the doting husband. Liam still recognized their approval, even though they didn't change the topics of discussion already going on around him to point it out.

As they all discussed the food options and whether or not they should eat before dancing or dance for a little while and then eat, Rylie finally settled down on his lap. She looped her right arm around his neck, reaching up with her left to play with his bowtie. "Why didn't you wear this on Saint Paddy's Day?"

"Because it wasn't in my wardrobe trunk back then," Liam lied, not wanting to admit to being so distracted by her joining the roster that he forgot to pull it out and change before they went to the Saint Patrick's Day party after the show in Baltimore back in March.

The suit had actually been part of his GWA wardrobe for years, but he hadn't worn it for promos, even on Saint Patrick's Day, since he'd started teaming up with Dion. Once they started teaming up full time, they'd had matching ring attire made, but it had all been in their chosen tag-team colors of red and black. Since Dion didn't have a green suit for them to be able to match, Liam hadn't asked the wardrobe department to put his in his trunk until earlier that year when he'd planned to wear it to the Saint Patrick's Day after-party. And since he didn't have his tag-team partner to coordinate a Halloween costume with this year, he'd opted to go with the leprechaun suit, so he didn't have to go shopping for a costume.

Damn, I should have suggested she wear the gold bodysuit she sometimes wears to wrestle, instead of coordinating her costume with the rest of Protection Detail. Even if we couldn't find a pot-o-gold costume for her to wear over it this time of year, the glittery gold outfit would have been enough to let everyone know she was dressed as my treasure. Of course, if we'd done that, then she'd probably figure out how I feel about her.

But maybe I should call her Mo Stór for our gimmick from now on? No, calling her "My Treasure" on TV would make my feelings for her just as blatantly obvious to my family as calling her Mo Ghrá.

Liam just hoped that his efforts to soak up some of the alcohol she'd already imbibed wouldn't sober her up enough to figure out exactly how he felt about her from how he planned on taking care of her the rest of the night.

Chapter Nine

Once they landed in San Diego, Josh drove Teagan thirty minutes north to meet his parents for lunch in his La Jolla neighborhood. He wasn't super nervous about the first time he'd officially present her as his wife, since his parents had actually met Teagan before at one of the many wrestling shows they'd attended over the years, along with everyone else on the GWA roster. But he was a little nervous about whether or not Teagan would like his great-grandmother's ring, which his mother was supposed to be bringing to him at the restaurant where they were meeting.

He'd actually had to talk his mom into agreeing that the heirloom ring was perfect for him to give his bride, since the large center stone wasn't a diamond. Yes, there were smaller diamonds set on either side of the emerald in the center. But since the ring he'd been thinking of was actually a cocktail ring that his great-grandmother had often worn on her right hand, and not an actual engagement ring, his mother had tried to talk him into using another heirloom wedding set instead. It wasn't until he reminded his mom that Teagan's ring name was Emerald that she finally understood his reasoning and agreed to have the ring cleaned and inspected to make sure it hadn't suffered any damage from wear and tear over the years.

Josh had actually been a little worried that if there was any damage, then the jeweler his mother took the ring to wouldn't have enough time to repair it before he got home to pick it up. But luckily, just a couple days after he'd first spoken to his mom about the ring, she'd called him back to let him know it was in pristine condition. Then he'd also had to figure out how to measure Teagan's ring size while she slept to make sure the ring was sized correctly to fit her. He just hoped that the chart, which he'd looked at online to give his mom the correct size based on the length of a string he'd wrapped around Teagan's finger, was accurate.

Fuck, it's gonna suck if it's still not a perfect fit and we have to get it resized again, Josh thought as he parked his seafoam green 2017 Chevrolet Colorado Z71 Hurley at the restaurant. *But if I give it to her as soon as we get to the house in a bit, then maybe we'll have time to stop at the jewelers to find matching bands and take care of any resizing before we have to be at the arena. Yeah, that'll work, even if we have to pick up the ring on the way out of town in the morning, so the jeweler has time to resize it again.*

Since the GWA had a house show that night, and not a live televised event, they were able to coordinate their schedule with the local time, instead of having to report to the arena three hours early to work the show and still be live on air in the Eastern time zone. That meant they had a full five hours free in the middle of the day between when they landed and when they had to report to the arena, which Josh hoped would be plenty of time to drive to and from La Jolla, have lunch with his parents, visit the jeweler, and still have time to christen some of the new furniture in his house with his wife.

"Are you sure we didn't need to stop by the house and freshen up before meeting your parents here?" Teagan looked nervous as he helped her down from the vehicle.

"Don't worry, Wifey," Josh assured her, brushing his lips over her temple as he placed his hand on the small of her back to escort her into the restaurant, and not bothering to remind her that he had to get the new override keys to be able to get into the house before setting up their biometrics in the new system. "You look beautiful. And your sexy dress doesn't have even a single wrinkle from the flight in from Phoenix. Well, other than the ones that are supposed to be there for that little ruffle thing."

Josh ignored the way she rolled her eyes at him, knowing that if anyone would notice if there was a wrinkle out of place, it would be him, since he'd struggled to keep his eyes on the road while driving, wishing he could continue examining every square fucking inch of her athletic curves in the stunningly sophisticated green sheath dress she'd chosen to wear that morning. She'd actually swapped it out the night before from her wardrobe trunk that the GWA costuming department kept stocked with different options for her to wear in the ring and during promos, specifically because she wanted to wear something different from the dozen or so business casual outfits she usually traveled in, when she officially met his parents as their daughter-in-law.

While the choker neckline didn't allow any kind of view of her cleavage, Josh loved the way the sleeveless dress showed off her sculpted shoulders and arms. And the tailored fit highlighted her silhouette beautifully, stopping at just the right point on her knees to keep her modestly covered while still giving him a decent view of her luscious long legs. *Fuck! I've gotta stop staring at my sinfully sexy woman, or I'm gonna walk up to the table with a boner. And my folks will never let me live it down if they notice I'm tenting my slacks.*

Thankfully, thinking about his mom and dad was the perfect antidote for the constant hard-on he sported whenever he was anywhere near Teagan, so he didn't have to be embarrassed when the hostess led them to the table, where his parents were already waiting for them.

Josh barely got his mouth open to reintroduce his wife to his parents before his mom jumped from her seat and practically tackled Teagan with her welcoming hug, her whimpered greeting coming out so softly that Josh couldn't comprehend it.

"Guess I don't have to make introductions after all," he chuckled, reaching out to shake his dad's hand, while Teagan awkwardly returned his mom's embrace, whispering her own greeting in return.

He was surprised to feel the ring box in his dad's palm, expecting it to be his mother who passed it along to him. But he supposed it probably worked better to get it from his dad while Teagan was distracted by his mom. He quickly put the box in his pocket before pulling out a chair for Teagan. "Alright, Mom, you've gotta let go of my bride, so we can actually sit down and eat before they kick us outta the restaurant for making a scene."

As soon as Connie released Teagan, she slipped around her to give Josh the same treatment she'd given his new wife, blubbering as she hugged him. "I'm just so excited to finally have a daughter, especially one who's so talented, beautiful, and strong enough to keep you in line."

"I think you mean daughter-in-law, not daughter," Josh chuckled as he hugged his mom. "Since I'm your son, you calling her your daughter makes me sound like some kind of creep for marrying my sister."

"Oh, stop." Connie lightly slapped Josh's arm as she pulled out of his embrace to go back to her seat, wiping away what he assumed were happy tears as she rounded the table. "You're the only one who thinks anything weird like that." She turned to specifically address Teagan as she continued while they all took their seats. "I mean, seriously, daughter or daughter-in-law, the feelings are the same regardless of whether the relationship is biological or by marriage, so why bother making a distinction in the titles?"

"I don't know," his dad interjected with a smirk as he crossed his arms over his chest and leaned back in his chair. "If Josh keeps making things weird, maybe we should claim Teagan as our daughter and him as our son-in-law."

"I suppose we could do that." Connie tilted her head as if deep in thought. "But I'm not sure Teagan's parents will appreciate us trying to pawn Josh off on them."

"It's just my mom, and considering how well they got along when we were in Baltimore last month, I'm sure she won't mind the trade," Teagan chimed in with a smile and a shrug.

"Yeah, she's already said I can call her Mama Pam, so I'm sure she'll claim me, even if you guys don't anymore," Josh teased, draping his arm around Teagan's shoulders, so she couldn't punch him for the lie.

"She told you to call her Pam instead of Ms. Shields," Teagan protested, turning her head to glare at him. "*Mama* was never mentioned that day."

"Yeah, but since I have two moms now, I figured I have to differentiate them somehow," Josh joked, smirking as he watched his mom from the corner of his eye to see her reaction to his next words. "So, I figured I'd have Mama Pam and Mama Connie, so they'll know which one of them I'm talking to whenever we get the whole family together for holidays."

He was happy to see his mom's lips turn up in an affable smile.

"You mean like Aiken calls one of her dads Papa and the other Daddio?" Teagan arched an eyebrow at him, but she couldn't hide the slight upturn of her lips that let him know he was amusing her.

"Exactly," Josh nodded, grinning widely.

"I can live with Mama Connie," his mom agreed, picking up her menu and waving it back and forth to point to both Josh and Teagan. "But I expect both of you to use it from now on."

"But you can both stick to calling me Dad," Cole asserted, uncrossing his arms to also pick up his menu, though he only directed his next comment to Josh. "If I hear a single *Daddy Cole*, I'm disowning you."

Josh was glad they hadn't even ordered their drinks yet, knowing if he'd just taken a sip, he'd have spit it across the table as soon as he heard the way his dad emphasized the words "Daddy Cole" by raising his voice a few octaves to sound more feminine. "Yeah, I'll leave that one for Mom…Mama Connie."

Damn, it's gonna be hard to remember to call her anything but Mom. Hopefully, she won't come up with any of her crazy, off-the-wall punishments for me if I screw it up all the time.

While his father lightly chuckled and shook his head, his mother just rolled her eyes at him before opening her menu and changing the subject. "So, since I had to pick out all new furniture for your house, I hope you don't mind that I redesigned all the upstairs bedrooms as kids' rooms. Don't worry, I left your office space downstairs as an office for now. But I think once you decide to start having babies, you'll probably want to swap it and the nursery space, so you'll be on the same floor until the kids are a little older."

Fuck! I should have let Cal take care of refurnishing the house, Josh realized as he felt Teagan stiffen under his arm at the mention of them having babies. *But I was too busy thinking about how Mom would be better at dealing with Sarah, and it never even crossed my mind that she might use this opportunity to start pushing for grandbabies.*

"You didn't need to do that," he groaned, removing his arm from around his wife, and picking up his menu as the server approached their table. "But I guess it's fine if you just put twin beds upstairs for now. That'll keep the guys from wanting to crash with us whenever we're in town, so we can enjoy the honeymoon phase of our relationship for the next few years."

Thankfully the server arrived to take their orders then, so any discussion of when they might start a family was tabled. Josh just hoped he could keep his mother from bringing it up again later. He, at least, wanted to have the opportunity to talk one on one with Teagan about her thoughts on having kids, and what kind of timeline she had in mind for having them to lessen the impact of being pregnant and giving birth on her wrestling career, before discussing their potential children with their parents.

While he would be happy with however many children she wanted to have, and whenever she wanted to have them, Josh and Teagan hadn't really discussed the topic yet. Well, other than the very brief discussion they had in bed one night about continuing to use two forms of birth control, just to make sure they didn't have an oops baby while she was at the high point in her career. *Hell, for all I know, she might not want kids at all. Or maybe she'd rather keep wrestling until we're both too old to have babies, and then adopt some older kids once we retire.*

Knowing he'd be happy as long as he still had Teagan as his wife, no matter what she decided about children, he pushed those thoughts aside and ordered lunch. As soon as the server walked away, he changed the subject once again, hoping he wasn't opening a different can of worms by doing so. "So, if you've furnished more than just the master bedroom and main floor living space, I guess that means the cleanup is all done. Did you have any problems with the Nashes when you filled them in on what happened?"

"No, not at all." Josh's dad shook his head. "In fact, Bill insisted on covering all the cleanup, repair, and replacement costs for everything. He now has Sarah working in his office to reimburse him."

"And Kelly insisted she move back home, where she has to abide by the same rules she had as a teenager, until she's fully paid them back and grown up enough to be trusted living on her own again," his mom added.

"I really don't see how they'll be able to control a twenty-four-year-old woman like that," Teagan scoffed, shaking her head and looking rather irritated. "I mean, that's the same age I was when I joined the

GWA, and I certainly didn't listen when my mom tried to talk me out of a career in wrestling. So, I know there's no way I'd have moved back in with her at that age."

"Yeah, but you wouldn't have thrown a temper tantrum and destroyed someone else's property the way she did either," Josh pointed out.

"And with the security cameras catching some of her tirade, she really only had two choices," Cole added, just as their drinks were delivered. "Move home, see a therapist, and work off the damages, or spend up to three years in jail and pay restitution plus up to fifty-thousand dollars in fines."

"Whoa! I thought vandalism was a misdemeanor, and she'd only get a slap on the wrist or maybe some community service." The sentence his dad had just laid out for what Sarah had done shocked Josh. "And I thought the security cameras you put on the house were all outside. How'd they catch some of what she did when it was mostly breaking knickknacks and stuff throughout the house?"

"It's only a misdemeanor if the total amount of the damages is under four-hundred dollars," Connie explained. "But if the damages are over four-hundred dollars then it can be charged as either a misdemeanor or a felony, depending on the other circumstances of the case. And anything over ten-thousand dollars in damages is automatically a felony, and Sarah went way over that."

"And you're right. We only installed outdoor cameras when we put in your security system. But when she finished using a butcher knife on all the indoor furniture, she went outside to do the same to the patio chairs." Cole's expression made it clear how stupid he thought Sarah had been for not remembering the cameras were motion activated. "And she made several trips back and forth from inside, trying to fill the pool with the stuffing from all the pillows and couch cushions, so it was very clear that her path of destruction wasn't limited to what was caught on camera."

Holy shit! Why didn't any of them mention anything about her using a butcher knife before now? I thought she just broke whatever she could by throwing it across the room, or maybe bought a can of spray paint to deface the furniture and bigger stuff she couldn't break with her bare hands.

"Don't worry, dear," Connie cooed, reaching over to pat Teagan's hand reassuringly. "I replaced the whole set of chef's knives in the kitchen, even though the police only confiscated the one she left stabbed into the bed in the master as evidence."

Teagan's eyes widened as she turned to glower at Josh, clearly as worried by what his parents were saying as he now felt. "Are you sure we didn't need to keep one of those security teams with us while we're in town?"

Fuck! Maybe we shoulda kept talking about us having babies, Josh thought, suddenly worried that he shouldn't have listened to his dad's reassurances that Sarah wouldn't turn into another psycho stalker like the guy who'd injured Dion a couple weeks ago. *At least when babies were brought up, she just stiffened up a little, and didn't look like she's scared outta her mind like she does now.*

"I mean, I'm more than confident I can defend myself if she shows up unarmed and tries something stupid to sabotage us," Teagan continued, morphing into her fearless, badass Emerald character before his eyes. "But none of my wrestling training covered how to disarm someone carrying a weapon like a butcher knife. And even though I love watching shows like **Criminal Minds**, **NCIS**, and **FBI**, you know I'm sitting there telling the victims not to do something stupid to put themselves in danger. And now I'm thinking that going in your house, where a crazy bitch cut up your furniture with a butcher knife, without a bodyguard, might be doing something stupid to put both of us in danger."

Yeah, maybe we should have Dad check out the house or call in a bodyguard team, if he has any available. And maybe give me a refresher course on the self-defense stuff he taught me back when I was a kid and he'd first started Parker Security Systems.

"Oh, dear," Connie exclaimed, bringing her hand to her chest in a show of stress. "I think we might have given you the wrong impression of Sarah by mentioning what she used on the furniture." She cut her eyes to Josh before questioning him further. "Didn't you tell Teagan about all this when it first happened?"

"Yeah, I told her the same thing Cal told me," Josh defended his description of the damages as he reached out and grasped Teagan's hand, hoping to comfort his obviously upset wife. "That she tore up our marriage license and left it among the rubble of what she destroyed. But nobody ever sent me any pictures, so I figured she'd thrown breakable shit at the walls or whatever, maybe dumped out the actual trashcan in the middle of the living room, or spray painted derogatory messages everywhere. But I didn't know anything about her using a butcher knife on the furniture. If I had, I'd have taken it as more of a threat, and probably would have insisted on pressing charges, as well as hiring a security detail for while we're in town. Especially after almost losing a friend to a psycho stalker just a couple weeks ago."

"I'm sorry. I thought Cal already sent you copies of the photos the police took," Cole apologized, shaking his head. "And I never even thought to ask if you wanted a copy of the surveillance tape. But after seeing all kinds of cases like this over the years, when I've had to work with the cops to give them video evidence, I'm positive that Sarah only used what was easily available at the time, and wasn't trying to send any kind of threat that she'd attempt to stab either of you. You just didn't have any spray paint in the house, so she couldn't graffiti up the place."

Josh felt a little better after hearing his dad's professional opinion, especially since Cole had clearly watched the video of Sarah when she was in the middle of her tirade to be able to fully comprehend her actions. But since he hadn't told Teagan about his dad's full background and had only glossed over the family business as an alarm and security camera installation service provider, he wasn't sure Teagan felt the same.

"But even though that was my initial impression," Cole continued, "after you told me about Allissa being attacked and Dion being injured, I went over and had another talk with Bill, Kelly, and Sarah. I specifically pointed out how her use of a knife could be construed as a threat against your lives, and made it clear that if she comes within a hundred feet of either of you, the deal will be off and charges will be pressed. Bill assured me then that she'll basically be on house arrest while you're in town and would be constantly supervised until the psychiatrist they hired deemed her issues under control."

His dad stopped talking as their meals were delivered to the table, but continued as soon as the server walked away. "But if it'll make you feel better, I can have a couple of my guys go clear your house and shadow you for the rest of your time in town."

"Your guys?" Teagan tilted her head curiously as she cut into her salmon, appearing a little less trepidatious than she had previously.

"Yeah, Dad owns Parker Security Services," Josh explained, picking up one of his fish tacos.

"You told me that," Teagan stated after swallowing her first bite. "But I thought you said they install alarm systems and security cameras. You didn't mention anything about him being able to provide bodyguards, which is why I thought we should've had the Avington guys come with today since they're already at the arena."

"Yeah, we don't do as much personal security as Byron's group does, but I've got a few guys I can call in when we get a special request for it," Cole clarified.

"Wait, you know Byron Avington?" Teagan looked at Josh's dad, surprised by that tidbit of information.

"Yeah, we were SEALs together back in the day," Cole chuckled. "And the security field is kinda close knit, so we have a solid network to refer clients to when they move or if they have needs we don't typically cover. So, when I decided I was getting too old to put up with being shot at and wanted to focus more on the technological aspects of home and corporate security, I started referring a lot of the bodyguard and armed security guard jobs to Byron. In return, he refers tech installs to us, and if he gets a job that needs both, then we work together to meet all the client's needs."

Teagan turned and chopped Josh's chest. "All this time, you made me think you were just gonna have your pacifist mama try to keep Sarah from spreading rumors online by shaming her like a bad puppy, when you were really having your badass SEAL dad put the fear of God in her."

"Ouch!" Josh rubbed his sore pec from her epic, Ric Flair–esque chop. *Guess I should have told her more about my family, instead of letting her think we're all pacifists. I mean, yeah, we'd rather try to make peace first before jumping into a fight, but we're not hippies or true pacifists, so she probably should have known that.*

"Oh, I did threaten to post pictures of her cleaning up the house like those pet-shaming photos all over social media," Connie chuckled. "But I didn't have to actually do it because she turned over her phone, laptop, and cloud passwords, so Cole could wipe all copies of the marriage certificate from her accounts."

"Yeah, we knew Dad had wiped it from her stuff," Josh reminded them. "'Cause he called to let me know he kept a copy on his computer, and asked before sending it to Cal, so he could add Tea to all my accounts and will and stuff."

Now that they knew they didn't have to worry about Sarah being a threat to them while they were in town, Josh could feel Teagan relaxing beside him. Their conversation turned to lighter topics, like the possibility of the four of them going surfing early the next morning. Teagan made it clear that she'd gladly come watch Josh and his parents surf, but she'd rather lay out on the beach than get in the water, especially since she wouldn't have time to take out her braids to wash the saltwater out of her hair, do the various oil and deep conditioning treatments her hair needed after being in braids for the last month, and still make it to the plane in time for their flight to Los Angeles.

I wonder if she wraps her hair up like she does before a shower when she doesn't want to get it wet, and then wears a hooded wetsuit, would she still have to take the braids out to get all the salt out of her hair? Or could she just do the gentle braid wash like I've seen her do in the shower? Or would she have to wear a drysuit to be certain she didn't get her hair wet at all? I know we don't normally wear them for surfing, but maybe she'd still have the range of motion in one to surf, as long as she doesn't fall off the board and have to swim in all those heavy layers. I'll have to ask her later which she might want to try. And maybe plan a stop at the surf shop to buy her a wetsuit while we're already out going to the jewelers for wedding bands.

~~~

Teagan was a lot more relaxed when they left the restaurant than she'd felt on the way there. Having met Josh's parents before, she should have known she had nothing to worry about, but she'd still been a little nervous that they wouldn't accept her as Josh's wife, even though she had no idea why she'd been afraid they wouldn't like her. When Connie greeted her with tears of joy as she welcomed her to the family, though, Teagan soon relaxed, enjoying feeling included in the
~~~

lighthearted banter she'd previously only witnessed between Josh and his parents whenever they visited at a GWA show.

She'd also appreciated how Connie and Cole both tried to set her mind at ease when they were discussing the Sarah situation. She still didn't agree with the decision not to press charges for the vandalism of Josh's house. But since her name wasn't on the deed to the property, she supposed she didn't really get a say in the matter. *Although, maybe my name is on the deed now. At least, that's kind of what Josh implied when he mentioned sending a copy of our marriage certificate to his attorney. I should probably clarify what all he added me to, so I can find someone in Maryland to add Josh to all my stuff, too. Can the entertainment attorney I've had review my contracts do all that? Or will I need to find an attorney who specializes in some other area of the law? Unless, maybe Josh's attorney can do it all from here?*

She hadn't thought about needing to do anything with her bank accounts, property deed, or anything else before, thinking she needed to wait a little while to make sure she and Josh could make their marriage work long term before changing all that stuff. She hadn't even thought about changing her last name on anything either, but now she supposed she should probably talk to her husband, so they could decide on their next steps together.

As she watched her in-laws pull up beside her and Josh in the driveway of his peach and gray craftsman style home, so Cole could clear it for her peace of mind, Teagan wondered if she should bring any of that legal stuff up once Josh's parents left. Or if she should talk to Josh about his feelings for Sarah first. The fact that he still didn't want to press charges against her, even after hearing the full extent of what she'd done, made Teagan leery about whether or not her husband was capable of being all in when it came to their marriage.

Oh, she knew Josh cared about her. And she definitely knew that he lusted for her. But no matter what her friends had told her they overheard a couple weeks back about him being in love with her, she just had a bad feeling about how open his heart was to falling in love with her because she was afraid Sarah might already own at least part of his heart. Which totally sucked, since she knew she was totally head over heels in love with Josh.

"Hang tight," Josh instructed, squeezing her hand before lifting it to his mouth to brush his lips over the back. He then got out of the vehicle and joined his dad a few feet away at the tailgate of the truck.

Teagan couldn't hear what was said before Cole walked away from Josh to go in through the front gate, instead of opening the garage door in front of them and entering the house that way. Josh then walked around to the passenger side of his parents' Lexus RX Hybrid and leaned his arms on the passenger door to talk to his mom through the open window. Teagan could see Connie holding up her cell phone for Josh to see something on her screen, but from her position in Josh's truck, she couldn't see but part of the back of the phone in Connie's hand and had no idea what they were viewing.

Based on the stern expression on Josh's handsome face, however, Teagan couldn't imagine it was anything good. *Surely, she's not showing him the security footage Cole mentioned at lunch, right? Not without me right there to see it, too.*

Teagan unbuckled her seatbelt, opening the door to the truck to get out and go see for herself. "What are you guys watching?"

Josh met her at the back of his parents' Lexus RX Hybrid before she even made it halfway around to where he'd been standing. "Not watching anything," Josh sighed as he wrapped his arms around her, preventing her from getting close enough to see Connie's phone screen. "Mom just did a quick video call with Kelly Nash to verify that Sarah is still on house arrest."

"And why aren't you letting me see this proof for myself?" Teagan gripped the sides of his waist, trying to push him out of her way.

"Because it was uncomfortable enough having to listen to her apology," Josh groaned, tightening his hold so she couldn't get away. "We don't need to make it worse by you going all Emerald Stone and cutting a scathing promo on her."

Teagan was torn between feeling elated that he knew her so well that he could predict exactly what she'd have done, and feeling dejected because he hadn't wanted her by his side when he confronted the other woman. Considering all her earlier thoughts about the possibility of Josh having feelings for Sarah, unfortunately, she was leaning toward the latter.

Obviously, she means more to him than he's letting on. Why else wouldn't he want us to present a united front to show her that our marriage is solid and squash her delusions about breaking us up so she can be with him?

Even though she wanted to confront him about how he really felt about Sarah right then, Teagan held back, not wanting to give her in-laws the impression that she was a hothead. Oh, she knew she was easily riled up and prone to hotheaded behavior, but she didn't think the Parkers needed to see that side of her so soon. If she and Josh were going to have any kind of chance of staying together long term, she needed to stay in his parents' good graces as long as possible. Or at least until after the Sarah situation was fully behind them and Teagan felt more secure in Josh's feelings for her.

Thankfully, Cole returned then, letting them know the house was clear before handing the new override keys to Josh, and having them each scan in their fingerprints into a handheld device that was apparently linked to Josh's house somehow, so they'd be able to use the new keyless entry system. They said their "goodbyes" to his parents before Josh surprised her by scooping her up into his arms bridal style right there in the middle of the driveway.

"Josh! What are you doing?" Teagan screeched, instinctually wrapping her arms around his neck.

"Carrying my bride over the threshold." Josh grinned as he jogged down the sidewalk, through the archway that led into his yard, and all the way up to his coral colored front door, which his father had apparently left unlocked so Josh would have an easy time taking her through it without even having to stop to scan one of their fingerprints on the new lock. "It is tradition, after all. And yeah, I know I probably should have done this when we were in Baltimore, too. But I figured I lost my chance to do it right, when I didn't do it the first time we walked in your house 'cause we hadn't seen the certificate yet to know, for sure, we were officially married."

Teagan almost forgot all her earlier worries as she enjoyed her husband's playful side coming out as he kicked the door closed behind them. He only paused his playfulness momentarily to lift her legs up a little higher so he could arm the alarm and relock the front door. Then he was right back to his happy-go-lucky self as he carried her through the foyer that opened up into an open-plan living and dining room space, which almost mirrored the layout of hers back in Baltimore. The difference being that when someone walked into her home, they entered straight into the space to see the dining room and kitchen on the left with the living room space on the right, but when someone entered Josh's home, they entered the great room from the foyer with the living room directly in front of them, the dining room on the right, and the kitchen tucked in beside the foyer. If they'd had similar design styles, she'd have felt like she was entering a larger version of her space back home from the hallway that led to the stairs and bedrooms.

Their design styles weren't the same, though, which was quite evident as Josh spun her around to give her a three-hundred-and-sixty-degree view. Where she stuck to neutral browns and grays accented with white trim, Josh's home had more of a beachy feel. He still accented the space with white trim and built-in bookshelves, but the walls in the great room were more peach in tone to match the outside of the house. He also had various accent pieces in ocean blue and seafoam green, which were probably what gave her the feeling that he, or more likely his mom, was trying to coordinate the space with the view of the ocean out the glass-paned doors that appeared to be able to fold completely open all along the back wall.

She had to admit that she was impressed with the ocean view from the back of his house, only turning away from it when Josh finished his quick jaunt around the room by sitting down with her on his lap on a white sofa, which faced the stone fireplace on the left side of the room with a big screen television above it.

"I know I should probably go get our stuff outta the truck and show you around the place, but now that we're finally alone, I can't wait another minute to kiss you, Wifey." Josh cradled her face in his hands as he pressed his lips to hers.

Teagan couldn't resist momentarily giving in and kissing him back. But her trepidation about Josh's feelings for Sarah derailing her future with him was just too great for even his passionate kiss to completely wipe from her mind. Considering how his kisses normally cleared her head of all conscious thoughts about anything but making love with him, she was more than a little concerned about the power of her fears.

"Wait, we need to talk before we get too carried away." Teagan broke off the kiss, pushing off on Josh's chest as she tried to stand from his lap.

"Talking is overrated," Josh protested, gripping her hips to hold her in place. "But if you insist, I'll only agree as long as you stay right where you are, so we can get back to the kissing as soon as the talking is over."

"Josh, this is serious." Teagan shook her head, not wanting to risk getting carried away on a wave of lust and not being able to adequately express her thoughts. "I need some distance from you to be able to say what I need to say."

"And I need you as my touchstone to be able to get through any serious discussions," Josh argued, smirking sexily in an obvious attempt to convince her not to get up off his lap.

Is that why he kept holding my hand or discreetly touching me all through lunch earlier? And why he does the same during all our pre-show meetings with the rest of the GWA since we found out we're married and decided to try to make it work?

"Well, since I can't let you distract me with your dick poking into my hip, we're going to have to compromise," Teagan suggested, pointing to the sofa cushion beside where Josh was sitting, where her heels were currently resting. "How about I sit there and you can hold my hand for a touchstone?"

"I don't suppose it matters that I like distracting you with my dick?" Josh arched an eyebrow at her, but he released his grip on her to finally let her stand as he huffed out his acquiescence. "Fine, you can sit over there for now. But once this conversation is over, I fully intend to have you back on my lap. Only without our clothes in the way, so you can straddle me properly."

God, I hope you still want that after this conversation, Teagan thought as she moved to sit beside him on the sofa.

Once she was seated, Josh reached over and clasped her hand, smiling and wagging his eyebrows suggestively. "So, what's so important that we have to talk about it before we get started christening all our new furniture?"

"Is that why Sarah destroyed your old stuff?" Teagan unintentionally blurted, too appalled at the thought of Josh and Sarah fucking on the sofa that used to sit in the very same spot they were in right then to delicately ease into the conversation the way she'd planned. "Because you'd christened it all with her?"

"Oh, God, no!" Josh's face contorted in disgust, which might have helped ease some of Teagan's jealousy, at least a little. "I've told you, I only ever thought of Sarah as Ben's little sister, and a half-decent assistant. We were never even close enough to share a friendly hug, so there's no way we'd ever do anything even remotely similar to the images I'm sure you're conjuring in your mind."

"Then why won't you press charges against her?" Even though he seemed so adamant that he wasn't ever attracted to Sarah, Teagan couldn't fathom there was any reason other than having feelings for her that might justify his not wanting to prosecute her for destroying his home. "After hearing just how crazy she went, cutting up all your old furniture and leaving a butcher knife stabbed into your bed, the only reason that makes sense for you not wanting to press charges is that you have feelings for her. And if you…" Teagan couldn't say the L word she was thinking, not when she was talking about Josh and another woman. "…care so much about her, then I don't know that there's enough room left in your heart for me. So, it makes me wonder if we should even bother trying to make our marriage work."

"Oh, Tea," Josh sighed, shaking his head before pulling her hand up to his lips and kissing the back of it. "It's precisely because I don't care about her that makes me indifferent about whether she's punished or not. Just as long as she leaves us alone, her existence on this planet means nothing to me. And I figured the fastest way to get her to leave us alone is to just drop it, which is exactly what I did on that call a while ago."

"But if you talked to her and let her apologize, you didn't really drop it," Teagan disagreed, even though she wasn't completely certain what had transpired on that call.

"I didn't speak to her, though," Josh elaborated, squeezing her hand. "Mom turned the phone to show me that Sarah is at her parents' place in Catalina. And when she saw me on the screen, she started apologizing. But then I saw you getting out of the truck and walked away without saying a word to her."

"Oh." Teagan wasn't sure how to respond to the new information Josh was imparting. On the one hand, she was thrilled that Josh had basically walked away without giving Sarah the time of day. Hearing that made it clear her fear that Josh had feelings for Sarah was completely unfounded. But on the other hand, she was worried that him ignoring Sarah might cause the crazy woman to try something else to get his attention. "You don't think you not even acknowledging her apology will set her off to try something else, do you?"

"No, I don't," Josh reassured her. "Ignoring her shows we couldn't care less about her. But pressing charges now might just show her she's getting to us enough that she'd want to escalate the situation even further. Trust me, washing our hands of this situation and letting Dad keep an eye on things from now on is the best way to handle it."

"Okay," Teagan conceded, hoping he was right.

"Now, let's get on to the more important topic," Josh smirked as he slid off the sofa to get down on one knee, releasing her right hand to take her left instead. "You, my dear Teagan, don't have to worry about sharing space in my heart with anyone else. Well, maybe a little with Mom and Dad, and any kids we might decide to have in the future. But you, Teagan Zira Shields-Parker, are the only woman I have any romantic feelings for. I'm in love with you, and only you, now and forevermore."

Teagan was so shocked by him declaring his love that it took her a moment to realize what he was doing, when Josh reached into his pants' pocket with his right hand, pulling out a little black box, which he deftly opened one-handed to present her with an exquisite emerald and diamond ring. The square-cut emerald was the main stone, with two smaller but still fairly large round-cut diamonds on either side of it, all set atop a gold band.

"Oh, Josh," Teagan gasped, covering her mouth with her right hand, and really hoping he intended to place that gorgeous ring on her left ring finger.

"I know neither of us remember our wedding night well enough to be sure, but since the pictures show we used Chastity's rings, I'm pretty sure we skipped the whole proposal part of the process. So, I figured we should have a bit of a do-over. I would have done this last month when we first found out we're married, but I had to wait 'til we were here so I can give you this ring. It was my great-grandmother's, my mom's grandma's, ring that I remember her wearing often when I was a little boy. It wasn't her engagement ring, but I always thought it looked nicer than her wedding set. And now I know that's because I've always had a thing for Emerald Stone, even a good twenty-plus years before I met her."

Teagan chuckled at the sweet but sappy way he incorporated her ring name into his proposal with an emerald ring.

"So, my beautiful bride, the woman of my dreams, who I love with all my heart, will you stay married to me, forever and always?"

"Yes, Josh, my handsome hubby, the man I love more than mere words can express," Teagan gushed, nodding her head as she spread her fingers to give him room to put the ring on her finger. "Yes, I'll stay married to you, forever and always."

Josh slipped the ring out of the box, dropping the box to the floor so it was out of his way as he slipped the ring on her finger. Teagan was surprised to see that it was a perfect fit. As soon as the ring was in place, Josh lifted his hands to her face once more, holding her in the position he preferred as he sealed their bond with a passionate kiss.

Teagan wrapped her arms around her husband, returning the ardent expression of their love lick for lick. She finally allowed the drugging quality of Josh's kiss to wipe all other thoughts from her mind, relishing the feeling of being in their bubble of nirvana, where only the two of them existed. When he broke off the kiss to speak once more, it took her a moment to comprehend his words.

"I was thinking that after we officially consummate our marriage now that you're wearing my ring, we might leave here an hour or so earlier than we need to leave to get to the arena on time, and stop at the jewelers to pick out matching wedding bands."

When his words sank into her brain, Teagan couldn't help but chuckle. "Yeah, I think we've already consummated our marriage about fifty times over. But if you think this time will be the *official consummation*, we should probably do it in a bed."

Since they only made love in a bed about half the time, often opting to find creative locations at the various arenas where they had shows, or utilizing all the various surfaces in their hotel rooms, especially the bathrooms, traditional sex in a bed was kind of a novelty for them. But if they were going to recreate the traditional events they'd missed out doing on their wedding night, then Teagan thought wedding night sex should be in a bed.

"Naw," Josh disagreed, unzipping the back of her dress. "Our first time in each of our homes needs to be on the couch. And if you think it has to be in our bed to be the *official consummation*, then we should probably save that for tonight when we get back from the show, when we have our wedding bands on, too."

Teagan couldn't argue his logic as Josh peeled her dress down her arms, exposing her lace Capri Sea green, Sexy Tee Wireless Bandeau Bralette from Victoria's Secret. Especially when he trailed his lips down her neck, stopping periodically to lightly suck on her skin as he worked his way down to the top of her bra.

Yeah, I suppose we should have a do-over of our first time, Teagan decided as she started working the buttons on Josh's emerald green button-down, which matched her outfit, as soon as her arms were free of the dress. *So I can let him take the lead this time, and see how many more orgasms I could have had back then if I hadn't tried to run the show. And at least, if he rips off the thong that matches this bra, I won't have as hard a time picking up a replacement as I am with the La Perla panties he ripped off me in New Orleans.*

As soon as she had his shirt unbuttoned and tugged free of his black slacks, Josh shrugged it off. Then he unclasped her bra, dropping it on the floor with his shirt and the ring box. He showered her breasts with his oral affection, even as he gripped her hips and lifted her up until they were both standing beside the sofa. He pushed her dress and her panties down her legs, while Teagan worked on unbuckling his belt and unfastening his pants. She shoved his pants down, taking his boxer briefs with them, not thinking about him needing to get a condom from his wallet before losing them.

Josh toed off his shoes and socks as he lifted her in his arms, spinning around to retake his original seat on the sofa with her straddling his lap, and continuously worshiping her breasts with his mouth. The fact that she still had her strappy green stiletto sandals on, the same way she'd left her shoes on the first time they made love at her house, wasn't lost on her.

"Oh, Josh," Teagan moaned, arching her back from the exquisite feel of him sucking and lightly biting her nipples. She rapidly lost control of her body, grinding her pussy over his shaft with wild abandon as she ran her fingers through his shaggy blond hair. "Please, I need you."

Obviously understanding what she needed, Josh slid one hand from her hip to cover her ass, lightly teasing between her cheeks with his middle finger. He also moved his other hand from her opposite hip, bringing it between them to stroke her clit with his thumb while pushing two fingers inside her.

He spread her arousal from her dripping wet opening in both directions, coating both her clit and her puckered back hole. Teagan hadn't ever wanted to experiment with back door action before. But she couldn't deny how Josh's light teasing back there made her feel decadently dirty in the most carnal and hedonistic way.

Teasing her tightest opening, combined with the way he was finger-fucking her pussy, stroking her clit, and sucking on her tits, Josh took practically no time at all to work Teagan up to her first climax of the afternoon.

"Oh, yes, Josh, Josh, Josh," Teagan panted repeatedly as the waves of euphoria washed over her.

"Fuck, Tea," Josh groaned, barely lifting his mouth from her breast. "I love making you come."

As soon as she started to come down from her orgasmic high, Teagan ran her hands down over his strong pecs and the ripples of his muscular abs, wanting to tease him a little with a hand job before she finally got him inside her. "I want to make you come, too, Hubby."

"Oh, fuck, yeah," Josh voraciously agreed, gripping her hips once more to slide her down his thighs, so they could both watch as she wrapped her hands around his thick dick.

She wasn't sure how much of the moisture on his cock was his precum, and how much was her cream that had dripped down to coat him. But either way, she appreciated the lubrication as she squeezed and stroked his cock with her right hand while lightly rubbing his balls with her left.

"Swap hands, Wifey," Josh commanded, not taking his eyes off the action to look her in the face while he gave the order. "I wanna see the ring that shows your mine on the hand jerking me off."

Teagan did as she was told, no longer surprised by how much wetter she got every time his voice deepened to that bossy tone. She didn't have as much grip strength in her left hand as she did in her right, but Josh didn't seem to mind that the pressure lightened when she switched hands, obviously getting off more on seeing that ring on her hand while she stroked him than from how tightly she squeezed his cock. To be honest, she also relished catching a glimpse of her ring every time she moved her hand up to cover just the head of his dick.

"Fuck, that's so hot," Josh gutturally grunted, reaching up to play with her breasts, while she kept stroking his cock.

Teagan unconsciously rocked her hips, needing the friction of rubbing her pussy on his thigh.

"Fuck, I love how responsive you are, Tea. I barely touched your tits to get your greedy pussy humping my leg."

"I need your big dick in that greedy pussy," Teagan purred, eager to be stretched open and filled by his girthy cock.

"Hmmm, we'll get to that eventually, Wifey," Josh mewled, lifting her off his lap and twisting to lay on his back on the sofa. "But first I need to eat your pussy and fuck your mouth. Now show me what a good wife you are by sitting on my face while you suck my cock."

"Yes, Sir," Teagan cooed, quickly moving to straddle his head as she bent to wrap her lips around the bulbous crown of his cock. Since she didn't think he could see what she was doing while licking her pussy, she wrapped her right hand around the base of his shaft to stroke the half of his dick that wouldn't fit in her mouth, and went back to using her left to play with his balls, not wanting to risk squeezing them too hard with her dominant hand while in the throes of the orgasm she was sure Josh was about to give her.

Josh didn't waste any time giving her further instructions, gripping the globes of her ass in his hands to hold her in place while he devoured her. He ravenously ate her out, alternating between licking, sucking, and fucking her with his tongue until he worked her up once more.

Teagan enjoyed his oral affection so much that she had a hard time focusing on what she was doing, coming close to choking when she tried to swallow more than half of his eight-plus-inch length as the inner walls of her pussy clamped down on his tongue. She vaguely recognized the need to back off and breathe as she spasmed and writhed, soaring over the edge for the second time.

Josh knew exactly how to take care of her to prolong the orgasm, not stopping until she was totally spent and collapsed on top of him with his cock still in her mouth. "Fuck, Teagan," he groaned, somehow picking her up and flipping her around, so she ended up on her back on the sofa. "I can't wait any longer."

Teagan felt like a rag doll, limp and unable to move on her own as she recovered. But she somehow mustered the energy to speak. "Yes, Josh, need you now."

"I'm all yours, Teagan Parker," Josh smiled, wrapping her legs around his waist, and leaning down to kiss her as he sheathed his cock in her pussy. He worked his way inside her slowly, allowing her plenty of time to stretch around his girthy erection without feeling even the slightest twinge of pain. Once he filled her to the hilt, he broke the kiss to growl, "And you're all mine."

"Oh, yes, Josh," Teagan agreed, wrapping her arms around her husband now that she'd caught her second wind. "All yours."

What started out as slow and sensual lovemaking soon turned into a passionately primal mating, with their bodies instinctually syncing up the rhythm of their gyrating hips. Teagan lost all track of time as Josh took her up and over the edge several more times before finally joining her in a synchronized climax. They cried out each other's names as their bodies convulsed in their mutual pleasure, with each ripple of her pussy milking a spurt of his cum from his cock.

It didn't take long after Josh pulled out of her to collapse beside her, so he didn't squash her into the sofa, for her to realize that they'd forgotten a condom. As they were regularly tested for everything as part of their jobs with the GWA, Teagan knew they were both S.T.I. free. And since she was on the pill, she didn't think they had to worry about an unplanned pregnancy either, so she wasn't too concerned at the realization. Well, other than worrying slightly about how to clean their cum stains off the brand new white sofa.

"Um, Josh, do you know if you have any upholstery cleaner here?"

"No clue." Josh pushed up on his elbow to look down into her eyes. "Why?"

"Because I think we just christened your brand new sofa with a fairly big cum stain."

Josh sat up then, looking down between her legs. "Fuck! I forgot a condom!"

"It's fine," Teagan assured him, reaching out to take the hand he wasn't running through his hair in hers. "We know we're both clean, and I'm still on the pill, so I don't think we have anything to worry about. Well, other than possibly damaging the sofa cushion."

"But we said we should still use two forms of birth control, since neither of them are one-hundred percent effective." Josh looked frantic, making her worry that he might not want kids. Thankfully, he quickly quashed her fears as he continued rambling. "As much as I want us to have a family in the future, I don't want to mess with your career to have them. That's the whole reason why I've tried to be diligent about always wearing a condom. Hell, I know how much your career means to you, so much that I'd be happy to adopt instead of asking you to take time off to give birth. And I'm gonna feel like the world's biggest ass if my screw up just now means you can't wrestle for the next nine months."

"It wasn't your screw up," Teagan protested, shaking her head as she sat up. "I was the one who shoved your pants to the floor without grabbing your wallet for a condom."

Josh reached down and grabbed his boxer briefs out of his pants on the floor, wadding them up and pressing them against her pussy to catch any of his cum that hadn't already dripped out.

"Seriously? You couldn't go get a towel?" Teagan chuckled, knowing that the material that was pressed against her most intimate area was clean, having only touched the inside of his pants and not the floor.

"These were clean and right here," Josh shrugged, "so I figured they'd work for now without interrupting our discussion."

"Fair enough," Teagan agreed, smiling at her impish husband. "But as I was saying, neither one of us thought about a condom, so there's no reason for you to feel bad if I end up pregnant. I mean, even two forms of birth control aren't always one-hundred percent effective, so unless we want to stop having sex, there's always a chance of making a baby. And I'm okay with that if it happens. And hopefully, if it does happen, it'll just push Rick to hire more talent for the women's division. Which he really needs to do, so we can all take turns being off having babies without cutting all the women's matches from the cards."

She knew Rick was planning to sign the Goddesses tag team that had tried out a couple weeks earlier, but they had to wait until their current indie contract was up before they could join the GWA roster. But two more women in the division weren't enough, especially when they couldn't actually start until the beginning of the next year.

"You're really okay with having my babies?" Josh looked over at her with hopeful, puppy-dog eyes. "Even if it means taking time off from wrestling?"

"I'm more than okay with it," Teagan informed him, smiling brightly as she leaned over to brush her lips over his cheek. "In fact, I'm kinda looking forward to it."

"Me too," Josh grinned before claiming her mouth in a soul-searing kiss. He didn't let the kiss linger, however, breaking it off as soon as her toes started to curl. "But we can't keep hanging around here practicing making those babies, 'cause we've gotta get cleaned up and dressed to go buy some upholstery cleaner along with our wedding bands. And maybe a wetsuit for you."

"Why do I need a wetsuit?"

"So you can go surfing with us in the morning," Josh started. "I think with a hooded wetsuit and wearing your shower cap under it, you might be able to get in the water without getting your hair wet. But we can look at hooded drysuits too."

As he rambled on about the differences between wetsuits and drysuits and detailed his thoughts on the best way to protect her hair from the saltwater, he scooped her up and carried her past the kitchen and dining room into what Teagan assumed was the master suite, where the walls were painted in a light aqua blue while still maintaining the white trim that she'd seen in the other parts of the home. He carried her through to the ensuite bathroom, which also had white cabinetry, only topped with sandstone solid surface counters, instead of the seafoam green marble of his kitchen counters and island, and a slightly darker brown glass bowl sink that resembled a seashell. There was a walk-in jacuzzi tub beside the glassed-in shower across from the vanity and the toilet, which was separated from the vanity by three-quarters of a wall for a little bit of privacy without actually closing it off behind a door.

Oh, yeah, I'm going to enjoy relaxing in here whenever we have to take time off for maternity and paternity leave. And apparently, I'm going to learn how to surf, too.

Chapter Ten

Monday, November 11, 2019, Los Angeles, California

After having Aiken in his bed every night for the last two-and-a-half weeks, Brent felt their relationship was turning out way better than he'd expected. He'd felt guilty after their first time having sex, worried that he'd let his baser urges override his ability to think before acting, causing him to take things too far when he wasn't sure he was capable of falling in love or that he'd be able to fully commit to their marriage the way she deserved. But over the last two weeks, when he'd been completely unable to resist his wife, he'd overcome those guilty feelings, knowing it was just residual fear of being like his mom that kept him from going all in with Aiken. It took several discussions with his dad and all the married guys, and the one soon-to-be married guy, on the GWA roster to help him sort through everything in his head, but he now believed he was capable of love. It might still take a little time for him and Aiken to both develop the full extent of their feelings for one another. But as he recognized he might already be falling for her, he could definitely see them both falling head over heels for each other sometime in the near future, so they could really make their marriage work for the long term and start planning for their life together after their wrestling careers were over.

Since realizing he was most likely falling in love with his wife, and not just confusing his feelings of friendship and lust toward her for love, he'd started implementing some of the advice his fellow wrestlers had given him about romancing her, which seemed to be working very well for pushing her to fall in love with him, too. At least, if the way they connected nightly in bed was a good barometer of their relationship, anyway.

While neither one of them had come out and expressed their love for one another yet, he knew they were both getting close to the point that they wouldn't be able to hold back those three little words much longer. In fact, he'd had to stop himself from saying them several times in the heat of the moment while he was buried balls-deep inside her.

He still wasn't completely certain he understood all the idiosyncrasies of being in love and expressing his feelings to Aiken, even after talking with several of the guys about their relationships over the last couple of weeks. But if he'd learned nothing else from observing all the happy marriages of his coworkers and friends, he'd clearly figured out that in the middle of sex was not the best time to share that sentiment for the first time. So, he was biding his time, waiting until he could pick up the perfect ring to give his bride before planning a romantic dinner to tell Aiken he was falling in love with her for the first time.

He'd originally thought about taking her shopping for wedding bands while they were visiting her dads, thinking it would be nice to bring them along on the shopping trip since they hadn't been able to attend the wedding. But after seeing Josh and Teagan's rings, which they were sporting on Sunday when Josh's parents came to the arena for the GWA show, and hearing that Teagan's engagement ring was a family heirloom handed down from Josh's great-grandmother, Brent first wanted to look over the family rings, which he'd recently remembered his dad had in an old jewelry box stashed in the attic, before going to buy something new with less meaning. Now, as he followed Aiken's directions to turn off the Sunset Strip to head into her West Hollywood neighborhood, Brent was second guessing his plans.

When she'd first told him she lived in her dads' guest house in West Hollywood, he'd known her neighborhood was probably a little fancier than the one he'd grown up in. But he'd associated West Hollywood with more of the club scene, specifically some of the famous music venues he'd enjoyed visiting whenever the GWA was in Los Angeles. He'd also believed that part of the city encompassed a variety of neighborhoods, ranging from the slums to maybe an upper middle class socioeconomic designation. So he'd assumed she lived in one of the upper middle class neighborhoods and the guest house was originally a detached garage that had been converted into a mother-in-law suite, as some of his neighbors called their garage apartments back home. He hadn't really thought her neighborhood included any big, fancy mansions. In his mind, those were relegated to places like Beverly Hills, or maybe over on the beaches of Malibu. But as they drove up through the hills of her neighborhood, passing more than a few large buildings he assumed were modern mansions hidden behind tall fences and shrubbery, often with a hundred feet or more of frontage between the various gates to enter the properties, Brent realized just how wrong his assumptions had been.

Maybe I should take her shopping for rings today, after all. 'Cause there's no way she'll be happy with the jewelry my ancestors could afford when she's used to such opulence. Yeah, she'll have to take off a massive rock when she wrestles, but she'd have to take off whatever rings she wears, even if we just went with plain gold bands.

"That's my house." Aiken pointed to a white building he could clearly see over the tall shrub row edging the road. "But you have to drive around to the gate at the other end of the property to park."

While he could only see the roof line and what he assumed was the second story, or maybe the uppermost living area, if the home stretched down the side of the hill for more than two stories, Brent soon realized that her dads' house was larger than most of the other homes in the area, and it was possibly the biggest home in the neighborhood. The vast building was at least as long as a football field, and appeared to curve around to match the line of the road. He counted to realize that there were three separate houses on the other side of the street between where she first pointed out they'd arrived at her home and where she ultimately instructed him to pull through the gate, which she opened with an app on her cellphone.

Fuck! This place has to be at least ten times the size of the house I grew up in. Hell, after growing up here, there's no way she'll wanna look at houses in Dad's neighborhood back in Portland when we finally retire from wrestling.

While Brent was technically a multi-millionaire from saving and investing the majority of his GWA salary, there was no way he could afford a home even half the size of this one. Well, at least, not anywhere in the Los Angeles area, anyway. Maybe he could have something similar built in the middle of nowhere, where property values were much lower and construction costs were a lot cheaper.

Not that he'd ever feel comfortable living in such a huge home. Hell, he thought the big houses the Hunters had built on their family property in Heart's Destiny were too big. And even combined, he didn't think James and Dean's houses were as big as this place. While the Pearson home only appeared to be a quarter of the size of the Heritage House portion of the Hunters' Bed and Breakfast, Brent didn't think a single-family residence needed to be one-fourth the size of the boutique hotel.

But then again, he'd grown up in a two-bedroom, one-bath house, which wasn't quite two-thousand-square-feet of living space, in what he considered a modest middle-class neighborhood. And then he spent most of the last decade living out of his suitcases in hotel rooms that weren't exactly huge, even though he always requested king suites to have a big enough bed that his feet didn't hang too far off the end. So, what did he know about how big a house needed to be for a family to be comfortable?

Hell, he still listed his dad's house as his primary residence, not feeling it was necessary to buy a house and pay utilities and upkeep on a place he only visited a few times a year. He'd paid off his dad's home loan years ago, when his GWA salary first hit the seven-figure range. So, his dad insisted he stay there whenever he was in Portland, making it clear Brent would inherit the place one day anyway.

Since he hadn't thought he'd ever get married or have a family to need a bigger place, Brent didn't see the point in buying another house, unless living with his dad became a problem once he retired from wrestling. But even then, he'd always thought he'd buy something close to his childhood home, just far enough away that they'd have some privacy for hookups, but would still be close in case of emergencies.

Exiting their rental car and walking over to a short set of steps that led down to the glass front door of the home, Brent realized Aiken would never be happy living in a small house, like his childhood home, or the one he'd imagined possibly buying one day in the same neighborhood. *Maybe I should talk with the Hunters about how much their cabins cost to build? Surely, I can get used to living in an eight-to-ten-thousand-square-foot house, if it'll make her happy.*

Even if he could convince her to compromise on their lifestyle as a couple when they retired, and settle down in a house somewhere between the over the top opulence of her dads' estate and the tiny two bedroom he currently shared with his dad, Brent was afraid he'd never be able to provide for her in the nature she was accustomed to. That fear suddenly made him wonder if they'd actually be able to make their marriage last. Yeah, they'd probably be fine as long as they were both still wrestling, but that would only be for the next five or ten years.

Fuck! Is she gonna leave me if I have to retire before she does? Or if I have to live in Portland to take care of Dad in his later years? Not that that'll happen anytime soon, since he's only in his mid-fifties, but still, it won't give us much time after we retire from the ring to possibly have a family.

Unless we retire much earlier than our late thirties or early forties like I was planning. I mean, I'm not planning to get shot like Dion, but accidents happen in the ring all the time, so it's not like this career is guaranteed to last a certain number of years. And hell, it's practically certain that I'll end up having to take care of Dad when his health starts to decline, just like he had to take care of Granddad back when I was a kid.

Thinking back on that time in his life made Brent wonder if his dad's need to care for an elderly parent might have had something to do with why his mom left. *Fuck! I don't want history to repeat itself with Aiken leaving me the same way Mom left Dad and me.*

Brent had to shake off his negative thoughts as soon as Aiken opened the door and announced that they'd arrived.

"Papa! Daddio! We're home!"

"Aikey Baby!" Shawn Pearson squealed as he ran up the stairs right beside the front door. Luckily, Aiken was standing in front of Brent, so she got the first bear-hug greeting when he reached them.

Guess this place is at least three stories, Brent realized as he noticed another set of stairs going up to the level he'd been able to see above the privacy fencing and hedges.

Shawn didn't leave Brent out, though, practically tackling him as soon as he'd released Aiken. "And our strapping son-in-law! Welcome to the family."

"Thanks," Brent chuckled, awkwardly patting the flamboyant Black man on the back to return the embrace. Since he'd met Aiken's dads before, in addition to having spoken to them a few times on the phone in the last couple of weeks, he'd expected the standard handshake greetings they'd shared in the past, not the same kind of affection they bestowed on their daughter. Not that he had a problem with hugging Aiken's dads, but he just wasn't used to that level of affection from his own dad, so it felt a little strange to him.

Thankfully, when Theo finally made it up the stairs, the older man greeted Brent with the handshake he'd been expecting before greeting his daughter with a hug and kiss on the cheek. They made small talk about the traffic on their trip from the airport to the house as they walked into a spacious living area, which in addition to a wall of photographs of Aiken at various points in her life, had a glass wall all along the back of the house, so they could look out over the city of Los Angeles. Brent made a mental note to have Aiken tell him all about each photo later as he took a moment to really look at Aiken's dads, realizing they were a good five or ten years older than his dad. It wasn't just the extra lines around their eyes and extra silver in their hair that made him think they were older. They also already appeared frailer than his dad, with the thinness of their shoulders and arms emphasized by their impeccably tailored dress shirts.

While they'd mentioned trying to make time to work out in their home gym during one of their phone calls with Aiken in the last couple of weeks, Brent was pretty sure that if they did manage to get in a workout, then both men focused more on cardiovascular exercise, rather than the weight lifting required to maintain muscle mass. Shawn obviously came the closest to matching Harlan Crockett's two-hundred pounds, but at somewhere around five-foot-eleven or maybe six-foot tall, he was still a few inches shorter than both the Crockett men's stature of six-foot-three. Whereas Theo was no more than five-foot-ten and a good fifty or sixty pounds lighter than Brent's two-hundred-and-thirty pounds.

If they actually did manage to schedule in more heart healthy cardio in their busy schedules, then they might be able to stay healthy a little later in life than Brent's granddad had. But if they didn't also add in some kind of strength training, Brent could see how aging would be detrimental to their quality of life.

Aw, hell. Here I've been worrying about how Aiken will handle me having to take care of my dad when he reaches retirement age and starts physically deteriorating, when her dads are a lot closer than my dad is to possibly needing our caretaking. While I hate the thought of any of our dads getting too old and frail to take care of themselves, I guess I won't have to worry about her not understanding when I have to be in Portland to take care of Dad. 'Cause we'll probably have already gone through it twice over with her dads.

Brent felt like an ass for his morbid thoughts when he should be paying attention to the conversation with his fathers-in-law. But he was soon brought out of his mental musings by a Hispanic woman about his age, wearing what appeared to be a chef's uniform, alerting them that lunch was ready to be served.

Holy fuck! I knew Aiken said they had a housekeeper, but I thought she meant they used a cleaning service like I have go by Dad's every week to take care of the stuff he doesn't have time for, like dusting, mopping, and deep cleaning the bathroom. She never mentioned a personal chef. Or any other household staff, which they probably have to have to take care of the pool, spa, landscaping, and who knows what else in this place.

"Oh, Carlotta, what are we having for lunch?" Aiken excitedly took his hand to lead the way into an open concept dining room and kitchen combination that also had a full glass back wall to look out over the pool and below to the city of Los Angeles.

Damn, I bet that view is gorgeous at night. Well, maybe, if all the lights aren't blocked by smog the way the view is during the day.

"Pescado con salsa verde striped sea bass with piquillo crema and cherry tomatoes," the chef informed them, waiting until they'd each taken a seat at the table near the back wall before serving their meal, beginning with Theo and Shawn Pearson.

"Yum! One of my favorites," Aiken gushed as Carlotta placed her plate in front of her.

"Smells delicious," Brent added, smiling at the woman as she placed his plate in front of him. The presentation of the two pieces of fish rivaled that of a high-end restaurant, with a few halved cherry tomatoes nestled in some kind of sprouts on top, as well as a couple beside the fish in the drizzle of sauce on the plate. But regardless of the immaculate job of plating and the fabulous smell of the spicy sauce, Brent didn't think it was anywhere near enough food to fill him up until dinner in catering at the arena later.

No wonder they're so thin. It's hard to maintain any kind of muscle mass while eating only tiny portions all the time.

And hopefully, they won't be offended if I stop at a drive-thru on the way to the arena later, so I can fuel up before our match run-throughs.

Feeling unsophisticated for his voracious appetite was only part of the reason Brent felt uncomfortable. He also felt like a giant trying to sit in a child's chair. It wasn't just that the padded sides of the chairs felt tight against his sides, either. The fact that they were so low that he had to extend his legs under the table to keep from hitting the bottom of it with his knees also made it clear that the fancy furniture wasn't built for a man his size. And he was actually on the smaller side of average for the guys on the GWA roster. While there were a few guys who barely cleared six-feet tall and two-hundred pounds, and a few who were six-foot-six or taller and weighed in at two-hundred-and-seventy pounds or more, the majority of the men on the roster were between six-foot-three and six-foot-five and weighed somewhere between two-hundred-and-thirty and two-hundred-and-sixty pounds.

Damn. I wish we'd have brought some of the guys with us to visit with her dads. It'd have been funny as hell to see Magnum trying to sit in one of these chairs. And maybe if we'd have brought a few of the guys I'm used to hanging out with, then I wouldn't feel like such an outsider sitting here with just Aiken and her dads.

Even though he'd let Aiken talk him into wearing a burgundy tie to match her dress, along with his khaki slacks, white dress shirt, and brown blazer, Brent felt completely out of place and woefully underdressed for sitting down to such a fancy meal, regardless of the fact that he was the only one there in a jacket and tie. His unease only heightened when a younger guy, dressed in all black like a waiter or possibly the chef's assistant, appeared to present a bottle of wine to Theo before pouring it into their glasses.

"Just water for me, thanks." Brent covered his glass with the palm of his hand as the waiter approached him.

"Oh, do you not drink any alcohol since Vegas, or is wine just not your thing?" Theo questioned, raising an eyebrow inquisitively at Brent, making him feel like the older man was questioning whether or not he was an alcoholic, who'd decided to quit drinking after getting married while he was too drunk to remember it. "We have some specialty beers and a full bar of various liquors downstairs, if you prefer something else."

Brent removed his hand from his glass as the waiter returned to the table with a water pitcher in hand, allowing the man to fill his glass. "Neither. I just don't drink anytime I have to drive within a couple of hours, or before wrestling. And since I have to drive to the arena as soon as we're through with lunch, and wrestle tonight, I won't drink anything but water, protein shakes, and Gatorade until after the show's over. But I'll be glad to check out your bar once we get back here later."

"Oh, good, then we can get your opinions on the wines we're considering for your wedding reception," Shawn chimed in with a grin. "I know you're going to your friends' wedding on your Thanksgiving break, but do you think we'll be able to schedule something for your Christmas break? And we need to know how many of your family and friends will be coming in for the festivities, so we know if we have enough bedrooms here for everyone, or if we'll need to reserve a block of hotel rooms to have rooms for all of them."

Brent was glad he'd just taken a bite of his fish, so he had a moment to think before replying to Shawn's barrage of questions about a reception he'd had no idea her dads were planning. While he agreed that they probably needed to do some kind of party to help the Pearsons feel like they were part of their daughter's wedding, Brent still felt like they needed to wait a little longer to make sure the marriage was going to work for the long term before planning anything like that. Even though he was pretty sure they were both falling in love with one another, he still wasn't convinced that love would be enough to make their marriage last.

"Papa," Aiken sighed, shaking her head, and looking slightly embarrassed by the way Shawn seemed to be putting them on the spot without any kind of forewarning. Brent wasn't sure what her objection was to the party Shawn wanted to plan, but he was glad she was the one speaking up to keep him from having to reveal his trepidation about their marriage to Aiken's dads. "I told you already that I think we need to wait until next year to plan anything like that. I want everyone in the GWA to be able to come to our celebration, whenever we decide we're ready to have one, especially the other couples who got married the same day we did. And that can't happen until after Liam and Rylie quit talking about getting an annulment, which they're currently planning to do over our Christmas break."

"But I thought you said you have a plan to put a stop to that nonsense while you're at your other friends' wedding at the end of the month." Shawn smiled mischievously at Aiken. "So, we should still be able to plan the reception for your Christmas break."

"Yeah, we've got a plan, but we're not sure it'll work yet. And even though I know Rylie is on board with trying to make her marriage work, Liam's being extremely stubborn about wanting an annulment. So, I think it'll take more than having them room together that week, and having them act like they're happily married to keep from having the town matchmakers try to set them up the whole time we're there, to convince him to drop his current plan to dissolve the marriage."

"Wait, I thought you and Teagan were working with the matchmakers in Heart's Destiny to try to get Liam and Rylie together that week?" Brent was confused, knowing Aiken and Teagan had intentionally talked to the women in Dean and Allissa's families when they were at the *Halloween Horror* show to start setting up their plans.

"Yeah, we are, but Liam doesn't know that," Aiken explained with a conniving grin. "Which is why we've reinforced the line Rick fed him about needing to act happily married while we're there to keep them off his back. It's not going to stop any of the matchmaking plans, but it'll make it easier to get Liam to go along with them because he'll think he has to keep acting like he's madly in love with Rylie. We're just hoping that by the end of the week, he'll realize he really does love her and wasn't really having to act the part."

Considering the way the girls plan to let Rylie get super drunk on Halloween to force Liam to have to take her back to her room at the hotel hadn't ended the way they wished, Brent wasn't as confident in their next scheme to be successful either. Oh, yeah, Liam had taken Rylie back to the hotel that night, but he'd also stopped her from drinking more than her first three alcoholic drinks, while sobering her up with food for the rest of the time they were at the club. So, by the time they all went back to the hotel, it was clear that she didn't need his assistance to get to her room.

In fact, it seemed like that plan had just given Liam more confidence in his ability to pretend to be the doting husband in public, while not actually changing his mind about annulling their marriage. So if the ladies were planning a whole week of similar setups, Brent didn't believe they'd have any kind of effect on Liam. But he wasn't about to burst Aiken's bubble by stating as much aloud. Instead, he focused on his meal, only half listening as Aiken and Shawn brainstormed matchmaking ideas for their friends.

"Theo, darling, you really should try to schedule your meetings with Becky Burleson that same week, so I can be there to help with all the matchmaking plans," Shawn implored, reaching over to place his hand on Theo's arm. "I know seeing the town they're based on will really help solidify your vision for the *Devine* and *Heart's Desire* movies you're working on with them. And after reading the books and the screenplays for *Kissing Kat*, *Winning Rhonda*, and *Ronnie's Runaway*, I'm dying to check out that formalwear shop. And I just know that kitschy store Britches-N-Boots will have just what I need to outfit all the cowboys in *Heart's Desire*, so I'll only have to focus on recreating the eighteen-hundreds wardrobe for the ladies."

"Oh, are you both working on the movies for Kay and Brook's books?" Aiken appeared to be almost as excited about the possibility of her dads working with their friends as she was about all the matchmaking plans they were coming up with for Liam and Rylie. "And the real name of the store in Heart's Destiny is Boots & Britches."

"Yes, we are," Theo confirmed without commenting on the stores in Heart's Destiny or Shawn's desire to visit them. "But I doubt we'll be able to coordinate a trip out there to check out the possible filming locations until the end of the year, or maybe the beginning of next year, when our director's schedule clears up."

"Well, even if you can't make it while we're there at the end of this month, I'm sure Mandi Hunter, who runs the B and B, will hook you up with the other matchmakers in town, Papa, so you can help them out with all their plots for the locals," Aiken giggled, grinning at Shawn before redirecting her gaze to Theo. "And they might even be able to help you with casting some of the locals for any of the scenes that require equestrian skills, or at least they'll work with your lead actors to make sure they have the competency with horses, since I know proper training is a must for you with casting."

"Yes it is," Theo agreed, smiling at his daughter. "In fact, I've been working with David and Tonya over at Blue Thunder to start casting for the *Devine* series, since the lead actors in *Winning Rhonda* are professional wrestlers and there are a lot of wrestlers as background characters throughout the series."

"Oh, really? How are they? I haven't talked to Tornado or Lightning in ages," Aiken gushed.

"Doing good," Theo replied. "They both asked about you and wondered if you'd be interested in coming back to take one of the roles we're casting."

"Like I have time with our crazy GWA schedule." Aiken turned to look directly at Brent before explaining, "Blue Thunder Wrestling Academy is the group I trained with to become a wrestler, back when I thought I was only going to do enough training to play a wrestler in a movie."

"Yeah, after how she hated gymnastics and dance as a little girl, we never thought she'd ever pick a career in something as athletic as professional wrestling," Shawn chuckled.

"But thankfully, I grew out of my klutzy phase sometime between high school and college, so the wrestling training didn't lead to anywhere near as many injuries as gymnastics or dance did when I was a kid," Aiken laughed along with her papa. "So I enjoyed it a lot more and found my true calling for my career."

"If I'd have thought about you being friends with the authors who originally wrote these characters, I'd have asked you to get passes for David and Tonya to come to the show tonight to meet them," Theo said, shaking his head. "Or at least the one who works with you, so she could describe the characters in a little more detail. But I suppose it's too late for that now."

"Yeah, since they're also friends with Rick, they can probably still get backstage passes for tonight's show," Aiken pointed out. "But since Kay's off this week, you'll have to settle for having me introduce them to all the wrestlers her characters are based on to give you some basic ideas about casting. Then you can call her later to find out which of us she's planning to use for inspiration for the main characters in the *Intergalactic Wrestling Federation* series she's started writing, so you can cast those characters in the earlier movies with actors who will want to come back for lead roles in the next series. Although, based on the title of the first book, I think it'll be about Rick and Fiona. Or rather their book counterparts, Rob Richards and Finley Harris."

"She's been using us as inspiration for her books?" Brent wasn't sure he liked the idea of being included in the character list for Kay's romance novels, especially now that they were being made into movies. "Please tell me she's changed our names enough that it's not obvious who we are."

"Oh, yeah, she's changed our names," Aiken grinned. "But it's still pretty obvious who's who. At least to those of us who know she's based her characters on us."

"Oh, you have to tell me which characters are based on the two of you," Shawn squealed, obviously excited by the prospect of a movie character based on his daughter. "And what's the name of her first book in this new series?"

"In her books, I'm Amber Peterson, using the ring name Amber, and Brent is Clint Bunyan, using the ring name Bunyan, which really works better for the lumberjack gimmick," Aiken teased, her lips turning up in a mischievous smile. "And the first book in the new series is going to be ***Booking the Boss***, which is perfect for Rick and Fiona's story, since as the GWA owner, he's our head booker, and she's an English teacher."

"Oh, I wonder what she'll name a book about the two of you, if she decides to pen your love story?" Shawn pointed back and forth between Brent and Aiken with his fork.

"If she sticks to the alliteration I've seen on a few of the titles for the books Aiken's been reading, and writes about the other two couples who got married when we did in the same book, I'm sure it'll be something like ***Vexed in Vegas***," Brent chortled, really hoping he was wrong and he would never appear as a main character in one of Kay's romance novels.

"Considering how confused we all were about whether or not we got married, that's a pretty accurate title," Aiken giggled. "But thankfully, our marriages were only truly aggravating to Rick, and maybe Liam. And now that we've revealed them through the GWA, Rick's not even all that grumbly about them anymore."

Brent felt a twinge of unease at her words, knowing he'd been extremely aggravated by the thought of being married when they first found out. While he'd definitely come around in the last month, he still wasn't a hundred percent certain his and Aiken's relationship would be able to stand the test of time, especially after seeing the drastic differences in how they were raised.

"And hopefully, all our matchmaking efforts will help your friend Liam see the light too," Shawn added with a glowing smile. "So we can finally celebrate your nuptials along with your friends, and Kay can write about all your happily ever afters for Daddio to make them into movies."

Brent plastered on a smile, hoping neither his wife, nor his fathers-in-law, could tell it was fake. Or that he still felt uncertain of his future with Aiken.

~ ~ ~

Wednesday, November 13, 2019, Portland, Oregon

"Are you sure you don't want to go check-in at the hotel with everyone else, and have Dad meet us there for lunch, instead of going to his place?"

"No, I want to stay in your bedroom tonight, just like we stayed in my room night before last," Aiken reassured her husband for what felt like the dozenth time since they boarded the plane in San Francisco that morning to fly into the private airfield in Portland. She wasn't sure why Brent seemed to have changed his mind about staying at his dad's house that night like they'd planned, but she was getting tired of having to repeat herself every time he tried to waffle on their sleeping arrangements for the night.

That's so not like him. Normally, he's very decisive and never seems to change his mind once he makes plans like this. But come to think of it, he hasn't really acted like himself since we had lunch with Daddio and Papa when we first got to L.A. a couple days ago. Did I miss something about that visit that made him uncomfortable? Or did seeing me with my dads give him some reason to think I'm going to offend his dad somehow?

300

"I did tell you there's only one bathroom in the house, right?" Brent reminded her, again, as he drove through Portland. "And it's small. So small that we won't be able to shower together like we do most mornings. And we have to share it with Dad, so we'll have to come up with a schedule for all of us to get ready on time to leave in the morning."

"So, I'll shower and blow dry my hair at the arena tonight after I wrestle to keep from having to take time to do it in the morning," Aiken offered, starting to wonder if his trepidation had anything to do with her taking a super long bath while they were in L.A., where she had access to her jacuzzi tub. "That way it'll only take me fifteen minutes in the morning to empty my bladder, brush my teeth, and put on the bare minimum of makeup before I can get out of your way."

"And the walls are really thin, so even though the bathroom is between my room and Dad's, we can't do anything we don't want Dad to overhear," he added, not even acknowledging the snarkiness of her words, almost like he hadn't even heard her.

As she glanced over at him, she noticed him tightening his grip on the steering wheel until his knuckles paled, making him seem reluctant to even exit the highway. Thankfully, he did at least take their exit. Though she wouldn't be surprised if he looped around to get back on the highway to go back toward the exit everyone else had taken to go to the hotel.

"Considering you refused to disrespect my dads by having sex with their daughter while we were under their roof the other day, even though there was no way they could hear us in the guest house from their bedroom in the main house, I didn't expect us to do anything he shouldn't overhear anyway." Aiken took a long look at her husband, trying to figure out what he wasn't telling her about why he didn't want to spend the night at his dad's house. "What's really going on, Brent? Why don't you want me to go to your dad's house? I know it's not because you don't want me to meet him, since I've met him before and we've talked on the phone a few times in the last couple of weeks. So, have I done something in the last couple of days to make you have second thoughts about us? Or maybe I just acted like too much of a diva while we were in L.A., and now you think I'm gonna act like a bitch if I have to wait my turn for the bathroom?"

"No, it's nothing like that," Brent sighed, turning into a neighborhood with quaint tree lined streets that reminded her of someplace she'd see on a sitcom or maybe a Hallmark movie. "It's just that my house is nothing like yours. It's tiny, like smaller than your guest house tiny. It's also old and outdated, with furniture that he's had since at least the nineteen-nineties. While Dad's good about keeping it up and making sure everything works, he only remodels when something breaks so bad that it's absolutely necessary. And even then he sticks to the basics and doesn't really upgrade to the amenities available in the twenty-first century. There aren't any fancy smart home features or jacuzzi tubs. Hell, there's not even a tub, just a plain white tiled shower stall that doesn't even have room for a bench. Though I did convince him to upgrade to a rain shower head in the ceiling, when a burst pipe in the wall forced him to remodel the bathroom a few years ago, so we'd quit having to duck under the standard shower head that was there when I was growing up."

"Brent," Aiken breathed out his name, finally realizing that he was embarrassed by his childhood home because he was comparing it to hers in his head. "I know we're still getting to know one another on a deeper level than the coworkers and sorta friends we were before. But I'd think that even only knowing me on a superficial level for the last five years, you'd have realized by now that I don't care about how big your house is, or if the furniture is as old as I am. I want to see it because I want to know you better. I want to see where you grew up and hear stories from your dad about your life before we met, like the ones my dads shared with you the other day."

"Well, that's good," Brent chuckled lightly as he turned into a driveway and parked behind a large blue pickup that was parked in front of what appeared to be a detached garage. "'Cause Dad'll definitely talk your ear off with stories about what a hellion I was as a kid. But I still think you'll be more comfortable if we stay at the hotel tonight and not here."

"How 'bout we go in and have lunch, but leave our bags in the car?" Aiken suggested, trying to find a compromise, so they weren't having their first fight as they walked into his dad's house. "And then if you still want to stay at the hotel tonight after we eat with your dad, then we'll stop and check-in at the hotel on our way to the arena later."

"Yeah, that'll work," Brent sighed out his agreement, just before he turned off the ignition and got out of the car.

She knew he preferred her to wait in the car for him to get her door, so she did just that, realizing he wasn't as agreeable to her compromise as she'd hoped, when she saw him rip the hair band off of his low ponytail to run his hand through his hair as he rounded the front of the vehicle. *Smile, Aiken,* she mentally told herself, as Brent opened her car door and held out a hand to assist her from the vehicle. *Maybe he'll relax a little when he realizes he has nothing to be embarrassed about. Considering how nice the landscaping is, I'm sure he's over exaggerating the negatives about the inside of the house.*

They walked along a gravel garden path between obviously well-tended flower beds to bypass the backyard, which was also mostly gravel and appeared to contain several raised planters and seating areas, to get to the back door of the house. Considering she needed a coat with the high temperature in the low-to-mid fifties, she was surprised to see that there were still flowers blooming and that the beds weren't just covered in mulch awaiting the next year's plantings.

As they stepped through the back door, which was even with the yard, Brent immediately turned to the right to usher her up a few stairs, which curved to the left, instead of going straight through the door just across the lower landing. Since it was a fairly cramped stairway, she immediately opened the door at the top of the steps to enter into the kitchen of the home.

She instantly realized what Brent meant about it being outdated, with the only updates being those that were absolutely necessary. Since the stainless steel stove, refrigerator, and microwave were the only modern looking items in the kitchen, she assumed they'd had to be updated in the last few years. The walls were painted plain white, as were the upper cabinets, while the lower cabinets were painted an olive green that she didn't think had been in style since the 1970s. But even though the style of the cabinetry was old fashioned, it was all neat and clean, not showing any reason he should feel embarrassed about the condition of the home.

I wonder if the previous stove and refrigerator were that same color green? No, surely they wouldn't last forty years to just be replaced recently.

"Hey, Dad, we're here," Brent called out as he closed the door behind them.

"Be right out," Harlan hollered back, right before she heard a toilet flush and the water turn on in what she assumed was the bathroom somewhere on the other side of the house.

Brent ushered her past a breakfast nook tucked into the space between the back entrance to the kitchen and the dining room, which they walked through past a hallway and into the living room. As she glanced at the padded chairs around the wooden dining table, and then got a closer look at the southwest-patterned living room furniture while Brent hung their coats on a coatrack by the front door, Aiken thought Brent might have been off by a decade in estimating the age of his father's décor choices. Clearly, the style of the furniture was more likely from the 1980s. Or at least, it was reminiscent of the set pieces the theatre troupe she'd joined the summer between high school and college had used, which supposedly hadn't been upgraded since the eighties.

But regardless of the age of the furnishings, it was all well-kept and spotlessly clean, which she knew wasn't easy in a home with white walls. The hardwood floors weren't even showing any signs of the wear and tear she expected, knowing Brent had probably scuffed up the floors as a child much worse than she had, based on the activity level differences she'd noticed between boys and girls in her coworkers' children over the last few years. And she'd actually gotten in trouble for leaving marks on the floors while roller skating indoors when she was a kid. *But I suppose the area rugs in the highest traffic areas could be covering up any scuff marks. Or maybe protecting the wood to prevent any damage in the first place.*

Overall, she felt like Brent's childhood abode was exceptionally homey, even if it was very masculine. So, she was still at a loss when trying to figure out why Brent didn't want to stay there that night, when Harlan joined them. Brent's dad was just as tall as he was, but he was also a little softer than his son, not quite as muscular and with a little bit of a paunchy belly. While the two men shared the same hair and eye colors, Harlan kept his hair cut short in a more traditional men's haircut and was clean shaven. While he had a few more lines around his eyes than Brent, Aiken believed looking at Harlan's face gave her a glimpse of what she'd see if Brent ever shaved his beard.

"I stopped and picked up a bucket of carnivorian chili at Portland Kettle last night on the way home," Harlan informed them as he came out of the hallway and through the dining room to join them in the living room. "Figured you'd want your favorite meal, since you're only here for a short time and won't be back for another six weeks or so."

"Chili is your favorite meal?" Aiken questioned, surprised Brent hadn't mentioned it at any point in the last few weeks.

"Carnivorian chili from the Portland Kettle is my favorite take-out meal when I'm here," Brent clarified, shaking his head. "And if they run out of the carnivorian chili, their vegetarian chili is an acceptable replacement. Chili from anywhere else is questionable about whether or not I'll like it. And I don't really have a favorite meal overall, just a few that are my favorites at certain places."

"Wow, it must be really good if you're willing to eat the vegetarian version," Aiken laughed, knowing Brent tended to fill his plates in catering with mostly meat and seemed picky about which vegetables he'd eat.

"That's only because the first time he ate it was when he came to my company Christmas party, which was catered by the Portland Kettle, and didn't realize the first bowl he'd scarfed down was the vegetarian chili until he went back for seconds and checked out what was in some of the other kettles, instead of just going back to the first one," Harlan chuckled as he ushered them back to the kitchen. He then pulled a gallon-sized container from the refrigerator and sat it on the counter.

"They didn't have the cards up in front of the kettles the first time, so I didn't realize there were other options," Brent elaborated, reaching into a cabinet to pull out three large bowls and plates.

Once Harlan placed a square container on the counter beside the bucket of chili, along with a tub of margarine, and Brent grabbed utensils, they each dished up their bowls of chili and slices of cornbread. They took turns microwaving their meals to reheat them while pouring glasses of soda to drink. Though both Harlan and Brent referred to it as "pop" when deciding on which flavors they each wanted. That led to a lively discussion about how different parts of the country referred to soft drinks, and a funny story about how Brent thought he was being offered drugs the first time he went out after a show in Georgia and was asked if he wanted a Coke.

"Hey, don't laugh at my naïve idiocy," Brent huffed, though he couldn't hide the slight upturn of his lips when Aiken couldn't stop laughing. "I was only twenty-two, on my first trip out of the Pacific Northwest with the GWA at the time, and the way the guy was acting all sketchy didn't make me think he was offering me a pop when he asked if I wanted some Coke."

"I'm sorry, I just can't believe you were ever so sheltered that you didn't know most people call Coca-Cola, Coke," Aiken chortled, unable to stop laughing. "Especially when you were at a bar, where you were presumably ordering a drink."

"Yeah, I knew Coca-Cola was also referred to as Coke, but this place seemed way to wild for him to be offering me something so tame." Brent shook his head. "It was kind of a goth bar, or maybe a punk rock bar, so everyone who worked there was in all black and wearing platform boots and way more eyeliner than necessary, even the guys. So, no, I did not think I was being asked if I wanted a Coca-Cola when the guy literally tapped the side of his nose when he made the suggestion, especially when the rest of the guys were all ordering beers and shots with names that sounded like street names for other drugs."

"It sounds like the rest of the guys took you there as a way to rib the newbie on the roster."

"Probably." Brent finally gave in and laughed along with her. "But if it was meant to be a rib, it was one of the tamer ribs for back then, and not nearly as vicious as they were most of the time."

"Really?" Aiken hadn't ever known any of the little pranks the wrestlers pulled on one another were ever vicious, just funny ways of bonding as a crew.

"Oh, yeah, back before Rick took over and came up with the code of conduct we all have to follow to keep our jobs, the pranks weren't limited to just being silly and stupid ways of teasing our friends," Brent explained, as they went back to eating now that they weren't at risk of choking on their food from laughing. "In fact, some of the older guys were especially malicious, trying to get anyone who might take their main-event spots to get fed up and quit. Hell, I can't tell you how many times my airline, hotel, and rental car reservations were canceled in the first six months I was with the company. Keep in mind, this was back when each of us was responsible for making our own travel arrangements, so they all knew where I'd booked things because they'd recommended the places they'd used for years. Well, eventually they recommended the decent places they typically stayed, but only after first ribbing me by recommending roach motels for the first couple of weeks. Thankfully, I smartened up and started checking out the web reviews before booking anything, and then learned who I could trust to actually give me good recommendations. But after Dion took me under his wing and helped me figure stuff out, the cancelations got so bad I was seriously worried about getting fired for missing a couple of TV tapings and a pay-per-view because of the guys fucking with my travel."

"Oh, em, gee," Aiken gasped. "How'd you get it to stop? Or did you have to wait until Rick took over to stop it?"

"No, it was a year and a half after I joined the company when Rick took over, bought the company plane, and finally set it up so the company books everything but our trips home for breaks," Brent explained. "But when Richard called me into his office in New York to talk to me about missing shows, I explained exactly what was happening. He then set me up to travel with Rick, who helped me figure out which one of the guys was calling and impersonating me to cancel my reservations, and let me get my revenge by convincing his dad to book me in a shoot match with the main culprit before firing him."

"That was when you called to thank me for sending you to every wrestling and martial arts class at the rec center when you were still too young to come home after school by yourself and thought you were too big to go to day care like a *little baby*, wasn't it?" Harlan chuckled before popping his last bite of cornbread in his mouth.

"Yeah, it was," Brent grinned, nodding at his dad. "I might not have been able to use all those fighting styles I learned back then while wrestling on the school teams, but they sure came in handy for kicking Jarrett's ass in a way he had no idea how to counter."

Aiken didn't recognize the name of the former wrestler who'd messed with Brent. She didn't even know if it was his first name, last name, or ring name. But that wasn't too surprising since she hadn't really paid attention to professional wrestling until she started training for a movie role after college. Since it was clear that he'd already been dealt with and there was nothing she could do to retroactively defend her man, she opted to drop the subject, wanting to hear more about Brent's childhood instead.

"Okay, Harlan, you have to go back and tell me more about Brent thinking he was too big to go to day care," she prompted before taking another bite of the truly excellent chili.

"Well, right after his mom left when he was in kindergarten, I had to find childcare for the afternoons while I was still at work," Harlan started, a wistful smile spreading on his face. "And the easiest thing was to enroll him in the day care center down the block that picked up several other kids from his school every day. Of course, this was right after we'd made such a big deal about him being a *big boy* to get him excited about going to school. And I didn't realize it at the time, but there were also a few of his classmates, who were already showing bully tendencies and picked on any of the kids who got on the *baby bus* to day care, instead of having their moms pick them up, or going to a different after-school program that didn't have babies painted on the side of the bus that picked them up. So, being the hothead he was, Brent ended up in a few fights with them to prove he wasn't a *little baby*, and almost became the first kindergartener to be expelled from school."

"And you thought teaching him better ways to fight was the way to deal with his behavior?" Aiken didn't think that sounded like the best parenting strategy.

"No, I wanted to take away his video games and tried to convince the principal to put him in detention instead," Harlan chuckled. "But she told me about the martial arts program at the rec center and how it helped her grandsons learn to channel their tempers. She also told me about the after-school program through the rec center that included martial arts and other classes. So, we compromised with a three-day suspension from school and a week of no video games for his punishment. And I switched him to the rec center program immediately. I still had to take those three mornings off work 'cause the rec center program was only available after noon, except for school holidays when they had an all-day program. But it did help him channel his anger. And when the bullies came back to school after their suspensions, they no longer had a reason to pick on him."

"Oh, they still tried to pick on me a couple of times," Brent chimed in with a grin. "But once I demonstrated the first kata I learned in karate, and pointed out that I was learning even better ways to fight than I'd known when I beat them up the first time, they decided it was in their best interest not to pick on me or any of my friends who still went to day care on the baby bus."

"And you didn't get in trouble for beating them up again?" Aiken found that hard to believe.

"Oh, no, I didn't beat them up again. I demonstrated a kata on the playground."

Aiken gave her husband an incredulous look, needing him to elaborate further for her to understand.

"A kata is a sequence of strikes, kicks, and blocks that are done to demonstrate the mastery of the forms, so the sensei could assess when we were ready to move up a belt. But they're choreographed like a dance, or maybe something you'd do in a Tai Chi class, so whoever's performing the kata never actually strikes anyone. Honestly, I think it was all the times I screamed, *'Kaia,'* during the kata that scared them more than seeing my very novice moves."

Aiken couldn't help but chuckle along with Brent when he smirked impishly.

"I'm still surprised you never put a hole in any of the walls with the way you stomped around the house punching and kicking the air all through elementary school," Harlan laughed, picking up his empty dishes to take them to the kitchen sink.

"Are you kidding? After sensei cut his hand in class while punching through a board, I knew I didn't want to risk hurting myself by actually hitting anything," Brent laughed as he picked up his dishes and joined his dad at the kitchen sink.

As the men washed their dishes by hand, Aiken quickly finished the last few bites of her lunch.

"Why don't you have your truck in the garage, Dad?" Brent asked Harlan, obviously looking out the window over the sink to see their vehicles.

"'Cause I picked up a sixty-nine Mustang convertible a couple of weeks ago, and have it in there now," Harlan replied, just as Aiken finished eating and carried her dishes to the sink to join them.

"Seriously? Why didn't you say something when you got it? What kinda condition is it in?" Brent seemed excited about the classic car, focusing more on looking out the window than on drying the dishes his dad had just washed.

"Why don't I take over on clean up duty while you guys go out there?" Aiken suggested before Harlan could answer. She took the bowl and towel from Brent's hands. "So you don't drop and break these dishes in your hurry to go see the car."

"Thanks, Princess." Brent barely brushed his lips over her temple before rushing out the back door, not even bothering to go grab his coat from the living room, where he'd hung them earlier on the coatrack by the front door.

"You can leave these here and I'll finish them up when we get back in," Harlan offered, rinsing the dish soap from his hands.

"I don't mind finishing them up," Aiken smiled at her father-in-law. "And I think I even remember where they all go to put them away."

"Well, okay then," Harlan smiled back before turning and following his son.

Aiken took her time finishing up the dishes, watching out the window as Brent opened the garage door before Harlan was even halfway across the yard. Since it was only three plates, bowls, cups, and spoons, along with the serving spoon and butter knife they'd used to prepare their individual servings, and Harlan had already washed two of the bowls and plates, it didn't take her long to wash, rinse, dry, and put away everything.

Once she'd wiped down the table where they'd each sat, she decided to explore the house a little bit, needing to find the restroom while she knew it was unoccupied. Since the door was open at the end of the hall, it was easy to find for her to do her business while waiting for the men to come back inside. After she finished and washed her hands once more, she peeked into the two bedrooms, since those doors were both open.

Assuming the room at the back of the house was Harlan's since the bed was unmade, she only glanced in there momentarily before going to get a closer look at the room she deduced was Brent's. Once she stepped inside, she found the one wall in the house that wasn't painted white.

For someone who claims to not have a favorite color, it seems strange that he'd have a navy blue accent wall in his bedroom. Though I suppose it could be Harlan's favorite color, since it's the same color he painted the brick fireplace in the living room. But with all the wrestling and martial arts trophies on that bookshelf, this is obviously Brent's room.

She walked over and looked at the items on the shelves, noting the only books were biographies of various athletes, including a few professional wrestlers. At least, she assumed they were wrestlers' biographies based on the pictures on the book covers. *I guess he wasn't kidding about not really reading anything else.*

The rest of the shelves were filled with framed belts, presumably from those martial arts classes they talked about earlier, a few framed photos of Brent and Harlan, along with pictures of a much younger version of Brent with friends and teammates, and some mementoes of the various phases of his life, like a mini football from a local high school and his GWA action figure.

I guess he's more sentimental than he lets on, she realized, hoping to get him to tell her about everything on the bookshelf at some point that afternoon. *I wonder if our marriage license or one of the pictures from the chapel will end up framed on this shelf one day soon?*

Not wanting to miss out on possibly hearing more of Brent's childhood stories from his dad, she decided to go out and join them in the garage. *With as excited as Brent seemed about that car, I bet they could easily lose track of time talking or tinkering with it, so going out to listen to boring car talk is probably the only way I'll make sure we're not late getting to the arena.*

She stopped in the living room and put on her coat, taking Brent's with her just in case he finally realized his slacks and button-down weren't sufficient to combat the cool temperature outside. She followed a secondary path through the backyard this time, wanting to check out the flowers in the raised planters before she got to the garage, so she'd have another topic to discuss with Harlan.

She stopped momentarily at each of the raised beds, mentally making notes of the various fall colored flowers to be able to ask what each of them were. When she got to the last raised planter at the corner of the garage, however, she stopped dead in her tracks from overhearing the discussion between Brent and Harlan.

"…when I couldn't honestly look her dads in the eyes and say for sure that I'm in love with their daughter."

"So, does that mean you're still thinking about getting the annulment?"

"I don't know." Brent paused a moment before he finished answering his dad's question. "But I have to wonder if it's not best to go ahead and end the marriage now before more feelings get involved, instead of dragging it out until one of us retires and we go off in separate directions with our lives."

"What makes you think you're gonna go off in separate directions after you quit wrestling?"

"Wrestling is the only thing we have in common, so once we don't have that, I'm sure even our sex life will start to fizzle out to where it can't sustain us."

"Are you sure that's all you have in common? Didn't you say you had a great time on your dates, even when they were at places neither one of you would normally enjoy going?"

"Yeah, but, fuck, Dad, I only dropped my plans for an annulment and started *dating* her, if you can even call hanging out with her as a friend, *dating*, because Rick suggested it, so we could keep all the women safe without them getting pissed at us for thinking they couldn't defend themselves when that stalker escalated his threats," Brent groaned, sounding pissed about having to spend all that time with her. "It was just the easiest way to make sure she didn't keep getting a rental car all to herself, so she wouldn't be vulnerable off on her own. And it was supposed to end once the stalker was caught, not drag on forever."

"And you don't think you would have changed your mind about the annulment, if your boss hadn't made that suggestion?" Harlan inquired.

"I don't know," Brent started to reply.

Aiken didn't stick around to hear another word from her husband, turning and running back to the house as quietly and quickly as she could in her heels. She was grateful the shutters were closed on the window into the garage, so she knew they hadn't seen her. *And hopefully, I'll be back inside before they figure out what they might have heard of my retreat, so they won't catch me crying.*

She was careful to quietly shut the back door as she reentered the house, and rushed to put their coats back where Brent had previously hung them. Then she ran into the bathroom, turning on the faucet to cover the sounds of her sobs.

I knew the last few weeks were too good to be true. But why the hell didn't he just tell me he didn't really want to make a go of our marriage, instead of lying about wanting us to try dating? If he'd have explained that Rick didn't want any of us riding alone because of the stalker, I'd have been fine with riding with him or some of the other guys. Or hell, I could have tagged along with Emerald and Josh, or Chastity and Protection Detail, or any of our other coworkers just to get to and from the airports, hotels, and arenas without interfering in their dates.

For that matter, he could have come clean about why he wanted to date me when I said something about it feeling like we were just friends after that first week. I'd have been fine with just riding together to stay safe, instead of pushing for more in our relationship, if he'd said something then. But no, he had to go along with exploring our chemistry and showing affection for one another, so I actually fell for the big jerk.

Was that just because he wanted to get laid? Is he so cold-hearted that he doesn't care that I gave him my heart at the same time I gave him my body? Does he not realize how bad it's going to hurt me when we end our marriage?

For that matter, why hasn't he gone back to pushing for the annulment since the stalker is no longer a threat? Is it just because he wants to keep getting laid while we're booked in this married gimmick for the next few months?

If that's what he thinks is going to happen, he's got another think coming! We are definitely going to stay at the hotel tonight now. And we're going back to separate rooms, too!

~~~

As soon as his dad joined him in the garage, Brent knew he needed to take advantage of the few minutes Aiken was occupied in the house to talk to his dad about his confusing feelings for her, assuming they

313
~~~

could review his dad's latest hot rod restoration later. Or that they could quickly switch topics, if necessary, whenever they heard Aiken coming out of the house. *Naw, she's not interested enough in classic cars to come out here. She'll most likely stay inside, where it's warm, and go snooping around my bedroom.* Brent grinned at the thought while opening the garage door.

"Since when are you interested in my hobby of tinkering around with old cars?" Harlan asked, stepping into the garage just a few seconds behind Brent. "Hell, you won't even buy a car, since you think it's a waste to let it sit while you're on tour."

"I've always been interested in your hobbies, Dad." Brent popped the hood of the rusty red Mustang. "In fact, I kinda thought I'd be out here working alongside you when I get too old to keep wrestling. Besides, wasn't it you who taught me that it was a waste of money to pay full price for a new car, plus the extra insurance each month, for it to just sit and depreciate when I'm not here to drive it?"

"Yeah, you might be right about that," Harlan admitted, leaning back against the tool bench and crossing his arms over his chest as he observed his son. "But that doesn't explain why you suddenly seem all excited to check out *this* car. The way you're acting kinda makes me think you're just using it as an excuse to get away from Aiken for a few minutes."

"It's not that I wanna get away from her," Brent sighed, walking over to the passenger side of the car and leaning on the fender, so he could face his father to talk, while appearing to be looking under the hood, as he kept an eye on the garage door to see Aiken, if she should happen to come outside without him hearing the screen on the backdoor squeak. "I just wanted to talk to you about her, or rather my feelings for her, without her overhearing."

"Oh-kay…" Harlan drew the word out, clearly intending it as a prompt for Brent to start talking.

"I'm confused 'cause it seems like my feelings keep changing," Brent admitted. "And I'm not sure if that's because I'm falling in love with her, or if I'm confusing friendship and lust for love. Like, how am I supposed to know for sure that I'm not just thinking with my dick?"

"Well, when all your blood flow is going there instead of your brain, it can be kinda confusing," Harlan laughed. "But that's why you need to think about how you feel when you're not focused on having sex with her. How'd you feel about her when we were eating lunch a few minutes ago? How'd you feel when you were at her dads' place a couple days ago? How do you feel when you watch her wrestle? Or when she's approached by other guys to sign autographs?"

"When we were eating lunch earlier, it felt like I was sitting there with my two best friends," Brent confided, making sure his dad knew he was still the person Brent considered his first best friend, even if he felt like Aiken was quickly working her way up to an equal best friend status. "And when I watch her wrestle, I feel proud of her for her talent, both as a fellow wrestler in the ring and as an actress when she's cutting promos and taping vignettes to air on TV."

Brent paused to blow out a harsh breath before admitting to the negative feelings he had when thinking about the other two situations his dad mentioned. "I feel jealous as fuck whenever fans hit on her. Hell, even just watching her sign autographs for the women and children at the fan expo a couple of weeks ago, I hated that they were getting all her attention instead of me."

"So you felt possessive of her?" Harlan arched an eyebrow inquisitively. "Not just protective because the stalker hadn't been caught yet?"

"Yeah," Brent huffed, irritated with himself for how he'd felt like he'd had some of the same thoughts about Aiken as stalkers did for their victims. "And the worst part is that I had some of those same thoughts and feelings when we were with her dads on Monday. But most of the time we were there, I just felt like I wasn't good enough for her."

"Why the hell would you think you're not good enough for her?"

"She comes from mega money, Dad."

"So? You both do the same job," Harlan growled. "So, you probably make about the same amount she does, if not more, since you've been with the company longer than she has."

"I'm not concerned about our current incomes. I'm uneasy about being able to live up to the standards her dads have set for her while she was growing up. Her dads' house is nothing like this place." Brent waved an arm around to indicate he was referring to the house, as well as the garage they were standing in, before practically slamming his hand back down on the fender of the car. "Hell, their *estate* is like ten times the size of this place, with nine bedrooms and over a dozen bathrooms, and so many extra rooms that they have a whole nightclub in the lower level, along with a gym, and even a room just for meditation. Hell, they have a five-car garage and outdoor parking for at least five more cars. And don't even get me started on the hundred-foot-long pool and thirty-person jacuzzi spa. Not to mention the fucking sand volleyball court. Even if I could wrestle for another fifty years, I'll never be able to afford to buy her a house like that. So, even if I *am* falling in love with her, I'm not sure it'll be enough for us to stay married when I can't provide for her in the manner she's accustomed to."

"It won't be if you just give up and don't commit to working on your marriage every day for the rest of your life," Harlan pointed out. "And that starts with accepting the fact that you won't have to provide her with a house as fabulous as her dads', 'cause it sounds like she's already gonna inherit one eventually. Now you just have to decide if you love her enough to want to live there with her one of these days."

"I don't know, Dad," Brent sighed, shaking his head. "I don't know if I'll ever feel comfortable there, especially after feeling like shit when I couldn't honestly look her dads in the eyes and say for sure that I'm in love with their daughter."

"So, does that mean you're still thinking about getting the annulment?"

"I don't know," Brent admitted, hanging his head in shame. "But I have to wonder if it's not best to go ahead and end the marriage now before more feelings get involved, instead of dragging it out until one of us retires and we go off in separate directions with our lives."

"What makes you think you're gonna go off in separate directions after you quit wrestling?"

"Wrestling is the only thing we have in common, so once we don't have that, I'm sure even our sex life will start to fizzle out to where it can't sustain us."

"Are you sure that's all you have in common? Didn't you say you had a great time on your dates, even when they were at places neither one of you would normally enjoy going?"

"Yeah, but, fuck, Dad, I only dropped my plans for an annulment and started *dating* her, if you can even call hanging out with her as a friend, *dating*, because Rick suggested it, so we could keep all the women safe without them getting pissed at us for thinking they couldn't defend themselves when that stalker escalated his threats," Brent groaned, feeling like a jackass for starting his relationship with Aiken under false pretenses. "It was just the easiest way to make sure she didn't keep getting a rental car all to herself, so she wouldn't be vulnerable off on her own. And it was supposed to end once the stalker was caught, not drag on forever."

"And you don't think you would have changed your mind about the annulment, if your boss hadn't made that suggestion?" Harlan inquired, using the tone of voice Brent recognized as the one his dad always used when he was trying to make whoever he was talking to realize they were wrong.

"I don't know," Brent grumbled, honestly unsure if he'd have eventually come to the realization on his own that his attraction to Aiken was more than just the fleeting desire to fuck that he'd felt in the past. "As different as things feel with her compared to other women I've *dated* in the past…" He coughed to cover for using the word "dating" to describe his series of random hookups with ring rats before he was married. "…I'd like to think I'd have eventually smartened up and asked her out for real. And even if I hadn't started dating her before the stalker was caught, I think my fear for her safety when I heard those gunshots would have clued me in that I might really feel more than just lust and friendship."

"So, does that mean you've finally realized you're actually in love with her?" Harlan smirked when Brent finally lifted his eyes to look at his dad, instead of continuing to stare down at the rusty fender he was leaning on. "'Cause based on everything you just said and the way you couldn't take your eyes off her the whole time we were having lunch, it's pretty damn obvious to me how much you love her."

While looking at the earnest expression on his father's face, Brent suddenly realized he wasn't just starting to fall for Aiken. He'd actually fallen in love with her, whether or not he wanted to admit it to anyone else just yet.

Holy fuck! I think he's right. I'm in love with Aiken!

Hell, I'm not even sure what it means to be in love, other than worrying more about her than anyone or anything else on earth, and wanting to keep her all to myself so I can protect her from ever being hurt in any way. And that's definitely not the romantic love I'm sure she wants from her partner. But damn, I'm willing to learn whatever I have to, so I can be the romantic partner she needs.

"You need a few more minutes to wrap your mind around that? Or are you just waiting for me to impart all my wisdom about how to go about convincing your bride to stay married to you?"

"No offense, Dad," Brent chuckled wryly. "While I think you are by far the greatest role model I could have for how to be a father, I'm not sure you're the best person to advise me on how to romance my wife."

"Yeah, well, if you'd asked my advice back when I was your age, I'd have agreed with you," Harlan snorted, obviously finding humor in Brent's veiled reference to his parents' failed marriage. "But I've learned a lot in the years since Lisa left. And I know now that her leaving had nothing to do with me not being romantic enough. Yeah, I probably could have taken her out on the town more often, or bought her little thinking-of-you gifts every week, instead of only getting her stuff for birthdays and Christmas. But instead of buying her cut flowers that were just gonna die in a few days, I planted flowers for her, so she'd get to see them grow all season, and I told her 'I love you' every day. Those were the last three words I said every time we parted ways, whether it was as I left the house for work each morning, or just before we hung up after talking on the phone at random times throughout the day. I always wanted to make sure those were the last words she heard from me, just in case something happened and I didn't get to say them again. Even at the end, when practically every conversation ended up in a fight, I still said, 'I love you,' as my final words to her."

"If you were that romantic with her, why the hell did she leave?" When he thought back, Brent remembered his dad always ending conversations with those three words, but he'd kind of thought they were meant to be sarcastic when his parents were fighting. *Hell, he still ends all his phone calls with me by saying "I love you," so now I do the same with him. So, why the fuck didn't I realize he wasn't being sarcastic when he said them to Mom back then?*

"Because your mom grew up in an abusive household and it skewed her perception of a lot of things, especially relationships. She misunderstood my desire for her to stay home with you when you were little, and then not go back to work when you started school, as trying to control her and keep her dependent on me. When I really just wanted her to have her days free to pursue her favorite hobbies and be available whenever you were sick or needed a chaperone for field trips or other school activities. Hell, I wouldn't have had a problem with her getting a part-time job if it was something she was really passionate about and the hours coincided with when you were in school."

Harlan paused to take a deep breath and blow it out before continuing. "But the only places she wanted to apply were restaurants and bars, where she'd have to work nights and weekends, instead of spending our family time together. I didn't understand it back then, but I later found out that she had problems with self-esteem and depression, and wanted to work as a cocktail waitress because she needed more than just me telling her she was attractive to even half-ass believe it."

"How'd you find that out later?" Brent was curious about how his dad could figure out anything about his mom when neither of them had seen or heard from her since 1993.

"About ten years ago, when you insisted I get with the times and get on Facebook, I looked her up." Harlan shrugged, like it was no big deal. "She didn't have a profile then, but her best friend did. And she filled me in on how Lisa bounced around between bar jobs and boyfriends for several years before getting busted for drugs and spending some time in rehab and a mental health facility."

"Have you kept tabs on her since then? Do you know where she is now?" *Is she still in a mental health facility? Is that why she hasn't ever tried to contact me? If so, who's paying for it? Do I need to take over her expenses now, since as her son, I'm her only living relative?* With all the other questions running through his head, he didn't have the time or mental capacity to question whether or not knowing his mother's mental health issues had triggered her leaving all those years ago would change his perception of the past or his fears for his future with Aiken.

"I tried, but about five years ago, the one time Lisa called me to make amends as part of her program, she made it clear that it was best for her mental health to move on with her life and not look back." Harlan's melancholy expression made it clear to Brent how hard it was for his dad to accept his mom's decision. "I made it clear she'd always be welcome here as part of our family and that we hold no ill will toward her, but she needs to be the one to make the decision to get in touch again. And even then I told her I love her just before we hung up."

"And if she does show up here one day, are you really willing to give her a second chance to break your heart?"

"Absolutely. She's the love of my life, Son, so if she were to ever show up here again, I'd romance the hell outta her to try to get her to want to stay."

Is Aiken the love of my life? Do I love her enough to wait for her if she ever left like Mom did? I don't know, but I sure as hell hope so. Only I hope she thinks of me as the love of her life, too, so she'll never wanna leave me.

"Why didn't you tell me all this before now?" While he understood that his dad probably needed some time to work through all his feelings after learning this new information, it seemed like he should have easily done that in the last ten years, since he'd first looked her up. Or at least in the last five years, since he'd actually spoken to her. *Hopefully, it won't take me as long as it took him to come to terms with this new info, so I can get past my fear of Aiken leaving me a lot sooner than five or ten years from now. I mean, I know she doesn't have the same mental health problems Mom did, or still does, so I really shouldn't worry about our marriage repeating their history. But I could have inherited some of that shit from Mom, so I still have to wonder if I'll ever flip out and need to be hospitalized. And if I do, how will that effect things between me and Aiken?*

"'Cause I figured you were dealing well with not having her in your life, and I didn't want to get your hopes up that she might come back, when I'm pretty sure that's never gonna happen."

"And why didn't she call me when she was making amends as part of her program? Shouldn't I be included in the list of people she needed to call and apologize to after the way she just took off without even saying goodbye?"

"I tried giving her your phone number for just that reason, but she wouldn't take it." Harlan cringed. "She said something about the program having exemptions for making contact with any kids the participants gave up for adoption, which she felt included you since she'd signed over her parental rights in our divorce. At the time, I assumed it was a blanket statement that the facility covered with everyone to protect any kids whose adoption records were sealed. But now I have to wonder if she knew about it because she had other kids that she put up for adoption over the years."

"Fuck," Brent groaned. "Are you saying I could have siblings or half-siblings out there somewhere?"

"Well, she didn't mention any specifically, but it is possible."

"Maybe I should have done one of those DNA tests some of the guys did a few months back, so I might one day find them." *But hell, if they're as fucked up in the head as our mom, maybe I don't want to take that chance.*

Brent really didn't want to get into that debate with his dad, though, knowing he needed time to let all this new information about his family sink in before he could rationally make a decision about whether or not he should try to find out more about his possible siblings. "How the hell did we go from you offering me advice about me and Aiken to discussing all this?"

"Beats me," Harlan chuckled and shrugged. "But I'd much rather go back to talking about your beautiful bride and how I think you need to go about telling her you love her for the first time, so you can start following my best advice by saying those three little words to her daily."

"Yeah? And how do you think I need to go about doing that?" Brent smirked at his dad, knowing the old man probably had a doozy of an idea.

"Since you got married without all the usual bells and whistles beforehand, I think you need to surprise her with a romantic proposal for staying married, like while you're out at a candlelight dinner, where you can have the room filled with roses or her favorite flowers, and her dads and I can witness it from a nearby table. And I have just the rings for you to use." Harlan pushed off the tool bench he was leaning against and stepped out of the garage to go to his truck.

Brent was surprised when he opened the passenger door and reached into his glove box. "I was actually going to ask you if you still have that old jewelry box in the attic I could go through to find a family heirloom to give her."

"Yeah, well, I saved you the trouble of going through all that old junk," Harlan beamed as he handed Brent the small blue ring box he'd just pulled from his glove box. "These were my parents' wedding rings, which I just had professionally cleaned and checked to make sure the setting wasn't loose in the engagement ring. I didn't know your ring sizes, so I could only estimate that Granddad's band would fit you by checking on my hand. But you can get Grandma's rings resized if they don't fit Aiken."

Brent opened the box to see three gold rings, two of which were matching plain gold bands, with one obviously much larger than the other. The third ring was an obviously older design that he wasn't sure how to classify. He thought most engagement rings were diamond solitaires, but since the small central diamond on this ring had chips of what he thought might be more diamonds on either side of it, he didn't think it was a true solitaire. But since there were two of those little chips on either side of the center stone, which couldn't be more than a carat, and probably wasn't even a full carat, Brent also knew it couldn't be classified as a three-stone ring, which was what Aiken had told him Teagan's ring was after seeing it Sunday night.

His fear that his family heirlooms wouldn't be flashy and expensive enough for Aiken returned tenfold, but Brent wasn't about to share that feeling with his dad. "They're perfect, Dad. But I'm not sure when I'll be able to set up a special dinner with you and her dads flying in to be there when I give them to her. I'd do it one day over our Thanksgiving break, but I don't want to take the spotlight off of Dean and Allissa during all their wedding festivities. Maybe we can schedule something over our Christmas break?"

And that'll give me plenty of time to figure out if I should give her these rings and tell her their history, or if I should go buy something with a bigger diamond. Or if I should call her dads and have them help me pick out something they know she'll love, since I'm sure Shawn knows her taste in jewelry way better than I do.

"Or maybe you could schedule it on your next pay-per-view weekend, so all your GWA friends can be there too," Harlan suggested with a smile, slapping Brent on the back.

"Yeah, maybe," Brent agreed, hoping the month until the **Christmas Chaos** show would be enough time for him to decide on the right choice of rings. Even though he wasn't sure he'd use them,

Brent walked over to his rental car and put the ring box in the bottom of his suitcase, where hopefully Aiken wouldn't find it. "But for now, we should probably go back inside before Aiken comes out here and catches us plotting my proposal."

"Damn, Son, I didn't even think about the possibility that she might still be standing by the sink to see me giving you the rings." Harlan looked over his shoulder at the window over the kitchen sink.

"Since we both had our backs to the house when we were at your truck, and then the trunk obscured her view when I put them away, I doubt she saw anything." Brent reassured his dad as they walked over and closed the garage door. "But I'll be sure to stealthily grab my cufflinks out of my room before we leave, so if she asks, we can say that's what you were handing me, so I'd have them in case I need them for the wedding in a couple of weeks."

When they walked back in the house, they quickly figured out that they wouldn't have to come up with a cover story for Aiken, since she wasn't anywhere near the kitchen. Hearing water running in the bathroom, Brent assumed she'd been in there long enough that she hadn't seen a thing, since washing her hands would be the last thing she did before coming out after using the restroom. But Brent still took advantage of her being otherwise occupied to get his cufflinks from his top dresser drawer and put them in his pocket, just in case.

"So, I'm guessing you didn't bring your bags in 'cause you're not staying the night here." Harlan arched an eyebrow at Brent when he returned to the living room. "Is that 'cause you're still in the honeymoon phase and want more privacy than you'll have here? Or because you've finally decided you're too old to stay the night with your dad?"

"Definitely the privacy thing," Brent chuckled as he sat down on the sofa to face his dad, who was leaned back in his favorite chair with his feet propped up on the ottoman. He ignored the ick-factor of how well his dad knew him to recognize his reasoning for wanting to stay at the hotel instead of his home. But considering he and his dad were so much alike and hadn't ever had a problem discussing sex in the past, he wasn't really as creeped out about his dad knowing what he wanted to do with Aiken at the hotel as he would be if he was sitting there talking to one of Aiken's dads. *After having to fight the urge to make love to her on Monday night and feeling like an ass for wanting to do it in her dads' house, I'm not about to do anything to make Aiken feel as weirded out as I did then, especially when we can stay at the hotel and both feel much more comfortable making love.*

Damn, I really must be in love with her, since I'm thinking about sex as making love instead of fucking. And now I really want to hurry over to the hotel, so maybe we can sneak in a quickie. "In fact, since we came straight here from the airport, we probably need to go get checked in at the hotel before we have to report to the arena. You don't mind meeting us there later, do you?"

"No, I don't mind," Harlan grinned, just as Aiken finally joined them. "I may be old, but I still remember what it's like to be newlyweds. So, I wouldn't dream of interfering with you two going off for a little *afternoon delight* before you have to be at work."

"Oh, no, we don't have time for anything like that," Aiken spluttered, blushing profusely at his dad's veiled reference to them sneaking in a little hotel sex.

Fuck, that sweet, innocent blush is sexy as hell. But damn, she must be really embarrassed 'cause usually her eyes don't turn red too.

"Not if we don't hurry," Brent teased, wagging his eyebrows suggestively at his wife, before standing and grabbing their coats from the coatrack between the sofa and front door.

Before Aiken could protest any further, Brent helped her put on her coat, while making sure his dad had the proper credentials to be able to park in the performers' lot and get past security to come straight into the backstage area, instead of having to deal with the crowds and waiting for the doors to officially open like a typical GWA fan. He then ushered her out the door to their car.

As soon as he pulled out of the driveway, she broke the silence that had settled between them. "Do you think there's any chance that the hotel still has two rooms available on the GWA reservation?"

"I don't know," Brent replied, suddenly worried that seeing his childhood home had clued her in on just how much better she was than him. *Fuck! Did I prematurely start trying to banish my fear of her leaving me?* "Why?"

"I suppose it depends on if Rick has notified the travel department to only book us in one room, huh? Or if they even book you a room here, since you don't normally stay at the hotel in Portland." Aiken kept talking in a bland, flat tone that he'd only ever heard from her one other time — when they first found out they were married and she told him to let her know what he found out about the requirements for an annulment. She didn't even seem to register that he asked her why she was wondering about the room availability. "Well, hopefully, they'll still have a couple of rooms available, even if we aren't able to check-in on the GWA reservation."

"Why do we need two rooms, Aiken?" Brent hated that he'd raised his voice and practically barked out the words, but it was the only way he felt like he could get her attention right then. *Please don't say it's because you're done with me.*

"Because I heard you talking to your dad earlier, and think we need to go back to separate rooms and start researching our annulment options."

Fuck! No! Fucking, fuck!

How the fuck did I not hear her come outside? Or go back in? Or walk across the gravel in those heels to get close enough to the garage to overhear us without me being able to see her?

"Well, you obviously didn't hear the whole conversation, or you'd know I just needed to talk shit out with Dad to clear up my confusion about how I feel about you before deciding to ask you to stay married to me forever!" Brent paused to take a deep breath and try to rein in his temper, not wanting to blurt out those three little words in the heat of the moment.

"No, I didn't feel it necessary to stick around after hearing how you lied about not wanting the annulment and only dated me because Rick asked you to. Since you made it clear that you don't want our relationship to drag on forever, I walked away to keep from fighting with you in front of your dad and any of his neighbors, who might have taped it to send in to CNZ."

"I never said I don't want our relationship to drag on forever," Brent argued, cutting himself off before he dug himself a deeper hole by trying to explain his earlier poorly worded statement. *Calm down, asshole! Don't make it worse by getting pissed. That'll just give her another reason to not wanna give me a chance to win her back.*

"No? Then what didn't you want to *drag on forever*? Those are your exact words, Brent. So what did you mean by them?"

"I meant the stalker situation, not us dating. I just worded it wrong because I was venting about how guilty I felt for starting our relationship under false pretenses, and being too much of a blind idiot to see I wanted us to be more than friends and coworkers before we started *dating*," Brent admitted with a sigh. "But regardless of how we started, or if I had unrecognized feelings for you before, I've definitely developed deeper feelings for you in the last few weeks."

"No," Aiken interrupted, holding up a hand in the universal symbol for stop. "Don't you dare say a single word about falling for me since we found out we're married. After the way you lied to me already, I won't believe those words right now."

Yeah, I know now is definitely not the right time to say "I love you" for the first time.

"Then give me a chance to show you how I feel before you start looking into annulment options," Brent pleaded, hoping he hadn't blown his only chance with her. "I understand if you still think we need to go back to separate rooms for a little while, but please, let me keep taking you on dates, so I can prove myself to you. So I can prove that I don't want to end our marriage, and I desperately want to plan our future together."

"You want to plan our future together?" Aiken glared at him skeptically.

"Yes," he replied vehemently. "And I'm not just talking about the next few months. I want us to plan the next fifty or sixty years together."

"And what exactly do you see in our future?"

"Wrestling until you're ready to retire, then houses in both L.A. and Portland, so our kids can spend time with all three of their granddads," Brent stated matter-of-factly, letting the fact that he'd just decided he wanted children with her sink in as he envisioned the future he wanted with Aiken as his wife. "And I want at least two kids, so they never feel like a lonely only the way we did growing up. I don't care if we have them biologically or adopt them or have a combination of biological and adopted children, but I want us to spend quality family time together as much as possible."

Brent surprised even himself with his words. But the more he thought about the vision of their future family he'd just described, the more he felt the need to make it a reality. He held his breath as Aiken examined him cautiously from the other side of the car. *Please,*

Princess, say you'll give me a chance to show you that we're meant for one another.

"Fine, I'll give you time to prove yourself," Aiken conceded, her lips barely turning up slightly at the corners after he mentioned them having kids together. "But we're definitely going back to separate hotel rooms and starting over with dating. That means going back to just basic friendly affection, holding hands, hugs, and chaste kisses only. Nothing sexual or even mildly passionate until you prove that's not all you want from our marriage."

"Deal," Brent agreed instantly, not wanting to give her the chance to change her mind.

I guess this means I have a lot more than a month to decide about our wedding rings. While I'll have to sneak a text message to Dad, so he doesn't start looking at flights for our **Christmas Chaos** *weekend, I think I'll still hang on to Granddad and Grandma's rings, just in case. Even if I can't give them to her, maybe having them in my suitcase will act as a good luck charm to help me convince her that I love her.*

Chapter Eleven

Josh was surprised by how Teagan seemed to be rushing him to get into the lobby of the Hunters' Bed and Breakfast as soon as they got into town for all the festivities leading up to Dean and Allissa's wedding, which was now just a little over a week away. Instead of waiting for him to come around and open her door, she jumped out of the car as soon as he had it parked and hurried ahead of him, not even pausing long enough to give him a peck of a kiss, like they always did when they parted briefly. Granted, that was usually backstage when they had to go to their separate locker rooms, or when one of them had to perform, but he still missed their usual see-you-in-a-little-while kiss when she left him in the car to go in the B and B without him. When he caught up with her, and found her huddled with Allissa, Fiona, Rick, and Mandi, whispering about room assignments for all three Vegas couples, he soon figured out that her frenzied behavior was because she was finalizing plans to play matchmaker for their friends.

He was a little surprised to see that their boss was obviously on board with whatever matchmaking shenanigans the ladies were suggesting. But then again, after witnessing Rick and Fiona's whirlwind romance at the beginning of the year, he probably shouldn't have been. Rick's devotion to Fiona and desire to do anything she asked of him was written clear as day on their previously stoic boss's face. After experiencing all the changes in the GWA since Rick took over from his father and divorced his first wife, Josh was glad to see the boss happy and really letting down his guard to have fun with the crew again.

While Rick had never really stopped being the fun-loving guy with his daughter that he'd been with everyone back when he was wrestling, he'd definitely distanced himself from the rest of the GWA roster. But since having Fiona in his life, he seemed even happier than he'd been when Josh first met him as a fellow wrestler. But then again, back when Josh first joined the company, Rick had been married for a couple of years and was traveling without his family to perform on all the shows. So, even though he joked around with the other wrestlers, his home life wasn't as jovial as his professional life.

While Josh completely understood why Rick had to put that professional distance between himself and everyone who worked for him when he took over as the owner of the GWA, he was also glad to see that having the right woman in his life seemed to be having a positive influence on his ability to joke around and be a friend to all his employees and not just the boss. In fact, witnessing the positive changes in Rick's life, since meeting, dating, and marrying Fiona, was probably one of the reasons why Josh was able to drop his no-dating-coworkers rule when he'd found out he'd married Teagan.

Hell, I hope following his lead, and going along with whatever matchmaking plans Teagan has for this week, won't come back to bite me in the ass.

Watching as the other two couples who got married in Vegas finally entered the lobby of the boutique hotel, however, he wasn't so sure whatever Teagan and her matchmaking friends had planned would be as successful as he was sure his wife intended. After all the talks they'd had the last few weeks, he was positive Liam would fake being happily married just enough to keep up appearances this week. Then he'd go back to avoiding Rylie most of the time as soon as they left town. Well, other than when they had to work together on the GWA shows, anyway. So, Josh was certain Liam would be pissed about having to room with his wife all week and wouldn't end up leaving Heart's Destiny being happy he was married to Rylie the way Teagan hoped.

Josh wasn't just concerned about how Red and Chastity were probably going to fight back against having to spend any extra time together this week, either. While he'd thought Crockett and Amethyst had started developing feelings for one another after starting to date for the first month after they all found out about the weddings, he'd noticed that their connection seemed to have cooled off quite a bit since they'd visited both their families while the GWA traveled the west coast loop a couple weeks back.

Of course, he'd also thought the majority of the heat he'd seen between them the first couple of weeks was just Crockett acting interested to keep Amethyst safe because Rick had asked all the men who worked for him to watch over all the women and children after Allissa's stalker started escalating his threats. But then, when all that came to a head at the end of October, and the guys had sat down to talk to Liam, Crockett was pretty adamant that he'd developed real feelings for Aiken, especially when Liam pointed out that he could stop playing bodyguard all the time now that the stalker was no longer a threat.

In fact, when Josh had noticed that they'd started rooming together after that weekend in New Orleans, he'd really thought that meant they'd decided to make a go of their marriage. But then after their tour stops in L.A. and Portland, when Josh assumed they'd spent time with both their families, since he saw Aiken's dads at the L.A. show and Crockett's dad at the Portland show, they'd reverted back to getting separate rooms. They still rode together between the airports, hotels, and arenas, and resumed going on midday dates once the restrictions on those were removed after the stalker was dealt with, but they weren't nearly as glued together backstage as they'd been between New Orleans and Los Angeles.

Fuck! I hope it's not a homophobic or racial thing with Crockett's dad. Josh didn't think Brent actually had issues with Aiken being Vietnamese and adopted by a gay couple, with one of her dads being Black and the other being white, since he'd never expressed any discomfort with working with anyone in the GWA, regardless of race, gender, or sexual orientation. But Josh had only briefly spoken with Harlan Crockett a handful of times over the years in the almost a decade that he and Brent had both worked with the company, so he didn't know the older Mr. Crockett's views on such things. *If that's the problem they're facing in their marriage, then none of Teagan's schemes to push them together this week are gonna help them fix it. Hell, short of trying to convince Crockett to cut his dad out of his life, if he has a problem with Aiken or her dads, there's not really anything any of us can do to help them work things out.*

Assuming that would be exactly what his beautiful bride would expect him to do, if he mentioned what he'd noticed about their friends in the last couple of weeks, Josh decided to keep his thoughts to himself as he finally stepped up to the desk to get them checked in at the bed and breakfast. *But maybe I can distract her from any other plans she might try to pull me into tonight with a little faux punishment for her interference in our friends' marriages. I know she's not into any kind of hardcore BDSM, but with how her pussy gushes whenever I get commanding and step out of vanilla sex territory with a little light kink, I have to wonder if she'll enjoy a light spanking and maybe a little punishing-my-naughty-housewife role-play.*

Considering his cock stood at attention from just the thought, Josh was glad Teagan's conversation with her co-conspirators had to be cut short, now that their four matchmaking targets were in the room. But when she tried to dawdle after he got their room assignment, he decided to put his plan into action immediately, just so he didn't risk anyone but Teagan noticing how he was tenting his slacks. "Come on, Wifey," he commanded, lowering his voice the way he knew made her panties wet instantly. "We have some things we need to…discuss in our room right now."

"But I'm waiting until the girls get their room assignments, so we can make plans to meet up for dinner," Teagan argued, looking back and forth between Josh and their friends, who were near the back of the line of GWA wrestlers waiting to get checked in.

"Yeah, you're gonna hafta plan to meet them for breakfast instead of dinner," Josh insisted, reaching out to clasp her hand to pull her away from the front desk and back out the front door to their car, so they could drive around to the larger of the two B and B buildings, where their room was located. "'Cause we're gonna be ordering room service for dinner tonight and not leaving our room until tomorrow morning."

While the bed and breakfast hadn't had a room service option the first time they'd been there the year before, Josh knew they'd added it on a limited basis since the addition of the full-service restaurant downstairs in the Heritage House building. Before that, they'd had to order pizza or burgers from the restaurants in town and have them delivered to their room. Of course, he'd also managed to get room service before it was officially offered by getting the right member of the Hunters' family on the phone to place a food order, and they'd made sure it was delivered to his room. So he was certain that if he called after their normal room-service hours, he could still get food delivered to his room whenever he and Teagan were ready to eat while taking a break from their sexual escapades.

Teagan's eyes widened as she seemed to catch onto what he had planned, but she grinned brightly as she willingly followed him, calling out behind them to their friends, "See you guys in the morning at breakfast!"

"Remember, the breakfast buffet is only from six to ten," Mandi Hunter shouted back at them. "So, if you don't make it down by then, you'll have to go to the restaurant in the Heritage House, or head back over here to use the kitchen in this building to make your own."

Josh knew the building the Hunters referred to as the Heritage House was the huge building they'd refurbished the previous year to accommodate all the wrestlers and GWA staff who came to Anthony and Kay's wedding. But he had no idea if they'd actually named the building that had originally housed the first iteration of the bed and breakfast. Not that he was sticking around to ask anyone right then.

After already spending three of his previous holiday breaks in Heart's Destiny for various wedding festivities in the last year, this fourth time checking in and driving around the property to the other building before getting out their luggage and going to their room felt almost like an ingrained habit. With all the GWA wrestlers and staff getting married here recently, Josh realized he'd actually spent more time in the Hunters' Bed and Breakfast than in his own home, and more time in Heart's Destiny than any other city or town in the last year. Thankfully, thinking about that was enough to deflate his cock before they had to get out of the car and carry their luggage through the Heritage House and up to their room on the second floor, so he didn't have to worry about any of the staff bustling around noticing his aroused state.

"Whoa! Josh, you're going to have to slow down some," Teagan complained as soon as they were loaded down with their luggage and started walking from the car to the building, pulling back on his hand, presumably to get him to stop dragging her behind him as if she was another piece of luggage. "There's no way I can run up those stairs in heels without tripping and breaking something."

"Sorry," Josh apologized to his wife, stopping in his tracks to let her set the pace for how fast they walked into the building and up to their room.

"It's okay." Teagan grinned at him now that they were walking at a more normal pace, instead of speed-walking, as they picked up their rolling suitcases and started up the half-dozen outside stairs to the main entrance. "But what is it we need to discuss that's got you in such a rush this afternoon?"

"I think you know already," Josh smirked, arching an eyebrow at her as he stopped at the top of the stairs to open the door for her to precede him into the building.

"Well, I think I might have an idea," Teagan teased, glancing over her shoulder at him as she walked past him. "But since we didn't have to fly out of Lubbock until after lunch, it's only been about four hours since we did *that* before checking out of the hotel, so I can't imagine you're in such dire need that you can't wait until after dinner."

"Really?" Josh quickly caught up to her, dipping his head to whisper in her ear, so nobody around them could hear. "After the way you kept rubbing your hand on my leg, both on the plane and in the car, you don't think I'm in dire need for you now?"

"That little bit of touching is all it takes to get you revved up? I'd have thought you'd have learned to control yourself better than that by your age. I mean, don't most men outgrow their quick-draw phase when they leave their teens?"

"Oh, Wifey, I think I've more than proven over the last few weeks that I'm no Quick Draw McGraw," Josh growled near her ear, keeping his voice low and guttural. "But your touch is extremely potent, so even if you just accidentally brush up against me, I'm instantly amped and my cock pops up to take you for a ride. But there's a big difference between being easily aroused by you and jizzing in my Jockeys. And maybe you should remember that before your teasing earns you more of a punishment than I'm already planning to give you for interfering in our friends' marriages."

"What?" Teagan spun on her heels, catching him in the shin with the corner of the rolling suitcase she was pulling behind her. He'd thought he was safe from it, since they'd carried or pulled their luggage on the sides opposite of each other, leaving their hands free in the middle to walk hand in hand as they often did everywhere they went. But somehow it managed to bypass her as she spun to slam into his leg.

"Ouch!" As he saw a couple of kids walking out of the restaurant with their parents, Josh barely managed to keep from cussing at the pain caused by her hard-sided suitcase.

"You *did not* just say you plan on punishing me like a child," Teagan hissed, not seeming to notice that she'd injured him.

"Definitely not like a child." Josh smirked, shaking his head as he stepped around her giant green Samsonite, and trying to ignore the throbbing in his shin as he continued toward the grand staircase that led to the upper floors. When she caught up with him, so he could speak where only she could hear him, he added, "More like a naughty wife."

Teagan opened her mouth as if to reply, but quickly snapped it shut. Josh observed her through his peripheral vision, as they both paused to lower the telescopic handles on their rolling luggage to carry them up the much larger flight of stairs than the few steps they'd already traversed outside. Based on the way her eyes flared and her breathing quickened, Josh was pretty sure she was way more aroused by the idea than even she expected. Neither of them said anything more as they made their way up the stairs and down the hall to their room.

Josh knew his wife well enough to know it was best to wait her out before laying out all the things he had planned out in his head. She needed time to process the basics of what he was suggesting to decide if it was something that interested her enough to try. Then if she didn't flat out refuse, they'd have to discuss the more intricate details of what he had in mind before deciding if she really wanted to try something new. She was the same way whenever she planned out a wrestling match with a new opponent, or even if one of the women she'd worked with for years wanted to try a new maneuver. It was actually observing her choreographing her matches for the last few years that clued him in on how he'd need to approach adding anything even slightly kinky to their sexual repertoire.

"Okay, what exactly did you have in mind?" Teagan finally asked, after they entered their room and mostly organized their things. She crossed the room and took a seat on the end of the bed.

"Primarily, I thought about how hot you'd look bent over the end of the bed for me to spank you, and then fuck you from behind," Josh admitted, making sure she noticed how he raked his eyes over her body from head to toe as he leaned against the dresser just a few feet away. "But I figured we'd have to do a little role-play to set the scene, which is why I came up with the idea to say I'm punishing you for interfering in our friends' marriages, instead of focusing on ours."

"And what if I don't like being spanked?" Teagan arched an eyebrow at him.

"Then we skip it and I'll just fuck you from behind," Josh shrugged. "I know you love it when I bend you over the nearest flat surface and push your skirt up outta the way 'cause I can't wait to take you, so we're both gonna enjoy it whether we add the spanking or not. I just thought it might be fun to try and see if you like it. No big deal, either way."

"So, you're not really upset with me for scheming with the local matchmakers to try and help our friends end up as happily married as we are?"

"No," Josh chuckled, walking over to sit beside her on the bed, joining their left hands so he could appreciate the sight of their wedding rings together. "I'm a little concerned that you might not get the outcomes you want from these little schemes, but I'm not upset in any way. Hell, I'm hoping you'll surprise me by coming up with the perfect plan to make sure all our friends are as happy as we are, so we can enjoy hanging out with all of them again."

"Okay." Teagan nodded, brushing the pad of her thumb over the band on his hand as he did the same with her rings. "But how hard are you planning to spank me?"

"Not nearly as hard as you slap my arms or chop me in the chest whenever you get riled up," Josh smirked. "Or even a tenth as hard as you hit me in the shin with your suitcase downstairs a few minutes ago."

"Oh, God! Did I hurt you? I'm so sorry. I didn't even realize it hit you." Teagan looked down at his legs, her expression appearing troubled, and maybe slightly confused, by not being able to see the evidence of his injury through his pants.

"I'm probably gonna have a hell of a bruise, but I'll live." Josh released her hand and lifted his pant leg, so they could both see where his skin was already discolored from his normal tan to a dark red from the blow. "Thankfully, we've got ten days before I'll have to figure out how to cover it up to wrestle."

"With the way you wrestle barefoot, instead of wearing boots and shin guards like the rest of us, we'll probably have to go by a beauty supply store this week to find some makeup that will cover it without clumping up your leg hair," Teagan suggested as she leaned forward and examined his leg. "Maybe one of those powdered mineral foundations or the airbrush stuff will work?"

"Yeah, I'll let you figure all that out if the bruising hasn't faded by this time next week," Josh chuckled, thinking letting his wife put makeup on his lower leg sounded way better than his original plan of having Doc tape him up, and then having to endure the pain of ripping the hair off his leg to remove the tape after wrestling.

"I suppose injuring you could be another reason you need to spank me," Teagan cooed, lightly running her hand over his bruised shin before sitting back up. Josh didn't think the gesture was meant to be teasing, but with all his blood flow redirected to his cock, he no longer felt any pain at the site of the minor wound. "Though maybe for that I should lay over your lap, so you don't have to stand on your injured leg. And then maybe I should get on my knees and service you with my mouth to apologize."

Fuck! Maybe she did mean to tease me by stroking her hand over my shin.

"My leg doesn't really hurt that bad, but I'm game for combining our plans to see what positions we like best." Josh tried to hold back his smirk, putting on a stern expression to test the waters for how ready Teagan was to get started on the role-play. "If you're ready to accept your punishment, Wifey, you need to strip before you start apologizing."

"Yes, Sir," Teagan agreed coyly, standing to remove her red dress and reveal her matching red bra and panties.

"Fuck," Josh groaned, his dick throbbing at the sight of his sexy wife. His ache for her was so intense he unconsciously reached down and squeezed his cock through his pants to momentarily feel a little relief. "You're gorgeous. But even as hot as you look in red lace, you need to quit stalling and finish stripping before you earn more than the ten swats I have planned for you."

"May I ask how you came up with that number for my punishment, Sir?" Teagan cooed as she reached around behind her to unfasten her bra before letting it drop to the floor.

"Five for focusing on our friends' marriages instead of ours, and five for hitting me with your suitcase," Josh replied, unfastening his slacks so he could stroke his cock without grinding his zipper into his rigid flesh. "But now that I'm really thinking about it, maybe I should add another five for throwing a fit when I first mentioned punishing you."

"No, please, Sir, I don't think I can even handle ten swats," Teagan pleaded as she pushed her panties down her luscious long legs. Then she dropped to her knees and reached for his cock, which was poking out the top of his boxer briefs. "I'd rather you fuck my mouth instead."

"Oh, no, I'm not gonna fuck your mouth, Tea." Josh gripped her wrists to keep her from touching him and making him blow his load too soon. "You're gonna show me how sorry you are by sucking my cock. But only after I'm finished spanking you. Now lay over my lap and take your punishment like a good wife."

"Yes, Sir," Teagan agreed breathily as she stood, giving him a glimpse of her glistening wet pussy before she draped herself over his lap.

With his left hand on her upper back to make it feel like he was holding her in place, Josh ran his right hand over the round globes of her fuckable ass. Thinking about how bad he wanted to fuck her in every hole made his dick twitch against her side. He ran his hand down between her thighs to feel how wet and ready she was for him, taking a moment to finger-fuck her while giving her the rest of his directives for accepting her punishment.

"So, fucking, wet already. Such a naughty wife, being this turned on by just the thought of being spanked. But this is a punishment, not a reward, so you'd better not come from me swatting your ass." He spread some of her arousal up between her cheeks to lube up her asshole for him to work his thumb in up to the first knuckle while still finger-fucking her pussy with his middle and ring fingers. "You're not allowed to come while you're sucking my cock either. If you're a good wife, accepting your punishment and apologizing while holding back your orgasm, I'll let you come on my cock when I fuck your sweet cunt. But if you're a naughty wife and come before I'm balls-deep in your pussy, then instead of fucking your cunt, I'm gonna fuck your tight asshole. And I won't stop until you come at least as many times with me in your ass as you come while being spanked and sucking my dick."

Her pussy gushed as she moaned her agreement. "Yes, Sir, Josh."

"Hmmm, Sir Josh, I like that. It sounds rather regal. You should call me Sir Josh anytime we're playing like this."

"Yes, Sir Josh," Teagan whimpered, wiggling her hips until she'd taken his whole thumb in her ass.

Josh could tell she was getting close to coming and since he'd only specifically mentioned that she couldn't come while he was spanking her and she was sucking his cock, he pulled his digits from her body, not wanting her to sneak one in and then claim it didn't count to get out of anal. While he would never force her to do something she truly didn't want to do, based on how she always came harder whenever he teased her ass while they were making love, he knew she'd love anal if he was ever able to get her over the taboo aspect of it to take more than the tip of his dick in her tightest hole.

Before she could vocalize a protest for him withholding her orgasm, Josh lightly slapped his palm on the fleshiest part of her ass.

"Oh!" Teagan jerked over his lap, probably more from surprise than from the sting, since he'd only barely tapped her.

"You need to count your swats," Josh commanded as he watched his precum drip on the side of her back. "Then thank me for it and ask for the next one, Teagan."

"One," she panted out breathlessly. "Thank you, Sir Josh. May I please have another?"

"Such a good wife," Josh praised, bringing his hand down a little harder for the second swat before massaging it in to ease any residual sting.

"Two. Thank you, Sir Josh. May I please have another?"

Fuck, I hope I can hold out and not come until she has me in her mouth.

It only took four swats before Teagan faltered in her counting, crying out her orgasm as her pussy soaked his pants to the point that he felt the moisture through the fabric. Josh took advantage of her euphoric state to work his thumb back in her asshole, knowing he'd have to open her up enough to take his thick cock.

"Such a naughty wife. You didn't even make it halfway through your spanking before you showed me how much you want my cock in your ass."

"Yes, please, Sir Josh, fuck my ass," Teagan begged, rocking her hips to take more of his thumb in her anus.

"I will," he promised as he worked a second digit into her tightest opening, wanting to take her right back to the edge before pulling out and slapping her ass some more. "But first we have to finish your spanking and see how many orgasms you have with these next six swats."

"Isn't it eleven more swats, Sir Josh?" Teagan questioned, writhing on his lap as he finger-fucked her ass.

"That's right, I did add an additional five, didn't I?" Josh couldn't contain his grin at how she'd gone from not thinking she'd like being spanked to actually asking for more than he'd originally planned.

"Yes, Sir Josh." Teagan turned her head to smile up at him. "And I earned every single one of them, so I'll only learn my lesson if you give me all of them."

And he did just that, making her come three more times from the spanking, which he alternated with preparing her ass to take his cock, using the combination of her arousal and his precum that coated her low back to lube her up enough to take three of his fingers in her asshole. "Alright, my naughty wife, get on your knees and clean all this precum off my cock."

"Yes, Sir Josh," Teagan purred as she gracefully got into position on her knees between his spread legs. She pulled his slacks and boxer briefs down out of her way before running her tongue from his balls to his tip, lapping up the trail of precum that had oozed down between their bodies.

When she got to the head, she swirled her tongue over his most sensitive spot where the shaft met the ridge, making his dick twitch in anticipation of the pleasure she was about to bestow on him. Then she closed her lips around him and sucked him to the back of her throat, totally blowing his mind.

"Fuck, Teagan, I'm so turned on from spanking you and playing with your ass that I'm not gonna be able to hold back much longer."

Josh gathered her braids in his clean left hand, holding them out of the way so he had a full view of her plump red lips wrapped around his cock. "So, as much as I love watching you mark me with your lipstick on my dick, we probably need to skip straight to bending you over this bed and getting out the lube, so I can actually get in your ass before I blow."

Instead of popping off his dick like he expected, Teagan doubled the suction as she gripped the base of his shaft in her right hand and his balls in her left. While she continued bobbing up and down on his length, she made it clear that she was also shaking her head "no" at the same time.

I suppose I do need the recovery time to finish preparing her ass before I fuck her there. Especially if I wanna hold out long enough for her to come four more times while I'm in her ass.

"Fuck, Teagan," Josh growled as his balls drew up just before his orgasm exploded through him, shooting rope after rope of his cum down Teagan's willing throat. "Fuck, yes, swallow every drop, Teagan."

Josh collapsed back on the bed, needing a few minutes to recover, while his wife licked every inch of his dick completely clean.

"Thank you for my snack at the end of my punishment, Sir Josh." Teagan lightly kissed the tip of his cock before standing and going to dig through their toiletries bag.

"Yes, well, I have to make sure you get enough protein in your diet," Josh chuckled, barely able to muster the energy to sit up and start unbuttoning his shirt.

"Where'd you put the condoms?" Teagan questioned as she stood there holding the bottle of lube they'd picked up a couple weeks earlier.

"I left them in La Jolla, since we decided we don't need them anymore."

"Well, then you'd better put your clothes back on and run to the store for some before you fuck my ass."

"Why would I need to do that?" Josh looked at his wife in confusion. "Even if we were still doubling up on the protection methods, I can't get you pregnant by coming in your ass."

"No, I'm not worried about that." Teagan rolled her eyes at him. "But after deciding that I want us to try anal, I asked Kori if there's anything I needed to know to prepare, since I figured she's getting it in both holes when she's with both her husbands at once. And while she recommended an enema to clean everything out first, I don't want it to be a cum enema like Fiona warned us about, no matter how funny Kay thought that would be for a book scene. So, since you don't seem to have the ability to pull out before you come, the only way your dick is going in my ass is if you have a condom on to keep from making a disgusting mess."

Did Fiona shit on Rick when he came in her ass? No, I don't wanna know the dirty details of my boss's sex life.

"I'm so glad I'm a man," Josh blurted, trying to block out the mental images of his boss and coworkers that she just put in his head. "'Cause our locker room talk isn't nearly as disturbing as it sounds like goes on in the women's locker room. And now that you've put those repulsive images in my head, we have plenty of time to pick up condoms later, 'cause it's gonna be a few days before I can block them out enough to be able to fuck your ass."

<div align="center">~~~</div>

As she sat down to dinner with Brent and their coworkers, Aiken struggled with her mixed emotions about sharing a room with him again after spending the last nine nights alone in bed. After what she'd overheard at his dad's house, she'd felt so hurt by his lies that she honestly didn't think she'd ever trust him enough to want to sleep with him again. But after that first night not sharing a room with him, she'd realized that she'd been wrong, missing having him to cuddle with much more than she expected after only spending eighteen nights with him. Now she wasn't sure how to handle their first night back in the same room, especially since they hadn't discussed all the details of what she overheard for her to make a rational decision about whether she wanted to forgive him or not.

I should have insisted we talk about everything with clearer heads the next day. But no, I had to get all excited about seeing the **Sleepless in Seattle** *houseboat on our midday date at Lake Union and decided to let him follow through with showing me how he feels with romantic date ideas instead. Now we have to go back to sharing a* *room with only one bed, when we haven't actually worked anything out.*

"So, when is Big D going to be here?" Rylie's question pulled Aiken from her thoughts.

"Sometime tomorrow at the earliest," Liam replied. "He had a doctor's appointment today, so he couldn't make his travel arrangements until he finds out if he's cleared to fly or not."

"Yeah, I was hoping we'd hear from him by now," Dean added, pulling his phone from his pocket. "So we'd know if we need to go get him 'cause he's still grounded. But I suppose now's as good a time as any to call him and find out what the doctor said today."

Dean swiped across his screen a couple of times before laying it on the table. Apparently, he put it on speaker mode, since Aiken could clearly hear the sound of it ringing through to Dion's phone.

"Hey, Dean," Dion spoke from the phone laying on the table. "Sorry, I forgot to call you earlier to let you know I won't be there until tomorrow."

"That's fine, D. But since we're all here at dinner and wondering when we'll see you, I figured you wouldn't mind me calling and putting you on speaker, so everyone can hear the plan, instead of you having to deal with a dozen calls to tell each of us later. I'm guessing that you planning to be here tomorrow means you don't need us to come drive you over, right? Does that also mean the doctor cleared you to fly?"

"No, I'm still not cleared to fly." Dion audibly sighed over the phone. "But after talking to him about this trip for your wedding and how you said I've been there a lot over the last year, the doctor thinks it might help me get some of my memories back if I spend more time there. So Dare's gonna drive me over after we drop Mama Marcel off for her cruise in the morning. Then we're gonna stay through the end of the year."

"Do we need to let Ma know to extend your reservation for the B and B?" James asked, looking around like he might be looking for his mother, the proprietress of the boutique hotel they were all staying in while they were in town.

"No, we called Mandi already," Dion informed them. "And in addition to changing my appointment to pick up my tux to Monday, she's already reserved an additional room for Mama Marcel, since she'll be flying in once she gets back from her cruise."

Aiken assumed his original appointment had been for the next day, when she and everyone else in the bridal party were scheduled to go to Destiny Dresses and Benny's Formalwear for the final fitting for their wedding attire. *Hopefully, that'll still give them time for any adjustments or alterations before the wedding next weekend. With such a large bridal party, I can't imagine how rushed the shops will be to get those done, especially when the work week is interrupted by a holiday. Maybe it's a good thing Papa wasn't able to come this week. While he might have been able to help with some of the alterations, he probably would have slowed down the overall progress by talking Mr. and Mrs. Benson's ears off about movie wardrobes.*

"Did the doctor give you any idea when you might be cleared to fly again? Or how long it'll be before you can wrestle again? I'm getting tired of having to work a whole match instead of having my partner there to give me a breather," Liam quipped, leaning away from Rylie as he directed his words toward the phone.

Oh, no, that doesn't look good. She's so tense and him pulling away is just making it worse. Obviously, our plan to try to convince him they should give their marriage a chance isn't going well so far.

"Yeah, ya might wanna have Rick assign you a new tag-team partner." Dion's voice sounded dejected, which was extremely out of character for him. "At this point, he's basically said the only way he'll clear me to wrestle again is if this trip triggers me to get all my memories back and miraculously clears up all my other concussion symptoms, so I'm no longer at risk of second-impact syndrome. But even if I start to get some of my memories back, he doesn't think all my symptoms will ever go away completely, so my days in the ring are most likely over."

Oh, God! What's he going to do if he's not able to wrestle anymore? And what the hell happened to the "he's going to be fine" that we were told in the hospital that day? Still having symptoms that will keep him from wrestling isn't anywhere near fine!

Aiken noticed Liam reaching over to take Rylie's hand upon hearing the news, making her wonder if her earlier assumption about them was premature.

When he realized they had Dion on speaker phone, Rick walked over and joined in on the conversation. "Regardless of whether the doctor clears you to wrestle or not, Dion, you'll always have a job as a booker waiting on you whenever you're ready for it."

"Thanks, Boss. And I'll probably take you up on that just as soon as I'm cleared to fly, so I don't go stir crazy sitting at home."

Aiken was relieved to know Dion had a secondary plan in place, but hearing his potential career option if his wrestling days were over made her think about what she might want in her future after wrestling. *Brent did say he wants kids in our future. I wonder if he'd be on board with being stay at home parents when we hang up our wrestling boots? Or would that make him stir crazy the way Dion thinks he'll be until he can come back as a booker?*

"Oh, we're not waiting until then," Rick chuckled, drawing her back into the conversation from how rare it was to see their stoic boss laugh. "While you're in town this week, I expect you to bring me a list of ideas for how to keep the tag titles on Red Velvet for a few more months without you having to step foot in the ring."

"Like sending different wrestlers down to the ring in my place every time Red has to wrestle?" Dion chuckled. "Or taping a bunch of vignettes of me bringing you doctor's notes about why I can't wrestle yet?"

"Exactly," Rick agreed. "But you also have to work in how Red can win Chastity's managerial services on his own, too."

"Since we have that show in San Antonio on our first day after the break, do you think we can tape a few of these vignettes to have D send proxies to the ring for a few weeks?" Liam released Rylie's hand as he actively got involved with how to bring his best friend back to the GWA. "Even if we only get a half dozen of them, that should give D until the *V-Day Massacre* to get cleared to fly with us to do them live or change the angle."

So, he's only reaching for her when he gets bad news? Is that good or bad for them as a couple? I mean, it seems like he trusts her to be there for him while he's dealing with negative emotions, but he needs to share the good ones with her too.

"Yeah, Red, we might have to wait and see how I do on this trip first. If I get my memories back and my headaches and blackout spells go away, then I'll gladly tape anything like that. But I don't want to commit to anything 'til I know I can do it without having an episode."

Yeah, I don't know much about concussions, but even I know that getting his memories back won't miraculously cure his other symptoms. If anything, it'll be the other way around. He won't get his memories back until his brain heals enough that his other symptoms start going away. And even then, he might not get all his memories back.

Even though she didn't think it sounded like Dion would ever rejoin the GWA roster as a wrestler, and maybe not even as a booker, she kept her opinions to herself, not wanting to upset any of her friends, and especially her husband, who'd reached over and taken her hand upon hearing that Dion might not be up for coming back in even a limited basis anytime soon. Knowing how Dion had been one of the wrestlers who took Brent under his wing when he first started with the company, Aiken knew him not coming back had to be hitting her husband hard, too. And regardless of anything else going on with them, she wanted to be there for him as a friend while he dealt with his feelings.

Isn't that kind of what he was trying to do with me for the last week and a half? Being there as my friend while I took the time I needed to come to terms with him lying to me about why we started dating in the first place? And was his lie really that bad? I mean, he did keep me safe that whole time. And spending time on those dates helped me develop deeper feelings for him, so maybe he really did start falling for me too. If he hadn't, why would he have spent the last week and a half taking me on friend dates again?

Granted, she knew he was trying to be romantic with each of the dates he'd planned for them since they left Portland, but even the romantic dates were too public for them to really be able to talk to one another. So she still felt like they were just friend dates, even though he'd snuck in a few deeper kisses than the chaste ones she'd agreed to. He'd also been mostly successful in picking places for their outings that made her feel like he'd really paid attention to her likes and dislikes whenever they'd been alone to talk before the incident in Portland, which made her feel like he had really started to have feelings for her other than friendship.

She especially enjoyed their dates to places like the Major Tom restaurant on the fortieth floor of a skyscraper in Calgary, Alberta, Canada, where they could see the whole city while eating lunch. And strolling hand in hand through the Nicolaysen Art Museum in Casper, Wyoming, where they found they had similar taste in artwork. But he'd also failed miserably with things like the Segway tour of Billings, Montana, which was extremely uncomfortable with the biting cold whipping under the hem of her long skirt, even before they had to stop halfway through because of a thunderstorm. Not that he had any control over the weather to make it more enjoyable. But maybe he should have thought to schedule outside activities like that in the summer when it wasn't so cold, and picked an indoor activity that day instead.

But even though most of those dates were enjoyable, she still missed the time they'd spent alone, when they could talk without anyone overhearing them. While they could still do that to some extent whenever they drove between the airports, arenas, and hotels, that time was limited and usually not long enough to get into the deeper topics they really needed to discuss. Not like when they'd roomed together, when they'd gotten into the habit of spending those last few minutes before going to sleep just talking, and often ended up staying up hours later than they should've just enjoying each other's company.

Sometimes they'd discussed the highs and lows of their day, especially when one of them felt they needed another opinion about their matches. Other times they'd talked about their childhoods, of their high school and college experiences. And occasionally they'd conversed about nothing of in particular importance, like whatever movies they each wanted to go see whenever they had some time off to actually visit a theater. But while their previous nighttime discussions hadn't been as important as the state of their marriage, Aiken had missed those talks for the last week and a half.

Maybe we can take advantage of having to room together this week to talk like that again, only about the important stuff we didn't have time to talk about in the car since Portland. Even if it's not enough for us to decide to try again, we have to talk things out before we can choose either way. But I really, really hope he can explain himself better this time, so we might have a chance at having that future he described.

Aiken missed the end of the conversation with Dion by being lost in her thoughts. But she quickly tuned back into what was going on around her when Rick bent down between her and Rylie, then motioned for Liam and Crockett to lean in, so only the four of them were able to hear his next words.

"You guys really need to run into San Antonio in the morning and get some engagement rings for the ladies and wedding bands for all four of you. There's no way the Matchmaking Mommas will buy that you're happily married when all four of your left ring fingers are bare."

"No problem, Boss," Rylie sputtered, obviously realizing she'd forgotten to swap her mother's rings to her left hand before then. She quickly moved the rings from her right hand to her left before removing the plastic spacer from her dad's ring and handing it to Liam. "I've got ours covered now."

The action of Rylie removing that spacer caused Aiken to have a flash of memory from their wedding night, when she'd had to put the spacer on Rylie's mom's rings because they were a size or two too big for her finger. *I guess that explains how they didn't look too big in the pictures, even though Rylie and I aren't the same ring size.*

"Actually, your dad's ring is a little too tight for me to feel comfortable wearing it all week," Liam balked, handing her back the ring. "So, I'll go in the morning and pick up a plain gold band for me."

When Rick turned to look directly at her and Brent, Aiken let her husband answer to their boss about their bare ring fingers. "We'll take care of it before morning, Boss."

"Whatever works for each of you is fine," Rick agreed. "Just make sure you all have a ring on before you go anywhere else in Heart's Destiny, including your appointment tomorrow to pick up your tuxes and dresses."

As Rick walked away, Rylie put the spacer back on her dad's ring so it would fit on her right pointer finger and put it back on her hand. While Rylie tried to cover her feelings with a blank expression on her face, Aiken could clearly see how much it hurt her that Liam refused to wear her dad's ring.

Yeah, things are definitely not going the way Rylie wants them to. Maybe we can sneak in some extra lingerie shopping while we're getting our dresses tomorrow, so she can entice him more once they're alone in their room?

As they went back to eating dinner and her friends all carried on the conversation at their table, Aiken found herself reflecting on what she needed to do to get her own marriage back on track, not even paying enough attention to the meal to remember what she ate for dinner. *Instead of worrying about Rylie and Liam, I need to think about getting some lingerie for myself tomorrow. Yeah, we need to talk things out first, but once we do that, I need to be prepared to start practicing for making those babies he said he wanted.*

She'd originally felt like a naïve schoolgirl for backing down on her resolve to end things with Brent when he mentioned wanting to have kids with her. But even though she was hurt when she first found out why he'd originally asked her on a date, she couldn't stop herself from feeling like the reason didn't matter all that much, if their friend dates eventually led to them both developing deeper feelings for one another and wanting the same things in their future. *But does his mentioning wanting kids really mean we both want the same thing for our family?*

Her dads had raised her to be strong and independent, career minded and a hard worker. Oh yes, they wanted grandbabies eventually, but they also wanted her to have a well-rounded life that included both a family and her career. So she felt a little guilty for imagining the day when she and Brent both retired from wrestling to spend the rest of their lives playing with their kids and living off the residual income from their investments instead of working.

It wasn't that she didn't love her job. She absolutely loved being a professional wrestler, considering it the best acting job available because she didn't have to keep going on auditions to line up new roles every few months, like she had when she was trying to break into Hollywood. And while her five-million dollar a year contract with the GWA wasn't nearly in the realm of the highest paid Hollywood actresses, it was well above average for the majority of film and television actors in supporting roles, which was most comparable to her role on the GWA's weekly television show since she didn't hold one of the championship titles. But thanks to her dads, and then the Hunters, who both had degrees in finance, when they joined the roster a couple years after she did, all helping her to invest the majority of her income, she was financially well off enough that she didn't have to keep wrestling once she started having kids.

After seeing both Holly and Shauna still battling to lose the baby weight a year after their youngest children were born when she first started with the company, Aiken didn't think she'd be eager to get back in the ring after giving birth. And she didn't even want to think about how they'd had to nurse their babies right before wrestling and still had to put pads in their bras to keep from having visible breast leakage while in the ring.

Yeah, if I ever have a biological child of my own, whether that's with Brent or not, I'll definitely be done wrestling then. Honestly, even if we decide to adopt, I'd probably want to take some time off to help the child adjust to being a part of our family before letting anyone else watch them while I'm in the ring.

I mean, I know Kay and Anthony were off for maternity leave when they first adopted Antonio, but I really think it was having them at home with him twenty-four-seven for the first few months that helped him feel secure in their family before being surrounded by our crazy GWA crew. Well, that and having two big sisters to keep him occupied while Anthony's flying the GWA plane and Kay's moving around to help out with all the other kids.

Honestly, after seeing how Tia watches over all her younger siblings when her parents are working, and how that family transformed the scared little boy I met in May, when we were in Heart's Destiny for Randi and James's wedding, into such an outgoing, well-adjusted child by the time they came back from Kay's maternity leave in September, I kind of want to ask Kay to write a parenting how-to book, so I can learn her secrets before having or adopting any kids of my own.

All her thoughts about potentially having children soon brought her around to thinking about how many she wanted and trying to picture her future family. *I know Brent said he wants at least two, but I wonder if he has an upper limit on how many kids he wants. I mean, I can't see myself giving birth to more than two. And let's be real, if it's really painful to have the first one, then two might be pushing it for my pain tolerance. But knowing firsthand how many kids out there need families like I did, I could definitely see myself adopting as many kids as I'm legally allowed to, even if I have to find a house as big as or bigger than my dads' to have bedrooms for all of them.*

The longer she sat there trying to picture her future family, the more she knew she wanted Brent by her side to raise those imaginary children. *But that can't happen if we don't talk through our issues and figure out how to make our marriage work. If we can even work things out when I'm still not sure I'll believe him if he ever tries to proclaim his love for me. I mean, I know it's possible that he's fallen for me as much as I've fallen for him, but I just don't know if I'll ever be able to get over the fact that he lied to me before to believe him in the future.*

"It's okay, Princess," Brent whispered in her ear, bringing her out of her head and back to the moment with the rest of the GWA crew. "I know you're not into action-adventure movies, so we can skip checking out the new movie screen in the local theater tonight." He brushed his lips over her temple before leaning back in his seat and redirecting his next statement to the rest of the people at their table. "Sorry, guys, we're gonna skip the movie tonight."

"Oh, come on, ya'll have to come along," Randi pleaded. "Allissa and I aren't into the crazy car chases and outlandish spy stuff either, but getting to see Rafe Kincade on the big screen makes up for all that."

"Ya know they have to put him on the big screen to make him look as tall as a normal guy, right?" James grumbled, eyeing his wife dubiously as he motioned around the table at the rest of the women. "But like most of those Hollywood actors, he's probably so short that ya'll would all have to look down at him if you ever met him in person, even without your heels."

"I doubt he's so short that even Aiken wouldn't be able to wear heels without looking over his head," Randi protested, rolling her eyes at her husband as she pointed out that Aiken was the shortest person at the table.

Allissa pulled her phone out of her handbag. "Let's look him up online to see just how tall he is."

"Oh, yeah, and maybe find some of the shirtless pics they're using to promote *Secret Spy*," Rylie added, pulling her phone from her wristlet and leaning over toward Aiken like she was going to share the view of the shirtless pics with her.

"He's five-foot-nine, which is the average height of men in the U.S., and two-and-a-half inches taller than the average for men in Mexico, which is where he's originally from," Allissa informed them.

"How the hell did he end up with the last name Kincade if he was born in Mexico?" Dean leaned over to look at Allissa's phone.

"Kincade isn't his birth name," Allissa explained, rolling her eyes. "He was adopted after immigrating to the U.S., apparently by a movie producer with the last name Kincade, who helped him get started in the movie business. Not that any of that matters as much as knowing his height. So now we know that as long as Randi and I stick with heels no more than three inches high, we won't tower over him."

"Ooh, and I can get away with a four-inch heel," Rylie cooed as she swiped through pictures of the actor on her phone.

"And lucky for me, none of my heels are more than six inches," Aiken added, bumping shoulders with Rylie and enjoying the jealous expression on Brent's face that matched the rest of the guys around the table. "So I won't have to worry if Daddio ever casts him in a movie for me to get to meet him."

"Oh yes!" Randi squealed, leaning across the table to high-five Aiken. "If that ever happens, you've gotta hook us all up for a set visit."

"Of course," Aiken agreed as she slapped her palm against Randi's. "Maybe I'll suggest him to Daddio for one of the films he's working on with the Burlesons."

"Nope, not gonna happen," Brent scoffed, shaking his head. "I can't believe I've found a reason to be happy that Kay's based all her books on us and the Burlesons, but he's way too scrawny to play any of us in those movies."

"He could fill the role of Missile or Cannon," Rylie suggested, referring to the two shortest male wrestlers on the roster, who were still right at or just under six feet tall. "But unless Kay writes a book with them as the male leads, I doubt an actor of his caliber would agree to fill a supporting role."

"He'd still need lifts in his shoes to fill either of their roles," Liam chuckled. "And that'd be dangerous as feck if he actually had to get in the ring and pull off some of Missile's acrobatic moves."

Aiken tried to imagine pulling off one of the aerial maneuvers Missile was known for while wearing her heels and cringed at the realization that it would definitely end in a broken ankle.

"Not that any of that matters for why we can't go tonight," Liam continued, discreetly looking down at his left hand, which was resting on the table. "We've got to wait until we go get rings in the morning before we can go out where word might get back to the Matchmaking Mommas that we're not wearing them."

"You could just make sure your left hands are in your pockets 'til the lights go down for the movie to play," Dean suggested with a smirk.

"Yeah, like that won't look suspicious at all," Brent chortled, shaking his head at Dean. "No, we'll just call it an early night, so we can get up extra early to go to San Antonio and be back before our appointment at the tux shop."

So much for staying up talking things out tonight, Aiken thought, as they all settled their bills and stood to leave the restaurant.

Once they got up to their room, Aiken decided to get a better idea of how early they needed to get up the next morning, so she could decide whether or not to bring up the things they needed to work out in their marriage. So, as she sat down in the chair by the desk to take off her shoes, she asked, "How early do you think we need to go to San Antonio tomorrow?"

"Probably pretty early, since our appointment for our tux and dress fittings is at eleven," Brent sighed as he loosened his tie and walked over to the closet, where he pulled out his garment bag, presumably so he could change for bed. "If we decide to go all the way to San Antonio to buy new rings. But we could just use my grandparents' rings, so we don't have to rush around in the morning."

"Your grandparents' rings?" Aiken was confused by the statement, unaware they had an option other than going to buy new rings. *Did he pick them up when we were in Portland? If so, why didn't he say something before now? I mean, pulling those out on the way to the hotel would have proved he was being honest when he claimed he wanted to ask me to stay married, when I thought he was lying again.*

Duh, Aiken! Because I was a bitch and tried to break up with him, instead of letting him explain what I overheard and really trying to work things out. It's no wonder he didn't trust me enough to mention the rings, when I've been making him go back and start over with just friendly dates, instead of talking things out with him like an adult.

"Yeah, one of the things I had to talk to my dad about in Portland was if I should give you my grandma's wedding set or go buy something new that would be bigger and flashier," Brent admitted as he removed his tie and placed it around the neck of the empty hanger he'd removed from the bag. He laid it on the bed beside the garment bag before unzipping one of the accessory pockets on the bag and pulling out a Tiffany blue box. "Well, technically, I'd wanted to ask him if we had any family heirloom rings I could give you, or if I needed to go buy something new once we figured out how to make our marriage work. But when I brought it up, he gave me this box and told me how he'd already had my grandparents' rings professionally cleaned and made sure the setting was still solid on the engagement ring."

"And then I was a bitch to you when we left there…"

"No, you weren't a bitch," Brent interrupted her. "You were rightfully upset about me not being completely honest with you. Hell, I've been pissed at myself for the same thing. But when Rick first mentioned us dating our wives, I really didn't think I was capable of ever falling in love, so I figured we'd just hang out as friends until the stalker was no longer a threat, and we'd still get an annulment eventually. I was so fucking stupid then that I actually thought we'd both leave the marriage unscathed with our friendship intact. Hell, I didn't just think we'd still be friends, I thought we might be closer friends than we were before. But now I know better. Now I know that if we don't work out, then I'm going to be a miserable bastard for the rest of my life and will have to retire early 'cause there's no way I'll ever be able to sit by and watch you start to date other guys, or God forbid, actually find your Prince Charming and get remarried."

Aiken opened her mouth to reply, then promptly closed it, too in shock over his words to form any of her own for a few moments before finally stuttering out, "Wha-when did you figure all that out? Just since we were in Portland? Or just tonight when we were talking about the possibility of me meeting Rafe Kincade one day?"

"I started figuring it out a week after we started *dating*," Brent claimed as he took a seat on the end of the bed, sitting as close to her as he could without actually sharing her chair. "Remember when we were working out and you called me out on how our dates didn't feel like couple dates? When we talked about our chemistry and I said I didn't want us to be like my parents?"

"Yes," she nodded, as Brent reached out with the hand not holding the ring box to take her hand in his.

"At that point, I thought I was only capable of feeling a fleeting lust for you like my parents had when they were together. I mean, it made sense to me at the time that as their kid, I was only capable of developing the same kinds of feelings they were, and since they didn't seem to be able to love one another, I didn't think I was capable of falling in love with you. But then I talked to my dad when I got back to my room. And he started telling me all about how I come from a long line of Crockett men who fell in love only once in a lifetime, but when they fell it was hard and fast. For the first time in over twenty-five years, I heard him say he loves my mom. That's when I started to realize that if he's capable of still loving her after all these years, then maybe I'm more like him than her, and capable of feeling love too."

"But what I heard of your conversation with Harlan made it seem like you still didn't think…" Aiken trailed off, unsure how to finish her sentence since she couldn't recall the exact words of any of his statements where he actually said how he thought he felt about her.

"Yeah, that was just one of many conversations I've had with Dad and a few of the guys over the last couple of months, when I was trying to figure out if I was confusing feeling friendship and lust for thinking I was falling in love. But after hearing what Dad learned about Mom's life after she left us, and seeing the truth of his love for her when he said he'd take her back even after everything she's done, my feelings for you became crystal clear." He paused and looked down at their joined hands.

Aiken held her breath, anxiously expecting him to declare his love right then and knowing that she'd been wrong earlier when she thought she wouldn't believe him.

"I know we've still got a ways to go before we rebuild the trust between us that we'll need to make our marriage work. But I want you to know that I'm willing to do whatever it takes to work through my issues, so we can have a long happy life together."

"Okay," Aiken sighed, feeling slightly disappointed that he hadn't declared his love for her right then.

"And that starts with total honesty from now on, even if I know it'll most likely piss you off, like implying that you aren't capable of defending yourself by insisting you never go off by yourself so I can protect you in case another stalker starts targeting the GWA."

"Yeah, I don't know if you've noticed," Aiken smirked, "but since the incident in New Orleans, the only times I've even gone to the bathroom without at least one of the other women accompanying me to the locker room was when we were at our dads' houses or I was in my hotel room, which you've been checking for boogiemen before allowing me to stay in them without you."

Aiken had thought it was a bit of overkill for him to keep checking their rooms once the stalker was no longer an issue. But after talking to the other women on the roster to find out that their husbands all still did the same thing (with the exception of Liam, who'd apparently pawned the task off on Protection Detail for Rylie), she figured it was a task still mandated by GWA security in case any of them picked up another stalker.

"Yeah, my overprotectiveness is one of the things Dad pointed out to prove my feelings for you are the real deal," Brent chuckled and shrugged.

"Yeah? What else did you and Harlan talk about that day to make your feelings for me crystal clear?" Aiken hoped asking more about their talk would get him to share those feelings with her, desperately hoping he was as in love with her as she was with him.

"A lot of stuff actually." Brent looked back down at their joined hands and rubbed his thumb over her knuckles. "Starting with all the things I'm afraid might come between us."

Like what? Aiken barely stopped herself from blurting the question, knowing she needed to let Brent take his time to feel comfortable before expecting him to reveal his fears to her.

"The biggest one being that I won't be able to provide the lifestyle you're accustomed to because I'm a simple man from a humble background, who'd rather wear jeans and flannel shirts than all the suits I have to wear now, and I'm nowhere near good enough for you."

"Well, then once we leave the GWA, you won't mind me trading in all my dresses and skirts for yoga pants, so we should get along just fine." Aiken reached over with her free hand to cup his face as she leaned in and pecked her lips against his. When she pulled back, she added, "Your worth as a person has nothing to do with material things like that. Neither one of us is better than the other. We've just had different experiences in life."

Brent smiled at her, but his smile didn't reach his eyes. "So, one-hundred percent truth time. I'm still not sure if I should give you these rings, or go shopping in the morning for something bigger and flashier, 'cause I'm still not sure which you'll like best."

"Brent," Aiken sighed, hating that he still seemed to believe she was so shallow that she'd rather have a big expensive diamond than a smaller ring with much more sentimental value because of his family history. "Is any of the jewelry I wear regularly big and flashy?"

"No, but that's because you only wear the smallest body piercing jewelry that can't be removed without special tools, so you don't have to worry about losing it in the ring or having it rip delicate areas if it catches on something."

"Well, that is a benefit to my choice in jewelry, but that's not why I don't wear anything big and flashy. I only wear small pieces because I don't like gaudy jewelry that's too big for my petite features. So, even if you decide that you don't want me to wear your family heirlooms until we're certain we'll spend the rest of our lives together, I don't want you to buy anything that's going to make me feel like I'm lifting weights every time I move my hand, like Teagan's rings. And honestly, if questions about us are what's holding you back from opening that box and putting those rings on my finger, then I'd rather we go pick out some cheap costume jewelry in the morning, since it'll just be to get through this week and not what I'll want to wear for the rest of my life."

"Well, I didn't think I was holding back for any reason other than thinking they wouldn't be good enough for you," Brent sighed, releasing her hand and closing both his hands around the ring box while resting his elbows on his knees. "But now I'm wondering if maybe it wouldn't be better to go buy something less meaningful for this week, so I have time to get over all my fears for us before giving you these."

"Then that's definitely what we should do." Aiken smiled sadly. "But I also think we need to discuss all these fears, so I can help you work through them. Can we do that while cuddling in bed, like we used to do at the end of the night, only with our pajamas on?"

"Yeah, we can definitely do that, Princess." Brent smiled as he stood and put the ring box back in his garment bag without ever letting her see the rings inside. "I'll even let you take the first turn in the bathroom to change."

They spent the rest of the evening cuddling as Brent told her all about his fears of possibly having some of the same mental issues as his mom, and how they might affect their relationship in the future, as well as not knowing what to do about the possibility of having siblings he'd never met. They didn't resolve anything immediately, but as she drifted off to sleep in his arms, she was hopeful that they would work everything out in the end.

<p style="text-align:center">~~~</p>

What the hell was I thinking when I agreed to play the role of Liam's devoted, loving wife the whole time we're here? There's no way this plan is going to work to convince him that we should give our marriage a real shot. Rylie's confidence in the plan to try winning over her husband to want to stay married to her kept falling as she followed him up to their room.

After the awkward, silent ride from the airport, Rylie knew Liam wouldn't have a hard time ignoring her whenever they had to be alone in their room at night. And since he'd proven on Halloween that he could act like the doting husband while they were in the club, even going so far as to take care of her so she didn't get as drunk as she'd wanted, then easily walked away from her at the hotel without so much as a backward glance, she was certain he'd ace his part for the next ten days. Meanwhile, she was falling apart inside because shutting off her feelings wasn't as easy for her as it was for him.

Eating dinner with him and their coworkers in the hotel restaurant had proven that point clearly. Thankfully, the other couples they were seated with were able to carry most of the conversation, so she'd mostly sat quietly beside Liam without feeling like she had to do too much to sell their happy marriage to the locals in attendance. *If all the events are like dinner was tonight, only with Teagan and Josh also acting as a buffer between us and the rest of the town, then maybe I can handle it. Well, as long as Liam doesn't do like he did on Halloween and have me sit on his lap again.*

She was still mortified about how her first three drinks had already lowered her inhibitions enough that she kept wiggling around to rub her ass on his dick that night. *Thank God, the water and food sobered me up enough to realize what I was doing, so he didn't figure out that I was actually jealous about him flirting with those ring rats and trying to get him to flirt with me instead. If he knew how I really feel about him, instead of thinking I was just mad about him not selling our gimmick, then I'd be absolutely too mortified to be around him and would have to quit the GWA.*

When Dean called Dion in the middle of dinner earlier, Rylie felt almost as uncomfortable as she had on Halloween. Yeah, she was curious about the extent of his injuries and if and when he'd be cleared to come back to work. But she still didn't think it was right for them to have left him on speaker, so everyone in the room overheard Dion's private medical information as he answered all the guys' questions about his symptoms. But before she could excuse herself to go to the restroom for a moment, so she didn't feel guilty for sticking around to listen, Liam reached out and took her hand. Just like on the day Dion was shot, she felt the need to stay right where she was to support Liam as he dealt with the fallout of that traumatic event. So, even though she wanted to give Dion and those closest to him a little privacy at that moment, she'd simply squeezed Liam's hand, hoping the comforting gesture was enough to give him the strength to face the emotions he had to be feeling right then.

As Liam opened their door, she wondered if they might need to talk more about Dion's injuries and the likelihood of him ever returning to the GWA. *Yeah, I'm not busting Liam's bubble of hope that his best friend will come back on tour with us. Getting him to see me as his life partner while we're here this week is going to be hard enough. I don't need to give him another reason to be pissed at me and push me away. So if he brings it up, I'll just try to quietly be supportive and not mention that I don't think D will be coming back to the GWA, even as a booker.*

"Since I have to get up extra early to go get a ring in the morning, I'm gonna call it a night and try to get some extra sleep now," Liam informed her, stepping over to the closet and removing his suit jacket.

"Since you're using your mom's rings, I'll try to be quiet when I leave so you can sleep in."

"Oh, um, okay, thanks." Rylie felt awkward as she stood there watching him gather a few things before stepping into the bathroom. While he was going through what she assumed was his nightly routine, she gathered her favorite sleep shorts, tank top, and hair scarf, along with her toiletries, planning to go to bed immediately, so she didn't keep him up by trying to watch TV or read a book. Her sleep attire wasn't overtly sexy like some of the items in her suitcase, but she didn't want to be too obvious that she was trying to entice him by wearing a baby doll nightie to bed on their first night in town.

When Liam stepped out of the bathroom in only his boxer briefs, however, she was very tempted to swap out her sleepwear. But since his underwear covered more of him than the short tights he sometimes wore to wrestle in the summer, she decided not to say anything about his sleepwear, or change her own, walking into the now vacant bathroom to get ready for bed.

As she removed her makeup, brushed her teeth, and applied her nightly moisturizer, she thought about how he'd embarrassed her by rejecting the use of her dad's ring in front of all their friends and their boss. *Since when does he remember Dad's ring being too small for him? Unless he remembers more of that night than he's let on? If so, does he remember enough to verify if my dream about telling him how special these rings are was real or not?*

And if that was a real memory, and not just something I dreamed up, is his refusal to wear Dad's ring his way of telling me that he's serious about wanting the annulment because he doesn't love me?

Yeah, that's probably the message he's trying to send without blatantly saying it. It was stupid of me to think using Mom and Dad's rings to marry him was a sign that we could be as in love and committed to one another as my parents were from the moment they met until they took their last breaths.

But maybe his rejection of the ring is just what I need to make sure I stay on my side of the bed tonight and don't try to lure him into having sex with me again by using my vibrator once the lights are out.

Who am I kidding? Yeah, his obvious rejection of me is definitely enough to keep me from pulling out my vibrator and trying to tempt him. But once I'm asleep, I'll forget all about it and my horny hoo-

hah will take control. Maybe I should request some extra pillows to build a wall between us to keep me from cuddling up next to him in my sleep? Hell, even that probably won't be enough, if I have one of my normal nightly dreams about making love with him.

Once she finished changing her clothes and wrapping her hair, along with everything else she could think of to dawdle in the bathroom, so hopefully he'd be asleep by the time she returned to the bedroom, she found out she didn't have to order extra pillows. Liam had shoved all four of the pillows on the bed to the middle, only laying his head on half of one of them with his back to the center of the bed, so he wouldn't even partially see her over the wall of pillows.

Rylie quickly put away her things, making sure her dirty clothes were bagged up to go to the front desk to be laundered the next day. Then she walked around to the side of the bed farthest from the door and crawled in, only taking one of the pillows back to her side and leaving the two extras and the half that Liam wasn't using in the middle between them.

Since Liam's eyes were closed, she didn't bother saying "goodnight" as she reached over and turned off the lamp on her bedside table, which was the only light he'd left on in the room. It took a lot more time than she preferred for her to fall asleep, tossing and turning and hoping she didn't wake Liam.

When she awoke a couple hours later, she was surprised to see light coming from the bathroom. *Maybe he woke up in the middle of the night and needed it to see to get back in bed? Or he thought I might need it to see to get back to the bathroom, in case I woke up in the middle of the night too?*

Since she wanted a drink of water, she was grateful he'd left it on, so she could see to walk over to the mini-fridge in the room and get a bottle of water without having to turn on the bedside lamp and possibly wake him up. When she got to the refrigerator, however, she quickly realized Liam was actually up and in the shower, totally forgetting what she was standing there for at the moment.

She couldn't stop her eyes from wandering over to the bathroom door, which was open enough for her to see his reflection in the bathroom mirror clearly through the three-inch gap. The clear shower doors did absolutely nothing to hide the perfection of Liam's naked body, as he stood there with his eyes closed under the spray while stroking his impressive dick.

Since her only sexual experience with Liam had been in her mostly dark hotel room in New Orleans, when she'd only been able to feel his body and could only barely make out the shape of his face in the low ambient light coming in around the curtains, Rylie appreciated actually being able to see all of him in that moment. His dick was definitely as thick as she remembered feeling almost a month before, but it was surprisingly longer than she'd thought during their one night together.

Holy shit! He's at least nine inches. Why'd he only give me about two-thirds of it the night we made love? Clearly he strokes all the way to the base when he jerks off, so I know he would have preferred to go balls-deep instead of holding back that last three inches.

Did my little wince from stretching around his girth make him think I couldn't take more? Is that why he hasn't made a move to do it again? 'Cause he thinks I can't handle all of him? Is that one of the reasons why he wants to end our marriage, because he didn't enjoy it that night since he wasn't able to go balls-deep at first and didn't realize I just needed a minute to adjust before he could?

If so, how the fuck do I show him I want all of him? How do I show him I'm able to take every inch, so next time it will be just as good for him as it was for me?

Thinking their one time together wasn't nearly as amazing for him as it was for her was almost enough to stop her from creaming her panties while watching him stroke his cock. But when he moaned something in Irish as he squeezed just below his crown, her pussy gushed in response, causing her to wonder if she should join him in the shower.

Could I possibly prove I can make it better for him by stripping down and surprising him with a blow job? Or will he put a stop to things before I can get in because the shower door opening would alert him to my presence?

Before she could decide what to do, Liam came, shooting his load on the shower door while crying out, "Moh store. Is too moh graw. Moh an-um cair-ah."

Did he just say, "Kara," as in the baker here in town who makes all the cakes for the weddings we've been at here? Or does Cara in Irish mean the same thing it does in Italian, so he's just using it as a term of endearment for whatever random woman he's fantasizing about? If that's the case, then he was probably thinking about Jen while he was jerking off, since she's the woman he's been paired with every time he's been here and not Kara.

No matter who he was fantasizing about, Rylie knew she couldn't let him catch her watching him, since it was most definitely not her he was calling out for when he came. So, she rushed back over to the bed, sliding quietly back under the covers and completely forgetting her earlier plan to get a bottle of water.

I guess I'll be scrapping all my plans for flirting with him this week and trying to tempt him to fuck me again. Now if I can just figure out how to fall out of love with him, so I don't leave here with a shattered heart after suffering through everything going on for the wedding.

Chapter Twelve

Saturday, November 23, 2019, Heart's Destiny, Texas

As she walked into Tully's Roadhouse with Josh, Teagan hoped the free flowing alcohol would be enough to keep the locals from noticing the strange vibes she'd felt from her fellow Vegas brides all day. Apparently, Aiken and Rylie hadn't had as fabulous a time as she had the night before, and the cracks in their marriages were really showing. She just hoped that she was the only one who noticed because of her close friendships with them.

And hopefully, the plan to have them room with their hubbies isn't going to blow up in my face this week.

Teagan felt slightly guilty for spending their first evening in town up in her room with Josh, instead of being there for her friends when they clearly needed someone to talk to about their marriages. While Aiken claimed that she and Crockett were back on track after talking the night before, Teagan wasn't convinced by her bestie's performance at their dress fitting earlier in the day. But then again, they weren't alone at the time, so they couldn't get into the details about why Aiken had forgiven him for lying about why he wanted to take her on their first date.

Who knows? Maybe I'm reading too much into the fact that they just got plain silver wedding bands instead of picking out an engagement ring too? Maybe they really didn't see an engagement ring they both liked when they were rushing around shopping this morning? And maybe having to share a room last night really was enough for them to realize that they both developed feelings for one another on those dates, so it doesn't really matter why they originally started going on them? Either that, or they banged it out with an angry fuck, and just haven't had time to get to the sensual connection of make-up sex yet. So, once they get to that, then I'll finally stop thinking they're projecting weird vibes.

"Don't have too much fun without me, Wifey," Josh growled, as they stopped at the group of tables that had been pushed together to form one big table, where the local ladies were already gathering.

"And just how are you going to punish me if I do?" Teagan teased, referring to how much fun they'd had when he spanked her the night before.

"I think you know exactly how." Josh ran his hand over her ass and lightly squeezed, reigniting the memories of the momentary sting from the previous evening. "Even though I'm not sure it's much of a deterrent."

"Hmmm, sounds like an incentive to me," she taunted as she ran her hand up his torso, enjoying the feel of his muscular abs and pectorals under the soft material of his blue dress shirt, which perfectly matched his eyes.

Before he left her to go into the back room with the rest of the guys, he dipped his head and kissed her passionately. Teagan eagerly opened her mouth to accept the invasion of his tongue, wrapping her arms around him and running her fingers through the back of his hair.

"You guys might wanna sneak off to the storeroom before you go any farther," Dane Bennington quipped as he walked by. "It's the last door at the end of the hall, but you'll have to do it against the door to hold it closed 'cause there's no lock."

"I don't even wanna know how you know that," Teagan replied, as soon as Josh broke their kiss.

"But we might check it out later." Josh wagged his eyebrows suggestively before releasing her completely to head into the back room with the rest of the guys.

As Teagan took a seat with the rest of the ladies, she noticed Aiken and Crockett parting with a much more chaste kiss than the one she'd just shared with Josh. *But other than leaving the hospital last month, they've always kept their PDA pretty chaste, so maybe I was wrong in the vibes I thought I felt from her earlier.* When Rylie plopped down in the seat beside her, however, Teagan knew she wasn't wrong about there still being problems between her and Liam.

"Ugh! When will the first round of shots be here?" Rylie glared at her husband, who'd stopped to speak with Jen Burleson for a moment before going to the back room.

Damn! No wonder she's in a pissy mood.

"Right now," Becky Burleson replied, motioning for the waitress carrying a tray of drinks to start with Rylie as she distributed them.

"You don't have to worry about my sister," Julie Burleson informed them from her seat across the table. "She was only congratulating him on his marriage to you."

"How do you know that?" Rylie downed the first shot she'd been handed before replacing the glass on the tray and picking up a second. "You weren't even over there when they were talking."

"We're twins, and sometimes it feels like we share the same brain because we have the same thoughts," Julie shrugged. "In fact, I bet the first thing she does when she gets back from the bar is congratulate you next."

Sure enough, just a few seconds later, Jen stopped to hug each of the Vegas brides and offer her congratulations on all their marriages before walking around the table to take the seat between her sister and cousin Becky. "As soon as the preggo mocktails get here, we'll get started with all the toasts to the new brides and the bride-to-be."

Preggo mocktails? Teagan was confused by Jen's words since she took one of the Blow Job shots that were being passed around to all the ladies. But then she noticed Randi's friend Amy, who looked like she was about to give birth any minute now, and remembered that Charlotte had announced her pregnancy at Rick and Fiona's wedding in July. *Oh, yeah, I guess they can't really drink the shots we requested.*

"Oh, shit, are you knocked up too?" Teagan blurted when Julie was served one of the non-alcoholic drinks, along with her cousin and future sister-in-law.

"Yes," Julie chuckled wistfully, "with twins."

Before Teagan could ask who the father was, Randi kicked off the toasts to Allissa. "Everyone raise your glass to our beautiful friend and my soon-to-be favorite sister-in-law, Allissa!"

"Don't let Diana hear you say that," Kay chuckled, playfully chastising her sister.

"Diana's not here." Randi rolled her eyes at Kay. "And if she wants favorite sister-in-law status, she's gonna hafta come visit more than once a year."

"Who's Diana?" Aiken asked, looking around the room.

"She's Randi and Kay's brother's wife," Becky quietly informed them. "The only times she's come down here are when they each got married, but she's really quiet and reserved, so I'm not surprised you didn't meet her at James and Randi's wedding."

"Anyway," Randi continued, raising her voice to be heard over everyone interrupting her. "I want to be the first to welcome you to the family and congratulate you on marrying the second best looking Hunter man."

"Dean and James are identical twins," Allissa giggled. "So, how can you rank Dean second?"

"Technically, James and Dean are tied for second," Randi clarified, smirking. "PopPop is number one."

Even grumpy Rylie laughed at Randi's playful gibe at her husband and his twin.

"Oh, yeah, that makes sense," Allissa nodded her agreement as she clinked her glass with Randi's.

They all tapped their glasses with at least one of the women nearest them, calling out their "congratulations" to Allissa before downing their shots. Several more rounds of various shots and test-tube shooters were delivered and passed around before Becky offered the second toast.

"Okay, we'll get back to toasting Dean and Allissa in a minute. But first we need to congratulate Chastity and Liam, Amethyst and Crockett, and Emerald and Surfer Josh. Thank you all for biting the bullet and taking those guys off the market, so our moms have fewer men to try to match us up with against our wills."

"You're welcome?" Teagan tentatively offered, unsure if Becky's toast was as complementary as her wide smile implied.

"Seriously, after all the times we've had to sit with your guys at weddings and holiday celebrations for the last year, we consider them friends and want nothing but the best for them, which is what we know they found when they married each of you," Becky added. "Congratulations. We're happy for all of you."

They all clinked their glasses once more before downing another shot. Or in Julie's case, taking another sip of her mocktail before leaning over to have a whispered conversation with her sister. Teagan and the rest of the ladies took turns offering toasts to Allissa and Dean, until the party was interrupted by Dion's arrival.

"Jewel!" Dion shouted, drawing the attention of everyone in the room as he stalked over toward their table.

What the hell? Dion never raises his voice like that, so whoever he's calling out to must have really made an impression on him. I wonder if it's the woman the guys mentioned that he's been dreaming about? Teagan didn't have to wonder long as he quickly made his way around the table and stopped right beside Julie's chair.

"No!" Julie held up a hand in the universal sign for stop. "Don't you dare call me that after ghosting me for the last month!"

Oh shit! Is she the woman he's been dreaming about? And is she pregnant with Dion's babies?

"I didn't ghost you, Jewel." Dion didn't sound like his normal, confident self as he spoke. "At least, not on purpose. I was injured and can't remember how to contact you."

"Oh, I heard all about your injury," Julie yelled, shaking her head at him. "From my cousin! When he got home four days later! But he was too late for me to be interested in hearing what happened, since I saw the news reports the day it happened and tried calling you. Do you know what I found out when I called you, Dion?"

Dion shook his head, as everyone around them looked back and forth between him and Julie, like they were watching a tennis match.

"I was told never to contact you again," Julie seethed. "That you didn't need to be bothered by a *ring rat* trying to take advantage of your injury to con you out of your money. Well, newsflash, *Dark Chocolate*, I'm a Burleson. I don't *need* your fuckin' money. And after being treated like shit when I called, concerned about you possibly being shot, I don't *want* you in my life. Or my babies' lives." Julie pushed her chair back slightly and placed a hand over her belly, revealing an obvious baby bump, which Teagan hadn't noticed earlier because it had been hidden by the table. "So, go hang out with your boys in the back, and stay the hell away from me while you're in town this week."

I guess that's why she hadn't left her seat since we got here. She probably didn't want to spend the whole night answering a bunch of questions about her babies when her baby daddy could walk in any second. And I stupidly asked the first one earlier, with plans to ask a lot more once all the toasts were done. No wonder she and Jen started whispering to one another and quit talking to the rest of us. I'll have to apologize to her later for not knowing when to keep my trap shut.

Dion opened and closed his mouth a few times, like he was trying to figure out how to respond to Julie's words, before swaying on his feet.

"Dare, I need to lie down." Dion reached out and grabbed his brother's arm.

Damn, I must really be distracted to have not realized Darius was standing right beside him.

"I'm sorry, D. I think I screwed up when I answered your phone while you were in the hospital," Darius stated as he helped Dion walk back toward the door.

The rest of his words were drowned out by the music and whispers of all the women around them. But Teagan was too worried about the way Julie was flushing after the altercation to try to hear anything more from the Davises, thinking raising her blood pressure so high couldn't be good for her babies.

"Oh my gawd, are you okay, Jules?" Jen screeched the question as she assessed her sister.

"Was that Dion's brother?" Cait inquired as she turned to watch the two men leave the bar. "And did he just say something about answering Dion's phone while he was in the hospital?"

"Yeah, that was Dion's brother," Teagan replied, nodding at the woman she felt like she'd befriended back in October. "Dare had Big D's phone for the first couple of weeks after he was injured because one of the main rules of the concussion protocol is *no screen time*."

"So, it could have been him that answered Dion's phone when Julie called him that day after we heard what happened?" Cait questioned, leaning around Becky to visually check on Julie, who was rubbing her temples like she had a headache.

Probably from the sudden spike to her blood pressure. Hopefully, her sister knows what to do to help her get it back down, 'cause even though I know high blood pressure isn't good for the babies, I don't have a clue what to do to help her.

"Yeah, probably," Aiken replied, when Teagan was too focused on Julie to continue her explanation. "D was out cold for a while after…you know. And when Dare came out to tell us he'd woken up a couple hours later, he didn't remember anything. So, I'm sure he wasn't able to answer his phone if anyone called him after hearing what happened."

As Aiken, Allissa, and Randi continued filling in the locals on the rest of the timeline for the day Dion was shot, and the Burleson women gave them more details on Julie's phone call that day, Teagan focused on Rylie, who was apparently as rocked by Julie's revelation as Julie appeared to be by seeing Dion again. Rylie downed the other three shooters in front of her before reaching over and taking one of Teagan's.

"Whoa, Chas, you're going to need to slow down or Liam's going to have to carry you out of here tonight." Teagan reached out and clasped Rylie's hand, stopping her from grabbing yet another shot.

"Excuse me," Julie blurted as she stood, not continuing to explain why she needed to be excused as she took off toward the hallway that led to the bathrooms.

I guess it's kind of obvious why Julie needs to go splash some water on her face after that. But why is Rylie so upset by Julie having hooked up with Dion? Unless, maybe because she thinks Liam hooked up with Jen one of the times Red Velvet was paired up with the twins for wedding events in town?

"Not tonight, Em. I need to forget right now, not…whatever." Rylie pulled her hand from Teagan's, waving it around haphazardly before turning to flag down the waitress while obviously avoiding looking over at Jen. "Can I please get another tray of those shots over here?"

"Which do you want next, the Ankles in the Air, Sex on the Beach, Blow Job, Panty Dropper, or Lick My Pussy shots?"

Teagan couldn't help but chuckle at how the waitress maintained a straight face while listing out the drink options. *Hopefully, she'll pick something other than the Blow Job shots, since the others all have significantly less alcohol in them. I know she wants to forget tonight, but getting blackout drunk isn't really a good idea.*

"Not a Blow Job," Rylie replied with a wry grin. "I'll stick to the Lick My Pussy shots for the rest of the night, so my man will easily figure out what I want to happen when we get back to our room tonight."

Oh, shit! Was that a dig at Jen? Or is Rylie really planning to step up the teasing with Liam?

"I'd better go check on my sister." Jen gave Rylie a guilty look as she stood before turning toward the head of the table where Allissa was seated. "Congratulations, again, Allissa."

With that, she walked away, heading down the same hallway Julie had a few moments before. Becky, Cait, and Charlotte followed her, presumably to go comfort Julie and try to get her to return to the party.

"Wow, I know I'm not as close to the Burlesons as I am to my GWA crew, but I thought they liked me enough to stay for more than a few minutes of the party," Allissa quipped.

"They haven't left," Kay reassured Allissa. "They're just going to make sure Julie's okay, but they'll be back."

"I guess there's been a lot more going on between Big D and Julie than any of us knew about," Randi added, shaking her head in obvious confusion about what just happened.

"Maybe we should get some of the guys to go check on D," Teagan suggested, thinking he seemed to be just as shaken up as Julie had been, if not more so.

"Yes," Aiken agreed, standing and motioning for Rylie to join them. "Come on, Chas, we need to go tell our hubbies what happened, so as D's closest friends, they can go check on him together."

As they stood to go into the back room, they noticed the Burleson women coming back from the restroom. Becky, Cait, and Charlotte rejoined the party, but Jen and Julie said their "goodbyes" and left.

"Guess we'll skip the games and go straight to the dancing," Allissa shrugged as she and Randi also got up to go fill their men in on what happened.

While Rylie was reluctant to join them at first, she dutifully followed Teagan and Aiken into the back room, where the guys were all gathered around the pool tables. But only after she took the whole tray of shots that the waitress somehow had time to deliver.

"Damn, that's some fast service," Teagan commented, surprised by the speed at which the waitress had fulfilled Rylie's request.

"Yeah, we've got a system worked out for these parties," the waitress, whose name tag read "Melissa," chuckled, pointing over at the bar. "After figuring out which shots are ordered most at these things, Leo started putting together as many trays of them in advance as he can, so we just have to go grab a tray out of the cooler for most of them. And it only takes a couple of minutes to top a tray with whipped cream for the ones that can't be completely premade."

While she thought the setup was smart on the part of the bar, she wasn't so sure Melissa handing Rylie a whole tray of what looked to be about two-dozen test-tube shooters was such a great idea. Granted, the test-tubes held about half the volume of a standard shot glass and each one was clearly less than an ounce, which then had to be further divided between the coconut rum and various juices, so it was probably less than a quarter of an ounce of alcohol per shooter, but still twenty-four of them added up to quite a lot of alcohol for one person.

I'll have to make sure we each take a couple of these to keep her from drinking all of them by herself.

While she hadn't thought any of them had a drinking problem, and considered the night they got blackout drunk in Vegas a fluke because it was one of the few times anyone she knew drank more than one or two drinks in a night, with the others being at previous bachelorette parties, Teagan was starting to get worried about Rylie using alcohol to numb her feelings recently. *But is it really a problem since the only time I've seen her drink excessively when we weren't all drinking a little more than normal was on Halloween? Yeah, she's had a couple more than the rest of us tonight. But hell, I'd probably want to drink a few extra tonight, too, if I thought I was sitting at a table with a woman Josh had hooked up with in the last few months.*

Deciding to just keep an eye on her friend and talk to her about her drinking at another time, when she was sober enough to have a rational conversation, Teagan pulled two shooters out of the slots on the tray Rylie sat down on the table closest to where Josh, Crockett, and Liam were standing while watching Anthony Burleson and Magnum play a game of pool.

Damn, Anthony might only be an inch shorter than Magnum, but he looks like a beanpole when they're standing side by side because of not having near as much muscle mass.

Turning away from the pool game, she handed one of the shots off to Josh before slipping her arm around his waist and softly telling him, "I thought you might want to try a Lick My Pussy shot."

"Are you trying to give me ideas for later, Mrs. Parker?" Josh crooned as he tapped his test-tube shooter against hers and promptly downed it. "'Cause you're a lot sweeter than that shot."

Instead of replying, Teagan swallowed her own shot of the tropically fruity drink and grinned at her husband's compliment.

"No, she's stealing the Lick My Pussy shots I ordered to give Liam ideas for later," Rylie snorted before throwing back two shooters at once.

"Aw, thanks, Moh Graw." Liam brushed his lips over Rylie's temple before pulling a shooter from the tray. "But I really can't drink this many shots and still be safe to drive back to the B and B later, so we need to share with the rest of our friends."

Rylie managed to pull two more shooters from the tray before Liam passed it around for Aiken, Crockett, and a few others to each take a shot. She and Josh each took a second before the tray migrated around the room and Liam offered a toast.

"To Dean and Allissa, may you be blessed with the luck of the Irish all the days of your lives. May your troubles only be wee ones, and when you're blessed with wee ones, may they be only as mischievous as a leprechaun. I wish you many years of lying…in each other's arms, stealing…kisses and moments alone, and celebrating it all with lots of drinks with friends."

As soon as they all raised their glasses or shots and offered another round of "congratulations" to Dean and Allissa, Teagan felt they needed to quit wasting time and tell the guys about what happened with Dion and Julie. But she still didn't get the chance to pull them aside immediately.

"That one wasn't bad," Dean chuckled after they all drank. "But I still like the one about being rich in love and poor in sorrows better."

"What's he talking about?" Aiken asked before Teagan could.

"Since he has so many groomsmen, we've all been trying out different toasts, so we can narrow it down to just the ones Dean thinks his parents and grandparents will like best," Crockett clarified.

"And hopefully, we'll have the best ones refined enough that we won't be sick of repeating them by the time D gets here to offer his and help us choose an order for giving them at the reception," Josh added.

"D's already been here and left," Teagan informed them, blurting it out way more bluntly than she'd intended.

"What? How'd we miss him?" Liam turned to look toward the archway that led back to the front room of the bar.

"He just came in long enough to say a few words with Julie and then Dare had to help him walk back outside," Teagan explained, just before Liam bolted toward the front of the bar.

"Why would he stop just long enough to talk to Julie and then leave without saying a word to any of us?" Josh questioned.

"I imagine it has something to do with the shock of finding out Julie's pregnant," Teagan elaborated. "And maybe because he's starting to get some of his memories back, since he called her Jewel instead of Julie."

"Wait," Crockett interjected. "Jewel is the name of the woman he's been asking us about since he woke up in the hospital, isn't it?"

"Yeah, it is," Dean agreed, as Allissa nodded along at his side. "But he swore that first day that it wasn't Julie. Are you sure that's who he was talking to?"

"Oh, yeah, it was definitely Julie he was referring to," Allissa assured her fiancé.

"And she's pregnant? Do you think D's the father?" Josh questioned.

"Who's pregnant with D's baby?" Liam asked as he walked back up to their group. When they all stared at him instead of answering, he finally motioned with his thumb over his shoulder and added, "I'd have just asked him, but he wasn't in the parking lot by the time I got out there and he's not answering his phone."

"Julie's pregnant," Teagan replied.

"And we think Big D's her baby daddy because he called her Jewel," Aiken added with a half shrug, "which set her off to start yelling at him about being rude when she called him while he was in the hospital. But after talking to Becky and Cait once D and Julie both left the table, I think she actually talked to Darius that day, and not Dion. Only Julie doesn't know that and thinks D broke up with her."

"Do you think they were just seeing each other on our breaks 'cause it was convenient? Or do you think they were really serious about each other and that's why D's been dreaming about her?" Josh asked the group as a whole.

"It's more likely that it started out as a no-strings break fling, but then it turned into more," Crockett replied as he hugged Aiken to his side. "D might not have realized how much she meant to him until after he was injured, but with how he's asked us about her practically every time we talked to him in the last month, it's clear he's developed feelings for her."

"Feck, I knew I saw Julie at a couple of our hotels in California back in August," Liam exclaimed, shaking his head. "But D convinced me that I was just imagining a face I recognized on one of the hundreds of thousands of blondes in the world. I bet she was out there to meet him, which is why he went straight back to the hotel instead of going out with us after the shows."

"Are you sure it was in August?" Aiken's eyes widened as she looked over at Liam, who just nodded in agreement. "That's when Burleson Incorporated bought out the studio Daddio and his friends started. I bet she used that deal as cover for why she had to be in California at the same time we were, so she could see Big D without anyone figuring it out."

"But why wouldn't he tell any of us, so we could help him see her more often?" Dean wondered aloud.

"Probably for the same reason we agreed to the whole friendship ruse with Jen and Julie in the first place," Liam pointed out. "So everyone would keep wondering if we were more than friends or not and keep the Matchmaking Mommas confused as to whether or not their schemes were working, so they wouldn't keep playing musical chairs with the twins and every eligible man to come through town."

"With the way the Matchmaking Mommas have had you and D paired with Jen and Julie for every wedding event for the last year," Dean tilted his head as he examined Liam, "I have to wonder how long D and Julie have been more than just friends?"

When Liam only shrugged in response, Aiken answered Dean's question. "From what Cait and Becky said, they've been hooking up since Kay and Anthony's wedding."

"Feck, I wonder how many of the other times he went back to the hotel early were because she'd come to meet him while we were on tour? And why the feck didn't he tell me, so I could help him come up with excuses to get out of the arena early on nights we weren't wrestling? Or fill Dare in, so she woulda been welcomed by his family instead of…what exactly happened on this phone call she was pissed about?"

"Apparently, Dare accused her of being a ring rat and a gold digger and blocked her from D's phone," Teagan informed them, completely understanding why Julie was pissed, especially if she still thought it was Dion who'd answered his phone. "But hopefully, once she finds out it was Dare and not D that she spoke to, they'll be able to work things out to get back together. 'Cause no matter what she said tonight about not needing him in her or her babies' lives, I can't see Big D walking away from his family without a fight."

"Naw, D won't make it into a fight," Crockett disagreed, shaking his head. "He'll negotiate and kill her with kindness until she gives in and takes him back."

"True," the guys all agreed.

"I just wish I knew what to do for him," Liam sighed as he took a drink from the water bottle sitting on the table in front of him.

"I think all any of us can do is be here for him if he wants to talk," Dean offered.

"And make sure we invite Julie to all the group activities we have planned this week, so he gets extra chances to talk to her besides at the formal wedding events," Allissa added.

"And we probably need to come up with some other ideas for advancing our angle, since he'll probably want to stay here instead of taping the vignettes we were talking about last night and coming back on tour as soon as he's cleared to fly," Rylie added, looking around the room. "And that's going to take a lot more alcohol for me to do tonight, so I need to find our waitress."

Teagan started to object, but Rylie walked away before she could form the words.

"Don't worry, I've got her," Liam assured Teagan and the rest of their friends before following Rylie.

"I suppose we should get back to the party," Dean suggested. "You still have games to play, Darlin'? Or can I take you for a spin around the dance floor?"

"Yeah, I think I'd rather dance than have Randi blindfold me and hand me creepy paper penises for the Pin-the-Dick-On-the-Dude game." Allissa placed her hand in Dean's before they walked back toward the front room, where the dance floor was located.

"How about you, Princess? Wanna dance? Or try to beat me in a game of pool?" Crockett motioned toward the now empty pool table, where Anthony and Magnum had apparently finished their game.

"Oh, Brent, don't you know by now that there's no such thing as *try* when it comes to me?" Aiken smirked at her hubby. "I will absolutely beat you at a game of pool."

Left alone with her husband, Teagan looked at Josh to find out what party activity he wanted to join in on.

"Hey, Wifey, what do you say we go check and see if that storeroom is vacant?" Josh smirked, obviously reading her mind.

"Absolutely, Hubby," Teagan grinned, taking his hand, as they weaved their way through the people at the pool tables before skirting their friends on the dance floor to head down the hallway beside the bar.

The farther they got down the hall, the quieter the music from the front of the bar became, making it all too easy for them to hear the sound of bodies slapping together and against the wooden door of the storeroom. "I guess we're too late," Josh chuckled, redirecting her back in the direction they just came and wiggling his eyebrows suggestively. "But on one of the times I've been here in the last year, I heard about some trails over by the bowling alley. How do you feel about pretending we're teenagers again and going parking?"

"Oh, I've heard about those trails." Teagan decided to tease her husband a little to find out if he'd ever hooked up with one of the locals on the trails the Walkers told her, Aiken, and Rylie about back at Randi and James's wedding reception. "But I heard they have gates to block out anyone the Walkers haven't given the code, so unless you've been there before to have the code, we'll have to find someplace else to go parking."

"No, I don't have the code." Josh shook his head, looking slightly disappointed for a moment before his lips turned up in a smile. "But I bet the new trails the Hunters just cleared out to start preparing the different fields for the vineyard will be just as deserted this time of night. And we don't need a code to go parking on them."

"Let's go find out," Teagan grinned, not about to give Josh a reason to wonder if she'd ever been on the local make-out trails, the way she'd just momentarily feared he had, by mentioning that Luke Walker had told her the code while trying to talk her into going home with him after the wedding back in June.

She hadn't gone home with Luke, or verified that the code he told her would actually work, so she didn't see any reason to possibly upset Josh by sharing the story. Especially when they could quite possibly go over to the trails right then and find out she'd been given bad information. Since she didn't even let Luke walk her out of the reception or give her a kiss goodnight, there was no reason to cause any strife between him and Josh over something that happened over two months before she and Josh got married.

They didn't say anything to any of their friends as they snuck out of the party, even though she wasn't sure they'd make it back later to keep everyone from speculating about where they'd gone. Teagan wasn't even worried about needing to stay and help their friends work on the issues in their marriages, like she had earlier in the day. All she cared about in that moment was finding someplace to be alone with her husband to show him how much she loved him.

As soon as they were in their rental car and driving along the mostly empty streets of Heart's Destiny, Teagan slipped the shoulder strap of her seatbelt over her head, so she could lean over the center console and tease Josh with her hands and mouth while he drove.

"What are you doing, Tea?" Josh questioned as she moved his lap belt to be able to unfasten his slacks. "You need to stay in your seatbelt."

"I'm still in the bottom part of the seatbelt," Teagan assured her husband as she freed his cock and started stroking him. "And there's nobody else on the road this late at night here, so I figured this would be the only time I'd be able to safely give you road head."

"Fuck," Josh groaned, as she swirled her tongue around the head of his dick while stroking his shaft with her hand. He made an adjustment on the steering wheel, moving it up to its highest position so she had plenty of room. "Thank fuck the roads in town are on a grid. If there were curves between here and the hotel, your hot mouth would cause me to wreck."

Teagan couldn't help but smile as she lapped up the precum oozing from his tip before closing her lips around his cock and sucking him as far back as she could without triggering her gag reflex. Instead of pulling her braids out of the way to watch what she was doing like he normally did when she sucked his cock, Josh kept both hands on the steering wheel the whole time she bobbed up and down his length. He only released his white-knuckle grip with one hand to push her hair over her shoulder when he stopped at a red light. But as soon as the light turned green, his hand went right back to the wheel.

"Fuck, maybe we should've just pulled around behind the bar," Josh moaned, as Teagan continued to run her tongue over the most sensitive parts of his cock while maintaining the perfect amount of suction. "I know it's only five miles from the bar back to the main entrance of the Hunters' property, but…oh fuck, that feels so good."

Teagan almost laughed at how he was trying to talk to distract himself so he wouldn't come, but she couldn't with his dick in her mouth. Instead, she smiled as she lightly grazed his shaft with the edge of her teeth.

"Oh, fuck, yes, Teagan, just like that." Josh rocked his hips as he thrust up into her mouth, slightly revving the engine with each upward stroke. "Since there's so many lights at the main entrance, I'm gonna hafta double our driving distance to go in the side gate, so nobody will see us."

Teagan alternated swirling her tongue along his shaft as she moved down his length with lightly dragging her teeth against him as she pulled up.

"Fuck, fuck, fuck. I'm not gonna make it to the vineyards before I blow if you keep doing that, Tea."

Good, Teagan thought, not slowing even slightly as she felt Josh turning the car, presumably to go to the side entrance of the Hunters' property. *Then we'll have time to move to the backseat while you recover. 'Cause there's no way we'd both fit in one of these front seats, especially with the steering wheel in the way on the driver's side, which is exactly where you'd expect me to climb on you if we didn't take the edge off first.*

After a couple more turns, Teagan heard the crunch of gravel under their tires, which let her know he'd turned off the paved roads of town and onto the gravel road from the west side of the property that led to James and Dean's houses. A few seconds later, Josh slammed on the brakes and threw the car in park. "Fuck it. This'll have to do 'cause I can't wait to be inside you any longer."

Josh gripped her braids with his right hand, pulling her up off his cock, while reaching down beside the seat with his left hand and fiddling with the handle until he moved the seat back as far as it would go, and then reclined the back of the seat until he was almost lying flat. "Get over here and ride me, Wifey."

"Josh, we won't both fit in the driver's seat," Teagan protested, lightly chuckling at her predictable husband as she sat up and unfastened her seatbelt. "We need to move to the backseat where we'll have more room."

"Don't worry, Wifey, we'll both fit," Josh disagreed, stroking his cock while waiting on her to mount him. "This first time's gonna be quick, so we'll move to the backseat for round two."

"I think you're just trying to make sure I end up with bruises on my knees to match the one on your shin," Teagan joked as she hiked up her skirt and removed her panties before crawling over the center console to straddle Josh's lap.

"If you end up with any bruises from this, I'll be sure to kiss them and make them all better when we get up to our room later," Josh promised as he rubbed the head of his cock over her clit several times before lining it up with her soaking wet slit for her to slide down on his shaft. "Unless you have someplace else you'd rather I kiss you later."

"Oh, you'll be doing a lot more than just kissing my pussy later," Teagan declared as she took his dick inside her, reveling in the exquisite stretch as he filled her up.

He hadn't been lying about the first time being fast. He only waited long enough for her to adjust to his size before he gripped her hips and bounced her up and down his length in time with his thrusts up into her. When it was clear that he was much closer to the edge than she was, Josh slid one hand over so he could circle her clit with the pad of his thumb. That little bit of friction was all Teagan needed to push her over the edge, especially when she looked out the windows to realize that Josh had parked along the side of the road that she knew their friends would have to drive down to get to their houses after the party.

While she didn't like the thought of any of their friends seeing either of them naked, the thought of being caught when they were clearly having sex while mostly covered added an air of excitement to their coupling. It was just enough to send her over the edge in mere moments.

"Oh, fuck, yes, Josh," she cried out as her whole body spasmed in orgasmic bliss.

"Teagan," Josh groaned as the convulsions of her inner walls from her climax triggered his release deep inside her. "Fuck. I love you."

"I love you, too, Josh," Teagan panted out breathlessly as she collapsed forward on top of him.

Josh wrapped her in his arms, kissing her passionately as they shuddered with each aftershock.

When she finally caught her breath, Teagan pushed up into a sitting position on top of him once more. "You'd better find us a much more secluded spot than this before you join me in the backseat for round two."

With that, she crawled over him into the back of the car, not even bothering with a seatbelt.

"Yes, ma'am," Josh chuckled as he adjusted his seat back into an upright position and shifted the car into drive. "But you'd better pay attention to how many turns I make, so we can find our way back to the hotel later."

Hopefully, we won't get too lost and miss the wedding shower tomorrow.

Liam felt overwhelmed as he followed Rylie back up to the bar in the front room of Tully's. Between his lack of sleep from the nightmares he'd been having for the last few weeks, his guilt for taking his wife to the bar where he'd kissed another woman, having that woman be the first to congratulate him on his marriage as soon as they got there, everything he'd just learned about his best friend, not being able to catch up to Dion to see how he was doing, and now having to try to keep Rylie from overindulging and getting so impaired that she inadvertently let on to the locals that they weren't as happily married as they wanted everyone in Heart's Destiny to believe, he had way too much on his mind to be able to deal with everything at once. *Since I can't do anything to help D 'til he calls me back, and I can't go back*

in time to prevent the kiss with Jen, I guess I'll just try to keep Rylie sober enough that she won't break kayfabe tonight. But maybe not so sober that I'll wake her up if I have another nightmare tonight and have to turn on my bedside lamp to see that she's perfectly safe and sleeping peacefully before I can try to get some more sleep.

"I need another tray of those Lick My Pussy shots," Rylie ordered, as soon as Leo acknowledged their presence at the bar.

"Don't you think you should maybe have a bottle of water before the next round of shots? You know, alternate equal amounts of alcohol and water, so you can enjoy more of the party without drinking so much you get sick or pass out?" Liam looked to Leo for backup, but the bartender just turned his back and pulled another tray of shots from the cooler. *Feck! Doesn't he realize he needs to be more responsible and not overserve her?*

"Yeah, maybe, if these were full-sized drinks," Rylie argued, rolling her eyes at him. "But they're tiny, so I have to drink a whole bunch of them to equal a whole bottle of water. And I'm not going to drink them all myself. I'm taking them over to the table to share with the rest of the girls while we play dick games."

Leo handed Rylie another test-tube tray, which she promptly thanked him for before turning to walk back over to the table where a few of the ladies had sat back down to take a break from dancing.

"Don't worry, man," Leo informed him as he put a bottle of water in front of Liam. "She's not completely wrong about the size of these shots. After realizing how many rounds the women went through at the first of these parties last year, we switched to the test tubes for most of them to limit the amount of alcohol they were able to consume. And we steered them toward doing shots of mixed drinks that are mostly juice, so for any of the drinks in the test tubes, they have to drink like eight of them to equal the alcohol content in a standard drink. Only the Blow Job shots are full-size drinks now, since the whipped cream on top doesn't really dilute the alcohol content of the amaretto, coffee liqueur, and Irish cream. But because they're so much stronger than the other drinks, we tend to limit them to two or three rounds all night, usually just the first and last rounds, and maybe one other round in the middle if they're requested."

"Yeah, I kinda wondered if the one I drank in the back even had any alcohol in it," Liam chuckled, remembering the splash of what tasted like tropical punch when he gave his last toast.

"If you only drank one, then it probably wasn't enough to even register on a Breathalyzer," Leo laughed, "even if you held it in your mouth while taking the test. When we did the math while modifying the recipes to make them in batches, we figured out there's less than a quarter ounce of Malibu in each of those fruity shooters."

"With as heavy as Leo goes with the orange juice in the Ankles in the Air shots, I swear they have more vitamin C than alcohol," the waitress teased as she walked behind the bar and got three more trays of shooters out of the cooler to take over to the ladies.

"Still, I should probably get over there to make sure my wife doesn't finish off a couple dozen by herself," Liam excused himself, taking both his half-full bottle of water and the full bottle Leo had just served him over to where Rylie was sitting with several of the other ladies.

"Alright, ladies, now that we have more drinks, it's time to start the Drink-If game," Randi explained, holding up a card that Liam couldn't read from where he was standing. "I'm going to read the list and we each have to take a drink whenever one of the statements is true for us. Drink if you've known Dean or Allissa for over twenty years."

"Am I supposed to drink on this one, since I've known myself all my life?" Allissa asked, turning to Randi for clarification as all the local ladies at the table took a sip of their full-sized drinks or downed a shooter.

"Yes, 'cause it's Dean *or* Allissa. If it had been Dean *and* Allissa, then none of us could drink," Randi clarified before going on to the next item on her list. "Drink if you've known Dean or Allissa for less than a year."

Again, the local ladies took a drink, along with Rylie and Randi.

"Hey, Randi, I don't think you were supposed to drink then," Liam pointed out as he sat down beside Rylie, "since it's been more than a year since we all met you at the hotel in Tulsa."

"I didn't meet Allissa then, though," Randi disagreed. "I didn't meet her until I started with the GWA after Thanksgiving break last year, so I still have a few days before I'll officially know her for a whole year."

"My bad." Liam held up his hands in surrender. "Carry on."

"Drink if you're related to Dean or Allissa." Once again, Randi and a few of the local ladies took a drink.

"Geez, Leigh, did you write these out so you can drink for almost all of them?" Rylie questioned, holding a shooter in each hand to be ready for her next time to take a drink. "Or did you actually include some for the rest of us to get to drink along with you?"

"I didn't write any of them," Randi defended. "These are all things I found online, so yes, there are some that work for everyone here. In fact, even Liam has to drink for this next one. Drink if you're in the bridal party."

"Wait," Allissa held up her hand to stop them from drinking as she looked around. "We need to get the rest of the bridal party up here for this one. Where are Amethyst, Emerald, and the rest of the guys?"

They paused the game long enough for Kay to go in the back room and round up most of the bridal party. "I think I saw Emerald and Surfer Josh go outside earlier. I thought they were just getting some air. But it's been a while, so now I wonder if they left?"

"Those freaking horndogs are probably making out in their car," Amethyst giggled. "I'd suggest we go out and interrupt them to bring them back in here, but I doubt either one of them would be embarrassed enough to stop, and I really don't want to see that."

"Naw, Josh knows the police chief is in here, so I doubt they'd risk getting arrested for public indecency by staying in the parking lot," Crockett corrected his wife. "They're probably back at the B and B by now, unless they found someplace closer that's private enough to go parking."

"Do you think they know the gate code to get to the trails?" Dean questioned.

"I doubt it, since none of us wanted to hook up with Surfer Josh because of him sharing the same name as one of my brothers," Becky replied, shaking her head.

"But the Walkers told us the code at Randi and James's wedding reception, so I'm sure Emerald knows it," Rylie interjected, sending Liam's blood pressure skyrocketing from the thought of one of the local men hitting on his wife.

As everyone else around them decided to not wait on Josh and Teagan to come back to finish the game, Liam remembered back to the reception on the first of June to figure out which of the Walkers the local matchmakers had paired up with Rylie. *Fecking Leo! No wonder he was so nice to Rylie earlier and eagerly handed her a couple dozen shots right before Melissa carried several more trays of them to the rest of the ladies.*

Liam didn't even realize he'd stood from his seat before he was back at the bar, getting in Leo's face. The only reason he didn't reach over the bar and grab him by the shirt was because his hands were full with the bottle of water Leo had just served him and the half-full bottle he hadn't finished yet. "You gave my wife the code to the spot you all go to fuck?"

"Whoa! Dude!" Leo held his hands up in a placating gesture. "That was months ago, when I didn't know there was anything going on between ya'll. Hell, I thought you were dating Jen then, so even though it was obvious she was crushin' on you, I thought I might be able to help her move on since the crush appeared to be one-sided. But she turned me down flat and told me she'd only use that code if you took her out to the trails."

"Feck!" Liam backed down then, stomping out the front door, and hoping the fresh air would help calm his temper.

I knew from the first moment we met that she was just as attracted to me as I am to her. But I didn't think it was obvious to anyone but the two of us. And I stupidly thought that as long as we never acted on it, then I'd be the only one with a broken heart when I retire from the GWA and leave her to finish out her career. But if her feelings for me are obvious to even Leo Fecking Walker, who's probably only spent a total of four or five hours talking to her whenever we've all been in town for weddings, then my rejection of us being a couple is probably hurting her as much as it is me.

And hell, considering women are much more in tune with their emotions than men, or at least all the ones I know are, she's probably hurting a hell of a lot more than I am. And I feel like I'm fecking dying from not being able to be with her. Feck! Feck! Feck! I hate hurting her!

But what the hell else am I supposed to do? If we take advantage of the time we have left before I retire to fuck as often as possible, we won't fuck each other out of our systems, like some of the guys suggested. It won't feel like fucking with Rylie. It'd be making love, just like it was last month. And more of that will only make our feelings for one another stronger, and the pain ten times worse when I go home without her.

And that shit will be a lot harder to endure than even the hell of trying to keep from waking her up when I have a nightmare while we're sleeping in the same bed. But I guess at least being able to see her safe in bed beside me when I wake up from the nightmares will make them go away faster. Hopefully, long before I retire and have to spend the rest of my life waiting to see her on TV every Tuesday to know she's safe.

At least, seeing her in bed beside me last night helped me get over the nightmare faster. Even if it was hard as feck to stop myself from pushing that pile of pillows out from between us and waking her up to talk her into making our marriage real until I retire. But even if losing myself in her sexy little body would help me forget the nightmares, I don't want her to think the only reason I want to be with her is to deal with my trauma from everything that happened at **Halloween Horror**. *'Cause that's definitely not the case, no matter how it might already appear to her since the only time we've made love was that night.*

Besides, making love with her again might not do anything to stop the nightmares, but it'll definitely leave me with a broken heart when we have to go our separate ways in a couple of years. And probably even more pain than I'll feel if we just make a clean break now. So, no, I definitely can't give in to my physical desire for her and have a temporary fling.

I just need to get through the rest of this week, keeping as much physical distance between us in bed as possible. And when I wake up fighting my lust for her, I can take the edge off by getting up to go jerk off in the shower once she's asleep, like I did last night. But, feck, I doubt even my best fantasies about fucking her while jerking off will be enough to keep me from missing her like crazy once I'm in Belle Harbor and she's still traveling the world.

Liam didn't know how long he paced around the parking lot, trying to get his wild thoughts under control. But it must have been at least a couple of hours, since he'd finished off both bottles of water. In all that time, he was able to cycle at least three times between talking himself into spending the rest of his career making love with his wife, and then talking himself back out of that plan and into deciding once more to end everything between them now, so their breakup wouldn't hurt as much as he knew it would if he had more time with her. All the while, spinning the Claddagh wedding band he'd bought that morning on his left ring finger and wishing it was something he could wear forever.

When the first few couples exited the bar to call it a night, he quickly realized he'd spent way too much time outside, instead of watching over Rylie for the rest of the party. *Feck! I'm such an arse,* he mentally berated himself as he reentered the bar and tossed his empty water bottles in the closest recycling bin. *I should have stayed inside to help keep Rylie from getting so drunk she'll have a hangover in the morning, instead of throwing a temper tantrum like a spoiled child.*

He quickly spotted her at the jukebox, swaying on her feet as she repeatedly pushed the button to scroll through the menu of songs. "I wanna play *Shots* again," she slurred, clearly having consumed way more shots than water while he was outside, before singing off key. "Shots, shots, shots, shots…"

"Sorry, Mo Ghrá, we'll have to save the rest of the shots for next time." Liam looped his arm around her waist to keep her from falling when she spun on her heels at the sound of his voice.

"Liam," she shouted as she threw her arms around him. "There you are! You missed the blow jobs, but datz oh-tay cuz I'll give you one when we get to our room."

I fecking wish, Liam thought, knowing he couldn't allow her to suck his cock while she was obviously inebriated, even if he had come close to talking himself into enjoying their sexual attraction during his limited time with Rylie while pacing around the parking lot.

"She's talking about the last round of Blow Job shots," Randi clarified with a giggle as she leaned heavily on James. "Well, the ones you missed anyway. I think she has other plans for when ya'll get to your room."

I guess, at least, if she's been talking about giving me blow jobs for the past couple of hours, she's still selling our marriage, instead of alerting the locals to our annulment plans. But feck, if alcohol is truth serum like I've always heard, then getting her to sign the papers is gonna be a lot bigger problem than I thought. And if I force the issue, I'm gonna hurt her so bad that she'll probably never forgive me, and

I'll end up in the same situation as my brother with never getting my second chance with my one true love.

"I made sure I's good at 'em by doin' the ones the preggo ladies couldn't. Did you know preggo ladies can't give blow jobs? Their hubbies must be so sad, waiting 'til the babies are born before getting blow jobs again."

"They can still give blow jobs, they just can't have Blow Job shots because of the alcohol," Kay clarified as she and Anthony walked by on their way to the door.

"Oh, good, then we can still has babies," Rylie slurred, running her hand over his abs as she shuffled along beside him, while he aimed her toward the door where everyone else was exiting.

Feck! Do not even think about how fecking hot a pregnant Rylie would be, Liam chastised himself, futilely trying to keep from imagining her round with his child.

"Who's driving? And how much did you have to drink?" Bobby Burleson asked each couple before letting them exit the building.

"I'm driving," Liam replied for him and Rylie. "And I had one beer and a test-tube shooter at the beginning of the night and two bottles of water since then."

While he hadn't been responsible for driving anyone else home from one of these parties in the past, Liam already knew the drill for limiting alcohol and switching to water early in the evening to be able to drive away at the end of the night whenever the police chief was in attendance. He'd just rode with Dion or one of the other guys if he'd over imbibed in the past.

"You actually drank one of those fruity things?" Bobby gave him a skeptical look.

"Yeah," Liam admitted with a half shrug, still holding Rylie up with his other arm. "I'm not sure if it was the one with more vitamin C than alcohol or not, but Leo assured me it wasn't enough to even register on a Breathalyzer, even if you'd tested me right after I drank it."

"Considering it takes over a dozen of those things for Brie to get a buzz," Bobby chuckled, "he's probably right if you only drank one."

Once Bobby was assured that Liam was sober, they left the bar to head back to their room at the bed and breakfast. Rylie babbled about babies with his eyes and hair and her complexion for about half the trip, which didn't do anything to help him shore up his resolve to end things with her the way he still thought he needed to in order to lessen both of their heartaches in the end. Then she promptly fell asleep, lightly snoring the rest of the way back to the hotel.

Guess it's probably safer for me to carry her upstairs, anyway. Between those fuck-me heels and the way she shuffle-walked out of the bar, she'd never make it up the stairs without tripping, so I'd have ended up carrying her anyway, even if she was awake right now.

He hit the lock button on the key fob as soon as he got the passenger door open, so he could put it in his pocket. Then he got the keycard for their room out of his wallet before he lifted her from the car, knowing he'd need to have it in hand to open the door to their room without having to put her down first. Once he unfastened her seatbelt and scooped her up into his arms, he kicked the passenger door shut before striding from the parking lot to the grand front entrance of the Heritage House. He had to lower her legs slightly to open the main door into the building, while still maintaining his grip on the keycard so he didn't accidentally drop it.

"Hmmm, you smell so good," Rylie purred as she rubbed her face against his neck, where he'd rested her head against his shoulder when he picked her up. "It makes me wanna lick you all over."

"Feck," Liam groaned when he felt her tongue teasingly tracing circles on his pulse point, picking up the pace as he crossed the lobby.

"Did she just lick you?" Teagan questioned from somewhere behind him.

Liam didn't slow down long enough to reply, even though he kind of wanted to ask where she and Josh had been after skipping out of the party several hours earlier.

"Oh, look at how he's rushing to get her up to their room," she continued gushing, obviously not that far behind him as they all made their way up the stairs. "I guess my plan to have them room together is working better than I thought."

I knew when we were given single rooms yesterday, instead of adjoining rooms like we usually get when we're here, that it had to be more than just a way to convince the Matchmaking Mommas that we're happily married. But I didn't realize we should have been more worried about the matchmaking antics of our peers than the Matchmaking Mommas of Heart's Destiny.

He couldn't take the time to straighten out his misguided coworker right then, though, because he still needed to get Rylie into their room and try to get her to wake up enough to take some over-the-counter pain relievers and drink a bottle of water to stave off the hangover she was bound to have in the morning. So, Liam ignored his friends as he fumbled with the keycard until he got their hotel room door open and was able to carry Rylie over the threshold.

He placed her on the bed before going to gather the supplies, which he placed on the bedside table while he took off her shoes. "Rylie, sweetheart, you need to sit up for a minute and take some ibuprofen."

"No, need to lay here and kiss you." Rylie reached out for him, but she didn't open her eyes. "If I rest while you lick my pussy, then I can wake up to give you a blow job."

Liam took a step back from the bed, grateful he'd been at her feet already, so she wasn't able to get ahold of him and pull him onto the bed with her. While he was raised to never take advantage of a woman while she was impaired, he wasn't a saint. If she pulled him down on her side of the bed and kissed him, he wouldn't be able to resist kissing her back. He'd most likely get up before letting it go farther than that, but as she whimpered about needing him to make love to her, he quickly lost all confidence in his ability to resist her.

"There's water and ibuprofen on your bedside table," he informed her before turning and walking toward the bathroom. "I'll just be a few minutes in the bathroom, but that should give you enough time to take those pills and gather your stuff to change for bed."

Liam promptly closed the door behind him, and prayed he'd get his dick to deflate while brushing his teeth so he could actually empty his bladder before going back out to get in his side of the bed. *You're not getting any tonight, so you can go to sleep now,* Liam mentally scolded his cock as he stripped off his boots, jeans, and button-down shirt, brushed his teeth, and washed his face. *If you go down now and don't embarrass me while she's still awake, then I'll jerk you off in the shower once she goes to sleep, just like last night. I know that's not nearly as enticing as the blow job she offered you, but she's too drunk to consent to that tonight, so my hand will have to do.*

Once his dick reluctantly receded back into his boxer briefs, Liam emptied his bladder and washed his hands before carrying his clothes out to put them in the dirty laundry bag in the closet. He noticed that

Rylie had taken the ibuprofen and drank half the bottle of water on her bedside table, but she hadn't waited for him to vacate the bathroom before getting ready for bed. Her hair was wrapped in the same silk scarf she'd used the night before and she was under the covers. He didn't know if she'd changed clothes or not, but he assumed she had, so he wasn't about to wake her again to go brush her teeth.

He turned out the lights by the door and bathroom. Then he walked to the other side of the room to pull the curtains closed over the window and turn off the lamp on Rylie's bedside table. Finally, he walked back around to his side of the bed and shut off his bedside lamp, after lying down and turning his back to the mountain of pillows piled up in the middle of the bed, which he'd put there the night before to keep them on their own sides of the bed.

Unlike the night before, however, the room wasn't completely quiet, even though he'd verified everything was turned off. *What the feck is that buzzing noise? Is that the air conditioner? No, it can't be, not in November. Unless, maybe Rylie turned on the heat, since it is in the low fifties overnight here this time of year?*

Liam was just about to get up to go feel for airflow by the opening to the ducts, when Rylie moaned and he felt the slightest movement from her side of the bed. After rolling to his back, so he had more surface area of his body in contact with the mattress, he realized that the buzzing sound coincided with the pulsing rhythm of vibration that he could barely feel through the mattress. *Holy shit! Is she using her vibrator?*

"Hmmm…ooh…yes…" she moaned, rocking the bed as she seemed to really enjoy fucking her toy.

Feck! I wish I'd left the lights on, so I could see what she's doing. Liam's cock jumped to attention, obviously eager to trade places with whatever she was using to pleasure herself. He couldn't stop himself from gripping his dick and squeezing it tight over his boxer briefs as he rolled to face her, trying to see what she was doing over the pile of pillows between them. Unfortunately, all he could see in the sliver of moonlight coming in around the edge of the window was her hips rising and falling under the blankets. *You absolutely can, fecking, not move these pillows outta the way and join in.*

"Ooh…aah…mmnmm…" The way she kept moaning in pleasure made it impossible for him not to shove his hand in his boxers and stroke his cock, matching his rhythm with that of her bouncing hips. *If she can use her vibrator under the covers while I'm in bed with her, then it's okay for me to jerk off under the covers at the same time, right?*

When he looked at her face, it was obvious she had her eyes closed. But Liam wasn't sure if that was because she was actually asleep, or if she was just so lost in the erotic play that she couldn't keep them open. *If only the bedding wasn't in the way, so I could see exactly what she's doing.*

As if she'd just read his mind, Rylie pushed her covers down to show off her bountiful breasts in a pale lace-trimmed silky nightie with thin spaghetti straps. With it mostly dark in the room, Liam couldn't tell if it was white, light pink, or maybe a pastel yellow, but it was definitely lighter than her warm copper complexion. He was so entranced by watching her breasts bounce as if they might pop out of her nightie that it took a moment before Liam realized she'd kicked the blanket and sheet down far enough to expose her naked lower half, with the bottom of the nightie pushed up over her belly. Between her legs he could see the bright purple plastic of what he assumed was a rabbit vibrator, since the bunny ears were pressed on either side of her clit.

Well, feck, that description makes a lot more sense now that I'm seeing it in use.

Liam knew it was wrong to keep watching her as she moved the shaft of the toy in and out of her pussy, but he couldn't look away. He also couldn't stop stroking his cock, too turned on by the sight of her pleasuring herself to completely suppress the urges of his body. It took every ounce of self-control he possessed to just lay there and jerk his dick, when he really wanted to shove the pillows out from between them and take over fucking her with the toy before finally replacing it with his cock.

"Oh, yes, yes, yes," Rylie cried out as her body convulsed as she reached her release.

That toy didn't make her squirt like I did, though, Liam silently gloated as he watched her shiver with each aftershock. *Too bad I can't go help her out with that now.*

Once she seemed to have recovered from her orgasm, Rylie pulled the toy from her body and rolled to cuddle the pillows between them, slapping him in the chest with the still vibrating toy. She didn't open her eyes, or pull up the covers, snoring lightly as she mumbled, "Liam."

Feck! Was she fantasizing about me that whole time? Or was she asleep for most of it and dreaming about me?

Knowing the toy would need to be cleaned and recharged before she could use it again, Liam took it from her hand before getting up to go preserve her dignity by covering her up, so hopefully she wouldn't be embarrassed when she woke up half naked and flashing him in the morning. Then he used the flashlight on his phone to see as he dug through her suitcase to find the box and charging cable for her toy before carrying it into the bathroom, where he could turn on the light to figure out how to turn the thing off.

Since she had the original packaging for the Jack Rabbit Signature vibrator, he flipped through the booklet that came with it to make sure it was safe to clean with soap and water before cleaning it up for her. Realizing it was waterproof and still partially charged, however, quickly gave him an idea.

I need to make sure the battery is almost completely dead before I plug it in, so I don't shorten her toy's battery life by overcharging it. And while the dick part does absolutely nothing for me, I bet I'd enjoy those rabbit ears moving up and down my cock like I imagine she'd lick me.

Liam promptly dropped his boxer briefs and carried Rylie's vibrator into the shower with him, adjusting the water temperature before turning the toy back on. Holding the toy by the short handle at the base of the shaft, he ran the rabbit ears over the head of his cock the way he envisioned Rylie would swirl her tongue. But that grip weirded him out when he accidentally hit the button to cause the fake cock that had been inside Rylie just a few minutes earlier to thrust against his dick.

Fecking hell, Liam groaned, quickly turning off the thrusting action and spinning the toy around to use the shaft as a handle instead. *I wanna figure out how it might feel if I use this with her, like maybe give her the fantasy of two dicks with the toy in her ass and me in her pussy, with these bunny ears tickling my balls, not feel like I'm fucking another guy.*

With that thought in mind, he slid the rabbit ears down his shaft, pausing momentarily when the vibrations hit his most sensitive spot before moving them down to his balls. With his free hand, he used the pump on Rylie's bodywash to squirt a little of the product labeled "Amazing Grace Intense" into his palm. Then he appreciated her fruity floral scent as he stroked his cock with the soap acting as lube.

Feck. Hers works so much better than mine, he thought as he worked his dick with one hand while running the rabbit ears of her vibrator over his balls with the other. Between her scent surrounding him and his fantasy of fucking her pussy with his cock and her ass with her toy, it didn't take long before he shot his load all over the wall of the shower.

"Mo Stór, is tú Mo Ghrá, Mo Anam Cara." *My Treasure, you are My Love, My Soulmate.* "Feck, Rylie," Liam groaned in both Irish and English, as spurt after spurt of his cum exploded from the end of his dick. Rylie's toy stopped vibrating just before he lowered his hand, allowing it to dangle at his side while he shuddered with each aftershock from his orgasm.

This doesn't feel nearly as good as it did when I came while balls-deep inside her. But hopefully, it'll be enough to help me stay in control the rest of the night, so I don't do anything inappropriate while she's still too drunk to consent.

Liam cleaned up the mess he made in the shower, soaping up her toy and making sure it was clean and dry before plugging it in to charge on his bedside table along with his phone. *I should probably set an alarm to get that put away before Rylie wakes up in the morning, so I won't have to explain why it's on my bedside table instead of hers.*

Chapter Thirteen

Rylie felt like death warmed over when she woke up after overindulging at the bachelorette party the night before. She was half buried in the pile of pillows stacked down the middle of the bed, with one of them pressing against her core, where she'd obviously humped it when her dreams of Liam turned carnal. *Guess it's a good thing we put these here, so I just humped the pillow and not Liam. While jumping him in my sleep might show him I want to make our marriage real, sex isn't the only thing I want our relationship based on, so I don't need to make it too easy for him to get in my panties.*

Thinking about her panties, she assessed her body before opening her eyes, needing to know if she'd left them on or if she'd taken them off to use her vibrator the night before. *Oh, God, was I really so drunk that I thought it was a good idea to get out my rabbit while Liam was in the bathroom, hoping he'd join in when he caught me using it? Or was that all a dream?*

Fuck! My panties are missing! So maybe it wasn't a dream after all? Maybe he did spend a little time on my side of the bed, showing me just how much better he is than my vibrator? But if that's the case, why did he go back to his side of the bed and leave these pillows between us?

Unless maybe it was just a dream, and I only used my vibrator last night? That would explain why I'm not wearing panties and why my hoo-hah isn't sore like it was after sex with Liam last month. But if I used my rabbit while just fantasizing about Liam, then where's my toy now?

Damn, I really need to stop drinking so much that I can't remember what I did the night before to know what was real and what was just in my dreams. I thought I did pretty good by sticking to the fruity test-tube shooters for most of the night, since they don't knock me on my ass like the Blow Job shots. But apparently, they were strong enough to make me less diligent as the night wore on, so I probably had more than just the first two Blow Job shots I remember from our first round of drinks. At least, she assumed that's why her head was pounding and she didn't remember anything after finishing the Drink-If game.

"I'm going to head down and get us some breakfast while you shower and get dressed." Liam's words startled her into jerking her eyes open and looking over to see him placing his wallet in the back pocket of his dark gray slacks. He then buttoned the matching suit jacket to mostly cover his white dress shirt and navy-blue tie. "Do you have any preference for something that'll help with your hangover? Or that might help settle your stomach?"

You taking that suit back off and coming back to bed. Shit, Rylie, don't say that to him!

"Only if you can find me a chocolate chip muffin with half the chocolate chips replaced with aspirin," Rylie joked, glancing around the bed to make sure he couldn't see her vibrator, since she still didn't know if she'd actually gotten it out to use when she changed for bed and wrapped her hair the night before, or if she'd only dreamed she had.

"Yeah, I don't think they make those," Liam chuckled. "But I left a bottle of ibuprofen on the bathroom counter, so you can take a couple of those and still have all the chocolate chips in your muffin."

"Thank you." Rylie would have appreciated him acting more like the friend she'd recently missed if she'd been able to think straight with her head pounding.

"No problem," Liam smiled before turning and leaving the room.

She rubbed her temples for a second before getting up and going into the bathroom, where she promptly emptied her bladder before taking two ibuprofen and chugging an entire cup of tap water. Then she brushed her teeth before going back to look through the bedding for her vibrator.

"Where the hell is it?" Rylie questioned the empty room after stripping the blanket, top sheet, and all the pillows off the bed. When she still didn't see it, she quickly put everything back on the bed, so hopefully Liam wouldn't notice she'd frantically searched the bed for her favorite toy. "Did I really only dream about using it last night?"

As she pulled out her favorite red dress and undergarments from her bags, she checked the pocket she kept the toy in, only to find that she hadn't even returned the box to the usual spot after the last time she used it. "Shit, did I forget to pack it before we left Lubbock on Friday?"

With no time to look any further, Rylie carried everything she needed to get dressed into the bathroom and started her shower. "I must have left it in Lubbock, right? And then just dreamed about using it with Liam last night since it wasn't in my bag. I mean, it's not like he'd have found it in the bed this morning and then went through my bags to find the box and hide it all from me. So, I had to have just been dreaming that I used it to tease him until he fucked me last night, right?"

Once she convinced herself that she had to have lost her favorite toy before she arrived in Heart's Destiny and had to room with Liam, Rylie quickly ran through her morning routine. She was dressed and ready to go as soon as Liam returned with her chocolate chip muffin, which she ate in the car on the way to the church.

While she hadn't been back to a Catholic church since losing her parents, feeling disillusioned with religion when none of her prayers saved their lives, Rylie found she enjoyed her visits to the non-denominational church in Heart's Destiny, when she'd been there for all the events surrounding the two weddings she'd attended over the summer. She wasn't sure if it was because she'd matured in the almost seven years since she lost her parents, or if it was because this church was nothing like the one she'd attended with her parents for years, but either way, she found comfort sitting on the pew and listening to the pastor's sermons.

This time, sitting next to Liam, as the preacher gave a sermon about how husbands and wives have to work on their marriages by forgiving one another for the little things, was no different than the previous times she'd attended the services in Heart's Destiny. She still felt comforted, like her parents were watching over her from Heaven. And maybe they were whispering in Fiona's dad's ear for him to know the exact messages she needed to hear. While the need to forgive Liam for his attitude since they found out they got married resonated with her, she hoped he heard the underlying message that loving each other and working together to make their marriage work was a choice they each had to make daily, so maybe one day he'd change his mind about the annulment and choose her instead.

She still wasn't certain that he could possibly return her feelings, but after seeing how he and Jen had pretty much ignored each other after their brief interaction at the beginning of the party the night before, and realizing Liam and Kara never even seemed to notice one another's presence at the party or church this morning, she was starting to wonder if she'd been way off in her fears after watching him jerk off Friday night.

He said some of that same stuff in Irish the night we made love too, so maybe it was just terms of endearment that he meant for me? Maybe he was thinking of me when he stroked his cock in the shower Friday night?

But if that's the case, why is he still so dead set on getting an annulment? Is that because he doesn't think our feelings for one another are strong enough to be true love? And even if he thinks it's just lust, why aren't we taking advantage of rooming together this week to satisfy that lust? Is he afraid it'll turn into more if we have sex more than once, and he doesn't want to risk falling in love with me? Or is he possibly trying to keep me from turning into a clinger by giving me false hope through sex?

But if that's what he's trying to do with all the distance between us when we're alone and the constant talk about the annulment whenever our future plans are brought up backstage or on the GWA plane, then shouldn't he try to get by with as little PDA as possible this week, even when he's trying to sell our happy marriage?

Hopefully, the way he kept his arm around my shoulders all through the service and held my hand as we walked from the chapel to the fellowship hall are signs that he might be leaning toward giving us a real shot, Rylie thought as they took their seats with the rest of the bridal party, both Allissa and Dean's parents, and Dion and his brother for the wedding shower. *And maybe the PDA now isn't just him acting the part of the loving husband because there are so many people watching us.*

Leah Mae Wright

With her head pounding again due to her hangover, she couldn't keep dwelling on her relationship with Liam. That would just lead to her reading every little thing he did as a sign for how he felt about her. So, Rylie mostly kept quiet as everyone made small talk while waiting for lunch to be served, only speaking when someone directly addressed her.

As it was her first chance to really observe Dion since he'd been shot, she decided to let most of the conversations around her go in one ear and out the other, so she could focus on observing any differences in him as a result of that day almost a month earlier. While she wasn't as close to Dion as the rest of the GWA crew, Liam was his best friend. So, as Liam's wife, she felt like it was her responsibility to understand what was going on to be able to help her husband deal with his feelings if Dion wasn't able to come back to work.

Are the girls right that he only acted so out of character last night because of the shock of finding out Julie is pregnant? Or is he dealing with more repercussions of his injuries than he's mentioned on the couple of calls I heard last week?

Like her, Dion was also being quieter than normal and letting everyone else carry the conversational load. Until he randomly laughed for no apparent reason.

"What's so funny?" Dean asked Dion.

"Just thinkin' 'bout how Mama Marcel's gonna wanna move her fortune telling business to town when she gets here next week," Dion grinned.

"Oh, I wish we'd have thought to have her here for the haunted hayride last month," Dean's mom, Mandi, interjected, turning to look at Allissa's mom. "Windy, don't let me forget to get with her next week when she gets here to see if she's interested in booking sessions with the retreat groups we have coming in January."

"Why do I have a feeling Mama Marcel making friends in this town is gonna be a bad thing for me?" Darius looked back and forth between Dion and the two older women at the table.

"Well, you did say you wanna spend some time with the hotties you saw in the bar last night," Dion chuckled.

Since he's referring to the brief time they were at Tully's like he remembers it, maybe I'm wrong about how bad his injuries are affecting him now.

"Yeah, that was last night, when I thought they were like the party girls in NOLA," Dare defended. "But seein' 'em all in church this morning has changed my perspective."

"Too late, Dare," Dean laughed. "You're on the radar of the Matchmaking Mommas now, so ya might as well prepare yourself for gettin' hitched."

"Just be glad you're meeting them in Heart's Destiny and not out in Vegas," Liam quipped from beside Rylie as he wrapped his arm around her shoulders once more. "Here the Mommas just manipulate situations, so you'll end up sitting with the woman they wanna match you up with at every public event they can. But out in Vegas, Windy and Kandi will get you drunk and rent a limo to take you to the county marriage license office on the way to one of the chapels, so you actually end up tying the knot."

Wow, I guess I was wrong in thinking he actually believed some of the things we said about being just drunk enough to lower our inhibitions and allow us to act on our feelings for one another when we announced our wedding news at **Halloween Horror**. *Clearly, he still thinks we were coerced into getting married and didn't do it because we both secretly wanted to, like I want to believe.*

"Don't listen to them, Darius," Windy argued, shaking her head at Liam. "We just wanted to take some pictures at the marriage license bureau and with an Elvis impersonator at one of the chapels to stir up a buzz on social media, and maybe push Allissa and Dean into getting hitched. But we had nothing to do with any of these yahoos saying 'I do.' That's all on them."

"Sorry, we're not buying that line anymore," Liam objected before Rylie or anyone else who'd gotten married in Vegas could put in their two cents. "Since none of us were ever charged for the licenses or ceremonies, I'm betting it was you who paid for all of them."

"And when I called to find out how to get copies of any pictures or videos, it was you the woman at the chapel described as the woman who picked up all our hard copies of the ones she ended up having to email us," Josh added, pointing straight at Windy.

"Fine, yes, paying for everything was my wedding present to each of you," Windy admitted, holding her hands up in surrender. "And I have all the photos and videos at my place in Dead End, but you'll have to wait until the next time you're here for a break to get them, since they're being boxed up with the rest of my stuff and shipped out here once I pick a house to officially move."

Rylie looked at Liam, who leaned back in his seat like he was gloating. *But admitting to paying for everything and picking up our hard copy pictures and videos as a wedding present isn't the same as confessing to forcing us down the aisle. It's not like she had a gun to our heads to make us get married. We still had to willingly sign the paperwork, walk down the aisle, and say "I do" before anything became legal. So, Windy might have given us the idea, but we're each still responsible for deciding to tie the knot that night.*

"With you not remembering the last couple years, how do ya know you didn't get married when these guys did?" Darius asked Dion, bringing Rylie back out of her head with her curiosity over Dion and Julie's relationship.

"Because Jewel wasn't there," Dion insisted.

"Are you sure she wasn't?" Liam arched an eyebrow at Dion. "It was one of the nights you went to the hotel early, so it coulda been one of the nights she snuck into town to see you without any of us knowing about it."

"Trust me, as often as I've dreamed about those hotel room rendezvous in the last month, if I'd have married her, I'd have remembered it in my dreams," Dion asserted. "Besides, both Dare and Mama Marcel woulda known if I got a marriage license in the mail like ya'll did."

From the look on his face, it seems like he'd be thrilled if he had married Julie. Much more thrilled than Liam is with being married to me. Hopefully, they'll be able to work things out, so he can have a happy family with the woman of his dreams.

"Wait." Teagan held up a hand to stop the other conversations going on around the large table. "Are you saying the only memories you have of the last two years are your hotel room hookups?"

"Yeah, and they're all with Jewel," Dion confessed, glancing over toward Anthony for a moment before looking back toward Rylie and Liam.

At least, Rylie first thought he was looking at her and Liam. But when she looked closer at his eyes, it was obvious he was looking past them, presumably at the table behind her and Liam, where Julie was sitting.

Aw, he can't keep his eyes off her. I hope someone tells Julie how lucky she is to have a man who obviously adores her. I'd give just about anything to have Liam look at me that way.

"And Jewel is Julie?" Aiken clarified.

"Jewel is that beautiful blonde in the purple sweater dress," Dion confirmed, lifting his chin as if to point her out. "Who is apparently too pissed off to talk to me because of Dare bein' a dickhead when he answered my phone while I was unconscious and having a CT scan the first day I was in the hospital."

Rylie glanced over her shoulder to verify that Julie was indeed wearing a purple sweater dress, making sure their assumptions were all correct. Even though she'd been positive Dion was dreaming about Julie after the scene at the bar the night before, she wasn't sure how much her alcohol consumption had clouded her assessment of the situation.

"So, it wasn't you she spoke to that day?" Kay voiced the question that all the ladies had pondered the night before.

"No," Dion replied, shaking his head while looking over at Kay and Anthony.

"It was me," Darius admitted with a heavy sigh. "And after dealing with reporters calling nonstop and having to get hospital security to remove a couple of women who'd snuck in the back way to his room in the ER, I was a colossal ass when I answered the call. And I followed the angry ass routine with the dumbass move of blocking and deleting her from his phone."

I knew Julie had to be confused last night when she accused Dion of being the ass on the phone. Hopefully, it won't take long before she's willing to hear him out to realize it was all just a misunderstanding. I might not like that Liam was paired up with Jen every time Dion was paired up with Julie at events here, but I still want Dion and Julie to get their happily ever after, especially since she's pregnant with his babies.

"Lemme guess, D," Crockett chuckled. "You're so chill 'cause Dare got all the hothead genes in your family?"

"Something like that," Dion replied with a smile at Crockett before turning back to face Anthony and Kay. "If I'd have been able to answer my phone that day, I woulda begged for her to come to NOLA to help me try to remember more than the few flashes I'd had of her while I was knocked out. I'm hoping that, now that I've found her and figured out who she is besides my Jewel, that we can pick up where we left off before I lost my memories. And I can show her that even when I forgot everything else, I didn't forget how much I love her."

Aw! Talk about true love.

"Oh, wow, that's so romantic." Randi placed a hand over her heart as she looked at Dion before turning to her sister, Kay. "It sounds like something you'd put in one of your books. A love so strong that even amnesia can't erase it. You'll have all your readers swooning if you pen their story next."

Rylie nodded, fighting not to tear up as she agreed with Randi's sentiment.

"Yes, well, we'll have to see how everything plays out before I decide who to write about next." Kay smirked as she eyed each of the couples who'd gotten married in Vegas, obviously considering each of them for her next book to give Dion and Julie more time to work things out.

Yeah, that next book better be about Josh and Teagan or Crockett and Aiken, Rylie thought as Randi redirected the flow of the discussion.

"Why didn't ya'll tell us about Julie being pregnant before we found out at the party last night? I thought sisters share everything, so I shoulda been in the loop, even if you didn't want me to tell anyone else."

Oh, damn, Randi's right. Kay and Anthony would have found out on one of their days off, so they could have warned all of us not to say anything to upset her before the party last night.

"That's my fault," Anthony admitted, holding up a hand to stop Randi from continuing to question her sister. "After Julie had to tell the family about the twins at Halloween before she was ready, I made Kay and the kids promise not to tell anyone else, so she could be the one to reveal her pregnancy news on her own timeline."

"D is the dad, though, right?" Liam questioned, not seeming to notice that Dion had zoned out and didn't seem to be paying attention to the conversation. "Is that why she waited to tell any of us until after he got to the party last night, so she could tell him first?"

Based on what she heard of Dion and Julie's brief conversation the night before, Rylie didn't think that was the case, since she hadn't come out and said specifically that Dion was her baby daddy. But she didn't think it was any of her business, so she kept her mouth shut.

"I don't know what was said last night." Anthony shook his head. "So, I don't know what order she told anyone."

"She actually told me first," Teagan admitted sheepishly, "when I asked if she was knocked up because she waited on a mocktail instead of taking one of the shots we were passing around for the first toast."

Before anyone else could chime in to rehash the events of the night before, Darius waved a hand in front of Dion's face, apparently trying to get him to pay attention to the conversation. "Hey, come back to earth, D." When Dion finally looked over at his brother, Dare continued, redirecting his comments to the rest of them. "Ya'll have to excuse my brother. Since the TBI, he tends to zone out like this whenever he gets to thinking too hard, or trying to force a memory."

I guess he's still dealing with more concussion symptoms than he mentioned Friday night on the phone, Rylie realized, smiling sympathetically at Dion.

"Sorry," Dion apologized, looking slightly embarrassed by the brief zone-out episode. "I should have just asked everyone I met in the last couple of years to reintroduce themselves, instead of trying to figure out who's who."

"Oh, dear," Mandi gasped. "You did say something about one of your symptoms being that you don't comprehend things as easily as you used to, and I didn't even think about how that would affect you in trying to remember all the names I went over with you on the phone last night. I should have continued with the introductions after church the way I started them this morning. I'm so sorry. I didn't realize."

"No need for you to…be sorry. I'm the one who should…" Dion took a longer pause before continuing, obviously struggling with his words. "…be sorry for being a…bad guest."

"Dude, you're not a bad guest," Dean argued, shaking his head at Dion. "If anything, we're being bad friends by acting like nothing's changed, when we could be doin' things like extra introductions and talking about the other times you've been here to help you get your memories back."

They quickly went around the table, reintroducing themselves, so Dion would know who he was talking to as they finished eating lunch. He'd still need to be reintroduced to the rest of the people at the wedding shower, but Rylie felt a little better about observing him now that he at least knew her name, even if he had no memory of meeting her before.

"So, if you don't remember the last couple of years, you probably don't remember being here for either of our wedding showers." James pointed between him and Randi, then over to Anthony and Kay.

"No," Dion shook his head. "The church feels familiar, but I don't have any specific memories of being here before."

That must be so disconcerting. Memory loss is scary enough when it's just a night or two after drinking heavily. I can't imagine how frightening it must be to not remember years of his life like that.

"The first time was a year ago," Dean stated.

"Technically, a year and a week," Anthony interjected, bobbing his head from side to side before turning to smile at his wife. "Since it's our one-year anniversary today."

"Sorry, guys, I didn't even think about ya'll wantin' to spend the day off by yourselves to celebrate today," Dean offered, looking embarrassed at not recognizing the date.

"Don't worry about it," Anthony waved off Dean's concerns. "We've got plans to leave the kids with the grandparents tonight for our private celebration. And we wanna be here for ya'll the same way you were here for us last year."

"Well, we at least need to have an extra toast," Dean suggested, lifting his glass. "To Anthony and Kay. I hope this is the first of many happy anniversaries."

While Rylie didn't feel as guilty as some of her peers around the table probably did for not realizing it was their anniversary, since she hadn't known them then, she still joined in as everyone at the table wished Anthony and Kay a happy anniversary. After that, Anthony told Dion, and everyone else at the table who hadn't attended their ceremony the previous year, about his and Kay's wedding shower, which was apparently the first time Dion attended the Heart's Destiny Community Church. Rylie wasn't surprised to hear how much it resembled the other wedding showers she'd attended since joining the GWA.

"Was that the first time I would've met Jewel?" Dion questioned.

"No, that was the day before at the barbecue on the ranch," Kay clarified with a warm smile. "I didn't see the first moment you saw each other, but Hazel and Susan said they saw more sparks flying than horseshoes while ya'll were playing."

"Yeah, I was playing in that game with them and Jen," Liam shook his head, making Rylie inwardly cringe at the mention of one of the times he'd been paired with the other woman. "And I didn't see any sparks, so I think the Matchmaking Mommas were seeing what they wanted to see."

Or maybe you were too busy hitting on Jen to notice, Rylie thought jealously, hating that she reverted to those thoughts when she'd almost talked herself into believing they were only friends.

"Dude, none of us knew she was comin' to visit him on the road either," Crockett pointed out, disagreeing with Liam. "So, obviously, they were good at covering their feelings from day one."

"I don't know," Surfer Josh bobbed his head from side to side like he was trying to decide how to word his thoughts. "I thought he had to be into one of the girls when he followed them over to the horses to go on a trail ride."

And I'm pretty sure it wasn't a horse Liam rode that night, Rylie's inner jealous bitch grumbled.

"No way!" Darius reached over and slapped Dion's shoulder. "My brother rode a horse?"

Several people at the table nodded, as Rylie tried to hide how she was inwardly fuming over what she was picturing happening between Liam and Jen several months before she even met him.

"Please tell me someone got pics," Dare implored.

If so, please don't have them with you now. Hearing about all this is bad enough. I don't need to see photographic evidence of how well Liam and Jen hit it off from the first day they met.

"Ma might have one that Philippe took," Anthony shrugged, turning to look at his wife for confirmation. "But I don't remember anyone taking pics with their phones that day."

"No, I wanted to sneak a few pics of Randi that day, but every time I thought about pulling my phone out, Charles gave me the evil eye and I figured it was best not to get caught pervin' on his daughter within a few hours of meeting him," James chuckled.

"Yeah, while it was clear the moms all wanted to match us up with their daughters, the dads all made it clear that we'd better be on our best behavior," Liam added, smirking. "Jon mentioning the need for a rifle on that trail ride made it clear that I didn't wanna do anything to piss him off, including getting out my phone to take pics. 'Cause if I accidentally took one he thought was inappropriate or could be used to prove his threats in court, he'd just shoot my phone to destroy the evidence. Right after shooting me."

Huh? Maybe I was wrong about what he and Jen did together then. Rylie smiled as her opinion oscillated back over to the possibility that Liam and Jen were only friends.

"Yeah, I'm kinda surprised Uncle Jon hasn't mentioned his gun collection to Dion yet," Anthony chuckled.

"Ya'll are gonna hafta fill me in on whose dad has a gun in this town, so I don't accidentally hit on the wrong woman," Darius joked.

"All of them," Anthony, James, and Dean replied in unison.

"Never mind," Darius sighed, shaking his head. "Let's just go back to talking about the wedding showers D's been to here."

And they did just that, including both the ones Rylie had attended, as well as the one in September for Charlotte and Ian, which apparently Dion and Liam both attended. When Liam removed his arm from around her shoulders as they discussed the wedding festivities over their Labor Day break, just a couple of weeks after they'd gotten married in Vegas, Rylie had to wonder what happened that week that made him act like he felt guilty for something.

Do I even want to know if he slept with her then? It's not like he knew we were married at the time. So, can I really be pissed if he cheated on me?

Yes. Yes, I can. Especially since I haven't been with anyone else since I met him, even though we never claimed to be more than friends until after I found our marriage certificate in my mail.

As they finished eating and started mingling while the tables were rearranged for the Newlywed Game, Rylie thought long and hard about her feelings for Liam and what she wanted for them going forward. *I need to quit with all these schemes to try to get him to see me as his wife and just point blank ask him if the reason he's so adamant about us getting an annulment is because he has feelings for Jen. No matter how much I love him, we'll never work if he's in love with someone else.*

Hell, even if he claims to not be in love with her, we won't work if he's slept with her since we got married. That would kill any trust that

I had in him to the point that we could never get enough of it back for us to even go back to being friends like we were before.

Now I just have to figure out whether I should ask him when we get back to our room tonight, or wait until after this week is over, so I don't fuck up Allissa and Dean's wedding if whatever I find out makes it impossible for me to even walk down the aisle beside him on their big day.

Yeah, I should probably wait 'til at least the second, when we're in San Antonio and back in separate hotel rooms.

~~~

After all the commotion at the wedding shower, with Randi's friend Amy going into labor and all the Burlesons leaving with her to welcome the newest members of their family when Amy and Justin's twins were born, followed shortly by Dion and Darius leaving to deal with another of the passing out spells Dion had started having every time he got overwhelmed since being shot, Brent was relieved to not have anything else planned for the rest of the afternoon and evening. While he knew he and Aiken would still have to figure out what they wanted to do for dinner later, he hoped they'd be able to spend most of the time in their room, finally finishing the conversation they'd started Friday night.

While they'd managed to get changed for bed and laid there cuddling while he told her what he'd learned about his mom, they'd both been too sleepy for him to fully explain how what he'd learned increased his fears for their future as a couple. Then, the next morning, their trip to the mall in San Antonio ended up causing them to run late to their fittings, which in turn delayed the whole wedding party from getting to the barbeque the Hunters threw for lunch. After that, they had the bachelor and bachelorette party, and couldn't really spend any time talking once they got back to their room because Aiken was exceptionally sleepy after drinking.

Maybe we should have just used my grandparents' rings, Brent thought as he spun the silver band on his left hand while following Aiken up to their room. *But I wanted us to finish our talk and be one-hundred percent sure about us before I even let her see them. And*
~~~

besides, all three of our dads would be pissed if I'd cheated them out of seeing me slide those rings on her finger, like I already cheated them out of being at the wedding. So, I guess it's not a big deal for us to wear these for a few weeks. And getting these gives me time to make sure my grandma's rings are Aiken's size in time for if I decide to fly our dads to New York for the **Christmas Chaos** *weekend.*

"Is it bad that I kind of want to change into comfy clothes and veg out in front of the TV until the next time we're scheduled to meet everybody for the group activities the Hunters have planned?" Aiken questioned, as Brent opened the door to their room.

"No," Brent chuckled as he quickly did a walkthrough to make sure nobody had snuck into their room while they were at the church for most of the day. "Other than wanting to turn on the TV, I'm right there with you."

"Oh?" Aiken looked at him quizzically, as he motioned for her to enter the room before he shut the door and flipped the latch that acted as a secondary lock. She walked over to the closet and pulled out a change of clothes as she continued speaking. "Do you want to just go straight to napping? Or do you have something else in mind to occupy us besides mindless television?"

"While a nap does sound tempting, I thought we might use this free time to finish the talk we started Friday night." Brent followed her lead, loosening his tie before completely removing it as he joined her at the closet. He grabbed a pair of sweats and a t-shirt from his bag, preparing to change as she stepped toward the restroom to go first.

"I agree. We definitely need to finish that conversation." Aiken smiled at him before she shut the bathroom door between them.

Fuck! I hope this talk will be enough for us to quit having to go to separate rooms to change clothes, Brent mentally groaned, grabbing a hanger from the closet and carrying everything to the closest side of the bed, so he could quickly change before she returned to the room. Normally, he hung up his suits and anything else that had to be dry cleaned as he took it off. But in his rush, he just tossed everything on the bed, wanting to at least have his sweats on before she came back and got the wrong idea by catching him standing there buck naked. *Even though I'm sure seeing me naked isn't near as arousing for her as it is for me when I see her naked, or even just imagine her naked like she probably is in the bathroom right now, I don't want her to think I'm planning on us doing more than talking this evening.*

Just the thought of her stripping off her dress while only a few feet away in the ensuite bathroom was enough to engorge his cock to the point that he worried he should have grabbed his jockstrap before putting on his sweatpants. *Fuck, maybe I should look into getting some of those compression boxer briefs James and Dean were joking about Liam needing the other day, so I can quit having to wear a cup outside the ring.*

Brent had always preferred going commando, only wearing an athletic supporter as part of his wrestling gear because it was a habit he'd developed in his amateur wrestling days when he was a kid. Thinking back, he realized that he'd only worn underwear as a little kid until about six months after his mom left. Since his dad apparently also preferred going commando, he hadn't thought it necessary to replace Brent's underwear when he outgrew them, instead teaching his son how to move his dick away from his zipper to prevent possible pinching injuries.

Damn, I bet Aiken will make our boys wear underwear, Brent thought, starting to put his dry-clean-only clothing on the hanger, while catching a glimpse of her dark purple panties under her lavender sleep shorts, as she bent over to put her shoes in their protective bag in the bottom of her suitcase. The fact that he'd just imagined having two little boys that were a mix of the two of them didn't faze him one bit. Since he'd finally admitted to himself, and to her, that he wanted a family with her at some point in the future, he'd gotten used to the images that randomly popped in his head of their someday family. And the only time he freaked out was when he envisioned them having little girls, whom he'd need to protect from all the horny boys in the world. *But I guess I can't really complain about that, since I'd want to dress our little girls like nuns.*

"What's that look for?" Aiken's question brought him out of his mental musings, making him realize he was now scowling. "When I first walked in here you were smiling, but in the few seconds it took me to put away my dirty clothes and shoes, you switched to looking pissed off."

"Sorry." Brent consciously forced a smile back on his face.

"Are you upset because you're thinking about us talking now?"

"No, not at all," Brent huffed to stifle a chuckle, shaking his head. "I was actually thinking about you changing in the bathroom and me needing to put on a jockstrap to keep from tenting my sweats, which led to me thinking about how Dad taught me to keep my dick away from my zipper when he first taught me to go commando. And then I thought about how you'd probably make our sons wear underwear, and I can't complain about that 'cause if we have daughters, I'm gonna wanna dress them in full nun's habits."

"Yeah, Papa will never let you get away with that," Aiken giggled, walking around to crawl up on the other side of the bed from where he had his stuff laying. "At least, not unless they land roles in the remake of *Sister Act*."

Brent laughed along with her as he finished putting his stuff away, now that it was prepared to send off to be laundered. "I'm sure it won't matter if we have boys or girls, Shawn will teach them to dress way more fashionably than me."

"You know he'd gladly pick your wardrobe anytime you want, right?" Aiken informed him, as he joined her on the bed, laying on his side and propping his head on his hand so they could talk face to face. "And I don't think he'd grope you as much as Dean's meemaw did when she measured you for your wedding tux. Maybe?"

Her mischievous expression didn't do much to make him feel like she was joking.

"Yeah, I'll be sure to go back and ask Benny for a copy of my measurements while we're here this week, so I'll have them if Shawn ever needs them," Brent chuckled, feeling a little self-conscious at how Aiken's papa had proclaimed his crush a couple weeks earlier.

"So, since you're still thinking about us having kids someday, does that mean you're no longer worried about passing on your mom's mental health issues?"

"Honestly, I hadn't even thought about that possibility," Brent admitted, rolling onto his back to stare up at the ceiling as their conversation turned more serious. "I was too worried about developing the same issues myself and how that could screw things up for you and me to realize they could skip a generation and affect our kids."

"Do you really think her issues are hereditary and not just a product of her upbringing?" Aiken rolled closer to him until she could lay her head on his shoulder.

Brent wrapped his arm around her and held her against his side as he replied. "I don't know. Dad said she grew up in an abusive household, which is what he thinks skewed her view of relationships and messed with her self-esteem, so maybe it's not hereditary. But he also said she had a problem with drugs, so I don't know how much that impacted her other issues. And while I've never had an issue with being addicted to drugs or alcohol, some people would say the way I became obsessed with wrestling as a kid and focused exclusively on training to be a professional wrestler as a teen was a form of addiction. Hell, since my career is still my primary focus in life, I'm sure there are some people who'd say I'm still addicted to wrestling. And if that's the case, then maybe addiction is a hereditary trait that I inherited from my mom, only I'm addicted to something positive and won't realize just how bad I'm hooked until I start going stir crazy when I can't wrestle anymore."

"How long has your dad worked for Oregon Logging?"

Brent had to take a moment to do the math, knowing his dad had started with the company when he was only eighteen, several years before Brent was born. *Shit, he's fifty-six now, so he's only a couple years short of forty years with the same company.* "Thirty-eight years, but he hasn't done the same job all that time."

"No, I know he's worked his way up to management and doesn't actually cut down the trees anymore. But he's not only worked in the same industry for most of his life, he's also worked with the same company all that time. So, if you want to say you're addicted to wrestling because you evolved from amateur wrestling to professional wrestling and worked for a couple of smaller promotions before you joined the GWA, then you have to think he's addicted to the logging industry, too. And since he's never changed companies, then he's even more addicted to the logging industry than you are to wrestling. And if that's the case, then Daddio is addicted to making movies, and Papa is addicted to fashion, and I'm addicted to acting." Aiken pushed up on her elbow to look down into his eyes. "Having a passion for something or feeling a calling toward a specific career isn't an addiction. Honestly, the closest thing I'd say you might have to an addiction is your preference for strawberry protein shakes. But even that's not really an addiction because you'll drink a chocolate, vanilla, or banana shake if there aren't any strawberry right on top in the cooler in catering."

Brent felt a little better after listening to Aiken's perspective on the possibility of him inheriting his mother's negative issues. "I suppose you're right. And maybe her addiction issues were triggered by her trying to self-medicate to deal with her other problems. But if her depression and self-esteem issues were caused by the negative environment she grew up in, do you think I'll always have abandonment issues because of the way she left when I was a kid?"

"No," Aiken disagreed, shaking her head. "'Cause you recognize that you have abandonment issues, which is the first step to getting help for them, so they won't go on forever. Besides, she's the only person who abandoned you. Your dad stuck like glue. And now that I know why you acted like an idiot instead of just falling head over heels for me instantly, I know that eventually you'll realize I'm stuck to you like glue, too. And once you realize that we're not letting you go, you'll be cured of your abandonment issues for good."

Brent couldn't help but smile as Aiken leaned down and brushed her lips over his. He slid his hand up her back until he weaved his fingers through her silky black hair, holding her head in place so he could deepen the kiss. While he knew he needed to break off the kiss to tell her he loved her, Brent couldn't stop plundering her mouth with his tongue as she moved up to straddle him, grinding her pussy on his cock while pressing her perky tits into his chest.

Fuck, if we don't stop this soon, we're going to go way past the limits she set for while I'm trying to prove I want more with her than just sex.

Brent tried to do the right thing and pull away, but as the scent of her wild summer apricot hair products and lotion surrounded him, he lost all his will to resist her, especially with her acting so sexually aggressive at the moment. *I've never eaten a fucking apricot in my life, but if they taste half as good as they smell on her, they may replace strawberries as my favorite fruit*, he thought as their tongues tangled passionately. *And fuck, she's gotta be okay with us blasting through her boundaries, since she's the one who took this from just a simple kiss to dry-humping like teenagers, right?*

He momentarily felt bereft when Aiken broke the kiss to push up into a sitting position, unsure what to say to move them back to talking instead of continuing with the make-out session until they were both naked, sweaty, and satiated. While he'd desperately missed making love to her since they flew out of San Francisco, and currently had so much of his blood flow redirected to his overly engorged cock that he couldn't see straight, Brent knew he had to wait until she specifically said she wanted to make love before they took things any further.

"We have too many clothes in the way," Aiken informed him, grinding on his cock once more as she stripped off her purple tank top to expose her perky tits.

Even though he'd always thought like most typical guys that bigger was better when it came to breasts, Brent had realized since being with Aiken that size didn't matter nearly as much as he'd once thought. He now preferred the responsiveness of Aiken's tawny-pink nipples, which pebbled beautifully in the center of her A-cups.

Brent wanted to join her in tearing off his t-shirt to feel those taut little nubs pressing into his pecs, but he hesitated before doing so, needing to make sure she was really ready for them to add sex back into their relationship before he removed the barrier of his clothing. "Are you sure, Princess? We can still wait to make love…"

"Yes, I'm sure, Brent." Aiken pushed his t-shirt up his torso until he crunched up to help her strip it from his body. When he reached behind his head to pull the shirt off, Aiken hopped off of him and the bed, standing to strip off her shorts and panties. "Now, hurry up and lose the sweats, so I don't have to wait any longer to ride your cock."

Brent didn't have to be told twice. He eagerly bridged up to shove his sweats down his thighs. Before he finished lowering his hips, or even got the chance to sit up and shove his pants the rest of the way off his legs, Aiken rejoined him in the bed, moving to straddle him once more. He quickly kicked the sweatpants the rest of the way off, not caring where they landed, as Aiken gripped his dick and rubbed the head through her dripping wet folds.

"Fuck, Aiken, you need to move up here and sit on my face, so I can eat your pussy first." Brent tried grabbing her hips to keep her from taking him without any foreplay, knowing he needed to open her up enough that his size wouldn't hurt her.

"No, not this time, Brent," Aiken protested, squeezing her knees into the sides of his hips in an effort to prevent him from moving her. "Trust me, I'm warmed up and ready for you already."

Brent moaned in pleasure as her pussy ring rubbed along the side of his cock when she started to take him inside her. *Fuck, she feels even better than I remember.* As he looked down to where their bodies were joining as one, he realized why. "If you're sure," he reluctantly relented, hoping his size wouldn't be too much for her to take without adequate preparation. "But we at least need to get a condom first, Princess."

"No, we don't," Aiken contradicted, shaking her head as she sank lower on his dick. "We're both clean, and I'm still on the pill, so this is the next logical step to show our trust in one another that we'll faithfully honor our wedding vows. Unless you don't trust me yet? Or aren't sure about only being with me…"

"No, I trust you completely," Brent interrupted her, thrusting up into her to prove his words were true, as the velvet feel of her inner walls on his cock made him forget any possible reason why they'd previously needed a barrier between them. "And I don't ever want to be with anyone but you, Aiken, my wife, for the rest of my life."

He bit back his declaration of love, as she sank farther down on his cock, smiling as she leaned forward to press their lips together once more. Reveling in the feel of the hard tips of her tits pressing into his chest, Brent deepened the kiss, wrapping his arms around her to limit her range of motion until he was able to slowly work his dick all the way inside her tight cunt. While he knew in the middle of sex wasn't the right time to tell her he loved her for the first time, he wanted to show her how he felt by gently making love to her.

He tenderly squeezed her ass in one hand, only mostly holding her hips still as he rocked his pelvis up and down, giving her a little more of his dick on each upward stroke until he finally bottomed out inside her. He slid his other hand up her back until he reached her hair, running his fingers through the long, soft tresses in much the same way she was playing with his wild mane.

After realizing how much she liked playing with his hair in bed, Brent had started wearing it down more often, instead of always pulling it back in a queue whenever he dressed up for traveling with the GWA, or as was the case that morning, for going to church. Since the only time he'd ever stepped foot in a church was when he attended with the rest of the GWA crew for wedding stuff, he'd previously followed the Hunters' lead in how to style his long hair, assuming they knew the proper etiquette for such things since they both had long hair and went to church every Sunday when they were in their hometown. But since the only time he'd seen either of them wear their hair down in church was when James wore his down for his wedding, while Dean still pulled his back as a groomsman, Brent felt like he was being a little rebellious as he'd sat through the service that morning before the wedding shower. But when Aiken reached over and ran her fingers through his hair, he quickly decided he didn't care what anyone else thought about his choice of hairstyle.

Feeling her play with his hair now as he made love to her only solidified his desire to wear it down for her as often as possible. *Who fucking knew I'd be just as aroused by her running her hand through my hair as I am when she touches me anywhere else? Well, anywhere but my cock. Fuck, after this, I'm never going to want to wear a condom again.*

Brent released her hips, allowing her to sync up her movements with his thrusts, as he caressed the smooth skin of her side until he could work his thumb and forefinger between them to tweak her diamond hard nipple. Obviously wanting to give him better access, Aiken broke their kiss to sit up, lightly tugging his hair and making his cock twitch inside her.

"Fuck, you feel amazing, Princess." Brent crunched up to lick her other tawny-pink nipple while continuing to softly roll the first one between his thumb and forefinger. He swirled the tip of his tongue around the tight nub before wrapping his lips around her whole tit and sucking the way he longed to have her suck his cock.

Holy Shit! Brent momentarily froze at the realization that his feelings for Aiken were so strong that he wanted to get over his teenage trauma to let her give him a blow job. He hadn't trusted anyone to get their mouth near his cock in the last fifteen years, since his first and only blow job experience, when he was sixteen, and the girl had both puked and bit down on his dick. *She must really be* **The One** *if I'm imagining her doing that and not freaking the fuck out. Guess I'll have all the proof I'll ever need that I'm in love with her, if I* *can ever block out the memories of the puke and pain to actually let Aiken suck my cock.*

"Oh, Brent," Aiken moaned in pleasure, grabbing handfuls of his hair to hold his head to her chest, as he pulled back to flick her nipple with his tongue before drawing her firm flesh back into his mouth. "Feels…so…good. You're gonna…make…me come."

Brent dropped the hand in her hair to rub the pad of his thumb over her clit, knowing the magic button to push to instantly set her off. "Come for me, Princess," he growled against her skin, only releasing her titty from his mouth long enough to give the order before sucking the taut tip once more.

"Oh, Brent, Brent, Brent," Aiken cried out as her pussy squeezed his cock in a vise-like grip that almost forced him to join her in the orgasm.

Oh, fucking hell! We're definitely not going back to condoms after this.

It took every ounce of Brent's concentration to hold off his release as he endured the best erotic torture of his life, feeling her creamy cunt gush on his bare cock as her inner walls gripped and released his dick with each new wave of her climax. As soon as she went limp in his arms, releasing her grip on his hair, Brent flipped them, so she was on her back in the middle of the bed, and he finally had the freedom to move that he needed to really pound into her. He pulled her legs up so the backs of her knees rested on his forearms as he gripped her hips, then pushed up on his knees so he had the leverage to stroke his full length in and out of her pliant pussy.

As she recovered from her first orgasm, she couldn't do anything more than lay there and take it as he plundered her beautiful body. Brent barely leashed his inner beast, needing to animalistically mate with her while also not wanting to hurt her in any way.

"Tell me if it's too much, Aiken," he commanded, his voice sounding more gravelly than normal, even to his own ears. "I need you so bad, but I don't wanna get too rough."

"Not too rough," Aiken panted out as she reached up and ran her hands over his abs and pecs. "Fuck me harder, Brent. Please. I need it too."

"You're the fucking perfect woman, Aiken," Brent growled as he picked up the pace, pounding into her pussy like a man possessed. "Perfect for me. All mine."

"Yes, Brent," Aiken shouted, as her inner walls started fluttering with the beginning waves of her next release. "I'm all yours, Brent, and you're all mine."

"Every fucking inch of me, Princess. Yours, forever," Brent swore, as the contractions of her tight pussy milked his cock. He couldn't hold back any longer, plunging in as deep as he could go to fill her cunt with his cum. "Fuck! Aiken! I love you!"

He would have mentally chastised himself for shouting out his first declaration of love in the throes of their mutual climax, but he was too mentally drained to realize it at the time.

"Yes, Brent, yes. I love you, too."

It wasn't until after the aftershocks all passed and he collapsed beside her on the bed that he realized what they'd each just said to one another for the first time. *Holy fuck! Did that really just happen? Am I really that much of a dumbass that I couldn't tell her at a better time?*

"So, um, since we've finally had make-up sex and shared our feelings for the first time, does that mean we can trade out these rings for the ones in your garment bag?" Aiken held up her left hand and pointed at the silver band on her finger.

"Nope, not yet, Princess." Brent turned his head to peck his lips against her temple. "I've got to figure out when we can get all our dads together first, so I don't cheat them out of seeing me slip the real rings on your finger, like we already cheated them out of being there for the wedding. So, we'll just have to keep wearing these until our Christmas break, and figure out if we want us all to meet in Portland, L.A., or somewhere in between to celebrate the holidays." Brent didn't mention the plans he just decided to put back in place for the **Christmas Chaos** weekend, wanting to surprise Aiken with his "proposal" and their dads' attendance at the event.

"Like maybe booking a ski lodge at Lake Tahoe from the twentieth to the twenty-seventh for our first family Christmas, then sending our dads back home, so we can have a short honeymoon over New Year's?"

Leah Mae Wright

"If that's what you want, I'll make it happen," Brent eagerly agreed, hoping to find a secluded cabin with a hot tub for him and Aiken while their dads all stayed at the lodge, so he could get some alone time with her over the first week of their honeymoon and not just the second after their dads left.

Chapter Fourteen

Aiken was still flying so high on the endorphin rush of the night before with Brent that she wasn't even the slightest bit irritated that Mandi Hunter had come knocking on their door to ask them to help put together the wedding favors she hadn't had time to do before everyone arrived for the festivities. After making love the first time, and finally sharing those three little words she'd been holding back before their misunderstanding in Portland, they laid there and talked some more before starting over with round two. They not only planned their first family Christmas and honeymoon, but they'd also discussed more of what they each wanted for their long-term future together. After discussing how they both wanted to build their family with a combination of biological and adopted children, and agreed to determine their house size based on how many children they eventually ended up with so they could each have their own bedroom, they circled back to what Brent wanted to do about finding out if he had any siblings or half-siblings out in the world. He was still torn between trying to track down his mother to go and point blank ask her if she gave birth to anyone but him, or just doing an online DNA test to see if anyone popped up on his match list. But no matter what he ultimately decided or how his relationship with his mom and potential siblings turned out, Aiken knew she'd be there to support him as he dealt with everything because they were now fully committed to one another.

But I still think it's ridiculous that he won't even show me his grandparents' rings until our dads are all with us for Christmas, so they can be there for the first time I see them. I mean, shouldn't he want to make sure the rings fit now, so we can get them resized this week while we have time off in the same city in case it takes more than a day to adjust them?

Although, I suppose he does know my ring size now after going to buy these bands, she thought as she caught a glimpse of the ring on her finger as she started filling the next gift bag with a bottle of coconut water and a personalized reusable water bottle commemorating Dean and Allissa's wedding before passing it to Brent, who added granola bars, candy, and chips to the wedding favor bags. *So, I suppose he could just take them to the local jewelers and double check that they're already a size six, or have them resized to a six, without me having to actually try them on.*

"I swear, these were all done and ready to pass out when I walked by this room Friday night," Liam grumbled as he stuffed several packets containing ibuprofen and Pepto Chewables in the wedding favor bag in his hand before passing it to Rylie, who added an assortment of coffee pods, tea bags, and packets of energy boosting water additives to the bag. "And since they seem to be things to help with hangovers and spending the week in the B and B, you'd think they'd have given them out as welcome kits when we arrived, instead of as wedding favors. Honestly, it makes me wonder if the Matchmaking Mommas took them all apart, just so they could make us spend the next couple of days putting them all back together."

"Why would they do that?" Josh may have asked Liam the question, but the way he looked at Teagan, as he took the favor bag she passed him before adding hand sanitizer and Emergen-C packets to finish filling the bag, made Aiken wonder if her bestie had been in on the plan without telling her.

Based on the way Mandi had practically assigned them seats where each couple sat beside their spouse on three sides of the rectangular workspace in the middle of the room, Aiken was pretty sure Liam was correct in his assumption that their favor bag stuffing duties were a set up for all three couples, even though only Liam and Rylie really needed to be set up with their Vegas spouses.

"For the same reason they made us sit with certain people every time we've been here in the last year," Liam scoffed, "so we have to spend time with our spouses."

"No, if they were trying to set us up, they'd send each couple off to do a different task, so we'd be alone where we could get naked." Teagan rolled her eyes at Liam's probably pretty accurate assumption. "Besides, with everything we saw Saturday night when we went exploring the area they're preparing to plant the vineyard, I'm sure Mandi just had too much on her plate to realize these would have been better to give out before the bachelorette and bachelor party. And she probably thinks they'll be just as beneficial after the champagne at the wedding."

"Yeah, I can see how some of these things will be useful after the wedding, especially when we change hotels Monday before the show in San Antonio and won't have stocked mini-fridges in our rooms like we do here at the bed and breakfast. But I also could have really used some of these things yesterday morning," Rylie agreed. "And I swear, if I ever go to another bachelorette party here, I'm skipping the rounds of Blow Job shots. I don't know why I'm able to drink the fruity shooters all night long and barely feel a buzz, but I seem to get super drunk from only one Blow Job shot."

"It's because those shooters are mostly juice and hardly have any alcohol in them," Teagan chuckled as she took a favor bag from Rylie and added makeup remover towelettes, breath strips, and lip balm. "But the Blow Job shots are nothing but alcohol and a dollop of whipped cream."

"And you had way more than one of them Saturday night," Aiken added, laughing along with her bestie as she remembered how Rylie started the night off with two Blow Job shots and ended the evening with another half dozen of them.

"Well, lucky for me, the only times I've ever had them were when we were here for bachelorette parties," Rylie wrongly claimed. But Aiken wasn't about to mention that she'd remembered the ladies switching to Blow Job shots in Vegas after choking down the first Irish whiskey shot Windy had ordered a round of at the *Sin City Showdown* after-party. "So unless the Matchmaking Mommas convince Sawyer, Blade, Kade, or one of the Benningtons to marry a local girl, I won't have to worry about resisting them again. And we all know none of them are getting married anytime soon."

"You never know, they might," Aiken chortled, remembering how the ladies in the room had plotted to convince the Matchmaking Mommas to target their single male coworkers this week.

"You do know we've all been invited to Justin and Amy's wedding events over our Christmas break, right?" Liam arched an eyebrow at his wife, making Aiken wonder if he was challenging her to attend with him, instead of going to meet with attorneys in their hometowns to start on their annulment that week, like he'd previously commanded for him and Rylie.

Oh, oh, oh! Is our plan working to show him he wants to stay married to Rylie?

"Yeah, but since we barely know them, Aiken and I are planning our first family Christmas and our honeymoon during our Christmas and New Year's break," Brent interjected before Rylie could reply to Liam's challenge, making Aiken almost want to kick him under the table to get him to stop throwing a monkey wrench in the plans to keep Rylie and Liam together. "So we won't be coming to Heart's Destiny that week. And since only a few of us seem to be more than acquaintances with Justin and Amy, I doubt most of the rest of the GWA roster will be attending their wedding either."

But if we only spend the first part of our holiday break with our dads, I bet Papa will convince Daddio to come here that weekend. If the movies they're working on with the Burlesons aren't enough to convince him, then I bet Papa will insist on representing me and Brent at our friends' wedding while we're off on our honeymoon.

"Yeah, we weren't planning to come here for Christmas," Teagan jumped into the conversation, motioning between herself and Josh. "But if Big D is able to convince Julie to give him another chance, then we'll probably be back for their wedding festivities sometime next year. Plus, I've been thinking that maybe we should schedule a vow renewal here, since we missed all the parties and our families missed our wedding. Maybe over our Independence Day break or maybe the Labor Day break, since those are the closest to our one-year anniversary?"

"That's a great idea, Tea," Josh beamed at his wife. "We know Mandi and the other Matchmaking Mommas can pull it all off in a week, and it'll keep our moms from feeling like we're playing favorites if we pick somewhere other than Baltimore or La Jolla to have it."

"That's why we picked Lake Tahoe for our family Christmas, instead of L.A. or Portland," Aiken pointed out, agreeing with the idea to pick a place in the middle of where each of their families lived, and Texas was about as close to the middle between Massachusetts and California as Teagan and Josh could pick. But she was also a little envious that her friends were planning to do a vow renewal and have all the parties that she and Brent had also missed out on.

But it would be rude to ask if we could join them in doing everything that same week. Especially since it would only really make sense for us to combine our wedding celebrations if it was all of us who got married in Vegas participating. And since we have no idea if Rylie and Liam are any closer to staying together after having to room together this week, now is definitely not the time to broach the subject.

"Since D's probably going to be living here now, planning something here would make sure he can attend, too, even if he doesn't get cleared to fly before you get it planned," Brent added.

"Feck," Liam huffed, roughly shoving his assigned items into the next gift bag before passing it on to Rylie. "Now that he's gonna be a dad, he'll probably stay here instead of taking the booker job Rick offered him, even when he gets cleared to fly again. So, we're gonna hafta rethink all our promo plans we had for him to tape on Monday."

"Do you think Rick will want to change our angle again if D decides not to come back?" Rylie asked Liam.

"Not too much, I don't think." Liam ran a hand through his short brownish-red hair. "It'll probably just end up with me having to hold tryouts for a new partner 'cause D had to retire, instead of D sending in proxies to cover for him while he's continuing to recover. And honestly, that might end up working out even better, so I can claim the trial-partner's losses don't count since I'm the only legitimate tag-team champion, and in order to win the titles, Protection Detail will have to pin me."

"Oh, we should definitely pitch that idea to Rick just as soon as we finish up here," Rylie suggested. "Unless you think we should find Dion first to verify his plans before we present this alternative option to Rick."

"Actually, since I heard Rick say something yesterday about meeting with Dion today," Liam replied, stopping their production line of bag stuffing to stand up, "we should probably go find both of them right now, so Rick has the whole week to decide on what promos we need to shoot to lead into *Christmas Chaos*."

"Okay," Rylie agreed, also standing and walking out of the room with Liam.

"Speaking of things we need to take a break for, we should probably go check with Mandi to see if she has one of our holiday breaks free for us to book our vow renewal next year." Josh stood and extended his hand to Teagan, who eagerly agreed and followed him out of the room.

"Do you think any of them are planning to come back and help us with this?" Aiken watched, as their friends left without mentioning how soon they'd be back, before turning to Brent. "Or do you think we're going to get stuck stuffing all these bags by ourselves?"

"Liam and Rylie might come back when they can't find Rick 'cause he has plans with his in-laws today that made him change his plans with D," Brent shrugged, as his lips turned up in the slightest smile. "But I'm betting Josh and Teagan are sneaking off to find someplace a little risqué to fuck, like they do at almost every arena."

"So, should we finish up our part of these bags and just pile them up on the corner of the tables between you and where Liam is supposed to be? Or do you think we need to do all their jobs too?"

"Well, there's not really much room for them to pile up on the corner of these two tables," Brent smirked as he took the bag Aiken had just finished from her hand and set it down beside the boxes of supplies he'd been pulling from to fill them. "So, maybe we should go with option three."

"I only gave you two options," Aiken pointed out, not bothering to continue working as they talked. "What's option three?"

"Option three is shutting and locking that door, so they can't walk in on us while we're taking advantage of being left alone to take a break, too."

Aiken could tell by the gleam in Brent's forest green eyes that he was planning on some semi-public sexcapades of their own once he locked that door, so he was sure nobody would actually see them in the middle of the act. "Are you thinking about a naked break, Mr. Crockett?"

"I absolutely am, Mrs. Crockett," Brent grinned, wagging his eyebrows suggestively as he stood to go shut and lock the door.

As Brent stalked around the four tables that had been pushed together in the center of the workroom to get to the door, Aiken looked around to figure out where they could get comfortable for their amorous activities. Unlike the parlors that were set up for hotel guests to gather and relax, this room was very utilitarian, without a single sofa or other soft piece of furniture to be seen. This room was obviously normally only used to store extra tables and chairs when they weren't being used in the ballroom or one of the meeting spaces that could be set up for conferences and such. Luckily, it was also big enough to provide table space to put the wedding favor bags together along with plenty of room to store the boxes of items to go in the favor bags.

In addition to the four rectangular tables that had been pushed together in the middle as a workspace with the extra boxes of supplies stowed beneath them, there were four more rectangular tables lining two of the walls, which was where they were instructed to stack the completed favor bags. And the other two walls were lined with tables and chairs stacked on rolling carts, presumably to make them easier to transport to the rooms where they were needed for the various events hosted at the bed and breakfast.

Obviously, we can't do anything near those carts of folded up tables and chairs. At least, not without risking knocking stuff down and possibly ending up with a black eye or two from rogue chair legs.

And with half the supplies and bags scattered on the worktables, we probably shouldn't do anything here either. So we don't end up with crushed bags, or with some of those smaller items stuck in places they shouldn't be.

Not that these chairs are comfortable enough for us to do anything here anyway. I guess that leaves the three tables that are still empty because we haven't finished with very many of these bags yet. Hopefully, they're strong enough to hold both our weight, so we don't have to explain how we broke one.

Aiken cringed as she imagined breaking one of the tables as if it was gimmicked for a wrestling match.

"What's that expression for, Princess?" Brent eyed her dubiously as he walked back toward her after locking the door. "If you're not into this here, where someone could come back to check on us and figure out what we're doing when the door is locked, then we can go up to our room for our break if you'd rather."

"No, the thought of possibly getting caught makes it more exciting." Aiken shook her head as she stood from her seat and met her husband halfway across the room. "Especially since I know Liam and Rylie don't have a key to get in, and they're the only ones likely to come back anytime soon."

"Then why were you making the same face you get whenever someone botches a move and you're worried they might be injured?" Brent reached out and rubbed the worry line between her eyebrows before taking her in his arms.

"I was just trying to figure out where we can get naked in here without risking an injury." She waved a hand toward the two side walls lined with the rolling carts. "Or possibly getting wedding favors stuck in places we don't want them." She waved her other hand toward their worktable. "And decided our only option is one of the empty tables where we're supposed to put the finished bags. But then I wondered if they're strong enough to support both of us, and pictured it collapsing under us like one of the tables you guys use to slam each other through at ringside. So my worried face was probably from thinking I don't really want to take that bump while naked."

"Don't worry, Princess," Brent chuckled as he picked her up and carried her over to one of the tables in question, sitting down on it with Aiken straddling his lap. "Those spots require partially pre-cutting the table first. And even then, it still takes two guys my size or bigger putting all their weight behind the slam to get it to break. So, with just you and me on a table that's not gimmicked, there's not much chance of it breaking. But if it makes you feel better, you can be on top, so I'll take the brunt of the impact if it does break."

As much as Aiken loved riding her lumberjack, she'd rather not take a chance on either of them getting hurt or accidentally damaging one of the Hunters' tables. She decided to tease her husband a bit before making her suggestion, though, kissing him briefly before trailing her lips along the upper edge of his beard until she was close enough to whisper in his ear while he brushed his lips down her neck.

"Or maybe you can just lean against it while I'm on my knees sucking your cock."

"Fuck, Aiken," Brent groaned, rocking his hips to grind his hard dick against her core. "You know you don't have to do that."

While he'd gone down on her practically every time they made love, he hadn't let her give him a blow job yet. At first, he'd claimed he was too impatient to get in her pussy for why he didn't want to take the time to let her reciprocate the foreplay. But when she'd persisted in trying to go down on him, he'd finally explained that he'd had a bad experience with his high school girlfriend getting sick only a couple minutes into his first blow job, which had made him leery of repeating the experience ever since.

"Brent, besides the fact that I'm not an inexperienced teenager with no clue how far I can go before triggering my gag reflex, I've also seen how thoroughly you wash yourself in the shower every morning, so I know there's nothing dirty under your foreskin to make me sick. I want to taste you, and I know I'm going to enjoy sucking your cock as much as you enjoy eating my pussy. So you can trust me to do this without any chance of puking."

"It's not that I don't trust you to do it without throwing up," Brent sighed, lifting her off of him and waiting until her feet were both on the floor before he stood up and paced away from her. "But after spending over an hour worried about what kind of infection I could get because I couldn't clean her vomit off my dick until after I dropped her off and drove home where I could shower, I'd just rather we were actually in the shower when we do this for the first time."

"Really? Then why haven't you let me suck you off one of the times we've showered together?" While Aiken knew a traumatic event as a teen could lead to irrational fears as an adult, Brent's reactions to her suggesting giving him a blow job didn't add up. Yeah, the thought of not being able to do more than wipe off the majority of the vomit for more than an hour was gross, but it wasn't like it was something painful, so she didn't think it was bad enough to cause such a harsh reaction from him.

Unless maybe there were chunks stuck under the foreskin that whole time? But since he'd made it clear when he originally told her the story that he didn't actually get an infection like he'd feared at the time, it didn't seem like it was traumatic enough to cause him to never want to get another blow job for the rest of his life. *And if it was so traumatic, then he would have lost his boner when I brought it up. But did he? No, he humped me like he was excited at the thought. So obviously his dick is on board with the idea of getting blown. Which means there's got to be another reason that his brain shuts me down when his cock is clearly eager for me to shower him with kisses. So, what the hell is he not telling me?*

Aiken stood there patiently watching while Brent paced around the room, mumbling to himself and running his hands through his hair. She felt terrible for ruining the mood, especially since she'd never really enjoyed giving blow jobs all that much in the past. But for some reason, she almost frantically craved sucking Brent's cock. *It's probably only because he won't let me. I bet if he ever does agree, I'll realize it's no different with him than with anyone else and won't want to do it anymore.*

"Let's just forget I brought it up," she finally broke the silence between them, walking back toward her seat to go back to stuffing favor bags, "and finish putting these things together, so we don't have to work on them again tomorrow."

"No," Brent disagreed, stalking over between her and the worktable to prevent her from going back to their previous tasks. "I'm not doing anything more with these bags until the others get back down here to do their share of the work."

"Okay, then what do you want to do while we wait?" Aiken wasn't about to suggest anything sexual again when he was still clearly upset over her last suggestion.

"First, I want to apologize to you for being an ass." Brent reached out and brushed her hair behind her ears before cradling her face in his palms. "I'm so sorry, Princess. I don't mean to take my hang-ups out on you, and I'm really gonna try to stop doing that, especially when I know you just want to show me you love me by doing something most guys would enjoy."

As Brent dipped his head to kiss her, Aiken wrapped her arms around his waist, returning the kiss with equal passion. Pressing her body into his as he trailed his hands down her neck, shoulders and back until she was wrapped in his arms, she could feel that he was still aroused, making her wonder if semi-public sex was still an option for filling their time. *Maybe, but only after I apologize too.*

When they finally broke the kiss to take a breath, she did just that. "I'm sorry too. I know that's something you don't want to do, so I shouldn't have brought it up."

"No need to apologize, Princess."

Unfortunately, Aiken was still too curious to just let the subject drop. "I just can't understand why it's such a big deal for you. I know you said it was traumatic. But honestly, every time I try to picture it in my head, I feel like it's more slapstick comedy than terrible teenage tragedy. And since your cock seems to be on board with the idea, I just can't figure out why you're not willing to try it."

Brent closed his eyes as he sucked in a deep breath and lifted his face toward the ceiling, not releasing her from their embrace, but clearly taking a moment to think before replying. Aiken just squeezed him tighter, turning her head to press her cheek into his firm chest.

She felt his lips brush over the top of her head before he finally spoke. "The puke wasn't really the traumatic part," he admitted. "She bit me and didn't release the bite enough as she pulled her head back, so she left scrape marks from her teeth that were almost two inches long. And I was so freaked out by the puke that I scrubbed a little harder than I probably needed to, which just made the abrasions worse. I don't know if you remember the pain of falling and scraping your knees as a kid, but I always thought scraped knees were the worst kind of pain until that night. Let me tell you, scraped knees are nothing compared to similar abrasions on your dick."

"Ouch," Aiken cringed in sympathy. She couldn't really relate since she didn't have a dick, but she assumed it would be similar to rubbing sandpaper on her clit.

"Yeah, I had to keep pushing the foreskin back to coat my cock in Neosporin several times a day for the next couple of weeks. It was horrible. And I was too embarrassed to tell anyone about it, so I still had to wrestle in the meet with our biggest high school rivals the next day instead of being out on the injured reserve."

"Please don't tell me that was the only time you lost a match," Aiken pleaded, finally understanding why it was so traumatic for him.

"Actually, no," Brent chuckled. "I ended up with the fastest pin in North Portland High School's history 'cause I couldn't stand being in my singlet and cup any longer. Coach was pissed that I went straight to the locker room and changed into loose sweatpants within seconds of being awarded the win, instead of immediately sitting back down with the rest of the team to cheer on the rest of the guys. But I didn't care. I needed to replace my scratchy jock and singlet with the softest material I could find to keep from making the pain worse."

"Yeah, I'm sure," Aiken agreed, thinking about how uncomfortable her panties were for the first couple hours after going for a Brazilian wax, which she did once a month. "But since it's the teeth that are so traumatic for you, what if I do this first?"

Aiken opened her mouth and contorted her lips to cover her teeth, causing Brent to break out laughing. "Yeah, no, don't do that. That's too freaky looking, and kinda reminds me of seeing my granddad without his dentures."

"Are you saying we're going to have to wait until we're old and gray and I can take my dentures out before you'll let me give you a blow job?" Aiken joked, not acknowledging the fact that he'd just compared her to his granddad.

"Yeah, I guess," Brent laughed. "If I can even still get it up when we're that old."

"If not, I'll take you to the doctor for a prescription for Viagra," Aiken bantered back as an idea popped into her head for how she could help him get over his fear of blow jobs. "And in the meantime, maybe we can come up with our own form of exposure therapy, so you won't have a heart attack when I finally lose all my teeth and can take you in my mouth."

"Exposure therapy? Like watching blow job videos online to see that they don't normally end painfully?"

"Yeah, we can do that too," Aiken agreed, nodding her head as she reached out and rubbed her hand over the bulge in Brent's slacks. "But I was thinking I could give you a hand job, while on my knees, as if I was going to suck you. And maybe, since we don't have anything down here to use as lube, I could lick you like a lollypop to use my saliva without actually taking you in my mouth."

"Yeah, that hand sanitizer might be okay down on the shaft, but I bet it'd burn like hell if it got in the tip." Brent cringed, obviously realizing they didn't have any other options for lube without going up to their room.

"Do you think we could try letting me lick you, as long as I promise to only use my tongue?"

"Yeah, I could probably handle you being on your knees to give me a hand job," Brent conceded as he took her hand and led her back over to the empty table along the outside wall of the room. He leaned back against the edge as he negotiated the rest of their plans with her. "And as long as you just use your tongue, I can probably handle letting you lick me. But only if you're naked, so I can look at you if I need a distraction to keep from having an anxiety attack."

"Then we should probably close those curtains, so nobody can see in the window." Aiken lifted her chin toward the window behind the table a few feet down from where they were standing, which looked out over the gardens at the back of the Heritage House, as she released his dick to unbutton her purple blouse.

"Absolutely," Brent agreed, rushing to close the drapes on all the windows along the outside wall, even the ones she didn't think were close enough for anyone to see them in the corner of the room. As he stalked back toward her, he unfastened his dark gray slacks, dropping them to the floor before getting back into position. He then removed his light gray button-down shirt, tossing it on the table beside them in almost exactly the same spot she'd just laid her blouse and bra.

Aiken stepped out of her shoes and shoved off her black yoga pants, which were made to look like dress pants, along with her panties. As soon as they were both naked, she dropped to her knees and reached for Brent's cock with both hands. She was tempted to lean in and press her lips to the tip in a gentle peck of a kiss, but since she'd promised to only use her tongue, she refrained, not wanting to give him any reason to tell her to stop.

She stroked him gently at first, knowing she'd need to lube him up before getting more vigorous, as she examined him closely to see if there were any scars left from his previous bad experience. She didn't see any at first. But then she remembered how he'd said he had to push the foreskin back to put antibiotic cream on the scrapes, and knew she'd have to look closer once he was fully aroused.

"Fuck, that feels good," Brent groaned, gripping the edge of the table as if he needed it to ground him, or keep him from gripping her hair and pulling her head away from his dick. "But you definitely need to lube me up some."

Aiken stuck her tongue out, barely touching him with the tip first to make sure he could handle it before she went any further. When his dick twitched in her hand from the first touch of her tongue, Aiken looked up at Brent's face to make sure her whole man was okay with her doing more, and not just his cock.

She could tell he was still nervous, but she took his smile as encouragement to continue. She swirled just the tip of her tongue down the side of his shaft before flattening out her tongue and licking back up from base to tip.

"Fuck," he groaned, as she used her hands to spread the trail of saliva she left in her wake around his excited member.

Aiken followed that first lick with several more passes of her tongue, coating him completely before stroking him more vigorously with her hand to get him fully aroused. After his cock seemed to grow until the head jutted out a few inches from his foreskin, she went back to swirling the tip of her tongue over his most sensitive areas while stroking the base of his shaft with her hands, noticing only the faintest white lines, which she wouldn't have ever guessed were from an injury if she hadn't known the whole story.

"Stop, Aiken," Brent demanded only a few minutes into the modified blow job, reaching down to grip her under her armpits and lift her off her knees. "I can't take anymore. I need in your pussy now."

Aiken assumed he'd sit on the table and she'd straddle him to make love, but Brent surprised her with another idea.

As soon as he released her, Brent stepped to the side, commanding, "Get up on the table. On your hands and knees, facing the wall, so I can eat your pussy and fuck you from behind."

She was so excited to try this new position that she didn't have the heart to tell him that she was already so turned on from licking his cock that she didn't really need the foreplay before he fucked her. She just quickly clambered up on the table, spreading her legs and arching her back as she got into position, eagerly anticipating his next move. She didn't even think about how her arousal dripped down onto the surface of the table. And if she had, she wouldn't have cared even the slightest right then.

"Damn, Princess, you're soaked already," Brent bluntly stated the obvious as he ran his fingers through the wet folds of her sex. "Did licking my cock turn you on this much? Or are you just getting excited about me licking your pussy now?"

"That's all from licking you," Aiken admitted, rocking her hips as he inserted two fingers inside her. "I don't need you to lick me first. I just need your cock inside me. Now, please, Brent."

"Since you're begging so nicely, I'll skip eating your pussy this time," Brent concurred, pulling his fingers from her body before replacing them with his dick. He took his time working his way inside her, allowing her time to stretch around him before speeding up his strokes. "But once we get upstairs later, I wanna use eating your pussy as my distraction while you lick my dick some more."

"Yes, Brent," Aiken cried out, already feeling like she was about to come after only a few thrusts of his cock inside her. "Oh, fuck, yes, Brent!"

"Already? Damn, Princess," Brent growled, reaching around to flick her pussy ring with his finger while rubbing her clit with his thumb. With his other hand, he teased her nipples, spreading his big hand across her chest so he could rub one with his thumb and the other with his finger. "I'm just getting started. And I think I'm gonna make you hit double digits before I finally fill your pussy with my cum."

With his hands stimulating all of her external erogenous zones and his cock rubbing and tapping her internal love-buttons, Aiken couldn't stop coming, with one orgasm rolling straight into the next. "Oh, Brent, yes!"

Aiken tried to keep count, but it soon became almost impossible to tell when one orgasm ended and the next climax began. She just thought he was getting close to his goal of getting her orgasm count up to double digits. But when he bent over her back and trailed his lips and tongue down her spine from the base of her skull to the middle of her shoulder blades, then worked his way back up with his soft hair almost tickling along her sides, her whole body convulsed in the most explosive orgasm of her life, causing her to completely lose count as she floated on a cloud of ecstasy. She was so lost in the euphoria, she couldn't even whimper his name, barely making unintelligible sounds as she flew over the pinnacle.

"Fuck, yes, Aiken!" Brent shouted, as she felt him plunge deep one last time before he filled her pussy with his seed.

Aiken wasn't sure how long they stayed in that position with her still on her knees, even though she'd bent her arms to rest in a modified version of child's pose from yoga, while he was bent over her back and still buried inside her, but it felt like hours before their bodies stopped twitching with each aftershock. When he finally pulled from her body, Brent rolled to lay on the table perpendicular to her with his head by her shoulder.

"Damn, Princess, with the way you just drained me, I think we're gonna need to take a nap before we can stuff any more of those bags."

"Yeah, I'd come cuddle with you for that nap and just have you wake me up when the others get back, but even that's gonna hafta wait until I can feel my legs again."

~~~

As Liam and Rylie searched for Dion and Rick in all the public spaces of the first floor of the Heritage House, he thought about how Dion not coming back to the GWA was going to impact their angle at **Christmas Chaos**. For the last month, they'd played off Dion's absence as a temporary thing, hinting on all their TV spots about just moving the winner-takes-all match between Red Velvet and Protection Detail to the December pay-per-view. Liam had just been wrestling singles matches while waiting on his partner to return, thinking they'd figure out a temporary partner for him if D wasn't completely ready to return by then. He'd actually been looking forward to taping a few vignettes with Dion on Monday to have his best friend picking his proxies for their matches, since he was taking longer to heal than expected. But after seeing Dion zone out a few times at the wedding shower the day before, Liam wasn't sure his friend would be able to handle the pressure of taping the promos they'd discussed on Friday night. Now that those plans might not be an option, Liam wasn't sure he really wanted to continue with the same angle.

Oh, he knew he at least had to go through **Christmas Chaos** with a temporary partner to drop the belts to Protection Detail. But with his best friend basically being forced into an early retirement from the ring because of his injuries, Liam hated the thought of replacing him to form another long-term tag team. And while they could possibly get by with temporary partners to make the angle work through the **Saint Valentine's Day Massacre** show, he'd need a more permanent partner for the six- to twelve-month angles Rick liked to run for title feuds,
~~~

especially since they'd been planning on swapping Chastity's managerial services every two months or so with the long-term angle they'd previously decided on.

Maybe I can just lose both the titles and my wife at **Christmas Chaos** *and go back to singles competition for the last few years of my career? And let some of the younger guys fill the tag-team spots, so Rick won't have this same problem when I retire, with finding a new partner for whoever he wants to team me up with now.*

Thinking about that option reminded him that the GWA would be in New York City for the whole *Christmas Chaos* weekend. *Feck! There's no way I'll be able to keep my family from figuring out the Vegas marriage angle isn't a work if they come to* **Christmas Chaos**.

But then again, none of them have mentioned the angle since we announced the marriage at **Halloween Horror**. *Granda hasn't even said anything about my Irish terms of endearment since then. Just like everyone else in the family, his only texts have been about how Dion's doing and if I'm coming home for the holidays. Hopefully, their avoidance of asking about the angle is because they all believe we're just faking the marriage for the GWA, and not because any of them know we really got married.*

Since none of them have even asked about **Christmas Chaos** *tickets or backstage passes, maybe I'll get lucky and they won't come that weekend. If they don't come to* **Christmas Chaos**, *they can't talk to anyone in the company who might let it slip that I really got married.*

I'm still going to have to flat out lie to their faces if they ask about the angle while I'm home for Christmas and New Year's, but at least I won't have to ask any of my friends to lie to them. Or explain why I want to get the marriage annulled.

"Are you sure Rick and Dion were supposed to be meeting here today?" Rylie's question brought him back out of his mental musings, as they entered the library after walking through several parlors and the restaurant.

"Yeah, that's what they said right before D left the wedding shower yesterday," Liam replied, scanning the room and being surprised that there wasn't anyone but the two of them in there. "Maybe we should go check D's room? You know, just in case they're meeting there so D doesn't get as overwhelmed as he did yesterday while they're talking about contracts and stuff."

"Yeah, that's probably where they're meeting," Rylie agreed, following along dutifully as they left the library.

Liam couldn't believe how comfortable it felt to have her by his side as they meandered through the halls of the hotel. Somehow, in the last twenty-four hours, they seemed to have settled back into the easy friendship they'd had before finding out they were married.

After the awkwardness of the ride into town and their first night rooming together, Liam hadn't thought it would be possible for them to actually pull off the act of being happily married. Then, when he'd found matching Claddagh wedding bands when he went shopping Saturday morning, he couldn't resist buying both of them, even though he didn't think he'd ever give Rylie hers. Although, after the show she put on in their bed after the party Saturday night, Liam had been very tempted to try talking her into making their marriage real for the rest of their time in Heart's Destiny.

But since he woke up Sunday morning and realized how hard it would be to give her up after having her for a whole week, he knew he couldn't do it. He'd scrapped his plan to wake her up with her vibrator before pushing for more, hiding it in the bottom of his suitcase with the Claddagh wedding band he'd bought her, so she'd never know what he'd witnessed while she was inebriated. He knew she was probably searching for the toy, but he couldn't put it back in her things until it was time for them to check out of the bed and breakfast and go back to staying in separate rooms because he knew he'd never be able to resist joining in if he saw her using it a second time.

Then as he was sitting through Pastor Harrison's sermon about marriage and forgiveness before the wedding shower, the portion of the sermon about being thoughtful and kind when dealing with your spouse's feelings really hit him hard, as did the section about how your spouse should be your best friend. With those words still rattling around in his head, Liam knew he couldn't keep up the asshole act with Rylie, even if it was only in his head to try to keep his mental distance while pretending to be her loving husband in front of the town matchmakers.

The fact that he'd basically slipped back into the friend zone with her so easily wasn't all that much of a surprise to him after all that. But the way he felt so comfortable reaching over to lay his arm across her shoulders while they were sitting together at the wedding shower, or how natural it felt whenever he held her hand or put his hand on the small of her back, like he was now as he guided her through the hotel while they were looking for their boss, however, were quite surprising. Well, with the exception of when he'd had to remove his arm from around her shoulders at the wedding shower while reminding Dion of their time in Heart's Destiny over their Labor Day break because of his guilt over kissing Jen. That was when he'd decided he needed to find a Catholic priest in San Antonio to hear his confession and absolve him of his guilt.

I should have thought to do that Saturday morning when I was there to buy our rings. Now I'm either going to have to find a reason to drive all the way back into the city by myself, or wait until next Monday when we leave here to go to the hotel there before the show. And I'll still have to find some time to sneak away alone, when I know Rick is planning on us spending all our free time setting up promos for whatever we decide to do leading into **Christmas Chaos**. *But then again, it might be better to go to confession after this week, so I can ask for forgiveness for all the times I'm perving on my wife while we're rooming together.*

But is innocently touching her like I am now really perving on her? I know watching her use her vibrator when she didn't know I was watching, and jerking off to fantasies of her every time I shower, are things I should probably confess to a priest. But this is more a case of needing to feel close to her and not in a sexual way, so is it okay?

Before then, he'd thought his desire to touch her all the time stemmed from his sexual attraction to her. But none of the ways he'd touched her in the last twenty-four hours were sexual in any way. Oh, he still had to get up and go jerk off in the shower after she went to sleep because of how bad he wanted to fuck her. But the platonic touching he kept doing felt like it was solely based on his need to feel connected to her.

What the feck is up with this need to touch her that has nothing to do with sex? Is that just because I miss my time as her friend? Or is it because I feel more than just sexual desire for her? Like maybe it's because I'm in love with her? He didn't have time to figure it out right then as they arrived at Dion's room.

After they knocked and got no answer, Rylie suggested, "Maybe we should check the other building? Maybe Mandi or whoever she has working the front desk will have seen them leave?"

"Yeah, maybe," Liam agreed, leading her back down the hallway to the grand staircase in the center of the building.

Just as they got to the bottom of the stairs, they found Mandi Hunter walking into the building on her way toward the restaurant. "Hey, Mrs. Hunter, uh, Mandi," Liam called out, still feeling awkward calling the older woman by her first name, even though she'd been telling him to for the last year. "Have you seen Dion or Rick this morning? I know they were supposed to be meeting today and we need to sit in on part of that meeting to discuss our angles before we go back on tour."

"Yeah, I think they had to put that off, so Rick could go with Fiona to the baby doctor today," Mandi replied with a smile. "At least, that's why Kathy said she'd have Britney with her today. We're all praying for them to get some good news soon."

"That's right," Rylie interjected, her voice sounding hopeful. "Fiona said something about looking into other options if her P.C.O.S. treatment didn't work to clear the path for the old-fashioned way. My mom had the same problem, which is why I'm an only child, 'cause if those options were available back then, they weren't affordable."

Liam was shocked that Rylie knew so much about their boss and his wife's family planning issues. He knew they were trying to conceive, but he hadn't heard anything about a medical issue preventing them from easily getting pregnant. *I guess the ladies share more in the locker room than we do.*

"Oh, I bet your parents consider you their miracle baby," Mandi gushed.

"Yeah, they did," Rylie smiled sadly. "I just wish they'd have gotten a couple more miracles, so they'd still be here with me."

"Oh, I'm so sorry." Mandi pulled Rylie into a motherly hug. "I know nobody will ever be able to take their place, but if you ever need a little mothering, you let me know. Even if I'm busy, I know at least a dozen other women here in town who'll gladly adopt you for as long as you need us."

As Liam watched the exchange, with Rylie returning the embrace while thanking Mandi, he knew his ma and granny would probably offer the same, if he ever quit being a chicken shit and told them about his wife. *Feck! I can't think about that right now. If I do, I might talk myself into thinking giving her a family again will make up for being selfish in wanting to keep her as mine, instead of letting her pursue her career.*

When the ladies released each other and wiped a few tears, Mandi finally turned to him and updated him on Dion's whereabouts. "Dion went with his brother down to Dean's. I think he was going to make sure Allissa approved of his tux before getting a workout in."

"Oh, okay, thanks," Liam sighed, wishing he hadn't gotten up early that morning to go for a run, so he could use the workout as an excuse to catch up with his best friend and talk through their angle options. "I guess we'll go back to stuffing favor bags then, and catch up with them later."

"Thank you so much for doing those," Mandi thanked them again, much the same way she had earlier that morning when she'd shown them to the room and assigned them the task. "I've just got so much going on right now, I can't keep up with it all. But knowing ya'll will do a hundred or so a day between the other activities we have scheduled takes a big load off my mind."

"No problem, we don't mind at all," Rylie lied for them, waving goodbye to Mandi as she took Liam's hand and started walking down the hall toward the workroom they'd left less than a half hour earlier. "But since we only got about fifty of them done so far this morning, we really should get back to it, so we'll be free to meet up with everyone this afternoon."

Liam followed along dutifully, biting his tongue to keep from saying anything about the obvious set up to one of the Matchmaking Mommas. When they got back to the room, they quickly figured out from the closed door that they were probably done stuffing favor bags for the day.

"Did everyone else leave when we did?" Rylie questioned as she tried to open the door, only to find it locked.

"Yeah, I heard Josh and Teagan talking about going to find Mandi as we were leaving," Liam shared. "But when I looked back, they went down the hall between here and the restaurant that leads to the back garden, so I don't know if they found her or not."

Before Rylie could reply to ask about the other couple that had been in the workroom with them that morning, they heard Aiken and Crockett, who were clearly taking advantage of having the room to themselves.

"Yes, Brent! Oh, fuck, yes, Brent!"

"Already? Damn, Princess, I'm just getting started. And I think I'm gonna make you hit double digits before I finally fill your pussy with my cum."

"Oh, God, I did not need to hear that," Rylie chortled, jumping back from the door she'd just been trying to open.

"Yeah, me either," Liam agreed, dragging her by the hand through several parlors to get to an exit from the building where they wouldn't likely run into Mandi again, or find Josh and Teagan in a similar position to what he assumed Crockett and Aiken were doing in the workroom.

"Where are we going?"

"To get lunch," Liam replied without slowing down as she ran along beside him. "And maybe call or text Dion and Rick to schedule a time we can all talk about our angles."

"Shouldn't we just go back to the restaurant for that?"

"Not without having to explain to Mandi why we're back so soon," he elucidated, just as they finally got to the exit at the end of the building. Too bad it was the opposite end of the building from the parking lot. "And before you ask why I didn't hit the nearest exit, it's because I'm pretty sure Josh and Teagan went that way to find a place to fuck in the garden, which I don't want to see. Hearing Crockett and Aiken was bad enough."

"Good point," Rylie giggled. "So, where are we going for lunch?"

"Someplace in San Antonio," Liam decided. *Hopefully, with a Catholic church nearby so I can spend some time in the confessional. Feck! I should probably set a daily appointment with the priest while we're here.*

<div align="center">~~~</div>

"Why are we heading out into the garden? Mandi is probably up at the front desk or in her office, not out here."

Josh just shook his head at his clueless wife while searching for the perfect place to fuck her. His only requirement was that it was secluded. Other than that, any flat surface would do. Horizontal or vertical didn't matter. Even the angled benches in the gym had provided memorable experiences for them. For that matter, a surface didn't have to be flat. They'd had a blast on an exercise ball the last time they were alone for a workout.

"Yeah, and she probably has no idea what her schedule will be like six to eight months from now, so we don't need to rush to book anything. That was just the first excuse I could think of so we could sneak away while all the families with kids are off at Sea World and there shouldn't be anyone in the garden to catch us taking a fuck break."

"Yeah, we should probably wait and see if Big D and Julie need one of those weeks for their wedding before we book it anyway," Teagan grinned, as they made their way through the garden paths, trying to find a private location. "Even if he convinces her to get back together while we're all here this week, I bet she'll want to do like Amy and wait until after their twins are born to have the wedding, so she doesn't have to worry about outgrowing the wedding dress. And since we don't know exactly when she's due, we can't be sure that'll happen in time for them to get married over our Memorial Day break, so they might want to do it one of the same two weeks we're thinking of. And they should have first dibs since Julie's from here and all."

"True," Josh agreed, when he finally saw an opening in the hedgerow at the end of the building, pulling Teagan into an alcove around the southeast corner of the boutique hotel, between the brick wall and a tall shrub row, where they likely wouldn't be seen, even if someone looked out one of the nearby windows. He wrapped her in his arms as he pressed her back against the wall, protecting her from the rough brick with his arms, or rather protecting both of their skin with the long sleeves of his Henley. "But we can think about all that later. Right now, I just wanna fuck my wife."

"Oh, you do?" Teagan wound her arms around his neck as she pushed up on her toes.

"I do," Josh confirmed, dipping his head and meeting her upturned lips with his own.

Josh took his time, savoring the sweet taste of Teagan while listening to make sure they were completely alone. While he loved the idea of semi-public sex, he didn't want to risk anyone else seeing his sexy wife in the throes of passion. It wasn't just that he wanted to avoid any potential public indecency charges and keep anyone else from seeing her naked body. Thanks to her love of wearing dresses even on their days off when they could dress a lot more casually, he knew he could prevent those possibilities by remaining mostly covered. All it took to keep anyone from seeing anything, even if they caught them in the act, was just pushing her dress up in the front, her panties to the side, lowering the front of his jeans and boxer briefs only enough to free his cock, and fucking her while standing. But he still didn't want to risk getting caught because her O-face was meant to be only for him.

"Can't wait any longer, Hubby," Teagan insisted, pushing him slightly as they broke the kiss, so she could move her hands down to unbutton his jeans.

"As you wish, Wifey." Josh could only smile at his take-charge woman, knowing she needed to be in control once in a while, and he was secure enough in his masculinity to let her have that control when she really needed it.

He took a step back to give her easier access to free his cock, not caring when he felt his shirt snag on the shrubs behind him. He pushed all three layers of the front of her green cotton dress up from the mid-calf length until he could see to move her green lace panties to the side. Then he ran his fingers through her dripping wet pussy, making sure she was ready for him, as she finished unfastening his jeans and shoved them and his boxer briefs down just far enough to free his cock.

Keeping his hands under her skirt to hold it up, he slid his hands over her thighs, gripping the backs of them to lift her up. She wrapped her legs around his waist and her arms around his neck, as he slipped his cock into her tight, wet heat. Once she was fully seated on his dick, and he knew she had ahold of him enough that she wouldn't fall, Josh released his grip on her thighs and repositioned his arms around her, so he could push her back against the wall once more.

He didn't really need the assistance to hold her up while he pumped his hips to fuck her. But with the limited space between the bushes and the wall, he wanted to make sure he didn't pull back too far and end up with a branch violating his ass. And the best way to do that was to make sure he kept his arms firmly against the wall, protecting both of them.

"More, Josh," Teagan pleaded, writhing against him as she tried to get him to up the intensity. "Harder, deeper, please, Josh."

Josh tried adjusting his strokes, going faster while staying deeper inside her, only pulling out slightly before shoving his way back in. He dipped his head to suck on her neck, instead of explaining why he couldn't pull out as far as he normally did.

"No, not deeper the whole time," Teagan groaned, clearly getting frustrated with his shorter strokes. "I need you to pull out farther, like you normally do to hit my G-spot before slamming back into my cervix."

"Sorry, Tea," Josh chuckled against her skin, wishing he had room to do exactly what she was asking for. "The only way that's happening this time is if we spin around, 'cause I'm not into being fucked in the ass by this bush. So, take your pick, short but deep strokes, or our normal longer strokes with a boxwood figging?"

"Don't even joke about figging of any kind." Teagan's eyes widened as she tugged on his hair to get him to move his head back enough that their eyes could meet. "I may be cool with you playing back there, but other than you, only properly sanitized toys are going near my back door."

"Exactly, and since my ass is only available for your fingers, I'm not going to risk pulling back too far and figging myself, either."

"What if I move my legs down to protect your ass and we try to find a happy medium?" Teagan adjusted her legs to do just that, hooking her ankles together so her heels rested on the meatiest part of his ass.

Seeing the determination in her eyes, Josh conceded to try pulling out a little farther. "Tell me if any branches touch you," Josh insisted as he slowly pulled out, not wanting to risk scratching up her legs or feet.

"Stop there." Teagan grinned when he was able to pull out about two-thirds as far as he normally did. "It's not quite enough for the tip to rub across my G-spot, but the ridge does, so I'll still get more stimulation than just the shaft. And I don't feel any leaves or branches touching me yet, so I think we're safe."

"Yeah, it's actually the ridge that's rubbing over it when I do this to make you come," Josh informed her as he swiveled his hips to circle her G-spot with his coronal ridge, stimulating every bumpy spot on the front inner wall of her otherwise smooth pussy.

"Oh, yeah, that's what I needed," Teagan practically purred, her head falling back against the wall. Thankfully, she didn't fling it back hard, so he wasn't worried about the possibility that she'd hit her head against the bricks roughly enough to cause a concussion.

"Easy, Wifey, that brick looks like it might be a bit rough on your braids."

Teagan smiled as she leaned her head forward once more, releasing her grip around his neck to reach up and pull her braids forward over one shoulder. She protected her hair by putting the braids between their chests before resting her head on his shoulder, so neither the brick nor the bushes would snag it. "Guess I should carry a scarf to wrap my hair before we try garden sex again."

"I'll try to remember to remind you of that next time," Josh chuckled as he lowered his mouth to her now exposed neck, kissing and suckling her golden brown skin right over her rapidly beating pulse as he sped up his thrusts and hip swivels.

"Fuck, Tea, you feel amazing," he murmured against her skin, loving the feel of her tight, slick pussy. Teagan was the only woman he'd ever trusted enough to go without a condom. And now that he knew how glorious it felt without any barriers between them, he almost dreaded having to put one on again to fuck her ass. *But I will for her. I'll do anything for her.*

As Josh felt the first flutters of her impending orgasm, he thrust back inside her forcefully, grinding his pubic bone against her clit when the end of his dick met her cervix. He knew exactly what she needed from their lovemaking. *And it isn't for us to be quiet like she tried to claim our first time together.*

"Fuck, Teagan, I love the way you squeeze my cock when you come. You're so fucking tight. So fucking wet. You're absolutely perfect, Wifey." Josh kept his voice low, growling the words in her ear, so he wouldn't draw attention to them if anyone happened to be walking around the grounds. "I can't get enough of you. I need you so bad, I don't think one lifetime will be enough. I love you, Teagan, so fucking much."

"Yes, Josh, yes," Teagan whimpered as her whole body convulsed with her powerful release. "I love you, too."

Between her words of love and the feel of her inner walls clamping down on his cock, Josh couldn't hold back his own release. As his balls drew up, he thrust as deep inside her as he could get, filling her up with rope after rope of his cum. "Fuck, yes, Teagan."

They were still clinging to one another as the aftershocks washed over them, when they heard a door open nearby, then the voices of a couple of their friends. Josh lifted his head and turned to the left just in time to see Liam and Rylie walking down the stairs about twenty feet from where Josh and Teagan were still connected.

"And before you ask why I didn't hit the nearest exit, it's because I'm pretty sure Josh and Teagan went that way to find a place to fuck in the garden, which I don't want to see. Hearing Crockett and Aiken was bad enough."

"Good point," Rylie giggled. "So, where are we going for lunch?"

"Someplace in San Antonio," Liam declared.

Thankfully, their voices faded as they walked toward the front of the building instead of back toward the garden, so Josh didn't think their friends had seen them. But he still waited until he could no longer see or hear them before he pulled out of Teagan and lowered her feet to the ground.

"You don't think they saw us, do you?" Teagan reached down and adjusted her panties back in place before smoothing the skirt of her dress down her legs.

"No, they didn't see us," Josh assured his wife as he tucked his dick back in his boxer briefs before pulling them and his jeans back up into place and fastening the jeans. "I looked as soon as I heard them and only saw the backs of their heads. Besides, we kept everything pretty well covered. So even if they had, they might have figured out what we were doing, but they wouldn't have seen more than what looked like us hugging 'cause the hedges are thick enough that they blocked everything but maybe our heads and shoulders, even if they looked down from the top of the landing."

"Good," Teagan sighed, looking toward the stairs one more time before slipping out from behind the hedgerow to walk along the garden paths. "What do you think happened when they went looking for Rick and Dion to make them need to get out of Heart's Destiny for a little while?"

"I'm not sure," Josh shrugged, taking her hand as they strolled back toward the door where they'd exited the building. "Depends on who all they ran into besides Rick and Dion."

"You think they might have run into a bunch of the locals and needed a break from pretending to be happier together than they are?" Teagan's voice sounded worried, almost like she felt a little guilty for being in on the plans to push Liam and Rylie together.

"No, most of the people they'd have to pretend for still had to go to work today, so I doubt they're going to San Antonio for a break," Josh tried to reassure his bride. "Besides, whether it's here or in San Antonio, they're still spending time alone together, so maybe this is a good thing for the two of them in the long run."

Josh wasn't certain that Liam would give up his plans for an annulment after spending time hanging out with Rylie, since he'd never acted on his attraction to her even when they'd hung out as friends before the Vegas weddings. But after finding out that sex hadn't worked to change his mind either, Josh didn't know of anything else that might work to get Liam to quit being a dumbass and stop blocking his own happiness.

"Maybe," Teagan finally agreed, just as they made it back to the door they'd exited less than an hour before. "They have been acting more like they used to the past couple of days, so maybe they just needed to reset their friendship before trying for more. Although, now that I know they're heading out of town instead of just taking a quick break from working on the wedding favors, I kind of feel bad for leaving Aiken and Crockett to handle putting all of them back together."

"I still can't believe you volunteered all of us to put them back together," Josh chuckled as he opened the door for her to reenter the building before him. "Or that you got Rick to help deconstruct them in the first place."

"Well, at the time, I thought it would be a good way to get the six of us in a room, so we could help talk them all through the issues in their marriages," Teagan defended her actions as they walked back to the workspace Mandi had set up for them to put the five-hundred gift bags back together.

Before they reached the door, they heard the distinct sound of skin slapping against skin, along with a few grunts and whimpers that quickly clued them in on what Liam had referred to hearing as he and Rylie left. But it was Brent's shouted, "Fuck, yes, Aiken!" that made Josh decide it wasn't quite time to go back to see if their friends needed any help finishing the favors.

"Yeah, I don't think they need us to help them talk through their issues," Josh chuckled, tugging on Teagan's hand to redirect her toward the restaurant. "So, maybe we should go get lunch before we try again to come back and finish the work you signed us up for, Mrs. Parker."

"Yes, lunch sounds like a great idea," Teagan agreed with a little giggle. "Especially since we've all worked up an appetite, so they'll probably come to the restaurant to refuel and let us know that it's safe to come back here to finish up."

Chapter Fifteen

Brent wasn't sure what his friends were thinking when they suggested a bowling night when there weren't enough lanes for even half the GWA crew to participate, much less all the wrestlers, their families, and a fairly large group of local residents. But since he and Aiken had bailed on the horseback riding that morning to spend some private "riding" time in their room, they felt like they had to make an appearance at Lover's Lanes. Thankfully, the bowling alley also had a bunch of tables set up between the snack bar and lanes, so they were able to sit and have a bite to eat while observing their overly competitive coworkers and friends being shown up by several of the kids.

As he sat at one of the tables, munching on nachos, Brent had to lean over to the next table to ask Rick about the game that included the boss's daughter, her best friend Tia, the two Canadian members of Protection Detail, and the Bennington brothers. "Are Protection Detail and the Benningtons just really bad bowlers? Or has Tia taught Britney how to do her crazy physics calculations, so they're basically undefeatable?"

"Maybe a little of the latter," Rick chuckled as he watched his daughter throw a strike. "But I think the guys are intentionally throwing the game to earn the sympathy of the single ladies in the next lane."

"And you and Anthony are both okay with your daughters being the wing-women to the biggest players on the roster?" After hearing more than a few lectures about behaving appropriately around all the GWA kids over the years, and especially seeing how overprotective both

Rick and Anthony were as their daughters became teenagers in the last year, Brent was surprised to see the thirteen-year-olds being left mostly unsupervised with their parents either at one of the tables or bowling on another lane with some of the other kids.

"Only because I know everyone on the roster knows better than to do or say anything inappropriate," Rick replied with a smirk. "And Anthony is in between them and Cooper's boys."

"Don't believe his overprotective papa talk," Fiona giggled, leaning into Rick so she could talk around him. "Since he knows seeing him with Britney was part of what attracted me to him, he's now hoping some of the single guys will settle down when my friends see them interacting with the kids, like they might be good fathers one day."

"Seriously? Losing to a couple of teenage girls is supposed to make them look good as potential fathers to their kids?" Brent thought it made them look more like potential pedophiles, which was why he was always polite to the kids but not overly attentive, so none of his friends would get the wrong idea about him. Obviously, he spoke to the kids whenever they spoke to him first, which was how he knew about Tia's use of physics to analyze any physical activities because she'd specifically asked for his stats to do the math while watching his wrestling matches. But he never initiated those conversations, and they were all usually when the kid's parents were nearby, either backstage or at events like this.

"Oh, yeah," Aiken, Teagan, Rylie, and Fiona all replied in unison.

Brent looked at his wife, surprised she'd joined in with the other ladies in stating that opinion.

"What?" Aiken arched an eyebrow at him, obviously seeing the questions in his expression. "Seeing a man build up a kid's confidence is hot. In fact, I think I started falling for you on our first date when you let Connor and Cody teach you what they knew about Edgar Allan Poe."

Brent didn't bother mentioning that he still didn't understand half of what the boys had said that day. All he really remembered was that Poe had a thing for birds and most of his work was rather morbid. *And how Connor pointed out that if I'm trying to scare her into my arms, I'd be better off taking her to a horror movie 'cause poems aren't scary enough to make her jump and want to hide her eyes in my chest while I protect her.*

Leah Mae Wright

Damn, now I understand why Anthony is bowling in the lane between his and Rick's daughters and Cooper's sons.

"We need new opponents," Britney complained as she plopped down in the empty chair at Rick's table and took a drink of what Brent assumed was her pop, since food and drinks weren't allowed on the lanes. "Those guys are too busy flirting with the women in the next lane to give us any competition."

"Maybe you should recruit couples then," Rick suggested, pointing with his thumb at the table where Brent was sitting with Aiken, Josh, Teagan, Liam, and Rylie. "None of these guys have bowled yet, so I think it's probably their turn."

"You guys wanna come play with me and Tia?" Britney popped out of her chair and over to their table. "There's only six spots for names, but we can do teams of two, so all eight of us can play if you want. But only if you promise not to be all kissy like Tia's aunts and uncles were earlier."

"We just need one more couple," Tia called out from the lane. "Uncle James and Aunt Randi agreed to play with us, but only if I bowl left handed to make it fair."

Brent wasn't close enough to see Tia roll her eyes, but her expression as she shook her head made it clear, even to him, that she was pulling the typical teenager move.

"So, yeah, I guess we'll just need two of you now, and then the other four can come down for the next game," Britney pointed out. "So, who's gonna be first? Lilie, Teash, or Crocken?"

"I guess we're all official now, since we've been shipped," Aiken giggled. "Release the Crocken!"

Brent couldn't help but laugh along with his wife, as several people in the bowling alley apparently understood her classic movie reference and shouted it back at her.

"Wait, how come they get a cool name like Crocken and we're Lilie?" Liam protested. "Shouldn't you use both their first names or both their gimmick names instead of his gimmick name and her first name?"

"We don't know Crockett's first name, so we had to go with Crockett, and we didn't like Crockethyst or Amett." Britney replied with a shrug.

"It's Brent, so you could have gone with Bren or Aint," Liam suggested. "And you know both our first names and our gimmick names, so you could have come up with something better than Lilie. That sounds like we're a flower and not a couple of cool people."

"Would you have preferred Ryam? Or Redity? Or Chased?" Britney questioned Liam. "'Cause we can still change it, but only if you guys beat us in this next game."

"Lilies are my favorite flowers," Rylie chimed in with a smile at the teenager. "So, I don't mind Lilie."

"Oh, yeah, we're definitely going to beat you at bowling," Liam declared, ignoring Rylie's comment as he took her hand and pulled her up as he stood to follow Britney down to the lane where Tia, Randi, and James were already waiting.

"If you do get reshipped, I vote for Chased," Brent joked.

"I second that vote," Josh agreed. "Though now that I think about it, I think we should be reshipped as Jogan 'cause it sounds more badass than Teash."

"If you do that, then I'm gonna pitch a movie to Daddio titled *The Jogan Chased by the Crocken*," Aiken chortled.

"Are you thinking this'll be a monster movie, like all the *Godzilla* movies?" Brent questioned, chuckling. "Or is that the name you're suggesting for the book Kay will probably write about the six of us? 'Cause to be honest, if a main character is gonna be based on me, I'd kinda prefer it to be in the monster movie."

"Ooh! Kay!" Aiken waved over the writer, who was walking back from the snack bar, carrying a tray of drinks and snacks. She dropped off the refreshments at the table closest to where her husband and children were bowling before coming over to see what Aiken needed. "We have a book idea for you. How do you feel about writing fantasy romance with mythical monsters as your main characters?"

"It's not a genre I've thought about writing before," Kay shrugged as she took a seat in one of the empty chairs at their table. "But I bet Becky knows some authors who might be interested, since she's been curating a list of different genres to make their books into movies." Kay looked up past the rest of the occupants at the table, smiled, and waved at someone Brent presumed had just arrived since she was looking toward the door. "In fact, she's here now, so why don't you tell her your idea, too."

Soon, they were joined by Becky and Jen Burleson, and all of the ladies at their table and Rick's table beside them started talking about the possibilities for a monster romance they could make into both a book and a movie. Since Brent wasn't really interested, he tuned them out, instead listening to the conversation going on at the next table, where Dion had joined Rick.

Damn, when did D get here? Brent wondered, suddenly wishing he wasn't sitting with his back to the main entrance of the bowling alley.

"Sorry, Boss, I don't think I'll be able to, um, do those promos on Monday," Dion apologized to Rick.

"If it's a problem with being back in the arena, we could maybe shoot them at the B and B this week," Rick suggested. "And obviously we'll get whatever counseling you need to be able to get over the PTSD and handle being in an arena again without having flashbacks to the shooting before we expect you to travel with us for the booker position."

"No, it's not that," Dion sighed. "Since I don't remember anything about that day, the only thing that will bother me about being at the arena will be that I can't get in the ring."

"Are you thinking those blackout spells you mentioned are going to be a problem?"

"That's part of it," Dion agreed, but Brent could clearly see him shaking his head in the negative. "But not the biggest problem."

"Okay." Rick didn't say anything more, obviously waiting for Dion to explain his situation instead of speculating further.

"I can't think as fast as I used to," Dion finally admitted, after a really long pause in the conversation. "I'm losing words. And when I can't find them, I feel overwhelmed, and that triggers a blackout. Hell, it's happening now. I know there's a word for what the camera does while we're…*doing* promos. And a better word for *doing* that I can't find right now, but they're both lost to me. And with as slow as my brain is working right now, I don't think I can get into my Dark Chocolate character to even read a prepared statement without looking like an idiot."

Fuck! D shouldn't be dealing with this shit! He's too good a guy to have to suffer like this.

"Okay, I think I understand now. Do you think it would help if I told you the words I think you're missing right now? Or would that just make you lose more words?"

"Hell if I know," Dion chuckled. "But it can't be worse than playing charades with Dare to try to tell him what I wanted for dinner that first week. So please tell me what you think I'm missing now, and maybe I'll be able to quit stressing about these words before I lose any more."

"Yeah, I imagine you had a pretty hard time trying to act out shrimp gumbo," Rick joked, causing even Brent to chuckle at the mental picture.

"Thankfully, gumbo is one word I haven't lost," Dion laughed.

"Well, I think the words you're looking for now are cutting and recording," Rick replied. "As a performer, you're cutting a promo and the camera is recording it. But doing made enough sense I knew what you were talking about. Does the doctor have any idea how long it'll be before you quit losing words like that?"

"No," Dion sighed once more. "He said the aphasia can completely go away once my brain heals some more, or it can be a problem for the rest of my life. Same with the blackouts and zone-out spells, which he thinks are some type of seizure, even though none of the seizure meds stopped them. Which is why I know I'll never be able to wrestle again."

"But you are still interested in the booker job once these things clear up enough that you get cleared to fly?"

"I was…" Dion drew out the second word, obviously having a "but" that he hadn't vocalized.

Damn, if he's not even coming back as a booker, the GWA really won't be the same. And since he's not even doing the promos they talked about last Friday, Rick is going to have to come up with another tag team sooner than I thought. I wonder if it would help him to scrap mine and Josh's feud to team us up now? Or would he rather drag out the proxies for Dion long enough for us to get in a couple of big matches to sell how we've earned each other's respect enough for our tag team angle to make sense?

"But until I talk to Jewel, I don't know what I might end up doing in the future."

Leah Mae Wright

Yeah, I think Liam was right yesterday when he said Dion will probably want to stay here in Heart's Destiny now that he's going to be a dad. And even though it'll suck for the rest of us in the GWA to miss working with him, I completely understand and agree that staying here and being a dad is his best option.

"Speaking of Jewel," Dion stood from his seat and blocked the path of Jen, Becky, and Kay, who'd apparently finished their conversation with Aiken and Teagan and got up to walk across the room. "Where's Jewel, urh, Julia?"

"She's not coming tonight," Becky replied, looking extremely uncomfortable talking to Dion.

"She already had other plans for tonight before we found out about this." Jen waved her hand around to encompass the bowling alley.

"Can you at least give me her phone number, so I can call and schedule a time to talk to her while I'm in town?" Dion pleaded, looking so dejected that Brent wished he had Julie's number so he could give it to the man.

"Nope." Jen pushed her way past Dion, followed closely by Becky.

Kay paused and put her hand on Dion's forearm, smiling up at him sympathetically. "When she's ready to talk, she'll reach out to you. Just give her a little time."

"Thanks." Dion obviously tried to turn his lips up in a smile at Kay, but it was clearly a sad smile.

Brent felt terrible for his friend and former mentor, wishing there was something he could do to help fix Dion's current situation. At the same time he felt sorry for Dion, he was grateful that he and Aiken had worked out their issues, which didn't seem nearly as complicated as what Dion was going through with Julie.

"Hopefully, Kay will talk some sense into Julie and the rest of the Burlesons, so they won't keep treating Big D like shit for something he didn't do," Teagan scoffed.

"I just wish there was something we could do to help him," Aiken agreed.

Before any of them could come up with the right words to show their support for their friend, Dion flagged down his brother and left.

Fuck! I bet not being able to get any information about Julie, on top of the stuff he just told Rick he's dealing with, was too much for him, so he's leaving to avoid having one of those spells in front of everyone.

Knowing he wouldn't want to pass out in front of most of the people in attendance that night either, Brent completely understood why Dion left. But understanding didn't change how much he hated seeing Dion suffer with all he was going through.

I might not be able to do anything to help D, but I can offer at least one idea to Rick to help the GWA deal with the fallout.

"Hey, Rick, I have an idea I wanna run by you," Brent called out, inviting the boss to move over to their table, so Aiken, Josh, and Teagan could all hear his idea at the same time.

Rick turned his chair, not exactly moving toward their table, but at least redirecting his focus there. "Yeah, what's that?"

"I know we just started our feud," Brent motioned between himself and Josh, "but I was thinking maybe we could cut it short to tag team instead. Ideally, we'd get in matches at **Christmas Chaos** and **Saint Valentine's Day Massacre**, at the very least, to sell earning each other's respect before deciding to team up to reunite our wives. But if you end up scrapping the angle to have proxies fill in for D in the Red Velvet and Protection Detail feud, and need a new tag team immediately, we could swerve the fans by teaming up now and claiming we talked things out off camera."

"Talking things out off camera won't work," Rick disagreed, shaking his head. "But even without Dion making an appearance, we can probably drag out the proxy angle with Liam long enough for you guys to end your rubber match at **No Remorse** in a double count out after your ladies convince you to quit fighting each other and team up."

"Oh, I like that idea," Aiken gushed beside Brent.

"Me too," Teagan agreed. "Especially if I get to talk my man into joining us on the dark side."

"Well, you will be replacing a heel tag team," Rick pointed out with a grin.

"And I look forward to the challenge of working heel for the first time in my career," Josh grinned back.

"Damn, Josh, how'd you manage not to turn before now?" Brent thought back to all his time in the GWA and realized he'd turned at least three times in the same amount of time Josh had worked solely as a babyface.

"What can I say? I'm just that well loved by the fans," Josh bragged, smirking.

"Whatever," Brent scoffed, turning back to Rick. "I thought it might help you keep your numbers even by pulling both a heel and a face from the singles ranks too, but I forgot to account for me and Liam basically swapping positions on the singles and tag-team divisions."

"Yeah, but with Cooper talking about retiring from the ring to help me out with some of my responsibilities so I can be off for paternity leave next year, this will still keep my numbers even. Well, for the men's divisions anyway. Even with the two new women starting in January, we still need at least one more woman to be able to even out the women's division between heels and faces."

Before they could discuss anything more about possible future additions to the roster, Liam and Rylie returned to their table.

"Alright, Teash, it's your turn to try getting reshipped," Rylie pointed over her shoulder with her thumb in the direction of the bowling lanes. "Hopefully, you'll have better luck than we did."

"Don't worry, Lilie," Brent teased Liam as he stood and took Aiken's hand to pull her along with him. "Since we don't want to be reshipped, we'll use our victory to reship you as Chased."

"Yeah, good luck with that," Liam laughed. "I think the only way anyone will be able to beat Tia is if she has to bowl blindfolded."

"Seriously, I used to feel like I was a decently intelligent person," Rylie chuckled, shaking her head. "Maybe not smart enough to think to use physics to plan how to throw the ball, but at least smart enough to understand it if Tia explained her formula. But after trying to follow along as she recalculated to account for throwing the ball with her weaker arm, I now remember why I barely squeaked by with a C in all my high school math classes."

Yeah, I'm not going to be the one to suggest blindfolding Anthony and Kay's teenage daughter. So I guess I'll just hope I don't get beat too bad.

~~~
~~~

Rylie tossed and turned for the fifth night in a row, suffering from sexual frustration while listening to Liam jerking off in the shower. Well, she assumed it was the fifth night in a row, not really remembering Saturday night after too many shots at the bachelor and bachelorette party. *It's at least the fourth night since we've been here, even if I passed out cold and slept like a log in my drunken stupor Saturday. And after what Randi and Allissa told me I said about blow jobs as we were leaving the party, I'm sure I was sexually frustrated that night too, even though I can't be certain Liam jerked off in the shower then. But since he has every other night we've been here, I'm pretty sure he did. If only I could find my vibrator, so I could get a little relief while he's jerking off in the shower now.*

She desperately wanted to search through all her bags to see if she'd just put her vibrator in a different spot in her rush to leave Lubbock on Friday, but the only time she had alone in the room for the last few days, Liam was either in the shower or had just run downstairs for food, so she didn't have time to do a thorough search and put everything away before he caught her in the act. And she really didn't want to have to explain to him why she'd gone crazy and pulled absolutely everything out of every bag she owned in her frantic search.

She'd also thought about ordering a new vibrator after seeing Ashlyn at the bowling alley and knowing the It's My Pleasure consultant probably had one in stock she could pick up while she was in town. But since she and Liam were supposed to be playing the roles of newlyweds in love while they were in Heart's Destiny, she was afraid placing that order would send up too many red flags. Yeah, she knew her friends had supposedly recruited the local matchmakers to help her win Liam over, so the older generation of ladies in town probably knew her marriage was only a legal technicality. But she had to keep selling it as real to the younger women, who might be rooting for her and Liam to implode because they were friends with Jen.

Nope, I don't even want to think about how Jen might be recruiting her friends to try to come between me and Liam so she can have him back. I'd rather plan for how I'm going to get a new vibrator before our Christmas break, 'cause I can't go another month without an orgasm, so I can't wait to replace it until I can actually have time alone to go to the adult store in Atlantic City where I got my first one.

Leah Mae Wright

Since I'll still be riding with Liam to our show in San Antonio on Monday, finding a store there is out. But maybe I can get some alone time on Tuesday in Austin to go shopping. Now I've just got to figure out how to get through the next week of sexual frustration.

I suppose I could just use my fingers now to get a little relief. If I stay under the covers, then I'll be able to stop as soon as I hear the shower turn off and Liam won't know what I'm doing. But there's no way I'll be able to relax enough to actually get off when I'm listening for every little sound he makes to keep from being caught.

Then again, if he does catch me, maybe he might be tempted to replace my fingers with his cock. Yeah, there's no way that'll happen. No matter how much I dream about him wanting me as much as I want him, his desire for an annulment makes it obvious that he's not interested in me. At least, not that way. And since, for the last couple of days, he's been back to acting like the friend he was before we got married, I don't want to do anything to rock the boat and send him back into asshole mode.

The day before, when they'd gone to San Antonio for lunch, they spent a couple hours walking around and taking a boat tour of the River Walk. They'd had a pleasant but somewhat superficial conversation, making her feel like the old Liam was back. Unfortunately, that version of Liam kept them firmly in the friend zone, not even holding her hand as they strolled along with the rest of the tourists.

Too bad there wasn't an adult toy store in the mall where he dropped me off while he went to confession at one of the local Catholic churches.

When they got back to the B and B and rejoined their friends in putting together the wedding favors, he maintained that friendly distance between them. The only time he touched her at all was when they were in the hotel restaurant for dinner that night, where several members of the older generation of locals stopped by their table to congratulate them on their nuptials. And even then, it was only to reach over and hold her hand briefly or put his arm around her shoulders. None of those affectionate gestures could be construed as anything sexual between them, no matter how her traitorous body responded at the time.

The same could be said for earlier that day. While they were in the stables for the staff to help them get comfortable with the horses for the trail ride Dean and Allissa arranged, he was still only affectionately friendly, but not overly demonstrative of their supposed love, while there were strangers among them. Once it was just the GWA crew on the trail as they rode the horses, he included her in the conversation, but didn't do any of the things the other couples did, like pulling his horse up alongside hers to steal a kiss.

Not that he'd stolen a kiss at any other point in their time in Heart's Destiny. Even when they were bowling earlier that night and the other couples around them were giving kisses for good luck between frames, Liam had stuck to verbal good luck wishes and hand holding while waiting for their turns actually bowling. He spoke more as if they were a real couple, but his actions were clearly much more friendly than romantic. Of course, he also didn't repeat the asshole action of speaking to Jen without Rylie being close enough to hear the conversation, like he had at the beginning of the bachelor and bachelorette party, apparently finally understanding how that might appear to the rest of the people they were trying to fool into thinking their marriage was strong and happy.

Rylie still wasn't sure how to read Liam's relationship with Jen. They weren't acting nearly as close as they had at all the summer wedding events she'd witnessed them attending together. But she had to wonder if the distance they kept between them was all an act because he was trying to keep her family from figuring out Jen was the real reason Liam wanted to annul his marriage to Rylie.

Not that acting like he's happily married to me now will help him win them over so they can get together again after we dissolve our marriage. If he wants to be with her, then shouldn't he be playing up how we didn't know we got married and that we're ending it, so her family will be sympathetic to his drunken mistake and accept him into the fold later? And honestly, if he wants to be with Jen, then when she got there tonight was when he should have reverted to his asshole behavior with me.

But then again, he probably wouldn't want to do that publicly either, not if he wants to stay in the Burlesons' good graces. So, if he was going to revert to asshole mode, I guess the only time it would make sense is when we're alone here in the room. Like maybe this morning, when we woke up wrapped in each other's arms with our extra pillows shoved to the floor?

Thinking about that morning, she almost wished he'd have acted like an asshole instead of apologizing if he made her uncomfortable while acting totally indifferent about the intimate position they were in when they awoke. *Or was his indifferent act kind of a mild version of his asshole mode? I mean, true asshole mode would have been shoving me off of him and jumping out of bed while acting disgusted to have touched me. And while that would have hurt, it would have helped me strengthen my resolve to not throw myself at him this week. But him not seeming to care one way or the other about how we woke up hurt me just as much, only it still left that little sliver of doubt about his sincerity, so I'm still feeling hopeful that he might one day love me.*

Of course, ideally, I'd have rather he'd showed some cracks in the walls he's putting up between us, so I'd know to keep trying with him. Especially since we both know my nipples were hard and my pussy was wet because of the way we were practically dry-humping in our sleep. So it woulda been nice if he'd have at least pretended his morning wood was because of me and not just a normal biological occurrence that happened daily, regardless of whether he shared a bed with someone or slept alone. At least, if he'd acted like he was attracted to me, I wouldn't feel too nervous about him catching me in the act to play with myself now.

Then again, if he'd lied about being hard for me only to make me feel better this morning, then the rejection now would hurt even worse, if he caught me in the act and didn't want to do anything to satisfy both of us. UGH!

As if she wasn't already frustrated enough, she heard Liam grunting in Irish again, making it clear he was reaching his peak right then, even though he was clearly trying to keep his voice down because she couldn't clearly understand anything he said. Irritated by him obviously getting off while she was suffering with sexual frustration, on top of being confused by what was really going on between him and Jen, and why he was possibly calling out Kara's name as he came, Rylie sat up in bed and flipped on her bedside lamp.

I can't wait until after Allissa and Dean's wedding to clear all this up, or I'll definitely ruin all the festivities by going crazy wondering and flipping out in public to find out! But maybe if he clears up my

460

confusion now, I'll be over my anger and frustration in time to keep from making a scene the next time we all have to be in the same room.

She sat there fuming as she heard him continue showering for almost ten minutes before finally turning the water off. It took him another five minutes to dry off, urinate, wash his hands, and put on his boxer briefs before he finally walked out of the bathroom.

Damn! Does he have to look so freaking hot in nothing but boxer briefs?

"Rylie!" Liam gasped in shock at seeing her sitting up in the bed, stopping in his tracks about halfway across the room. "What are you doing up? Did I wake you when I went to the bathroom?"

"No, Liam, you didn't wake me," Rylie bit out venomously, unable to stop herself from letting her jealousy show, even as she couldn't take her eyes off his chiseled abs and pecs over his eggplant colored boxer briefs, which left little to the imagination. *No! Do not get distracted by how hot he is! Stay on topic!* "I haven't gone to sleep for even a second tonight, so I heard absolutely everything you did in the hour you've been in the bathroom. Just like I heard you last night, and Sunday night, and Friday night. And I'm pretty sure the only reason I didn't hear you Saturday night was because I was drunk enough to actually sleep through all your Irish endearments and calling out Kara's name when you came. Though I have to say that surprised me. I really expected you to call out for Jen then."

Liam at least looked apologetic and maybe a little embarrassed when she first started her tirade, but his smirk at the end ruined her enjoyment of his initial reaction. "I wasn't calling out for a woman named Kara," he chuckled as he closed the distance between them and sat down on his side of the bed. "I said moh an-um cair-ah, which is Irish for 'my soulmate,' not a specific person's name."

While Rylie was relieved to know he wasn't holding a torch for the local baker, it still hurt to hear he was calling out for some nameless, faceless woman, instead of grunting "Rylie" because he'd been fantasizing about her while pleasuring himself. *Obviously his soulmate still isn't me, or else he'd have made a move for the real thing, instead of jerking off in the shower alone.*

"What do the other things you say in Irish mean?" Rylie couldn't believe she'd just blurted out that question, instead of asking the harder ones about him and Jen. *Yeah, right. I'm just too afraid of*

461

what his answers will be when I finally woman up and ask about what's happened between him and her. So, I'd rather find out what he said the one night we made love, in the insane hope that I can construe it to mean that night meant something to him, too.

When he arched a curious eyebrow at her instead of answering her, she tried to repeat the words she remembered hearing the last few nights. "Moh store? Is too moh graw?"

"Wow, your pronunciation is excellent," Liam smiled. "You almost sounded Irish just now."

Rylie fought not to roll her eyes at him as he stalled before answering her.

"Moh store means 'my treasure' and is too moh graw means 'you are my love.' My granda calls my granny, moh graw, my love, as his pet name for her."

That's what he called me the night we made love in New Orleans. Can I really believe that's because he cares about me and was using it as a pet name? Or is it just a generic term of endearment that he uses no matter who he's fucking, so he doesn't have to worry about forgetting a random ring rat's name? Or worse, is it the term of endearment he's been using for Jen, and he just used it with me because in the dark he was able to pretend he was with her that night when he was hurting so much?

While they hadn't actually discussed what happened in the middle of the night in New Orleans, Rylie assumed the sex hadn't meant as much to him as it had to her. He was so devastated that day when Dion was injured that she was certain he just needed the physical outlet to release some of his mental pain. She tried desperately to be understanding and not read anything into the encounter, knowing she'd done something similar by sleeping with her ex-boyfriend while dealing with the grief of losing her parents. But now that they had a little distance from the traumatic events of that day in October, she wondered if maybe they might both benefit from discussing what it meant for them.

"You called me moh graw in New Orleans."

"I did," Liam agreed, disarming her as he smiled once more.

"Is that because it's your go-to term, so you don't have to remember the name of whatever woman you're fucking?"

"Nope." Liam shook his head, leaning in slightly closer to her. "That night in New Orleans is the first time I've ever said those words when I wasn't mimicking Granda to practice my Irish accent."

"Oh." *Geez, Rylie! Oh? Really? That's all I can think of to say right now? What a totally fucking lame response.*

While his words weren't confirmation that he only thought of her when he said the same things while jerking off in the shower, Rylie couldn't stop herself from hoping that's what he meant.

"Yeah, oh," Liam chuckled. "That's almost the same thing I thought when I first realized what I said that night, except I added a feck after the oh."

"Because you regretted it?" *Please say no. Please say no,* Rylie mentally chanted after accidentally blurting her first thought.

"No, I don't regret that night. At least, not the physical act or what I said in the heat of the moment." Liam sighed and ran a hand through his hair nervously. "The only thing I regret about that night is that we were both in a state of shock and not capable of seeing how sleeping together would complicate things for us going forward before we made that decision."

"You mean because we consummated the marriage while sober, so now we can't use being drunk when we got married as grounds for the annulment?" Rylie wimped out before asking if he was referring to more than just their legal complications, not wanting to be the only one to admit to feeling like their lovemaking was a physical manifestation of their feelings in a moment when they were both vulnerable.

"Feck! I didn't even think of that possibility," Liam groaned, dramatically flopping forward to land face first on the bed, burying his face in a pillow.

Liam's histrionics distracted Rylie from her thoughts of love. Knowing he was faking his hysterical response to lighten the mood, she turned in the bed to pick up one of the other pillows between them, hitting him in the back with it. "Quit being a drama queen."

"Sorry," Liam smirked up at her as he rolled to his side, the pillow on his back falling to the floor. "I just needed a moment to freak out over not only being disowned by my family for getting married in Vegas instead of the church, but now also probably being excommunicated by the church if we have to get a divorce instead of an annulment. But since only the two of us know what happened in that hotel room in New Orleans, I doubt it'll be an issue, so I think I'm okay now."

Or we could prevent both by staying married and renewing our vows in the church. As much as that was what she longed to have happen between them, Rylie wasn't about to voice that suggestion out loud, not wanting to admit to being in love with him until he told her he loved her first. And since she didn't believe that would ever happen, she knew she had to tell him what she'd learned in her research while searching for an attorney.

"Not according to the New Jersey attorney I had a phone consult with a couple of weeks ago," Rylie admitted, hating that she'd even gone through the appointment without being brave enough to even mention it to Liam beforehand, so he could have been on the video call with her. "She said we'll have to prove that we've been living separately and haven't appeared to have accepted the marriage even once after we sobered up. When she found out we've worked it into an angle and broadcast it around the world that we're married, she made it clear that in New Jersey, we'd have to get a divorce, not an annulment. Apparently, it doesn't matter that we used our ring names when making the announcement, since the judge could obviously tell it's us if they see the tapes of our shows. She couldn't say for sure if that's the case in other states, but she made it clear that as far as she knew most states have strict requirements like that."

"So, it doesn't matter if we've consummated the marriage or not? If the judge, or a court reporter, or bailiff, or whoever else might be in the courtroom is a GWA fan and saw our last month's worth of TV, they'll refute our grounds for an annulment?"

"Yep, pretty much," Rylie confirmed as she laid down on her side, so they were now face to face as they talked with only the pillow down by their legs between them.

"Why the hell didn't Boyle tell me this when he scheduled my appointment to meet with someone in his family law department?" Liam huffed, rolling onto his back to look up at the ceiling. "Unless maybe it's different in New York, and he thinks we can show the court the difference between the scripted world of pro wrestling and the real world?"

Since she didn't know who Boyle was, Rylie couldn't answer him, assuming his questions were rhetorical. So, instead of trying to reply in a placating manner, she opted to point out the upside to not being able to get an annulment, hoping to get them both a little sexual relief for the rest of their time in Heart's Destiny. *Even if it's not enough to convince him that we can really fall in love and make our marriage work, I'll regret it if I never make love with Liam again.*

"So, since the annulment ship has already sailed away without us, what do you think about us easing both of our sexual frustrations by adding some benefits to our renewed friendship while we're stuck sharing a bed this week?"

~~~

Feck! Liam mentally shouted, feeling torn over how to respond, all thoughts about how impossible it would be to keep his family in the dark if they had to get a divorce flittering out of his head the instant she mentioned adding "benefits" to their friendship. While in his head he knew the honorable thing would be to keep his hands and his dick to himself, his hard-as-a-rock cock was clearly voting for rolling over and ravishing Rylie right then and there. And his heart wasn't capable of casting the tie-breaker vote.

On the one hand, he knew making love with her again would feel amazing and make this week so much more bearable. But on the other hand, he also knew it would only amplify his feelings for her and absolutely shatter his heart when their time together was over.

"Feck, Rylie, I wanna say yes to all the benefits," Liam groaned, wishing he'd gotten under the blankets to hide how his dick eagerly responded to her. He rolled to his side to face her, hoping to conceal his cock by over rotating his hips to press it into the mattress instead of leaving his dick aimed at the ceiling. "But there are other complications we need to consider first. Sex with friends and coworkers isn't like one-night stands with ring rats or a no-strings week-long fling with some random person you won't have to see again after it's over. Feelings get involved and things get messy. When it inevitably ends, those messy feelings can lead to tension among the group and a hostile workplace. Not to mention the possibility of a

465
~~~

broken heart. As much as I want you, I don't want to risk the negative outcomes any more than we already have."

"Have I done or said anything in the last month that made you feel like what happened in my hotel room in New Orleans led to any of these *negative outcomes*?"

"No," Liam reluctantly admitted as their eyes locked on one another, her intoxicating floral scent enveloping him and muddying his thoughts. "But with everything else that happened that day, our one time together was more like a moment out of time. And even that one time required us to take a step back from our friendship for a few weeks to reset everything back to normal. Repeating it now without the crazy adrenaline roller coaster we were on then would make it real, and make it more likely for those issues to crop up."

"No, Liam," Rylie huffed, disagreeing with him as she reached over and poked his shoulder with her French-manicured long fingernail. "It wasn't the adrenaline or even the trauma that day that kept me from turning into a stage-five clinger and causing all this tension and drama you're afraid of. It's the fact that I was raised better than that. Do you know that I'm still friends with every guy I've ever dated? From the first boy who kissed me in kindergarten to the man I broke up with in February when I found out I had a shot at a spot on the GWA roster, and everyone in between, whether I had sex with them or not. We may only check in on social media now, but I still consider every one of them friends, whom I'd gladly meet up with for lunch or invite backstage at a GWA show to catch up. I've never had a bad breakup, and I'm not about to let my only bad breakup be with you. But since I lost my vibrator, there's no way I can get through the rest of this week, listening to you jerk off in the shower without joining you. So, you either need to help a girl out, or take me shopping in San Antonio for a new rabbit."

Liam felt an irrational surge of anger at the thought of Rylie meeting up with any of her ex-boyfriends, even if she met them backstage at a GWA show, where he could easily intimidate them into staying away from her. Luckily, the feel of her nail scoring his skin redirected his thoughts to all the places he wanted her to scratch him with her talons, just as her final few sentences clicked in his brain.

Shit! I've got to tell her about her vibrator and give her that option as an out before I take advantage of what she's offering.

"Yeah, um, speaking of your vibrator," he muttered sheepishly as he looked at her with his best imitation of puppy-dog eyes. "I kinda hid it in my suitcase after you used it Saturday night."

"You what?!" Rylie screeched, her eyes widening and her jaw dropping in shock, as she pulled her hand back as if she was creeped out by touching him after his revelation.

"You were using it when I came to bed," he admitted, half-shrugging with the shoulder not pressed into the mattress. "At first, I thought the buzzing sound I heard was the heater. But then, when you kicked the covers off, I was mesmerized by the show you put on for me, even though I felt like a jackass for watching you when you were drunk and had your eyes closed, so you didn't know I was watching."

"Oh my God, did you do more than just watch? Is that how you ended up with it?" Rylie appeared to be torn between being mortified at the thought and hopeful that they'd made love again.

No, I've got to be imagining that. Even though she just suggested adding benefits to our friendship, she'd never want to be with someone who'd take advantage of her while she was too drunk to consent.

"I just watched until you were done and slapped me in the chest with the still vibrating toy," Liam confessed, rolling more onto his side so he could hold up both hands in surrender. "Then I got out of bed, covered you up, and used the flashlight on my phone to find the box and charging cord in your suitcase so I could clean it up and charge it for you." He paused to take a deep breath before continuing. "But then when I got in the bathroom where I could read the instructions to figure out how to turn it off and if it was waterproof so I could clean it with soap and water, I decided it was probably best to completely kill the battery before recharging it."

"Are you saying *you used my vibrator*?!" Rylie's eyes widened as her voice rose. "Like, did you seriously stick my rabbit in your ass?"

"No, there were no insertions!" Liam shook his head vehemently, making sure she knew his back door was a no-go zone. "I just rubbed the little rabbit ears over my balls while jerking off and imagining what it would feel like if you were taking both me and the toy at the same time. And when I was done, I thoroughly cleaned it before charging it overnight."

Damn, I hope she doesn't point out my double standard for anal right now.

"But instead of giving it back the next morning, you hid it in your suitcase?" Rylie eyed him curiously, obviously confused by his behavior. "Why?"

"So I could avoid the embarrassment of admitting to all that," Liam chuckled before turning serious. "And because I knew I wouldn't be able to resist doing more than watching if you pulled it out again this week."

"Was New Orleans so bad that you don't want a repeat?" The vulnerable look in Rylie's topaz eyes was heartbreaking.

"New Orleans was amazing. Well, our part of New Orleans was amazing." Liam pushed up on his elbow as he ran a hand through the longer hair on the top of his head, trying to figure out how to explain his thoughts to her before finally resting his head on his hand. "Feck, Rylie, after New Orleans, I think our attraction to one another is pretty damn obvious to both of us. But attraction and desire aren't enough when we're in such different places in our lives."

"You don't think we could build up to more if we tried?" The hope he saw in Rylie's eyes was almost enough to make Liam cave. "And how are we in different places in our lives? We both wrestle for the GWA and are literally in the same place twenty-four-seven, even if we're in separate hotel rooms everywhere but here this week."

No, I can't be selfish and ask her to walk away from the career she loves to raise a family with me.

"We could probably convince ourselves that we feel more than we really do for a little while," Liam lied, knowing he was madly in love with her. "But as soon as I retire and stay in New York while you keep traveling for your career, we'll realize we were wrong. If you were ten years older, or I was ten years younger, I'd love for us to give this a shot. But I'm already starting to feel my ring skills declining, so there's no way I can keep wrestling 'til I'm fifty to travel with you. And I also can't ask you to quit wrestling in a couple of years to stay home with me, when your career is just getting started. We'd just end up resenting one another if we tried either of those options. So, I'd rather enjoy being friends with you than risk ruining our friendship by thinking with my dick and acting on the attraction again, only to have you hate me in the long run."

"And you don't think we can do friends with benefits while also getting divorced? Did you not hear me earlier when I said I don't do bad breakups?"

"Yeah, I heard you, but I just don't know how that would work. Are we talking just for this week while we're rooming together? Or randomly hooking up whenever we get the urge until I retire? What about whenever you're in New York with the GWA after I retire? Are we really going to try a long-distance friends-with-benefits relationship for the next fifteen years, or however long it is before you're ready to quit wrestling? There's just too many variables for it to make sense to me."

"We could limit it to just this week if you want," Rylie offered with a sigh. "So it's not too confusing when we do the divorce over our Christmas break. But if it was up to me, I'd rather we just play it by ear and stop hooking up whenever it no longer works for one of us."

If it was up to me, we wouldn't do the divorce, or annulment, and instead we'd figure out a way to never be apart, so I could fuck you at least twice a day for the rest of our lives. But I can't ask you to sacrifice your career to be with me.

"Is that how you managed to have no bad breakups in your past?"

Rylie seemed to contemplate his question for a moment before finally replying. "Yeah, maybe. It might also be that I'm counting everyone I ever kissed or went on one date with, even if it was obvious there was no chemistry and we were better off as friends from the get go, as well as one-offs, when we both knew there were no strings and it may or may not happen again. There've only actually been three guys, where we got serious enough to be exclusive for it to count as a real breakup. And all three of those relationships started out with the caveat that we were honest with each other and ended things before moving on, so we could maintain the friendships. And that's all I'd ask from you if we decide to hook up again. That we'd be exclusive from now until one of us is ready to move on and we'd be honest and end things first before hooking up with someone else."

"I hope you know seeing our marriage certificate made us exclusive from that moment on, even though I was a total asshole that day." Liam knew he should confess to his failed make-out session with Jen right then, but he couldn't bring himself to ruin the moment with Rylie. Not when they were so close to possibly making love again.

"Yes, you were," Rylie laughed, making him smile. "But I was in so much shock that I don't even remember my cab ride to the arena after seeing that certificate in my mail, so I can understand why you freaked out, too."

"I'm still sorry for the way I reacted," Liam apologized. "But it was hard to come to terms with having the woman I've been lusting over for months dangled in front of me, when I knew it wouldn't work because of our age difference."

"Geez, Li, don't say it that way," Rylie whined, rolling her eyes at him. "That makes it sound like you're old enough to be my dad or pervy uncle. Ten years isn't that big a deal, especially since you don't act like you're even a day older than me. It's simply a career timeline difference. And honestly, I'm not planning on wrestling 'til I'm forty, like everyone seems to think is the cut-off age for delivering a quality match. So, you may retire in a couple of years, only to have me come knocking on your door a couple years later to let you know I've retired too."

Feck! If she's seriously not planning a long career, maybe we could give this marriage a go?

"Really? Do you have an age you're thinking you'll be ready to stop touring and settle down?"

"Not a specific age, exactly. But with the risk of injuries cutting our careers short, it could be anywhere from next year to five or six years from now. But hopefully, it'll be long enough that I can save up enough of a nest egg to not have to worry about trying to start over in a new career." Rylie shook her head. "But I don't see myself wrestling much past thirty, so I might have a shot at having a family. And with my increased risk of P.C.O.S. because of my mom, even that might be pushing it. I mean, just look at Fiona. She's only twenty-eight, and she's already having problems conceiving. And from the things I've overheard when she was talking to Kay about ideas for book scenes, I'm pretty sure she and Rick fuck like bunnies, so it's not from lack of trying."

Like they dress up as furries? Or they just fuck often enough that they should reproduce like rabbits? Feck, now she's got me picturing Rick dressed as the Easter bunny and hopping around chasing Fiona.

"Yeah, I don't want to know anything about what goes on between our boss and his wife," Liam grimaced, holding up a hand to stop her from putting any more of those images in his head.

"Is that face because you're picturing them with my rabbit vibrator now?" Rylie giggled.

"No, but that's not much better than the Easter bunny costume I was picturing," Liam laughed along with her. "But now I have to reset my brain, so the only rabbit image in it is of you and your rabbit vibrator, like I saw Saturday night."

"Or you could get it out of your suitcase and take a new mental picture," Rylie suggested. "Up to you if it's only from listening while I'm using it in the shower, or if you want to join me and give adding benefits to our friendship a shot."

Feck. I really should give her vibrator back and wait until we've talked some more to make sure our future plans really line up before I make love to her again. But do I really want to take a chance on not getting to be inside her again, if that talk ends up with her thinking I'm trying to talk her into retiring and having my babies before she's ready? And what if she doesn't want to stay married and have her family with me? Hell, even if she's open to that possibility, will meeting my crazy, overbearing family scare her off?

And how will we deal with it if she has fertility issues like her mom? Will she be okay with adopting, so I don't have to watch her suffer through painful treatments that might not work?

Feck, if I don't agree to this friends-with-benefits arrangement now, will I even get the chance to talk to her about all those issues? Or will she write me off as a bad bet and move on? I definitely can't take that chance, 'cause there's no way I'll survive seeing her date someone else between us ending our marriage and my retirement.

Feck, it's gonna hurt like hell when she decides I can't have her anymore, Liam thought, still not sure he could believe they might want to retire around the same time to have more than just a short-term fling. *But I'm damn sure gonna enjoy every second I can spend naked with her until then.*

"You promise we won't have a bad breakup?"

Rylie nodded once. "Absolutely."

"I'm gonna hold you to that, Mo Ghrá." Liam reached over to cup his hand around the back of her neck, being careful not to disturb the scarf around her hair. Then he leaned across the center of the bed, and pressed his lips to hers, no longer able to resist the pure pleasure she was offering him.

Rylie returned his kiss with equal passion, running her hands over his chest and shoulders before winding her arms around his neck. When she pulled him even closer, Liam relished the feel of her soft breasts pressed into his pecs. The soft cotton of her red tank top did absolutely nothing to disguise the way her nipples hardened almost instantly.

As he savored her sweet taste, Liam decided to skip the toy and just take her to the shower for their first round. Wrapping her in his arms, he rolled them to the edge of the bed before pulling her legs up on either side of his hips and standing.

"What are you doing?!" Rylie squealed, her lips only lifting a hair's width from his, so their breath mingled as they talked.

"Carrying you to the shower, so the water running will muffle your screams to keep from waking our neighbors." Liam adjusted his hold with one hand cradling her ass and the other supporting her back as he walked from the bed to the bathroom.

Rylie wrapped her arms and legs around him, grinding her pussy over his cock as she clung to him. She offered no protest as he claimed her with another scorching kiss. Unfortunately, once he turned on the light in the bathroom, he realized they'd have to break apart long enough to remove their clothes before they could actually get in the shower.

"As sexy as these little shorts and tank tops are on you, we really need to start sleeping naked to make this easier," he grumbled as he released her, lowering her bare feet to the floor. Liam made quick work of removing her red tank top, enjoying the view of her voluptuous tawny brown tits and her diamond hard terra-cotta nipples, which he ached to get his mouth on once more.

"Yeah, I'm not the only one who's overdressed for the shower," Rylie chuckled as she reached for his boxer briefs, lifting the waistband up and over his erection before starting to push them down.

"I said *we* need to sleep naked, not just you," Liam pointed out as he grabbed the waistband of her red and black plaid shorts, bending at his hips and fighting to push her shorts and red thong down at the same time she was squatting to remove his underwear. He only got her shorts down to her knees, before she sank down on them, effectively taking her clothing out of his reach until she returned to standing.

He wanted to remove the scarf around her head, so he could enjoy the view of her braids cascading down her back as he fucked her from behind. But he knew that with as adamant as she was about protecting her hair while she slept, she'd probably object to getting her hair wet, too.

But feck, I'd love to grab a handful of her braids to guide her head up and down as she sucked my cock.

As if she'd just read his mind, Rylie didn't wait for him to step out of his undershorts before releasing them and reaching for his dick. She gripped his shaft with both hands, unable to completely encircle his girth with only one, as she lapped up a drip of precum from his tip before wrapping her full lips around the head of his cock.

"Feck, Rylie," Liam moaned at the exquisite feel of her sucking him to the back of her throat, running his hands over her scarf-covered head and resisting the urge to thrust into her mouth. "Your mouth feels amazing, but this isn't what I planned."

After bobbing up and down on less than half of his nine-inch length, Rylie pulled back to spread her saliva down the rest of his shaft. "You got to taste me last time, so it's my turn to taste you this time."

Liam wasn't about to argue as she closed her warm, wet mouth over his cock once more, eagerly sucking as much of him as she could handle while stroking the rest with her hands. Her total lack of finesse made it obvious that she didn't have much, if any, experience sucking dick. But her enthusiasm more than made up for the occasional scrape of her teeth over his tender flesh.

Within minutes he was fighting to hold back his orgasm, which was surprising considering how hard he'd just come while jerking off and imagining he was fucking her less than an hour earlier. Not wanting to come without her, Liam reached down and grasped her under her armpits, lifting her to her feet.

"Sorry, if that wasn't any good, it was my first time," Rylie rambled, looking slightly embarrassed by her admission.

Holy feck! I'm the only man she's ever had in her mouth? Liam felt a sense of male pride he'd never known before, praying things would work out for them, so he'd be the only man to ever have that experience with her for the rest of their lives.

"That was perfect, Mo Ghrá." Liam smiled reassuringly at her as he brushed his lips over hers. "So good I was about to come, and I don't want to come until you do."

"Oh," she smiled back, as Liam pointed her toward the shower while he stepped out of his boxers and over to his Dopp kit to get out a condom. She grabbed a plastic shower cap from her toiletry bag, putting it on over the silk scarf she already had protecting her hair before stepping over to the shower enclosure.

Once he had a condom in hand, he followed her as they stepped into the enclosure, closing the door behind them. She turned on the water and adjusted the temperature, leaning to the side to keep her head out from under the spray, even though her hair was doubly covered. *I guess getting her braids wet is a bigger deal than I thought.*

"Do we need to move this back to the bed, so we don't mess up your hair?" Liam placed the condom on the shelf in the shower, wanting to spend some time worshiping her beautiful body before using it.

"No, we're good as long as it's covered," Rylie grinned, stepping away from the spray and closer to him, teasingly running the tips of her fingernails over his abs. "But if my shower cap is a turnoff, I suppose I could take it off and wash my hair this morning. But if I do that, then you'll have to cover my part of the favor prep, so I can go to the salon in town to sit under the hair dryer for a couple hours to get my braids dry."

"Yeah, I have a feeling that if you take that shower cap and wrap off now, you'll spend a lot more than a couple hours at the salon to fix how bad I'd wreck your hair. So it's probably a good thing that I think your shower cap is sexy as feck."

Rylie giggled at his cheesy line, making him smile even more. Liam gripped her hips and pulled her body into his, lifting her so he could kiss her without having to bend down to account for the eleven inch difference in their heights. Rylie wrapped her arms and legs around him, rubbing her smooth pussy along the underside of his cock and coating him in her cream, as they passionately kissed once more.

Feck, I'm never gonna be able to give this up. I'm just going to have to train harder, so I can keep wrestling for five more years, so we can retire at the same time to start our family. Rylie is mine. I've just been an idiot for fighting fate the last few weeks.

Liam shoved all thoughts of the future out of his mind, focusing exclusively on worshiping his woman, in the hopes of giving her so much pleasure she'd never leave him. He broke the kiss and trailed his mouth down her neck as he lifted her higher, needing to memorize every inch of her tawny beige flesh. When he reached her buxom bosom, he flicked his tongue across her nipples before sucking one into his mouth, eager to turn her terra-cotta tips a deeper shade of rosy russet. The desire to mark her with his mouth was something else he'd never experienced with anyone but her. But he knew he'd have to keep the hickeys limited to areas she could cover with her clothing to maintain kayfabe for her Chastity gimmick.

"Please, Liam, don't tease me too long," Rylie begged, trying to wiggle her way back down to his cock, as he savored her other nipple. "I need you inside me now."

"Yes, Mistress Rylie," Liam taunted, lightly nipping her with his teeth as he turned to press her back against the wall of the shower while reaching for the condom he'd left on the ledge in the corner by her bodywash. "Oh, wait, that's not right. I'm not a sub and you're not a Domme, so you're gonna hafta wait for me to decide when you're ready for my cock."

Considering they both knew the wetness she was rubbing on his upper abs had nothing to do with the water flowing from the shower head, it was pretty obvious that he wouldn't be making her wait much longer. But he did take a little more time than truly necessary to keep worshiping her tits while blindly donning the condom.

As much as he wanted to talk to her about the possibility of one day having no barriers between them, after being exposed to Allissa's stalker's blood only a month earlier, he wanted more than just the one negative test he'd taken since being exposed before he took the chance with her health for his first experience with condomless sex. While technically he and everyone else exposed that day had been informed that the tests of Marcus Gardner's corpse had also come back negative, Liam knew it was possible for someone to contract a disease and be contagious while still testing negative because they were in the initial incubation period. So, just to be on the safe side, he was waiting out the three-month incubation period before considering himself safe.

Not that he was going to mention that to Rylie right then. He'd just keep protecting her while hoping their sexual relationship would continue long enough for that discussion to become necessary.

Once he'd sheathed himself in the latex, Liam popped his mouth off her reddened flesh. He then reached around her leg to use his fingers to make sure she was opened up enough to take him before lowering her down on his throbbing erection. Ideally, he'd have preferred to give her at least one orgasm first, but when he was easily able to slip three fingers inside her, he realized the initial orgasm before sex wasn't necessary. *Which means I get to be inside her for every one this time.* "Hmmm, I guess you are ready for me, Mo Ghrá."

"So ready," she practically purred as the head of his cock breached her lower lips. He relished the feel of his first stroke inside her, looking into her sultry topaz eyes as he connected them as one.

"Fuck me, Liam. I need your big dick, hard, fast, and deep. Now."

While Liam normally preferred to be in charge during sex, he had no qualms with obeying her orders right then. But only because he'd already bottomed out inside her, so he knew she could take all of him without any discomfort. Unlike their first time together, when he'd had to keep his strokes shallow and only give her half his dick until her orgasms relaxed her enough to take all of him. He gripped her hips once more to lift her up and almost completely off his cock before slamming her back down and impaling her to the hilt.

It only took a few strokes like that before her whole body convulsed with her first orgasm of the night. "Oh, yes, Liam," Rylie cried out, digging her nails into his shoulders as the already tight walls of her pussy clamped down on his cock.

Liam pressed her back into the wall once more, holding her in place as he thrust his hips like a jackhammer, fucking her through it until her first climax rolled into the next. Being inside Rylie again was pure heaven, feeling even better than he remembered. She writhed and rocked her hips in perfect time with his rhythm, instinctually syncing their movements.

The pleasure was so intense that Liam felt almost mindless as he peppered her shoulders and neck with kisses while praising everything about her. He was so lost in his own world with Rylie that he didn't even realize they were still in the shower until the water hitting his side turned cold. Even then, he just reached over and turned it off, continuing to fuck her through orgasm after orgasm as he babbled in a mix of Irish and English that he wasn't sure made a lick of sense.

Rylie's whimpers and moans weren't any more coherent than his ramblings, with the exception of a loud shout of his name every once in a while. Neither one of them had a second thought about how loud they were being in the middle of the night, not even considering they might wake their friends in the neighboring rooms.

Liam wasn't sure how he held off his release for so long during the best sexual experience of his life, but he somehow held it back until Rylie went limp in his arms, unable to move from being so satiated. Knowing she would be unconscious any moment, if she wasn't already, Liam thrust in as deep as he could one last time, basking in the euphoria of filling the condom with more cum than it could hold.

"Mo Stór, is tú Mo Ghrá, Mo Anam Cara. Mine. My Rylie." *My Wife*.

Chapter Sixteen

Teagan felt like a glutton after eating way too much of the delicious Thanksgiving dinner put on by the bed and breakfast and the town's most prominent families. She normally tried to avoid overeating like that, needing to maintain her figure for wrestling. But since Thanksgiving only happened once a year, she couldn't resist splurging, especially when the town of Heart's Destiny brought out some southern foods she'd never tried before.

I just hope this meal didn't add an extra ten pounds to the ten pounds the camera is going to add on Tuesday.

"Do we really have to get up and go be social right now?" Rylie questioned as half the people at their table got up to go mingle, leaving only the three Vegas couples still sitting there. She rubbed a hand over her belly as she leaned into Liam's side. He wrapped his arm around her and pulled her closer before brushing his lips over her temple. "Shouldn't we listen to the advice the new moms at the next table were given about resting when the babies rest, even if ours are only food babies?"

Teagan was surprised to see the whimsical expression on Liam's face as he looked down at Rylie's stomach before patting his free hand to his own. "Do our food babies count as twins if we each carry one?"

Those two have certainly acted more affectionate the last couple of days. I wonder if that means our plan is finally working?

"Maybe, but I think that would make them paternal twins," Rylie replied, reaching over to run her hand over Liam's abs.

"I think you mean fraternal," Teagan corrected her friend, wondering if someone had spiked her tea to make her mix up her words like that.

"No, I figure if the daddy carries one, then it doesn't matter if they're identical or fraternal, the one he carries is paternal." They all chuckled at Rylie's lame joke.

"If only our men could carry the human babies and not just food babies," Aiken sighed. "After seeing how uncomfortable Amy was Saturday night and Sunday before she left the wedding shower, there's no way I'd be able to have twins unless we could each carry one."

"Yeah, that's not happening, Princess," Crockett chuckled as he wrapped his arm around Aiken's shoulders and hugged her to his side.

"Lucky for you, I don't think you're likely to have twins unless you're a twin," Teagan pointed out. "And if that had been the case, then I think your dads would have adopted both of you."

"Yeah, they would have, if they were told everything back then," Aiken agreed with a sad smile. "But they weren't given much information about my biological family, so it's entirely possible that they could only afford to keep one child and had to give me up when I surprised them."

"Sounds like we both need to do those DNA tests to find out if we have any siblings out in the world," Crockett suggested as he brushed his lips across the top of Aiken's head.

"Since when do you need to do one of those tests?" Josh asked, eyeing Crockett dubiously.

"Since I found out my mother may have given up any other kids she had after she left me and Dad." Crockett explained with a shrug.

As Crockett filled them all in on the issues his mom had that caused her to leave the family over twenty-five years earlier, Teagan felt grateful for the normal family she married into. While she'd only met Josh's parents so far, he'd told her all about his aunts, uncles, and cousins, all of whom sounded completely normal. The only family skeletons they might have crop up one day were from her not knowing her father. But even then, she'd known his name and had looked him up online years earlier to find out he'd died without any known family, so she didn't think there'd be any major revelations in the future.

But if he didn't know about me, then it's possible he had other kids he didn't know about, too. Shit! That means I should probably do one

Leah Mae Wright

of those tests to find out if I have any other siblings, too. But can I handle having another Kijana in my life?

Before she could decide one way or the other, three local ladies she hadn't met before approached their table. Unlike the casual and comfortable clothing most of the locals wore around them, or the dignified and demure dresses Teagan had seen on all the ladies at church or one of the more formal events in town, these three were dressed as if they were going to the club instead of a celebration of the holiday geared toward families. Their short skirts and low-cut tops reminded Teagan of how Allissa's mom, Windy, and her friend, Kandi, had dressed when they first came to a GWA show back in August. But since they'd officially moved to Heart's Destiny, Texas, even the two former brothel workers were dressed more conservatively than these three.

Why do I have a feeling this is going to turn into a joke that starts off with, "a blonde, a brunette, and a redhead walk into Thanksgiving..."

"So, I hear we missed out on our turns being fixed up with the three of you," the raven haired woman stated while eyeing up each of the men left at the table before zeroing in on Liam.

"It's too bad ya'll got married 'cause we coulda had a really good time together," the redhead added, stepping a little closer to Josh.

Teagan glared at the woman, but didn't say a word in response. She was too focused on trying to figure out the best way to throw out the trash without causing any damage at the bed and breakfast, so the ballroom would still be pristine for Allissa and Dean's wedding reception in a couple of days.

"Well, ya'll missed out, but I didn't," the bleached blonde, whose brown roots were showing, giggled as she placed her hand on Crockett's shoulder. "I was smart enough to jump the line and take my turn without waiting on the old biddies in town to give me a shot. Ain't that right, Crockett?"

Oh shit! Teagan's eyes darted to her bestie, curious about how Aiken would respond to this woman's claim.

"Unless you want that hand broken, you need to take it off my husband," Aiken warned the blonde, straightening in her seat as she stiffened up to prepare for a fight.

"Whatever." The blonde rolled her eyes, but she lifted her hand, obviously realizing that, even though Aiken was the smallest among them, she was more than capable of following through with the threat. "Gimme a call when ya get tired of the old ball and chain, and we'll have a repeat of our Fourth of July fireworks."

As the blonde kissed her hand and went through the motions of blowing the kiss to Crockett, the brunette started to extend a similar invitation to Liam. "It might not be a repeat for us…"

"…but ya'll are all welcome to call us when you get bored and are ready for real women," the redhead finished for her friend, obviously intending for Josh to take her up on the invitation.

Before they could walk away, Rylie spoke up. "Li, remind me to thank Jen for being such a good friend and keeping the local skanks away from you before we were married."

Teagan had to smile at Rylie for trying to find the silver lining to all those past fix-ups, especially since she knew how jealous she felt over all the time Liam had spent with Jen. But when she noticed the murderous look on Aiken's face, she decided then was not the time to joke about sending thank you cards to all the women who'd been fixed up with their men in the last year. Instead, she schooled her features and stood, preparing to implement her plan to physically remove the three troublemakers from the premises. Clearly understanding her intentions, Rylie and Aiken also stood to assist her.

"Is there a problem over here?" They were all surprised by the barking voice of Bobby Burleson, the local police chief. He was followed to their table by his sister Becky, brother Josh, and Josh's girlfriend Cait.

"That depends on your definition of a *problem*," Teagan bit out, glaring at the redhead. While she had nothing against women who openly enjoyed sex, or even with women who made their living in the sex industry, she had major issues with women who blatantly hit on married men, especially her man. "And what we're legally allowed to do to defend our husbands when they're being harassed by whores."

"There's no problem, Bobby," the blonde cajoled, holding up her hands in surrender. "We were just inviting these guys to a party later, not harassing anyone."

"More like soliciting our husbands for sex," Aiken scoffed as Rylie nodded her head in agreement. "So you can fix the problem by arresting these three."

"Technically, since they didn't specifically ask for money in exchange of their services, I think the worst he could charge them with is indecent exposure for dressing like streetwalkers in front of all the kids here today," Teagan pointed out, retaking her seat, so she didn't risk an assault and battery charge for following through on her original plan now that law enforcement was there to handle the situation. Aiken and Rylie followed her lead and sat back down as well.

"Actually, I can't even do that unless one of them bends over and exposes anything more," Bobby corrected her before turning to speak to each of the unwanted women standing around their table. "BJ, Jackie, Melody, I think it's time for the three of you to go home and stop bothering the guests at the hotel before you get banned from coming to other events here."

"And put on some warmer clothes, so your frozen nips don't poke anyone's eyes out," Becky added with a smirk, causing several chuckles around the table, as the three interlopers turned and stormed off.

"Well, damn, that was totally anti-climactic," Josh Burleson huffed, slapping a hand on Bobby's shoulder. "I was looking forward to seeing how you were gonna arrest them without actually having to touch them to slap on the cuffs."

"Me, too," Becky agreed with her brother. "After how many times he's said he wouldn't touch the Thirsty Threesome with a ten-foot pole, I couldn't wait to make him eat his words."

"Naw, I wouldn't have had to touch 'em," Bobby smirked at his siblings before waving a hand at the occupants of the table. "I'd have just deputized these lovely ladies and let them subdue the perps until Jagger could get here with extra cuffs."

"So we didn't have to stand down and let you take over?" Teagan arched an eyebrow at Bobby. "We could have taken them outside and taught them not to hit on married men?"

Bobby just smiled and shrugged as the Burlesons all took a seat.

"You're right, Cowboy," Cait chuckled, looking over at her boyfriend. "Bobby is going soft in his old age."

"I'm not goin' soft," Bobby grumbled.

"Yeah, ya are," his brother disagreed with a huge grin. "You were just gonna let these ladies get away with a beatdown. But back on my birthday, when the Threesome was after me and Jake, I offered to let Cait borrow one of my guns to run them off while testing to see if silicone was as effective as Kevlar."

"Normally I'm against gun violence, but I kind of like the way you think, Josh B." Aiken reached over to fist bump the former Navy SEAL.

"Seriously?" Bobby gave his brother an incredulous look.

"Don't get too excited," Cait giggled. "He only offered me the BB gun, so you wouldn't have to arrest me for murder if I followed through."

"Yeah, Bobby's not going soft," Teagan's husband Josh chimed in. "Teagan alone would have caused more damage to all three of them than a BB gun, without even breaking a fingernail. So, siccing three trained fighters on them would have been overkill."

"I didn't see you trying to hold us back." Teagan turned her glare on her hubby. "Or speaking up to run them off."

"Of course not," her husband chuckled, leaning over to peck her lips with his. "I think it's hot that my Wifey is such a badass that I can continue to be a gentleman and not have to fight a woman 'cause I know you've got it handled. The only way I'd step in between you and a fight would be if it was with a guy. And even then, I'd have to sit back and watch for a minute before deciding if you really need my help or if you're just toying with your prey."

"What exactly did they say to get ya'll riled up?" Becky asked, looking around at the wrestlers. "We weren't close enough to hear anything, but from past experience, I knew when I saw them approach your table that it wasn't going to end well."

"They started off commenting about missing their turns at being fixed up with our guys," Rylie explained.

"Oh, please," Becky scoffed, rolling her eyes. "Our momma might not ever outright say anything bad about the Thirsty Threesome or BJ's older sister, but she'd never try to set anyone up with one of them."

"If only she'd known about Tammi Jo before my junior year of high school," Bobby groaned as he hung his head. "It woulda been mortifying to have Ma warn me off her, but that lecture woulda been a thousand times better than dealing with all the crazy shit she pulled after the one time I was dumb enough to go there."

"You're talking about the sister of one of the three who were just here?" Teagan needed clarification about who was who.

"Yeah, the blonde, Barbara Jean, who got her nickname BJ for her fondness of giving blow jobs more than for her initials, has an older sister, Tammi Jo, who Bobby was a moron and hooked up with right after he turned eighteen and moved into his own house," Josh Burleson explained.

"She thought it actually meant they were dating and literally tried to move in with him," Becky added, smirking over at her oldest brother. "That's why we now have gate codes to get on the ranch."

"But as a junior in high school, he thought he was cool for getting with all the senior girls," Josh Burleson continued. "And way too cool to listen when his freshmen brothers tried to warn him about the three girls in our grade, who made it clear they wanted to sleep their way through every guy in school. So it's his own fault for not realizing one of those girls had a crazy older sister, who set her sights on him."

"That's because I didn't see anything wrong with girls enjoying active no-strings sex lives the same way we all wanted to back then," Bobby huffed, shaking his head at his brother. "And it wasn't until after I hooked up with Tammi Jo that you mentioned how they targeted specific guys to make life hell for the girls they'd been dating."

"Why the hell didn't any of you guys warn us about the crazy chicks we needed to avoid the first time we came to town?" Crockett asked, nervously looking back and forth between the Burleson men at the table.

Oh shit! Could what that BJ chick said about hooking up with him on the Fourth of July be true? Teagan locked eyes with Aiken and knew her friend wasn't handling the news very well at all. But instead of blowing up about it the way Teagan probably would if she was in Aiken's shoes, her friend was quietly fuming while refusing to make a scene. *Oh, there's going to be a hell of a conversation in their room later. One that might just end up with Aiken coming to room with me tonight and poor Josh having to go deal with Crockett.*

"Because we knew Ma and her friends wouldn't fix ya'll up with any of them," Bobby shrugged. "And after word got around town about 'em back when we were all in high school, they've all pretty much quit trolling in town, so we didn't think it would be a problem. Besides, they're the type most single guys are looking for, down for just about anything with no strings attached. So we figured the only way one of ya'll would go there was if you were players, who wouldn't want to get serious with our sisters or cousins anyway. And while we might not be best friends with certain people, pretty much everybody in town is fairly non-judgmental. As long as they're not hurting anyone or causing trouble, we're happy to live and let live."

"And it's just those four who never outgrew the high school mean girl phase of life," Becky chimed in, sounding way more optimistic than Teagan thought was appropriate for the topic. "Jackie and Melody's sisters are both normal. In fact, Jackie's sister Carrie teaches at the middle school, and ya'll've met Melody's sister Melissa, who's the best waitress at Tully's."

"Wow, she's really nice. I'd have never guessed she's related to her slutty sister." Rylie's lip curled in disgust as she referred to one of the women who'd just left, presumably the brunette who'd targeted Liam since she most resembled the waitress Becky mentioned.

"Where do the rest of them work, so we know where to avoid for the rest of the time we're in town?" Liam questioned the locals.

"I don't know about the Thirsty Threesome, but Tammi Jo works as a cashier at the H.E.B.," Cait replied as she looked over at Bobby and shrugged. "Brook warned me not to go through her line the first time we went shopping for the ranch."

"I bet she did," Bobby chuckled and stood. "Speaking of my lovely wife, I'd better get back over to her and Maddie, so I can take over baby duty while Brie gets first dibs on dessert."

"He's really just leaving so he doesn't hear about what BJ, Jackie, and Melody do again, since he can't police the internet to shut it down," Josh Burleson chuckled.

"I take it they aren't doing internet sales like Ashlyn does?" Teagan wondered aloud, thinking the sex toys Ashlyn sold for It's My Pleasure would be right up their alley.

"Oh, that's what they claim, but the specific products change every time someone asks about them," Becky replied, shaking her head. "And they won't give any of us the web addresses to their sites, which makes no sense if they're really selling candles, cookware, or makeup, like they've each said at one time or another."

"Jake actually got a web address out of them at our birthday party," Josh Burleson smirked, referring to his twin brother. "But since they're not underage, or being recorded without their consent, and there are firewalls in place to keep minors and anyone who doesn't pay for the privilege from seeing their videos, it's perfectly legal to provide content for porn sites with their webcams."

"If it's legal, why does Bobby want to shut it down?" Teagan's husband Josh questioned the other Josh at the table. "That doesn't seem to go along with his 'live and let live' speech a minute ago."

"Because he's had to rescue women who've been trafficked and forced to do some of the things they do willingly and a lot worse," Josh Burleson explained, slightly frowning. "And he's afraid they're making themselves targets for the traffickers to come back to this area. We might not like their bitchy attitudes or the fact that they don't respect the boundaries of relationships, but they're still Heart's Destiny girls, so it's his job to serve and protect them, just like the rest of our neighbors and anyone who visits our town."

While Teagan wasn't all that surprised to hear the outrageously flirtatious women who'd accosted them a little while earlier were webcam girls, recording themselves in their bedrooms for horny guys around the world to pay for seeing them, she also didn't begrudge them for doing something they enjoyed to make a living. But apparently, the news bothered Aiken. All the color drained from her face as she clasped a hand over her mouth.

"I'm going to have to skip dessert," Aiken choked out before standing and running for the nearest exit.

"Aiken, Princess," Crockett called out after her, following hot on her heels. "I promise I'm not on any of those videos."

"Oh fuck." Josh Burleson looked mortified as he pointed with his thumb over his shoulder in the direction Aiken and Crockett fled from the ballroom. "Did he…?"

"We don't know what he did," Liam cut off his question before he could finish it, clearly trying to hold out hope that Crockett had kept his dick in his pants.

"But that bottle blonde implied she hooked up with him on the Fourth of July," Teagan's husband Josh informed the other Josh at the table, shaking his head. "But since we were all hanging out together at Dean's for a workout and then at the fireworks that night, I'm pretty sure she was lying."

Since she and the other ladies at the table had gone with the group to hang out at the River Walk in San Antonio that day, assuming they'd see a bigger fireworks show in the larger city, Teagan didn't know what any of the guys at the table did on Independence Day. But as Dean and Allissa returned to the table with plates of pie and cake, Liam confirmed what Josh had claimed.

"Yeah, Crockett was with us the whole day," Dean agreed, once they'd filled him and Allissa in on the reason they were questioning the events so many months later. "The only person I saw leaving the town square with someone outside the GWA was D. And come to think of it, I kinda wondered why he caught a ride back to the B and B with Julie instead of riding back with us. But I just chalked it up to the Matchmaking Mommas' shenanigans back then. And now we know it was probably one of the nights they hooked up."

As they all got dessert and the conversation continued around her, Teagan went through the motions of picking at a piece of pie, too worried about her best friend to really taste what she was eating. *Hopefully, they'll talk things out quickly and Aiken will come back in here to let me know she's okay. Otherwise, I might just have to track her down and check on her before going to our room for the night.*

~~~

As he followed his wife out of the hotel ballroom and up to their room, Brent felt like the biggest dick on the planet for not protecting Aiken from a run-in with one of his previous hookups. Granted, he hadn't even remembered the chick's name that he'd banged in the back room at Tully's back in July, but he still should have warned Aiken of the possibility of running into her when they came to town. But since he'd only seen her that one random night he went out that wasn't for one of the wedding events that week, and she hadn't attended any of the other town festivities at any other point in the last year that he'd been coming to Heart's Destiny for friends' weddings, he'd thought she was a ring rat, who'd only come to town because of the hype about Rick
~~~

Leah Mae Wright

and Fiona's wedding being there, and not a local. He'd intentionally not hooked up with any of the local girls he'd been fixed up with, knowing things would get awkward if he ran into them on his return trips to the small town. So, he hadn't expected this to be a possibility.

I guess I just got lucky that in the last couple of months we haven't run into any of the ring rats I hooked up with and don't remember from all my years in the business. But fuck! I was honest with Aiken about when my last hookup was, so I don't know what else I could have done to prepare her before now, short of giving her specifics. And I know neither one of us want to hear the details of anyone we banged in the past.

"Aiken, Princess, please talk to me," he pleaded, surprised at how fast she was able to run up the stairs in four-inch heels. Even with his much longer stride length, he had to jog to keep up with her. Well, to mostly keep up with her. With the view of her heart-shaped ass in the fitted purple dress she wore being right at his eye level, he didn't mind at all being a few steps behind her as they made their way up the stairs.

"I will when we get to our room," she hissed, not even turning to look at him as she reached the landing and swerved around a family he didn't recognize, who appeared to be on their way down from the third floor, while she continued to the hallway leading to their room.

"Excuse us," Brent apologized to the family as he also swerved around them to keep from mowing them down in his haste to catch up with his wife. He didn't say another word until after she unlocked their door and they both entered the room. "I'm sorry, Aiken."

She didn't acknowledge his apology as she beelined for the bathroom, not even taking the time to shut the door before she hit her knees and retched into the toilet.

"Oh, fuck." Brent instinctively joined her on the tile floor, pulling her long, silky, black hair into a messy ponytail and securing it with the rubber band from around his wrist to keep it out of her way. He then stood and grabbed a clean washcloth, wetting it with cold water and ringing it out so it wouldn't drip down her back as he held it against the back of her neck.

When she finished losing her lunch and flushed, Aiken turned her head to look at him, pointed at the washcloth he was still holding at her nape, and asked, "Where'd you learn that trick?"

"I have a vague memory of my mom doing this for me when I got sick as a little kid," he admitted, releasing his grip on the rag when she took it to wipe her mouth. "Although, now that I think about it, I think she might have been trying to get my fever down more than trying to stop me from puking. Sorry if it didn't help as much as I thought it would."

"No, it helped a lot, which was why I asked because I hadn't ever heard of it before." Aiken stood and brushed her teeth, obviously wanting to get the taste of puke out of her mouth before they talked.

Brent left her in the bathroom in case she needed privacy for anything else, going to sit on the end of the bed and wait while worrying about what made her throw up. *Was that just because of what that blonde bitch said? Or could she be sick because of a birth control failure? I mean, it's only been a month since our first time together, and we used condoms and her pills for the first couple of weeks. Then we spent a week and a half not having sex before going down to just her pills since we've been here. Surely using two methods of birth control for the majority of the times we've made love makes it highly unlikely that she's pregnant, right? And even if they both failed, doesn't it take longer than a month before morning sickness kicks in?*

Watching Aiken strip the rubber band from her hair and shake out the long mane as she walked out of the bathroom, Brent imagined her round with his child, causing his lips to turn up in a huge smile. *Fuck, the timing would suck because of having to talk about what just happened downstairs, but I'd be elated to know we're having a baby.*

"How can you smile like that right now?" Aiken glared at him, stopping as she got to the bed and trying to hand him the rubber band.

"Just imagining a wonderful reason for why you might have just puked," Brent admitted, taking her hand and pulling her onto his lap without bothering to replace the rubber band around his wrist. He ran his hand over her still flat stomach. "And hoping you're carrying more than a food baby right now."

"Oh my God, Brent! I am not pregnant!" Aiken shoved his hand off her belly and stood, stomping around the bed to sit down in the chair by the desk in their room and slip off her shoes. "I got sick because I ate too much and got queasy at the thought of you having shot a porno with that big boobed, blonde skank."

"I did not shoot a porno with her," Brent swore, turning to face Aiken as he pled his case for forgiveness for the things he did before they were married. "I didn't even leave the bar with her, much less go to wherever she has her webcam set up."

"But you did hook up with her on the Fourth of July?" Aiken tilted her head curiously, examining him while awaiting his answer and fiddling with the rubber band still in her hands.

"Technically, it was the third, not the fourth, because I was back here *alone* before midnight." Brent shook his head, hating that he could only deny the date and videography, but not the hookup. "And there weren't any cameras in the back room of the bar."

"Are you sure she didn't record it on her phone?"

"Yes, I'm sure," Brent huffed, really wishing he didn't have to get into specifics to reassure his wife. "'Cause her phone fell out of her back pocket when she took off her jeans, and not realizing it was on the floor, I accidentally stepped on it, rendering it completely useless. The hookup was so lackluster that I don't even remember it or her name, but I do remember being glad I had enough cash in my wallet to pay her for a new phone right then, so I didn't have to meet up with her again to go buy her a replacement."

Aiken surprised him by laughing then and shooting the rubber band at him from across the room. As it bounced off his chest and landed in the bed, she explained her laughter. "Oh, Brent, I think you got doubly screwed that night. From what I just saw of BJ downstairs, I'd bet her phone was broken before you met her and she just used you as an easy mark for getting an upgrade. Did you even look to see if it was repairable? Or did you just give her enough to cover the latest iPhone?"

"Considering it was in a couple dozen pieces after I stepped on it, I can't guarantee it didn't have a cracked screen beforehand, but it was clear it was unrepairable after being stomped on by my size twelve work boots," Brent chuckled, glad Aiken was laughing about the incident instead of still acting pissed about it, even though he still felt like he owed his wife a huge apology. "But I still wish I could go back and undo everything that happened that night, so you wouldn't have had a reason to get sick just now. Hell, if I could, I'd go back and undo all my random hookups with ring rats, so there'd be no chance any of them could come back to haunt us later. But unfortunately, I can't. All I can do is tell you how sorry I am for being such a dog before we got married and promise that's all in the past. There's been no one but you since over a month before we got married, and there'll be no one but you for the rest of our lives. I love you, Aiken. Only you. And I don't want my stupid past mistakes to come between us."

"I know that, Brent," Aiken smiled, giving him hope that they'd be able to move past this little setback. "And I love you, too."

"So you forgive me for the stupid stuff I did before we were married?"

"Yes, and technically, you'd already told me your last hookup was during our Independence Day break, so I really wasn't all that surprised to run into her here. Although I am surprised to find out you'd hooked up with someone who goes by the nickname BJ, considering your aversion to blow jobs."

"Yeah, the more I think about it, the more I think the reason I didn't remember her name is because she didn't mention it. 'Cause there's no way I'd have hooked up with her if she'd said anything about blow jobs." Brent shuddered at the thought of anyone but Aiken's mouth getting anywhere near his dick. And even with Aiken, he still needed to limit her to just licking him and not actually sucking his cock. "Hell, I practically break out in hives every time Blow Job shots are mentioned when we're out partying."

"Yeah, I hadn't noticed before Saturday, but after you telling me about your teenage trauma, I understood why you took a bathroom break when those came out at the end of the night." Aiken smiled reassuringly. "But now I'm a little worried that associating blow jobs with your last hookup before we got married will set us back in your exposure therapy. She *was* the last hookup before we got married, right?"

"Yes," Brent admitted with a sigh, knowing he had to forewarn his wife that she might not be the only one-night stand they might run into while they were in Heart's Destiny. "But there were a couple others here in the last year, so if there's another rodeo in the area this weekend, we could run into one of them if we go back to Tully's."

"Are you telling me you didn't sleep with any of the women you were fixed up with here, but you picked up tourists at Tully's every time you were in town for a wedding?"

Leah Mae Wright

"I haven't ever *slept* with any woman but you," Brent pointed out, wanting to make sure she knew she was way different than anyone else he'd ever hooked up with in the past.

"You know what I mean," Aiken huffed, rolling her eyes at him again.

"I knew better than to fuck anyone I might run into again or who might read more into it than just two people needing a release," Brent shrugged, feeling like a total cad for his previous attitude about casual sex. "But when we were here for Anthony and Kay's wedding, Dean made it clear that on the nights we didn't have wedding stuff to go to, there'd be plenty of buckle bunnies passing through town with the rodeo, who'd gladly convert to ring rats for a few hours, since cowboys tend to smell like their horses. Honestly, that's what I thought BJ was back in July. Either that or a ring rat, who only came to town after hearing about Rick and Fiona's wedding being here that week. She certainly didn't act like any of the other local women I've met here, so I thought I'd never see her again, just like all the others."

"My God, Brent, do you have any idea how many women you've screwed in your life? Or even remember any of their names?" Aiken's eyes widened as she shook her head at him.

"I remember Megan's name," Brent pointed out, referring to the high school girlfriend who'd been his first when they were both virgins. Of course, she was also the girl who bit his dick, so like the trauma, her name stuck with him. "And I remember your name, Aiken Thi Pearson Crockett. And as far as I'm concerned, yours is the only name that matters."

"So, me and the dick biter are the only names you remember?" Aiken sighed, closing her eyes momentarily. "You're a terrible horndog player, Brent Allen Crockett."

"I'm a *reformed* terrible horndog player, whose dick exclusively belongs to you now," Brent corrected her with a grin. "Besides, I bet you can't remember the names of every guy you've ever been with either."

"You'd lose that bet," she informed him with a smirk. "I remember all eight of them, while you've probably forgotten over eight-hundred women's names."

"Yeah, I might have been a dog, but I wasn't that big of a dog," Brent laughed, knowing his real number was probably somewhere close to a quarter of what she estimated. Not that he was going to give her his guess of how many hookups he'd had over the last fifteen years, since he'd started having sex when he was sixteen. Instead, he'd rather get them back to talking about their relationship. "So, am I number eight?"

"Yes, you're number eight." Aiken rolled her eyes at him again.

"Cool, I kinda like the number eight. If you turn it sideways, it becomes an infinity symbol, so it seems appropriate that I'm your number eight. Almost like it's a sign that we'll be together for infinity." Brent wagged his eyebrows at her.

"Yeah, I suppose that is a pretty good sign for us," Aiken agreed, smiling beatifically.

"So, Mrs. Crockett, what do you want to do for the rest of the afternoon? Is your stomach feeling up to going back downstairs to see if there's any dessert left? Or would you rather change into something more comfortable and cuddle up to watch a movie?" Brent wanted to suggest make-up sex as their third option, but if her stomach was still iffy, he didn't want to jostle her too much and make it worse.

"My stomach's fine, but I don't want to go back downstairs," Aiken asserted as she stood and gracefully glided across the room, stopping as she stood in front of him. "I was thinking we might order some ice cream from room service and spend the rest of the day incorporating dessert into your exposure therapy, so you don't have a setback."

"You wanna lick ice cream off my dick?" Brent's cock leaped to attention in agreement with the idea.

"Your dick is only one of the places on your body I want to lick ice cream off of," Aiken purred as she straddled his lap.

"And do I get to lick some of this ice cream off of you, too?" Brent dipped his head and trailed his tongue down the side of her neck, stopping to lightly suckle her pulse point as he felt under the fall of her hair to find the zipper on the back of her purple sheath dress.

"Of course," she agreed, loosening his tie, as he unzipped her dress.

"Yeah, I don't think I can wait long enough for room service to deliver ice cream," Brent groaned as he ran his hands over the smooth skin of her back. "But maybe we can grab a protein shake from the mini-fridge to lick off of each other instead?"

"You and your strawberry protein shakes," Aiken giggled, pulling his tie from his collar before unbuttoning his shirt.

"What can I say?" Brent shrugged, allowing her to push his shirt off his arms before reaching to pull her dress down in front to expose her braless breasts. *Fuck, I love it when she wears dresses with built in bras, so I have easier access.* "They work much better for maintaining my abs than ice cream. And I'm sure a shake will be just as tasty licked off your tits. But we should probably put some towels down to protect the bed first."

"Or we could just go stand in the shower for this, so we don't have to order fresh towels before rinsing off any residual stickiness," Aiken suggested, pushing off his chest to stand once more and letting her dress fall to the floor, revealing her sexy purple thong panties. "Or explain why the ones we have now are covered in pink goo."

"Good point," Brent chuckled as he stood, toed out of his shoes and socks, and dropped his pants before following Aiken, who'd only paused long enough to grab one of his premade shakes from the fridge before stepping into the bathroom.

By the time he caught up with her, she'd already stripped off her sexy purple thong and opened the protein shake. While she hadn't turned on the water, she was already standing in the shower, holding the pink drink in her hand, and waiting for him to join her.

"Damn, you're the sexiest sight I've ever seen, Mrs. Crockett." As he stepped into the shower, Brent took the protein shake from her hand. "But I bet you're gonna be even sexier once I paint your tits pink."

"How'd I know you were going to insist on going first?" Aiken teased him with a flirty smile, as he went down on one knee to get his mouth closer to even with her perky peaks.

"'Cause you know I'm gonna need the memory as a distraction when it's your turn?" Brent shrugged, pouring the cold liquid over her cleavage with one hand while spreading it around her whole chest with the other.

"Ooh, ooh, ooh, that's freaking cold," Aiken squealed, her whole body shivering, as her nipples pebbled even more from the drastic temperature difference than they already were from just being aroused.

"Aren't you glad we just went with a refrigerated shake instead of frozen ice cream?" Brent dipped his head and licked the strawberry shake from her nipples first before lapping up what he'd spread all over her taut mounds.

"Yeah, if we decide to try this again after ordering room service, we'll have to request the hot fudge sauce on the side, so we can eat the ice cream first and just use the warm sauce for foreplay."

Brent chuckled at her change of heart, not lifting his mouth from her breast to thank her for saving his dick from the possibility of shrinkage under the frozen treat. Once he'd cleaned up every drop of pink from her chest, he poured a little more on her torso, just below her breasts, letting it drip down across her flat abdomen. He had to sit completely down on the floor of the shower to lick her lower, but he didn't mind one bit. After cleaning up her midsection with his tongue, Brent lifted one of her legs to prop it on his shoulder before pouring just a little more over the top of her mound. Then he placed the remainder of the shake down on the bench behind her and lapped up the rest of the strawberry shake before it could drip down onto her folds.

While he assumed pretty much all food items were skin safe, he didn't want to take a chance on accidentally getting any inside her, where there was a possibility of causing a rash or yeast infection if it wasn't all properly washed away. So, he cleaned up what appeared to be every drop with his tongue before asking her to hand him the handheld sprayer and turn on the water. Once the temperature was adjusted for her comfort, he soaped her up with her apricot bodywash, then rinsed her off. Finally, he dropped the sprayer and dove in to really eat her pussy, licking over every lip and through each and every fold, making sure he didn't miss a single drop of her arousal.

Fuck, her cream is so much sweeter than that strawberry shake, Brent thought as he flicked her piercing with the tip of his tongue and inserted two fingers to start opening her up for his cock. After only a moment of focusing on her piercing, he redirected his tongue to spread more of her cream over her small but sensitive clit. It didn't take long at all with him targeting both her clit with his tongue and her G-spot with his fingers before her pussy gushed with her first orgasm.

"Oh, fuck, yes, Brent!" Aiken screamed, gripping two handfuls of his hair to hold his head in place as she ground her creamy cunt on his face. She chanted his name a couple more times before her voice became unintelligible as anything more than a grunting moan.

Brent lapped up every drop he could, reaching down with his free hand to give his hard cock some small semblance of relief. *I don't think I'm gonna be able to wait long enough for her to lick me before I have to fuck her.*

As Aiken's inner walls clamped down on his fingers, she dug her foot into the middle of his back, every muscle in her body contracting with her explosive climax. Brent felt so much satisfaction from getting her off that he had to stop stroking his dick to squeeze his fingers around the base like a cock ring to keep himself from coming with her.

He didn't stop sucking her clit and licking up her girl cum until she yanked his hair to lift his mouth from her sensitive nub. He lowered her leg from his shoulder, gripping her hips to make sure she was steady on her feet before releasing her to stand back up.

Aiken didn't wait for him to get to his feet before turning and picking up the remainder of the protein shake from the bench. She poured a little on his pecs, surprising him by swirling her tongue around the flat discs of his nipples until they pebbled like hers.

He'd never really thought of his chest as an erogenous zone before, but that was probably because, other than his first initial backseat fumblings in high school, he'd only ever taken his shirt off for sex with Aiken. While he knew seeing him shirtless in the ring was a turn on for a lot of wrestling fans, both female and male, by keeping his hookups in whatever club he'd been partying in when he met them, he'd avoided having to do more than lower his pants to his mid-thighs, so during his player days he wasn't usually shirtless with the women he fucked.

"Fuuuck," he groaned, wanting to enjoy each new sensation she gave him, even as his dick twitched with the desire to get inside her right then. He fisted his hands at his sides, fighting the urge to pick her up and impale her on his cock as he anxiously awaited her next move.

Aiken didn't disappoint, moving down to lick more of the shake from his abs after she cleaned it all off his chest. The sensual torture felt exquisite, even though she only touched his dick with the back of her hand to move it out of her way while she traced every groove in his abdominal muscles with her tongue.

"Oh, Princess, I didn't know you were such a tease."

"I'm not teasing you any more than you teased me," she countered, smiling up at him as she lowered herself to her knees while skimming the tip of her tongue down his happy trail until she reached the base of his cock.

Aiken then poured the remainder of the shake over the head of his dick, waiting for it to run down his shaft before lapping it up. He couldn't take his eyes off the sensual sight of her little pink tongue licking him clean. At least, not until his gaze landed on her amber orbs.

Fuck, her tongue feels amazing. I bet her mouth would feel as hot and wet as her pussy. If only I could keep from freaking out and flinching, which would probably end up with me scraping my own dick on her teeth.

He knew she was watching his face for his reaction, gauging how much he could handle, so she could stop before she pushed him to his breaking point. When her lips got closer to his cock as she flattened out her tongue to ensure she got all the creamy shake off his flesh, he unconsciously took a step back.

Fuck! Fuck! Fuck! Why can't I relax and enjoy this? Clearly my dick is eager, since I'm as hard as a rock and oozing precum.

"Sorry, I didn't mean to get my teeth too close."

"I know, Princess. And what you've been doing feels amazing. I just can't handle much more without something to distract me, so I can't see how close your teeth are."

"Okay, how about I clean you up and we try something different?" Without telling him what she wanted to try, Aiken grabbed the dangling handheld sprayer and waited for him to turn the water back on. She then sprayed him down everywhere she'd poured the shake earlier, soaped him up with her apricot bodywash since his was on too high a shelf for her to reach from her knees, and gave him a hell of a hand job as she cleaned him up.

Fuck! I hope she doesn't want to go back downstairs for dinner later, 'cause it's gonna be impossible to keep my dick under control when I smell like her.

Once she'd taken him to the point he was about to come, she rinsed off the soap. After he turned the water back off and she released the sprayer, she puckered her lips and peppered his thigh with pecking kisses. "Think you can handle that as long as I promise to keep my mouth closed?"

Brent's dick twitched again, which he took to mean the appendage was wholeheartedly on board with her idea. "Yeah, I think I can handle that," he agreed with a smile.

Aiken didn't reply, instead closing her mouth and puckering up once more. She softly pressed her lips against his balls, pulling back slightly before repeating the butterfly kisses until she'd covered his entire scrotum. Then she slowly worked her way up the shaft, lightly kissing every inch of him until she reached his crown. After pecking the tip, she pulled back and stuck her tongue out once more, closing her lips around the pink protrusion before lapping up the precum he couldn't control, swiping just the tip of her tongue through his slit.

"Fuck, Aiken," Brent groaned, gripping her under her armpits to lift her up before he lost control and shot his load in her face. "Can't wait any longer. Need inside you now!"

"Yes, Brent," Aiken eagerly agreed, wrapping her arms and legs around him, as he thrust his hips and filled her completely in one swift stroke. "Oh, fuck, yes!"

Sliding his hands down to grip her ass, Brent pressed Aiken's back to the wall of the shower and set a brutal pace as he fucked her dripping wet cunt like a primal beast. He crashed his lips over hers, claiming her with his kiss as much as with his cock.

As their tongues tangled in their carnal kiss, their sounds were limited to grunts, moans, and the slapping of skin against skin. But there was no need for words between them right then. Their writhing and thrusting bodies spoke volumes, physically affirming their passionate love for one another.

As her inner walls rhythmically squeezed and released his dick with each wave of her next orgasm, Brent gave up fighting his own release.

"Brent, Brent, Brent," Aiken chanted his name, digging her nails into the muscles of his back as she came.

Brent shoved his way inside her until he felt the tip of his cock breaching her cervix, then reveled in the feel of her tight pussy, milking every drop of cum from his dick until it filled her womb. "Fuck, yes, Aiken!"

I know she wants to wait until she's done wrestling before having babies, but damn, I'm gonna have fun testing her birth control while we're practicing making them.

Once the aftershocks died down and they both caught their breath, Brent couldn't resist asking once more, "Are you sure you're not pregnant?"

"Positive," Aiken replied, smiling sadly. "I got my period last week while we weren't sharing a room."

"Oh." Brent felt an unexpected loss, even though they hadn't actually lost anything.

"But if you're really that ready to be a dad, we can ask Kay and Anthony what they had to do to be able to adopt Antonio while traveling with the GWA, so we can start the process next time we're home for a holiday break." Aiken beamed at him, brightening his mood.

"Yeah, I think we have to pick a city to call home and actually set up a house there to be able to adopt," Brent pointed out. "So, have you decided between Portland and L.A.? Or are we still planning to have a house in each?"

"Actually, I was thinking we could look at houses in Lake Tahoe while we're there for Christmas, so we'll always be halfway between our dads."

"Excellent idea, Princess." Brent dipped his head and kissed his wife, looking forward to the rest of their lives together. "I love you. And I think we're gonna love living in Tahoe, even if we have to buy property with guest cabins for our dads."

~~~

After dessert and what seemed like hours, but was probably less than one, of awkward conversations with his wife and the various women he'd been seated with at all the social events he'd attended in Heart's Destiny over the last year, Josh was more than ready to spend the rest of the evening alone with Teagan in their room. It wasn't that he'd done anything with any of the women in Heart's Destiny to feel guilty about, having not even kissed any of them, but it still felt weird to have the local matchmakers previous attempts to fix him up mentioned so casually in front of his wife. Thankfully, of all the women he'd been previously paired with, only Charlotte had actually fallen for the next guy she was matched up with, so he didn't have to go on a lengthy tour
~~~

of the room to reassure anyone but Ian that there'd been nothing but cordial conversation between Josh and any of the local women. But now he still felt like he needed to reiterate that assertion with Teagan.

Hopefully, since we both walked up to our rooms at the same time at both of the last two weddings we've attended here, she'll know I didn't do anything more with my "dates" than she did with hers, even at the wedding last year that she didn't attend, so this talk won't last long. Then I can tell her my idea for a Christmas themed murder-mystery dinner with our families on our **Christmas Chaos** *weekend, before using our Christmas and New Year's break for the honeymoon we haven't gotten to take yet.*

"I want to check on Aiken before we go to our room," Teagan informed him as they reached their floor.

"Yeah, of course," Josh agreed, inwardly cringing for having completely forgotten how one of his best friends had ended up in the doghouse between dinner and dessert. *Fuck, I hope I was right about Crockett not actually hooking up with that BJ chick on the Fourth of July. 'Cause if I was wrong, I have a feeling I won't get any alone time with Teagan tonight, so she can console Aiken.*

Just as they reached the Crocketts' room and Teagan raised her hand to knock, they heard shouts coming from behind the door.

"Can't wait any longer. Need inside you now!"

"Yes, Brent! Oh, fuck, yes!"

Hearing the clear voices of both Crockett and Aiken, along with the very distinct sound of skin slapping against skin and thudding against a nearby wall, made it clear their concern for their friends' marriage was unnecessary.

"On second thought, maybe we shouldn't interrupt them," Teagan giggled, lowering her hand and turning away from their friends' door with a huge shit-eating grin on her face.

"I knew, even in his player days, Crockett had higher standards than to bang that BJ chick," Josh grinned as they walked across the hall and he unlocked their room.

"Oh, please, like those three weren't exactly the type both of you used to be all over when we'd go out after a show." Teagan rolled her eyes at him as she walked past him into their room.

"I can't speak for Crockett or Liam, but if you'd really paid attention the last few years, you'd know that the ring rats were all over me, not the other way around," Josh pointed out as he loosened his tie, ready to strip off his dress clothes and get comfortable. "I was merely being polite to them before going back to my room *alone* to jerk off to thoughts of you."

"Are you seriously trying to convince me that you haven't fucked a ring rat in the last five years? 'Cause I know for a fact that neither one of us was so enamored on the night we met that we immediately had to give up our one-nighters." Teagan sat down and removed her heels before padding over to the closet on her bare feet to grab a t-shirt and shorts.

"No, I freely admit to spending the first couple of years after we met, trying to get over my attraction to you by screwing around like a damn idiot." Josh shook his head in disgust as he thought about how empty those encounters had been, while removing his dress shirt and replacing it with a t-shirt. "But somewhere in that third year, it all started feeling wrong, like I was cheating on you even though we weren't together. So, I quit screwing around and only allowed back room and bathroom hand jobs and finger fucks on the nights you left the club we were in with some other guy. And hell, I haven't even done that in the last year."

"Oh, wow." Teagan looked shocked as she seemed to momentarily freeze in place while she untied her wrap dress. "That's about the same time I gave up one-nighters, too."

Josh arched an eyebrow at his wife, finding that hard to believe, since he clearly remembered her leaving clubs with other guys in the last couple of years, even when he could no longer bring himself to try to forget with a willing woman any longer. "Really? Then what were you hoping for when you went on your date with Dane? And what about the guy you left the *No Remorse* after-party with back in April?"

"That date with Dane was my attempt at getting over my crush on you with someone who didn't have your rules about dating coworkers," Teagan defended, finally getting her dress untied so she could change clothes. "And you already know that, other than the worst goodnight kiss in the history of kissing, it was as platonic as every time the Matchmaking Mommas tried to fix you up with one of the Heart's Destiny locals."

Josh swapped out his dress pants for sweats, putting away his Oxfords and dirty clothes while waiting on Teagan to finish answering his questions. Once they'd both finished changing and sat down in the bed, she finally explained.

"As for whatever his name was at the *No Remorse* after-party, he was just the last in a long line of guys that I only let walk me out to a cab or Uber before going our separate ways." Teagan turned to him with honesty shining through in her copper brown eyes. "I swear I haven't allowed more than a chaste kiss with anyone but you in the last couple of years."

On the one hand, Josh was thrilled to know she hadn't been with anyone else in years. But on the other hand, he felt guilty as fuck for the hand jobs and finger fucks he'd tried to use as a piss-poor substitute for her on the nights he'd been wrong about what she was doing after leaving the club.

"Fuck, I wish I'd have known you weren't fucking any of them." He slammed his head back against the headboard. "Then I coulda got my head outta my ass to throw out that idiotic rule a lot sooner and saved us both a couple years of frustration."

"Well, the good news is that it's finally the right time for us to be together," Teagan consoled him, leaning into his side and resting her head on his shoulder. "So now we get to spend the rest of our lives being totally, deliriously in love."

"True," Josh agreed, wrapping his arm around his wife. "And I fully intend to spend every night for the rest of our lives showing you how much I love you, and only ever want to be with you."

"Yeah, me too," Teagan smiled beatifically up at him. "But tonight, our lovemaking is gonna have to wait until after my food settles a little more. How do you feel about picking up where we left off binging *Criminal Minds* for a couple of episodes first?"

"That's fine," Josh agreed. "But before we start that, I have a couple of ideas I want to run by you."

Teagan arched an eyebrow curiously at him, but she didn't say anything, obviously waiting for him to elaborate.

"I thought we might want to invite both our families to come to New York for the *Christmas Chaos* weekend to celebrate the holidays early, so we can spend our break on the honeymoon we haven't taken yet. I thought maybe we could take everyone to a Christmas themed murder-mystery dinner, since we'll be in a hotel where neither of our moms will be able to cook a more traditional Christmas dinner.

Maybe even invite all our GWA family, too, unless you think it'll cause flashbacks for Allissa, Dean, or Liam."

"Maybe it'll be okay if we find one that's not about murder," Teagan suggested, nodding like she liked the idea. "Like we have to figure out who's sabotaging the toy production at Santa's workshop, instead of someone trying to kidnap or kill the big guy, so it's a mystery, but not too gruesome to trigger anyone or scare the kids if we invite everyone."

"Surely in a city the size of New York, we'll be able to find something like that, right?" The one Josh had already looked into only mentioned helping Santa figure out who was killing his elves, but he figured they had to have other options that would work for all ages.

"Oh, I'm sure," Teagan agreed, reaching over to the bedside table and grabbing her phone to start searching. "Where were you thinking you'd like to go for our honeymoon?"

"I was thinking one of the less populated beaches in Bali, so we can spend some time surfing, since that won't really be an option when we're in Denpasar City next year." Josh was excited about the GWA tour Rick had planned for the South Pacific in January. But even though they'd be there in the height of summer for the southern hemisphere, he knew the GWA schedule wouldn't allow near as much time for surfing as he'd want if he could get it, especially since they'd be sticking to the larger cities for most of the GWA shows, which weren't necessarily near the best surfing beaches in the world, even if they were on the same islands.

"I think you mean so you can spend time trying to keep me from drowning," Teagan chuckled, shaking her head as they both thought back to his one attempt at teaching her to surf so far. While his plan for a shower cap under a hooded wetsuit had worked well, her grace and skill in balancing on super tall stilettos hadn't translated to her being able to balance on a surfboard.

"Naw, it's just like any other form of athletics," Josh assured her. "You just need more practice than the couple of hours we had in La Jolla. After a week and a half on a beach in Bali, you'll be so good at standing on your board that you'll be ready for me to teach you a few trick moves."

"Like a real Alley-Oop three-sixty?" Teagan eyed him dubiously.

"Maybe." Josh wasn't certain Teagan would stay in the water long enough on their honeymoon to get that good, knowing they'd spend half their time finding places to make love, and she'd probably spend another quarter of their time getting spa treatments. But based on her athletic talent in a wrestling ring, he knew she was capable of getting there eventually. Probably with more like a couple of years of practice, instead of just a couple of weeks.

"Why do I have a feeling I'm going to have to take my braids out and convince whatever airline we take to let me bring several gallons of leave-in conditioner and other hair products on our honeymoon?"

"Don't worry, Wifey," Josh smirked. "You won't have to bring anything for your hair. Bali is known for some of the best spa retreats in the world, so I'm sure they'll have all the leave-in conditioner and other hair products you'll ever need while we're there."

"Oh, yeah, they are, aren't they?" Teagan smiled. "I guess you *were* thinking of what I'd enjoy too, and not just the surfing for you."

"Of course I was. I always want to make sure I'm taking care of you, Tea, especially on our honeymoon."

"And how are you planning on taking care of me tonight?"

"Since we're watching an episode of **Criminal Minds** first, I think I'll give you an orgasm for every dead body the team links to the unsub," Josh suggested, wagging his eyebrows at his wife.

"You do know that some of the unsubs on this show are credited with killing hundreds of people, right?" Teagan arched an eyebrow skeptically, even as her copper eyes lit with excitement at the possibility of him trying to deliver that many O's.

"Then we should probably warn Dean and Allissa that we might miss the rehearsal tomorrow," Josh teased, leaning over to trail his mouth from Teagan's shoulder, over her collarbone, up her neck, and finally stopping as his lips hovered over hers. "And maybe even the wedding on Saturday."

"Or maybe we'll just skip binging the show now and see how many times you can make me come in a twenty-four hour period, so we'll know if it's even possible to try your challenge on our honeymoon," Teagan suggested as she tossed her phone aside and wrapped her arms around his neck.

"I like the way you think, Mrs. Parker." Josh pressed his lips to hers, relishing the taste of sweet potato pie that blended perfectly with her warm vanilla sugar scent.

They might not have gotten to spend a full twenty-four hours making love before they had to leave for the wedding rehearsal the next day, but the record numbers of twenty-four orgasms for Teagan and five for Josh that they reached that night seemed like a good indication of how blissful they'd be for the rest of their lives. And Josh looked forward to trying to break those records daily on their upcoming honeymoon.

Chapter Seventeen

As they pulled into the church parking lot for Allissa and Dean's wedding rehearsal, Aiken was glad to see it was empty. While she knew it would fill up with more than just the vehicles for the wedding party before the actual rehearsal was due to start at five, she'd specifically suggested getting there an hour early to both Teagan and Rylie, so they might have a few minutes alone to catch up before being surrounded by the rest of their friends and however many locals had to be there to walk them through their parts of the ceremony the next day.

"Are you sure we needed to get here this early?" Brent questioned as he parked their car in the otherwise empty lot. "I swear, Dean said to be here at five, not four."

"The rehearsal is supposed to start at five," Aiken explained, glad to see the other two couples pulling into the lot and parking beside them. "But we wanted time to check out the bride's dressing room beforehand, so we're prepared for what we need to do to get ready at the hotel and what we have space to do here."

"And you haven't had a chance to get Rylie alone to find out if your plan to convince Liam not to go through with the annulment is working or not." Brent teased her with a knowing smirk before getting out of the car and walking around to open her door.

"Shuhh, don't say that too loud," Aiken whispered as she took his hand and stood from the car. "You'll give away our plans."

"Don't worry, Princess," Brent replied, softening his voice, so hopefully neither of the other couples getting out of their cars could hear him, as he leaned his mouth close to her ear. "I'm not about to out you for the little matchmaker you are, 'cause I don't want the guys to rib me mercilessly for helping you with your plans."

Aiken didn't take the time to explain that only Liam and the single guys would rib him, since Josh and the rest of the married guys were all just as complaisant with their wives matchmaking efforts, knowing that conversation would have to wait until she wouldn't be overheard.

"Do either of you remember how to get to the bride's dressing room?" Rylie questioned as the ladies led the way into the church. "All I remember from going to see Randi before her wedding is getting lost trying to get back to the chapel."

"Yeah, I think so," Teagan nodded before looking at Aiken, as if she could confirm that Teagan knew the way.

"That's why I suggested getting here early," Aiken chuckled as she looped her arms with the other two women and led them off to the left from the vestibule. "So we'd have time to get lost, find ourselves, and draw a map for tomorrow before everyone else arrives."

"I suppose we should check out the groom's dressing room too," she heard her husband suggest before they walked far enough away that they couldn't hear the guys.

"Yeah, lucky for us, I know the door to it is on the right side of the chapel, between the first row of pews and the altar."

"Was Liam in one of the other weddings here?" Rylie questioned as they walked past the hallway that led to the fellowship hall.

"No, I don't think so," Teagan replied, shaking her head.

"He probably just knows where the groom's room is from visiting Rick, James, or Anthony there before their weddings, like we did with Randi." As they weaved their way through the hallways surrounding the church offices to get to where she thought the bride's room was located, Aiken hoped her assumption would reassure Rylie that her husband hadn't previously escorted Jen Burleson down the aisle at another wedding here, even though she wasn't certain about who made up the bridal party for Charlotte and Ian's wedding in September.

"You're probably right," Rylie agreed, just as they finally reached the door she remembered led to the ladies' changing room. "He would have mentioned it if he'd been in one of the other weddings here."

"Considering how much they all talked yesterday about the other times they've been here and who they were matched up with at each event, I'm sure he would have said something if he got roped into walking with Jen at one of her cousins' weddings."

"That must have been after Brent and I left," Aiken mused, confused by Teagan's words, since her husband hadn't specifically mentioned names for any of the women he'd been fixed up with by the local matchmakers before they got married.

"Yeah, as we were mingling some more during and after dessert," Rylie confirmed, as they all looked around the small dressing room before taking seats at the long vanity along one wall. "And after hearing how Josh and Crockett were both fixed up with Charlotte and Becky Burleson and several of their friends, I'm not sure if I should be happy or concerned that Liam was only ever paired with Jen. Like were they really just friends and she saved him from hooking up with a half-dozen other local women? Or were they more and that's really why they were always paired together?"

"Well, even though Josh was paired up with several of the same local women as Crockett, he didn't hook up with any of them," Teagan admitted with a shrug. "But from what he said in our room last night, I think that was more about him not hooking up with anyone while he was fighting his attraction to me. So I don't know what it might mean for the probability of the local women wanting to hook up with your guys."

"What did Crockett say about that BJ chick after you left?" Rylie looked at Aiken curiously. "Or any of the other local women he was paired up with?"

"Based on the sounds Josh and I heard coming from your room when we came upstairs about an hour later," Teagan smirked, "I'm assuming he confirmed what Josh and Liam said about him being with them all day on the Fourth of July, so he couldn't have hooked up with her."

"Actually, he told me it was the third when he hooked up with her in the back room of the bar," Aiken admitted, shaking her head. "But he'd already told me his last hookup was here on our Independence Day break, so I can't really be upset about it, since I didn't have a claim on him then."

"Then why'd you run out of the ballroom looking so upset about it?" Teagan's eyebrows rose in a shocked expression.

"Because the thought that his last hookup before me could have been recorded and uploaded to her porn site made me so sick that I had to go puke up my lunch," Aiken admitted, almost tasting the vomit once more from just thinking about it again. "Thankfully, after I explained the puking wasn't pregnancy related, he assured me there was no way she recorded him."

"Remind me to come back to that pregnancy discussion after you elaborate on how he can be sure she didn't secretly record him." Teagan gave Aiken a pointed look.

"First, because he didn't go back to her place or wherever she has her webcam set up." Aiken held up a hand and counted off the reasons by extending a finger after each statement. "Second, because there aren't even security cameras in the back room at Tully's. And third, because he was apparently wearing those big clunky work boots he wears for his lumberjack gimmick, when her phone fell out of her pocket and he stepped on it, shattering it into a couple dozen pieces."

"Well, yeah, I guess that'll do it," Teagan laughed.

"Since he admitted he was still hooking up with locals as recently as July, did he say anything about hooking up with the women the Matchmaking Mommas paired him up with?" Rylie still looked nervous as she posed the question.

"Yeah, that he knew better than to fuck anyone he might run into the next time he was in town, or that wanted more than a one-timer in the back room of the bar," Aiken confided while rolling her eyes at her husband's previous opinion of casual sex. "So, he only hooked up with women he hadn't seen at any of the wedding events in town, and thought they were all out-of-town rodeo buckle bunnies, or ring rats who'd just come to town after it was announced that Rick and Fiona's wedding was going to be here. But just like Teagan said, what he did in his pre-wedding player days doesn't give us any idea what Liam might have done."

"Considering how much more affectionate you guys have been the last few days, I assumed you'd already asked him about what happened between him and Jen." When Teagan redirected her gaze at Rylie, Aiken followed her bestie's lead, really looking at their younger friend as Teagan continued. "But apparently, I shouldn't assume anything anymore, since you've clearly not talked to him about your concerns, or else you wouldn't look so worried right now."

"No, we haven't really talked about him and Jen," Rylie admitted sheepishly. "The one time I brought her up, I also mentioned Kara because I thought he was saying her name when he came while jerking off in the shower."

"Kara as in Kara's Kakes, the local bakery?" Aiken was confused, not remembering seeing Liam and Kara anywhere near each other at any of the previous events they'd all attended in town.

"Yeah, but I misheard him when he was saying, 'moh an-um cair-ah,' which means 'my soulmate' in Irish," Rylie explained with a self-deprecating eye roll.

"So, Liam becomes Red and starts speaking Irish when he comes?" Aiken laughed, finding that hilarious, even though it was more information than she really needed to know about one of her male coworkers.

"It's not like he's living the gimmick," Rylie scoffed, smiling even though she didn't seem to agree with Aiken that Liam's Irish orgasm quirk was funny. "I actually think it's kinda hot when he gets so carried away in the moment that his Irish comes out, especially when he calls me 'moh graw' while buried inside me."

"So the one-bed trope is working for you guys to do more than just sleep this week?" Teagan grinned. "Does that mean he's cancelling the annulment?"

"Oh, yeah, we're definitely doing more than sleeping in that bed this week," Rylie bragged, smiling brightly. "Not just in the bed, either. We've also enjoyed showering together and exploring for other places we can sneak off for a quickie. But we're still meeting with his lawyers to find out if we can do the annulment in New York, or if we'll have to get divorced like the New Jersey attorney I spoke to thinks."

"Wait, so you're having sex, but you're still going to dissolve your marriage? That doesn't make sense." Aiken looked from Rylie to Teagan, hoping her bestie might have more insight to share telepathically while they waited on Rylie to enlighten them.

"Yeah, we're just doing the friends-with-benefits thing for now," Rylie shrugged. "He basically explained that his push for an annulment isn't because he doesn't want me, but because we're at such drastically different points in our careers. He doesn't think we can maintain a long-distance relationship when he retires in a couple of years and I'm still touring. So, we're just going to enjoy each other as long as it works for us to be exclusive."

"So you're basically just going to be fuck buddies until he retires?" Teagan questioned much more bluntly than Aiken would have if she'd posed the question.

"If we don't implode before then, yeah," Rylie shrugged. "But I'm hoping that he'll keep wrestling for another five years, so we can retire together and get remarried. Or if he does retire before then, he won't jump into a relationship with anyone else, so we can hook up whenever I'm in New York, and then get together for real after I hang up my wrestling boots."

"You're really thinking of retiring in five years?" Aiken couldn't believe Rylie was planning such a short career. "That would be like us retiring in the next year, which seems like way too soon."

"Unless you have something else planned and are just using wrestling as a stepping stone." Teagan tilted her head as she studied their friend curiously. "Are you thinking acting or MMA?"

"Neither actually," Rylie confided, shaking her head. "I have a strong family history of P.C.O.S., so I'm hoping five or six years in the business will give me enough of a nest egg that I won't have to work while going through all the expensive treatments to try having babies before my ovaries completely quit working properly."

Knowing Fiona was currently dealing with the same condition making it harder for her to conceive, Aiken finally understood why Rylie planned to have such a short career in the ring. While Fiona could continue working in her position as a teacher after successfully getting pregnant, wrestling wasn't a profession any woman could continue during pregnancy without risking the health of their unborn babies.

"Did you tell Liam about your plans to retire early to have babies?" Rylie nodded her affirmative reply to Aiken's first question, so she tacked on a second to get her friend to elaborate. "And is he on board with wanting babies with you then?"

"I don't know," Rylie shrugged. "Right after I told him why I want to retire so early in my career, we kind of got sidetracked with talking about Fiona having the same issue and how she and Rick fuck like bunnies, which led to talking about Easter bunny costumes and my rabbit vibrator. Once we circled back to him watching me use it

Saturday night, we ended up having shower sex and didn't go back to the deeper discussion about what our fling means for us in the future."

"Yeah, you should probably talk to him about that," Teagan pointed out. "Right after you ask him if anything ever happened between him and Jen."

"Yeah, I know," Rylie agreed. "But right now, I just want to enjoy being with him and don't want to ask any questions that might end us while we're still sharing a room and have to appear happy for Allissa and Dean's wedding."

"Understandable." Teagan reached over and hugged Rylie before redirecting her gaze at Aiken. "Now that we know Rylie's plans for babies, what are the chances Crockett was right and you puked yesterday because you're pregnant?"

"Zero, zilch, zip, nada," Aiken replied, shaking her head at her friend. "Brent just didn't realize it wasn't possible because we weren't sharing a room last week when I was on my period."

"But you've worked past the issues that caused you to temporarily go back to separate rooms, right?" Rylie questioned, appearing relieved to no longer have the spotlight on her relationship for a moment. "You guys are good now? And planning to stay together?"

"Yeah, that was just me PMS-ing and overreacting to only hearing part of Brent's conversation with his dad while we were in Portland," Aiken explained, holding up her left hand to display the silver wedding band on her ring finger. "But we worked all that out. I just have to wait until we see all our dads for Christmas, so they can witness the moment Brent replaces these rings with his grandparents' rings that he won't even let me see yet."

"And you've talked about your future family plans?" Teagan questioned.

"Yes, unless we have a birth control failure before then, we're planning to wait until after we retire to try for biological children," Aiken confided, smiling at her friends. "But we haven't made any plans for when we're going to stop wrestling, assuming we'll make that decision when injuries or just general wear and tear on our bodies makes it necessary. So we want to start setting everything up so we can adopt sometime next year to go ahead and start our family."

"So, I'm the only one of us who's actually considering trying to have a baby next year, once Rick adds a few more women to the roster?" Teagan pouted slightly as she looked back and forth between Aiken and Rylie. "Since Randi said she's waiting at least five years and Allissa said she's waiting at least ten, I was hoping one of you would have babies about the same time I do, so we can raise them with built-in best friends."

"Well, considering our periods have started syncing up after working together the last few months, maybe your baby mojo will rub off on me, too," Rylie chuckled. "If I'm still enjoying my benefits with Liam when you decide to start trying, I wouldn't mind fate intervening to change my plans, especially if it means I won't end up having to go through fertility treatments."

"Yeah, we might want to warn Rick that he's going to need to hire more than just Amoura and Juno to keep the women's division strong while we're all out on maternity leave at the same time," Aiken decided. "'Cause even if our crazy synchronicity doesn't kick in for me to end up preggers at the same time as both of you, I'm hoping the first child we adopt is a baby so we won't have to take too much time off to get them used to being a part of our family before bringing them on tour. And depending on how long the process takes, we could adopt at about the same time you're planning to have your babies, so we'll all have kids close to the same age."

"Oh, goodness, are ya'll already blessed enough to be expecting?"

Surprised by hearing Fiona's mother's voice, they all three turned in the direction of the door.

"No, not yet," Teagan answered for them. "We were just discussing my plans to start trying next year, and wondering if the way our periods have synced up with us working so closely together might carry over to us each getting pregnant about the same time."

"It's possible," Kathy Harrison confirmed with a broad smile. "I got lucky with conceiving Fiona the old-fashioned way, even with my female issues, and I honestly think it's at least partially because we had a baby boom here in town that year. Hazel and Susan Burleson, Karen and Lisa Walker, and Hannah Thompson all had babies that spring and summer, too, along with quite a few other ladies here in town who had their babies just before or just after we did. None of the rest of us were quite as in sync as the Burlesons, who had their boys only a week apart, but I do think being around other pregnant women certainly helped the rest of us release the right hormones to make it happen easier. That's why I keep telling Fiona to spend as much time with the Burlesons as she can while she's home for the holidays, since they seem to be having another baby boom this year. Hopefully, between all the extra baby mojo and our constant prayers, she and Rick will have success with this first round of IVF and I'll get a new grandbaby next fall."

"Well, we aren't adding any extra baby mojo yet, but we're certainly keeping her and your future grandbaby in our prayers," Rylie beamed at the pastor's wife, as Aiken and Teagan nodded their agreement.

"Thank you," Kathy grinned back at them. "Now, we really must get ya'll out to the sanctuary to start the rehearsal. With so many people in the bridal party, it's going to take a little extra time to figure out how to best line you all up."

As they walked back through the church, they discussed the strange circumstances of having the shortest bridesmaid paired with the tallest groomsman and the tallest bridesmaid paired with the shortest groomsman. Apparently, that height discrepancy posed problems for maintaining symmetry for the photos.

"Yeah, well, we're just going to have to be asymmetrical, 'cause I don't think any of us are into husband swapping, even for a few minutes for the pictures," Teagan quipped, causing all the ladies to chuckle as they walked into the chapel, which had started filling up with their friends. "But I'm willing to wear shorter heels and you can put lifts in Josh's shoes if it helps fix the issue."

"You should have warned me that you're gonna try to make us all the same height for the pictures, so I could've practiced walking on stilts this last week," Kay chortled.

"No, we ordered the same shoes for everyone," Allissa informed them, shaking her head. "So shorter heels for me, Randi, and Teagan, and stilts for Kay and Aiken won't work."

"That's good, since I didn't volunteer for stilts," Aiken retorted, wondering how she got dragged into the joke since she wasn't the shortest woman in the bridal party.

"Since the guys are all a lot closer in height, why don't we line everyone up based on the ladies' heights?" Dean suggested.

"We can do that for everyone but the matron of honor and best man," Kathy agreed, directing Allissa, Dean, Randi, and James to take their positions at the altar. She then lined up Teagan and Josh to the outside of Randi and James, followed by Rylie and Liam, then Aiken and Brent, and finally Kay and Anthony.

As Mandi Hunter and Windy Walters approved the aesthetic appeal of their positions while standing up for Allissa and Dean's wedding, Aiken looked around at her friends and took a moment to appreciate just how happy they all were. Yeah, Rylie and Liam still had some things to work out. But based on the way they were looking at each other as they went through the motions to walk in and out of the chapel, Aiken was sure they'd eventually cancel their plans to dissolve their marriage and would live as happily ever after as the rest of the couples there.

~~~

Saturday, November 30, 2019, Heart's Destiny, Texas

Teagan was thrilled the night before, when the ladies were all informed that they needed to be at Dean's house by eight a.m. to have their nails, hair, and makeup professionally done by the local glam squad. While she knew there was no way they had time to completely redo her or Rylie's braids and still do everything else they had planned for the women of the bridal party and Allissa and Dean's families, she was still looking forward to a fresh manicure and not having to do her own makeup. She was also hoping for a chance to get Rylie alone while everyone else was having their hair done, so she could check on how her friend was doing after seeing how uncomfortable she was the night before, when Liam relayed more stories of the times he was fixed up with Jen while trying to help Dion get more of his memories back.

Her obvious discomfort last night, and Liam's total lack of noticing it, or that he was the cause, makes me wonder if what she's said about them having sex as part of a friends-with-benefits arrangement is all lies. Or at best, just wishful thinking on her part.

As the ladies took over the bar and family room on the lower level of Allissa and Dean's house, the guys were all instructed to go hang out at James and Randi's house for the day. Apparently, in addition to
~~~

scheduling the local beauty technicians for the ladies, the Hunters also had the local barber set up to trim the guys' hair and beards or do a professional shave, so they'd all look their best for the pictures.

"So, is this something you all do for every wedding here?" Windy asked, as she, Mandi, and Kandi sat in side-by-side chairs to be the first to get their nails done.

"I don't know that we do it for every wedding here," the brunette, who'd introduced herself as Lexi Wilder, replied as she started Windy's manicure. "But after the Burlesons started getting engaged, and our friends requested we put together a wedding package similar to the way we all got ready together before our high school dances, we've done a few."

"This is the first one where we've teamed up with Walt's Barbershop and sent one of Lexi's nail techs to work with the guys, though," the strawberry blonde, who'd introduced herself as Cassidy Reilly, continued for her friend as she worked on Mandi's nails.

"Yeah, Grandpa Walt didn't seem to understand why the guys couldn't just come to the barbershop earlier in the week whenever I asked him about taking care of the other grooms and their family and friends," the sandy brown haired woman, who'd introduced herself as Kayla Scott, chuckled. "It took his friend Mr. Rick asking for him to agree."

"It took me complaining about his five o'clock shadow showing in the pictures from James and Randi's wedding to get PopPop to explain to Walt about why the men all needed a proper shave on the day of the wedding," Meemaw Hunter clarified for everyone in attendance.

"We really should have scheduled something like this with the hotel spa before we took Chastity, Emerald, and Amethyst to the chapel in Vegas," Kandi pointed out, surprising Teagan by seeming to admit that their weddings had been pre-planned by the older ladies.

"I would have, if I'd have realized the men were going to insist on actually getting married, instead of just pretending for the pictures," Windy agreed with a sigh. "But we were already in the limo and driving down the strip by then. And those guys were in such a rush to get to the chapel that I doubt they'd have agreed to turn around and go back to the hotel for beauty treatments first."

"Wait, are you saying our husbands insisted we get married? It wasn't your idea?" Teagan wasn't sure she believed Windy's version of events for that night in Vegas.

"Well, I hoped taking the pictures would push all of you to admit to your attractions and maybe start dating and eventually get married," Windy admitted as Lexi finished her nails and directed her to move over to put her hands under a UV light to dry the polish. "But I honestly thought you and Amethyst would end up with Magnum and Trojan, so I was really surprised when Crockett and Surfer Josh both insisted on you really marrying them."

"Red and Chastity didn't surprise us one bit, though," Kandi added, smiling knowingly as she too moved over to dry her nails. "He might have been the last of the three to verbally stake his claim, but the way they were hanging all over each other before we even got in the limo, it was obvious he wanted more than friendship. It was almost like he was physically showing everyone he wanted to marry her before any of us thought about making it a reality."

Teagan watched Rylie for her reaction to Kandi's statement as Allissa, Randi, and Meemaw each replaced Windy, Mandi, and Kandi in the manicurists' chairs. Unfortunately, Rylie's blank expression didn't give her any clues about how her friend felt.

Is she happy that he physically showed his affection first? Or hurt because he was the last to say he wanted to get married?

"So, who actually suggested doing more than pretending for the pictures?" Aiken's question drew Teagan's attention back to the Vegas matchmakers.

"Crockett," Windy and Kandi said in unison.

"Really?" Aiken looked surprised by that revelation.

"Yes, you laid across his and Blade's laps and asked who was going to pretend to marry you first," Windy explained with a soft smile at Aiken. "And he told you that you could pretend all you wanted right then, but when we got to the chapel, you were marrying him for real. And you were so agreeable that you sat back up and kissed him right then and there."

"He even had a pet name picked out for you already, making it clear he'd wanted more with you for a while," Kandi added with a grin.

"Princess?" Aiken questioned, arching an eyebrow at the older women. When they both nodded in agreement, she let out a contented sigh as her shoulders dropped, seeming as if she felt more relaxed than she had at the beginning of this part of the conversation. "I didn't think he started calling me that until a couple of weeks after we found out we were married and started dating to see if we could work as a couple. I guess his dad was right about him having feelings for me before that he just hadn't recognized."

"How did our guys end up on board with the weddings?" Rylie asked, waving a hand between herself and Teagan.

"Within seconds of Crockett saying he and Amethyst were getting married, Surfer Josh told Emerald they were getting married for real, too," Windy explained. "And while they were kissing to seal the deal, Red said he and Chastity were too, telling all of us how they could work the marriage into the storyline between Red Velvet and Protection Detail to keep everyone from getting in trouble for the pictures."

Shit! Teagan could tell from the way Rylie flinched that she was upset by the way Windy made it sound like Liam had only jumped on the bandwagon with the other guys as a way to keep them from pissing off their boss. *Even if they were having sex this week, I bet she'll cut all that off after hearing this, especially if he can't reassure her that there wasn't anything going on between him and Jen on his previous visits here.*

"He might have said it was to keep everyone from getting in trouble, but the way you were making out and groping one another the rest of the night, it was obvious that wasn't his real reason for marrying you, Chastity," Kandi added, obviously noticing the same reaction Teagan had from Rylie.

"Oh my God! Did we cause a scene in the limo? Or worse, outside the limo, where we could have been charged with public indecency?" Rylie looked mortified.

"No, you were just leaning on each other a lot as you got in the limo and while we were riding around, and other than the kisses during the wedding, you just exchanged pecks where anyone else could see you," Windy tried to console Rylie. "It was Emerald and Surfer Josh who were groping each other in the limo, but she let go of his dick when they started kissing after agreeing to get married."

Teagan just shrugged as every eye in the room turned to her. Even though she didn't remember any of that happening, she knew herself well enough to know it was probably true. "What? I had to check out the goods before deciding to say yes to getting married, even if I didn't have enough privacy to take him for a test ride."

"I'm with Teagan," Kay chimed in, grinning. "Our momma taught us that a smart woman always takes a test drive to make sure she doesn't end up with a lemon."

"She was talking about buying a used car, not picking a man," Randi screeched, looking appalled at the thought of their mother having the same opinion of premarital sex. "But when she first met your in-laws, she agreed with the lessons Hazel and Susan taught their daughters about being wary of a bull giving the beef away for free because it's usually rotten."

"Oh, Hazel and Susan only told their daughters that when they were teenagers," Mandi clarified. "After our kids all finished college, they switched to suggesting pre-purchase exams like we do when buying a thoroughbred horse before choosing a mate for all their kids. I'm sure they only mentioned the rotten beef analogy for Tia."

"Yeah, well, when my mom spouted that line at me, she was referring to your son," Randi pointed out.

"And I'm forever grateful that you didn't listen to that lesson," Mandi chuckled.

"If we're going to talk about beef sticks, can we please talk about the beefcake wrestlers, who aren't our grandsons or our grandsons' childhood friends, who are almost like extra grandsons to us?" James and Dean's Grandma Joan requested. "I'm sure Kay needs specifics on size, curvature, and any piercings, so she can accurately describe them in her books."

"I don't really need specifics unless it's something other than long and thick, which is usually how I describe them in my books." Kay raised her hands and shook her head.

"Oh, em, gee! Are you telling me the piercings described in *Claiming Carlita* are based on what Charlotte told you about Ian's dick?" Teagan felt her eyes bug out as she turned to look at Kay.

"Technically, they're based on the piercings Char suggested for one of Ashlyn's products back before we knew she'd hooked up with Ian,"

Kay clarified. "But I'm only guessing that she got the idea from being with Ian."

"So, ladies, are there any details readers will want to know when Kay gets to your books?" Meemaw Hunter asked as she stood from her seat and took Windy's place under the UV light to dry her nails.

"Your standard description works fine for Josh," Teagan spoke up, not wanting to give any details about the special way Josh swiveled his hips to stimulate her G-spot, no matter what the other ladies were willing to share.

"It works for Liam, too," Rylie agreed.

"We can't vouch for that since we couldn't see Red's dick when they were dry-humping in the stairwell on their wedding night," Kandi added. "But if you're taking notes for your books, I will say that Chastity has the most perfect natural boobs I've ever seen."

"Well, of course, she is *Chas-titty*," Allissa and Randi joked at the same time. Not that any of them had the chance to reply to the standing gag about Rylie's ring name as the woman in question started grilling the former brothel workers about what they'd seen back in August.

"You saw us in the stairwell? That wasn't a dream?" Rylie appeared to be both mortified and shocked. "How'd you see us when we were alone? At least, I think we were alone from what little I remember."

"Well, I don't know what you dreamed happened, but when we went to the security room with our friend Chuck, you two were alone in the stairwell, dry-humping against the wall," Windy confirmed. "But it was clear you weren't actually having sex since Red stayed fully clothed and only pulled down the front of your dress and bra."

Teagan was at a loss for how to change the subject to help relieve Rylie's embarrassment at hearing she'd been exposed to both Windy and Kandi, as well as their friend Chuck, who was apparently a security guard at the hotel they stayed in whenever they were in Vegas. Thankfully, Aiken was a quick thinker and stepped up for their friend.

"So, um, is Brent being uncircumcised something you need to know for writing our book?"

Wow! Talk about TMI.

"Really? Does that make it feel different during sex?" Kay questioned, sitting down in the next empty chair for her manicure beside Grandma Joan. "Does he have to physically push the foreskin back or does he just grow out past it when he gets hard?"

"It doesn't feel any different for me, other than him being longer than anyone I've been with before. And I have to wonder if not cutting off the foreskin is why he's longer than average."

As Aiken filled the third seat beside Kay to get her nails done while answering the writer's questions, Teagan pulled Rylie aside, stepping over into the game room so they wouldn't be overheard, or overhear more than they wanted to know about Aiken's husband. "Are you okay?"

"Yeah, just learning a lot more than I expected this morning." Rylie still looked shell-shocked as she leaned up against a classic arcade game. "But I guess I should be grateful that screenshots from that security camera haven't shown up on the dirt sheets or CNZ."

"Yeah, that's at least one silver lining," Teagan agreed, hoping she wasn't about to make her friend feel worse as she pointed out what she thought was another. "And getting that hot and heavy before making it to one of your rooms shows that he was really into you. So whatever he said about making your marriage into an angle was probably just an afterthought and not the reason he wanted to make it real between you two. He probably just said it because he's a typical clueless male."

"True," Rylie agreed, nodding her head.

"And what Kandi said about your tits is a real compliment," Teagan pointed out. "I mean, I'm sure she and Windy have seen hundreds of naked women in their former profession, so for one of them to say yours are perfect is pretty high praise."

"Yeah, that's true, too," Rylie laughed. "I just wish their friend Chuck hadn't seen them. Or that I could be assured nobody else will ever see that footage."

"It was just us and Chuck in the security room that night," Windy assured them, joining them in the game room. "And we made Chuck delete the footage once you and Red got to your rooms, so you know it won't ever end up being seen by anyone else, or end up online. We wanted you to take a few fun pictures and take a chance on falling in love, not post anything that might actually cause a scandal for you or the GWA."

Leah Mae Wright

"We know," Teagan smiled at Allissa's mom, knowing the older woman's heart was in the right place, even if her methods back in August had been questionable. "And even though I wish we'd have been sober enough to remember our weddings, I do want to thank you for giving us the push Josh and I needed to quit fighting our feelings for one another."

"Oh good, I was afraid you'd all be mad at me forever," Windy smiled, her shoulders sagging with relief. "And I did try to sober everyone up with a trip through the Starbucks' drive-thru for iced coffee between the hotel and license bureau, but apparently it only worked long enough to make you appear sober to the officials who issued the licenses and performed the ceremonies. And then we switched to champagne for the ride back to the hotel and totally undid all the coffee."

Teagan could only laugh, as did Rylie beside her.

"Don't you ever change, Windy," Rylie chuckled as she leaned over to give Windy a side hug. "'Cause if you weren't the wonderful person you are, I wouldn't have taken my chance with Liam either. Thank you."

Teagan might not be convinced that Rylie and Liam were as well on their way to happily ever after as she and Josh or Aiken and Crockett, but all she could do right then was hope for nothing but the best for all three of their marriages.

I really hope they're able to take this friends-with-benefits thing Rylie said they're doing and turn it into a long and lasting marriage, so they can be as happy together as Josh and I are.

~~~

The whole day felt like an emotional roller coaster for Rylie. After the bumps and dips that morning from hearing both Windy's and Kandi's versions of the events of the night she married Liam, she'd felt like she was soaring on an emotional high while witnessing Allissa and Dean's wedding, especially since Liam was making eyes at her across the aisle as they were standing up for their friends. But then the reception brought more bumps and dips, starting with Rick roasting them for the Vegas weddings causing an online uproar. Then, seeing Julie and
~~~

Dion catch the bouquet and garter, and them unsuccessfully hiding their love for one another while posing for the pictures, Rylie couldn't stop her heart from plummeting at the realization that Liam and Jen had spent just as much public time together over the last year as Dion and Julie, when they could have easily fallen in love, too. On top of all the stories Liam had told about his fix-ups with Jen over the last week while trying to help Dion get some of his memories back, that realization brought back all Rylie's insecurities about her husband's relationship with the other woman. By the time she and Liam made it up to their room after the wedding reception, she was more than ready to get off the sickening ride.

Shit! I'm still going to have to ask him for help getting all the pins out of my hair from the updo Kayla did this morning with my braids, since there's no way I'll be able to find them all when I wasn't the one putting them in to know exactly how many were used and their general locations. But can I really handle having him touch me that much, when I'm still unsure if his heart belongs to her, or if I have a chance in hell of him ever loving me? Hell, dancing with him tonight was torture enough after noticing the way Jen kept looking over at him.

But regardless of how uncomfortable I'm going to be while he's helping me, I can't go to sleep with these pins in either. So, I just need to suck it up and ask for his help.

"Hey, you okay, Rye?" Liam questioned, running his hands down her arms as he stepped up behind her, where she'd basically stopped walking before even getting halfway across the room from the door.

"Yeah, just tired," she lied, mentally shaking off the goosebumps his touch caused. "It's been a long day and I still need your help getting all the pins out of my hair before I can even get comfortable to go to bed."

"Well, then we'd better get started." Liam dipped his head and brushed his soft lips over the junction where her neck and torso met, causing her body to tingle with arousal. "You wanna sit on the bed, so I can sit behind you and find all these pins?"

"Sure," Rylie agreed, rushing over to sit on the edge of the bed and kicking off the red heels that perfectly matched the floor-length asymmetrical cutout halter bridesmaids' dress she wore. She was grateful for the slit up the side that came almost to the top of her thigh, so she could turn sideways on the bed without her legs being confined by the otherwise fitted sheath.

Neither of them spoke, as Liam followed her across the room, unbuttoned his black tuxedo jacket, and sat down behind her with one leg hanging off the bed and the other bent up the same way hers was to keep his shoe off the bed. He carefully touched her braids, making it seem to her like he was feeling for the bobby pins more than looking for them.

"Wow, whoever did your hair is really good at hiding the pins holding it up," he chuckled before finally pulling the first one out.

"Yeah, she specifically mentioned using different colored bobby pins, so they'd blend with the hair around them and wouldn't be noticeable in any of the pictures," Rylie informed him, knowing Kayla had used several shades of brown and black bobby pins in her ombre extensions. "I just hope having to dig around for them now won't loosen the braids too much, so I can wait until our Christmas break to take them out."

While eight weeks was the longest she'd ever kept braids in, since starting to wrestle, they usually only lasted between four and six weeks. But she was really hoping to get seven weeks in this time, so she could give her natural hair over a week of rest when she didn't have to appear on television before putting in new extensions for the new year.

"I'll try to be extra careful taking them out," Liam assured her, using the end of the first bobby pin to help him work the next one out enough that he could grab it without pulling more than the pin. "Other than taking out your braids, what else do you have planned for our Christmas break?"

"Not much," Rylie shrugged, wondering why he was asking. *Does he want us to do something together for our break? Or is he just trying to find out if I'll be available to take a day trip into New York to sign papers in his lawyer's office?* "Mostly vegging out, cleaning my apartment, and maybe catching up with some old friends, if they're not off visiting family out of town. What about you?"

"Actually going home," Liam chuckled, "so my family will quit complaining about me spending all my breaks elsewhere for the last year. And other than my appointment with the family law attorney on the twenty-third, my family will have my schedule packed from the moment I arrive until it's time for me to fly out on the first with midnight mass, caroling, special meals for Christmas Eve, Christmas Day, and the Feast of Saint Stephen on Saint Stephen's Day, and probably a dozen different parties with our extended family and friends."

As he was talking, Liam removed enough of the bobby pins that he'd let down about half her braids. The way he mentioned spending all his breaks away from home for the last year only reinforced Rylie's need to ask him about what happened between him and Jen on each and every one of those breaks.

Screw it! If asking him about Jen leads to him stopping before he's removed all the bobby pins, then I'll just text Teagan to get her to help me make sure I don't miss any of them. Or maybe see if Kayla is available for an emergency braid removal tomorrow.

"So, you've really spent every holiday break here in Heart's Destiny for the last year?"

"Yeah," Liam sighed, continuing to fondle her hair in a way that caused her to tingle with each new braid he released. "It started out just for our Thanksgiving break for Anthony and Kay's wedding. But after seeing the matchmaking here didn't make me feel nearly as pressured as Ma and Granny's scheming, I agreed with D when he suggested we come back here for Christmas and New Year's to make those holidays easier on Jen and Julie."

"I know you came for our Memorial Day and Independence Day breaks because of the weddings, the same as me, but why'd you come here for our Labor Day break? Was that just to keep making things easier for Jen? Or was there more between you and her than just friendship?" Rylie held her breath as she awaited his answers.

"Honestly, by that point in time, I'd spent enough time with all the Burlesons that I wanted to be there for Charlotte and Ian's wedding as much as I wanted to be there for Jen," Liam admitted with another sigh, not responding to her question about there possibly being more between him and Jen.

An awkward silence settled between them as Liam continued removing the bobby pins from her hair without saying another word. Rylie kept her mouth shut too, hoping the tension would eventually get to him enough that he'd answer her without her having to ask again.

As curious as she was, she didn't want to come off as a jealous shrew by badgering him for answers.

"Okay, I think that's all of them," Liam finally announced, standing and handing her a handful of black, brown, and tan bobby pins.

"Thanks." Rylie smiled up at him as she took the bobby pins, stood, and walked into the bathroom. She wasn't sure if she'd ever need them again or not, but it wouldn't hurt to have them on hand for doing another updo in the future. So, she pulled a rubber band from her toiletry kit and wrapped it around them to keep them bundled together before putting them in one of the side pockets. She used the mirror on the wall along with the hand mirror in her bag to double check that all her braids were hanging freely without any other bobby pins still being caught up in one of them before winding them up and wrapping her head with a silk scarf.

They went through the motions of their nightly routine to get ready for bed without speaking further. Rylie wasn't sure if Liam bought her tired excuse from earlier for why she waited until he finished brushing his teeth before closing the bathroom door for privacy while changing for bed. But she hoped he'd realize she wasn't in the mood to make love again like they had for the last few nights.

When she finally finished putting everything away and walked around to her side of the bed, she found Liam already on his side, sitting up with his back against the headboard and wearing a pair of sweatpants and a t-shirt instead of just the boxer briefs he usually slept in.

"When you got your pajamas out, I figured that meant we need to finish talking before anything else," he explained with a shrug.

"Yeah, I kind of need you to finish answering my earlier questions before we can do anything but sleep tonight," Rylie agreed, sitting down facing him, wanting to tackle their issues head on.

"I swear, I've only ever thought of Jen as just a friend, nothing more." The dejected look in Liam's hazel eyes wasn't very convincing.

"There's never been anything between you two?" *Please, please, please, don't say yes to my next question,* Rylie mentally pleaded, knowing if there'd been more between Liam and Jen, then she'd be heartbroken. "Neither one of you ever made a move on the other, just to see if you could be more than friends?"

Liam closed his eyes and took a deep breath, the morose expression on his face giving away his answer without him having to say a word.

"Never mind," Rylie sobbed, feeling her heart shatter in her chest. "That expression tells me all I need to know. But honestly, Liam, if you really want to be with Jen, you should come clean with everyone here about how you feel, instead of pretending to be happy we got married. This ruse is just going to make it hard for the Burlesons to accept you into their family later. But if they know our marriage was just a drunk mistake and that you aren't in love with me, they'll probably forgive you."

"No!" Liam exclaimed, shaking his head as he slightly lifted his hand in her direction, almost as if he started reaching out for her but decided against it, and dropped his hand back to his lap. "You've got it all wrong, Rylie. I don't want to be with Jen. I've never wanted to be with Jen. My pained expression wasn't about whatever you think it was about. It's because I regret doing something stupid to try to get you outta my head."

"Me? What are you talking about? It was when I asked about you and Jen ever hooking up that you made that, that…" she waved her hand around in his general direction, "…face."

"Yes, you," Liam defended, even as he almost looked like he was tearing up. "Feck, Rylie, I've wanted you since March sixteenth, when I first saw you at ringside before your try-out match. But even though you're the hottest woman I've ever met…" His voice trailed off as he seemed to change his train of thought. "Hell, you're the hottest woman I've ever even seen, including all the models and actresses that I've only ever seen on TV or in pictures. But I still didn't think I could be with you, so when I was here over our Labor Day break, I thought maybe I could get you outta my head by being with someone else. So, when Jen flirted more than usual, I flirted back."

Liam paused, closing his eyes momentarily as he took a few deep breaths while gathering his thoughts. Unlike Liam, Rylie held her breath once more, anxiously waiting for him to finish telling her what happened between him and Jen just a couple of weeks after he'd married Rylie.

Oh God! We were married when they hooked up! I don't care if he knew we were married or not, that's still cheating. And I can't be with a cheater.

"After lots of flirting and a little bump and grind on the dance floor, Jen convinced me to sneak into the storeroom at Tully's."

"You fucked her in the storeroom at Tully's?" Rylie's eyes filled with tears, which she desperately tried to hold back from falling.

"No! Absolutely not!" Liam adamantly denied, once again acting like he wanted to reach out to her momentarily before pulling back. "We tried to kiss and epically failed. Hell, I'm surprised we didn't both have concussions from head-butting one another on our first attempt. And when I quit letting her be the instigator, and held her head in place so I could kiss her, it felt like I was kissing my granny. It was such a bad kiss that even with her grinding on me to try to push for sex, my dick didn't respond. I swear, if it was possible, it woulda turned itself inside out to get away from her because she wasn't you. I might not have known we were married then, but I still felt like I was cheating 'cause my dick only wants you."

"Really? You're trying to convince me that you and Jen only had a couple of bad kisses by lying about you only wanting me? Sorry, I'm not buying what you're selling." Rylie rolled her eyes at him before wiping under them, her anger not doing much to help control her tears.

"I'm not lying to you," Liam swore, his pleading eyes making her almost want to believe him. "I promise, every word I've said tonight has been the God's honest truth."

"No, I don't believe you." Rylie shook her head. "If you'd really wanted to be with me, then you'd have been happy to find out we got married, instead of acting like an asshole that first day. And you would have responded to my blatant attempts at flirting with you, so we could have been fucking for almost two months by now, instead of only for a few days."

"Not when I thought it would just lead to getting my heart broken when I have to retire and you'd still be wrestling for the next decade," Liam argued, shaking his head. "Remember, it did take you convincing me that you aren't planning a long career for me to agree to adding benefits to our friendship this week, and I only did that 'cause I'm hoping I can last five more years in the business so we can retire at the same time and give our relationship a real shot. And besides all that, I think my response to your flirtation has been pretty damn obvious, considering my wrestling tights don't exactly conceal how hard I get anytime I'm around you."

Thinking back to how glorious his bulge looked in his tights when they first started the flirtation angle, and especially how great it felt against her ass when she sat on his lap on Halloween and during the first few vignettes they shot to announce their marriage, she had to admit, if only to herself, that he did seem to reciprocate her attraction. *And his dick certainly hasn't tried to turn itself inside out to get away from me this week, so maybe he really is only into me.*

But no matter how much her heart was telling her to forgive him, or how bad her pussy was begging her to forgive his cock, her head was still filled with the lessons her mother taught her when she was in high school and found out her first boyfriend had slept with another girl when she wasn't ready to have sex.

"Once a cheater, always a cheater. It's better you found out before you had sex with him because a boy like that doesn't deserve the precious gift of your virginity, much less your heart."

"Not that any of that matters now," she finally huffed in response, no longer able to keep the flow of her tears down to a trickle. "You still wanted to have sex with someone else only a couple weeks after you married me. And even if you only shared a couple of bad kisses with her, you should have told me about them before having sex with me. Maybe not before New Orleans because of the special circumstances then, but definitely before we decided to try a friends-with-benefits arrangement this week. So, you can consider that over now. I'll still play my part tomorrow and whenever we're working a GWA show, but otherwise, I need my space and a lot of time before I'll be ready for us to even hang out as friends again."

With that, Rylie stood and gathered the extra pillows that had been tossed to the floor a few days earlier, stacking them down the middle of the bed once more before crawling under the covers on her side and turning off her bedside lamp.

"I'm sorry, Rylie."

With her back to him, she couldn't see if he was crying as hard as she was or not, but his anguished tone certainly sounded like it. Liam

Leah Mae Wright

turned off his bedside lamp, but she didn't feel the bed move as if he was laying down to try to sleep. Not that she could worry about whether or not he got any sleep when she was too busy crying her eyes out.

Yeah, I'm not going to wait to find out what his attorney says about the possibility of an annulment on the twenty-third. Just as soon as we land in San Antonio on the twentieth, I'm going to head to the commercial side of the airport and get the first flight home, so maybe I can get to the lawyer's office before they close to start the divorce.

Chapter Eighteen

Tuesday, December 3, 2019, Flying from San Antonio, Texas to Austin, Texas

Liam felt like shit as he buckled up for takeoff on Tuesday morning. He knew part of his unease was caused by a lack of sleep from his recurring nightmares, which he'd briefly banished for a few days the previous week while making love with Rylie. Unfortunately, they came back with a vengeance since their breakup Saturday night. Still, he could only blame the nightmares for a small segment of his distress. The majority came from the heavy burden of guilt he carried for causing their relationship's demise. He'd sat up half the night with tears pouring down his face after she told him their friends-with-benefits arrangement was over, wishing he could hold her in his arms and comfort her as he listened to her crying herself to sleep. But since both their broken hearts were his fault, he couldn't allow himself even the small amount of solace he'd have taken from consoling her.

Not that she'd have let me try to soothe her pain by holding her anyway. Feck, other than Sunday when we still had to act like we're happily married while we were still in Heart's Destiny, and yesterday when we sat down with Rick to plan today's TV spots, she hasn't given me the chance to even say "hello," much less try to make things right between us again. So I may as well face the fact that I blew my one and only shot with her. And now I'm doomed to spend the rest of my life with this irreparable hole in my chest where my heart is supposed to be.

Since he'd made the mistake of sitting in a rear-facing seat, he could clearly see her sitting several rows back, laughing at something one of the guys in Protection Detail said.

Feck, she's gorgeous when she laughs like that, Liam thought, trying to remember the last time he'd made her giggle so gleefully. *Maybe when we celebrated her birthday and I joked about not being able to find a big enough fake cake to jump out of in a Speedo?*

Thinking about celebrating Rylie's birthday over a week after her actual date of birth brought back all the guilt he felt after realizing that his time in the storeroom with Jen at Charlotte and Ian's bachelorette and bachelor party was technically after midnight, so those bad kisses had taken place in the wee hours of the morning on Rylie's September first birthday. *Yeah, she doesn't deserve to be saddled with an eejit like me.*

Feck, even if I hadn't let things go that far between me and Jen when I was blinded by beer goggles, I doubt my relationship with Rylie would have lasted anyway. I don't care what she says about wanting to stop wrestling after only five or six years in the big leagues of the business. I've seen how she glows with that natural high only performing in the squared circle can provide, so I know she won't want to give it up that soon. She may only have a ten-year career instead of the fifteen or twenty years most of us strive for, but she won't give it up in five to be able to retire within my planned time frame. So, we would've ended in a few years anyway.

At least now she has a chance to fall for one of the younger guys, so even when she does decide to take time off to have kids, she'll be able to come back and continue her career and tour with her family after their babies are born. Being able to continue her career like that will make her a lot happier with Magnum or Trojan, or maybe one of the Benningtons, than she'd ever be with me.

"Hey, Red, let's go upstairs and talk for a minute," Rick instructed, walking by Liam's seat toward the stairs beside the second set of restrooms on the plane and bringing Liam out of his thoughts.

"Sure thing, Boss," Liam agreed, unbuckling his seatbelt as he realized they'd taken off and already leveled out for the short flight to Austin. He followed Rick up to the top level of the plane, feeling slightly uncomfortable when he realized it was set up as a bedroom. "I wanted to talk to you, too, about ending this marriage angle at **Christmas Chaos** by having me job to Protection Detail. I think I'd rather just go back to working singles matches, so you don't have to scramble for my replacement in whatever tag team we might form now when I retire in a few years."

"I was actually going to talk to you about a heavyweight title run next year," Rick informed him, but the boss wasn't smiling the way Liam expected if they were really thinking on the same wavelength. "But we can't switch you over to singles until after *Saint Valentine's Day Massacre*, so we don't have to scrap everything we've come up with for Crockett, Josh, and the Precious Stones to team them up to fill the tag-team slot."

"Oh, okay." Liam understood the need to finish out their current feud before teaming them up, so he was willing to work with random partners for a couple more months. With the *Massacre* pay-per-view scheduled for the ninth of February, Rick really wasn't asking him for much, just an extra pay-per-view and six weeks of television appearances as Chastity's husband before his torture would be over. "So are we going to have whoever you decide to team up with me job to them this time and have me dispute the loss and rebook it for *Massacre*?"

"Actually, I think we need to have you go over at *Chaos* to win Chastity's managerial services," Rick disagreed, shaking his head. "Then at *Massacre*, we'll have your partner job and you claim that he could only lose the titles, not Chastity's managerial services, since she's your wife and you'd have to be pinned to lose her. That way we can book a heavyweight title feud between you and Vaughn with your wives feuding over the women's title."

"I don't know, Boss." Liam shook his head, knowing it would probably be uncomfortable for both of them to have to continue the marriage angle after they dissolved their union. "You know we're starting the legal process to annul our marriage over our Christmas break. We can probably fake it 'til February, but I don't know that we'll be able to pull it off for longer than that. Besides, won't I need to work with Cooper or Tank, since they're still feuding over the heavyweight title?"

"Actually, I've got a new three-man team trying out in a couple weeks, so if they end up signing, Tank will be going back to Heavy Artillery for a six-man feud. And Cooper is ready to retire from the ring and start booking."

"Seriously?" Liam was surprised by the news. Though when he really thought about it, he realized he probably shouldn't be, since Cooper was the oldest wrestler on the current roster. "I mean, I knew Dion decided not to come back as a booker, but I figured you'd just fill that position with another television writer."

"No, I won't be hiring another television writer," Rick bellowed obstinately. "I know Dad thought he needed someone more creative to help lure in viewers, but after the issues with Langston, I refuse to hire anyone who hasn't at least been trained to perform in the ring. I have too much else to juggle and don't have time to micromanage the booking team so we don't end up with any off the wall bullshit making it on a show."

"You mean like the bra-and-panties-dildo-on-a-pole match that made it on the pay-per-view right before Britney was born 'cause you and Richard were both back in New York on baby watch?" Liam teased his boss, forgetting to go back and repeat his objection to continuing the marriage angle once he moved back to singles competition.

"Exactly," Rick chuckled. "Which is why I'm so adamant that I only want to hire former wrestlers as bookers, and am going to be spending the next few months training both Cooper and Stone to handle some of my other duties, so I won't have to worry about the company when it comes time for me to take off for paternity leave. Which is actually why I asked you to come up here."

"Oh?" Liam waved around at the bedroom space surrounding them before arching an eyebrow at Rick. "Shouldn't Fiona be the one up here with you for this? 'Cause I don't have the right parts to help you make a baby."

"I don't need your help making a baby," Rick grumbled, shaking his head, even though he was clearly fighting a smile at Liam's quip. "But I do need someone who's going to be in New York over our Christmas and New Year's break to go pick out the pods that are being put up here and on our second plane that week. Apparently the ones we have on the lower level are no longer available and the sales rep I've been talking to can't tell me which option is most comfortable for guys our size because he's only five-foot-nine. So I'm hoping you won't mind flying home from San Antonio with the Yorks and meeting with the rep to actually try out a couple of different pod styles."

While Liam had known Rick purchased a second plane for the ground crew, so he didn't have to charter one each time they traveled abroad, he didn't realize they were cutting it so close to getting it customized before the South Pacific tour in January. He also assumed Derek York would have been the one tasked with assisting Rick with any airplane issues that had to be taken care of in New York, since that's where the pilot and his family lived. But when he really thought about it, he realized Derek couldn't do this task for Rick because the pilot wasn't quite six feet tall, either, so just being in New York for the holidays wasn't the only reason Rick gave Liam this task. While he wasn't the largest man on the roster, he was the largest of them who would be in New York at the right time. "Yeah, I can do that. I guess this means you're spending the holidays in Heart's Destiny this year? Do you want me to video call you while I'm there so you can give the final approval? Or will Richard be in the city to make the final decision after hearing my opinion?"

"No, Mom and Dad are going to be in Heart's Destiny, too." Rick shook his head, his normally stoic expression turning even more serious than usual. "And I won't be available for a video call, even though the appointment is on Saturday the twenty-first, so you'll have to make the decision and authorize the work that day. Then go back on the thirtieth to make sure everything is done before you fly back to Texas on the first."

"Are you okay, Rick?" Liam had no idea why his detail-oriented boss would suddenly appear worried about whatever he had going on that day that would keep him so busy he couldn't take a quick five-minute phone call, especially on a Saturday when they all had time off. "I mean, I know you probably don't want me to interrupt your family time for something like this, but it's not like you to appear worried about anything going wrong whenever you choose to delegate something."

"I'm not worried about anything going wrong with the planes," Rick reassured him with a tight smile. "We're doing our first round of IVF this month. And if everything goes as planned, I'll be spending Saturday the twenty-first worrying about my wife while she's sedated for the egg retrieval, and somehow trying to block out my concern for her long enough to give them a sperm sample at the same time."

"Oh, wow, okay." Liam was speechless, unsure how to respond to hearing his boss would be jerking off in a cup, even though it made perfect sense for why Rick wouldn't be available for a phone call that day. *And there's no fecking way I'm gonna interrupt him with a video call!*

"That's just the best-case scenario," Rick continued with a sigh. "Worst case, I'm going to screw up one of the shots I have to give Fiona between now and then, so when we go to their partner clinic in Indianapolis on the nineteenth, they won't be able to give her the shot to trigger ovulation and we'll have to skip the egg retrieval this month. Which means we'll have to take a month off for the next round, so they can do all the shots I'm giving her, and blood draws we're having Doc do and send to them when we can't get in with one of their partner clinics for this round in their office."

"Well, then, I'll be praying for your best-case scenario to happen," Liam assured Rick, hoping he was actually projecting positive vibes. "How soon after the retrieval will you know if it worked?"

"About three weeks." Rick ran a hand through his salt and pepper hair, which seemed to have a few more gray strands in it over the last couple of months. "It takes six days for them to combine my sperm with her eggs, and hopefully get viable embryos to either freeze or implant, so we tentatively have an appointment on the twenty-seventh for implantation. And then she'll have to take a pregnancy test no sooner than the tenth of January."

"Isn't that when we'll be on the South Pacific tour? Will she be able to get a pregnancy test if we're not in the US?"

"Yeah, but we'll still be in Hawaii that morning, so it won't be a problem for Doc to do a blood draw and overnight it to the fertility clinic if they don't have an affiliate clinic in Hilo," Rick explained. "Plus we already have a full box of the urine test strips we're planning to bring with us then, so she can test multiple times, just in case the urine tests can't detect it that early and it takes the lab some time to get us the results of the blood test."

Derek York came over the intercom in the plane to alert them to prepare for landing in Austin, so Liam and Rick both made their way back downstairs to retake their seats. Liam spent the rest of the flight thinking about everything he'd just learned and wondering if Rylie would have to go through all those same procedures to be able to have a baby one day.

Feck! If she has to do all that to get pregnant, maybe she won't want to do it while still traveling with the GWA after all. But that still doesn't mean she's going to be ready to fully retire to start trying for a baby at the same time I do.

Not that it matters now if she does, since I fecked up so royally that she won't want to have babies with me even if we do retire at about the same time.

~~~

Saturday, December 14, 2019, New York City, New York

"Seriously, Brent, why are you in such a rush to get down to the restaurant for breakfast?" Aiken grilled her husband as she practically ran to keep up with his long walking stride from their room. Since they normally only grabbed something from the continental breakfast to take with them on their way to the plane, and had only sat down to a full breakfast on their days off for a holiday break, his abnormal behavior this morning made no sense. "What's so special about this breakfast that we had to skip our morning…*workout*?"

"We didn't skip our morning *workout*, Princess," Brent chuckled, as they stepped into the elevator, smiling seductively as the doors closed to encapsulate the two of them alone. "We just did it a couple hours ago when I woke you up with my tongue."

"Yeah, but normally we still make love in the morning, even if we've had a middle of the night quickie," Aiken pouted, as Brent pushed the button for the ground floor before pulling her into his arms. Aiken placed her palms on his chest and looked up into his forest green eyes before continuing. "And we don't have to be at the arena for the fan expo for like three more hours, so I don't understand why you had to deprive me of my morning O's."

"I'm sorry, Princess," Brent half-heartedly apologized, brushing his lips over her forehead. "But I promise, I'll make up those orgasms

537
~~~

when we get back from the expo, so you'll be nice and relaxed before Josh and Teagan's Christmas mystery dinner tonight."

"While I'll happily take those extra O's, I still want to know why you're acting so weird this morning."

"Not weird, just have a surprise for you. One I think you're going to love, so just be patient for a few more minutes and you'll understand."

Thankfully, the elevator opened just as Brent finished his explanation, so Aiken quit badgering her husband and dutifully walked hand in hand with him out of the elevator and down the hall to the hotel restaurant. When they walked in, she was surprised to see the red and green poinsettias, which had been on every table the night before, had been replaced with flower arrangements in every shade of pink. There were pink roses, carnations, orchids, tulips, hyacinths, peonies, dahlias, hibiscus, and hydrangeas everywhere. And those were just the flowers Aiken could easily identify.

"Oh, Brent," Aiken gasped, covering her mouth in shock. "Are all these flowers my surprise? There's no way we can take them all with us when we fly out on Monday, if they'd even all fit in our room upstairs until then."

"They're only part of the surprise, Princess," Brent informed her as they were directed to a table in the center of the room. "And I was only planning on bringing one bouquet with us. The rest are scheduled to be delivered to the residents at a local nursing home this afternoon."

"Oh, Brent, you're such a wonderful, thoughtful man," Aiken gushed, pushing up on her tiptoes to return his earlier peck of a kiss, only on his cheek instead of his forehead, since she couldn't reach that far.

As they walked through the restaurant to get to their table, which held the largest of the bouquets, she finally noticed that their friends sat around every table in the room, with the exception of the one beside where they were supposed to be seated. "Daddio! Papa! Harlan! What? When? How?" She was so shocked to see all three of her and Brent's dads that she couldn't think straight to fully articulate her questions.

"Don't mind us, Aikey Baby," Papa instructed, motioning for her to turn around. "If you'll give your hunky hubby a minute, I think you'll understand."

When she turned away from the table where their dads were all seated, she found Brent down on one knee, kneeling beside the chair he'd obviously pulled out for her. "Oh, I really should sit down for this." She fanned her face with her right hand as she took her seat, allowing Brent to take her left hand in his.

"Aiken Thi Pearson Crockett, my beautiful Princess, I just couldn't wait another week to ask you to be mine forever," Brent started, removing the silver band from her left ring finger and swapping it over to her right before pulling a Tiffany blue box from his pocket. "Six months ago, I had no clue that I'd already fallen for you. Getting married and having a family weren't things I thought would ever happen for me. I thought love was something that only happened in movies and on television, and maybe for a select few real people, but it wasn't something I believed I was capable of, but I was so wrong. But then four months ago, fate stepped in, with the help of *a lot of Jameson...*"

"So much Jameson," Liam moaned, causing a chorus of chuckles around the room.

"And when I was too drunk to think with my brain, I followed my heart down the aisle with you. We've had some ups and downs since then, with me taking way too much time learning to follow my heart while sober. In our time together, I've learned that not only is true love real, but also that I'm capable of feeling it with you, more and more each day. I know people say 'I love you' so much that those three little words almost seem to have lost some of their meaning, so I want to make sure you know just how much I mean it every single time I say 'I love you.' My love for you is stronger than Edgar Allan Poe's obsession with birds."

Aiken couldn't contain her chuckle at his reference to their first date.

"My love for you is stronger than your love of classic movies. My love for you is stronger than my love of strawberry protein shakes. Hell, Princess, my love for you is stronger than my love for professional wrestling. I never want to spend a single day for the rest of my life without you by my side because without you I feel like I can't breathe. You're my best friend, my lover, the future mother of my children, the woman I want to grow old and gray with, my everything. Please, Aiken, will you marry me again in front of all our family and friends?"

"Yes!" Aiken exclaimed, eager for him to open that box and put their real rings on her finger.

"Before you agree, I have some…*special stipulations* for our vow renewal ceremony." Brent grinned at her mischievously. "I mean, we are professional wrestlers, after all, so like any major match, our wedding has to be gimmicked, even though it's a shoot and not a work."

"Of course," Aiken agreed, giggling like a giddy schoolgirl in her excitement.

"Our one-year anniversary is on a Tuesday, so I'm *proposing* that we renew our vows in the middle of the ring, live on the GWA's weekly TV show, with our families and fans in attendance, and totally, one-hundred percent sober this time. So, Aiken Thi Pearson Crockett, will you marry me again with those special stipulations?"

"Yes, Brent Allen Crockett, I absolutely will," Aiken beamed, as Brent opened the ring box and pulled out both a gold band and a dainty gold and diamond engagement ring, placing them both on her left ring finger. Once he was done, she removed the silver band from his left hand and moved it to his right, replacing it with his grandfather's gold band from the box. She lost track of the ring box as their lips met in a passionate kiss to seal their bond.

Aiken wrapped her arms around Brent's neck, opening her mouth for him to deepen the kiss. As his tongue tangled with hers, he pulled her into his arms and lifted her from her seat, standing and spinning her around with her feet floating a foot off the ground.

The room around them erupted in a chorus of cheers and congratulations, keeping them from taking things too far in front of their audience. Once Brent placed her back on her feet and released the kiss, they were surrounded by their fathers, who all took turns hugging each of them as they offered "welcome to the family" statements, as if this was the first they'd heard of an engagement.

As their friends joined in on the festive embraces, Aiken got an idea, grabbing Teagan's hand to keep her from stepping back too far when they released their hug. She scanned the crowd, seeking out Rylie and Liam while Teagan and Josh were still right beside her and Brent. Unfortunately, while they were both less than ten feet away from where she stood in the center of the room, they were on opposite sides of the space with several members of the roster separating them.

After what Rylie said happened between them after Allissa and Dean's wedding reception, I doubt they'll agree now. But since it'll be August before we do this vow renewal, they have plenty of time for Rylie to forgive Liam, so the two of them can get back together and join us.

"Since we're doing this in the middle of the ring on our anniversary, we really should have a vow renewal for all of us who got married in Vegas," Aiken suggested, pointedly looking at each of her friends.

"Oh, yes!" Teagan eagerly agreed, pulling Aiken in for another hug. "And we should do the same for the parties we're planning in Heart's Destiny, too."

"When are you planning parties in Heart's Destiny?" Dean asked, looking back and forth between Aiken & Brent and Teagan & Josh.

"Either for our Independence Day break or our Labor Day break, since they're the closest dates we have off to our anniversary," Josh clarified. "But we're waiting to schedule everything to let Dion have first dibs if he's able to convince Julie to marry him."

"Since he's been invited to help her move today, I think he's got a good chance of convincing her," Anthony chuckled.

Oh, good! Big D really deserves to get his happily ever after with the mother of his babies.

"Any chance they'll pick a Memorial Day wedding, so we can go ahead and book everything for July?" Josh inquired before Aiken could push for a response from Rylie and Liam.

"Considering the twins are due the day after Memorial Day, I highly doubt it," Kay informed them. "Even if she has them at thirty-eight weeks instead of the full forty, like often happens with twins, I expect Julie will want to do like Amy and take at least a month to lose the baby weight before squeezing into a wedding dress."

"It was Memmaw and Aunt Susan who invited him to help her move today, though," Tia pointed out while catching the pacifier her five-month-old brother spit out before her father could, even though Anthony was the one with baby Sam strapped to his chest in the cutest cartoon airplane covered carrier. "Aunt Julie hasn't even agreed to go on a date with D, yet, so I wouldn't hold your breath waiting for them to get engaged before you start planning something. With pregnancy hormones making her crazy right now, and for a few months after the babies are born until they go back to normal, she may not even agree to go out with him before the end of next year."

"You really need to monitor what she's learning in those online biology classes, Sis," Randi teased her sister, Kay. "My niece is too young to know about pregnancy hormones."

"Sorry, Aunt Randi," Tia sighed, shaking her head. "Between Mom, Aunt Brook, Aunt Amy, Aunt Charlotte, and now Aunt Julie, I don't need an online class to see that pregnancy hormones make women act like they've had a brain injury. That's why I've decided I'm just going to adopt my kids when I'm old enough to meet my Mr. Right and get married, so I don't lose IQ points when I'm really going to need them to keep up with everything for my family."

"Good plan, Tia," Anthony smirked.

Before the dads among them could point out that the only way the teenager could guarantee she never got pregnant was to never have sex, Aiken decided it was time to redirect the conversation. "Well, regardless, we still have a few months before we have to book anything, so we can wait and give D and Julie a chance to work everything out. Though I suppose we do need to get Rick's permission to have a triple wedding in the middle of his wrestling ring on his live TV show."

"Don't worry, Princess, I already ran it by the boss," Brent informed her, hugging her to his side. "Didn't I, Boss?"

"Yes, you did," Rick agreed with a chuckle. "And I agreed as long as you added that sober stipulation."

"That just goes for the renewal ceremony, though, right?" Brent questioned, obviously fighting not to smile. "'Cause if you meant for today too, then I need to make sure our waitstaff knows to use sparkling grape juice instead of champagne in our celebratory mimosas before they bring them out."

They all laughed when they noticed the servers entering the room carrying trays of what Aiken assumed were mimosas in champagne flutes.

"I think you're a little late, Crockett." Josh quipped as they all took their seats for the wait staff to pass out the mimosas.

"These are all made with sparkling grape juice," the waiter who served Aiken and Brent whispered, after Brent finished moving the large bouquet from the center of the table over to one side and scooted his chair around, so they could sit side by side, instead of across from one another. "Did we need to make some with champagne?"

"No, these are perfect, thanks," Brent assured the waiter, chuckling. "I was just joking around with our boss because we have to go to work after this."

The waiter nodded in understanding before informing them that the breakfast bar was ready whenever they were and walking away.

When Aiken looked over at Rick to make sure he knew they were all non-alcoholic, she noticed him rubbing his temples momentarily before turning and pointing at the bookers, Stone Fields and Ethan Abrams, then to Cooper Stafford, who was apparently planning to retire in the next few months to join the booking team. "I hope you're all prepared to keep the inmates from running the asylum when I go on paternity leave this summer."

"Oh! Em! Gee! Are you already pregnant?" Jaxon Nolan, the history tutor who worked with the kids who traveled with the GWA, and Fiona's bestie, squealed with excitement, bounding out of his chair to excitedly hug Rick's wife.

"No," Fiona replied, returning Jax's hug anyway. "We've got a couple more weeks before we do the implantation, and then it'll take a couple weeks after that before we can test to see if it works."

"But if it works on the first try, then Fifi won't be able to fly after our Independence Day break," Rick elaborated, "and we'll be grounded in Texas from then until the baby is born and both the baby and Fiona are cleared by the doctor to fly again."

After a brief discussion about how the other tutors would cover for Fiona and the bookers would cover for Rick, with both of them being available for video calls if there were issues only one of them could handle, Brent made it clear that the mimosas were non-alcoholic so their dads could lead off the toasts. Then everyone was instructed to fill their plates at the buffet.

Once they were all seated again and eating, Stone brought them back around to the discussion of incorporating their vow renewal into the GWA show. "How are we supposed to book a triple heel wedding in the middle of the ring without having the fans heckling them all through the ceremony?"

"You can't," Rick scoffed. "It'll have to be a triple face wedding, which is why I mentioned needing to plan several turns in the next couple of months."

"We can't turn heel until March when our condom sponsorship expires," Trojan pointed out, motioning between himself and his tag-team partner, Magnum.

"Yeah, but that's perfect timing for you to spend a month floundering after not winning Chastity back at *Massacre* before you decide being nice and playing fair isn't working for you anymore," Cooper enlightened the members of Protection Detail.

"And that also gives us a month after our second match against each other at *Massacre* to work things out and team up," Brent elucidated, motioning between their table and where Teagan and Josh sat. "So if we start feuding with the two of you, then your heel turn will push our face turn."

"If we do this, then the Goddesses will have to come in as heels, so we're not trying to turn them too soon," Aiken added, knowing Rick had mentioned having the new girls feud with the Precious Stones once they were a tag team again. She still thought it was funny that since the guys each only used one name for their gimmicks, Rick wanted them to take on the last name "Stone" as if they'd taken their wives' last names. And once they all came back together as a faction, they'd be known as the Stone Family instead of the Precious Stones.

"I agree," Rick nodded. "With having the Valors and Reds turn as well, we'll already have ten people turning this spring, so I think we're pushing the limit to what the fans will tolerate."

Aiken knew the "Reds" he was referring to were Liam and Rylie, since they'd slowly started using his first name for his gimmick again. Apparently, back when Liam first started wrestling, he used the ring name of "Liam the Red," and over the years it just got shortened to Red. Now that they were working in the married angle, they'd opted to say his name was Liam Red, so Chastity could take his last name and become Chastity Red.

"If you think that's too many turns at one time, I'm happy to keep working heel, if the Valors are cool with staying babyfaces," Liam offered. "Since we're annulling our marriage, we won't have to do a vow renewal, so it'll work better as a Stone Family thing, anyway."

Aiken looked over to where Rylie sat with Protection Detail, trying to figure out how her friend felt about not participating with the rest of them. Unfortunately, Rylie's tight-lipped smile looked more like a grimace, making it clear that she was hurt by Liam's declaration.

Ugh! I wish there was something I could do to get them back on the same page, like they were at least part of the week we were in Heart's Destiny.

"We'll keep that in mind as an option," Rick replied to Liam, turning his gaze to each of the bookers, which she knew was their boss's way of making sure they were all working together. "But we've got at least six months before we have to make a decision on turning you to make it a triple wedding or not turning you to keep it to just the Stones. And there's no telling what could happen between now and then that could totally change how we're planning on booking all your angles."

Since Brent and I fell in love in less than six weeks, I'm sure six months is plenty of time for Rylie and Liam to quit fighting their feelings for one another, forgive each other's past mistakes, and get their happily ever after, just like us and Teagan & Josh.

Epilogue

Liam's phone rang just as he got out of the shower. "Feck," he groaned, knowing he'd miss the call by the time he finished drying off, so he wouldn't drip all over the hotel carpet between the bathroom and bedside table, where his phone was currently sitting on the charger. Still, just in case it was his attorney's office calling to confirm his appointment on Monday, he rushed through toweling off, wrapping the towel around his waist, and running out of the bathroom. Unfortunately, he'd only made it halfway across the room when his phone stopped ringing.

"Hopefully, they'll leave a message with the direct line I need to call back to confirm." Liam didn't bother going to check the caller ID, turning around and grabbing a pair of boxer briefs from the suitcase he'd left on top of the dresser to start getting dressed for the day. Once he dried his dick and balls a little better than he had in the bathroom, he discarded the towel and put on the boxer briefs before reaching into his suitcase once more for a pair of black dress socks, knowing they'd match no matter which of his black or gray suits he chose to put on that day.

As he walked over to the closet to pick a suit, tie, and shirt for the day, his phone rang once more. This time, he was able to grab it, seeing Da flash on the screen just before he answered it on the second ring. "Good morning, Da."

"Oh good, you answered this time. I wasn't sure if you didn't the first time because you were already on the plane headed home, or if I called early enough to catch you still in bed." Brian Connery wasn't big on greetings and pleasantries, always seeming to be two or three sentences ahead of Liam whenever they started a telephone conversation, almost like his da had said his greetings while the phone was still ringing.

"I was actually in the shower," Liam clarified as he finally made it to the closet to settle on a medium gray suit, black dress shirt, and black and gray houndstooth-patterned tie.

"Good, good, then it's not too late for me to tell you to bring your wife home for the holidays with the family."

FECK! Does he know about the wedding in Vegas? Or is he just fishing to find out if there's any chance of making our wrestling angle real in the new year? Liam was torn about how to reply, knowing if he tried to lie and say the marriage was just a work for the GWA, then his da would be upset if he already knew the truth. But he also couldn't agree to bring Rylie home for the holidays and pretend they were a happy couple, when she was only speaking to him when they had to interact for their jobs. Even their car rides between the airports, hotels, and arenas they'd shared since **Christmas Chaos** had been quiet and somewhat awkward. *Guess I'll just have to go with honesty, then, since her discomfort with being around me would be obvious to him and everyone else in the family, if I miraculously convinced her to come home with me.*

"Da, we're not really a couple," Liam started, planning to explain that they were annulling the marriage, so he couldn't make plans like that for Rylie, when Brian interrupted.

"Quit being an eejit. I already know you married her in Las Vegas," Brian informed his son, sounding exasperated, even as he surprised Liam by not calling him out as a liar. "Rick called to see why you hadn't asked for our normal passes for the show you had here last week and told me all about it."

"Then why didn't you come to **Christmas Chaos**, so you could have personally invited Rylie for the holidays?" Liam didn't mean to vocalize the question, but he was so gobsmacked by finding out his da knew he'd gotten married that his mouth didn't get the message to keep his thoughts in his head.

"Oh, I thought about it," Da chuckled. "But after talking it over with the rest of the family, we decided to give you the time you needed to man up and come clean."

"So, this call is to let me know my time is up?" Liam shook his head, as he put his phone on speaker and sat it on the bedside table, so he could continue getting dressed. Once he put on his slacks, he donned his shirt next.

"Only because Rick called back to let me know you were planning to come home alone and file the paperwork for an annulment."

Fecking Rick! I guess D was right when he said he thought our boss was playing matchmaker after seeing him deconstruct the wedding favor bags we had to put back together last month.

"I think you both need to talk to the rest of the family, and maybe Father O'Malley, before you make such a final decision about your marriage," Brian advised, not seeming to comprehend that Liam didn't really want to talk about how he'd screwed things up with Rylie, especially if his da intended to include his brothers in that discussion.

But maybe I can talk to him about some of our issues now, so he'll understand why bringing Rylie home to talk with the rest of the family isn't an option.

"I think it's too late for that, Da," Liam confided with a sigh as he tucked in his shirt and put on his belt, not really wanting to mention how he'd screwed up by kissing Jen after he'd married Rylie.

"Do you love her? 'Cause it's not too late if you love each other."

"We're just friends, Da." As he looped his tie around his neck and shirt collar, Liam tried deflecting the question, not wanting to confess his love to anyone else when he couldn't say those three little words to Rylie.

"Ha," Da scoffed. "Friends don't have the chemistry the two of you show the world every week on TV. So if I were a betting man, I'd bet you're in love with her and just haven't told her yet. But that's okay, you don't have to say the L-word to anyone but her. Just answer with a simple yes or no. Do you love her?"

"Yes," Liam reluctantly admitted, bungling the knot in his tie and having to start over. "But sometimes love isn't enough. Not when we've got so many obstacles to overcome."

"Ah, that's where you're wrong, Son. There's no such thing as an obstacle that love can't overcome."

"She's ten years younger than me, Da," Liam started, hoping to convince his father that he and Rylie couldn't work, even though he really wished they could. "And she's only been with the GWA for nine months, so she's got at least another ten years before she'll be ready to retire, while I'm planning on leaving the business in the next two to five years. We can't exactly have a relationship and raise a family if I'm in Belle Harbor while she's still touring. And even if she were to decide she loves me enough to cut her career short and retire when I do, I don't want to risk her getting hurt by not feeling welcomed in our neighborhood because she's Black and not Irish, or having to put up with snide comments because we didn't have a Church wedding."

"I hope you're not implying we'd discriminate against anyone just because our family and community are proud of our Irish heritage," Brian barked defensively. "I know I raised you better than that. I don't care what color her skin is or where her family is from, she's a Connery now, so she's family. And family will never be made to feel unwelcome here."

Liam felt like an arse for even bringing up that possibility, knowing his family would never discriminate or make her feel unwelcome, even though the same couldn't be said for all of their neighbors.

"Is that why you're planning to spend the holidays apart? Because her family wouldn't accept you?"

"No, Da," Liam sighed, sitting down on the bed to put on his socks and shoes. "The reason we're not planning to spend the holidays together is because we only got married because we were drunk and some of our friends were getting married, so in our inebriated state we wanted to join in, but we're not really a couple. We've never even gone on a date, only hung out as friends. The fact that she doesn't have any family left has absolutely nothing to do with it."

Fucking a few times doesn't count as dates, right? And neither does going to our friends' wedding stuff together, since we were mostly pretending to be happily married and married people don't date, no matter what Josh and Crockett call their lunches and sightseeing with their wives.

"She doesn't have any family left?"

Liam could hear the mix of concern and compassion in his father's voice and knew he'd said the wrong thing to convince him that Rylie wouldn't be coming to Belle Harbor for the holidays. "No, she's an only child, whose parents died a few years ago when their car was hit by a drunk driver. From what she's told me, her parents cut off contact with their extended families when they didn't approve of them getting married almost thirty years ago. So she's planning on spending the holidays with her friends, whom she doesn't get to see often since she joined the GWA."

"If they're not off visiting family out of town."

Liam remembered Rylie's words from a few weeks earlier and hoped withholding the possibility that she wouldn't be able to catch up to any of her friends from his da wasn't considered lying by omission. *If so, then I guess I have something else to add to my confession while I'm home.*

"While friends like that are important and can feel like family sometimes, seeing them for the holidays isn't as important as getting to know her new family. So, you need to convince her to come here at least through Saint Stephen's Day, even if she wants to go be with her friends for New Year's," Da insisted, making Liam feel like he had no choice but to agree to ask her.

Feck! I know she's going to decline, but the only way he's going to let me off the phone, so I can meet Rylie in the lobby and get to the plane on time, is if I agree with him.

"Okay, Da, I'll ask her as soon as I see her this morning," Liam finally caved, making sure he had everything packed to leave the hotel before putting on his jacket. "But she's a grown woman with a mind of her own, so don't be surprised if she refuses."

"Tell her you love her, Son, and she won't refuse you. And maybe say it in Irish, because de ladies lahve de accent," Brian advised, putting on a stronger than normal Irish brogue before disconnecting the call.

"If only it were that easy." Liam chuckled self-deprecatingly as he finished gathering his things, preparing to meet Rylie in the lobby so they could ride together to the airport, since they had to keep up the pretense of being happily married in public after he "won" her managerial services at *Christmas Chaos*. "But as bad as I hurt her by stupidly kissing Jen, I know she'll only agree to come home with me if her presence in my lawyer's office on Monday will expedite our annulment."

~~~

As Rylie took a seat in the same quad with her fellow members of Protection Detail on the GWA plane for the first of multiple flights she had scheduled that day, she pushed aside her guilt for not waiting around in the hotel lobby for Liam and riding with her teammates. Instead, she started to question if the savings from booking a round-trip ticket between San Antonio and Atlantic City, instead of two one-way tickets from Memphis to Atlantic City at the beginning of their holiday break and then Atlantic City to San Antonio when it was time to go back on tour, was worth all the extra travel time. Granted, she didn't have to deal with the holiday crowd at the private airports the GWA used, but she still wasn't looking forward to having to deal with cranky passengers and potential airline delays for her commercial trip home and then again for the commercial trip back to meet up with the rest of the GWA crew.

Maybe I should consider spending my holidays wherever the GWA plane is from now on, she contemplated while tuning out the conversation between Harrison and Cameron. *If I book my stays in extended-stay hotels, instead of the nicer places like we use with the GWA, I bet the cost would be about the same as all the round-trip flights. And it's not like there's anyone back in Atlantic City that I'll be spending my breaks with, so it doesn't really matter if I don't go back there all the time. For that matter, I could probably have all my mail forwarded to the GWA headquarters and get a storage unit for what little stuff I have in my apartment, and save quite a bit more of my salary by not having to pay rent and utilities every month.*

Considering her first year GWA salary was more than four times the highest combined yearly income she'd seen on her parents' tax records after they passed, she knew it probably seemed silly for her to be so frugal. But knowing she'd most likely end up having to go through multiple rounds of costly fertility treatments to have a family one day, and would need to have enough money saved to live on while going through all the medical procedures and for at least the first few
~~~

months of her babies' lives, she knew she had to save as much as she could while working in the highest paid job she'd likely ever have. And if she was really lucky, her salary would increase every year as her coworkers had implied theirs had, so she could save up enough to not have to go back to a crappy secretarial job, like the ones she'd had to pay the bills while waiting for her big break in sports entertainment, until after her children were old enough to go to school.

Or maybe one of the investments the Hunters recommended will pay off big enough that I can be a stay-at-home mom, like I've always dreamed of.

While she'd always assumed that fantasy life would only be possible if she met her soulmate and they combined their lives, and incomes, to make it happen, she was now resigned to doing it all on her own, since her marriage with Liam had imploded. After meeting and falling in love with him, she couldn't imagine making a family with any other man.

If I can stay on with the GWA long enough to start earning those multimillion-dollar contracts I've heard about, so I can invest more and really make my money grow, then my dream just might be within reach, even if I can't get past the pain of breaking things off with Liam and have to use a sperm donor to have my babies.

Almost three weeks earlier, when she'd told him she needed space and time to deal with her feelings before they could even hang out as friends again, she'd really thought she'd be able to convince herself to forgive him, since they technically didn't know they were married when he kissed Jen. But every time she tried to get her brain to listen to her heart and pussy, so she could forgive him and try to have a real relationship with him beyond the brief friends-with-benefits thing they'd tried, her brain kept getting stuck on what he'd said about wanting to sleep with someone else to get over her. And her pain and anger at him for his utter rejection just made her resent the time she had to spend with him. Which she now realized was probably why she was in such a pissy mood when he was late meeting her in the hotel lobby earlier, triggering her to act out by riding with Protection Detail instead of him. Unfortunately, she didn't know how to get past her anger, making her wonder if they'd ever get to the point where they might have a second chance.

Regardless of the fact that he was as attracted to her as she was to him, that statement made it clear that he didn't love her. Or at the very least, that he didn't want any deeper feelings to develop between them, so he wanted to decrease the risk of one of them falling in love by getting his physical needs met with anyone but her. It made her feel like he was saying, "I think you're hot enough to bang, but you're not hot enough for me to only want to bang you for the rest of my life." Only without actually being man enough to say the words.

Since Jen Burleson was only a couple of years older than Rylie and was so ensconced in her family business in Texas that she'd never move to New York to be with Liam, Rylie had at least convinced herself that he hadn't been lying when he said he didn't want to be more than friends with Jen. Considering their age difference and career paths keeping them apart were the two things he blamed for why their marriage couldn't work, she had to assume the same would be true for him and Jen. Combined with how epically bad Liam had described their two attempts at kissing, Rylie felt like an idiot for ever being jealous of the other woman.

But regardless of no longer believing those two kisses in September were grounds for breaking things off, she still couldn't bring herself to forgive him and ask to start over with their friendship, or possibly try for more, because the reason behind the attempt at being with another woman was the actual issue she had a problem with.

Is that because I'm afraid friendship is all we'll ever have? Or am I just trying to protect myself from a bigger broken heart later, if he rejects me again when I tell him I'm ready to move past friendship to something more?

Rylie was so lost in her thoughts that she didn't realize the plane had taken off until Liam appeared beside her seat, wearing a gray suit and black shirt, which almost perfectly matched her outfit.

"Can we go talk privately for a few minutes?"

Shit! I bet he's pissed that I didn't wait in the lobby for him this morning like I was supposed to and rode to the airport with Cameron and Harrison instead of him.

"In a plane full of people?" Rylie arched an eyebrow curiously at him, unsure how they could have a private talk unless they both went into one of the lavatories. *Gross, no, not happening.* "I don't think that's possible 'til after we land."

Leah Mae Wright

"Actually, we can go upstairs or to the back galley and not be overheard," Liam pointed out.

Rylie had only realized the plane had an upstairs a couple of weeks earlier, after seeing the staircase when Rick opened the door in the middle of the plane, which she'd always thought was a closet, before he and Liam disappeared up those stairs. Since she'd been in the back galley before to get bungee cords for securing her largest suitcase, she opted to go upstairs, wanting to see the previously unknown space. When she got to the top of the stairs and saw the top level was set up as a bedroom, however, she started to question if she'd made the right choice.

No, he just wants to talk, probably about how I broke kayfabe this morning by riding with Protection Detail. He didn't bring me up here so we can join the mile-high club. While intellectually, she knew Liam wasn't trying to get back in her panties, her hard nipples and wet pussy clearly hadn't gotten the memo. *Damn, I knew I should have worn pants today, instead of this gray skirt. Now I have to keep my legs crossed in case my thong can't contain the moisture, so he doesn't notice any drippage.*

Hoping he also wouldn't notice the prominent pebbling of her nipples under her black lace bra and thin stretch turtleneck, she squeaked out, "What did you want to talk about?"

"Rick asked me to take this plane back to New York and pick out the pods that are going to be replacing all this stuff up here, and filling up the second plane he just bought for the ring crew whenever we travel someplace they can't drive the trucks they usually take to beat us to the arena each day," Liam stated, not really getting into why she needed to know any of that information. But also surprising her by not berating her for not riding with him that morning, either.

So, this is our last chance to break in the bed and join the mile-high club?

"And I thought you might want to cancel your flight home to come to New York with me, so we can both meet with my lawyers Monday to find out what we need to do about the annulment."

Of course, he still thinks we can get his entertainment lawyer to convince the judge to give us an annulment instead of a divorce.

"Can't you just file everything and send the paperwork to my lawyer's office for me to sign? Or maybe just bring it back with you when we go back on tour, so I can sign it without having to hire a lawyer?"

"Yeah, I can if that's what you want," Liam sighed, shaking his head, which she took to indicate neither of those options were what he wanted to do. "But I thought it might be faster if we're both there on Monday, so maybe we can file and sign off on everything without having to take time off later to appear in front of the judge."

Don't cry, Rylie Ann. You knew he wanted to end the marriage as quickly and quietly as possible since the moment he found out, even when we were having sex and trying to see if we could eventually be more than friends with benefits. So this is not a surprise. There's no reason to cry over dissolving our marriage, no matter how much I wish we wouldn't.

Damn it! Damn it! Damn it! Why am I getting upset about ending our legal connection when I was just lamenting why I can't forgive him to be able to try to make our marriage real?

"Okay, I'll have to see if I can find a hotel that's not already booked up with the hordes of people from all over the world about to descend on the city for the holidays." Honestly, while she assumed she'd be able to find a place for the next few days and probably even through Christmas, she wasn't sure what her chances were of finding a hotel that would still have a room available through New Year's Day because of the ball drop in Times Square.

"You don't have to find a hotel," Liam disagreed, reaching out and stopping her from pulling her phone from her wristlet and doing a search on the plane's Wi-Fi. "I have a big empty house, where you can have your choice of guest rooms."

"And how are you going to explain my presence there to your family, when they're dragging you off to all the parties and stuff you mentioned a few weeks ago?" *Surely, he's not suggesting introducing me to his family, just in time to tell them we're ending our marriage.*

"Actually, my family already knows about you," Liam admitted sheepishly. "Da called me this morning and insisted I bring you home for the holidays. That's why I was late getting down to the lobby and missed meeting up with you to drive to the airport."

Rylie's jaw dropped in shock at hearing the news that his family knew they were married, totally missing the fact that he thought her riding with Protection Detail that morning was his fault. *Is that because you finally told them we really got married in Vegas? Or because the matchmakers in your family are hoping to push us into making our gimmick marriage legal?*

"I didn't tell them," Liam blurted, holding his hands up in surrender, and making her wonder if he'd just read her mind, or if she'd actually voiced the questions she'd thought were only in her head. "Apparently, Rick called Da when I didn't request passes for the family to **Christmas Chaos** and he told them about us."

Rylie had to wonder if Rick calling Liam's father was part of the matchmaking Fiona had talked him into while they were in Heart's Destiny for Allissa and Dean's wedding. But she wasn't about to mention that to Liam at the moment, knowing he'd be as irritated by that as he was about them having to share a room and reconstruct the wedding favors.

When she didn't immediately respond to his revelation, Liam continued telling her all about his conversation with his father that morning. "Apparently, the whole family is eager to meet you, so I wouldn't be surprised if Ma and Granny have a welcome-to-the-family party planned already. I'm just not sure if they'll try to spring it on us before or after the intervention Da mentioned to try to help us work through our issues, so we'll call off the annulment."

"He actually mentioned an intervention?" *Are they really trying to keep us together? Or hoping an ambush by the whole family will scare me off?*

"He didn't call it an intervention, exactly," Liam back peddled, shaking his head. "But he suggested we wait to decide on an annulment until after sitting down with the family, and possibly Father O'Malley, to discuss everything. At first, I thought he meant the whole family, and was absolutely against it because there's no way I want to hear my brothers' opinions on our marriage. But now that I think about it, I'm pretty sure he only means for us to sit down with him, Ma, Granda, and Granny, so they won't take a chance on my single brothers bringing any anti-marriage views to the table."

"And you want us to sit down with your parents and grandparents to discuss our marriage?" Rylie found that hard to believe, considering how adamant he'd always been about getting the annulment.

But if there's a possibility that they can help us work through our issues, shouldn't we try it? Even if their intervention isn't enough to change his mind about the annulment, maybe the women in his family can help me figure out why I'm having such a hard time forgiving him when I'm still madly in love with him.

I mean, I know it won't be the same as if I could still talk to my mom about everything, but a mother-in-law seems like the closest I'll ever have to getting Mom back. Not that I imagine Liam's mom is anything like mine was. Or that she'll want a close relationship with me like I had with Mom. But it's possible she'll be as open to mothering me a little when I need it as Mandi and the other women of Heart's Destiny were last month. And if not, then I'll just make another stop for a motherly hug from Mandi when we fly back to San Antonio on the first.

"Honestly, I don't know what I want," Liam huffed, running his hand through the longer strands of hair on the top of his head and making it stick up in all directions, instead of sweeping forward and off to the side as it normally laid. "That's not exactly true. I know I want us both to be happy. I just don't know how to make it happen without disappointing anyone else I care about. If my family or Father O'Malley can share the wisdom of their experiences to give me the insight to make us all happy with whatever happens next, then I'm willing to listen. But I'm also afraid that sitting down to discuss everything with them will just lead to more disagreements and none of us being happy with whatever we decide to do going forward."

Rylie's heart broke from the anguish in Liam's voice. She wanted to do or say something to comfort him, but she had no idea what might be effective without muddying the waters between them even more than they already were.

Joining the mile-high club will make us both happy, her pussy suggested.

No, sex is why everything is so muddy now, her brain argued.

Just hug him and tell him we'll go meet his family, her heart pleaded. *And maybe his family matchmakers will have better luck than the ones in Heart's Destiny, so we can get our happily ever after for Christmas.*

I don't agree with the hug yet, but going to New York is our best option, her brain chimed in once more. *If his family can't convince me to forgive him, then we'll at least be able to get a clean break by taking care of the annulment paperwork all at one time.*

"Okay, I guess I'm cancelling my ticket to Atlantic City, then," Rylie finally conceded, wondering if she could do it online from the plane, or if she'd need to wait until they landed to actually call the airline. "Will I have enough time on the ground in San Antonio to take care of that before we take off again?"

"Yeah, plenty," Liam assured her with a smile. "We're not flying to New York until tomorrow morning."

Thankfully, she knew Rick kept a block of hotel rooms booked for the first night of any of their breaks, so any of the talent who couldn't get an immediate flight out to their hometowns would have a place to stay. *At least, I don't have to room with Liam tonight. And hopefully, I'll be able to stay in his guest room without losing the fight with my libido to sneak into his bed, if we decide to go ahead with the annulment.*

No, hopefully, we'll work things out and spend every night in his bed for the rest of our lives, her pussy and heart chorused in unison as Liam led the way back down the stairs for them to take their seats for the rest of the flight.

Does thinking of my subconscious inner voice having three distinct personalities as various parts of my body mean I'm having some kind of psychotic break? If so, then I think I now understand why so many romance authors have their main characters tell their love interests, "You drive me crazy." 'Cause if I'm going crazy, Liam has definitely been the man to drive me there.

Liam and Rylie's story continues in **Winning Rylie**.

Coming Next in the GWA

<u>*Winning Rylie*</u>

After getting married while drunk in Las Vegas back in the summer, Liam and Rylie spent months fighting their mutual attraction to one another. Until fate and their matchmaking friends intervened to push them together. Unfortunately, their combustible chemistry wasn't enough to keep them burning up the sheets past the fall, and a winter cold front seemed to be hitting their marriage.

As Liam filled in for their boss and took the GWA plane to New York City for upgrades over the end of the year holiday break, Rylie accompanied him, presumably so they could both sign off on the paperwork to dissolve their marriage. But neither one of them were prepared for the mischief and magic of Christmas with the Connerys.

Would spending their break with his big Irish family bring them back together for their happily ever after? Or would they start the new year as newly single people?

DISCLAIMER: This multicultural, age gap, forced proximity, friends-to-lovers, drunk Vegas marriage, sports romance contains profanity, graphic sex scenes, struggles with infertility issues, and reconciling their lives with their religious beliefs. It is intended for adult readers (18+) who are not easily offended.

Coming Next in Heart's Destiny

Destined for Deanna

JJ Burleson met the woman he knew he was destined to marry a few years ago. They spent a wonderful week together at a conference, with JJ planning to propose before it ended and bring her back to his hometown. But for some unknown reason, Deanna Wolfe ended their fling before he could get the words out, leaving him heartbroken.

Deanna had fallen head over heels for JJ when she first met him. But after a whirlwind week with him, she had to end things because she knew she could never give him the family he wanted in the future. She went home and tried to make herself forget the younger man who'd stolen her heart, but it was difficult when her boss at OK Oil kept going head to head with JJ for deals they both wanted for their companies. While she never had to see him, it was still difficult for her to hear his name whenever Burleson Incorporated won a contract her boss wanted.

When JJ's cousin married Deanna's best friend, their longing for one another only got worse because she could no longer avoid seeing him whenever her friend invited her to family events. Especially when she learned that their breakup led him to study the kinks they'd both been curious about years ago.

Somehow she managed to keep her secrets, if not her distance, from JJ for over a year after they ran into one another again. But when Burleson Incorporated bought out OK Oil, JJ moved out of his small hometown to take over as her boss in Tulsa. Fighting their destiny was a lot harder when she had to report to him daily as his executive assistant.

DISCLAIMER: This second chance, older woman, younger man, he falls first, office romance contains profanity, graphic sex scenes including BDSM, and flashbacks to an abusive past, pregnancy loss, and forced infertility, as well as a hostage situation when her former abuser breaks out of prison and comes for revenge. It is intended for adult readers (18+) who are not easily offended.

Books by Leah Mae Wright

Heart's Destiny Series

<u>A Brief History of the Founding Families of the Fictional Small Town of Heart's Destiny, Texas</u> – Free on Book Funnel
<u>Courting Kay</u> – Anthony Burleson and Kay Lee
<u>Courting Kay Bonus Scenes</u>
<u>Wrestling with Randi</u> – James Hunter and Randi Lee
<u>Bobby's Bride</u> – Bobby Burleson and Brooklyn Barns
<u>Adoring Amy</u> – Justin Burleson and Amy Lawton
<u>Charlotte's Wedding</u> – Ian Campbell and Charlotte Burleson
<u>Joshin' Around</u> – Josh Burleson and Cait Campbell
<u>Dion's Dream Girl</u> – Dion Davis and Julie Burleson
<u>Destined for Deanna</u> – JJ Burleson and Deanna Wolfe (Coming Soon)
Lights, Camera, Ashlyn – Darius Davis, Ashlyn Lawton, and Cade Starling (Coming Soon)

Galactic Wrestling Association Series

Glossary of Professional Wrestling Terms – Free on Book Funnel
Fighting for Fiona – Rick Robertson and Fiona Harrison
Dean's Darlin' – Dean Hunter and Allissa Walters
Mistakenly Married? – Liam Connery and Rylie Long, Brent Crockett and Aiken Pearson, & Josh Parker and Teagan Shields
Winning Rylie – Liam Connery and Rylie Long
Blade's Botched Bump – Brandon "Blade" Braddock and Caitlyn Sullivan (Coming Soon)

About The Author

Leah Mae Wright lives in Florida with her husband and fur babies. Her head has been filled with romantic stories for as long as she can remember, beginning with fairy tales as a small child growing up in Oklahoma, and carrying through to countless ideas of her own throughout the years as she has moved around to live in several different states. Now that her children are grown and life has slowed down, she's letting them out of her head, so they can join the libraries of her fellow fans of romance. Leah's literary world is a wonderful place that has no Covid, no real politicians, and a few unreal towns. Her favorite part about her characters living in her literary world is knowing that they are guaranteed a happily ever after.

You can keep up to date with Leah's future book plans at:
www.leahmaewright.com – Be sure to sign up for the Newsletter to receive emails about new releases, sales, and freebies.
www.facebook.com/LeahWrightAuthor
www.amazon.com/author/leah_wright
https://www.instagram.com/leahmaewrightauthor/
https://www.pinterest.com/LeahMaeWrightAuthor/

Provide your feedback to the author at:
Leah's Literary World Facebook Group
LeahWrightAuthor@gmail.com
Leah@LeahMaeWright.com

You can also review Leah's books on Amazon, Goodreads, Bookbub, and Fictiondb.